"In *Six Bits*, author Michael
emotion, sweeping the read
twists. This book is not to b

MW01127617

**Author of, De Gaulle: Lessons in Leadership
from the Defiant General**

"This book wore me out—in a thrilling and unsuspecting way! Just when you think you have the plot figured out, author Michael Ringering sends you careening down a different path. The story is an incredible look at how some forget those things most important in life, and the price they're willing to pay to keep their family together. A wonderful read."

—**Jed Mescon, news anchor, WRCB-TV, Chattanooga, Tenn.**

"*Six Bits* is a simultaneous thrilling page-turner and heart-warming tale that weaves the threads of redemption, love and forgiveness throughout its pages. The story is one of self-discovery and transformation, as the main character must confront the dichotomy of who he is and who he would like to be. The author does an excellent job immersing the reader in the story. I laughed; I cried. At times, I shouted at the characters. Yet long after the last word was read, I continued to relive the journey of redemption that unfolds within the pages of this novel."

—**Dr. Christie Kleinmann, assistant professor, Lee University,
Cleveland, Tenn.**

"*Six Bits* is a page-turner that takes the reader on an exciting and emotional rollercoaster ride. The author provides just enough clues for the puzzle pieces to fit, yet you are surprised and overwhelmed with the outcome. If you're a fan of Capra's *It's a Wonderful Life* or Dickens' *A Christmas Carol*, you'll definitely want to place this book on your Christmas wish list!"

—**Rachel Oesch, former news anchor,
WDEF-TV, Chattanooga, Tenn.**

"*Six Bits* is a story that immediately draws the reader into the lives of each character and keeps your attention throughout."

—**LaTrice Currie, news anchor, WRCB-TV, Chattanooga, Tenn.**

"I found myself reflecting on my own life choices as I followed the author's protagonist through this Dickens-esque tale. The characters' interactions truly have the reader examining those things most important in life, while being thoroughly entertained."

"This story begins along the genre of a James Patterson novel before seamlessly transforming the reader to an era more befitting the works of Charles Dickens. The reader is kept transfixed as to how the author will tie all the elements together, as he embeds you in the transformational journey of Jack London Clarke—a man who rediscovers a life he always had, but never knew."

"I read this book twice, and am certain I will read it again and find an emotion I missed. There is a simple magic in author Michael Ringering's writing style; the way he draws the reader close to his character and places you in each scene and location. You literally feel as if you are a part of his main character's quest. *Six Bits* grabs your attention from the first page and fills your spirit with every possible emotion. You will pick this book up and not want to put it down. I look forward to more of Michael's novels!"

"*Six Bits* is a compelling novel that allows you to experience an emotional and spiritual journey with the main character, Jack London Clarke. This book is vividly written, and has a depth and complexity to the plot that continues to draw you in to the very last sentence. I thoroughly enjoyed this book and highly recommend it.

"From the brevity of the book's title, you cannot begin to imagine the complex journey author Michael Ringering has planned for you. The character building is superb, the plot complex and mesmerizing, and the message universal."

"*Six Bits* is a touching story filled with hope and goodness; very well written. I was so drawn into the story and its intense plot, I felt as if I, too, had become a character in the book."

"*Six Bits* is a riveting story about a man on an improbable search for himself and his family. Author Michael Ringering so completely pulls the reader into the depths of his main character's journey, the book becomes very difficult to put down. You will laugh, cry, and rage along with the characters—but you will not be able to resist turning to the next page!"

"Two wonderful worlds collide! Wrapped into one intense story of destiny and purpose, *Six Bits* is a modern day twist of *It's A Wonderful Life* and *A Christmas Carol*. Author Michael Ringering draws you into another world where you become a living part of the drama, the jealousy, rage, and ultimately experience amazing love and true redemption. You will not want to put the book down and will love the many surprises along the way. I am a better person after indulging myself in the story, as it drew me closer to those I love and appreciate the most. Life is precious and so fragile."

"I loved this book and thought the storyline was very imaginative and creative. Just when you think you have the plot figured out, the author delivers a twist that sends you on a new adventure. The writing is excellent; the story definitely keeps the reader intrigued and wanting to turn the page. *Six Bits* is an imaginative, well-written book that I highly recommend."

"*Six Bits* is an emotional read with an unsuspecting plot and several amazing twists. The book ignites thoughts of 'family versus all other things in life,' keeping the reader on edge throughout. Can we each remember when career became more important than family?"

"This book is a must read! You will laugh, you will cry, and be moved. Prepare for a wild ride. You will be glad you took the trip."

"*Six Bits* is an excellent novel that captivates from the beginning. Author Michael Ringering does an excellent job detailing each character and the many different settings, making the reader feel as if they are in the story. The book was hard to put down, and left me thinking about the characters and plot when I was not reading it. A great book and a must read!"

"*Six Bits* is a riveting tale that keeps the reader guessing and turning pages. We thoroughly enjoyed this book and would highly recommend it to anyone who likes a great story."

"*Six Bits* will forever change your outlook on life—an absolute must read! You will hate the main character almost immediately, cry with him as he faces his demons, and grow to love him as he transforms his life. A great story on every level."

SIX BITS

by

Michael Ringering

Published by Autumn Leaf Publishers (www.autumnleafpublishers.com)
Publishing Agent—Keith Provance
Edited by—Erin Reder, Bridget Garland, and Cindy Kimbrough

For information regarding permission to reproduce selections from this book, please e-mail: autumnleafpublishers2@earthlink.net.

Cover design by Michael C. Ringering

Scripture quotations used in this book are taken from *The Holy Bible,* King James version.

ISBN: 978-1-936314-59-1

Printed in Canada

14 13 12 11   10 9 8 7 6 5 4 3 2 1

For my loving wife, Teresa,
my incredible, supportive family,
and my extended families
the Logans, Palermos and Schanbachers.
This was possible because of you.

ACKNOWLEDGMENTS

In 2004, I had the pleasure of working for LaVERDAD Marketing and Media in Cincinnati, Ohio, and its founder, former Green Beret, and Procter & Gamble Company marketing and branding executive, Mike Robinson; a man I consider a true friend and mentor. Early on in my employment, Mike shared with me his strong belief in the concept of there being "power in numbers."

Although it seemed logical and simple enough, it was not until I witnessed the strategic manner with which Mike put the concept to use that I realized the true benefit in bringing diverse partnerships together to achieve common goals and interests.

This novel—*Six Bits*—is a prime example of there being "power in numbers." I say this, because I had so many people willing to preview the manuscript and offer their reactions and suggestions. This being my first published novel, I could not bypass the opportunity to thank all those who helped and have meant so much during this process. Of course, it always starts with those closest to you.

First, there was no one more inspiring or instrumental in helping me get through this process than my wife, Teresa. Her love of literature reignited my own passion for the written word and inspired my drive to complete this project. She accepted many evenings alone while I hammered away at the keyboard, yet pushed, persuaded, and supported me when I needed it most. As my time at the computer intensified, especially during the last two years, so did her urging. Her faith in my abilities never wavered, nor her confidence that this moment would one day arrive. I thank her for her love and patience, and for sharing this dream with me.

I must thank my sister, Patty Tomerlin, brother-in-law, Jay Tomerlin, and stepmother, Susie Ringering. Although I had originally not intended on letting anyone read the book until complete, I thought it wise to get feedback while going through the process, in hopes of lessening the editing on the back end. They each read along as

I wrote, sometimes waiting months in between chapters. For anyone who has started a book, put it away for three months, picked up where you left off, then repeated that process over a couple years' time, I'm sure you can appreciate how very difficult that is, especially when tasked to catch errors and inconsistencies. Their commitment and feedback kept me between the lines I had defined for the storyline.

Knowing the challenges I'd be facing as an unknown author peddling a 195,000-word manuscript, I knew for certain I had to eliminate as many x-factors in this process as possible in order to get the attention of an agent or publisher. One of those potentially catastrophic factors is submitting copy poorly written and littered with errors and inconsistencies. Fortunately, due to my line of work, I've developed relationships with many copy editors over the years and managed to secure the services of three of the best, in my opinion. Erin Reder, a longtime dear friend and colleague from my days working with the Cincinnati Reds; Bridget Garland, friend, colleague and current editor of the *East Tennessee Medical News*; and my publisher's editor, Cindy Kimbrough, each did an incredible job getting me through the process and helped to deliver a clean manuscript.

I'm sure most will agree, we are very little without the love and support of our families. I'm so blessed to have immediate and extended family members who understood and appreciated how important this project was, then offered support and assistance in ways I could not have expected or anticipated. My brother, Johnny Barnerd, whom I consider one of the finest men I've had the pleasure of knowing, was a true source of inspiration, support, and feedback, and one of the biggest "fans" of my work that I know. I want to thank my mother and stepfather, Jack and Judy Barnerd, and my father, Clint Ringering, for their ongoing support and feedback, and for providing me with the necessary life tools to get to this moment. I could not have done this without them. I would like to thank my sister-in-law, Becky Baysden, for her support and encouragement; my uncle, Larry Ringering, who provided counsel for an important scene in the book; and my aunt Sharon Ringering, for her critique and suggestions.

Speaking of family, I'm equally blessed to have developed great friendships with many of those who I work with at University Surgical Associates. My sincere thanks to Sonya Westbrooks, Tyra and Greg Gray, Kayse Rigsby, Melissa Hale, Marsha Bock, Cindy Shoemaker, Carol Davidson, Teri Elliott, Angie DeBord, Dr. Shauna Lorenzo-Rivero, and Heather Mixon for taking time to review the manuscript and offer feedback.

Close friends and colleagues who went way beyond the call include my two best childhood friends, Mike Logan and Dr. John Kell; my dear friend and literary mentor, Linda Provance; my publisher, Keith Provance; longtime family friend, Mae Kasten; and Sam Derusha. I'd also like to thank business colleagues and associates Melissa Pendergrass (Parkridge Hosptial, Chattanooga), Rachel Oesch (former news anchor, WDEF-TV, Chattanooga), Jed Mescon (news anchor, WRCB-TV, Chattanooga), LaTrice Currie (news anchor, WRCB-TV, Chattanooga), Steve Porter (sports editor, *Alton Telegraph*), Dr. Christie Kleinmann (assistant professor, Lee University), and Carmen Garland (Murray State University). A special thanks to Mr. Palmer Solberg, who so kindly detailed his life growing up in the Wisconsin countryside.

I offer you all my sincere and heartfelt appreciation for your support and willingness to walk down this path with me.

CHAPTER 1
December 22

"Who is she, Jack? I have the right to know who you're sleeping with."

Cocooned in several layers of blankets, swaying hunkered in a rigged-up rope hammock powered by a restless fidget, Jack London Clarke stared wide-eyed into the darkened rafters of the century-old post-and-beam constructed barn, contemplating the demand hurled at him not two hours prior.

A sting sliced at his cheeks from biting December air skulking through weathered gaps in the aged windows and maple slats encasing the structure. He watched each exhale drift from his lips and the condensation streams flow from his nostrils, as they seemed to freeze in mid-air, before drifting into the abyss as solid, elongated masses. He imagined their density robust enough to carry him off to another place and time.

The night had been a total wash, none more than the last forty minutes. Desperate for sleep—if for a moment—he gazed about the barn, unable to erase from his conscience his wife's suspicions perpetuating the accusation. Arriving home just beyond the stroke of midnight, infused with alcohol following an evening out entertaining clients, his plans included avoiding her altogether.

An oversized leather couch in the den of their renovated 1800's farmhouse served as his designated "bed away from bed" when returning home late in the evenings, and in many ways, a preferred winter nesting spot courtesy of a large stone fireplace dominating the far wall. The room was comfortable and intimate, in a ski-lodge sort of way, and was a place he had little trouble falling fast asleep in rapid fashion. This night had been no different. In the reflection of flames bursting high into the chimney, he'd pulled a cover under his chin, maneuvered into a cozy position, and fell into a deep sleep before the count of ten.

"Who is she, Jack? I have the right to know who you're sleeping with."

Appearing out of the shadows of a far corner, his wife's voice sliced through the silence with such startling effect, he leaped from the couch, confused and disoriented, almost plunging headfirst into the firebox. The planned attack induced a confrontation lasting three hours, spilling into nearly every room in the home. Intense verbal insults and varying accusations ranging from infidelity to leaving the butter dish riddled with toast crumbs, kept the couple at each other's throats. Reaching a point in the argument where the mood was ripe for a physical action, Jack stormed from the house to the barn and the one corner on the ten-acre plot he knew to be private—a place reserved for lazy Saturday afternoons.

Dawn was approaching, but Jack was unsure of the exact time. Dredging through the recesses of his memory, he searched for the last time he pulled an all-nighter, determining it to be a little more than four years ago on a snowy November morning when his twin daughters entered the world. Had this been any other day, he'd be encased in cozy flannel sheets under a goose down cover awaiting the soft sounds of Chicago's premiere jazz station to introduce the morning at a more desirable hour. The mere thought of starting the day on an empty tank only heightened his anger, prompting an expletive as he wondered just what his wife was thinking picking a fight in the middle of the night.

Jack dragged his eyes across the barn toward two giant double doors guarding the entrance. One of several barn cats, enlisted for rodent duty, sat atop a beam grooming the head of a purring offspring. Coming to the realization he'd have a better chance getting rest in his private office downtown, he pulled the blankets from his body—keeping one draped over his shoulders—steadied the hammock, then slid off. A hot shower was sure to provide a much-needed burst of energy and relief to his stiff and frozen joints.

Jack entered the kitchen to an immediate and welcomed upgrade in temperature. Navigating the pitch-black space toward the staircase leading to the upper level, he felt his body loosen as the chill mini-mized with each step toward the center of the home. Moving up the stairs then down the long hallway past his daughters' bedrooms, he slipped into the sitting room adjacent the master suite, traveled a small hallway to the entrance of the bedroom, and peeked around the corner to view the bed. It was empty. Brooke had either assumed his vacated spot on the couch in the den or slipped into bed with the girls. No matter, the scenario pleased him as his intentions were set on getting out of the house before she woke.

His shower was brief. The soothing hot water erased the chill and improved the movement in his many worn-out joints, but did little for his lethargy or mood. Moving through the spacious master closet, he grabbed at matching articles on first sight to assemble a casual outfit to serve his needs for the light day ahead. A quick pit stop in front of a massive floor-to-ceiling seventeenth-century gilded French mirror allowed for a haphazard effort to construct the beginnings of a Windsor knot in his purple tie.

Working to the rear of the chamber, Jack eased onto an antique butler's chair and made quick work of tying the laces to a pair of black leather dress shoes. Still bent over, looking between his legs, he noticed his wallet and its contents scattered on the floor under the seat, a vivid reminder that he'd thrown his suit pants in the direction of the chair sometime near the two-hour mark of the couple's bout.

Jack filtered through the mess in search of his driver's license, which he located alongside a rumpled copy of his insurance card. Also under the heap lay two credit card-sized items bonded together by years of close quarters. Separating the two items revealed a miniature, laminated copy of his college diploma and a picture he'd long forgotten.

Bringing the image close rekindled its origin immediately. Snapped by their realtor on a sunny, June afternoon, Jack held his wife close, posing with a "sold" property sign just after they'd completed the necessary paperwork to take possession of the old farmhouse. The pleasing comfort of her smile and excitement in her eyes stirred regret for the current rift between them. If only she'd concentrate on her duties serving as a mother and housewife, and less time questioning the means by which he provided their comfort and luxury. He studied the photo, and his wife, as if seeing both for the first time.

Regardless of their current strife, her natural beauty confused and mesmerized him. He'd tossed many a woman aside like a worn sock and not thought twice about it; with Brooke, it was always different. She'd cast a spell he was unable to break. The photo brought to mind the first time he saw her sea-green eyes and the way she made him work for her attention. Maybe that was her device against him. Maybe it was the manner with which she carried herself, or the way she could not see the beauty or sensuality in her incredible features as others did.

He drew his stare to a stained-glass window at the opposite end of the closet, contemplating the couple's future. He preferred they stay together, knowing any lawyer with a two-year degree or GED would get for her everything he'd worked so hard to attain. He'd invested a great deal of time grooming her in the ways important to his career, among partners and clients alike, and dreaded the thought of breaking in a new trophy. But if Brooke chose to test him, which he doubted she'd have the guts or means to do, he'd adjust to the single life better than she.

Jack again brought the picture to near the end of his nose. Brooke's beauty was undeniable, so too the attention he gained when entering a crowded ballroom, theatre, or corporate outing with her dangling on his arm. Although pleased how others envied him based on her physical attraction, he knew she too could claim the same benefit.

She adored his 6'5", 255-pound frame—this he knew—as she referenced many times the thrill she felt tracing the chiseled curves of his chest, abs, and arms with her fingertips. He'd instructed her at all gatherings to mention his former status as an All-American linebacker in college—citing the tactic as nothing more than a way to break the ice with strangers. He knew Brooke craved his attraction, as did every woman who crossed his path. He could not deny his lust for the attention of other women, especially when it occurred in the presence of his wife.

A self-proclaimed gym rat, Jack flaunted his physique as a trophy earned through iron will rather than a natural evolution. He'd surrendered to the world of barbells, dumbbells, and medicine balls in the seventh grade, necessitated by a skinny and underdeveloped frame, playground bullies, and a father unable to handle his liquor. His intent to break free from the control of others drove him to the weight room three times a day, every day, resulting in granite-like forearms and biceps, and a muscular back and chest no business suit could disguise. His wife adored his features as much as he respected hers. He was confident the current tussle between them would blow over as all others had. There was no way she could find anyone better or more attractive, and he knew it.

Moving from the butler's chair, Jack tossed the picture on top of his dresser, stuffed the wallet in his back pocket, and grabbed his suit jacket from off a hanger. Proceeding to the master bath, he paused upon noticing the warm glow of a chandelier in the makeup nook bursting in brilliant colors through a half-moon stained glass window above the opening.

"What the hell is she doing up?" he whispered in anger.

Jack inched closer. The first sign of Brooke's presence appeared as a shadow drifting across the floor in front of the entryway.

The nook situated in a corner of the upstairs once served as an exam room for a prominent Chicago pediatrician who treated patients in the home until his death in 1929. The space was just one of many upgrades Jack insisted on in transforming the broken-down, humble estate into a showpiece to flaunt in the faces of coworkers and friends. Upon reviewing the final blueprints of the upstairs renovation, he recalled a conversation with his wife from their second or third date. After noticing a small scar above her left eye, he asked of its origin.

Brooke described sharing a small bathroom with her five younger sisters for the first fifteen years of her life before her parents added on to their farmhouse. She recounted the ongoing fights, including those resulting in the loss of blood and need for stitches, precipitated by the close quarters and lack of privacy. Her battle scar was the result of her sisters' gang justice, resulting in a deliberate shove off a vanity stool into the corner of a small glass shelf near the bathtub when they decided her allotted time had expired.

The extent to which Jack updated and modernized the nook resulted in a sanctuary any woman would envy—a perfect blend of sophistication, elegance, and practicality. The space also conjured a few surprises. On more than one occasion, the couple heard the disembodied whispers of a young girl asking for an aspirin, and visions of an apparition hovering in a white coat standing over the vanity as if attending a patient.

Regardless, Brooke never felt threatened and viewed the space as very special—not because she no longer needed to bloody her knuckles to apply a simple coat of lipstick, but because her husband redesigned the entire space due to a conversation he'd remembered and one she'd long forgotten. The gesture meant a great deal to her at the time, but those days were no more. Jack was no longer *that* man and the area was little more than a space where she could wipe her tears in private.

Brooke perched crumpled on a brass stool in front of the vanity, lost in the words spilled between the couple just hours before. Sheathed in a pink chiffon robe, she fought against the sinking feeling her marriage was on less than life support. Gazing into the depths of a pewter encased mirror, she waded through what remained of their unfinished confrontation, recalling the many regrettable accusations hurled by both. Her eyes were bloodshot and swollen around the edges. Had there been a need to call the police, her husband would have found it difficult to explain her appearance.

Feeling a flush building in his skin, Jack knew sweat was soon to follow, as was a darkened ring around the collar of his shirt. Intent on avoiding round two, he was determined to breeze through the bathroom without making eye contact or uttering a word.

The sound of leather dress shoes folding at the toe and moving at an exaggerated pace caught Brooke's attention. She scanned up the mirror just in time to catch the reverse image of her husband rushing past toward the master bedroom. Maintaining her stare of the blank wall behind, she closed her eyes and called his name. Her voice was hoarse, scratching out like nails against a chalkboard. Waiting for a reply, she heard his footsteps slow atop the hardwood floor. "Jack," she called out again in a much sharper tone. Although faint, she heard his steps complete an about-face.

Angry his plan had failed, Jack stopped short of the opening, clutching the mahogany molding encasing the arched frame. Dropping his head, he rolled his eyes and clenched his lower jaw into his upper with a crushing force. Rocking forward just past the threshold, he expelled an exaggerated sigh to let her know he was there.

Brooke re-engaged the mirror, spying the profile of the man she considered the most handsome she ever knew. Aware of Jack's aphrodisiac-like aura, Brooke was seldom shocked as to its effect on the women he encountered. She herself had succumbed to his wavy brown hair, chiseled jaw with just the right amount of stubble bristling against the surface, and his sculpted physique. She knew too the possibility of one day having to confront issues of his infidelity.

His was a look she could not blame other women for wanting. His rugged edge, highlighted by a long Roman nose scarred at its bridge and misaligned from a collision on the football field, befitted a fron-tiersman or professional bull rider rather than a six-figure public affairs and marketing president. Despite the attention he received from other women, Brooke was jelly in his arms and longed for the love they once knew. She wondered what had happened to those days.

She turned from the mirror. "I want to know her name. You owe it to me and I deserve to know."

Jack stood his ground and said nothing. It was obvious the several hours the two sparred had proved futile. She swung full to face him, crossing one leg over the other, expecting an answer. Jack dipped his head around the corner to meet her stare, noting a similar expression to the one he viewed a few months removed from their wedding when he mistakenly called her by the name of an ex-girlfriend.

Brooke's long hair, black as polished onyx stone and void the first strand of gray, flowed soft over her left shoulder. The light from the chandelier above worked in diabolical partnership with two wall sconces to highlight a deep rut in her cheek where the decorative ribbing of a couch pillow carbon copied itself.

With her flowered robe open at the chest, Jack followed the v-shape of her face along her slender neck, then to the deep and tight crevice between her perfect breasts. Despite being thirty-five and the mother of twin daughters, Brooke maintained the look of a woman ten years her junior—even on her worst day. As if he were a stranger, she drew her hand to the robe and closed the gap. Jack expelled a sarcastic huff, knowing if he wanted it, he could take it.

"I'm not talking about this anymore, Brooke," he said. "I'm done. We've been through this a thousand times and I'm just done with it."

"You owe me an explanation."

"We went through this last night—for more than three hours. I've had no sleep—none. I'm tired of arguing and I'm tired of your stupid paranoia. There's no reasoning with you . . . I'm done."

"You and I both know something's going on. I'm not stupid. I want the truth, and I want it now."

"I don't know who called the house," Jack said, closing his eyes and gritting his teeth. "I deal with a hundred clients every day. Maybe it was a wrong number. How the hell should I know?"

"A wrong number? Are you kidding me?" Brooke said, shaking her head. "Is that the best you can do? The same woman calls *my* home four times asking for you and when I ask who she is, she hangs up on me. Do you think I'm a complete idiot?"

"How would I know if you're a *complete* idiot," Jack said with a sarcastic grin. "I have no idea who she was or why she called *my* house, okay? Jesus, how many times do I have to repeat it?"

"I pulled your shirts for the dry cleaners yesterday and three of them were reeking of a perfume not belonging to me. Did you bring home the wrong shirts or did you just happen to roll around on your office floor with a couple of clients?"

"I'm around women all day long; hell, our office alone is seventy-five percent female—you know that. You also know many of my clients are female. I can't help that every woman I come in contact with doesn't wear your exact perfume. *I* have to work, or have you forgotten who is responsible for all this luxury? Look around you. Look at all I've done for you and these kids," he said, his voice raising. "Look at all the shit you have; all those clothes and shoes in your closet. Are you driving a minivan? No, you're driving a $50,000 Cadillac Escalade. Are those girls lacking anything? They have more shit than all the children on this side of town put together. You wanted a rustic home; I bought you a rustic home. You wanted a pool; I built you a damn pool."

"I didn't ask for any of this, or have you forgotten?" Brooke fired back. "I was happy with the house as we found it. I didn't ask you to convert it to a million dollar estate. You did that for you—for your image and ego."

Jack continued his rant over her words. "Anytime you want to visit your family, I buy you a plane ticket. Everything you've needed, I've given and given without griping. I even gave you two damn kids. Do you think we'd have all this shit if you were responsible for supporting this family? You think your job working with the retards would support all this? What the hell else do you want from me?"

"How dare you," Brooke yelled. "What's the matter with you? Those children, every one of them, came from abusive homes and you know it. They're not retarded. How could you say something so vile? And our children? Is that what you think of them?"

Jack rolled his eyes, wishing he'd spent the night in his office.

"Those girls adore you," Brooke continued. "They cry at night when they don't see you before they go to bed. They cry when you leave without telling them goodbye. In the evening, they run to the window every time they hear a car go by the house. They look for you when it storms outside. They want to spend time with you. You don't touch them or hold them. When you speak to them, seldom as it is, you say the most despicable things.

"Last week, Julianna asked me what a cocksucker was. I almost fell off my chair. I asked her where she heard that and she said, 'Daddy says it all the time.' I mean, for God's sake Jack, do you not even get how irresponsible that is? I've resigned myself to the fact that the vulgar manner in which you speak to me will never change, but the children? Do you have such little respect for them that they must endure that abuse as well? You act as if they're nothing but inanimate objects, laundry; something you treat as you please when you have the time and something I'm supposed to take care of as I would any other household chore. Well, I've got news for you, the girls are not a load of laundry you deal with once a week. They need both of us. Do you have any idea what you're doing to them?"

Brooke paused to catch her breath.

The girls were her life and the sole reminder she was of any worth. A month before their arrival, she resigned from her position with a local agency providing counseling services for abused children. The pregnancy consummated on their honeymoon in the Caribbean, and following two weeks of severe morning sickness, the couple scheduled an ultrasound to confirm their suspicions. It was not until later that another routine check revealed a second fetus. Brooke was carrying the eleventh set of twins in her family's history—at least as far back as they could trace.

The pregnancy went off with few complications. Jordan reached the finish line first, nosing out Julianna by a minute and-a-half on a cold, snowy November morning. It was the first time Brooke had ever noticed any semblance of tearing in her husband's eyes, although he did not cry. She never saw him cry, not even the day he buried his mother.

"If you remember," she reminded, "I asked for a home, not a mansion. I asked you to be a husband, not the richest man in town. I didn't ask for a pool for myself. I needed it so I could better help the kids I was working with. I didn't ask for the fancy clothes or the shoes. I wanted a minivan because it would be much easier to drive and move the girls around town. You purchased the Cadillac because your ego would not allow for anything less. You didn't give a darn that a van would be more practical. You need me to have these things so the world can see what you've made of your life. I'm nothing more than something you pull out on occasions to prove to everyone you've arrived."

"Hey," Jack yelled, pointing his finger toward her chin. "You don't lecture me. You got it? You do not lecture me. You are the wife and the mother. It's your responsibility and duty to take care of those kids and whatever I need you to do. You don't lecture me and you don't question me. You just do as I say. Do you understand that?"

Brooke shook her head and dropped her chin toward the floor. "You just don't get it." Her voice faded and her eyes welled. "The only thing I've ever wanted was a husband I could love and grow old with and a family I could nurture. How did you ever misinterpret that?"

Jack rolled his eyes as silence washed across the space. He turned his focus to a large stained-glass window at the opposite end of the bathroom. Brooke waited for any sign he'd take back his searing words.

"I want to know who she is," Brooke demanded. "You owe me that much."

"I don't know what you're talking about and I don't owe you a thing. If you don't like it here, and don't like this marriage or the luxury I provide, then pack your shit and get the hell out and grub off someone else. Is that clear enough for you?"

Brooke stood from her stool and lunged at his forearm. "I want to know who you're having an affair with," she yelled, digging in her nails.

Jack slung his arm upward and toward her in an attempt to break the grip. The force of his movement pushed her onto her heels and into the stool, causing a stumble into the vanity table behind. Wincing in pain as her lower back connected against the edge of the marble counter, Brooke fell to the floor, attempting to reach the point of impact with her left arm. Jack reached to offer his help; she slapped his hand away.

"Just go," she whispered. "Get out of here and leave me alone."

Hovering above, Jack paused, shook his head, then exploded out of the room, burying a palm into the wall as he exited. The collision punctured the drywall, creating a crater the size of a softball, and sending a picture on the opposite side crashing to the hardwood below. Storming through the bedroom and adjacent sitting room, he slammed the door leading into the hallway.

Hunkered in a fetal position, crumpled on the floor, Brooke waited for the pain in her back to subside. The pain in her heart was much worse. Face down in a growing puddle of tears, she asked God why the only man she ever loved did not love her anymore.

CHAPTER 2

Jack stomped down the hallway, rubbing his palm and cussing under his breath. The aroma of fresh-brewed coffee drifting from the kitchen corralled his senses, dispelling his concern for his wife's condition. Disrupted by thoughts of their verbal exchange, he breezed past his daughters' bedrooms, oblivious to the fact they'd be leaving with their mother later in the day to visit their grandparents for Christmas.

He'd made a habit of checking on them as he left for the office the first year or so of their lives, but his ascension to the position of president of the firm's marketing division rendered that brief tradition a waste of valuable time. Upon reaching the landing at the bottom of the stairs, he descended the four remaining steps into the pitch-black kitchen, and with a final stride, caught the tip of the tail of the family's pet beagle, Peetie. The rescued vagabond yelped, sending Jack to his knees atop the frigid cobblestone floor. The dog scurried for the nearest corner where he buried his head. Returning upright, Jack flipped the kitchen switch, all the while cussing the beast for not having sense to move out of the way.

He hated the dog and the dog feared him. The mere sound of Jack's voice sent the animal racing out of whatever room in search of cover. Jack watched the dog quivering in the corner, shaking his head at the pathetic display.

"You piece of shit coward," he mumbled under his breath, before continuing toward a bistro-style coffee maker at the far end of the kitchen.

Jack's morning routine was now in a shambles. Bending low before a large, stainless steel coffee pot, he completed the final adjustments to his tie. Tracking his thick, scarred, but well-manicured fingers in the reflection of the steel, he made a quick repair before sliding the Windsor knot into its proper position against the pressed and starched lime-colored shirt. A flip of his collar and a final adjustment to a leather belt around his trim waist completed the sequence. Wide-awake, half-asleep, pissed off, or happy as a circus clown, the handsome thirty-eight-year-old father of two paused, as he did every morning, to digest the perfection of his own reflection. Cocking his head, he took one last look, concluding nothing more could improve the product.

Searching the countertop, a new wave of annoyance reddened his neck as he realized Brooke had failed to remember his clear instructions that his coffee mug be at the ready every morning, without exception. With an angered flip, he slung open a cabinet above the coffee machine in search of anything insulated. Lost in a world of tumblers and kiddie sippers, he fumbled through the unorganized mess, knocking several to the floor.

The ruckus of plastic flipping and flopping off cobblestone impeded Jack's auditory senses just enough that he did not absorb the chime of the home's doorbell. With cups coming to rest near his feet, the second chime caught his attention. As if poked with a stick, he jerked from inside the cabinet and shot a look toward the front entryway. Slamming the cabinet shut, he stepped at an exaggerated pace, reciting in his head the barb-laced greeting he was planning for the unwanted guest.

Stepping into the large foyer modeled after a sixteenth-century rotunda, he patted along the wall in search of the light switch as the visitor depressed the button a third time.

"All right, wait a second . . . Jesus."

A flip of a switch brought both foyer and porch into full illumination. Jack released the deadbolt and opened the heavy, sprawling door to an avalanche of frigid air. Its advance tore at him like an unsuspecting punch in the face, stinging the tips of his ears and nose. The landscape remained covered in the dark of pre-dawn, apart from a slight hint of purple hue nudging just above the eastern horizon. All was quiet.

Fighting through the wall of winter air, Jack diverted his attention to the intruder, a most peculiar looking fellow, standing erect atop the last step leading to the stone porch as if awaiting inspection. Preparing to fire an opening salvo, Jack took one look north to south then lost his train of thought. His strategic, explosive response expelled from his mouth as a harmless cloud of white condensation.

The squatty, egg-shaped old man struggled to focus through a thick patch of un-groomed eyebrows and wire-rimmed spectacles, looking as if they'd been mangled and bent back to shape. Ink-black pupils peered through half-fogged lenses cut from glass a quarter-inch thick. A wide, clownish smile revealed a mouth jam-packed with horse-sized yellowed teeth, framed by an unkept beard falling low below the chin. Wind-burned cheeks, expanded by the stretch of his grin, revealed deep canyons of wrinkles; a crimson-colored bulbous nose suggested this was a man who knew his way around a bar and a bottle. An imprint of an animal's hoof appeared as a dent on the left side of his face.

If he wasn't a hundred years old, then he was a scientific anomaly. Jack scanned him from head to toe. A black fedora cap two sizes too small perched tilted atop a pumpkin-sized head. He'd wrapped some sort of homemade earmuff contraption around the side of his head, covering less than half of two giant ears, one of which hung lower than the other. A plaid scarf wrapped so tight and so many times around his neck prohibited any natural movement from left to right. A heavy, unbuttoned wool coat covered a gray fisherman's sweater and bright red-and-white-striped suspenders were clipped to a pair of baggy, plaid knickers. Heavy wool socks merged with black leather shoes complete with pilgrim-like brass buckles, which finalized the uncoordinated ensemble resembling what one could order from a turn-of-the-century Sears and Roebuck catalog. The old man was either unmarried or widowed, because no woman would let him walk out of the house looking like that.

Jack concluded the old man had escaped from a mental ward or Santa's workshop. Regardless, he was not amused. Thinking it possible he was the butt end of someone's joke, he scanned his property in search of a van housing a hidden camera. He found nothing out of the ordinary.

"Is there something I can do for you, Mister?" Jack asked, his expression dripping with disbelief.

The intruder held a small postcard an inch from his face. Squinting, he asked in a slow, country drawl, "Is this the residence of Mr. and Mrs. Jack Clarke?"

"Yeah, what can I do for you?"

"What'd ya say?" the old man asked, extending his head forward, placing a gloved hand to his ear.

"Yes, this is the Clarke residence," Jack insisted, increasing the amplification. "What can I do for you?"

"Well," the old man began, "am I addressing Mr. or Mrs. Clarke?"

The words just passed his lips before the man cut loose a gut-busting laugh that bent him over at the waist and onto the backs of his heels. Jack crossed his arms and remained in an idle position as the old man teetered on the steps enjoying what he perceived as the funniest one-liner ever delivered.

Responding through the belly laughter, Jack identified himself as Mr. Clarke. Unsure if the man heard his response, he took advantage to survey the neighborhood a second time. Waiting in the frigid morning air, he endured the sporadic laughter before the man removed his cap and slapped it against his thigh.

"I'm sorry, Mr. Clarke. It's just a little joke I like to play with my customers. It gets me every time."

"Yeah, that's funny—well done."

"Wha'd ya say?" the man asked, squinting as if Jack had disappeared.

"I'm right here," Jack said. "I said it's funny . . . your joke was real funny. Why are you ringing my doorbell at six in the morning?"

The man steadied his body by grabbing at an iron baluster framing the steps. He replaced his cap and pulled himself up onto the porch.

"Well, Mr. Clarke, my name is Jubel Bigsby, of the Cartersville Bigsbys, and I work for the McClellan Delivery Service. I have a delivery for—"

"Cartersville Bigsbys?" Jack interrupted.

"What?" the old man asked, looking well to Jack's right.

"The Cartersville Bigsbys?" Jack repeated at a pitch sure to bring his neighbors across the street scurrying to their window. "Is that what you said?"

"Yes, sir, Cartersville," Bigsby replied, drawling out the "y" as if not wanting to let it go. The old man paused and cocked his head.

"Wha'd ya say?"

"What?" Jack questioned, looking as confused as the old man.

The man shrugged. "As I was saying, Mr. Clarke, I am—"

Jack tapped him on the shoulder. Bending close, fighting through an overwhelming odor of gorgonzola and horse manure, he caught the man's attention and asked in a loud and clear tone, "Could you take off the thing you have wrapped around your ears?"

Bigsby flashed a blank stare, gave a nod and pulled the homemade contraption over his head, knocking his hat to the ground. Jack recoiled as the man retrieved his cap. Returning upright with hat in hand, Bigsby reached for one of the columns supporting the porch roof and flashed an elfish grin after forgetting where he'd left off.

"Where was I?" he said to himself. "Oh . . . Well, Mr. Clarke," he said, pausing to mumble how much better he could hear, "my name is Jubel Bigsby, of the Cartersville Bigsbys, and I'm an employee of the McClellan Delivery Service. I have a delivery for you and the missus."

"I've never heard of the McClellan Delivery Service," Jack said.

"Well, we're a small outfit operating north and northwest of here, but I can vouch for the company. Been with 'em plenty of years now. We started out on horseback but have upgraded somewhat since. I enjoy delivering packages and letters, especially around the holiday season because—"

Jack interrupted what was sure to be a fascinating narrative, "Who sent the delivery? Where did it come from?"

Bigsby paused to allow his mind to recuperate from the several words he'd strung together and to catch up with his customer's latest request.

"Well, I'm sure I don't know that. It was sent anominally."

"What?" Jack asked.

"What?" Bigsby replied.

"Do you mean anonymously?"

"Well, if that means the sender wanted to keep it a secret, then yes."

"Was there any identification inside the envelope?"

"Well, ya see, if we open a letter or a package on the way to a delivery, we can get in a might bit of trouble. That sorta thing is frowned upon by my employer, the McClellan Delivery Service. I did it once and swore I'd never do it again; almost got relieved of my duties. I was just startin' out, ya see, and this feller, who was a good bit older, dared me to open this letter. Now my mother," Bigsby explained without taking a breath, "who was as saintly a woman as the good Lord ever put on this earth, taught me to mind my own business and abstain from inafearin' in the affairs of others. Well, that letter was sprayed with the sweetest smellin' sauce you ever did put a nose to, and we assumed it came from this feller's girlfriend, or something like that, because we happened to know he was married. And, oh, I guess I'd had too much to drink and was feelin' a bit sprite so I . . ."

"Mr. Bigsby?" Jack interrupted, extending an index finger near the man's face. Bigsby rambled on several moments before allowing his words to fade. "Can you please just hand over whatever it is you were sent to deliver? I'm in a pretty big hurry."

"Of course, Mr. Clarke," he said, annoyed his customer did not appreciate a good story.

Smiling in a way suggesting annoyance, he removed the glove from his hand, one finger at a time, all the while maintaining direct eye contact. Unsnapping the flap of a large and beat-to-hell leather satchel, he buried his entire arm, to the shoulder, into its depths where he fumbled for something near the bottom. His hand reappeared holding two envelopes, one much larger than the other.

"As I was sayin', Mr. Clarke, I was sent by my employer, the McClellan Delivery Service, to deliver these," he said, raising his stubby arms above his head, waving as if in possession of a winning lottery ticket.

"The small one's for you and the larger one is intended for the missus. That'll be six bits please." He dropped his arm, extended the envelopes toward his customer, and just as Jack reached in receipt, yanked them from his fingertips.

"Well, I don't know how y'all do things 'round these parts, but I'm obligated by my employer, the McClellan Delivery Service, to receive all monies in advance before handing over any products or parcels—that's the rule. Six bits please."

"Six what? What do I owe you?"

"That'll be six bits, please."

"What the hell is six bits?"

"That's what you owe the McClellan Delivery Service. We're not a free service. My employer would not be around long if that were the case. Ya see, if I don't collect, it could cause . . ."

Jack sighed. "I know you're not a free service. How much money is six bits?"

"Well, that's mighty peculiar," the old man said scratching the side of his head. "Where I come from, it's no more than seventy-five cents."

"What?" Jack asked, shaking his head.

"What?" Bigsby returned.

"Did you say seventy-five cents . . . for a home delivery?"

"No more than seventy-five cents," Bigsby corrected.

"Who charges seventy-five cents for a home delivery for Christ's sake?"

"Now, now there young fella," he said, waving a finger. "Don't be using the Lord's name. You're in enough trouble already."

"How can you charge just seventy-five cents?"

"Well, I don't charge that money myself. My employer, the McClellan Delivery Service, charges that money and I get paid out of the total profits at the end of the week. We've raised our rates a might but that's because things are so much more expensive these days. Ya see, how it works is, I deliver the packages and collect what my employer instructs me. Then, I take that money back to the station. It's all based on a system our forefathers—"

"I get it, okay? I get it," Jack said. "I don't understand how a home delivery could cost just seventy-five cents in this day and age. You people could put FedEx out of business."

"Who?" the old man asked.

"F-E-D-E-X. FedEx," Jack said.

"Well, I'm not familiar with them. Are they a local bunch? Did they start on horseback, too?"

"You've never heard of FedEx? How's that possible if you're in the delivery business? They deliver by trucks and planes?"

Bigsby offered a blank look as he scratched at the side of his head.

"Well, no sir, can't say I've heard of 'em, although I'm not used to these parts. You remember my employer, the McClellan Delivery Service, operates north and northwest of here. I heard some recent talk of a plane though, now where was that?" he said, looking down, tickling at his beard. "Somebody told me something about a plane; now who could have—"

"Mr. Bigsby, can you please just—"

"I know," Bigsby yelled, raising a finger, surprising Jack onto the backs of his heels. "This feller was putting on some sort of show near a corn field on the outskirts of this small town back home— Cumberland—and, well, something went wrong because that poor feller flew that dern thing right into this farmer's barn. Well, I don't have to tell you the hullabaloo it caused. Horses and cows, all of 'em, scattered all over the county, and well, the wife of the fella flying the plane was said to be having a little side deal with—"

"Mr. Bigsby," Jack said, snapping an arm toward the old man, "FedEx happens to deliver packages worldwide. They're everywhere."

"I see. Worldwide . . . hmmm," the old man mumbled, readjusting his lopsided spectacles and not buying for one second this FedEx outfit was bigger than his McClellan company.

Bigsby stood before him, smiling and rocking back and forth on his heels. Shaking his head, Jack reached into his pocket, plucked a crisp dollar bill from a gold money clip and passed the currency on to his agitator, receiving the envelopes in the exchange.

"Keep the change," Jack mumbled.

Bigsby accepted the currency, drawing it close to his face for inspection. He dispensed an exaggerated "Hmmm."

Jack peered over his shoulder. "Is there a problem?"

"Well, it's just about the strangest dollar I've ever seen," he said.

"What are you talking about?"

"I mean," Bigsby said, looking over the top of his spectacles as if scolding, "it sure doesn't look like any dollar bill I've ever seen." The old man reached into his pocket and pulled out a wad of very old looking currency. He fumbled through the bills, dropping several to the stone pavers below, before pulling out a dollar from the mess. "You see?" he said waving the currency in Jack's face, "there's an awful big difference."

Jack snatched the bill from the old man's hands. There was no question the bills were different. The design was unlike anything he'd seen before. The words "silver certificate" appeared in thick black print at the very top, as opposed to the "federal reserve" note script he was accustomed to seeing. It was puzzling, no question.

"Where did you get this?" Jack asked.

"Well, I'm not sure . . . must've picked it up yesterday in Clear Lake," he said.

"I don't understand. What do you mean Clear Lake? Where the hell's Clear Lake?"

"Clear Lake's a pretty fair distance from here," he continued, "north of course because, as you know, I am employed by the McClellan Delivery Service and we operate north and northwest of here. But I was in Clear Lake yesterday morning before heading this way and I'm pretty sure it's still there. It's a nice little town, sittin' real close to one of the best fishin' holes you ever dropped a bobber in. Do you like to fish, Mr. Clarke? Well, I just can't get enough of it. My mother told me I should a been a—"

Jack rolled his eyes as the old man rambled on. He wondered why the man had this money. None of it was adding up. Jack passed the ancient currency back into Bigsby's hand as the old man finished the conversation with himself.

"I'm sorry, Mr. Bigsby," Jack interrupted, "that's the only dollar I have."

"Well, okay, Mr. Clarke. If my employer, the McClellan Delivery Service, has a problem with this sort of money, I know where you live. By the way, here's your change," he said holding a coin Jack didn't recognize, and at the moment, didn't care to accept.

"Keep it," he said, turning for the front door.

"Well, thank you very much, Mr. Clarke. I'll be able to buy myself a sliver of cheese for dinner—maybe."

Jack shook his head and snarled his lip at the man's insinuation. Bigsby was sucking mental energy at an alarming rate and Jack could ill-afford a battle of wits. The old man offered a tip of his fedora, reattached the homemade earmuffs and stuffed the currency into the pocket of his knickers.

"Merry Christmas, Mr. Clarke," Bigsby said, stepping off the porch.

Jack watched over his shoulder as the man's fedora disappeared below the top step of stairs leading to the road. Re-entering the home with envelopes in hand, Jack felt the entire, bizarre exchange a bad episode of a soon-to-be-cancelled reality show. If this was a prank, someone had gone to great lengths to make it an elaborate one. Jack retraced his steps to the kitchen, so immersed in contemplation he forgot to shut the front door behind him.

A sharp, analytical thinker, he possessed an uncanny ability to make sound, accurate decisions with little or no warning or supporting background information. His ability to assess and decipher with precision—whether it be data, a perplexity, or a fellow human being—was deadlier than a special ops sniper from two feet away. It was this ability he rode to the very top of his industry.

Although many questioned his methodologies and ethics, Jack's tactics were hailed as cutting edge. He operated with an arrogance that, to the naked and unsuspecting eye, implied extreme confidence, passion, and a competitive drive. The attitude was a well thought-out strategy he spawned at a young age to compensate for a childhood marred with scars from being bullied and compromised by those he trusted most. His arrogance also was his weapon of choice for control-ling situations, circumstances, and those around him—including his wife. Coupled with his intimidating physical presence and handsome attributes, few held the necessary tools or mental capacity to challenge him head-on.

His most reliable attribute was failing him now. He struggled to connect the dots produced by the encounter. Nearing the kitchen table, an unlikely cry coming from the front of the house interrupted his assessment. It sounded first like a dog in distress. Still, he froze in his tracks and readjusted his head to assist in the identification process. Seconds later, the sound erupted again. It was no dog.

"That sounds like a damn horse," he whispered. Scurrying toward a large bay window framing the front of the property, Jack surveyed the street, now more visible in the budding sunlight. Scanning east toward the horizon, where the road cut into a soft curve fronting a steep embankment draped with 100-year-old oak trees, he could not believe the sight near the turn.

"What the hell?"

There sat Bigsby, with reigns in hand and a quilt blanket draped over his legs, perched atop a large wooden-wheeled carriage being towed down the street by two mammoth, white draft horses. The vehicle appeared a cross between an old "B" movie western stage and a royal carriage from jolly ole' England, with rear spoke wheels twice the size of the set in front, and a curved belly dragging close to the ground. Three open windows stretched along each side.

Jack let the envelopes slip to the cobblestone floor below. He tracked the giant team with mouth open as they pulled Bigsby around the bend and out of sight.

"What the hell is going on here? Who the hell is this guy?"

<hr />

Retrieving the envelopes, and without thinking, Jack tossed Brooke's envelope atop a pile of magazines and mail on the kitchen table and the other into his open briefcase on the island in the center of the room. Slamming the case shut, he grabbed his suit jacket off the kitchen counter before slashing through a door leading to a three-car garage. He was going to get some answers even if it meant chasing the old nut and his ponies down the street, out of the community and into downtown Chicago.

He raced across the garage, dodging Brooke's Escalade while guarding his step atop the uneven cobblestone underfoot. Tossing the coat and briefcase into the passenger side of his silver Hummer, he hopped in and set off in pursuit—failing to close the garage door.

Following the road around a sharp bend, he swung a hard right toward the main road. With no side streets branching off the half-mile winding shot, Bigsby would be easy to spot. Zigzagging down the tar and chipped pavement, guarded by mature elm and chestnut trees on either side, he passed through a short S-curve before the road straightened out, making visible the last quarter mile to the main road. He did not see a carriage in sight.

Racing to the end of the straightaway, Jack slammed on the brakes in time to pull behind a stone and brick shack housing the security company hired to protect the private lives of the entitled residents of Ridgeway Estates. He set the Hummer in park and jumped out.

The security guard on duty had just returned to his desk from raiding a small refrigerator under the cabinet in the kitchenette. With a two-day-old cherry-filled pastry in one hand and a steaming hot cup of black tar in the other, he settled in with his *Tribune*, easing the hot mug to his lips for a quick sip. He failed to notice the monitor to his right revealing a parked car behind the shack.

Just as the shot of hot brewed caffeine passed his lips, a hard rap on the Plexiglas window to the left startled the chubby rent-a-cop into spilling the liquid down the front of his fake policeman's uniform. The guard hopped from his chair as if on fire, swiping at the spill. Recognizing the familiar face, he whipped open the window.

"Good morning, Mr. Clarke. You're up early today. Is everything okay?" the man asked, brushing at his sleeve.

"Yeah, I'm fine; sorry about the coffee."

"No problem. I guess my wife can get the stain out. I'm sure you've probably heard she's having a bout with cancer right now."

"Well, we all have our own little problems, don't we," Jack replied.

"Yes, sir, I guess we do," he replied, dropping his head.

Jack knew the guards worked the residents to improve their bottom line around the holidays. Christmas bonuses were nearing and this particular guard was the worst of the bunch. It disgusted him the man would use his wife as a tool for profit.

"Did you happen to see an old man in a horse-drawn—" Jack stopped in mid-sentence; he hoped he'd done so in time.

The guard paused in mid-stroke of wiping, shooting a funny look. "What did you say, Mr. Clarke, a horse-drawn what?"

So focused was he in his search for answers, Jack had given little thought as to how that would sound coming from his mouth. He was now reminded of the many women in the community who stopped by to yap with the guards on their way in and out in hopes of obtaining information for later use. This particular guard could not be trusted with information. Jack rephrased the question.

"Has anyone passed through the gate this morning?"

"Not that I'm aware of. I just clocked in fifteen minutes ago. If you'll give me a second, I'll look at the sheet from the night shift."

"I'd appreciate it," Jack said, scanning the road back in the direction of his home in hopes of spotting the rig.

The guard pulled a clipboard off the wall and reviewed its contents. He scanned the list from the top, shaking his head as he neared the bottom.

"No sir, Mr. Clarke," he said from across the room, "no non-resident has passed through this gate in the past twenty-four hours." He moved to the window, catching Jack gazing down the road.

"Is there something wrong, Mr. Clarke? You look upset."

"No, no, nothing's wrong. I was expecting a delivery and was hoping to get it before leaving for the office. You sure nothing's passed here?"

"I just saw one car exit."

"Alright," Jack said, turning from the window.

"Sorry, Mr. Clarke," the man said, poking his Charlie Brown-sized head through the open window. "You have a great day now. If there's anything I can do for you, anything at all, you just let me know. 'Ole Nelson will take care of it."

"Save it, asshole," Jack muttered under his breath.

He slipped back inside the purring Hummer and swung the vehicle around. Scanning the scenery in all directions, he searched for any sign of Bigsby. Following the road swinging behind his property, he combed every field and side road, keeping a keen eye. Following thirty minutes of chasing the wind, he conceded. The old man had vanished.

Jack pulled the Hummer to the side of the road and thrust the gearshift into park. He slammed his palms against the steering column and yelled at the top of his lungs, "Sonuvabitch!"

Staring out the windshield, he replayed as many parts of the conversation with the old man as he could recall, searching his memory for a potential clue. The inability to have control over the circumstance was building toward a crescendo, challenging his vile temper. The echo of his curse moments before seemed to linger in the car without end. The slur resonated in his head, propelling a strange sensation that something was on the verge of breaking through to the forefront of his mind. It was right there on the tip, ready to bubble forth, but he just couldn't draw it out. Seconds later, a flashback hit him.

Recalling saying "Jesus Christ," "Jesus," or something similar during their conversation, he recalled the old man scolding him. Jack kept searching for the exact dialogue and dug out of the mish-mash Bigsby alluding he was "in enough trouble already." The recollection sent a chill to his bone as he sat contemplating just what the old man meant. Now his anger faded. His chest grew heavy, as he no longer considered the exchange a prank.

Confused by information now passing through his mind at warp speed, Jack realized that the most important piece of information was sitting not two feet from his current position. With both hands clamped tight to the steering wheel, the image of the envelope flashed before him, sending his stare toward the passenger seat and the black briefcase Brooke had purchased for his last birthday. Recalling he tossed the envelope into the case on the way out of the kitchen, he disengaged the two brass clips, revealing the faded and tattered envelope resting atop his company's quarterly report.

Covered with visible marks, scars, various postal stamps, and lacking a mailing address, the package appeared to have been on the hunt for its rightful owner for decades. He drew the envelope close, noticing a strange, musty smell. Wedging a finger under the flap, he sliced a rut down its length. The paper disintegrated with his stroke, sending tiny shards of aged stock floating to the leather seats and floorboard below.

Peeking through the slit, he discovered a folded piece of paper no bigger than an index card. The faded, pink slip was thin, of velum quality and appeared antique-like. Jack pulled at the piece, and despite its desire to remain bonded, coaxed the paper to separate. Upon spreading it open, he noticed the words 'Western Union' and 'telegram' centered at the top and printed in thick black script type above and below a circular logo in the shape of a black globe—complete with visible longitude and latitude lines. The header included the names 'Newcomb Carlton, president' and 'George W. E. Atkins, first vice-president.' On the upper left-hand corner, he noticed a form number: 1024.

The first line of the telegram underneath the logo displayed an apparent code of letters and numbers, with just the "X" and "B" identifiable. The next line revealed Western Union Station 66 in New Auburn received the telegram, but the state abbreviation was illegible. The type in the body was broken, with some characters smudged beyond recognition. The paper also had suffered severe water damage or staining from some unknown agent. He read aloud, making sure of each word.

```
MR JACK L. CLARKE=
1794 M-P-E ACR-S DRIVE    OAK BR-OK    IL-=

YOU MU-T ASCEN- -TAIRWAY   STOP

-OOR TO LEFT IS WH-RE SHE LAYS   ST-
```

```
I  AM  NOT  THE-E      S-P

TH-Y  HAVE  BE-N  CAL--D  BUT  SHE  M-ST  REMAIN      S--

N--T      -E-IV-RY    -O-A-    A-    2  P-

URGENT    STO-

MOD  =  DEC21-450PM-1923
```

"1923? What the hell? This is crazy."

The words floated from his lips in a confused whisper. Jack re-read the note, straining to make certain he was reading exactly what visible text displayed. The fifth line revealed the least. He thought he saw a '2' and a 'P,' but was not sure of that.

"Who the hell is M.O.D.?" Jack recited names of people he knew who might match those initials. "1923? This has to be a mistake."

A chill rippled atop his skin. He'd hoped for an explanation, not another undecipherable twist. He scanned the message again in search of anything that might make sense. How could a telegram with his name on it be dated 1923?

"There's got to be a good explanation for this. Jack and Clarke are common names. This is just a coincidence," he tempered.

Tossing the telegram to the passenger seat, he glanced to the rear view mirror. He looked like hell, felt like hell and contemplated for the first time in his professional life calling in sick.

But where would you go, he wondered. He could not return home, and spending the day at the club amongst those only concerned with the approaching Christmas holiday was not an option. He had but one choice.

His downtown office was his only safe haven and a place he could enlist the aid of the one person who could make sense of this senseless situation.

Guiding the Hummer to a clean pivot, Jack backtracked, scouring each street and offshoot for any signs of the phantom carriage. Blowing past the guard shack and onto the main road, he set his sights on the forty-five minute commute to Chicago's famed Magnificent Mile, contemplating how he could explain the first second of the last two hours.

CHAPTER 3

Soon after her husband had fled the room, Brooke fell into a deep sleep, curled in a ball on the carpet just inches from a visible stain where her tears had pooled. Resting half-naked atop a mound of her own hair, the slumber fell upon her due more to the lingering effects of the clinical depression she'd battled for months, rather than the strain of another argument with her husband.

A frigid, biting breeze creeping into the space sent a rush of goose bumps ruffling over her legs and chest. Her eyes shot open. Clearing the cobwebs, Brooke moved her fingers over her chest while gaining comprehension as to her position on the floor. Lifting herself up to gather her bearings, she extended an arm to move into an upright position. Her circumstance was made clear by the sharp, stabbing pain in her back. The recollection of the exchange with Jack flooded her senses.

This was not the first time an argument between the two resulted in a physical action. Jack's temper served him well between the lines of competition but not so much in their marriage. Less than a month following the birth of their daughters, the two sparred over a dress he'd demanded she wear to a cocktail party.

The black, backless petite silk gown cut down the front in a v-shape slitting to the naval, exposed half of each of her breasts and created a cleavage crease visible from every angle. Jack loved her streamlines and sculpted curves, even telling her once her figure could drive men to war. When Brooke refused her husband's demand, she paid with a sharp backhand to the mouth and spent the rest of the night alone with an ice bag over her bloodied and swollen lip. In the wee hours of the next morning, she packed a suitcase and left for her parents' farm.

Brooke reconciled only after Jack promised he'd enter an anger management program—which he did—then quit following the first session. Returning against her father's wishes created a deep and ongoing rift between her family and her husband.

Brooke secured a grip on the countertop then eased onto the vanity stool. Swiveling toward the mirror, she stretched her hips from side to side, experimenting with the stability of her lower back, before maneuvering her pelvis inward toward the vanity, arching and stretching in cat-like fashion. To her relief, there was little discomfort. *Just a deep bruise,* she thought.

Spreading and stretching her fingers, she ran both hands through the length of her hair, clearing the velvet-like strands from around her face before redirecting them to the center of her back. Graying skin and deepening wrinkles reflected the stress and exhaustion created by the couple's worsening circumstance.

Her despair reached a new plateau during the sleepless night, as thoughts of suicide and the manner with which she could accomplish the deed flashed through her mind. At one point, not long after her husband stormed from their home, she settled on the edge of their bed holding his pistol. Knowing it was kept loaded she released the safety and brought the piece against her temple. With her finger on the trigger and her hand shaking, she began to sob at the thought of her two most prized possessions having to carry on alone.

Brooke soon returned the pistol to its safety box, knowing she could never leave her daughters with a man who loved them less than he loved her. She spent the next hour buried in a wad of Kleenex reconciling her life and marriage. Remembering her father's words that no man willing to cheat on his wife was worth the salt of a single tear, she vowed if it was another woman Jack wanted, another woman he could have. But it would not come at the cost of her babies.

Unable to tolerate the cool air nipping at her calves any longer, Brooke lifted off the stool intent on finding the source of the cool air invading the home. The chill grew upon entering the master bedroom, feeling as if the temperature was dropping with each step toward the hallway. The thermostat displayed 59 degrees. The furnace was running.

Brooke rushed across the hardwood to the large stone fireplace engulfing the opposite wall. She pressed a button embedded in the stone, popping the firebox to life and sending a wave of welcomed heat infiltrating into the frigid space. Cozying up to the opening, with arms extended, she absorbed the heat into the palms of her hands. The urge was strong to climb into the large maple rocker near the hearth were she read her girls their bedtime stories, but she knew once settled, sleep would soon follow and there was just too much to do before their departure to her parents' home for the holiday.

Securing her robe, she entered into the hallway, easing across the old hardwood slats to minimize their creaking. Pausing near the end of the run, she stopped to check in on the girls, certain they were nestled together in the same bed. Like clockwork, one would sneak into the other's room sometime after midnight, where they'd spend a few moments giggling before falling fast asleep. Brooke peeked in the first door on the right, finding Julianna's bed empty. Moving one door down, she smiled at the sight of her two angels sleeping back-to-back, dead to the world.

Descending the hall staircase, startled at seeing her own breath, Brooke turned at the landing and noticed the many plastic cups and mugs scattered over the kitchen floor, and the door to the garage pulled wide open. Scurrying across the cobblestone, she pushed on the door to close it but felt a strong pressure pushing from the other side. Poking her head beyond the threshold, she gasped at the sight of the center garage door wide open. She depressed the button to close. Knowing her husband was upset, concern took hold as she wondered what would cause him to bolt in such haste that he'd leave the home unsecured. Although nothing he did surprised her any longer, this was out of character, no matter his mood. While correcting Jack's miscues, she registered Peetie's absence.

"Peetie," Brooke called. "Where are you boy?" When he did not respond, she conducted a quick search of the garage, mudroom, and laundry room; she saw no sign of him. Knowing the dog could hear food hitting the bottom of his bowl from the farthest reaches of the home, she sprinkled a few chunks of food from well above the bowl, ensuring optimal reverberation. She peeked around the corner and into the kitchen, calling out his name again when the dog did not appear.

"Peter, where are you?" As the echo of her voice died out, she caught the faint, familiar jingle of his collar. Waiting and watching, she dropped the cup of food from her hands, surprised at seeing him enter from the direction of the front door and foyer.

"What in the world?"

Brooke emptied the remaining three-quarter cup of food into the bowl. Sidestepping Peetie as he rushed into the room to bury his nose, she scampered toward the foyer.

"God, Jack," she yelled, stabbing for the doorknob. "What in the world were you thinking?"

Engaging the deadbolt, now convinced something was terribly wrong, Brooke's natural concern for her family sent her rushing to the phone in the kitchen. Grabbing the receiver, she punched in the first three numbers of her husband's cell phone before stopping mid-stroke of punching the fourth. No matter how much it hurt, no matter how much she wanted to know he was safe, he'd have to deal with whatever issue he was facing on his own. Right or wrong, she could not be there for him any longer. She dropped the receiver atop the cradle, absorbing guilt she knew did not belong on her shoulders.

Moving to the opposite side of the room, collecting a spoon as she passed the kitchen island, she poured herself a cup of coffee, staring at the whirlpool forming as she stirred in heavy cream. She hated the life she was living, and for the first time, realized the gap between the life she was living and the life she'd dreamed of as a little girl might never be reconciled. She thought of the many tears shed for a man she no longer recognized and a relationship she knew was on the brink.

Brooke ached over the devastation Jack's behavior was having on the girls' fragile and impressionable minds and the relationship she was certain he was having outside the marriage. His indifference at placing his daughters in the middle of the most horrible of circumstances was more than she could stand, and the distance he was creating—whether on purpose or by a change of heart—painted a scenario for which she could draw but one conclusion: his love for her and the life they shared was over.

A cold paw to the back of the leg extracted Brooke from the depths of her coffee cup. Bending toward Peetie, she dealt a soft pat atop his head and a quick rub behind an ear. Moving to the landing, she set in motion the mental inventory of the things needing completion before their journey. There would be no flight out of O'Hare today.

Brooke exited the kitchen, paying no attention to the aged manila envelope sitting on top of a stack of mail with her named scribbled in pencil. Calling her trusted friend to follow, she headed up the stairs with Peetie on her heels to begin the painstaking task of packing for a one-way trip.

CHAPTER 4

Jack was pleased to find the section of the underground parking garage reserved for upper management at Morgando, Rossi, and Associates all but empty.

The miserable commute only added to his already scrambled morning, thanks to some poor slob in a Maserati finding it reasonable to change lanes by passing underneath the trailer of a fast-moving semi. With traffic edging along slower than the lines at Disney, he used the additional twenty minutes to dissect the words spoken between him and old man Bigsby to determine how it was possible the telegram applied to him.

An immense relief settled upon his chest as he pulled below the sixty-five story high rise where his firm laid claim to floors thirty-five through forty-three. The two things he needed most were access to the Internet and his personal assistant—the latter more so, as she was a living, breathing Nancy Drew and the one person in the firm he could trust above all others.

Emerging from the garage into the corporate lobby, Jack blew past the front desk receptionist—a woman of forty years' employment—ignoring her general existence and blessings for a great day. Day after day the woman wished every employee and guest God's blessings, and day after day Jack failed to respond. When she lost her husband to cancer the previous year, forfeiting all her possessions including home and car to pay for his treatment and subsequent funeral, the firm offered assistance with a sizeable donation. Jack was the lone employee to decline assistance, citing the importance of "not setting a bad precedent."

Traveling but a few paces down the hallway, he entered the office of his assistant, which guarded the entrance to his private corner suite. Pissed she was not already there and had not returned his call from thirty minutes ago, he burst through his office door intent on starting the investigation without her.

The view upon entry to the 900-square-foot private office, an added benefit upon being named the firm's youngest president, offered the finest panoramic view the fine old city offered. Hovering above the congested insanity of Lake Shore, adjacent to the company's main conference room and corporate library, the elegant, glass-encased office overlooked the endless, blue expanse of the sixth-largest freshwater lake in the world, appearing as an artist's canvas, grabbing and tugging at the eye through a 14-foot-high by 35-foot-long glass portal. From massive tankers, sailing vessels of all types and colors, skiers and kayakers, to awe-inspiring sunrises and the many faces of Mother Nature, it all created an interactive playground Jack found hard to ignore.

The space was a sanctuary from the trials of his personal life and was loaded with numerous elegant comforts and conveniences, including a personal full bathroom, wet bar, private exercise area, plasma televisions, mahogany hardwood floors, and two walls of glass panels merging at the northeast corner. From behind his desk, the view north spanned some of Chicago's most historic landmarks. During the summer months, the Navy Pier offered 3300 feet worth of young female suburbanites and tourists clad in skimpy outfits and bathing suits, which he enjoyed through the view of a large pair of field binoculars.

Jack pulled his cell phone from the pocket of his suit jacket to redial a number he'd attempted several times during the commute. There was no answer. He dialed his assistant's number for the third time. Although upset she did not answer, he was not surprised. She was no doubt knee-deep in the sales aisle at Saks or in one of the clothier's dressing rooms, as was most every other woman employed by the firm.

The December 21 shopping spree coincided with a longstanding tradition at the company dating back to the 1940's. Founder and CEO John Morgando, Jr.—known as John Junior by friends and colleagues— closed his five-person advertising agency on the 21st to attend the funeral of his childhood friend who, along with 21 other officers and 394 enlisted men, perished into the depths of Pearl Harbor while serving on the *U.S.S. Oklahoma* that fateful Sunday morning. Every year since, the day served as a marker for the start of the company's holiday season that included a swinging party at the elegant and historic Palmer House Hotel, followed by six days of paid vacation for all.

John Junior used the tragic death of his dear friend to remind his employees of the importance of being with friends and family during the holidays. Although staff could do with the time off as they pleased, all were expected to make an appearance at the party, along with their spouses and children. The partners spared little expense, splurging on a smorgasbord of delicacies from around the globe, ice carvings, a fifteen-foot-high champagne waterfall, presents for all who attended, and as a special gift for the firm's youngest family members, a visit by Santa and a live reindeer. John Junior always found a way to surprise by booking a well-known national act for the evening's entertainment.

Jack was certain his trusty sidekick was out spending her hard-earned money on another evening gown. Samantha was to him as Watson was to Sherlock; as Sundance was to Butch. His personal assistant for more than six years, she was someone he trusted with all aspects of his professional life and many of his personal life.

Jack had few friends, male or female, but Samantha had earned his trust soon upon her employment. She was loyal and committed, and her intrepidity to express where she stood on any topic, whether he inquired or not, was useful in decision-making. She was sharp as a razor, witty to a fault with a strategic perspective—a seamless alignment with his business style.

She was slender and attractive, and appeared to be more of a European descent rather than Midwest USA, confusing those around her with black, seductive eyes—encased in black Nine West designer glasses—and mid-length, straight cut black hair. Her body was of athletic build and shape; a result of her days as a track and field standout in college and now maintained by hiking, biking, and swimming on the weekends.

Upon graduating at the top of her class at Northwestern University, Samantha spent her first four post-graduate years pumping out a series of successful spy and mystery novels, which benefited from a national public relations campaign developed by Jack's division. Her interest in public relations strategy and marketing, and a penchant for creative writing, combined with his appreciation for her communication skills, mastery of the English language, and photographic memory, made their joining forces inevitable.

Over time, they developed a strong alliance and a personal relationship mirroring that of siblings. Ear-splitting altercations were an occasional by-product of their intense personalities. She dealt with his holier-than-thou air and despicable, vile vocabulary, and he with her inability to concede on any level, and propensity to throw objects when pissed off. When it came down to business, both fed off each other's energy and challenged one another to bring their very best to the table.

Taking a seat behind his desk, an ostentatious solid cherry and marble-inlay beauty, Jack waited for his computer to awake from its slumber. The telegram was burning a hole through the right side of his brain, as it lay unfolded in the middle of his desk. A whalebone letter opener in his right hand tapped out a random cadence as he flashed glances between the phone, the telegram, and his computer. His obsession to get answers rendered him oblivious to the many other events taking place around him this day.

Following a brief moment of inactivity, the laptop flickered to life, exposing a multitude of desktop icons popping up on the center flat screen of a three-screen system. Stabbing at his mouse, he clicked atop his web browser icon and waited. The browser did not respond. Navigating to his email icon, he ripped off a double-click hoping the company's servers would not deny his need for information. Following several seconds, a message popped up, indicating a server error. Jack tapped the intercom button on his phone and punched in the number for the IT department.

"This is Jack Clarke," he said with slicing authority. "I'm having trouble connecting to my email and the Internet."

"What? Accounting? Well, what the hell's the number for the IT department?" Jack redialed.

"This is Jack Clarke. I'm having trouble getting my computer online this morning."

"I'm sorry, Mr. Clarke," a shaky, adolescent voice responded. "We installed new software on the server and have not yet rebooted the system. It will be another thirty minutes or so."

"Don't you think it might be a good idea to send out an email to let everyone know your plans to shut down the server?" he questioned.

"Umm, we did, Mr. Clarke. We sent it out about 4:30 yesterday afternoon." Thinking for a moment, Jack recalled the email and realized his mistake. He offered no apology.

"When you get it up and running, I want you to call me, pronto . . . do you understand? Don't you dare make me have to chase you down over this issue. I can assure you I can make it very difficult for you to find employment in this town."

Jack slammed the butt of his hand atop the phone and ran his fingers through his hair in frustration. Swiveling ninety degrees to the left, he leaned back and dropped his heels on the corner of the desk.

Reaching for the telegram, he pondered its meaning for what seemed like the millionth time, before dropping it into his lap. He peered over the tips of his shoes in search of a target on the horizon to assist the filtering process.

Despite its encroachment, Jack considered Lake Michigan a trusted friend; a place where he offered opinion for debate, queries for answers, and affirmation for the man he thought himself to be. He spoke aloud in the direction of the great expanse during moments of strategic contemplation and analysis, and like a trusted friend, the Great Lake always saw things his way; it's where he ruled the world.

Spying a blinking, amber light in the distance—likely on the bridge of a tanker—he watched the vessel moving at a snail's pace from north to south just below the eastern horizon. He glanced at the telegram one last time before locking onto the beacon's steady tempo. He soon entered into deep thought, posing questions aloud regarding the morning's encounter.

"Why would he say I was in enough trouble already?" Jack whispered. "And why would he say it so matter-of-factly?" He paused in hopes the Great Lake would supply an answer. It did not.

"Horses pulling a carriage in the middle of winter in Oakdale . . . how could he have traveled down the main road without being seen and disappear without a trace?"

Jack could not reconcile the antiquated currency, the old man's clothing, the way he talked, walked, rambled, or the fact he charged just seventy-five cents for a delivery. None of it made any sense—especially the telegram. Growing impatient with the computer situation, he continued tracking the beacon to the edge of the window where he would soon lose sight. The ring of his office phone interrupted his search for another target upon the lake.

"Umm, Mr. Clarke, this is Devin in IT," the boy said, his voice shaking. He waited for a reply, but got none.

"Well, sir, we're having trouble getting the server back up and running and it may take some time before we have it ready to go. I will keep you posted."

"How much time?" Jack demanded.

"We may be looking at one or two this afternoon."

"Dammit, Darren, is it going to be one or two?"

"I'm Devin, sir . . . I think you better count on two."

"You people are worthless," Jack yelled into the receiver before slamming the phone hard atop the cradle. He wondered how much worse his luck was going to get.

He swiped his face in frustration as he looked again to the telegram. He searched through a mental list of contacts for anyone with the initials M.O.D, although it didn't matter because he was certain he didn't know anyone with those initials now or in 1923.

"Why urgent?" he questioned. "Who's lying in the room?" His train of thought snagged at the sound of a set of keys landing hard on the desk outside his office. Seconds later, the bright glow of florescent lighting burst to life, breaching his doorway. It must be Sam.

Jumping from his chair, Jack headed for her office at an exaggerated pace, storming through the doorway like an angry bull. He glared as she stashed her purse in a cabinet in the credenza behind her desk.

"Where the hell have you been, Sam?" he shouted, causing her to bump her head on the knob of a cabinet just above.

"For crying out loud, Jack," she yelled holding her head. "What's the matter with you?"

"I've been trying to call you since seven o'clock this morning," he yelled, slapping his hand on the molding secured to the doorframe. "Why haven't you returned my calls?"

"I don't have my phone with me, you stupid jerk."

Wincing with pain, she held her head and crawled into the desk chair she'd pushed aside moments before. "I dropped it off yesterday to be fixed. It's supposed to be ready tomorrow. What's your problem? I'm sorry I didn't respond in a timely enough fashion. I was busy cleaning the magic carpet in my bottle."

"I need to talk to you. Something bizarre has happened and I need your help."

"What, were you pleasant to someone today and now you're finding it hard to cope?" she shot back, searching her palm for blood.

"Dammit, Sam. This isn't funny. This is serious, and I don't need any of your smart-ass comments."

"For crying out loud, just give me a minute," she yelled back, placing a tissue on the point of contact. "I need to check my email first."

"Don't bother. The server's down and won't be up until later this afternoon."

"How do you know that?"

"Because *I've* been here for close to thirty minutes," he mocked.

She pulled the tissue from her head, revealing a dab of blood, "You know, this day comes just once a year. I didn't hear you complaining last year when I didn't come in until almost noon . . . oh, right, how could you? You were in Florida playing golf."

"Never mind that . . . I need your help and I need it now. This is important. Come into my office," he demanded, stomping off.

"Sure, no problem . . . just as soon as I finish bleeding to death," she said under her breath.

"What?" he yelled over his shoulder.

"I said your fly's open, you jerk."

Jack stopped and looked down—sure enough.

Sam gathered herself, retrieved a notepad—something she carried for looks more than anything else—and headed to his office. She slowed her pace upon seeing him sitting behind his desk with both hands cupped around his face, staring down at a piece of paper. He wasn't the type, at least in her experience, to appear the least bit worried, much less fearful. Pissed off and angry, yes, but never in a state of panic or uncertainty.

To see him like this was a first. She knew of his marital issues and the problems he sometimes encountered dealing with his personal life, but when it came to knowing his craft, he was Genghis Khan. He was a naval destroyer among canoes, a nuke among firecrackers. When a problem presented, he was first out of the foxhole, often forcing her to pull on his reins.

She jutted forward to the edge of her chair to bring his face into focus. "What in the world's the matter with your eyes? Did you have a couple of shots of who-hit-John this morning? They're so bloodshot."

"Never mind about my eyes. And watch it," he said, pointing a finger, "I'm not in the mood." Jack picked up the telegram and viewed it for several moments before letting it float back to the top of his desk. He allowed Sam a moment to settle in her chair as he grappled for composure. She had a way that could light him up with very little effort and it annoyed the hell out of him.

"It's important you know I'm not making up what I'm about to tell you, okay? I mean, I need you to understand this shit is real. I also need you to promise you won't tell a soul, at least until I can figure it out. Okay?"

"Sure, Jack," she said. "It'll go to the grave."

"Well, it all started a little before six o'clock this morning. I was in the kitchen getting ready to leave and the doorbell rang. When I went to answer the door—"

His explanation was cut short in mid-sentence as his private phone line erupted like two orchestra cymbals clapping together from two feet away. Jerking toward the console, he eyed the incoming phone number on the display panel. It was a number he recognized and a call he was expecting.

"Hold on, I need to get this," he said, bypassing the speaker button and lifting the handset.

"Yeah, this is Jack," he said, shooting a quick glance at Sam.

"Uh-huh . . . What the hell are you doing calling my house?"

Sam's eyebrows stretched to her scalp as Jack swiveled his chair away from her view. Easing from her position, she retreated from his office, pulling the door shut behind her.

CHAPTER 5

How apropos, Brooke thought, fighting through another rush of tears as she stared at the fallen picture. Positioned in the corner of the master bedroom adjacent to the wall now scarred by the palm of her husband's hand, the image lay upside down atop slivers and chunks of broken glass reflecting bright, rainbow-like swatches of color from the aura of a massive chandelier hanging from the ceiling.

Slumped on the edge of the bed, she recalled hearing something fall to the floor as Jack hammered the wall, but did not remember the sound of breaking glass. The image of the once happy couple, snapped at a private island in the Caribbean, was her favorite among all the photos taken during their wedding and subsequent honeymoon. At the time, the moment was the realization of a dream.

Staring at the now upside-down picture, Brooke recalled the love they shared as they posed for a local photographer while sitting on the deck of a yacht in front of the most beautiful sunset God ever painted. With Jack resting his chin on the top of her head, she positioned herself against his chest with her hands wrapped around his forearms.

The photographer made a living taking pictures of tourists and snapped just the one image of them. He collected fifteen bucks and a mailing address, assuring the couple the picture would arrive within the week.

The honeymoon proved more than a precursor to wedded bliss. Still tentative and lacking confidence she could give herself to her husband in full, Brooke's mind and spirit opened as Jack responded with a cautious and loving respect. He was careful not to push her too far too fast. His warmth and sensitivity produced an arousal she'd never known, and for the first time in her life, Brooke felt free of the bonds that had been holding her back. His tender ways allowed her to surrender to the passions she knew were buried somewhere deep within. It was his understanding that provided her hope, and each time they made love, her confidence soared.

She recalled their search for the island's most private places where they could make love without notice. Closing her eyes, Brooke could feel their bodies melding together in perfect unison.

She loved the curves and dips of the sculpted muscles in his arms and abs; the density of his chest; the feeling in her fingertips as she glided her hands over his back. She'd never felt more cared for in her life, and she could not wait for the honeymoon to conclude so they could begin life as husband and wife.

Brooke wiped at the tears trickling down her cheeks and chest. Eight months had passed, maybe more, since their last sexual contact, which came only after he came home drunk and forced the issue. She struggled against his advance but was unable to fight off his determination. It felt like rape. What he gave her in the beginning of their marriage, he stole in the end. The thought rekindled memories she'd hoped to bury forever.

Although she feared her husband's temper, she also knew the power of his allure; it had grabbed her the moment they met and was something she feared she could never overcome. She knew he resented her sexual inadequacies. She struggled to find the switch that would allow her to become what other women were, but it was something beyond her reach.

With her palms resting atop her knees, Brooke rolled through the many questions plaguing her, desperate to find answers. She'd spent her entire life dealing with issues concerning appearance, caused in part by the embarrassment she was forced to endure as her beauty was flaunted by family and friends alike. She'd also yet to reconcile the single event that stole her innocence.

In the days of her youth, the majority of her social life was spent fighting off unwanted advances of every testosterone-charged idiot in the county, causing a withdrawal from friends and the social scenes most girls her age enjoyed. As a result, Brooke acquired few female friends other than her sisters, who at times also grew jealous of the fuss everyone made. She endured the advances of men well beyond her in years, including those of a blood relative.

Two weeks removed from her fourteenth birthday, Brooke traveled with her family to an uncle's 400-acre livestock ranch where her father's family celebrated their first reunion in more than twenty years.

Owned and operated by the family for more than a century, the property grew over time with the addition of several outbuildings used to house the many animals her uncle raised and sold. Brooke wandered off from the back lawn of the farmhouse where relatives, and relatives of relatives, gathered for the two-day event. Enamored with the many animals on the property, she set out with a pencil and notepad with the intention of cataloging the different types for an upcoming school science project. She enjoyed a thorough search of each barn, spending a fair amount of time observing before moving on to the next building.

Late in the afternoon, she ventured into the property's original main barn where her uncle kept several laying hens, a few goats, and some hogs. The building sat less than fifty yards from a small watering pond frequented by several hundred head of Herefords and a prize Angus bull, and camouflaged by large oak trees and various fruit bushes planted on either side.

The barn's interior housed individual fenced-in pens, nesting boxes, a large hayloft, and a section near the back corner where her uncle stacked piles of grain and hay bales to just short of the rafters. An aisle four feet wide remained between the grain and slatted walls. Brooke did not notice the smell of smoke when first entering the space, but after a few moments spent examining a large sow feeding her piglets, caught wind of the strange scent. The odor was unlike anything she'd encountered before. Her inquisitive nature got the best of her.

Peeking around the corner of the grain pile, she noticed a small puff of smoke pushing into the aisle at the opposite end. Advancing, she crept halfway down the aisle as smoke continued to billow from behind the stack. Pausing at the sound of movement, she attempted a retreat but was surprised from behind by a distant, older cousin who grabbed a chunk of her dress. Pulling her close, he drug her behind the pile and slung her to the ground.

Lying face first in a shallow layer of grain and hay, frightened beyond the ability to move or speak, Brooke let go a sudden gasp as the weight of the man came crashing down upon the small of her back. Grabbing a fistful of her hair, the cousin leaned down near her ear and took a whiff of her scent. She began to shake, but did not utter a word.

Reeking of whiskey and the strange odor, he moved close to her ear, pulled tighter on her hair and whispered that if she made the least little peep, he'd slit her throat. Brooke heard the snap of a button and noticed a steel blade out of the corner of her eye.

Fighting through another rush of tears, her attacker drug the blade across her cheek and whispered, "I'm gonna make you a woman today."

Pulling away, he rubbed his nose and chin across her cheek, taking in deep breaths as he adjusted toward her neck. Brooke felt the release of her hair then the weight of his body lift from off her back; a much-needed burst of air entered her lungs. Hoping he was having second thoughts and would go on about his way, tremors of panic shook her bones at the clinking sound of a belt buckle coming undone. Her mouth drained of saliva as she felt the man adjusting himself over her body.

Without warning, he ripped the plaid skirt from her waist, exposing her bare legs to the crisp fall air. Goose bumps erupted across her body.

Brooke felt her attacker's hands move over her calves before she again felt his weight drop on top of her back. Continuing his hands up under her sweater, he pushed below her bra strap then plunged down her side. His hands were cold and as coarse as sandpaper. His touch was painful, causing her to jerk as he massaged and pinched. She wanted to scream, but his weight was too constricting.

Keeping one hand under her bra, he removed the other to pull his own pants from his waist. Brooke could feel him rubbing against her underwear. She whispered a plea for him to stop but the request only increased his thrusting. Moving off and adjusting again above her, she felt his hand slip toward her hip. A quick jerk sent her underwear to below her knees.

Brooke's sobbing intensified at the thought of her worst nightmare coming true. Her attacker did not stop despite the convulsions sweeping over her. Reaching down, he spread her legs. With his free hand, he cupped her mouth and rammed his body forward. The motion was quick and the pain intense. Brooke expelled a grunt. As the man prepared to repeat the motion, her heart skipped as his body went stiff. Brooke heard the faint sound of someone calling from across the meadow opposite the barn. It was her mother's voice.

The man dropped close to her ear and warned he'd come in the night and kill her and her sisters if she mentioned the incident to anyone. He pushed off her body and fled from the scene, pulling at his pants. Brooke did not move and did not say a word. She heard the sound of a barn door slam shut and heavy footsteps flee in the opposite direction. Her mother's voice rang out again, this time from near the front of the barn. Holding her breath and her body stiff, she allowed her mother to pass, before replacing her clothes.

Shaking beyond control, Brooke wept in solitude in a corner of the barn until dusk. The attack, accompanied by the man's threats, forced her adolescent mind to abide by his order.

As all traumas do, the incident left a scar so deep and profound she would never be the same. She left the confines of the barn a different person. As years passed, she went out of her way to avoid bringing attention to herself, including buying oversized clothes and going without makeup whenever possible.

By nature, Brooke was shy and introverted, and the physical advances she thwarted ad nauseum caused great uncertainty with her own sexuality. Sex and topics regarding sexual relations were never discussed at home. This was a failure on her mother's part, who suffered from issues of her own, to prepare the girls. Each was left to figure it out as best they could.

It was not until weeks before her twenty-fifth birthday that Brooke willingly surrendered herself to a man she thought loved her for all the right reasons. Her timidity, coupled with a lack of sexual education, left her with no imagination and little passion under the sheets. The beau, who'd promised her the world, was not prepared to live a life of passionless sex—no matter her beauty—and disappeared. She felt little attraction toward men until meeting Jack.

Working her way through college as an assistant for a local physical therapist, Brooke and Jack met following Jack's surgery to repair a catastrophic knee injury suffered on the first defensive play of the last game of his senior season. She recognized his name, as did everyone in the small college town, due to the national attention he received from the media, NFL executives, and scouts.

Jack tumbled into a deep depression upon hearing the news from his surgeon that he stood no chance of a professional football career. Brooke spent many hours with him following the surgery and soon fell for his incredible good looks and charm. He was the most handsome man she'd ever seen but was certain he'd have no interest in her. He was all the things she was not. She worked hard assisting his physical rehabilitation, but had a more profound effect on his psyche.

He surprised her when, on a grayed-over October day, he asked for a date. She felt certain she was not the right woman for him, knowing he could have any woman on this or any other planet he wanted, and so she tried to keep the relationship strictly on a professional level. Jack let a week pass before getting the nerve to call again. He managed to convince her to go for a single date. One date evolved into a string of several.

Little time passed before the couple became exclusive and moving toward a sexual relationship. The first time they made love surpassed any level of intimacy she thought possible; the way he touched and held her, opened her spirit and mind, propelling a desire to learn more. He opened doors and spaces previously bound and unavailable to her. He was the man she'd waited for her entire life. Sex was something she hoped to be soft, warm, and secure, and Jack made it that early in their relationship. It didn't take long, following their marriage, for it all to start falling apart.

She revealed her rape to her husband well after they'd consummated their marriage. Her refusal to dress as requested brought his wrath, as he expected her to appear a certain way in public, including wearing clothes revealing her body way beyond her comfort level. Jack wanted her to be someone she could not.

There was now little lovemaking between them, just compassionless, rape-like sex when he demanded or came home drunk. Confident her husband's sex life was active outside the marriage, her intimacy consisted of occasional self-pleasure. It was an urge that seldom struck, as it only intensified and magnified the lonely feeling in her core. When the urge was necessary, she focused her fantasies on days when the two made love, as opposed to recent years when it was just quick, detached sex to satisfy Jack's immediate urges.

Brooke struggled to accept her continued desires to fantasize about this man who'd taken so much of her for granted. Her love for him was deep. She longed for the warmth and security of his arms and prayed to God that He'd somehow intervene and restore her husband's love, but her faith waned with every altercation and unpleasant word between them. She could no longer wait for a miracle.

Brooke felt a shiver, recalling the moments when being together and being close were the most important things in their lives. She remembered how Jack could not wait to get home so they could touch. What happened to it all? It was something she could not answer but placed most of the blame on herself and her inadequacies.

Lifting herself from the bed, Brooke eyed the fallen picture as she passed on her way to the master bath. Disrobing in front of the shower, she fired up its fifteen jets and large raindrop showerhead and stepped onto the heated pebble floor. She positioned her body to receive a steady stream on the bruised area of her back, stretching as the water cascaded over and down her body. She was so tired, yet the hot stream rejuvenated her senses. Rocking back and forth, enjoying the many jets massaging her every inch, she felt the earlier chill ooze from her pores.

She reached for a sponge, doused it with creamy, rose-scented soap, positioning into a corner where stainless steel heads exploded hot, intermittent bursts. Her eyes flittered shut as she returned in her mind to the honeymoon island. She eased the soft object over her shoulders, down her arms, and onto her thighs, before guiding it behind to the small of her back, where she could almost feel her husband's skin against her own and hear the gentle crash of waves against a white-sand beach at dusk.

Drawing the sponge against her stomach, she worked the soap into her skin, breathing deep its soothing scent and exchanging in her mind the sponge for her husband's gentle touch. If only she was in his arms. If only he loved her . . . if only.

Brooke felt a light tingle release from her body as the hot water washed away stress and regret. Despite the water's soothing effect, she found the pain in her heart unchanged. Wiping away both water and tears, she released the hope she'd held that some way, somehow, their relationship could be salvaged.

Upon exiting the master bath, she noticed Peetie sitting atop the bed, wagging his tail with delight at the sight of her. She walked to the edge, appreciating his attention and loyalty, and rubbed the back of his ears. How wonderful, she thought, if he were but a frog and her kiss the magic potion needed to deliver her prince. Running her fingers down his spine, she stared into the blue of the gas flames on the opposite wall then viewed over her shoulder. Stepping to the near corner, she removed the honeymoon picture from its frame, brushed it free of debris, and, with Peetie at her side, crouched low in front of the fireplace.

She loved her husband but detested their life. No longer wanting to be a mere measure of his success and desiring something more for herself and her children, she released the picture into the flames, and with it, the bond binding her husband to their marriage.

CHAPTER 6

"What do you mean you dialed my cell number?" Jack yelled, whitening his knuckles around the phone's receiver. "My wife said you called the house four times. Don't lie to me.

"Couldn't you figure out what was going on after you called the second time? Well, don't call anymore until you learn how to dial the right damn number."

Jack slammed the phone receiver against the cradle, jettisoning a piece of plastic from off the console and across the room. His chest pounded to the rhythm of an unsteady beat. Viewing north, he ripped the knot loose from his tie and unhooked the top button of his shirt as a white-hot flush bubbled to the surface of his skin. Boiling mad, he focused on a group of men and a crane operator struggling to hoist an empty tourist ferry out of the Chicago River. Upon regaining his composure and a normal breathing pattern, he re-summoned Sam.

With tablet in hand, she resumed her position in one of four leather chairs arranged in a half-moon pattern in front of Jack's desk. With his head in his hands, he presented as a man in great distress.

"What in the world is going on, Jack?" she asked. "I've never seen you like this. Who was that on the phone?"

"It doesn't matter," he replied, turning in his chair toward the lake. He extended his legs and slouched deep into the soft leather.

"I know this will be difficult for you to believe, but like I said before, you just need to know I'm not lying. Something very bizarre has happened; something I cannot explain nor have answers to. It would help if our super geeks could fix the Internet . . . but until then, I'm stuck."

"What is it?" Sam said, agonizing over the suspense.

"It all started this morning. I was in the kitchen at about quarter to six, getting ready to leave, when the doorbell rang," he said, removing his tie and tossing it in a ball atop his desk. "I went to the door and saw this old man standing on the porch looking like he just wandered through a time warp—I mean the way he was dressed."

"What do you mean? What was he wearing?"

"Like early 1900's stuff . . . a black fedora, plaid knickers, black leather shoes with those giant Pilgrim buckles . . . items like that."

"Knickers? Are you kidding? Who wears knickers today and in the middle of winter?"

"I know, I thought the same thing. I've seen a few guys wear them on the golf course as a novelty but the ones on this cat appeared as every day wear."

"Was he from Clowngram?" she asked, struggling to keep a straight face.

"Was he from what?"

"You know . . . Clowngram . . . they have that catchy jingle . . . 'When you're down and need a clown, call a pro with a big red nose' . . . you know, that company who sends telegrams and messages by clown. They advertise everywhere," she said, failing at keeping a straight face.

"No, he wasn't from Clowngram," Jack snapped, unamused. "Anyway, you know how I feel about clowns."

"Too bad . . . seems you could use one right now."

"Dammit, can I finish?" he asked, throwing his arms in the air.

Sam nodded. Her grin agitated him.

"Anyway, as I was saying, he was very peculiar. He spoke in this long, country drawl and used phrases as if he were from another place and time. He said he delivered for this company called the McClellan Delivery Service, which he reminded me of in every sentence he spoke, but never said where they were located."

"Did you ask him?" she said, too caught up in the story to take notes.

"No, I didn't. I was so taken aback . . . I didn't think to ask. He said they worked north and northwest of here. He introduced himself as Jubel Bigsby of the Cartersville Bigsbys. I mean, who talks like that, right? He didn't say where Cartersville was."

"I'm guessing here, but you didn't ask him, right?" Sam said, enjoying an opportunity to poke at the beast with a stick.

Jack shot a menacing look. "I'm at my front door at six in the morning looking at a 90-year-old hobbit spouting off a bunch of crap on my front porch. I wasn't thinking detective work at the time. Now, do you want to hear the rest of this or not?"

"Okay, sorry," she said. "Speaking of Cartersville, I've been through Cartersville, Georgia, a couple of times on my way to Atlanta."

"Yeah, great. There must be a thousand towns in this country named Cartersville. Anyway, I don't know if he meant he's from Cartersville now or was born there. He said he was sent to deliver this."

He tossed the telegram across his desk, so engrossed in the mystery he let slip from his mind the second envelope given to him by Bigsby for Brooke. Sam was immediately intrigued by its antiquated appearance and scooped it up to inspect its front and back. Settling against the back of her chair, she labored over the smudged text, working slowly over each line. Jack watched her reaction mimic his own as she reached the bottom of the message.

"1923?" she said, moving to the edge of her seat. "This doesn't make any sense. I mean, the telegram looks like it came from 1923, but how can this be addressed to you? It has to be a joke or mistake."

Jack shrugged his shoulders.

"You must ascend stairway? Door to the left. They've been called, but she must remain . . . this is so bizarre. Who do you know with the initials M-O-D?"

"I don't know anyone who has those initials. I've been racking my brain."

"Could New Auburn be New Auburn, Illinois?" she asked, referring to the station where the telegram originated.

"I don't know. The state abbreviation is long gone. When he asked for payment, he said I owed him six bits. I didn't even know how much six bits was."

"It's seventy-five cents," she replied, matter-of-factly, still staring at the document.

"Really?" Jack said, shaking his head. "You don't think I know that now?"

"What delivery company charges just seventy-five cents?"

"That's what I said. But he just stood there rocking back and forth on his heels. He mumbled something about their rates going up. I said it would have cost at least twenty bucks for FedEx to deliver, and he didn't even know who or what the hell FedEx was. I explained it to him but he went off on some tangent about a plane and a guy who'd flown it into a barn in Cumberland . . . then there were all these animals running all over the place and—"

"Jack," Sam interrupted, "how old do you think he was?"

"If he wasn't a hundred then he was one candle shy—easy. He was very unsteady on his legs and smelled like dirty feet or an old box of cheese someone stashed away in an attic for fifty years. I'm telling you, this cat was a total nut job. But there's more."

She shot an excited stare. She just could not get enough of a good mystery.

"I gave him a dollar and he mentioned how strange it appeared to him. He reached in his pocket and yanked out this wad of dough. He handed me one of the dollar bills, and I noticed how much larger it was than the bill I'd given him. It was a different color and didn't have the same design or markings on it. He said he picked it up in a town called Clear Lake the day before. The words 'silver certificate' were printed at the top. It was very strange. Every bill in the wad looked the same."

"Well, I know the words 'silver certificate' were on bills at the turn of the century . . . no doubt on bills in 1923."

"How do you know?"

"I remember seeing an old dollar bill my grandfather framed in his workshop. I don't think it was his, but it was the first dollar someone in the family earned at some point. It was much larger than our money today and I do remember seeing the same script at the top of the bill."

"You're saying this guy's from 1923?"

"Well, no, of course not. I'm not suggesting he dropped out of 1923, but it sounds like his wad of cash was authentic."

"You'll think he dropped out of 1923 when you hear the rest of this." Jack viewed the lake to take a quick break. Sam was anxious for more.

Unable to spot anything of interest, he pointed to the bottom portion of the telegram. "What do you think the last line says . . . you're the text expert."

Sam flipped the telegram over to view the front. She took several seconds to examine the broken print.

```
MR  JACK L. CLARKE=
1794 M-P-E ACR-S DRIVE    OAK BR-OK    IL-=
YOU MU-T ASCEN--TAIRWAY   STOP
-OOR TO LEFT IS WH-RE SHE LAYS   ST-
I AM NOT THE-E    S-P
TH-Y HAVE BE-N CAL-D BUT SHE M-ST REMAIN    S--
N-T   -E-IV-RY   -O-A-   A-  2 P-
URGENT   STO-
MOD = DEC21-450PM-1923
```

"Well, the '2P,' is obvious; I guess it's referring to 2 p.m. The second word looks like 'delivery' to me. If that's so, I'd say the first word is 'next,'" she said, as Jack jotted it down on a yellow post-it note.

"The fourth word appears to be 'at.' Since 2 p.m. refers to time. The third word is tricky. If we're assuming 'next delivery,' the word 'today' would fit with the 'o' and 'a.' I can't think of any other like-word fitting into the character space there that would make sense. But it's just a guess."

"So, you see 'next delivery today at 2 p.m.'?"

"That's what it looks like to me, but like I said, it's just a guess."

"I'd say it's a pretty good one." Jack leaned forward to rest his chin in the palm of his hand. "So, something else is coming?"

"Appears so," Sam agreed.

"As he was leaving, he said he'd see me again soon."

Sam could see Jack's mind squirming and wanted to ask what he thought was coming, but hesitated when he shifted to meet her stare. His look was much like a child wanting to admit to breaking a window but not knowing how to start. She guessed there was more.

"What is it?" she asked, tilting her head.

He hesitated, unsure how she'd react to the rest. To this point, there was hard evidence. His word was all he had now. He proceeded with caution.

"I watched him walk down the sidewalk to the street and went back inside to the kitchen," he said, tapping a finger on the desk. "I heard a strange noise and thought it might be a dog yapping. But it wasn't. A few seconds later I heard it again. It sounded like a horse whinnying."

Sam cracked a smile as if she were listening to someone reciting a fairy tale.

"I went to the bay window in the kitchen and saw the old man riding down the road in a . . . in a black carriage being pulled by these two gigantic white horses." Jack rushed through the statement as if the words were burning his gums.

"What? Are you kidding me?"

"I'm telling you, it was the most bizarre thing I've seen in my life. I can't begin to describe how big these horses were. They looked like elephants without the trunks and giant ears. I've never seen domestic horses that damn big, certainly not coasting down our street at dawn. I mean, what the hell . . . a horse and carriage? Not to mention it was thirty-four degrees outside? And this guy is driving away sitting on a stoop near the top of the carriage, wrapped in a blanket. What spooked me most was, I got into the Hummer with the intention of chasing him down. I couldn't have been more than thirty seconds behind. I followed the road—you know, where it banks then cuts hard right and heads out to the main road—well, I followed it all the way out and there was no sign of him; none. I drove the entire community for forty-five minutes. Nothing. He was just gone. I stopped by the security shack and they said they'd just seen cars exiting. I mean, how crazy is that, right?"

Sam shook her head, staring right through him.

"How do two horses, a carriage, and one old goofy shit disappear into thin air?" he asked. "Another strange thing was—"

"You mean you're not finished?" Sam said, peering over the rims of her glasses.

"Yeah, there's more," he said, nodding. "I was frustrated by all this, of course, and at some point when I was talking with him I said 'Jesus' or 'Jesus Christ' or 'Christ'—something. Well, he stopped me and told me I should not use the Lord's name in vain as I—meaning me—was, and I quote, 'in enough trouble already.' Now what the hell is that?"

"Sounds like he was giving pretty good advice to me," she quipped. The comment drew a cold stare. "I don't know, Jack," she continued, "maybe he knew what was in the package. Was he referring to the next delivery?"

"No, I don't think so. He went on this extended rant about how his employer didn't allow for the delivery people to open envelopes, and how he came close to being fired once. He mentioned his mother and all kinds of other crap."

"What kind of trouble do you think he thinks you're in?"

"I don't know. Brooke and I are having some problems right now, but she sure as hell isn't going anywhere. I mean, where would she go, right? What bothers me is he said it so nonchalantly, it didn't click until well after our conversation."

The two sat with not a word between them; Jack trying to connect the dots and Sam questioning how he could have so much trouble at home with one of the sweetest, dearest people she'd ever met.

Sam removed her glasses and settled back against the chair. "You know, Brooke is such an incredible person, and for the life of me I don't understand how you continue to have so many problems. I mean she's beautiful, smart, a great mother, cares so much for you and the girls, she's—"

Jack pointed a finger in her direction. "I don't want to hear any of your comments regarding my marriage," he said, pointing. "You have no idea what it's been like for me. You are not there, so do not act as if you've the first idea of what you're saying because you don't know a thing. You're off topic."

"Why is everything about you?" she fired back. "Why don't you think of her for a change? Do you have any idea what her life is like raising two four-year-old twin girls, alone?"

"I told you, I don't want to discuss this. I have enough problems right now. I've given her everything. Without me, she's nothing; less than nothing. Her job is to take care of me, the kids, the house, and the things I need her to do—period. As I told her this morning, if she doesn't like it, she can pack her shit and get the hell out anytime she wants."

"What? You said that to her? God, Jack, have you lost your stupid mind? Do you know how horrible that is to say? You know, that telegram is making more and more sense because you belong in 1923; you'd fit in just fine with the way women were treated back then."

"Don't even start with your women's lib bullshit. I've worked my ass off to achieve success and have given her everything."

"What . . . were you sprung from the loins of some Neanderthal? Did you club her over the head when you proposed? She's not about material things; she could care less about those things. Nobody denies how hard you've worked, but why don't you look at things from her perspective?"

"I work hard and I provide—that's what I do. If it's not good enough, she needs to go and find a better life. I don't owe her any explanations. I don't owe her a damn thing."

"Guess what, you do owe her. It's called being married for crying out loud."

"Why do you have to say 'crying out loud'? Why can't you throw caution to the wind just once and drop an f-bomb?"

"For the same reason you cuss like a drunken sailor in search of a Saturday night whore; it's how I was raised," she said, looking at him, shaking her head. "If I ever do get that mad, though, you better hope to God you're not standing within the reach of my fist."

"Take it easy," he said. "It doesn't matter anyway. Where is she going to go? She wouldn't leave if her life depended on it. Nobody could do for her what I've done, and no one in their right mind would leave the kind of lifestyle she enjoys."

"You're a fool," Sam said. "And I'll tell you something else, you better be darn careful because I guarantee you're underestimating her. She might have put up with your nonsense this long, but she won't forever. You mark my word."

"What the hell do you know?" he said, unfolding his arms. "When was the last time you were married? I'll tell you when, N-E-V-E-R. You don't know the first thing about being married. You couldn't find the word in the dictionary."

"I'll tell you what I do know," she shot back, almost falling off the front of the chair. "I know I'm a woman and I know what women want; and it's not you—at least for the long term. I don't know how Brooke has done it all these years, because she's a saint in my book. If she leaves you, the women you'll get will be those with zero character and even less self-esteem. They may want you for thirty minutes under the sheets, although I doubt your attention span lasts beyond a couple seconds, but they won't want you a week later because no woman is going to take your crap very long—even the stupid ones."

"Well, maybe I don't want to be married anymore," he said, ratcheting down his voice to a near inaudible level.

"What?" Sam asked, her chin drawing against her chest. "What did you say?"

"I didn't say anything."

"No, please, tell me again because I can't believe my freakin' ears."

"I said maybe you should shut the hell up," he yelled.

Sam let rip a sarcastic laugh. Pushing out of the chair, she stomped to the window with hands on her hips. She paused several moments to absorb the view.

"Let me tell you something," she said, pointing a finger, "you'll never—and I mean never—find another Brooke on this planet. And what about the girls? What about them?"

Jack spotted a large vessel on the horizon riding deep in the water—likely loaded down with coal or iron ore—making its way to the center of his line of sight. He marveled at ships of this size and their ability to remain afloat with such heavy loads. He would often count the seconds it took the vessels to pass along his view. Like a small child watching a fire engine racing down the street, he was captivated.

Sam shouted his name, seeing she'd lost his attention. Her voice cracked like a whip causing his body to twitch. "You won't recover if she leaves you; you understand that, right?"

"It's not that I don't love her," he said in a much calmer tone. "She's just not what I expected."

"The wrong loaf of bread, is she?" Brooke scoffed. "Have you given any thought to the possibility you may not be the man she expected? No, because you're the alpha dog and the rest of us are just ragged mutts drifting around your great expanse hoping for the leftovers that fall from your mouth. It's always about you. I've seen people try to get close to you and you push them away. They try, but there's no way they can ever please you. Have you ever wondered why I'm the one person you can turn to? You don't have one male friend you trust. Why?"

The look on his face confirmed her claim.

"What? You don't think after all this time I don't know who you are and what you're about? Tell me, why I'm the only friend you have?" she asked.

"I don't want to talk about this anymore," he said. "I've got to figure out what's going on here and what's happening, okay? I need to figure out what happened this morning before I lose my mind. If you want to help, then help. If you don't, just leave me the hell alone."

Sam sighed. It was like talking to a golf club. "What do you want me to do?"

"I don't know. I don't even know where to begin. I can't do anything until we get the Internet back up and running."

Sam moved closer to the front of his desk, wondering if he could be so stupid as to let Brooke leave him.

"I'll be in my office if you think of anything," she said. Jack did not respond. He re-engaged the ship on the lake.

Sam glanced again at the telegram before floating it to the middle of his desk. Retreating toward her office, she stopped at the door.

"Jack," she said looking over her shoulder, "don't let Brooke and those girls get away from you. If you lose them, you'll regret it the rest of your life."

Sam pulled the door closed behind as she left him to his thoughts. Having skipped breakfast to ensure beating other holiday shoppers to the punch, she decided to get something to eat. Flipping through the blank pages of her pad, she wondered why she hadn't taken the first note. Tossing the pad on top of her desk, she headed for the café on the building's first floor.

Jack contemplated his assistant's parting shot, teasing his mind with thoughts of life as a divorcé. He'd have no trouble finding companionship. As far back as he could recall, he was tracked, tagged, and bagged by the opposite sex. Young, old, or very old, it didn't matter. From girls in his third-grade class chasing him around the playground in hopes of stealing a peck, to the twenty-two-year-old babysitter who seized his virginity when he was thirteen, to several rolls in the hay with the fifty-year-old divorced mother of a high school girlfriend, supply always exceeded demand.

Jack moved to the corner seam of his office where he planted a shoulder into the ninety-degree angle. Facing the lake, he scanned the desolate Monroe Harbor located 400 feet below his position. Hundreds of empty boat stalls, connected by long, concrete docks, settled in an ever-thickening layer of ice, anxious for the first sign of spring and the return of the many styles of watercraft to occupy the spaces for the summer months.

He inspected the small harbor and dock home to the Columbia Yacht Club, exploring the thought of freeing himself from the handcuffs of a souring marriage. Sam was wrong, and he knew it. He'd been on his own since the age of fourteen. He hadn't needed the help or support of anyone to achieve the success he sought or enjoyed. If he were destined to be alone, so be it; how would it be any different from what he'd always known? He would not mind the many advantages a single man could enjoy in such a big city, including not having to explain late nights out, perfume on shirt collars, strange telephone calls, or the guilt levied for being unable to attend parent-teacher conferences, dance lessons, slumber parties, and Christmas plays.

His eyes trailed along the demarcation line in the harbor separating frozen from free-flowing water. His thoughts of a bachelor's life regressed as the face of his wife flashed before his conscience. There was something about her he could never quite place, from the instant she'd laid her hand on the six-inch scar running across the surface of his knee. Hers was a unique way, something special prevented him from walking away without apprehension or the confidence he wasn't making the biggest mistake of his life.

Even now, after suggesting she leave their home, something in those words did not align; something was out of sync in his core. The annoyance of her mysterious hold only pissed him off further. The conflict clawed at his ego and stabbed at his belief that women were here to serve. He could not help but think how effeminate it was for a man, any man, to lose control of his own destiny because of a woman.

Jack's view of their problem was simple. Brooke's insecurities were the wedge between them—since day one. The problems in their marriage were her fault. At some point, he thought, she needed to face the issues of her past head on and in a manner to enhance their marriage and sex life.

They could deliberate for months the reasons for their troubles, but he was certain of one simple fact: if the union were to end in divorce, he'd be the one initiating the proceedings. He was certain Brooke did not have the guts to leave him, or remove his children, nor did she have the means to do so. Although he knew she suspected something and was very angry, in his mind, it was nothing a new outfit or fine piece of jewelry couldn't fix.

CHAPTER 7

The box once securing sixty-four pristine crayons lay open and empty atop a manila envelope situated on a stack of magazines and mail on the family's antique farm-style kitchen table.

Equally divided between Julianna and Jordan, the girls used every wax stick in the collection to complete their refrigerator-worthy artwork for Grandma and Grandpa. Coloring and finger painting were their two most favorite activities, especially around the holidays when the new Christmas coloring books hit the five and dime following Halloween. They could not arrive at their grandparents' house without offering a picture each.

Julianna, who was an inside-the-lines artisan and conscientious of using correct color schemes, placed the finishing touches on an image of Santa preparing to drop down some lucky child's chimney with trusty Rudolph at his side, watching in great anticipation.

Jordan knew no boundaries or color codes. She scribbled haphazardly over a cozy family room scene, complete with a Christmas tree adjacent to a roaring fireplace with several gifts jammed underneath its branches. Preferring an abstract approach, she colored her tree black with pink lights and an orange angel, the flames in the fireplace a soothing shade of teal, and the puppy sleeping just in front, a hunter green.

The girls adored Brooke's parents and could not contain their excitement when informed of a trip up north to the family farm. The 100-plus-year-old farmhouse, built by Brooke's great-grandfather, transported the girls to a magical wonderland they could not get enough of. The 150-acre spread offered wheat and sweet corn fields, golden pastures, endless dirt trails, turkeys, horses, chickens, ponds, lakes, streams, silos, and barns. They were unaware of their mother's plans of that being their new residence.

"I've never heard of a black Christmas tree anywhere in the whole wide world," Julianna barked to Jordan.

Standing guard over two grilled cheese sandwiches sizzling atop the island cooktop, Brooke released a playful grin at the sound of her daughter's serious accusation.

"How come?" Jordan asked.

"Cause."

"Cause why?"

"Cause they're green. Our tree's not black," Julianna reminded.

"I bet it could be black," Jordan insisted.

"Uh-uh, it's green."

"It's green, but it could be painted black."

"Who ever heard of painting a Christmas tree?" Julianna snapped.

"I bet I could," Jordan insisted.

"Could not."

"Could so."

"Girls," Brooke interrupted, "please finish your drawings and put the crayons back in the box. Your lunch is ready, and we need to leave here in a little bit."

"But I'm not finished Mommy," Jordan whined.

"That's okay sweetheart, you can finish it in the car."

"I'm finished with mine, Mommy," Julianna chirped.

"Okay. Please help your sister put the crayons away."

Jordan collected the coloring books, placing them on top of the manila envelope. Julianna collected the crayons, inserting each into the box one by one, according to color shade.

Julianna's development was progressing at warp speed. She was further along than Jordan when it came to cognitive and motor skills, and possessed a level of patience, maturity, and intelligence her mother found inexplicable. She was submissive in nature, but not afraid to stand up for herself when her line was crossed. Blue eyes and auburn hair were the two features obtained from Dad, but her smile, long arms, and mannerisms came from her mother's side of the family. She fired off a hundred inquisitive questions an hour, expecting immediate answers to each, and would continue conversing whether someone was listening or not. Her level of absorption was uncanny, to the point Brooke kept a keen eye on where she was getting her intel. Julianna adored Peetie, doting over him with great care. Her fascination with animals and insects convinced her mother she'd be the family's first veterinarian.

Unlike her sister's affable nature, Jordan was destined to become the first female to play in the National Football League. Possessing her father's intensity, stubborn nature, and athleticism, she butted heads with Brooke, having an inability to take no for an answer. She was very quiet, paid little attention to detail, and most often looked as if she was nearing the completion of some scheme, waiting for just the right moment to spring it upon the unsuspecting. She loved to run, tumble, and play rough, and enjoyed using Julianna as a tackling dummy. Brooke witnessed Jordan running into walls and doors without so much as a flinch or whimper. Her tolerance for pain was unlike any child her age. She detested Band-Aids, informing her mother she liked watching the red color coming out of her skin. Her black, silky hair, long slender neck, and green eyes carbon-copied Brooke's, but her smile, nose, chin, and wide shoulders belonged to Daddy.

With sandwiches in hand—one with crust, one without—Brooke set the appropriate plate in front of the proper daughter, and a container of strawberry yogurt opposite them. She pulled up a chair as the girls dove into their sandwiches.

"Mommy?" Julianna asked, initiating the round-table summit before Brooke had settled into her chair.

"Yes dear?"

"Will Aunt Faye be at Grandma's house?"

"I think so. I think all your aunts, uncles, and cousins will be there."

"What's a cousin?" Jordan asked.

"Well, a cousin is just a member of the family you're related to, but don't live with," Brooke explained.

"Is Daddy coming with us?" Julianna asked, looking to Brooke over her sandwich.

"Your daddy's very busy with work, sweetheart. I don't think he'll be able to join us this year."

"Will we see him before we go?"

"Probably not, sweetheart."

"How come?" Jordan asked.

"Well, he's working today."

"He's always working," Julianna said. Brooke breathed deep. She knew the disappointment her daughter was feeling.

"Do you think Santa will visit him, even though we won't be here?" she asked.

"I'm sure he will."

"Maybe Santa will give him a ride in his sleigh to Grandma and Grandpa's," Jordan figured.

"I don't think Santa will be able to do that," Brooke said, wishing Julianna would change the topic. "He has too many gifts to deliver. There would not be enough room for your daddy."

Julianna took a break to finish off the first portion of her grilled cheese. The three sat silent, flashing smiles at each other.

"I miss Daddy," Jordan said, breaking the silence and the smile on Brooke's face.

The pain in Brooke's heart intensified. She was doing all she could do to hide her emotions from both girls—mostly Julianna who possessed an acute sense of knowing when something was amiss. She'd anticipated tough, direct questions from them both and thought it would've started when she requested they fill a large, plastic container with some of their favorite toys to take with them.

Brooke was not at peace taking the girls in this manner and felt riddled with guilt for not telling them the truth as to her plans. She was not prepared to explain the situation, nor was she prepared for the potential damage it might inflict separating them from their father. She feared they'd someday blame her, but it was a chance she was willing to take. There was no way she was leaving without them, nor would she trust them in his care. She felt like a thief in the night.

Although her head told her it was the right decision, her heart fought tooth and nail. She prayed, hoping God might forgive her. She was convinced Jack loved the girls, but she had to admit, his lack of attention toward them raised doubts. His conscious, deliberate efforts to keep the relationship with them at arm's length baffled beyond her ability to comprehend. She attempted to uncover circumstances leading to the drastic change in his attitude toward the girls, but was unable to pinpoint anything of real substance. She only knew the epicenter of where his decline began, recalling a cold and snowy January day five years ago in the sleepy village of Redrock, Wisconsin.

Brooke knew little of her husband's family. She'd probed him for years, but he refused to offer any detail, even when they were very much in love. She sensed a level of embarrassment or shame he was harboring, but could never get him to confide. She knew nothing of his family tree, other than that he was an only child, his father passed when he was seven, and his father's parents were born somewhere in Europe. She also knew he left home at the age of fourteen and, as much as she could tell, never once spoke to or saw his mother again.

Jack never shared his mother's first name. He mentioned she'd worked as a waitress at several greasy spoons across the state before being struck down by a heart attack one morning while at work. Brooke recalled the trip to the funeral after Jack received a phone call from a private detective working on behalf of the Waushara County Coroner's Office. She anticipated meeting his family, but from what she could gather, no other relatives attended the funeral. Of the eight people weathering the cold and snow that day, not one acknowledged Jack's presence or extended a hand in sympathy. It was as if they were attending the wrong funeral or were there to offer moral support for someone else.

Jack showed no emotion the entire day and refused to attend the visitation prior to the burial service. They spent fewer than fifteen minutes at the gravesite before he insisted they leave. On their way out of the cemetery, a woman dressed in black approached Jack as he passed the hearse transporting his mother's body. The woman reached out to place a hand on his shoulder in a gesture indicative of intending to speak, but he moved through her touch as if she were an apparition. Brooke peered over her shoulder to view the woman. Tears streamed down her face. She looked to Jack but he offered no indication of the encounter. She asked who the woman was, but he did not respond. After stopping by the coroner's office to sign a few papers, the two returned to Chicago with not a word spoken between them.

"Mommy?" Julianna said. "Did you hear me?"

Brooke jumped, not realizing the several other questions fired off by her daughter in rapid succession.

"I'm so sorry, sweetheart," Brooke said, smiling. "What did you say?"

"I asked you if turtles take off their shells when they take a bath."

Brooke marveled at how Julianna's mind worked and had grown accustomed to fielding questions from her that came out of nowhere. Brooke laughed then offered an unsatisfactory reply. Julianna had a follow-up already on the way, despite a mouthful of cheese and toasted bread.

"Then how do they get clean?"

"Well, I suspect they crawl into a stream and fill up with water, shake a little bit, then let the water drain out when they crawl back onto the bank," she joked. Soon, all three were laughing.

"You're silly, Mommy," Jordan said.

Brooke cleared her spoon of the last bit of strawberry yogurt, stood from her chair and collected the girls' plates. She deposited the plastic Snoopy and Charlie Brown platters into the dishwasher, wiped down the grill and beckoned the girls to follow her upstairs.

"I want you both to make sure you've got everything you're planning on taking. Okay?"

"Okay, Mommy," Jordan said.

"Julianna," Brooke called out from the end of the hallway, "make sure you get Jordan's blanket out of her room. And don't go downstairs until I come get you."

"Okay," she yelled.

Passing the threshold into the master bedroom, Brooke checked the space as one would when conducting a final walk-through prior to exiting a hotel room. An empty feeling overtook her senses; as if she had been occupying someone else's space all along.

The room was cold and dark, befitting the feelings she was experiencing deep within. With a clear plastic container half the size of a suitcase clutched in hand, she was quick to peruse the nightstand adjacent her side of the bed. Picking over the lot, she packed several knick-knack-type items, the simple clock radio she'd owned since college, a couple of unread novels and a study Bible given to her by her great aunt upon her confirmation into the Catholic faith.

With plastic bin in hand, she moved into the master bath, clearing the vanity and its drawers of all remaining beauty and grooming implements. She conducted a similar appraisal and extraction of items on her dresser inside the master closet. She'd emptied her side earlier, leaving just a few wood hangers dangling unadorned on the racks. Having no more need for fancy dresses, low-cut evening gowns and expensive shoes, she packed the lot into four large garment boxes and dragged them one-by-one to the garage. Wanting to leave no questions as to her intent, she lined the boxes in a neat row in the middle of the bay where Jack parked his Hummer.

Having collected only those things necessary, Brooke scanned the bedroom in full before pausing at the sight of the broken picture frame in the corner. So many tears had spilled this day, she wondered how it was possible more were at the ready, and how she could so love this man who'd tossed her away like a used shop rag.

She rested her head against the cold molding of the bedroom door after pulling it tight against the jamb. She took a deep breath and allowed her emotions to release.

"Girls," she called out, still leaning against the door, "come on, we have to go. I want to get to Grandma and Grandpa's house before it gets too late." A muffled acknowledgement followed.

Having lost sight of their mother's instructions, the girls were instead enjoying trying to synchronize themselves to land at the same time while jumping on Julianna's bed. Upon hearing Brooke's plea, they steadied each other to a standstill, hopped off the bed, and resumed collecting those items they could not live without on such a trip.

Julianna grabbed Jordan's blanket as instructed and raced through the bathroom collecting a few essentials along the way, including their Winnie the Pooh and Tigger Too backpacks—one red, one blue.

Down the stairs and through the kitchen, Brooke hurried her daughters into the Escalade, making certain both were organized and tucked away in their car seats. She stepped behind the vehicle, opened the tailgate, and rearranged their several pieces of luggage, storage bins, and a large pet cage, to make room for three oversized boxes full of Christmas presents for the girls and her family.

"Girls," she said, leaning in the cab to start the engine, "I'll be right back. I left my satchel in the house. Don't move."

Brooke located the carryall draped over one of the seatbacks at the table and noticed also her daughters' coloring books and crayons atop a stack on the corner. Knowing she'd have plenty of time to catch up on her reading, she grabbed a grocery tote from off the kitchen counter and stuffed in the entire stack. Hurrying to the door, she paused to take one last look across the space. She'd left so much behind, but didn't need plasma screens, fine china, sterling silver, expensive artwork or fancy clothes; what she needed and wanted most was gone.

Stopping short of climbing into the humming SUV, Brooke's conscience posted one final objection to the manner in which she was fleeing. She eyed her daughters—both of whom were paying no mind as they giggled away over something one of them said—then over her left shoulder to bring the garage door into view. The pause was brief.

With her travel companions stowed, she eased the SUV down the driveway and into the street. Holding steady against the brake, she surveyed the front span of the stunning property, wiping away tears as emotion clogged her chest. With her heart aching, she pulled her head forward, released the brake and watched through the rearview mirror as the life she had dreamed of disappeared behind a bend.

Catching the smiles of her daughters in the rearview mirror, she contemplated her newfound freedom and the life she feared, waiting for them 500 miles away.

CHAPTER 8

Standing behind his desk with arms folded, Jack marveled at the massive bank of dense, black-gray clouds churning across the expanse of the northwest horizon, consuming the crisp blue of the sky on its march east. The system had gathered over the Great Plains, catching the forecasters napping, spawning blizzard-like conditions in four states. It was now on a collision course with a hard-charging Canadian Clipper and its frigid temperatures, descending from the north.

Temperatures were expected to fall throughout the afternoon with light snow by nightfall, and heavy, consistent snow over the next several days. It was expected to be the city's first white Christmas in three years, and the first twenty-plus inch dump in more than a decade. Travel would be treacherous, if not impossible.

Searching about the landscape, Jack noted the many changes in the few months since the trees paralleling the curvature along the lakefront announced the presence of autumn with their brilliant display of burgundy, gold, yellow, and burnt orange foliage. He tracked pedestrians bundled in heavy coats and scarves, scurrying in and out of the many shops and businesses scattered along his view, passing through condensation clouds of their own making.

He preferred the winter months over spring and summer, although he enjoyed the two-week stretch in May when the watercraft returned to the harbor. Had December been void of the Christmas holiday, the month would be his favorite. The commercial nonsense leading up to the day, perpetuated by two daughters whose constant reminders kicked in mere hours after removing their Halloween costumes, was nothing more than an annoyance. To Jack, Christmas was a cold reminder of pain and death, and despite having no choice but to go through the motions expected of every parent each December 25th, it held no meaning in his heart.

Turning from the brilliance of the budding storm, he swiveled his view due west, catching sight of an out-of-place pink flatbed truck traveling on Wacker Avenue toward the building. Watching as the operator snaked his way in and around traffic, cutting off vehicles as if he were alone on the stretch, he could not pull his thoughts away from the insanity of the telegram. He was unable to rid his mind of its eerie reference describing a woman lying in a room on the left of a stairway he was to ascend. Fighting his imagination, he again contemplated how the message could pertain to him and what logical possibilities or events could manifest that would place him in such a situation. Watching as the strange truck ignored a red light at the Lake Shore intersection, a familiar chime belting from his computer interrupted. His reaction was immediate, knowing the alert indicated an incoming email.

Grumbling a profanity directed at the boys in IT, he spun his chair in the direction of the laptop. The alert was better than a mid-afternoon energy drink and provided the jolt of current he needed. At the very least, he could spend the next forty minutes investigating online before the supposed next delivery. Stabbing at the wireless mouse on his desk, he summoned the laptop and docking station from hibernation. The computer screen flashed to life, making visible a login window requesting re-identification. Jack typed in his username and password, waited as the computer loaded the desktop icons, then double-clicked the Outlook button, sending the email portal into action. The page opened to a bright white, empty field.

"What the hell? Where are all my emails?"

His personal file folders, along with several unanswered emails, had all vanished, and had been replaced with a lone email identified in the

"from" column by a single, black "x." Glancing at his watch, he
concluded the message had arrived on the chime and was not some
system leftover. Jack clicked the "x" and watched as multiple screens
opened and closed in rapid succession, bursting in various bright, vivid
colors, before disappearing into a solid black screen. The icons on the
desktop disappeared, duping him into believing the system was on the
verge of shutting down.

The instant he redirected the mouse forward, a new window popped
into view, appearing much like an advertisement. Flashing red bars at
the top and bottom revealed reversed-out block capital letters: ATTEN-
TION JACK CLARKE! Following a half-dozen flashes, a message in
small black print appeared in the center of the screen. Jack read the
message aloud:

"Dear Mr. Clarke:

"A low spot along the lakeshore leads to a dock and fence line
beyond; follow the path ore' the dam to a field of cut stalk; the light will
guide you.

"Signed, M.O.D."

"What the hell? Dock? Fence line? Fields of stalk? What the hell is
this? . . . M.O.D?"

Jack recognized the initials as those on the telegram. He pulled the
folded relic from his pocket to confirm, although he knew it to be true
having memorized every letter, smudge and stain. Fighting through a
blast of paranoia and a lump twitching in his throat, he could feel the
hair on the back of his neck jump to attention, something he had not
experienced since a lighting strike came close to deep-frying him and
his brother-in-law on the thirteenth hole at Cog Hill two summers ago.

In a desperate move to identify the sender, he attempted to reply to
the message but was stopped cold as the computer froze, halting his
ability to navigate the page. The glowing green light on the wireless

mouse faded to black, rendering the component useless. Jack jumped from his chair, ran across the room and slung open the door of his office, sending it crashing into the wall behind. The collision between door and wall sent Sam bounding from her chair and a half-eaten tuna fish and pickle sandwich in her hand jettisoning across the room into the hallway.

"For crying out loud, Jack," she yelled, "what's the matter now?"

"Did you just send me an email?" he accused, thinking she was attempting some misguided humor.

Sam did not respond, instead searching the floor for the half sandwich no longer in her possession.

"Did you just send me an email?"

"What? . . . No. The server's down."

"No, it's not. I just got an email. Check your computer," he demanded.

She'd checked not five minutes ago and was unable to log on. Resituating in her chair, Sam double-clicked the Outlook icon with Jack crowding against her back looking over her shoulder. The program opened to a blank page followed by a pop-up message: Unable to connect, please contact office administrator.

"Shit," he yelled, just inches from her ear. He pushed on the back of her chair, launching her into the credenza, before retreating to his office. Sam jumped up in pursuit.

"Jack, take it easy. What happened?"

Standing at the corner of his desk, he picked up the receiver and dialed the IT department.

"This is Jack Clarke," he yelled. "Is the server up?" Jack slammed the phone down after having dialed the creative department.

"What the hell's the number to IT?" he demanded of Sam.

"4647," she responded. "Jack, what's wrong?"

He punched the speakerphone button, tapped in the four numbers, and pointed to his computer screen. Sam walked behind his desk and parked herself in his chair. The email remained frozen on the screen. She started reading.

"Melvin? This is Jack Clarke. Is the server up and running? Melvin, Devin, whatever. Is the server up and running?"

"No, not at this point, Mr. Clarke," the young man replied.

"Then how would you explain an email showing up in my inbox?"

"That's impossible, sir. There's no connectivity."

"Impossible? I just got an email and it's the only one in my directory," Jack shouted. "All the other emails in my inbox have disappeared."

"Is it left over from yesterday?" asked the young tech.

"No. It was dated today and timed at 1:17 p.m."

"I don't know what to say, Mr. Clarke. It has to be a leftover."

"How can it leak through if there's no connection?" The young man did not respond.

"I'll tell you what, Melvin, you walk your ass up here right now and take a look at it. Do you understand me?" Jack crushed the receiver onto its cradle. Sam spilled out of the chair and moved to the front of the desk. She did not say a word as her boss ran his hands through his hair, trying to catch his breath.

"Well?" he yelled, spreading his arms as if expecting Sam to have come up with an answer.

"I don't know, Jack. I don't know what it means. It doesn't make any sense."

He paused; his eyes were boiling. "Did you see the initials at the bottom?"

"Yeah. I . . . I just don't know what to say. Are you sure you want the IT guys to see this?"

Jack considered Sam's point. He'd not given thought he might have to explain more than he was willing to at the moment. He redialed the IT department and canceled the request for assistance. Easing back into the chair, he attempted to revive the mouse but it did not respond. Sam maneuvered in behind, suggesting he reboot the computer. Upon the machine returning to life, Jack navigated to the inbox where an error message declared the system could not connect to the server. The email was gone. Jack peeked over his left shoulder to view Sam's reaction.

"I guess the delivery came a bit early," he said. She peeked at her watch. It was 1:30.

"You know," Sam said, "those were instructions, as if someone is expecting you."

"Doesn't matter, because I'm not going anywhere. Brooke and the girls are . . . oh, shit," he said, checking the clock displayed on his computer.

"What is it?"

"Brooke and the girls are flying out this afternoon to her parents' house for Christmas. I forgot all about it."

"You're not going?" she asked.

"We talked about my meeting up with them Christmas Eve, but I've decided not to go."

"Oh my God," she said, hustling to the front of his desk, "you mean to tell me you're not spending Christmas with them?"

"Are you serious?" Jack replied, jumping from the chair. "Are you kidding me? I have all this nonsense going on this morning, including now receiving this email, which by the way, is not possible because the server is down, and your main concern is my travel plans for Christmas? Have you lost your stupid mind?"

"I'm just asking a question . . . jeez. I just can't believe you'd rather be alone than with your family. Do you know how crazy that sounds?"

"What the hell do I care what it sounds like. I wanted to stay home, but Brooke insisted on being with her family. I'm not about to spend another day with a bunch of in-laws who'd rather see me dead than alive. I'm not doing it. Anyway, do you see the sky?" Jack said, pointing behind him. "In about six hours, no one in this city is going anywhere. With all that's happened today, how could you expect spending Christmas with my family to be a priority?"

"I just don't understand why you have such a problem with Christmas," she responded. "Why can't you talk to me about it? It's the same thing every year."

Taking a step back, Jack crossed his arms and gazed across the darkening landscape. Even had the day not already offered one mental challenge after another, he could not broach the subject; not with her, his wife, anyone.

Sam knew her boss was swimming in a sea of anxiety, and she regretted requesting he engage in more conversation regarding his personal life. She felt she was piling on. She did not intend to cause additional mental strain, but the issue he had with Christmas drove her insane, and she hoped someday he'd confide in her. Clearly, this was not the day. Cautious with her stride, she eased behind the desk, sidled up next to him. Jack did not acknowledge her approach or surrender his position upon feeling her near.

Following a brief scan of downtown, Sam leaned forward beyond Jack's large frame to view his face. He stood erect, rocking back and forth on his heels, scanning downtown from street to sky. She noticed the muscles in his jaw pulsating. Backing away, she thought how odd it was to see him in this condition. *He is mortal,* she thought, as a bit of empathy surged through her conscience. She placed a hand on his arm in a show of support.

"Is there anything I can do for you?" There was no response.

"I know a lot of goofy things have happened to you today and I don't know what's going on, but I believe everything happens for a reason. I also believe God does not put on our plate what we can't handle."

Jack's expression morphed from a man with a lot on his mind to one whose honor was just insulted in public. He dipped his head toward her direction. Sam dropped her hand from his arm and shuffled a few steps to her right as the corners of his mouth tightened into a snarl.

"If God has played any role in this, I can assure you it's that of an antagonist," he barked. "Don't lecture me on the righteousness of God or the divine lessons he teaches us to foster some saving grace. It's all bullshit."

Sam dropped a few more steps away, caught off guard by his reaction to what she thought was an innocent statement chronicling her beliefs.

"I've prayed to God," he said, walking toward her, burying a finger into his chest. "I've dropped to my knees, praying to God, and He's heard nothing. He's abandoned me during times I've needed Him most and He's taken from me more than you, Brooke, or anyone else will ever know. Don't you dare lecture me on God. God doesn't give a rat hole about me. If He does exist, whoever or whatever it is, I will not be a party to paying homage to something that picks and chooses who gets anointed in this world and who gets screwed."

Sam could not have been more stunned and refused to believe her ears. Remaining fixed upon the anger and pain in Jack's face, she wondered just where it came from and what had happened to cause such disgust and distrust. Jack resumed his original pose; Sam stood rigid, unable to disengage. She felt a twinge in her chest for the obvious pain he carried, and had it not been for a soft rap on the molding encasing his office door, she would be wiping tears from her cheeks.

"Hello, Samantha. It's me, Charlie McDonald. May I come in?" The old man stood behind the threshold, offering a wave of his hand. Sam paused, looking at Jack as if he'd just admitted to a murder, before moving toward the door and engaging her friend with a smile.

"Hello, Mr. Mac. Please, come in."

The old man proceeded into the room, looking over the office's grand features with wide eyes. Sam met him halfway.

A trusted employee of the firm since 1949, Mac—as he was known around the office—was a welcomed sight and someone near and dear to Sam's heart. A decorated World War II veteran, he fought a hero's war as a member of the prestigious First Marine Raider Battalion in the Pacific theatre before suffering severe wounds during the invasion of Guadalcanal.

Following a lengthy recovery at a naval hospital, he returned to action at Tarawa where he lost his left arm to a bayonet wound sustained fighting off two Japanese soldiers as they attempted to skewer a couple of his injured buddies in a mortar pit.

In a chance meeting at a military function just weeks after V-J Day, he met John Junior and was offered a position with the agency on the spot. With work difficult to find for a returning war vet missing a limb, Mac accepted the offer of running the firm's mailroom and courier service, which he served more than fifty years. When Mac was no longer able to handle the rigors of running deliveries, John Junior arranged a position for him with the group managing the high-rise to run the building's security and information desk.

Despite being an employee of the management company, John Junior rewarded Mac's years of loyalty to the firm with a lifetime contract that would keep him on payroll until the day both he and his wife passed. To Sam, he was a second father.

"I'm sorry to disturb the both of you," Mac said, taking off his security cap.

"You're not disturbing us, Mr. Mac. It's great to see you." Sam placed her arms around his neck; the two enjoyed a prolonged hug.

"Hello, Mr. Clarke," Mac said dipping his head.

"Hello . . . what do you want?" Jack snapped, prompting Sam to shoot a menacing glare in her boss's direction. She did not appreciate the tone or his lack of respect. She placed a hand on the stub of what was left of her friend's arm.

"How are you today?" she asked. "I looked for you at lunch."

"Well, I'm sorry sweetheart," he said, disappointed. "I ran down the street to pick up some medicine."

"Are you feeling alright?"

"Oh, feeling fine," he said, tucking a manila envelope under the stump of his shoulder, catching Jack's eye.

"The medicine is for Gayle. She's not feeling well. Thank you for asking, though. I just stopped by to drop this off to Mr. Clarke," he said, nodding toward the envelope.

Sam noticed a nervous vein popping in Jack's neck as he stared at the parcel.

"That was very sweet of you," she said, diverting her attention back to her friend. "You should've called me though. I would have been happy to come get it."

"No problem. I needed to come up here anyway."

"We appreciate it, don't we, Jack?" Not hearing a reply, Sam peeked back over her shoulder. "Don't we, Jack?"

"Oh, absolutely," Jack responded, nodding in hurried agreement, looking at Sam rather than the old man. "Thank you." Jack tugged at his shirtsleeve to view his watch. Sam noticed his expression change and followed suit. Her watch indicated 2:00 p.m. on the nose.

"Well, it's my pleasure, son," Mr. Mac said. "I'll tell you, though, it was just about the strangest thing I ever saw."

Jack disengaged from his watch and thrust his head in the old man's direction. "What do you mean strange?" he asked.

"Well, this gentleman pulled up in front of the building in a very old flatbed truck. I've not seen a truck like that in fifty years."

"Was it pink?" Jack asked.

"Why, yes, it was. How'd you know?"

"How *did* you know?" Sam asked, spinning on her heels.

"I was looking out the window earlier and noticed it traveling down Wacker, heading toward the building."

"Well, pink it was . . . strangest color on a truck I've ever seen. Anyway, I got up from behind the desk and walked out to the sidewalk to let him know he was in a no-parking zone. He stepped out of the truck and we chatted for a moment. I was going to insist he get back in and park elsewhere but I just could not help myself and had to ask him about it. He said it was a '53 Chevy one ton.

"He opened the door and let me look inside. It was as if it had rolled off the assembly line just this morning. It was immaculate. I mentioned it was a real beauty and he said he bought it yesterday. I turned and questioned him. He said he bought it in some little town north of here. I asked him if he was joking and he said 'no' just as matter-of-factly as you please."

"He said north of here?" Jack asked.

"Yes sir."

"Did he tell you the name of the town?" Sam said.

"Yes, I think he did, but I can't remember. I'm sorry, Mr. Clarke," he apologized.

"He also was dressed pretty funny," Mac continued, "at least for someone driving such a vehicle. It was like a rented costume. I'd not seen those types of clothes in years. He was in a brown, wool striped, three-piece suit, with a white shirt and a very short tie tucked in between the buttonholes. He wore a black fedora and brown boots with laces tied all the way up. Those boots reminded me of what the dough-boys were issued during the Great War."

"A black fedora?" Jack asked.

"Yes sir."

"Do you recall what he looked like?" Sam asked.

"Well, he was middle-aged, I'd say early fifties and he wore wire-rimmed spectacle glasses. He seemed a nice enough fella. Had a notice-able dent on the side of his head."

"Is there anything else you can remember?" Sam asked.

"Well, he said he was heading back home but thought he might drive around the city a bit since he'd not been downtown for some time. He asked me to give this package to Mr. Clarke, here," he said, nodding to Jack.

"I don't know how it was he knew that I knew you, but he did and said you were expecting this. Then he asked for six bits for the deliv-ery. I'll tell ya, I hadn't heard that expression in fifty years. So, I gave him a couple bucks, figuring it must be something important you were waiting on. Then he got back into the truck. He also said to tell you he was sorry for ringing your doorbell this morning. He said—"

"He said what?" Jack yelled.

The abrupt change in Jack's voice startled Mac, causing him to retreat a couple steps toward the door.

"Jack." Sam barked, seeing her friend move away. She followed after Mac and patted him on the back to settle his nerves.

"Mr. Mac, are you sure that's what he said?"

"Word for word, sweetheart." The old man kept a cautious eye on Jack.

"But you say he was in his early fifties?"

"Well, I might be off a bit, but he was much younger than me. Maybe in his late fifties, but I doubt it. I'd say fifty-three or so."

Mac noticed a change in Jack's complexion. "I don't mean to pry, but is there something wrong? Did I do something wrong?" he asked, as his eyes darted back and forth between the two.

"No, not at all," Sam urged, as Jack moved toward the two to retrieve the envelope. "You didn't do a thing wrong. We appreciate your telling us about it." Sam smiled, hoping his concern would ease.

"My pleasure. Anytime I can spend a few minutes with you is okay with me." The three traded glances, unsure as to who should speak next.

"Well, I guess I'll be on my way," Mac said. "If I don't see you before you leave today Samantha, you have a nice Christmas with your family . . . you too, Mr. Clarke," he said, waving his cap.

Jack didn't hear a thing. He'd already turned from them and was a million miles away.

"Merry Christmas to you," Sam said. "I hope Gayle feels better soon. Are you two coming to the party tonight?"

"No, not tonight. She's just not up to it, and I don't want to leave her home alone."

"That's probably best; looks as if the weather's going to turn bad anyway. Well, I guess I'll see you when I get back next week. We have a dinner date for the 29th. Don't forget."

"I won't, honey. Gayle and I are looking forward to seeing you. You be careful going home now. I love you," he said, putting his arm around her.

"I love you, too."

Mac stopped short of the threshold as another nugget came to mind. He pivoted, holding his index finger in the air.

"You know," he said, "there's one other thing. When the fella drove off, I noticed some lettering on the tailgate of the truck. I think it said McClellan Delivery Service."

The two watched as Jack's chin dropped. Without moving, Jack asked if the man offered his name.

"No sir, he didn't."

"Did you ask him?"

"No sir, I didn't."

"Shit," Jack barked as he spun away from their view. "That's just great."

Had Sam been holding something—anything—her boss would be extracting it from the back of his skull.

"Mr. Mac," Sam said, "the town where the man said he bought the truck, could it have been Clear Lake?"

"No," he said, shaking his head.

"Does Cartersville ring a bell?"

"Yes, I think he did say Cartersville."

"Did you happen to see his license plate?" she asked.

"No, I'm sorry. I guess I'm no Dick Tracy, huh?"

"Don't you worry about it," she said. "We appreciate everything you've told us."

The old man gave her a wink as he exited. Sam walked to the door and slammed it shut.

"God, Jack," she said, stomping toward him. "What's the matter with you? You scared that poor man to death. Did you see how bad he felt?"

He did not turn from the window. Sam moved at an exaggerated pace to a position in front of him, forcing a face-to-face.

"I don't appreciate the way you spoke to him," she said, burying a finger into his chest. "He's the sweetest and dearest man on this planet and you should be so lucky to have him for a friend. You wouldn't be fit as a hair in his nostril. Why do you have to be such a stupid jerk sometimes?"

"Don't lecture me," Jack shot back. "Did you hear what he said? Did you hear his description of the man who delivered the envelope? He said the man apologized for ringing my doorbell this morning . . . the jackass who rang my doorbell was not the man he just described—not even close. Do you want to tell me what the hell that means? And I don't want to hear anything other than answers coming from your mouth."

Sam buried her fists into her hips. "I know this is unsettling, but you don't have the right to take it out on everyone around you. Mac has endured more hell on earth than you'll ever know and he's nothing but an innocent bystander. He deserves your respect. And why don't you watch your mouth around people, for crying out loud. You're so foul at times, it's unbelievable. Have you ever once strung together 'yes' or 'no' with 'sir' or 'ma'am' in your entire freaking life?"

"I'm sorry, that doesn't sound like an answer to me; it sounds like a statement. Did you happen to notice the time?"

"I saw the time," she barked, "but you have no right to—"

"That means the telegram was accurate and the email was just another piece of the puzzle. Do you have any idea how crazy this is and how crazy it's making me? And you want me to be concerned with how I'm speaking to people or using the English language? Have you lost your mind? For crying out loud," he mocked.

Sam gritted her teeth. "I know this is nuts; it's beyond nuts. I'm just asking you to calm down and stop chewing on people trying to help you."

Jack turned before she could finish. Any discussion other than the topic at hand was of no interest. Sam waited for him to acknowledge his poor behavior but it wasn't coming. His attention redirected to the manila envelope in his hands.

"Well?" she asked, her tone impatient. "Are you going to open it or not?"

Staring out the window, he passed the envelope off in her direction. He did not have the nerve.

Snatching it from his hands, Sam was quick to slice the flap with a finger. Peeking in, she noticed two pieces of cardboard-like stock sandwiching a thinner, copper-colored paper stock. Pulling out the three pieces, she discarded the envelope to the floor and separated the cardboard, revealing an old, black and white photo. Her gasp drew his attention.

"Oh my goodness," she said, her voice vibrant with excitement. "Unbelievable."

"What? What is it?" he insisted.

The photo, yellowed by oxidation and chipped and scratched along its edges, revealed a young girl holding a kitten, sitting on a front porch step. Sam inspected every square inch as she walked toward the couch on the opposite side of the room. Jack followed in her wake, straining to view over her shoulder.

"Look at this," she said, turning on a dime halfway across the room.

Jack searched the picture as Sam held it steady against her chest. He missed something she had not.

"Okay, so it's a girl with a black cat in her lap. What about it?"

"Jack," Sam pleaded, "look at the girl."

"Yeah, okay, so?"

"So? Are you kidding me?" she said, flashing the picture then looking to him as if he were not recognizing his own reflection. "Jack, it's Brooke."

"What?" He grabbed the picture from her hands and brought it close to his face. He was unable to see any resemblance. "You're crazy, that doesn't look anything like her."

"I'm telling you, it's her. What, are you blind?"

"I don't know what you're looking at. Brooke was born in 1970, not in the 1920's, which seems to be when this photo was taken. She's allergic to cats."

"Wow, you're super smart, Mr. Science," she jabbed, rolling her eyes. "I'm telling you, this is either Brooke or her twin sister. I guarantee you this is how she looked as a little girl. Have you not seen a baby picture of her?"

"No. None I can recall."

Big surprise, Sam thought.

"There's no way in hell it's her," he insisted.

Sam recovered the photo to take one last look. She was certain the girl in the picture was Jack's wife, or a close family member. She'd stake her sleuthing reputation on it.

Returning the photo to Jack's grasp, she noticed on the floor a small index card protruding from the envelope. She lifted the card to inspect.

"There's a note here," she announced, after flipping the card. "It has Palmer House and six o'clock scribbled in pencil."

Jack snatched the card from her hand, bringing it close to his face.

"There's no signature, just the hotel and time," he mumbled. "How the hell did he know we'd be at the Palmer House this evening? Is something being delivered to the party?"

Sam shrugged. "I don't know . . . I just don't know how to explain any of this."

"That means something else is coming."

"Sure sounds like it," Sam replied.

Jack tossed the card to the floor and reached for the photo.

"This picture doesn't have anything to do with anything. What means something is old McDonald describing a man claiming to have rung my doorbell this morning that looks nothing like the man I remember. Either your buddy is smoking crack or somebody is playing a game with me. And if I find out who it is, I'm going to knock their block off and beat their mother with it."

"Hey, you take that back," Sam fired back. "If Mr. Mac told you the man was fifty, then it's so. He hasn't told a lie in his life, unlike someone else I know."

"And, by the way, what's going on between you two?" Jack snapped. "I mean, Jesus, he calls you sweetheart, honey, tells you he loves you. What, is he your lover or something?"

"How dare you," Sam yelled stepping forward to close the gap. She pushed against his chest. "You're such a complete, stupid idiot. He's been like a father to me. At least I have someone who means more to me than myself. At least I have someone who cares about me because of the person I am. You're so freaking smart, the one person you have who cares anything for you, you've told to get out of your life. Don't you ever say anything like that about him again. Do you understand me?" Sam shot for the door.

Jack called her name. Reversing course, she moved a few short steps in his direction.

"What? You want me out of your life too?" she said, spreading her arms. "I'm not Brooke; I don't have to take your crap. You're lucky I've put up with your insensitive and self-serving nonsense this long. And

I'll tell you something else, you wouldn't last one week without me. Chew on that fathead . . . you're such an arrogant jerk." Sam grabbed a hold of the doorknob. "By the way, you owe Mr. Mac two dollars, cheapskate." With that, she stormed past the threshold, making sure to slam the door as hard as she could.

"Sam," Jack yelled again, this time over the echo of the crash of the door and the sound of her office chair slamming against the desk. He froze, waiting for a reply, all the while keeping a keen eye on the door.

The first ten seconds were the most crucial when she exited in a huff. On more than one occasion, she'd returned to launch an object in his direction. He received a set of keys in the side of the head a few years back when he fired a longstanding staffer. An electric pencil sharpener nearly took off his ear just last year when he called her a hack editor for missing a typo in a PowerPoint presentation he'd designed for an important client.

Jack kept his eye on the door as he moved toward his desk. He had no plans of underestimating her bad habit. He was certain she'd calm herself in a few hours. Like Brooke, he knew she'd not leave him. She, too, enjoyed the benefit of a decent lifestyle, thanks to his success.

Beginning to feel the effects of skipping breakfast and lunch, Jack's stomach grew uneasy, although it was hard to determine if a lack of food or his wadded up nerves were the cause of the guttural rumbles emanating from his midsection. A quick sandwich would be nice, but he had no intention of leaving the office. He could rely on Sam to bring him something when his days grew busy, but if he didn't want something imprinted with the sole of her shoe and spat upon, he was out of luck this day.

His mouth had dried to the consistency of a sand trap. A rising panic was building as he fought a growing paranoia fueled by mental exhaustion. He needed time to think. Now confident his assistant had passed on the opportunity for a surprise attack, he reversed course and walked toward a collection of highball glasses stacked in the shape of a pyramid atop the bar. He grabbed for the first glass and dropped in two cubes of ice, before unscrewing the top off a bottle of thirty-year-old scotch. Returning to his desk, he sucked down a quick, shiver-inducing shot, before planting himself in his chair.

He pulled the telegram from his pocket and placed it on the desk next to the photo of the girl and the hand-written note. Taking another swig, he wished now he'd printed the e-mail before it was lost. Regardless, the message burned permanently in his brain. Leaning back in his chair, he clasped his hands behind his head and scanned the three items, searching for a connection.

His struggles focused on the old man's description of Bigsby.

"How could the man be fifty?" he asked aloud. "This morning he looked as if he'd crawled from a crypt."

He did not need a photo of Brooke when she was young to conclude that she and the little girl in the picture looked nothing alike. Sam was nuts. None of it was making sense. Jack exhaled a partial sigh and laughed as he thought of the many surgeries the person responsible for this would be facing when this was over.

Spinning to the window behind, he noticed how dark the clouds had become, appearing now as a tsunami readying to level the city.

Attempting to escape for a few moments, he focused his view on the traffic bustling along Lake Shore. He followed the route to the intersection of East Ohio Street, where an image caught his attention, forcing him to the edge of his chair. Snatching his binoculars, he worked to focus the lenses, then watched as a pink, out-of-place flatbed truck turned left onto Lake Shore Drive and disappeared into the traffic heading north.

CHAPTER 9

"How in the world can it not be right here?" Sam yelled. "For crying out loud."

Having searched along the far wall near her door, she was now crawling on all fours, inspecting the deepest corners under her desk for any traces of the missing half sandwich.

Her frustration was at a boiling point, caused less by the unaccounted-for tuna on rye than the infantile stupidity of her boss. Surmising the sandwich had disappeared into the same dimension also claiming her socks on occasion, Sam pulled back onto her chair and adjusted clothing that had scrunched sideways during the tunneling. She'd hoped the search and rescue effort would distract her from the intense anger burning inside, but was disappointed it only added to her agitation.

Hoping to lower her blood pressure and erase from her mind the insensitive remarks Jack spouted about her dear friend, she sat still, attempting several self-help exercises she'd seen on Oprah. None proved helpful. Had Jack directed his frustrations toward her alone, the issue would have passed through her system like a nice helping of fiber.

Dealing with his verbal abuse was nothing a computer speaker or hand-held calculator to the back of the head couldn't remedy. But attacking a poor old man, an innocent bystander, a veteran—well, it was more than she was willing or able to concede. Although Sam knew her reaction was consistent with the moment, she felt anger and guilt drawing battle lines deep within her gut as she recalled her own parting shots before storming out of his sight. It never seemed to fail; when she delivered an insult at the exact moment she meant to deliver it, regret always followed.

She cared for Jack; even loved him—as a sister would a brother—despite the many reasons he gave her to question that loyalty. He did look after her and was a champion, on many fronts, for her advancement in the firm, including fighting for raises and the tools she needed to do her job. He was *the* best at what he did; better than anyone she knew in the industry.

He'd taught her so much, and she was thankful for the opportunity to learn. His ability to take clients from less than mediocre to overnight success stories through ingenious and groundbreaking strategies became the stuff of legend on the national scene. He was a patient teacher—which surprised her—and she appreciated his involving her in every step with their clients. Despite his ways, he also deserved her respect.

Now fiddling with the wireless mouse on the credenza, she contemplated all Jack had done for her; not just from a professional standpoint, but for her personal life. The time he bought her a round-trip ticket to Utah to attend the funeral of her grandmother, or when he picked her up at a truck stop in the wee hours of the morning when her car broke down on her way back from visiting her parents.

She considered the ludicrous circumstances he was facing and the obvious pressure crushing his psyche. She thought of his pain; his hatred of God and the reasons causing such a reaction. She knew he was carrying a heavy burden and wanted to probe and learn more, but he either didn't know how to talk about it or could not surrender to the habit of isolating himself from those wanting to get close. She wondered what had happened to him.

The idea he'd suffered something so traumatic as to turn his back on God, weighed heavy on her mind. It was not long before her anger traded for guilt.

Turning to the credenza, she placed the mouse back in its rightful position near the keyboard. An inadvertent touch of the scroll wheel launched the computer into action, and as her monitor flashed to life, she noticed the familiar miniature yellow envelope at the bottom right-hand corner indicating a new email had arrived. She'd checked the server connection not long ago, finding it deader than a doornail. The system appeared back online. The good news broke her moment of reflection, summoning the interest she shared in her boss's predicament. His strange encounter with Bigsby and the material evidence she witnessed was enough for the beginnings of a good novel. Never one to back away from a challenge or mystery, the situation was just too tempting.

More than fifty emails monopolizing her large LCD screen confirmed the server's connection. Filtering through the messages, scanning each for importance and priority, Sam responded to the half-dozen or so needing immediate attention before reaching for a notepad and pen to organize her thoughts. Another quick click of the mouse replaced her e-mail with a web browser.

It was times like this her eidetic memory paid dividends—a trait many in her family believed she inherited from her great, great-grand-father. A celebrated captain of the world's oceans, legend had it he needed only to view a nautical map once before setting out on a journey.

Sam attributed her personal success to the skill, including her stellar scholastic performance and minor success as a novelist. Her uncanny ability for recall proved both a curse and a blessing in Jack's world. Being able to extract exact details of clients' conversations and requests proved so invaluable that he made a point to include her in every discussion, meeting, and client encounter.

Her memory filled the gaps where his faded, making them a powerful combination when going after big game or holding clients accountable. On the other hand, God help him if he said anything he could not substantiate later, because she'd nail his rear to the wall.

Sam cleared a spot for her notepad then pressed a palm against her forehead. She processed the towns Jack mentioned and completed an inventory of the other names, dates, and data of the most significant elements of the incident so far. The image of the telegram appeared, as did the information printed on it, including its origination at a Western Union station in New Auburn. She trolled her memory for the other locations, jotting down Cartersville, Cumberland, and Clear Lake.

Just as her pencil lifted from completing the tail of the "e" in Lake, she drew her head upward and over her shoulder as a familiar aroma drifted into the space from the hallway. The scent was delicate, yet obtrusive and one she knew well.

"Oh God, please, not now," she whispered.

The sound of precious metal pinging against the steel frame of her office door sent her torso swiveling toward the hallway. Hoping it was someone else, she watched as slender, ring-clad fingers stretched around the corner, suggesting the visitor was positioning for a peek into the space rather than entering at a normal gait. Following a slight pause, long, straight auburn hair breached the opening, followed by the perfect facial features of Staci DiSano.

"Good afternoon, Samantha," she said in a soft, sultry voice. "I wasn't expecting to see you here today."

"Hello, Staci," Sam said, minus the pleasant and uplifting smile with which she greeted most all other co-workers. Eye contact between the two concluded in a flash, with Sam diverting her attention to the mess of paperwork, open files, and post-it notes on her desk. She felt no reason to engage in idle chatter with a woman given a job on a silver platter with no college degree, experience, or a brain in her head.

Executive secretary to and niece of firm partner Giuseppe Rossi, Staci was all of twenty-eight years old and stunning beyond the male animal's ability to resist. Natural auburn hair flowed to the small of her back over one shoulder, and atop large, round, medically enhanced breasts over the other. A slender, "v" shaped face flaunted natural bronze tones characteristic of an Italian heritage. Her lips were perfect, full and rose in color, complimenting large, brown eyes commanding attention.

She was a woman who got what she wanted with little more than a wink and a smile. She'd secured her position and inflated salary as a favor from one brother to another, and did little to endear herself to the other females in the office. The men? Well, they loved her; dumb as a chick-pea but perfect in every other way. Other than appearing on a few corporate billboards and print advertisements, she contributed little else toward the company's bottom line, which did not sit well with Sam. She believed one should earn their way to a six-figure salary, not be given one because of kin or the ability to stop traffic with fake boobs and a nice pair of legs.

"Umm, by the way," Staci said, pointing a finger toward the other side of the doorway, "did you know there's a sandwich out here against the wall?"

"Oh, is that where I left it?" Sam said, scratching her head in a deliberate attempt to mock.

"Did you leave it out there on purpose?"

"Yes, I did," she replied, matter-of-factly.

"Okay . . . well . . . would you like me to pick it up?"

"No, the rats will eat it. What can I do for you?"

Staci shook her head, unsure if Sam was joking. "Well, I just stopped by to see Jack for a few moments."

"He's pretty busy today. Can I tell him what this is about?"

"Nothing urgent . . . just a social visit you might say."

"I see . . . well, I will check to see if he's available."

"By the way, your outfit looks fantastic," Staci said. "I love how it highlights your figure."

Sam could care less. "Can I tell him how much time you need?" She looked up to see Staci staring in an almost mocking fashion. The woman made her skin crawl.

"Can I tell him how much time you need?" Sam again questioned.

"Oh, I'm sorry, just a few minutes," she responded, twitching as if breaking from a spell. "I also have a few documents Uncle Giuseppe needs him to sign."

"Oh, well in that case, go ahead on in. He's by himself." Sam returned to her computer, anxious to start the investigation.

Staci advanced through the office, thanking Sam with a smile and a sensual wink. She tapped on Jack's door twice then entered. As the door shut behind, Sam scrunched her face and wiggled as if a spider had fallen from the ceiling into her hair.

<hr>

"Letters from your girlfriend?" Staci called out.

Jack did not hear the knock or notice the door open as he sat slouched studying the evidence. Despite her clear inflection, her voice did not break his concentration. The clicking of her heels against the hardwood floor did the trick. With great haste, he grabbed the items displayed on his desk and stuffed them into the top drawer.

Jack looked upon the elegant vision approaching, finding immediate favor in the woman and her outfit. A cream-colored blouse fit snug against her torso; a silky skirt tight against her narrow waist, dripped over slender hips. And those legs.

"No," Jack said, readjusting himself in his chair. "Just some crap. What do you want?" he snapped, hoping to cloak his true desires.

Staci approached the front of his desk, gliding along as if modeling for a European designer before slipping into one of the soft chairs.

Pulling herself back, adjusting her posture, she watched as Jack peeked between her legs.

"I thought I would stop by to say 'hello.'"

"I don't have time to talk right now. I'm very busy," he said.

"It looks like it," she said, scanning the top of his cleared off desk. "Are you angry with me?" Staci dipped her head, smiled, and pierced his soul with her seductive eyes. She was a player and knew what men wanted. She used it to her advantage, learning early in life a beautiful, sexy woman held the keys to the ignition of the universe.

"Yeah," Jack said. "Pretty pissed."

"Jack," she said, crossing her arms, "do you ever remember giving me your home phone number?" He did not reply.

"I called the number you gave me. I can't explain how it rang to your home. How stupid do you think I am?"

"Pretty freakin' stupid to call four times before figuring out something wasn't right."

"I've met your wife once. I didn't know it was her. I thought it might be one of your flunkies. Anyway, the voice sounded different each time I called. I didn't know it was her."

"Do you know how much I have to lose if this thing gets out of hand?" he asked, pointing a finger in her direction. "Do you have any idea how much I'm worth?"

"I have just as much to lose as you do, if not more," she countered. "Honest, Jack, I would not have called had I known."

"I think we need to back off awhile until this blows over," he said. "Brooke is not stupid. She already suspects something, and I sounded like a complete idiot this morning trying to explain your phone calls to the house and the perfume on my shirts. She could wipe my ass clean off the face of this earth if she finds the right lawyer, and I'm not willing to take that chance at the moment."

"I thought you liked my perfume? I wear it because you bought it for me."

"Not the point," he yelled, turning to the lake. "I'm not about to lose everything over this."

"Jack," Staci called out in an affectionate tone. He did not respond. "Jack, look at me," she said. He turned from the window. His eyes planted squarely on her chest.

"We will do whatever you think is best, okay? I promise. No more phone calls." Staci rose from her chair and walked behind the desk. Reaching over the back of his chair, she ran her long, slender fingers down the front of his shirt, caressing his pecs before retracting her touch to rest atop his shoulders. She leaned into him, brushing the tip of her nose and soft lips against his ear, sending a wave of fragrance exploding through his nostrils and a shiver down his spine.

"I know you can't stay mad at me very long," she whispered, toying with him as if he were nineteen and she his college professor.

Her scent was intoxicating and face soft as mink as she grazed against the light stubble along his jaw line. He could feel her breasts against the back of his head.

Stepping back, Staci placed her hand on top of the soft Italian leather chair and tugged at its corner to pull him around to meet her. A canyon of cleavage settled just inches from his face. Reaching down, she took his hand in hers and kissed his fingers. With his hands moving about her body unimpeded, she closed her eyes and expelled a soft sigh. Grabbing a hunk of his shirt, she attempted to pull him from the chair to against her body. Jack felt her intent and stood to meet her.

Staci extended high on her toes, advancing toward his lips. Deep exhales and inhales echoed through the office as the two allowed their passion to burst forth. They kissed, grinded, and grabbed at one another for several minutes before Staci broke contact. She leaned back and flashed a satisfied smile; Jack released his embrace.

Stretching her body to reach his ear, she whispered, "I knew you weren't upset." Taking him by the hand, she led him around the desk to the bar, thinking a quick splash of brandy would do them both a world of good.

With mouse in hand and eyes glued to the computer screen, Sam amassed several interesting tidbits in her research. She searched the Internet for a site to assist in locating matching city names across the U.S. and stumbled upon one offering a complete database. Searching the first name on her list, the site returned twenty cities and towns named Cartersville. She printed the list and followed suit with the other names. Clear Lake returned seven, Cumberland seventeen, and New Auburn three.

She was relieved at the promising starting point. New Auburn appeared in two states—Minnesota and Wisconsin. After cross-referencing the other three names, she determined just three appeared in Illinois while all four appeared in Minnesota and Wisconsin. She contemplated her next step in finding a sensible connection. After careful deliberation, she concluded if she were going to purchase a new car, she'd do so in close proximity to where she lived. She searched the proximity of the cities to one another.

Searching distances from New Auburn, Wisconsin, to Cumberland, Wisconsin, the program estimated driving time as forty-three minutes—one-way—less than one hundred miles round-trip to buy a new car, which seemed reasonable.

Plotting the four cities in each of the states, she discovered the grouping to be within a fifty-mile radius of one another in Wisconsin.

Sam continued mining for clues, searching for the McClellan Delivery Service and the officials' names on the telegram: Newcomb Carlton, president, and George W. E. Atkins, first vice-president. She received no results in the search for the delivery service. Several archived articles appeared regarding Carlton, who was indeed the president of Western Union in 1923; at least she could authenticate the year of the telegram. Information on George Watkins referenced only an old-time professional baseball player for the St. Louis Browns.

She found no matches upon searching the name Jubel Bigsby and nothing to connect the city of New Auburn, Minnesota, or Wisconsin, as being an official Western Union office. Sam documented her findings in a spreadsheet and printed it out with the intention of showing Jack. She loved research and the ease with which she could find information with just a few clicks of the mouse.

Despite an elevated interest in the mystery, a large part of her insisted Jack should figure it out for himself. She was still very angry, but felt obligated to help if she could. Sam picked up her findings from off the printer and reviewed them for accuracy. She was anxious to share the results.

Not thinking twice that her boss had a visitor, Sam entered his office looking left in the direction of his desk. Seeing it vacated, she pivoted toward the bar after catching movement out of the corner of her eye. As her head caught up with the turn of her body, she lost her breath at the sight of Jack and Staci embraced in a deep, passionate kiss.

The release of the door went unnoticed. Sam stood paralyzed in complete shock, unable to utter a word. Jack's eyes cracked open just in time to see his assistant standing with her mouth open. Breaking free of Staci's embrace, he moved away as if Brooke had entered the space. He took a few steps toward Sam as she backpedaled toward the door.

"Sam, this isn't what you think," he said, racing toward her. The wet glare in her eyes and shock upon her face stopped him dead in his tracks, prompting an eerie silence known only to those who've experienced the calm before a tornado. Sam gritted her teeth and stormed out of the room. Jack swung around to Staci.

"Move out of the way," he demanded.

"What?" she asked, looking confused. "What are you talking about?"

"Move out of the way, dammit," he yelled, waving his arm at her in the direction of the window. Staci stepped aside not a moment too soon. Jack turned just in time to identify and dodge a glass paperweight waffling through the air like a Japanese shuriken death star. The object just missed wide right, but found a target beyond, shattering three bottles of booze and several highball glasses resting on the bar. Staci let out a faint scream; Jack dropped his arms from around his head to survey the damage. Sam slammed the door as hard as she could.

Jack motioned Staci toward the door. As the two exited his office, he pushed hard against her back to suggest she should keep moving and not say a word. She passed Sam without making eye contact.

Sam said nothing, ignoring them both, as she stuffed personal belongings into a large blue backpack. Jack stood at the doorway, watching her slam items into the bag.

"Sam," he pleaded, "listen to me, it's not what you think." She stopped long enough to offer a brief reply.

"I'm done with you . . . you piece of—" she stopped herself before rattling off an expletive. She chomped down hard on her jaw in an attempt to rein in her anger.

"I'll be back after Christmas to get the rest of my things," she said in a much calmer but more direct pitch. "I can't believe I felt sorry for you. Whatever bad happens to you from here on out, you've earned it and deserve it. Good luck, you freaking coward."

Sam ripped the bag from off her desk, tossed it over her shoulder, grabbed her coat and purse from behind the door and headed down the hallway.

"Sam," Jack yelled, following her into the hallway. "Listen to me, I can explain this."

His attempts to stop her were in vain. He watched helplessly as she disappeared around the corner and into the lobby. The last indication she was on the floor was the slamming of the lobby door leading down the stairs. Jack brought his hand to his brow. He'd messed up large and he knew it.

CHAPTER 10

For Brooke, no artist expressed the holiday season with more spirited energy than Nat King Cole. Lost in her favorite CD, humming and singing along with the master crooner, she stared out the driver's side window at the passing harvested wheat and cornfields as the landscape merged from the browns of fall to the white of winter. The sun remained above the horizon somewhere, but it was losing its cast to a legion of rolling clouds portending a snowstorm.

A northwest course took the family into the face of the system charging toward Chicago, as harmless spits of sleet changed to light, fluffy snow, accumulating on all but the pavement below. Viewing the digital gauge on the rearview mirror, Brooke was not surprised to see the temperature had dropped twenty degrees from where it hovered when she pulled from their driveway. Checking the mirror, Jordan and Julianna remained limp against each other's heads, having fallen fast asleep to the gentle humming of oversized tires on asphalt.

She adored the sight of their faces as they slept, wondering where their dreams had taken them. Rudolph was hard at work saving Christmas on the pop-down video screen in front of them, but the girls had lasted little beyond his chance meeting with Hermey the elf. The girls were great travelers, enjoying watching videos, playing car games, and singing. Although thankful they were resting, Brooke wished they were still awake. The interaction would benefit her mind, which now wandered back to thoughts of her husband and the life she was fleeing.

Brooke had spent so much time talking to God the past few years that she often broke out in prayer on a whim; sometimes speaking aloud without realizing location or proximity to others. The few friends she had began offering pitying glances. She feared God had grown tired of her constant requests for intervention, believing now her pleas had fallen on deaf ears.

Nevertheless, she continued appealing for His guidance, hoping some way, somehow, He would help Jack find his way back to her. Speaking over the holiday music, softly so as not to wake the girls, she prayed for her husband's safety and for his soul, and begged God to forgive her for the pain—if any—she would cause him for taking the girls.

The approaching dusk forced on the vehicle's automatic headlights, illuminating the snowfall. Brooke never tired of watching snow, believing it was the most peaceful and pleasant of Mother Nature's wonders. It reminded her of the many Thanksgivings and Christmases spent on the family farm.

Severe cold and snow was something one learned to deal with at an early age in Iron River, Wisconsin. It was common for temperatures to dip to thirty or forty degrees below in January, although Brooke recalled an August when the mercury eclipsed the century mark.

Less than an hour southeast of Duluth, Minnesota, Iron River, a community of 1,000, was in the heart of the state's "vacationland." Brooke's great, great-grandfather, an engineer who'd spent the first forty years of his adult life developing the country's thriving railroad system, purchased 400 acres in 1890, padding his fortune by raising cattle and horses, which he sold to the many logging companies invading the region at the turn of the century. She loved the farm, especially draped in snow, and recalled the fun she had with her sisters sledding, skating, snowshoeing, and cross-country skiing until they could no longer feel their limbs. She loved lying on her back in one of their many pastures, watching snow flitter to the ground in complete silence. It was during those moments she had dreamed of having a family and children of her own.

Following harvest in October, Brooke's daddy cut a path in the corn-field for the girls to play hide and seek and to use later in the winter as a path for sleigh riding. The family would hitch their two Shires, pack a sack full of cookies and thermoses of hot chocolate, and ride for hours.

With the girls still in a deep slumber, Brooke decided to take advantage and call home. Her parents would expect to pick them up at the airport. She knew her mother would be suspicious when learning their plans had changed. It was not a conversation she was looking forward to, and the reason she'd delayed it this long.

Anna would not be happy with the manner in which her eldest daughter was removing the children from their home, despite her visceral dislike for Jack. Brooke hoped she'd understand, despite her mother's unwavering Catholic opinion that divorce was sin.

In their nine years of marriage, Jack spent the equivalent of seven days with her parents and family, including the wedding weekend in Chicago. He knew very little about them and used his career as an excuse to avoid reunions, weddings, and holidays. He and Brooke's daddy, John, a former Marine and longtime farmer, enjoyed each other's company in the beginning, but that relationship cooled after Jack bloodied his baby's lip. The last time the two spoke, the old man threatened Jack's existence if he ever hurt his daughter again. John was also a devout Catholic but aligned more with the Old Testament in matters of revenge.

Anna did not condone Jack as her daughter's choice. The fact was, there would never be a man good enough for her Brooke, but she knew her daughter needed to make her own choices. Jack lost any hope of gaining his future mother-in-law's favor the first time they met. He phoned Brooke's father requesting his daughter's hand in marriage but was denied the blessing until the family could meet him. The couple decided to make a quick trip to the farm the next weekend.

After spending most of the first day in the fields together, and knowing from conversations with his daughter how much she loved him, John approved Jack's request to marry his eldest. Jack proposed in front of the family that very night following dinner. He placed a gaudy two-karat ring on her finger then embraced her for a kiss. Forgetting, perhaps, where he was and the company he was in, he held his wife close, dropped his hand from the small of her back and grabbed a handful of her rear.

Anna dropped her cup of coffee at the sight of the distasteful act and removed herself from the table. The departure brought an immediate halt to the celebration. Brooke chased after her mother into the kitchen. The two quarreled several minutes, highlighted by loud accusations and pots and pans hitting the floor. The argument ended with Brooke storming off—blowing past the rest of her family—and running upstairs with Jack on her heels.

Despite receiving an apology, Anna made few attempts to speak to Jack thereafter. Although Anna's objections began with his apparent lack of devotion to Christianity, or any religion for that matter, it ended with his foul mouth and abusive tendencies. Jack slipped with his tongue several times in their presence, drawing ooh's and aah's, as swearing was prohibited. As hard as she tried, Anna could not understand how her daughter could fall in love with such a vile-speaking man.

Brooke dug deep into a side pocket of her purse to retrieve her cell phone. Keeping a keen eye on the road, she checked the display window for messages, feeling foolish at the thought her husband might have sent a text. She navigated to her parents' phone number. Fighting through a bit of static, she could hear a ring on the other end.

Always slow to answer, John and Anna owned just two phones—both of the rotary variety—and not one of them connected to an answering machine.

Her father picked up the receiver on or around ring twelve.

"Hi Daddy."

"Well, hello sweetheart. How are you?"

"Fine Daddy, how are you?"

"Just fine, can't wait to see everyone. How are my little angels?"

"They're doing great. They can't wait to see you."

"Well, we can't wait to see them. When does your flight arrive?"

"I'm not flying, Daddy. I'm driving. We'll be there in about two hours."

"Driving? Why are you driving? Don't you know how bad the weather's turning up here? They're calling for thirty inches of snow over the next few days."

"I just wanted to drive. I thought it would be easier on the girls this time. Anyway, it sounds as if it's a good thing I'm coming in tonight."

"Well, you be careful and call me if you have any trouble. Do you want to speak to your mother?"

"Sure, is she near?"

"Just in the kitchen. You be careful, now, I love you."

"I love you too, Daddy." Brooke heard her father's hand cover the phone and call out to her mother.

"Anna, your eldest is on the line. She's driving in," he yelled.

"Hi, sweetheart, is everything okay?" her mother asked in a panic. "Why are you driving? What's wrong? Are the girls okay?"

"Hi Mamma, everything's fine," Brooke said, trying to remain calm. Her mother's voice sounded aged and exhausted. Although always soothing, Brooke knew the years were catching up with her. "I just wanted to let you know we will be in around eight-thirty or nine."

"For goodness sakes, Brooke, why didn't you call us sooner? Why are you driving, what's wrong? Something's wrong, I know something's wrong."

"Things have been hectic and I thought it would be too much trying to get the girls, their presents, and everything else to the airport. I didn't have the stamina for the hassle. Anyway, it sounds as if the flight had a good chance of being canceled."

"We're in for a wallop, that's for sure. I hope your sisters can make it in okay. I'm assuming, since you're driving, your husband's not coming?"

Brooke hesitated too long to snuff out her mother's concern. She did not want to lie, but also did not want to have this conversation at the moment.

"No, Mamma, he's not coming."

Brooke heard her mother place a hand over the phone and whisper something to her father.

"Brooke, this isn't like you. Just tell me what's going on."

"We can talk when I get home. I promise."

"Did he hurt you?"

"What? No, Mamma. Please, don't start in on Jack. He didn't do anything. Just let me come home and we can talk when I get there, okay?"

"Okay sweetheart. I'm worried about you."

"I know you are. I appreciate it, but I'm fine—really. Is everyone coming home?"

"Well, I think so," her mother said, sighing as if already exhausted. They're all planning to filter in tomorrow. I'm so tired and have so much to do . . . I just don't know if I'll have time to get the tree decorated. Your father found a beautiful one this morning over at John and Margaret Logan's farm. We have it set up, but you know how he is . . . just refuses to decorate a tree alone. Kaye and Darrin, Diane and Jeff and Gina will all be here around noon. Erin and Bobby won't be here 'til around four, and Faye and Michael said they'd be here before dark. We'll have a full house. I just don't know where I'm going to put everyone."

"Don't worry," Brooke said, happy the conversation had been redirected. "The girls and I will get up at the crack of dawn and help you.

They'll be happy to help Grandpa decorate the tree. You don't need to overdo it."

"Well, it's going to be hectic, but your father and I are so happy we'll all be together. It's just going to be a madhouse around here."

"What's Christmas without chaos, right?"

Her mother laughed. Christmas was a special event in their home and one the girls grew up appreciating and anticipating. It was Anna who instilled in them the love of the season and the spirit of being together as a family. Brooke wondered if her mother knew how special a gift it was she'd passed on.

"Well, I better get off the phone. The snow is getting worse and I need to pull off at the next exit to get some gas and something for the girls to eat. We'll see you soon."

"Where are you?"

"Right at two hours away."

"Okay sweetheart. Please be careful. Your father and I will pray for your safe delivery. Please give my little chipmunks a kiss. I can't wait to see how much they've grown."

"I will. I love you." Brooke hesitated, knowing her mother was still on the line. In the hundreds of calls home she'd made over the years, her mother never hung up first.

"Mamma," Brooke said, "would you and Daddy mind if the girls and I stay there a few weeks?" A long pause, followed by a faint sniffle, cemented Brooke's initial assessment she should've left well enough alone.

"Sweetheart," Anna said, fighting through cracks in her voice, "please tell me what happened."

"I will, I promise. The weather is getting worse and I need to concentrate on the road. Please, I promise as soon as we get home I'll tell you everything. Now's just not the time."

"Okay, sweetheart," Anna said, letting out a deep sigh. "You know you can always come home. No matter why or how long you need to stay."

"Thank you Mamma. I love you so much."

She heard her mother begin to sob as she pulled the phone from her ear. Brooke snapped closed the case, feeling regret for mentioning anything at all. She dropped the phone into her bag and glanced into the mirror. The girls hadn't moved an inch.

Although excited knowing she'd celebrate Christmas with her sisters and their families in the same place for the first time in a long time, she was dreading the news she'd be announcing. They would support her and be there to help dry her tears. But they could not fill the place in her heart she'd reserved for her husband, or ease the impending heartache his absence would create. She worried her problems would ruin their holiday.

Brooke noticed a highway sign approaching in the distance. A faint sigh broke from the back seat, sending her peeking over her shoulder. Jordan rubbed her eyes and stretched her arms. Her movement brought Julianna out of her slumber as well.

"How are my babies?" Brooke asked, smiling first, then turning back to view the road.

"Are we there yet?" Julianna asked.

"Not yet, sweetheart. We still have a ways to go."

"Mommy, I'm hungry," Jordan directed.

"Me, too, Mommy," Julianna copied.

Brooke checked her GPS to confirm Exit 135 included a restaurant and gas station. With visibility waning and the roads worsening, she left the highway under the direction of a bright white arrow pointing toward a ramp leading to the sleepy town of Cartersville.

CHAPTER 11

Sprawled against the cold, wet slate of his private shower, finding it difficult to enjoy the peace of being the last employee remaining in the office, or the hot water pelting a soothing rhythm against his backside, Jack rolled his forehead back and forth, cringing with concern that Sam would spill the beans to Brooke. The two were close friends, and combined with Sam's sense of duty, he was certain his wife would learn the truth sooner than later.

The steaming water fell short of providing total relief. Every muscle ached. His legs were weak, even stringy. His stomach, tangled and knotted, was hungry. His head felt heavy as his conscience waded through fragmented bits and pieces of information begging for elucidation.

If there'd been a bench in the stall, he'd be on it and asleep. The time on a large clock hanging above the toilet assured he would not make the party by five. In all his years with the firm, he'd arrived on time just once. Resting the crown of his head against the wall, he aspired to snap a finger and be transported home to his king-size bed, rather than preparing for a party he had no interest in attending. Were it not for the pending delivery, he'd have been on his way home hours ago. What was coming distressed him—considering his bosses and peers would be present—but that was not the reason his nerves were biting at him like a swarm of angry wasps.

If Brooke learned the truth, she'd have an open and shut case in court and could take everything he'd worked so hard to build. A jury would not slight a wife of an adulterer and mother of two small children.

As if getting out of bed had not brought enough turmoil, he now confronted his own stupidity for letting his passion run amuck. It was not the first time he'd entertained a woman in his office, but it was the first time he had done so during business hours, and the first time he'd been caught.

Staci's sexual appetite was at a level unlike any woman he knew. What she wanted, she took with authority. What she needed, she made certain there was no room for misinterpretation. She was more than willing to explore new pleasures and possibilities. Jack could not get enough of her sexual energy and desire. He was unaware of her long-term intentions or expectations and didn't care. He was not interested in love or companionship, just sex; incredible, loveless, raunchy sex. He wondered if his marriage would be different if Brooke's cravings were similar.

Swaying from side to side, allowing the water to massage the lines of his tense shoulders and back, he could not stop replaying the devastated look on Sam's face.

He knew her look when she was angry, shocked, or uncomfortable. The look he saw as he broke from Staci's grasp was unfamiliar to his eyes. He knew Sam was pissed off from here to the moon, but for an instant, he saw something else; a look he'd not seen before. He swore he saw tears building.

The thought puzzled him as to why she would succumb to tears at the site of his passionate embrace with another woman. Anger he could understand; rifling something at his head, no question, but tears? Adjusting to allow the water to pummel his face and chest, he wondered if she was jealous.

"What else could it be?" he whispered. "Maybe, deep down, she's in love with me."

Never short on self-admiration, he savored the possibility of wearing down and conquering another helpless lass. The thought brought a half-cracked smile, but disappeared as another concern surfaced.

"If she's jealous," he said, as if talking to someone standing right outside the shower, "will she try to get even?"

Although Sam was no office gossip nor one to get involved in water cooler politics and romances, this situation was an exception. If she quit, as she threatened, was it possible she'd spill to Mr. Rossi? Or maybe John Junior on her way out the door?

"What in the hell were you thinking?" Jack yelled, turning to the shower wall and smacking his palms against the stone.

The day rivaled both mentally and physically the worst day of his life. He wondered where it was all leading. The six o'clock delivery now forced its way past the vision of Sam's expression and the other items collected since he stood in front of his bathroom sink brushing his teeth.

The once soothing, methodic splash of water massaging his body was now an annoyance. Forcing his triceps into motion, he pushed off the slate and returned his body upright. Lifting his head, he directed his face into the gush one last time before disengaging the shower-head and jets.

Leaning back, he pushed the water from his hair; a motion he wished he could mimic to remove the clutter between his ears. Feeling a cool sting as the remains of the hot stream reduced to frigid, intermittent droplets, he stepped from the shower and onto a soft, padded cotton mat.

Jack reached for a towel opposite the stall. As his fingertips connected with the soft cotton, a blindsiding, unexpected vision evinced with the speed and brilliance of a lightning strike. Staggering, he stared at the floor below, at a blurry outline of a human figure lying face down, pinned under a pile of burning debris and pointing at something in the opposite direction. He could see the flames growing from underneath the body, clawing away at the figure's torso. As quickly as the vision appeared before him, it dissolved in a misty haze into nothingness.

Staggering to regain his equilibrium and unable to focus, he raked at the wall in search of the towel bar, missing his first attempt but managing a secure grip on his second. A bizarre, dizzy feeling and intense nausea struck. He dropped his head and expelled a slew of foam-filled acid to the floor.

As quick as the phenomenon struck, it passed. Returning upright, he released his grip as the vertigo dissipated and his vision restored.

His pupils wandered the room as the residual of the image burned in his conscience. It was so real, so vivid. A wicked, dead chill ripped through the space causing goose bumps from head to toe.

Jack wrapped a towel around his waist and another around his shoulders, before easing onto a padded bench just in front of a locker. The disturbing image created fear that something dreadful was on his family's heels. With the vision came the feeling someone or something was in the space watching him.

The graphic scene stirred his recollection to the last time he saw Brooke; on the floor of their bathroom in intense pain. Knowing she and the girls were on a plane headed north, he grew concerned the vision was a premonition. Either Brooke and the girls were in trouble, or he'd just been given a glimpse relating to the telegram.

Jack crumpled against the wall with head in hands. Bigsby was responsible for this; he was sure of it. Speaking aloud in an effort to drive home his point, he reassured himself he had no intention of hurting Brooke earlier in the day, and that she was the cause of her own fall. He recalled offering his hand to help but *she* slapped it away. Regardless, if this was Bigsby again trying to get his attention, he could not deny that hearing his wife's voice, if for a moment, would ease a portion of his troubled mind.

Jack dug through his locker for a clean set of undergarments then pulled a spotted tan tie and white shirt to accompany an olive-green and cream pinstriped suit. Dressing with haste, he finalized with a dollop of hair gel and a splash of cologne from an unmarked black bottle.

He exited the bathroom to a darkened cityscape and the growing brilliance of millions of Christmas lights scattered and strung across town. Lumbering to his desk, he eased into his chair to retrieve the information he'd stuffed into the top drawer. He inspected the telegram, the photo and handwritten note a final time before depositing them into a manila folder. Rising from his chair, he snatched his briefcase from the floor and his cell from its charger.

He tapped in the number for his wife's phone, pausing just shy of the hallway upon hearing the line pick up.

"We're sorry, the number you have dialed is no longer in service or has been disconnected. Please check with your local listing service for more information. This is a recording."

"What the hell?" Jack dropped the device from his ear, looking at it as if it had sprouted tentacles. "That can't be. She hasn't changed her number in years."

He opened his contacts app on the main screen and drilled down through sixty or so entries to locate Brooke's information. He confirmed the number and dialed again. The line answered on the fourth ring. He hesitated in anticipation of receiving a greeting.

Following many seconds of dead air, he offered a questioning, "Hello." He heard nothing but light static and crackle. Again he spoke, getting no response. Just as he prepared to hang up and dial the number again, a strange voice rose above the interference.

"What can I do for ya?"

The male voice caught Jack off guard. He stuttered, unable to transcribe his thoughts into words. Several seconds elapsed before his anger took control.

"Who the hell is this?" he demanded. There was no response.

"Who are you and what are you doing answering my wife's phone?"

"Your wife?" the man asked in a calm, monotone voice, dripping with country drawl.

"Yes, my wife," Jack yelled. "Where is she?"

"She's come home to me, Jack. As have the girls. After all these years, we're a family again."

"What? What do you mean? Who is this? How do you know my name?"

"What do you care?" the man asked, serene as a Sunday afternoon breeze. "Why don't you ask Staci? Ask Staci if she cares."

The words achieved the same result as a stun gun to the groin. Unable to muster an immediate response, Jack's mind spun out of control with confused paranoia. The crackle of the phone line increased as he staggered past the metal frame of Sam's office door. More moments slipped past as he pursued a rational explanation.

"Who are you?" he asked in a low voice, calmed by fear. "What do you want? Money?"

"I hope ya enjoy the photo I dropped by today. I'm willing to wager you don't have a picture of Brooke or the little ones in your billfold. Am I right? What a shame; it sure is. Don't call this number again. Your time has come and gone . . . jack . . . ass."

"Bigsby?" Jack yelled into the phone. "Answer me. What have you done with my family? What do you want?"

A familiar laugh exploded then disappeared just seconds before the line fell dead. The man's voice sounded much younger than that of the old man on his porch, yet the annoying cackle was dead on. Jack pulled the phone away from his ear and depressed the redial button. The line rang several times before connecting.

"We're sorry, the number you have dialed is no longer in service or has been disconnected. Please check with your local listing service for more information. This is a recording."

Jack was unable to swallow. An intense fear grabbed hold of his senses. Attempting to work through the incident, he hand-typed his home phone number in hopes Brooke had delayed the trip.

"Hello, you've reached the Clarke residence," announced the excited, giggling voice of Julianna. "We can't come to the phone right now, but leave your name and number and Mommy or Daddy will call you back. Goodbye."

Jack stumbled in behind Sam's desk, dropping his briefcase to the floor before planting himself in her chair. He reached into the manila folder to retrieve the photo of the young girl on the porch. Placing it under the direct light of a nearby lamp, he studied it again and was stunned to notice a resemblance he did not recognize when first viewing the picture.

"Why am I only seeing this now and not three hours ago?" he asked as a chill worked its way down his back.

Although certain the photo was not of Brooke, he acknowledged similarities. He rehashed the calm, nonchalant manner with which the man spoke.

"It has to be the man Mr. McDonald described this afternoon," he whispered.

Jack scoured the picture several moments. Contemplating a next move, his lone idea was to call Brooke's parents, despite its being the last thing he wanted to do. Moving to punch in the number, he paused, realizing he had no idea what it was. He checked his contact list; there was no entry for Anna or John Mayberry. A sliver of guilt passed through at the realization that his relationship with his in-laws had deteriorated to the point he cared little to have any contact with them at all. The feeling did not last long as he dialed information.

"Yes, hello. Wisconsin, please," he requested. "John Mayberry in Iron River."

Jack scratched the number on a post-it note then tapped it out on his keypad. Bringing the phone to his ear, he prayed the old man would answer. There was no one alive he feared more than Brooke's mother. At eighty years old and ninety-five pounds soaking wet, she intimidated and scared the hell out of him. If she answered the phone, he'd be hanging up. Knowing the couple did not own an answering machine, he did not plan waiting beyond five rings. He didn't have to.

"We're sorry, all circuits are busy. Please try your call again later. This is a recording."

He was at a dead end. There was no one else to call. He dialed Brooke's cell number one last time, ending the call before the recorded message could finish.

"What the hell do I do now?" he yelled, slamming his cell phone on top of the desk before thrusting his body hard against the back of the chair.

The office was cold, yet he could feel droplets of sweat building and dripping under his dress shirt from around the base of his neck. He loosened the top button and yanked his tie an inch or so south to provide some relief. He took a swipe at a bit of moisture building against his forehead, depositing the residue on the side of Sam's chair. Being in a position of indecision was unfamiliar territory.

In desperation, he reached beyond the practical. Knowing he had an eyewitness in Mr. McDonald, he could call the cops and have the man describe his experience with the owner of the flatbed truck and let Chicago's finest take over. He sprung upright in the chair, retrieved Sam's phone and dialed 911.

"Precinct one, what's your emergency?" The operator was calm and professional, but machine-like. The moment Jack heard her voice he knew he'd made a mistake. As quickly as his excitement erupted over a potential solution, his psyche deflated ten-fold knowing it was a reach. He dropped the phone to the cradle and shrunk in the chair.

"How in the hell can you explain one single aspect of this?" he said aloud. "You don't even believe it yourself."

Looking about the space, he noticed a single sheet of paper lying face down in the knee well under the credenza. He retrieved the document, recognizing the city names appearing in alphabetical order with corresponding mileage ranges to and from, set in columns to the right. He'd become so involved in the events of the day, he'd neglected to check the status of the network. Sam prepared a short brief below the data, conveying her hypothesis that the state of Wisconsin played a major role in the mystery. The detail with which she had organized the document sent his roller coaster of a conscience back to thoughts of her. The last thing he wanted was to replace her. And, what if she was in love with him? What then?

Although he agreed with Sam's final assessment, it didn't matter at this point. The aberrant phone call brought the game to a new level and the pending delivery was on its way, whether the state of Wisconsin played a role or not. Checking his watch, Jack noticed he'd have less than twelve minutes to traverse the mile-and-a-half to the Palmer House if he intended to be there by six. Placing Sam's document into a shredder under her desk, he fed the piece into the teeth of the machine, all the while attempting to focus on how this next chapter would play out.

Rising from the chair, Jack grabbed his briefcase, exited the office and headed down the darkened hallway toward the lobby and elevator. Stepping into the middle car, he moved to the rear and leaned up against the back wall. As the stainless steel doors clapped shut, he chewed on the one fact he knew for certain; if Bigsby showed his face at the party, there was no God conceived or contrived that could save the man from the wrath he intended to inflict.

CHAPTER 12

Wedged between two of her coworkers' husbands at the bar inside the Empire Room of the Palmer House Hotel, Sam rummaged through a brand new pocketbook searching for a few dollar bills, keeping steady watch over the flow of heavy cream dispensing into the Bailey's she ordered just moments before. Too much and it would taste like a bad glass of chocolate milk; the right amount would subdue the potency just enough to allow a couple more during the evening without fear of impairment.

Sam dropped several singles into an antique brass spittoon serving as the tip jar, then flashed the palm of her hand in the direction of the young pup tending bar, halting the top-off. At least ten years her junior, he'd tracked her from the moment she pushed through the crowd, attempting more than once to coerce her into a personal conversation.

By a mile, Sam was the most attractive woman in the place. A dark green satin and sequin dress falling just below the knees complimented her long legs and slender waistline. A conservative neckline revealed little cleavage, but cut low enough to accent a beautiful necklace of pearls, willed to her by her great-grandmother.

Sam received her drink, ignoring both a wink from the bartender and a suggestive smile from one of the many husbands drooling nearby. She turned to conduct an inventory of the more than 200 in attendance, caring little that she'd not seen the first sign of her former boss. Still reeling from witnessing Jack and Staci making out like a couple of adolescents in the basement at a teeny-bop party, her intention this night was to be seen, grab a quick bite to eat then be on her way home to East Alton for the holidays.

Sam looked forward to the party each year, enjoying most talking with employees whom she did not see on a regular basis. She loved getting to know their spouses and children, but most years, she spent the event serving as an impromptu party host and organizer. She assisted here and there to ensure everything went according to plan, and at the party's conclusion, coordinated taxis home for those too inebriated to navigate their own way.

Much like a tangled ball of twine, her insides were an unraveled mess. Knowing this would be her last Christmas party with the firm, she found conversation with others difficult. With her emotions running on edge, and fearing she could burst into tears at any moment, she chose to avoid communication beyond "hello" and "good to see you."

She found a quiet space near the main stage opposite the bar where she paused to sip her drink. It was perfect. Looking about the space, she watched co-workers mingle and argue over seating options and children running about uncontrolled. The ballroom was decorated in fine holiday fashion. Dominating the back wall were two, twenty-foot Christmas trees, complete with large model trains running beneath weaving through brightly wrapped Christmas packages. Garland draped against gilded dental molding near the ceiling sparkled with bright white, blue, red, green, and orange lights, casting a holiday glow that rendered the overhead can lights unnecessary. Giant candy canes framed every entrance; lighted plastic Santas, snowmen, reindeer, and carolers were placed throughout. Any other time and the scene would have filled her with a Christmas cheer that would last well beyond New Year's.

The image of Jack and Staci clouded an otherwise perfect scene. She tried to shake the sight from her memory but was unable to get beyond how the two held on to one another. The way their lips connected, the way they grappled at each others' bodies, the grinding motion as they rubbed together—it all added up to a betrayal she did not expect. It was hard enough coming to grips with leaving a job and company she adored, but separating from Jack, despite his shortcomings, was a tough pill to swallow. Although he'd never admit to it, Sam knew he needed her well beyond the job she did and support she offered. Other than Brooke, whom she doubted he confided in at all, she was the one real friend he had in the world. Her heart broke at the thought of his forcing her to abandon him.

Sam removed her glasses to catch a rush of tears. With mascara coating her fingertips, she rushed through the crowd toward the ladies' room. She did not notice her every move being tracked.

Traversing a short hallway, she approached the door to the women's restroom, pausing first to peek in to gauge the number of occupants. As best she could tell, the space was empty. Surveying the room's design, she released a sigh at the several, semi-private makeup vanities lining the far wall. Setting her sights on a position furthest from the door, she advanced with a tentative gait to minimize the thunderous echo created by her three-inch heels popping on the rough-cut slate floor.

Easing onto a small, padded stool, she emptied her pocketbook, scattering a few personal care gadgets atop the marble surface. Sam placed her head in her hands and began to cry. Her grieving did not last long.

The sound of toilet paper unraveling from behind sent her scrambling to regain composure. She peeked into the mirror through reddened, bloodshot eyes in search of the occupied stall. Grabbing at several tissues from a built-in dispenser, she dabbed at her face, blotting away tears and leftover mascara, before gritting her teeth in anger over not conducting a more thorough search of the space.

Reaching for a small travel case containing her mascara, she noticed in the corner of the mirror the door to the bathroom swing open. A figure entered, but with her glasses stowed, she was unable to identify the guest. Sam assessed the damage to her make-up. She decided to apply much less in order to expedite herself from the space. She heard footsteps closing in on her position and noticed the stool next to her pulled from underneath the vanity.

She reached for her glasses. The pain grieving her heart rushed to the background, clearing a path for an equal amount of anger to boil to the surface. Had she been a cussing woman, the first salvo fired would have melted the hammered copper panels above her head.

"What do you want?" Sam asked in a frigid tone.

Staci DiSano pulled a Kleenex and dabbed at the corner of lips caked with bright red lipstick. She appeared resolute in posture, but facially, exuded an image of ambivalence. She was not certain of her decision to confront Sam, or the reaction she'd receive, though she expected it to be tempered thanks to the artificial authority she enjoyed through her uncle.

She reached with both hands to redirect her hair behind her ears then offered Sam a teasing half-smile in the mirror. Turning, Staci eased one leg over the other, the care necessitated by her short blue skirt falling nowhere near the tops of her knees. A suggestive silk blouse flowered open, revealing her chest and a vast panorama of exposed cleavage designed to draw every eye. She placed an elbow on the corner of the counter, rested her head in the palm of her hand and appeared as if preparing to offer counsel.

"I know you're upset, Samantha, but I just thought we might talk for a few moments."

Sam shook her head, expelling a brief sarcastic laugh. "There's nothing we have to talk about. Leave me alone."

Staci extended her arm, placing a hand on Sam's exposed shoulder. "I want to tell you my side of—"

"No," Sam said, pulling from her touch. "I don't want to hear the history; I don't want to hear an explanation; I don't want to hear a sob story."

Staci recoiled at the rebuff of her touch and the anger in Sam's voice. Sam offered a chilled gaze through the mirror. Several moments passed as the two women dug in.

"You do realize Jack started chasing me the moment I was hired. I mean, I had not been at my desk fifteen minutes before he was all over me."

"You weren't hired, you were placed. Regardless, I don't care. You can paint this picture any way you want," Sam said, ratcheting down her tone, "it doesn't matter to me. You both make me—"

The slide of a latch on the stall door behind sent both women chasing after the sound. The wife of one of the firm's young copywriters emerged looking nervous and wanting more than anything to be somewhere else. All of twenty-two years old, the squatty, overweight woman knew she was in on a conversation not meant for her ears, and without making eye contact or washing her hands, she headed straight for the door as if the place were on fire. The women followed her path through the mirror, waiting until she disappeared into the hallway.

"I know you're upset, but my intention was never to hurt you. I'm very fond of you, I think you know that."

"Hurt me?" Sam asked, whisking her stool to the right. "Hurt me? Do you think this is about me? Tell me you're joking."

"What, you don't have feelings for Jack? I just assumed you were upset because you're in love with him."

"You've got to be kidding me," Sam said, too stunned to come up with something more her style. She belted a sarcastic laugh and continued, "I'm his assistant, p-e-r-i-o-d. There's never been anything between us, there never will be anything between us, and I can't believe you have the gall to suggest such a moronic scenario. What's the matter with you?"

"Oh, come on, you mean to tell me you don't find him the least bit attractive? Please. I mean, my God, he's so handsome, sexy, and passionate. Why then, wherever he is you are too? I mean, you don't leave his side. What other conclusion could I come to?"

"For your information, I'm a professional. I do what I'm told, when I'm told and to the best of my ability. If I'm where he is, it's because he's asked me to be there. It's my job. And by the way, the man I get involved with will have a precise understanding of the concept of loyalty and a depth to his soul far exceeding the length of his penis."

"Well, if you don't have any interest in him, why are you so upset? I'd hate for this to come between us."

"I'm sorry, this is not about you and me, nor will it ever be about you and me. This is about you and Jack and what the two of you are doing." Sam scooped up her belongings.

"Maybe it would be best if you just mind your own business. If you don't want to talk, fine . . . but you have no right to judge me. I can come to no other conclusion than it's because you're jealous."

Sam snapped around to within inches of her face.

"You don't get it, do you?" she said, escalating her pitch. "Don't you dare make this about me. This is about his wife and his two daughters. What's your freaking problem? Not one time have you addressed the fact that he's married."

"It's not my fault he's not getting what he needs at home, or his wife doesn't appreciate what she has."

Sam shot from her chair, positioning herself in a hover above her antagonist. "You've no right or point of reference to make such a comment," she yelled, pointing a scolding finger. "Brooke is one of the finest people I know. She's done an incredible job raising those girls, by herself I might add, and has put up with so much crap from Jack I wouldn't know where to begin. She's not the problem. He's the problem, and now you're the problem. You're right, though, he deserves you more than he does her."

"Meaning?" Staci said, rising from her stool.

"Meaning the two of you are meant for each other because your moral fibers are in perfect alignment."

"You're out of line. You have no right to speak to me that way."

"You're the one who's out of line. You're the one hooking for someone else's husband, not me."

"Hooking? What does that mean?"

"You're so smart, you figure it out. It doesn't matter anyway," she said, raising both hands in the air. "My former boss can do whatever he wants to do. I'm done with all this."

"What do you mean former?"

Sam flashed a sarcastic grin and shook her head. "Do you think for one minute I could ever work for him again? Brooke is my friend. I see her all the time. We talk once a week or so. Do you think I'm going to prance around as if everything is just fine?"

"So, you're going to tell her?"

Sam paused, uncertain how to answer. Brooke was a dear friend, and if the situation were reversed, Sam would want to know the truth herself, no matter how badly it hurt. But she could not help but wonder the effect it would have on the girls and the guilt she'd bear for being the one spilling the beans. A tremendous push-pull erupted inside. If she said nothing, would she be betraying Brooke just as her husband was? She was at a loss. She could not think of it now.

"I'm glad your concern is for your own rear end," Sam jabbed. "Why should you worry, right? Why should you concern yourself with the lives of a loving wife and two very young girls? This sort of thing happens every day, right?"

"I told you, I didn't start this. He did."

"I don't give a damn," Sam screamed, slamming the palm of her hand atop the vanity. It was the first curse word from her mouth since likening a cousin to a part of the male anatomy for dropping his drawers and peeing in the family pool. "I don't want to hear any more of this. The both of you make me sick. Just leave me alone."

Sam whisked her purse from the countertop, kicked Staci's stool into a stall door and headed for the exit. Attempting to stop her progress, Staci grabbed hold of Sam's arm as she passed, but released as Sam's flying elbow nearly decapitated her. Staci swung around and called her name.

Sam stopped short of crashing through the door. She dropped her head in pause, before turning over her shoulder. Staci swallowed at the sight of tears streaming down her cheeks.

"You're right about one thing," Sam said, through an emotional stutter. "I do love him . . . very much. But not in a way your pimple-sized, puss-filled brain could ever understand or his overinflated ego would ever accept."

CHAPTER 13

Jack made quick work of the few blocks separating his location and the Palmer House Hotel. With traffic lights working in his favor and the streets void of their usual heavy congestion, he was assured of reaching the party before the supposed six o'clock delivery.

A few quick turns brought him to the valet drop-off just opposite the hotel's main lobby. Bringing the Hummer to a stop, third in line, he noticed a small gathering of uniformed valet personnel huddled around a strange looking vehicle parked along Monroe Street.

Bursts of condensation clouds indicated a bull session was in progress—something of obvious vital importance, since no one was paying attention to customers waiting for assistance. Not in a patient mood, Jack stepped from the Hummer, tucked both pinkies into the corners of his mouth and ripped a deafening whistle across the lot. The noise reverberated through the half-enclosed parking area, gaining the attention of a young, gangly kid who dodged his way through parked cars to greet him.

"Sorry, sir," the young man said. "We've never seen a car like that and got a little caught up in it."

"I don't care," Jack replied. "I want this parked in the garage, and I would prefer that you not park another car on either side. I also want the mirrors pulled in."

"Well, we're pretty full tonight sir, but I'll see what I can do. Here's your ticket."

"How old are you?" Jack asked, scanning the high school-aged punk from top to bottom.

"I turn nineteen next month. I just graduated from—"

"Well, be careful," Jack interrupted, not interested in the boy's life story. "This vehicle costs more than you'll pay for your college education. If I find a scratch, you'll be working a fast food drive-through come morning, do you understand me?"

"Yes, sir. Thank you, sir." The kid took a cautious step backward, intimidated by his customer's attitude and size.

Jack flipped the keys into the young man's hands, grabbed his suit jacket from the back seat and walked toward the hotel's entrance, never reaching for his money clip. Pausing as he approached the lobby door, his interest piqued as to what was capturing the hotel crew's attention. Changing direction, he weaved through a smattering of parked cars before pushing his way between two attendants. He was not a classic car enthusiast but knew a Ford Mustang when he saw one—except this was unlike any Mustang he'd seen before.

The sparkling white beauty featured twin blue racing stripes from front to tail, a front and rear spoiler, twin intakes, and solid chrome mag wheels. Speaking to no one in particular, he inquired as to the year of the hot rod. An attendant viewing the car street-side was happy, even eager, to show off his expert knowledge of the fine piece of machinery.

"Man, this is a 1967 Shelby Cobra GT 350 four-barrel Ford Mustang. Just over 1,100 or so of these sweet rides came off the production line, and this one looks as if it rolled out of the plant this morning. Look at it; not a scratch on it."

Returning his view to the car, Jack made a connection with the man's description. He recalled the same account of a classic, immaculate vehicle he received from Mr. McDonald earlier in the day. Pulling at his shirtsleeve, he viewed his watch—5:57 p.m. He wondered if the deliverer was wandering around somewhere inside the hotel.

"Who owns this car?" Jack asked. The attendants eyed one another, gauging who would respond.

"Some guy drove up, hopped out and said he would be back in a few minutes," said a man twice the age of the other attendants. "Said he was dropping something off at one of the parties inside."

"Do you remember what he looked like? What he was wearing?"

The man searched his coworkers. With no takers, he went on to describe a man in his early to mid-thirties, wearing a long black leather duster and a black Fedora. He also noted the man was carrying a manila envelope.

"How long has he been inside?" Jack asked.

"Couldn't be more than a couple minutes," another attendant chimed. Turning from the group, Jack entered into a jog toward the rotating entry door. Pushing against the heavy, motorized glass panel proved futile in increasing its speed beyond its calibrated setting. Entering the lobby to a throng of well-dressed guests, hotel officials, and bellmen, Jack bobbed up and down as he moved across marble floors one moment, then spacious Persian rugs the next, scanning everyone wearing a hat. Moving left, he took notice of those huddled around the lobby bar before reaching a set of stairs on the opposite end.

Jack raced to the top to scan the crowd, making certain to check each guest thoroughly. The space was large, noisy, and mimicked in décor what one would find in an Italian cathedral. Finding no matches in the lobby, he considered both directions of the hallway before heading toward the ballrooms, all the while keeping an anxious eye on those he passed, including checking to his rear every few yards. Reaching the Empire Room, he blew past one of the young accounting clerks assigned to check in guests, ignoring her greeting and feeble attempt to stop his progress.

Appearing as a starved mountain lion in a pasture full of sheep, he waded through the party crowd, his eyes exploding to the size of half-dollars, searching for anything resembling a black coat or Fedora. Friend or foe, he acknowledged no one, including those attempting to address him. He circled each table, caring little about contact with the many children scurrying about his feet, swinging his head in violent fashion as he scanned in every direction.

Sam did not see her boss sweeping through the crowd as she searched the stage area for the Bailey's she'd left behind. Weaving around tables, moving in the direction of the bar, she noticed an opening near the dance floor and shot through the hole at an accelerated pace. She saw Jack break free from the crowd opposite and into the open lane, heading straight toward her. She stopped in her tracks and raised a palm.

"Jack, I don't want to speak to you, I have nothing to—"

He breezed past offering an "excuse me" as if she were a stranger.

Catching a whiff of his cologne in his wake as he passed, she glanced over her shoulder, stunned he did not recognize her, watching as he waded through the crowded room like King Kong through the forest. A glance across the ballroom at a large clock offered at least one explanation for his bizarre behavior. Despite her intentions of never speaking to him again, his obvious distress propelled her into help mode. She followed on his heels into the mass of partygoers.

"Jack," she yelled, trying to keep pace. "Jack, what's wrong?" Her voice was lost in a sea of conversation and the sound of Bing Crosby blaring from speakers above. Jack continued through the crowd. His intensity increased. He knew his target was in the room; he could feel it. Noticing acceleration in his pace, Sam entered in a half-jog in an attempt to catch up.

"Jack," she yelled again. Close enough now, she grabbed hold of his coattails with both hands. He stopped to see who dared halt his progress. He saw no one at first as Sam crouched to replace a lost shoe. Looking up as he looked down, he appeared to have no idea who she was. She grabbed him by both arms.

"Jack, what's going on? Why are you running through the crowd like this?"

His stare was blank, as if searching the depths of his memory as to just who the hell this woman was standing before him. Sam knew this look well; she was privy to it many times. His fixation and concentration on certain issues could oftentimes send him into a trance-like state which took him several moments to break from.

"Jack," she said again, looking deeper into his eyes, "what's going on? Why are you running through the crowd?"

"He's here," he replied, regaining recognition of her face." Breaking from her grip, he continued on his way. Sam ran along at his side.

"Jack, stop. Is it Bigsby? Are you talking about Bigsby?"

"I think so," he said, searching each face at a dizzying pace.

Working to catch her breath, Sam moved to face his front. "How do you know? What makes you so sure he's in this room?"

"There's a car out front; I know it belongs to him. I've got to find him."

"Why? You knew there was something else coming. Just wait and see what it is."

"I think he has Brooke and the girls."

"What?" Sam said, staggering backward.

"I can't explain it right now. I've got to catch this piece of shit bastard and find out what the hell he's done with my family."

Sam cringed as a dozen people and an unknown count of children paused upon hearing the expletives. She couldn't tell whose jaws were closer to the ground. Unfazed, Jack pushed off through those who'd paused. Sam hunched her shoulders and released an apologetic smile. Jack continued but a few steps before the firm's senior partner popped in front, cutting off his path.

Sam failed to notice the two men coming together. Her face planted into the center of Jack's back, forcing him into his boss, propelling his boss's martini down the front of his suit. Cowering in the shadows of Jack's 56-long suit jacket, Sam could feel her face turning several different shades of red. She peeked around his forearm to see John Junior wiping at a wet stain on his jacket, and a larger blot in the middle of his crotch. She winced with embarrassment. Jack moved away, exposing her to the world.

"I'm so sorry, sir," Sam said, bringing a hand to cover her open mouth. "I wasn't watching where I was going."

The old man cracked a grandfatherly smile. "Don't you worry about it honey."

"I should've been paying more attention. I'm very sorry, sir," Sam said, taking a step back. "I'll be happy to pay for the cleaning of your suit."

"Nonsense, Samantha," John Junior said, waving his arm in the air, sending a few remaining ice cubes from his glass into the forehead of an onlooker.

"Don't give it a second thought. You see this?" he said, pointing to a dark stain on the front of his red satin tie adorned with Christmas wreaths. "One of those little Mexican meatballs fell right off its stick not two seconds after I arrived this evening. My June always carries a laundry pen for just such emergencies. Before the night's through this suit will look as if I fell down in the street and rolled around in the garbage dumpster just for kicks. The alcohol probably cleaned something."

The crowd circling, all of whom gathered to see if the old man would lose a screw, roared with laughter at the self-deprecating joke. Sam returned a smile, thankful he'd deflected the embarrassment from her shoulders.

"Merry Christmas, Jack," John said, extending a hand while offering a slanted look reeking of suspicion.

"Merry Christmas, John. Sorry about your drink. I was walking way too fast."

"Walking? Hell, son, if you'd been walking any faster you'd have broken the world sprint record. I saw you come in tonight. Is there a problem?"

"No sir, no problem. I . . . I was just looking for someone."

"It sure looks as if it's important; I mean, the way you were moving through the crowd."

"I'm sorry, sir. I don't see them. I must've been mistaken."

"Are you expecting something?"

"No, not really," Jack said, his eyes darting about behind his boss's position.

John Junior sidestepped to a nearby table where he collected from a chair a tattered manila envelope larger than the one Jack received at his office earlier. Extending the envelope, Jack noticed a McClellan Delivery Service stamp on the back of the tab. He made certain not to react.

"Is this what you're looking for?" he asked.

"Well, yes and no. I wasn't expecting the package here at the party."

"Funny, the young man who gave it to me said you were expecting this by six—asked me for six bits for delivering it. I hadn't heard that reference in fifty years. So I gave him a couple bucks."

"I'll be glad to reimburse you, sir," Jack said, working over the crowd in search of a Fedora. "You say he was a young man?"

"Yes . . . well, near your age, maybe a little younger. He walked up, addressed me by name and asked if I could give this to you once you arrived. I don't know how he knew me or that I knew you, but he conducted himself as if I'd dealt with him before. I'm pretty sure it's the first time I've seen him."

"Do you remember what he was wearing?"

"He was a nice looking young fellow, dressed well. He was wearing a long leather coat—like those dusters you see in those old cowboy movies—and a black fedora. He was just over near the bar a minute ago," he said, squaring in the opposite direction. "Oh, yes, there he is, over by the door."

Jack's body exploded in a mass of tingles. He located the dark figure leaning with one foot against the wall near the door. With the Fedora pulled low over his brow and the collar of the black duster extending high beyond his neckline, his facial features were little better than a blur, other than a set of eyes blacker than death staring back. The path between the two, packed with partygoers just seconds before, parted like the Red Sea, creating a tunnel-like sightline between them. Bigsby's stare was cold and menacing. Jack could feel its intensity piercing his soul, sending his heart rate shooting through the roof.

Without breaking contact, Bigsby tugged the hat even lower before making a move toward the exit. His body disappeared into a black mist before sweeping through the doorway as if sucked by a vacuum. Within seconds, the cloud was gone.

"Did you see that," Jack yelled to Sam, pointing to the door.

Sam saw the man but did not see him disappear. She craned her neck around much taller guests to get a better look.

"Jack, what's the trouble?" John Junior asked.

A handful of people circled around the two, noting the desperate look spread across Jack's face. Mere seconds passed before Jack acted on his instinct to chase after the man.

"Excuse me just a minute, sir," he said in a tone a million miles away. As he hurried toward the exit, the crowd reclaimed the open lane in front, disrupting his progress. Pushing adults to the side and with children bouncing off his thighs like padded tackling dummies, he worked and weaved toward the door wondering how a party intended for seventy-five employees and their families equaled in attendance to that of a Beatles concert.

Jack fought his way through another wave of humanity milling about at the exit. Upon breaking free, he entered into a full sprint down the hallway toward the lobby. He reached the staircase and paused but a second to survey the crowd, before rifling across the lobby floor and through the revolving door. He arrived in the parking area just in time to see the tail lights of the Mustang disappear around the corner of the hotel.

Jack sprinted to the middle of the street, oblivious to the oncoming traffic and heavy snow falling, watching as the car zipped through the intersection of Wabash Avenue heading east. The roar of the 350-cubic-inch engine drowned out all other manmade noises, making clear the driver was not out for a Sunday drive.

In a final jab to Jack's now fragile mental state, he watched Bigsby extend an arm out the window and offer a sarcastic wave with the snap of his wrist. Seconds later, the vehicle disappeared from view.

Jack pulled his cell phone and dialed Brooke's number. With cars swerving and honking, and taxi drivers cussing him in their native tongues, he waited. The line picked up to an immediate, ear-splitting crackle.

"Bigsby," he yelled, "I'm warning you . . . you do anything to hurt my family and so help me I'll hunt you down all the rest of my days. Bigsby . . . do you hear me?"

Upon his threat, the crackle in the line vanished. Uncertain if the line was live, he yelled for Bigsby to answer.

"You can't chase a memory, Jack," a younger voice slithered, calm and cool. "Sometimes there are no second chances."

Jack swallowed deeply. "Why are you doing this?" he pleaded.

"I'm only taking what you've discarded."

"Where are they? I want to see them."

"I'm on my way to see them now. I'll make sure to give them all a big hug and kiss for you. So long Jack, and thanks. You've made me the happiest man in the world."

"No, wait . . . please . . ."

The line fell silent. Jack pulled the phone from his ear and dialed again. A recording indicated the number was no longer in service.

With waves of slush slapping off his suit pants, he watched the traffic lights stretching several city blocks change in unison from green to red. With the manila folder in hand, he retreated to the curb, knowing all too well his predicament was no longer a figment of his imagination or someone's idea of a cruel joke.

Stunned, Jack turned tail for the Palmer House lobby in search of a spot where he could view the contents of the envelope, concerned now that what lay inside would only widen the gap between himself and his family.

CHAPTER 14

"Excuse me, sir," a woman said, brushing Jack's elbow as she passed toting two suitcases twice her own size. Standing over the crowd like a lone, giant oak centered in the hotel lobby, Jack found himself among a throng of staff members and an influx of guests racing from one end of the Palmer House lobby to the other, dusting free of the snow that had gathered on his suit jacket. With a cerebral attack budding and his throat parched, he worked through the mass behind a passing bellman pulling an over-stacked luggage cart toward the lobby bar.

Jack peeled away upon reaching the half-moon-shaped marble counter and climbed atop a stool located closest to the wall. Pulling close to the bar top, he worked around the room, unable to expel the sensation that someone or something was watching him. The churning paranoia forced his nervous eyes toward the faces of those sitting near and rushing past. The open lobby, with its increased volume of guests, produced a deafening echo that accentuated the growing ache in his head. He placed his elbows on the edge of the bar to massage his temples.

Replaying the encounter with this latest version of Bigsby, he wondered aloud why the three characters appeared at different ages. Feeling the strain of an annoying kink at the base of his neck, he closed his eyes and rotated his head in an exaggerated circle. "What I need is a stiff drink," he said.

"Well, I can certainly help you with that."

Jack stopped in mid-rotation at the sound of the woman's voice. His eyes flashed open to find the bartender standing opposite his position.

"Are you okay?" she asked.

"I'm fine. It's been a long day and I've a monster headache brewing."

"I'm sorry. What can I get you to drink?"

Jack grabbed at the back of his neck to work his fingertips deep into the knot.

"What's the strongest mixed drink you're legally allowed to serve?"

"That's easy . . . a Long Island ice tea."

"I'll take one of those . . . with a splash of Diet Coke."

The woman nodded, "Coming right up."

Jack reached into his pocket for his money clip, extracting a credit card and placing it on the bar top. Within seconds, the woman returned with a large pilsner glass topped off with an orange slice and maraschino cherry.

"I've a couple aspirin in my purse," she offered, ignoring the hotel's policy concerning providing drugs of any sort to guests. "I can get a couple for you, if you like."

"No, I'll be fine. I just want a quick drink before I head home."

"Probably for the best. The weather is going to get nasty tonight, and I'm sure the drive to Oakdale will be a tricky one. Are you sure I can't get you a couple aspirin?"

Jack did not respond. Kneading his temples, he moved his fingers down over his sideburns to the base of his ears, never questioning how the woman knew he lived in Oakdale. Following several minutes of self-treatment, he opened his eyes to a field of morphing and moving stars. The illusion dissipated as he regained focus by examining other patrons bellied-up to the bar.

He noticed the bartender restocking a nearby bar caddy with maraschino cherries, olives, and lemon wedges. The slender woman appeared out of place. Somewhat attractive despite closing in on sixty, she was well beyond in years compared to the other waitstaff employed by the hotel.

Streaks of gray hair merged with dark brown, meeting at a bun at the top-back of her head. Her skin, olive in color and free of make-up, appeared soft but weathered, as if she had spent a good portion of her life on open waters. He could tell she took good care of herself, and although he could not recall when, he believed they'd met somewhere before. He found it troublesome remembering names—another reason he could not live without Sam—but never forgot a face. Catching his eye, the woman flashed a smile, revealing soft wrinkles around the eyes and shallow dimples on her cheeks. He knew that smile.

"Is there something else I can get you?" she asked.

Breaking from her smile, he asked with a perplexed look if the two had met.

"I don't think so," she responded, "but anything's possible. I've lived here almost six years but spent the majority of my life in Wisconsin."

"Is that right?" Jack perked up at the coincidence. "I was born in Wisconsin; a town called Redrock."

"I moved around a lot in my younger days," she said, wiping down the area in front of him. She paused to look over her shoulder to gauge the drink levels of her other customers.

"But, you never know," she said, smiling. "Maybe we met in another life. I believe in those types of things; I believe in the impossible. If you would excuse me," she said, raising a finger, "I need to settle a tab across the way."

"May I ask your name?"

"It's Grace." The woman smiled, nodded, and moved to the other end of the bar.

Jack swore he knew her smile but was unable to place it. Any other day he could figure it out in a snap. His mind bounced from Grace's smile to the image of young Bigsby staring him down in the ballroom.

"It was obvious he wanted me to get a glimpse of him," he said. "Why was that so important?"

Jack grabbed his drink, popped the cherry into his mouth, plunged the orange slice into the depths with an index finger then sent the frigid liquid rushing down his throat. The taste refreshed but triggered an intense throbbing in his left temple. He glanced at the envelope through the corner of his eye, staring as if it had called out his name.

The mere presence of it produced an anxiety reminding him of the days when his grade school report card arrived in the mail. In a move to delay the inevitable, he retrieved from his shirt pocket the post-it note scribbled with his in-laws' phone number. Following another swig of drink, he created a new entry in his phone's directory and dialed the number. The line rang busy; finally, a break, he thought. He would try again in a few minutes. He was certain his in-laws could put an end to the mystery of his wife's whereabouts.

Jack reached for the envelope simultaneous to taking another quick gulp of his drink. Separating the flap from the glue tab released a sharp, musty stench that forced his nose in the opposite direction. As the odor eased, he peeked inside, noticing a newspaper folded in half. The copper-tint of the stock, along with its weathered, decaying edges, suggested it was very old, and reminded Jack of newspapers someone would discover behind a centuries-old oil painting. The paper was brittle to the touch, and, as he removed it from the envelope, he noticed small, glass-like slivers detach from around its edges.

Jack inspected the envelope for any identifying dates or signatures. Other than the delivery service stamp, it was free of any marks. Tossing the envelope aside, he unfolded the oversized newspaper sheet once on the horizontal, then again vertically, revealing the relic's front side. The masthead identified the paper as *The Eau Claire Leader* and the edition as Tuesday Morning, December 25, 1923.

"1923?" he whispered aloud. "The same year of the telegram."

Jack scanned to his left below the masthead. The words "Merry Christmas" appeared in large, bold script letters above a winter scene. To the left of the word "Merry," his mouth fell agape at the sight of a sketched image of a horse-drawn carriage and rider. The resemblance between the caricature drawing of the carriage—complete with two giant, solid white horses and a driver tucked away under a blanket— appeared identical to Bigsby and his carriage.

"Unbelievable . . . it can't be," he whispered, contemplating the significance and how it related to the mystery.

The paper was loaded with local and national headlines. He scanned them all, just in case. The feature article titled "Santa Claus As We Know Him Today, an American Creation," included a photograph of three young girls sitting near a fireplace listening to the radio. He could determine no connection. He read the remaining headlines aloud.

"Germany requests modification of rum policy, details are sent to British; French airship held aloft by storm is safe; Washington rum scandal may go before congress; Cannon is freed of charges: Frame-up by enemies of baseball union; Sentenced Negro slayer to die; Air mail flier killed in fall; Man slays wife with ice pick; U.S. farm imports exceed exports for first time in history; Three burn to death at Superior; Two drowned on way to Christmas celebration; One killed, three wounded in bootlegger row." Jack thought them all very interesting, but saw nothing relative other than the date and the drawing.

"Wow, how interesting," Grace commented, startling Jack from the headlines. She placed his credit card atop a copy of the register receipt in front of him.

"I'm sorry, Mr. Clarke. I didn't mean to interrupt you. Do you collect old newspapers?"

"No, not really, it's just something someone sent me."

"I just love looking at old newspapers and magazines. Do you mind?" she asked, pointing to the paper.

"Uh, no," Jack hesitated, not really wanting to part with the piece, "but please be careful, it's falling apart."

Grace flipped the paper with great care. She hovered over it with hands to her side as if looking at a museum piece with clear instructions not to touch.

"Wow," she said, "Christmas Day, 1923 . . . over 80 years ago. I can't believe this paper has lasted this long." She scanned the headlines while Jack conducted a mental inventory of the material evidence now piling up. He wondered about the significance of 1923.

"Did you see this story of the man who killed his wife with an ice pick on Christmas Eve? Wow."

She filtered through the remaining headlines then turned the paper to view the opposite side. Jack examined her face, puzzled by the familiarity of her features and scrambling to recall where he'd seen her before.

Grace's attention was grabbed by the personals section.

"This is interesting," she said, reading the announcements. "Mr. and Mrs. Ted Vanderbie of Chicago and Mr. and Mrs. Roy Sampson of St. Paul are spending the holiday week at the house of Mr. and Mrs. H.F. Vanderbie." Feeling his eyes boring upon her, she lifted from the paper.

"I'm sorry, Mr. Clarke. I guess I'm getting carried away. Do you want your paper back?" she asked.

"No. I just can't get over the thought of meeting you somewhere before."

"I'm certain I just remind you of someone else," she said.

"It's more than that. I just can't put my finger on it. All I know is something stirs in my memory when I look at your eyes when you're smiling."

"At my age, I'll accept a good pick-up line anytime," she said, shooting a playful wink.

"Oh, no, I . . . I—"

Grace was quick to dispel any concern that she mistook the comment.

"I'm just teasing, Mr. Clarke. Anyway, my dating days are long over. As I said, maybe we knew each other in another life."

Jack dropped the subject, having no interest in giving a sixty-year-old woman the wrong idea. Continuing her scan of the personals, Grace browsed the paper in silence while he attempted a third time to reach his in-laws—another busy signal.

"Oh, my," Grace said, backing away from the paper. Her face gave way to an expression of puzzlement. With the pilsner glass settled against his lips, Jack stopped in mid-swig noting the change on her face and in her body language.

"What? What's the problem?" he asked, never separating the glass from his lips.

"Have you seen the back of this paper?"

"No, why?" Jack grew pale at the look on her face. She pointed to a large photo at the bottom right-hand side.

"I'm not sure about this, but it has to be a coincidence."

Jack studied her eyes with concern as he spun the newspaper clockwise, sending a few more slivers of its edges floating to the floor. He drew to the photograph, noticing the caption had long since separated from underneath the picture. The black and white image was a tad grainy, but in relatively good condition. Three mounds and part of a fourth—all covered in white sheets—showed on the ground in the forefront with a man kneeling over them. Another man stood behind the man kneeling. A crowd milled about in the background. Jack could see nothing to explain Grace's reaction.

"Okay," he said, looking up, "so what?"

"Look at this guy right here," she said, pointing to the man standing.

The soft, amber glow cast from the pendant light hovering above deepened the tint of the aged paper, making it difficult to see. Bringing the paper closer to his face, he felt a lump erupt in his throat as he reconciled Grace's reaction. She noticed his face draining color and his body language suggesting rejection of what his eyes were claiming as fact. She saw the wheels spinning as his eyes darted back and forth across the image. He settled the paper atop the bar.

"Are you okay, Mr. Clarke?"

"Impossible," he insisted. "There's no way that's possible, right? It's . . . it's just a coincidence." Jack turned to Grace for reassurance. She was unable to offer any comfort.

"I don't know what to say. It's very bizarre."

"I just don't understand. This makes no sense."

Jack noticed the stool to his immediate right being pulled from under the bar lip and the scent of Chanel No. 5 now teasing his nostrils. He knew who it was. Sam adjusted her dress before scooting forward. Grace reached for a fresh bar napkin and placed it in front of her.

"And what can I get for you this evening, ma'am?"

"I'll have a Bailey's on the rocks with light cream please," Sam said, reaching for her pocketbook.

Without acknowledging her presence, Jack tapped the receipt in front of him, instructing Grace to charge him. Sam didn't thank him; Jack didn't expect it. The two did not speak as he cupped his hands around his nose and mouth. He was near shock, exhausted and unnerved beyond rational thought. Sam could see he was a mere shell of his normal self, and awaiting the delivery of her drink, contemplated which subject to broach first. Her concern for her friend and his wife took precedence.

"What's happened, Jack? What's happened to Brooke and the girls?"

Grace hurried to deliver the Bailey's. Having overheard Sam's question, she positioned in between the two in anticipation of his response. Grace grew conscious of Sam's stare, realizing her potential interference.

"Oh . . . I'm sorry. I didn't mean to nose in. My name is Grace," she said, extending a hand to Sam.

"That's okay," Sam said, returning with a shake, happy Grace had recognized her error. "It's nice to meet you Grace. My name is Samantha."

"Nice to meet you, Samantha. Mr. Clarke was just showing me a strange old newspaper someone sent him. We've been talking for a while."

"No worry. I won't be long."

Grace traded glances between the two of them. "Well, if you'd both excuse me," she said, smiling.

Sam waited for the woman's retreat then peeked at Jack out of the corner of her eye. She grabbed her drink and adjusted her body in the opposite direction. "What happened to Brooke?" she asked, as if speaking to someone else down the line.

Jack released his hands from his face and sighed. He knew she would not leave until she got an answer.

"Some crazy, crazy things happened before I left the office this evening," he said, dropping his head.

"Really?" she said. "Shocking. I couldn't be more surprised."

Jack eased toward her, though she continued staring in the opposite direction. He knew it was open season and he deserved a couple shots, but he also knew she was the one person he could confide in. He continued, despite knowing she possessed a cache of one-liners set and ready for launch.

"I'll continue," he said, flipping a hand in her direction. He spilled over the details of the vision as he exited the shower and the strange exchange with Bigsby on the telephone, piquing Sam's interest.

"So, you're telling me all of the sudden you began to notice similarities between the girl in the photo and Brooke, when you hadn't before?"

"Yeah, that's what I'm saying. It was as if the conversation with Bigsby was some sort of switch or trigger. I saw what you were seeing when you first looked at it. Another odd moment was hearing the old man's laugh just before the line cut. It was as if the younger Bigsby had conferenced in the older on the call.

"I chased him out of the hotel and saw his car heading down the street. I called Brooke's number again and he picked up . . . said he was on his way to see them right now and that I'd made him the happiest man in the world."

Jack paused to take another shot of his drink. "I mean, Brooke was flying out this afternoon to her parents' farm," he said. "There's just no way in hell anyone got to her, the girls, and that stupid mutt between home and the airport. There's just no way. When I get through to her parents, I'm sure they'll have heard from her. If not, well, I'll have to . . ."

"You'll have to what?" Sam asked as he hesitated.

"Call the police, I guess. What else can I do? If I can't reach her and her parents haven't heard from them, I'm going to have to call someone."

"Oh, yeah—well thought out. I can hear that conversation right now," Sam said, in between a sip. "Do you know what the result will be? Have you seen that section in the paper where they report those wacky claims by people who have seen UFOs and ghost sightings? Your picture will be plastered right there. You can't call the police. What are you going to tell them?"

"What the hell else am I supposed to do?" he said, getting the attention of his fellow bar mates. "I arrive here and there's an out-of-place car parked along the street, just like what your buddy described this afternoon. I enter the ballroom to learn this guy has introduced himself to my boss. I then spot him watching my every move before he disappears into a mist. I chase him into the middle of the street then watch as he waves as he drives away. I have an original newspaper from 1923 with a sketch on the front of a horse-drawn carriage identical to the one the old man was riding this morning. I'm in a photograph on the back side of this paper. I encounter three men throughout the day, all different ages but claiming to be the same person. I get a telegram addressed to me from eighty years ago. I have a picture of some girl who looks like my wife, and I have a freakin' headache the size of Texas. Let's see . . . did I miss anything?"

"Jack, shhhh . . . calm down . . . for crying out loud," she said, whispering. "I don't know why this is happening, but I think you need to—"

"Hey, maybe if we wait around long enough Bigsby will drop back by for a drink and we can all have a few laughs." Jack placed his hands over his reddened face, waiting for the throbbing to pass.

Sam reached for the paper and located the photo. A cold shiver shot up her spine, inducing the hair on her arms to stand on end.

"Oh, that's incredible," she said under her breath. "The likeness is identical. And it's the clearest pixel set in the entire photograph."

Her body twitched upon remembering a small magnifying glass stored in a side pocket in her purse; the one she used to view old war photos Mr. McDonald brought to the office on occasion. Removing her glasses, she floated the small enhancer close over the image.

"That's amazing . . . it's you. It's just you."

Sam dragged the magnifying glass across the photo, searching for additional clues. Inspecting every square inch, she paused atop the face of the man kneeling. Pulling from the glass, she swept her hand across the bar top, recalling the moment in the ballroom when she spotted Bigsby standing near the door. She'd gotten a good look at him an instant before her view became blocked and he disappeared around the corner. Returning to the magnifying glass, holding steady on the image, she made a positive I.D.

"Jack?" she asked in a tone reeking with regret. With his head buried in his hands, he turned, peeking through a small crack in between his fingers.

"What now?"

"Did you look at the man kneeling on the ground?"

Jack's body deflated. He pulled his hands from his face and eased the newspaper from her grip. Sam offered the magnifying glass, which he accepted. Placing the loupe near his eye, he leaned into the photo for a closer look.

"Are you both okay? Can I get anything for you?" Grace asked as Jack continued his inspection of the picture.

Sam shook her head. "No, I'm fine. Thank you."

"Anything for you, Mr. Clarke?" Grace asked.

Jack dropped the magnifying glass to the bar and returned upright in his chair, folding his arms over his chest.

"Mr. Clarke?" Grace asked. Jack did not respond, as both women noticed his cheeks changing color again. Glancing in Sam's direction, Grace rotated the newspaper in front of her.

"Did he find something else?" Grace asked Sam.

"The man kneeling looks familiar to us."

Grace brought the magnifying glass against her eye. "Oh, my," she said. "I missed this. It looks like the guy who was here earlier."

"What did you say?" Jack dropped his arms and moved closer to the bar.

"I said it looks like the man who was here at the bar earlier this evening."

"What was he wearing?" Sam asked.

"Well, I didn't wait on him, but he was in a dark black coat and wore an odd-looking hat. He was a younger guy . . . pretty handsome. Well, I mean, he looks just like this man," she said, pointing at the photo. "He stopped at the bar and asked one of the staff what ballroom some party was being held in."

Sam tracked Jack's pupils as he focused on something off in the distance across the bar.

"What are you holding?" Grace asked.

"I'm not holding anything," Jack snapped. "It's not me."

Grace paused. "I'm sorry, Mr. Clarke. Of course, you're right. Did you notice this, though?"

"By the way, how do you know my name?" Jack accused. "I never mentioned it."

Grace dropped the magnifying glass, turned to Jack then to Sam. She smiled. "It's on your credit card, Mr. Clarke."

Jack released an annoyed sigh. Aware of his agitation, Grace offered a gentle, understanding smile. Rotating the paper back in front of him, she pointed to the bundle in his arms. Jack waved his hand. Sam grabbed the magnifying glass and pulled the paper toward her.

"Looks like some sort of blanket to me," she said, holding the magnifier just above the paper. "It's not very big. Wait a minute . . . look at this. It appears to be a child. Look, you can see a small head poking out." Sam pushed the paper in front of him and pointed.

Fed up with a new twist presenting every time someone viewed the paper, Jack grabbed it, folded it in half and stuffed it back in the envelope. Completing the task, he slammed the envelope atop the bar, rattling glasses and causing guests to jump in their seats.

"No more," he yelled.

The two women looked to one another, each raising their eyebrows.

"Well, unless there's anything else I can get for the two of you, I need to leave for my night job," Grace said. "It was very nice seeing you again, Mr. Clarke."

She leaned in close to him, catching his attention before advancing a warm smile.

"I hope you can work all this out," she said placing her hand on his forearm. "I'm certain this is none of my business, but I think I know your heart. Sometimes, though, we have to take two steps back to take one step forward. Good luck to you." Jack found her smile so comforting. He wished he could recall where they'd met before; now he might never know.

"It was nice meeting you Sam. Good luck to you."

"Nice to meet you, Grace," Sam said with a puzzling look. The two watched as Grace walked to the opposite end of the bar, slid an employee I.D. card through a slot on the cash register and collected a few personal belongings. She disappeared through an exit at the far end of the lobby.

"How long have you known her?" Sam asked.

"I don't know her at all; just met her tonight."

"Interesting."

"What?"

"Why did she say it was nice to see you again?"

"What? I didn't hear that," he replied.

"That's what she said."

"I just heard two steps back, one step forward, and good luck."

"What, am I deaf? I was sitting right here. I know what I heard," Sam instructed.

"Well, I don't know her. She said she's lived and worked here a few years. She looks familiar to me, but I can't place where we might've met."

"Ma'am?" Sam called to a bartender pouring a drink nearby.

"Yes ma'am, can I get you something?"

"No, thank you. Who was the waitress serving us tonight; the one who just left?"

"Uh, well, I think her first name is Grace, but I don't know her last name. Tonight was her first night."

"Working at the bar or the hotel?" Jack asked.

"I believe it was her first night, period."

"Hmm, that's interesting," Sam mumbled.

"I don't know who she is, okay?" Jack defended, annoyed at the look on Sam's face.

"Looks to me like she was flirting with you."

"Would you do me a kindness and drop it," he said. "I didn't ask for your opinion, and I don't really care at the moment. I have enough problems to deal with. I need to find Brooke."

"Why would you care where she is? Didn't you tell her to pack her bags? Maybe she did. Don't worry though, Staci's half-naked and waiting in the ballroom. You could finish in the bathroom tonight what you started in your office this afternoon."

And there it was. Jack knew it was just a matter of time. Pushing away from the bar, he rose from the stool, collected his credit card, and signed his name on the register receipt. He finished off the final drops of the Long Island, keeping an eye on Sam as he tipped the glass on end. She was ready to rumble, but there was no way he was jumping into the ring with her, knowing well he'd lose and lose huge.

"Hey," Sam yelled, "don't you walk away from me . . . don't you dare turn your back to me and walk out."

Ignoring her, Jack placed his glass on the bar and turned away.

"If you leave, I'm gone. Do you understand? If you don't tell me why you're doing this to Brooke and your daughters, I will be gone and will never look back."

Her voice was clear and he heard every word. Seeing his advance toward the exit, Sam jumped from her stool and grabbed hold of his arm in an attempt to spin him toward her. The sight of this slight, attractive woman trying to maneuver this giant man three times her size reignited the interests of those around the bar. Jack continued along his path unfazed by her grasp. Sam felt a nail tearing as it caught on his expensive suit material. Her feminine grip covered less than a quarter of his forearm and she released before suffering additional damage.

"I'm done, Jack. Do you hear me? I'm done with you."

Jack waded through the throng of people pausing to watch the confrontation, maintaining a fixed stare on the revolving door. He noticed a barrage of small bar cherries whiz past his head, exploding on the coats, hats and foreheads of those around him. A second volley bounced off the back of his jacket.

"How does it feel to lose your wife, your kids, and your best friend all in the same day? Was that soulless tramp worth it, Jack? How does it feel, you piece of crap? You'll never recover from this. Do you hear me?"

Sam grabbed another handful of maraschinos and launched them toward the door. Both bartenders on duty rushed toward her in an attempt to prevent another salvo. Sam grabbed another large handful before they managed to remove the bar caddie from her reach. A security guard at the far end of the lobby hustled toward the scene.

"Do you know how many lives you've screwed today?"

Jack could hear her voice breaking. With cherry juice running down the back of his neck and patrons stepping across the floor now spotted with tiny red orbs, he stopped in front of the door, waiting for the next open wedge.

"You're a coward Jack," Sam yelled at the top of her lungs. "You're a gutless coward."

He squared his body to face her. With her arm cocked, ready to fire another round, she paused upon seeing his face. Jack could see the welling in her eyes under the soft glow of the lighting above, and watched as she dropped her arm to the side, opened her fist, then released the remaining cherries atop the polished black shoe of the security guard.

Sam grew aware of the guard standing next to her and the several hundred sets of eyes burning a hole through her torso. Now regretting the harsh words hurled in anger, she could feel guilt seeping to the forefront.

Jack's body language did nothing to ease her conscience. Leaning against the bar stool, she covered her mouth and gave way to her emotions. Jack exited through the revolving door. With the assault over, patrons continued on their way, slipping and sliding through the cherry juice.

Sam buried her face in her hands and began to cry. After ten years, her relationship with Jack was over. She knew deep in her heart neither of their lives would ever be the same.

CHAPTER 15

Had Jack sat his bare ass down on an anvil in the middle of January in Alaska, it would not have been any colder than the leather seats of his Hummer. The frigid interior bit at his cheeks and hamstrings, surging through the thin material of his suit pants as if he were wearing nothing at all.

He guessed the punk who'd parked the car ignored his request for a garage spot and left the vehicle outside as retribution for being stiffed out of a tip. With the vehicle idling in the drop-off cove, he sat with hands tucked under his armpits, waiting for the heating element in the bucket seat to work its magic.

Leaning against the headrest, he tried to bury the last ninety minutes at the bottom of the very large minutia pile now building in his head. The eerie photograph in the newspaper accelerated the suggestion something evil was lurking at his doorstep and his family was in jeopardy. Piling on top of that, a newfound layer of paranoia stroked his conscience as he thought of life without Sam. The thought of losing her was sinking in—rapidly.

The turbulence of the day rendered him oblivious to the business of his office. He did not think once of clients, campaigns, strategic plans, or returns on investment. He wondered what effect Sam's departure would have on his staff and clients, and was concerned how this might affect his personal bottom line. He worked through a mental inventory of the thousand little things she did every day to keep his machine running. Although he had never acknowledged it publicly, the day he hired her was the day his career accelerated. She was much more than a confidant; she was a security blanket. She was an instrument he used to keep the staff on target and focused. She knew his every action and reaction; what he wanted before he wanted it; what he needed before he needed it; what he thought before he thought it. She knew him and could read him better than anyone. Her stinging words as he exited the lobby sliced straight to the marrow and he wondered if they were a coincidence, lobbed in the heat of battle, or had he allowed her to get so close she'd uncovered what he already knew about himself to be true.

"You are a coward," he whispered, opening his eyes long enough to see the condensation of his breath fog a portion of the driver's side window.

Sam's words rang like a lone bell in the steeple of a valley church on Christmas Day. He'd been called a coward before.

The schoolyard appeared in his mind as clearly as the snow blanketing the city around him. Jack closed his eyes. He could see his classmates circled around; the spring sun burning high and bright in the afternoon sky. Gloves, balls, and bats scattered in all directions; he could hear the taunts and jeers of those he thought of as friends, not enemies. There stood his adversary opposite, ready to strike. He recalled the taste of fear. It was dry and gritty as the dirt on the baseball diamond where he stood, more scared than he'd ever been in his life.

He visualized the back of his house, third from the end in a row of fifteen homes appearing identical on all sides, placed a few hundred feet beyond the school's property line. He saw his father standing at the back door, a half burned cigarette dipping from his lips and a Schlitz clutched in his fist. He recalled the color of his shirt, the steel blue of his cold, uncaring stare, and knowing he did not intend to intervene. The man stood as a spectator.

Jack remembered the forearm to the middle of his back that sent him face first into the ground, and the wave of dirt and grit rushing into his mouth. His opponent, two years older and twice his size, did not waste the opportunity. A hard kick to the side of Jack's head ignited a field of stars and an intense burn near his eye socket. A second kick to the same side of his face splintered his cheekbone. Tears gushed from his eyes, but he was not crying. Picked up off the ground by a classmate from behind, Jack saw through one eye a crease open in the middle of the crowd. He did not see his adversary's fist coming from the opposite direction. It connected squarely against his mouth. Struggling to remain upright, Jack spat out a pool of blood and the remains of several shattered teeth, and wobbled toward the opening between his classmates, ignoring sucker punches to the back of his head as he fled.

Stunned and staggering, he burst through the crowd toward his home to the calls of "chicken shit" and "sissy." He remembered the struggle to ascend the concrete steps of the back porch, and bursting through the door where his father stood waiting. He recalled hearing his father's voice and the words uttered in a rage.

"You piece of shit coward . . . don't you ever run from a fight again," the man screamed, before grabbing a wad of his son's hair. Jack felt his body lifted off the ground. His father slammed him headfirst onto the hardwood slats of the family's kitchen floor. Jack's next recollection was waking at the children's ward at Redrock Community Hospital, recovering from dental surgery and fractures to both cheekbones and eye sockets.

Jack opened his eyes and lifted from off the headrest. "You *are* a coward," he whispered again.

He placed his hands on his head, spread his fingers wide and pulled, caring little if a few clumps of hair happened to gather in his fingers. "How in the hell did you allow this day to get so out of control?" Of all he was contemplating, just two facts were clear in his mind: there was no question he'd misjudged Sam's intentions and no way she'd ever get over seeing him and Staci together.

A polite beep from the horn of a car behind provoked a quick peek into the oversized driver's side mirror. Noticing a limousine attempting to maneuver away from the curb, Jack dropped the gearshift, peered over his right shoulder and merged with the traffic heading east.

An inch-and-a-half layer of snow was mere child's play for the four-and-a-half-ton Hummer as he negotiated his way through downtown with ease to the Eisenhower ramp. Although driving beyond the speed limit posed no real threat, the snow was blowing horizontally and into the windshield, creating havoc with visibility and duping his senses into believing he was traveling in reverse.

Already exhausted, Jack struggled to remain alert as the rhythmic thumping of the windshield wipers pulled at his eyelids. Cruising in virtual silence, other than the faint hum of the mechanized component propelling the wipers, he hoped the peace would help cleanse his mind, or at the very least, ease the merciless pounding against his temples. He would enjoy no such luck.

The silence was deafening. Acting as a stimulant for thought rather than a depressant, it stirred his analytic tendencies into high gear. He fought off the urge to re-evaluate the day's events, but could not stop the advance of the many bits and pieces of facts entering from all directions and exploding like shrapnel between his ears. His inability to maintain mental discipline was pissing him off and his ire was growing exponentially. His anger reached a bowel-splitting level as he realized he'd breezed right past his exit, and as near as he could tell, by more than a couple miles.

An overturned semi at the next exit forced him another two miles down the highway to complete the necessary U-turn. The mental lapse cost forty minutes by the time he'd crept through backed-up traffic and made his way to the proper exit. Leaving the clean pavement of the Eisenhower for the untreated mess of Ridgeland, he turned north to travel the four miles to the entrance of his farm community. Travelers noticing the Hummer eased to one side to allow passage, before falling in behind to take advantage of the deep ruts the vehicle was plowing through the white blanket.

Jack attempted another call to his in-laws. The line was still busy.

"There's no way either of those two would be on the phone for three hours," he said, angry the break he thought he was getting was just another dead end. He engaged the vehicle's audio system, requesting it call information.

"City and state, please," a pleasant young woman asked over the speaker.

"I've been trying to reach a number in Wisconsin, but it's been busy forever. Could you check the line and let me know of any problems?" he asked. He gave the number and waited for the operator's update.

"I'm sorry, sir," she said. "There's a pretty significant weather event taking place up there, and the lines are down. I was not given any information as to when service would be restored."

"Weather event? What does that mean?" Jack asked.

"I'm not sure sir, but probably a snow or ice storm. Is there anything else I can do for you this evening?"

Jack cut the line without responding. Knowing calling the police might be his lone option left, he thought through ways he could explain the situation, but decided to wait until he returned home before taking further action.

Finally reaching his community's front gate, Jack buzzed passed a grounds crewman shoveling frantically along the sidewalk leading to the guard shack. In the countless times he'd passed through the front gate, the same questions stirred in his mind like clockwork. Why does a community filled with farmhouses spread over several hundred acres need a gate, a guard shack and a grounds crew? It was something Jack could never figure and something that irritated him each month when he paid the community fees bill. Despite his insistence that the amenities were all unnecessary, he rather appreciated it on this night, as the hard work of the grounds crew allowed him a quick and easy passage to his street.

Taking a right on Redbud, he slowed the Hummer to view the electrical holiday orgy outlining his neighbors' homes. Far removed from the day when outdoor Christmas regalia held any meaning, Jack marveled at the nonsense of it all; the strung lights, plastic Santa Clauses, reindeer, elves, snowmen, candy canes, blow-up figures and the like. Their intensity rendered the Hummer's headlamps and fog lights non-critical as he coasted by, spying each plot searching for the latest and greatest piece of holiday crap.

Other than a vacant Victorian waiting rescue from foreclosure at the very end of the road, the Clarke residence was the lone occupied dwelling along the spread-out stretch free of outdoor Christmas cheer. He was far too busy to decorate and too far removed from the true spirit of the holiday to care.

Jack stopped short of pulling into his driveway after noticing an eerie darkness to the home. Leaning over the dashboard, he observed the stone and cedar clapboard structure from top to bottom, searching for any sign of life. If he was not certain of this being his residence, he'd have guessed it was the home in foreclosure. Brooke always left the under-cabinet lights on in the kitchen—night or day—which, when left on in the evening, illuminated the giant bay window extending opposite of the kitchen table. And she never left town without activating the automatic light timers on the security system. He leaned into his windshield and searched every single window visible from the road. Not a hint of light anywhere; not even from the small nightlight he knew to be plugged in below the window in Julianna's room.

"The power can't be out," he insisted, spying through heavy flakes, looking up and down the road at the other homes burning brightly.

Jack guided the Hummer up the cobblestone drive. He reached for the garage door opener clinging to the visor, depressed the button and waited for the massive wood door of the middle bay to respond; it did not. He mashed the button again as the vehicle inched closer; still no response. Slamming the gearshift into park, he slid the opener free of the visor and extended it to near the windshield. Shouting an expletive, he flung the driver side door open and stepped from the truck into three inches of snow. He approached the garage door and pushed with both hands to check for any obstruction; it moved freely against the frame. He pressed the opener one last time without success.

Stomping back to the truck, he reached in to cut the engine, grabbed the two manila envelopes from the passenger seat and slammed the door as hard as he could. The aggressive, twisting motion of his upper body, combined with the steep slope of the driveway, caused his feet to slip from underneath. In a mere blink, he was en route face-first toward the snowy surface.

Grabbing hold of the driver's side mirror on the way down, he managed to contort into a position enabling a landing on his shoulder and side, rather than taking a facial. With snow drifting atop him, he lay motionless for several seconds attempting to regain the breath stolen from his lungs.

Pain radiated throughout every joint. Although he'd absorbed much bigger hits on the field back in the day, he was no longer twenty-one years old. The fall only accentuated the throbbing in his temples. As his breath returned, he bent his legs upward toward his chest and torqued his hips and back to check for any damage below his waist. Other than a stinger pulsing through his shoulder, he believed he could lift from the surface under his own power.

Jack rolled onto his left side, planted his elbow into the snow, and pushed onto one knee. Searching for something to support his weight, he reached for the tubular sideboards on the Hummer, pausing in mid-motion after noticing a flash of light out of the corner of his eye.

He squared his body to the house, turning his focus to the far side of the second story. A nervous shock swept through at the sight of the three windows in the master bedroom in full illumination. Fighting through the surprising jolt, he scrambled to his feet, keeping a keen eye on the window as he limped through the snow into the front yard.

Glaring at the windows in disbelief, he scanned diagonally down the front of the structure in search of any other signs of electrical life. He could see nothing, including the amber-colored dot identifying the location of the front doorbell. As his eyes reconnected with the lighted panes on the second story, a second jolt struck him as a silhouette floated in front of the curtained opening and paused. Jack saw a misty figure rotate toward the window and appear to drop its head as if looking down at him, before continuing on its way. The sight caused an explosion of current to rifle down his spine. The figure moved past the windows with a fluidity consistent with being suspended. Seconds later, the room went black.

Jack bolted toward the front door, applying the brakes just short of the first step leading to the porch after realizing he was not in possession of his key set. Lumbering back to the driveway, he hunched over the area where his body had fallen, searching for his key ring amidst the blanket of disturbed snow. He noticed the manila folder underneath the truck. Reaching for it, he was relieved to feel the cold sting of keys brush against his palm. Grabbing the set, he pulled himself vertical and scurried back to the porch.

With the porch shrouded in black, Jack angled toward the street, using the holiday glow of the house opposite to assist in identifying the correct key—if he had the key at all. The lone time he'd entered the home through the front door was the day he and Brooke took possession. Fumbling through the set of keys like a drunkard, a strange noise joined in unison with the jingling of the keys, causing an immediate pause. Unsure of its origin or direction, Jack cocked his head, repositioned his body and waited for the disturbance to return.

Several seconds passed before the suspicious noise again breeched the silence, this time revealing its location. Jack swallowed hard. The noise was emanating from inside the house, but Jack found it hard to believe what his ears identified as whistling. He moved close to the door, placing an ear to within inches of the jamb. Puzzled as to why the intruder did not attempt to cloak their presence, he could hear the ghostly trill increase in pitch as if moving toward the front door.

Dropping the manila envelopes, he picked through the keys before pulling free from the mass the one key he could not identify. He buried it into the keyhole; it seemed a perfect fit. Jack paused before engaging the tumblers to assess his first move upon entering the foyer. He'd bought a Smith and Wesson a couple of years prior, but the great equalizer was upstairs in the master closet under lock and key. He rolled through an inventory of the other potential weapons available near the foyer, visualizing how he might gain quick access to them.

He knew of an empty vase on a pedestal near the den and a small candelabra on an end table at the bottom of the stairs; neither of which he knew would pose any real threat to an intruder. He remembered relocating his golf bag to the back of the front coat closet, which was to the left of the stairwell and a mere fifteen paces from the front door. If he got through the door clean, he was sure he could get to a club before the intruder got to him, unless of course, the man was standing right inside with a gun. No matter, he was certain getting to those golf clubs was his best chance of taking care of the situation himself.

With a sharp flick of his wrist, Jack turned the key and burst through the giant maple door with his left shoulder in the lead. The heavy plank crashed into the wall behind with a resounding "thud."

Without hesitation or attempting to identify the whereabouts of the intruder, he raced to the closet door, sent it slamming into a small glass table opposite, and ducked inside. Fighting through a matrix of coats, boots and umbrellas, he found his golf bag tucked in the far back corner and extricated an iron. It felt like his favorite wedge.

Jack removed his suit jacket and hunkered low behind the coat rack with the club resting on his shoulder, He hoped the intruder would wander into the open, at which point he'd spring from the depths and plant the cold steel mallet into his skull. Peering over several of his wife's coats, he kept an eye on the floor for any visible shadows lurking. The house fell eerily silent, and despite the frigid temperature inside, he could feel beads of sweat forming over his brow and lips.

Seconds bled to minutes as he waited for the intruder's next move. He heard nothing stirring above on the upper level nor did he hear footsteps descending the staircase. With adrenaline running high and his patience growing thin, he inched forward from the depths to take a peek. As he reached to slide a coat from his view, the intruder made his presence known again; this time bellowing a blood-curdling cackle. It was coming from the second story at the top of the stairs.

Determining the exact location of the disturbance was less of a shock than the sound of the voice itself. Jack was certain he knew that laugh; he'd heard it no more than three hours ago on the phone. It was that of old man Bigsby. His fear washed away as anger took its place.

"What the hell is he doing in my house?"

Bolstered by a deep-rooted anger, Jack burst from the closet to the center of the foyer, gripping the club as if readying for a fastball down the middle of the plate. At first sight, all appeared normal.

Intending to swing first and ask questions later, he moved with caution to the short set of stairs leading to the landing, dragging his eyes across the horizon in search of anything moving. Reaching the first step, he was forced into an immediate retreat at the sight of a strange, phosphorescent, fog-like blue mist descending from the top of the stairs. The cackling continued.

Jack buried his back flush against the wall leading to the landing and crept up the stairs. Planting on the last step, he inched around the corner for a look. Sweeping up the staircase, he froze at the sight of a dense, undulating glob of blue mist hovering at the top. He blinked to clear his head. The moment his eyes reconnected, the cackling echoing throughout the house ceased and was replaced by an unnerving, steady hum identical to that heard when standing too near an electric trans-former.

Jack eased onto the landing with the golf club at the ready. His senses hinted he was not in danger, yet a nervous doubt percolated. Having no intent to provoke, he stood rigid, staring into the blue glob in search of any definition or outline to indicate what the hell it was. Seconds passed before he heard what sounded like metal cables stretch-ing and dragging across a concrete floor. He felt something wriggle across the tops of his shoes. His body froze.

His eyes dilated as he watched in horror the black, wrought iron balusters lining the staircase morph into slithering, snake-like tendrils. Cascading over and down the stair treads like running water, the steel fingers spiraled in a quick fury up and around his legs like a super-charged vine. The frigid steel constricted against his skin as the tenta-cles made their way to his waist, around his arms and over his chest, binding his limbs tight against his body. His terror heightened as he found himself unable to move a single muscle. Panic raced through his psyche as he struggled to free himself from the grip. Unable to draw another breath, certain asphyxia was soon to follow, a sudden, intense stimulation shock swept over his body, forcing his jaws to collapse. As the steel snake settled tightly around his neck, he felt something or someone commandeer his conscious thought.

As the shock intensified, images manifested at a crawl first, then progressed at lightning speed. Appearing sepia-toned and frayed around the edges as if aged photographs, the images zipped across his consciousness until a seamless stream was achieved. He could smell, hear and feel every component of what was taking place before him. Despite the vise gripping at his body, he could feel his legs churning as he raced from the baseball field, he could feel the stunned daze in his head from the initial kicks to his face, and could smell the dirt and sand below his feet. A flash appeared in the form of his father's face. Then with a scream of agony, he felt his eye socket and cheekbone shatter inside his skin. The pain was excruciating. As if caught in a continual loop, the tormenting video replayed in multiples. With each visualization of himself racing from the schoolyard fight and his father grabbing him by the hair, Jack was introduced anew to the mental anguish of the moment and the physical pain of the incident.

Reaching the edge of his sanity, close to a point he could take no more, a new clip emerged. Jack watched in slow motion the back of his hand connecting against Brooke's chin, sending her collapsing to the floor of their bedroom. The image replayed over and over, each time accentuating the feeling of his knuckles connecting with the softness of her skin and chin. As the reel slowed, Jack felt a final sensation pierce his chest upon seeing the shattered look in Brooke's eyes. At that instant, the wrought iron tentacles released their grip, sending him crashing to the hard oak landing below.

Jack rolled onto his side, gasping to expand his lungs to their full capacity. He opened his eyes to blinding, intermittent pops of bright blue magnificence, mimicking the brilliance of camera flashes from six inches away. He attempted to squint through the aura, but was unable to focus.

He lay prone for several moments, shaking off the pain stinging his face. The familiar motorized hum discharging from the top of the stairs remained. Opening his eyes again, this time to an improved view, he watched horrified as magnificent dots of color amassed from nothingness to manifest in a honeycomb pattern in the center of the blue goo, before the colors expanded outward.

Jack wiped at his eyes, refusing to believe this vision straight out of a Hollywood sci-fi thriller, as the mass manifested. His incredulity washed away when the glob rendered its final form.

"What the hell do you want with me?" Jack demanded, easing off the landing, rubbing away the pain on both sides of his face.

The specter's features were identical to that of old man Bigsby, other than a ghastly set of solid white, pupil-less orbs which now replaced the deep black eyes Jack remembered. Vertical cracks covered the specter's lips, as if the ghost had walked through the desert for weeks without hydration. The specter hung in the air listing from left to right, staring at nothing. Jack waited for a reply but received none.

"What did you do with my family?" he ordered in a more aggressive tone, convinced if the thing had intended to kill him, he'd be dead by now.

The ghostly torso hung suspended, bobbing up and down like a buoy in the ocean. Losing patience, Jack dipped at the shoulder, grabbing for the golf club. Spotting the shaft mere inches from his heel, he returned his gaze to the top of the staircase after collecting the club in his palm. Slow to get to his feet, he tightened his grip and proceeded up the stairs with no plan, but pissed off and exhausted enough to finish the standoff one way or another.

His first move did not pass without a response. Maintaining eye contact, the specter rotated to meet his stare head on, stopping Jack dead in his tracks. The ghost remained rigid with its arms stationary, as if glued to its sides. The white orbs expanded twice their original size before mutating black as ink and dead cold. It remained fixated on Jack, cocking its head from side to side, much like a dog trying to identify an unfamiliar sound. The eerie motion kept Jack at bay, as the apparition gazed straight through him.

Without warning, the figure released a chilling scream from a featureless mouth, causing Jack to release the club, crouch, and cover his ears. The instant the scream subsided, the specter fled down the hallway.

As the light faded from the landing, Jack followed, scaling the steps on his hands and knees. Reaching the top, peeking around the corner, he spotted the figure entering the master suite. Rising, he crept down the hallway to the door.

Entering the sitting room leading to the master suite, he expected to see the familiar glow of the spirit upon entry, but saw instead the bright colors of the holiday lights easing through the windows from across the street.

Turning the corner, he crept along a short walkway separating the master bedroom from the master bath. A soft illumination emitting from the doorway further slowed his pace. Upon entering the room, he was stunned to find the specter gone. In its place, old man Bigsby himself, dressed exactly as he remembered, stood in front of the fireplace, staring at something protruding from under the grate. Jack moved closer, pausing when he reached the first post of the couple's bed.

"What shall you do now?" the image said, pivoting in a single, fluid motion to face him. It was Bigsby's drawn out, country drawl, at least from what Jack could tell, but the image before him did not move its lips.

"I saw them burned. I saw them all burned and so will you. You will never be the same."

"I don't understand," Jack responded. "Where are my wife and daughters? Please, tell me."

"My time is up," the voice said. "I can do no more. The time for your concern has long since passed."

With that, the figure began to shake as if receiving an electrical shock before being sucked into the chimney as a silky blue mist. In a blink, the specter was gone, leaving behind an afterglow of millions of brilliant specks illuminating the firebox. Jack drew his stare to the grate. He pulled at the corner of a half-burned picture. He knew the photo.

Backpedaling to the bed, he eased onto its edge, holding the picture in one hand and grabbing hold of a bedpost with the other. Through the glow of light breaching the master bedroom door, he glanced over his shoulder to the wall where the picture once hung. He noticed its twisted frame atop a pile of glass. He brought the picture to his face, trying to visualize their positions and the look on his wife's face. He could not remember. He let the image slip from his fingertips as he grabbed at his forehead, knowing Brooke had tossed the picture into the flame. As if not quite tormented enough, the ghostly whistling resumed, this time coming from the direction of the front yard.

Springing from the bed, burning the last remaining fumes of energy in his body, Jack ran to the windows of the sitting room and threw open the blinds to investigate. For the second time in less than twenty-four hours, he saw Bigsby riding away in a carriage pulled by two large white draft horses.

Tearing out of the bedroom and down the hallway, Jack descended the staircase two steps at a time then flew through the front door, slamming it shut behind him. Sprinting into the middle of the street, he again saw no sign of the driver or carriage, other than a trail of wheel tracks and hoof prints.

Jack pursued the prints fifty paces before the trail fell cold. As if hitting an invisible brick wall, rig, rider and beasts of burden had disappeared again into thin air. Shaking his head in disbelief, his confusion grew as he turned toward his home. Every light in the house burned bright.

Staggering up the cobblestone walkway and stairs, he saw through the bay window the illumination of the under-cabinet lights emanating from the kitchen. The dot identifying the doorbell cast an amber hue across the covered porch; a glow shone in Julianna's room from her nightlight.

Feeling as if he'd just endured sixty rounds with every heavyweight boxer of notable significance, Jack grabbed the manila envelope from off the porch and stepped through the front door, setting off the home's security alarm. Locking the door behind, he limped to the den, reset the alarm and dragged his body toward the fireplace and the backside of the couch. Tumbling over its top, he fell unconscious before slapping against the soft Spanish leather, never noticing the answering machine atop his desk and the bright red light bursting in rapid succession.

CHAPTER 16
December 22

From whatever origins the ear-splitting, cracking sound had sprung, whether real or conjured in the dream swirling about his subconscious, it exploded with such resonance Jack awakened from his dead slumber after plunging from the comfort of the soft couch to the hardwood floor below.

Nearly gashing his head on the corner of a nearby coffee table, a semi-conscious state was achieved with the expulsion of a bellowing grunt from deep within his gut the moment skin and bone met natural knotty Australian cypress.

Jack's eyes burst open upon impact as he extracted himself in full from the dream state he'd entered hours ago. The fact he'd fallen from the couch and not his king-size bed upstairs proved the biggest shock. Now positioned with his cheek flush on the floor with his arms trapped below his torso, his comprehension lagging, he sifted through a few remaining cobwebs, attempting to make sense of what had happened.

To his surprise, his senses were restored in quick fashion, as was the recognition of his surroundings. Objects appeared through a haze, albeit positioned sideways. The illumination in the room suggested dawn was upon him. His senses also informed of the frigid temperature of the floor and room in general. He noticed the homey aroma of burnt hickory wafting from the firebox. The rigidity in his muscles reminded him of Sunday mornings following Saturday football, along with the slow, defiant response of his limbs to maneuver upon command. Every muscle and joint felt locked in place as if struck with rigor mortis, as he struggled to lift his chin from the floor.

Jack rotated to swap sides of his face. He moved his arms from underneath his body, flattened out then paused to allow renewed circulation to ease the tingling in the tips of his fingers.

Although stiff as a board, he assumed he'd captured at least a few hours of much-needed sleep as a feeling of renewed vigor eased through his body. He stretched his still tingling hands and arms outwards, pressing hard against the wood floor, setting in motion the sound of popping bones and crackling cartilage ripping through the silent, empty home. The simple motion to attain a position on his knees expended more energy than anticipated, as every movement needed to settle on the backs of his heels emitted some sort of sound unnatural to a warm body.

Upright and with hands on his thighs, Jack felt a substantial, internal band of pain encircling his upper chest and back, prompting recollection of the entire episode on the staircase. The previous day's events flooded in reverse as they'd happened, as if he were flipping backward through the pages of a book he'd memorized. Taking pause to wipe away deposits encrusted in the corners of his eyes, his mind teased with a suggestion it was just one crazy dream . . . except the recollections of the sights, sounds, and experiences were as vivid and sharp as the hardwood slats below. He knew it to be all too real.

Jack studied the large, handcrafted grandfather clock just left of the entrance to the den.

"Ten after twelve?" he questioned, squinting. "There's no way in hell it's midnight."

He could hear the gentle tick-tock of the large pendulum swinging side to side. He could only surmise the clock had stopped recently and not reset properly. He was certain the hands were at least six hours fast.

Resting again on his thighs, he paused to stretch and pop his neck before dragging his eyes to the two large lead-framed windows facing the front road. He peeked through a modest gap between the curtains and noticed the landscape appeared muted—inconsistent with what one would expect with the breaking of dawn.

Getting to his feet with the assistance of the corner of the coffee table, he moved to the windows, threw open the curtains and fell back onto his heels, stunned to see dawn had long since passed.

"It's not midnight, it's twelve in the afternoon," he whispered.

He conducted a quick scan of his property. Not a single manmade or natural object was spared a covering of snow. He guessed at least four inches had fallen already, and based on the black and blue of the clouds above, much more was on the way. He could not believe he'd slept fourteen hours.

Jack moved to the center of the room in search of his cell phone. There was no choice now but to call the police. Not seeing the device in open view, he perused the top of his desk and an adjoining credenza, catching in his periphery the blinking light on the answering machine.

Remembering the call he made to the house from his office, he disregarded the alert and continued scouring the other furniture tops and cabinets. Heading to the foyer, he scanned the room over his shoulder a final time for any sign of his phone.

Upon entering the kitchen, Jack's subconscious registered the light on the answering machine had blinked twice in succession, not once. Stopping dead in his tracks, he initiated an immediate about face.

Rushing to the desk, he depressed the replay button, and following a brief pause, was informed of two unplayed messages. Cueing the first, he heard dead air then the line cut. The next message proved more informative.

"Jack, this is Anna Mayberry, your mother-in-law."

"Oh, shit," he whispered, bringing a hand against his brow in frustration that he'd not noticed the light blinking last night.

"John and I are very worried about Brooke and the girls. She called us two hours out from the house to let us know she was driving and not flying. That was about four hours ago. I've tried to call her cell phone but cannot get through. The weather is very bad here and is getting worse.

"We have a lot of snow falling and are expecting some ice, too. Brooke said she was pulling off the road to get some gas and something to eat. The closest exit as we can tell is the Cartersville exit. We have not heard from her since."

Jack heard Anna's voice crack, followed by a long pause and the voice of Brooke's father telling her everything would be okay. "We called the police department and they have no reports of an accident in that area or on the highway. Please call us as soon as you can. We're very concerned."

Jack felt his stomach drop at hearing the name of the town of Cartersville. He knew the name and was flooded with the remembrance of the old man introducing himself as "Jubel Bigsby of the Cartersville Bigsby's."

The nightmare returned full circle as he connected the two dots. If flying, Brooke would have called his firm's limo service. Moving across the den, Jack eased into a half-jog through the foyer and kitchen. He whisked the garage door open and fell numb. The Escalade was gone.

Evaluating the space, he noticed eight large garment boxes lined up in the bay reserved for his Hummer. He assumed Brooke had swapped out some clothes or packed away a few of the girls' old toys and left the boxes there for him to stow. He did not think much of it, but moved to investigate nonetheless.

Ripping open the first box revealed every formal dress and gown his wife owned; all of which were familiar to him and ones he would consider almost new. Racing to rip open the remaining boxes he was puzzled to find every dress, suit, skirt, blouse, pairs of slacks, and dress shoes she owned—everything. He recognized it all. These were not old or worn clothes.

Jack paused to look over the collective stash. Sam's words of warning replayed in his head.

"This can't be," he said. "There's no way in hell she would leave me."

Sprinting back through the kitchen, he navigated the staircase and hallway to the master suite. Bursting through the French doors leading into the bathroom, he stormed forward into the closet and fell dumbfounded at the sight. Half of the space was empty—her half. A few wood hangers dangled about on the varying levels of hanging racks. Not one article of clothing remained.

Heat began to build on the back of his neck. A nervous flush swept across his face as he exited the suite and raced to Julianna's room. Although several toys remained on the shelves, many were missing. He inspected Jordan's room to find the situation identical. Both of the girls' dressers were empty of all clothing. He returned to Julianna's room, staring in disbelief at her vacated closet.

Backpedaling, Jack eased onto the corner of Julianna's bed, looking about the space, trying to convince himself Brooke did not flee their home with his girls in tow. Sam's warning competed with the words of his wife as she pleaded for his attention the previous morning, leaving him wondering now if he had underestimated her courage and resolve.

Jack peeked over his shoulder, bringing into focus a picture on Julianna's nightstand of a captured moment long since passed in his memory. Seeing both daughters sitting atop his shoulders as they traversed the crowd on Main Street at the Magic Kingdom produced an instant, empty feeling, equal to what he felt the day he abandoned his own childhood after walking out on his family some twenty-five years ago.

He consumed his daughters' smiling faces and the utter joy of their expressions and body language. He wanted to smile; he wanted to recall the feeling of their tiny bodies bouncing atop his shoulders. He wanted to hear their giggles at that very moment. He wanted to smell their hair and the violet-scent emanating from the soap their mother used to bathe them. He wanted to hold them against his chest.

Jack pressed his hands against his face. His fears had become demons he could no longer exorcise. Getting close meant abandonment; loving too much meant pain; trusting with your heart meant betrayal. His father's sins were like a noose cinching around his neck.

"I'm so sorry," he whispered.

The moment of self-pity sent him deeper into the photo and his daughters' smiling faces. The trials and tribulations of his youth replaced the reflection of that perfect moment in time. Were it not for a single voice pushing through to reach the surface of his reverie, the mental churning would have lasted much longer.

The voice of old man Bigsby pulled him from the nethermost corner of his thoughts, as the man's claim of Brooke and the girls' returning to him completed a circle he was unable to connect previously. Knowing now Brooke's last contact with her parents came as she was nearing the Cartersville exit could mean only one thing; somehow, some way, she and the girls had fallen into the hands of this lunatic and it had to be the man he saw at the party.

Despite the fact his marriage might be at the point of crumbling, no one was going to steal what was his. The delight he saw in his daughters' faces in the picture solidified the fear he felt for their safety. The sinking feeling of losing his family was replaced with a resolve that Bigsby had pushed his final button.

"Game over, asshole."

The urge to step into the shower, if but for a moment, was difficult to fend off. Jack feared he'd wasted too much time. Changing out of his suit pants and shirt, he stripped clean of his undergarments, replacing them with a fresh set. He shoved an extra set of each in an oversized duffle bag stuffed with spare clothes and bathroom accessories. He tossed his loaded Smith and Wesson on top, slong with a couple of extra clips.

Passing through the master suite, he paused at the sight of the burnt remnants of the photo he'd let slip of the floor. Hovering over the charred image, he attempted again to rebuild the picture in his mind but could not stir his memory enough to recreate his wife's position or the look on her face, despite having passed it every morning on his way to the bathroom. Fighting a percolating guilt, the sensation drained with a simple turn of his head.

"I saw them burned and so will you."

The ghoulish dictum replayed in full as Jack's eyes locked on the firebox where Bigsby's ghost hovered. He was desperate to know the connection between the warning and the previous vision that had appeared to him as he exited his office shower, and he felt a stir in his heart at the evil nipping at his wife's heels. He also knew this was no time to dwell on what *could* happen. Time was his enemy; haste his only friend.

With duffle bag in hand, Jack rushed through the upper level hallway, stopping only to retrieve the photo of himself and the girls at Disney. He hustled down the stairs, keeping as far away from the balusters as possible, grinding through his mind the possible location of his cell phone. Recalling that he had removed his suit jacket in the hall closet, he hurried to the foyer and stepped inside, wading through the jumbled mess. The suit jacket lay atop his golf bag; his cell phone was tucked in an inside pocket.

Backing out of the space, he dialed his in-laws' number, getting another recording relaying all circuits were busy. He called Brooke's number again—another recording.

Knowing the convoluted state of his mind, and that any careless mistake or indiscretion could hamper his efforts in finding his family, he replayed his mother-in-law's message again, writing down her every word with the care of a court stenographer.

He thumbed across the screen of his cell phone to launch a trip planner. He set the destination for Cartersville, Wisconsin.

"I-90, to I-94, to highway 53. Seven hours gets me there around eight-thirty," he said, under his breath, staring at the grandfather clock. He grabbed the manila envelope stuffed with clues from the couch, scanned the room a final time, and hustled to the garage.

Upon making contact with the kitchen door, a strange sensation hinted someone or something was standing behind him. Frozen, staring at his hand wrapped around the doorknob, he could feel a prickly tingle erupt on the back of his neck, as if a warm breath had passed over.

The instant the sensation dissipated, he initiated a slow rotation of his head to look over his shoulder, hearing what sounded like a soft voice whispering the word "daddy." The space behind him was empty. He viewed the room, but saw nothing, heard nothing else, and determined it was the voice of the young girl they'd heard so many times, albeit upstairs in the master bathroom.

Had he not witnessed a very real specter fifteen hours earlier, he'd have paid little attention. Things were different now.

Jack passed through the garage door with a nervous haste, then buried his knuckles into the pad controlling the garage door. The large maple panels sprung to life, belching out ear-splitting cracks as frozen joints popped upon separating at the horizontal turn.

A blast of winter wind sent snow sweeping in from underneath, followed by a stream of frigid air charging at twice the speed of sound. Jack got his first glimpse at the thick, white blanket of snow covering the Hummer. Dropping the duffle bag, he conducted a quick search for a broom.

Seeing the yellow handle wedged behind a trash container on a wall opposite, he moved in pursuit but stalled as a scratching sound from behind startled. He paused to hone in on its location.

Several seconds passed as he stood still, waiting for the noise to resume, all the while scanning the length of the wall separating the garage and kitchen. Concluding a mouse had found its way into one of the many boxes stacked near the door, he continued across the floor. The noise struck again, this time twice as loud. It was clear to him where the sound was emanating from. With head cocked, fixated on the kitchen door, he retraced his steps wondering just how big a rodent he was dealing with.

The scratching continued as he placed his palm over the doorknob. Not wanting any part of some rabies-diseased varmint shooting through the doorway and onto his neck, he kicked at the door simultaneous to twisting the knob. Utter surprise sent him back peddling.

"You've got to be kidding me. What the hell are you doing here," he yelled, slamming his arms against his thighs.

Peetie edged his graying muzzle around the corner of the door before passing over the threshold with his tail between his legs. The dog appeared just as shocked to see his master as Jack was to see him.

"This is just great."

Peetie paused at the top step, shaking either from the chill of the winter air or from fear at the sight of his archenemy. With hands buried in his hips, Jack contemplated the circumstances for which Brooke would ever leave the mutt behind. He whipped through a few potential ideas on where he could dump him for a couple of days.

With little time to waste and knowing he'd never get Brooke back if she found out he'd abandoned the dog, Jack realized he had no choice. He would have to bring the mutt along.

Stomping past the kitchen door, just missing kicking Peetie from his path, Jack scoured the utility room for the dog's travel bag, leash, and a food bowl. He was surprised to find them all missing. Grabbing a half-empty bag of food, he pillaged through a kitchen cabinet to retrieve a couple of Tupperware bowls.

He returned to the garage finding Peetie having fled from the top step. He searched the space but found no sign of him.

Clearing the Hummer took twice as long as expected, as six inches of snow lay atop a quarter-inch of ice. Jack picked the ice clean from the windows, working fast as the heavy, wet snow continued to fall from clouds appearing much darker.

He could not help but wonder about the condition of the roads north, but knew it didn't matter. This was his lone option left and come hell or high water—or twenty feet of snow—nothing was going to stop him from finding his family.

Tossing the broom across the garage floor, he collected his bag, coat, and the few accessories for the dog, then stowed the lot inside the toasty confines of the SUV.

He ripped a whistle in the direction of the front yard, despite no presence of paw prints in the snow, waiting to see if the dog would come out from under a bush or from behind one of the many large trees where he left his calling card.

With no sign of him, Jack conducted a final search and found Peetie jammed face-first in the far corner of the garage beyond the kitchen door, convulsing as if he were suffering a seizure. Jack scooped him from off the floor. The unsuspecting and careless action resulted in a stream of hot liquid shooting down his left forearm. Stretching out his arms in an exaggerated motion, he held the mutt far from his body, cussing as the dog cleared his bladder in response to having his midsection constricted.

"You worthless piece of trash," Jack yelled as a golden stream shot from the animal six feet across the garage floor. With the unexpected shower subsiding to a light trickle, Jack grabbed a shop towel and wiped down his arm and Peetie's underbelly.

Literally and figuratively pissed, Jack half-jogged out of the garage and tossed the dog to the passenger side of the idling Hummer. He climbed in smelling as if he'd not showered in three weeks. Clutching the steering wheel, he paused to catch his breath and calm his anger.

With so much time wasted, he was now certain arriving in Cartersville by 8:30 was no longer realistic. Angry, he turned to send a menacing glare to his unwanted passenger. Only the black, white, and tan patches of hair on his backside were visible. Peetie was buried face-first into the corner of the seat, trembling with fear.

The dog had been a thorn in Jack's side from the moment he learned of his existence. Eight months to the day of the couple's first date, Brooke found the pup in a ditch on the side of an old country road, half-dead and half-buried in bloodstained snow, unable to work his back legs.

Having been shot and dumped for dead, Brooke pulled Peetie from the snow, discovering his lower back and hindquarters riddled with buckshot. Unresponsive to her touch, she rushed him to an emergency animal hospital where she spent the remainder of the day with the dog as he clung to life. Although surgery was possible and there was a slight chance he'd regain function of his legs, it would be a long shot, costly, and a lengthy recovery.

The vet suggested the dog be put down. Brooke declined and assumed responsibility, opting for the surgical procedure. There was no way she was putting this poor animal down, regardless of the expense or burden thereafter. She saw something in his eyes during the vet's probing; a connection was made and she knew it was something special.

Jack knew she'd have trouble paying the vet bill on her salary and that she'd never ask for his help. He expressed his opinion that keeping the dog alive was crazy, but paid the three grand for the procedure anyway, knowing Brooke would sell everything she owned if need be.

A little reconstruction and a couple of steel rods later, and the pup was on the road to recovery and soon moving around under his own power. Brooke dropped him off at the vet's office each morning before work where he underwent physical therapy until she picked him up in the evening—another two grand out of Jack's thinning wallet. Jack saw only pictures of the dog, as he and Brooke were still living in separate cities at the time.

He met the $5000 reclamation project for the first time almost four months following the surgery. Although having no pre-conceived expectation as to the greeting he'd receive, he hadn't counted on being treated as a leper.

Peetie was uncomfortable with his presence the moment Jack walked through the front door of Brooke's two-bedroom apartment. He sat at the end of a long hallway leading to the kitchen, staring at Jack as if he were the man who'd popped him with the shotgun. He didn't bark, growl, or blink. He just sat and stared—nonstop. It was the first of many times Jack would see the classic beagle "vulture" pose.

Peetie avoided him the entire weekend, never approaching nearer than ten feet. Brooke was disappointed at his behavior but convinced Jack it was most likely a man who'd shot him and he was just being cautious. She assured his behavior would improve in time, but even she underestimated Peetie's resolve and distrust. Peetie softened his stance somewhat over the years, but never to the point of cozying up.

After coming home drunk one evening and stepping into a pond of diarrhea, Jack kicked Peetie across the den in a fit of rage. The encounter caused the dog to run for cover at the sound of Jack's voice or the reverberation of his footsteps.

Jack now looked again to Peetie cowering in corner of the passenger seat. He expelled a sarcastic huff as he set the gearshift to reverse. He could feel in his own seat the reverberation of Peetie's shaking.

"Hey, relax . . . Jesus," Jack scoffed. The sound of his voice sent Peetie jamming further into the corner. His convulsions intensified. Jack surrendered a sarcastic grin at the sight of the animal's pathetic display. As Peetie continued burrowing for an escape route, the memory of Jack's own display of cowardice erased the careless expression splitting his lips.

Having no explanation as to why the thought erupted at this precise moment, it stalled his mocking of the dog in an instant. He wondered if the dog's show of fear was any less pathetic or weak than what he'd felt or displayed on the playground that spring day. He recalled his own uncontrolled trembling the moment his classmates encircled his position and upon seeing the look of mastery in his adversary's glare. He wondered if he looked no different to his father than the dog appeared to him now.

The fear he'd felt, and the devastation of being abandoned and left to fend for himself, was something he swore he'd never forget. Had his father just reached out; had he just been a source of refuge. He wondered at the difference between his emotions that day and the dog's now. Was the dog, too, not a living, breathing creature who could express many of the same emotions he himself fought to corral his entire life? The realization was confounding, humbling.

Guilt flooded Jack's conscience at the absolute raw terror the animal was experiencing just by his mere presence. Jack recalled the night he planted his size thirteen-and-a-half shoe into Peetie's rib cage and the horrific yelp expelled as the dog was sent crashing into a bookcase across the room. The sensation of Peetie's side giving way against his foot produced a disturbing churn in his stomach.

Jack turned to his passenger again. Reaching across the storage console separating the front seats, he settled his fingertips atop Peetie's back. The gesture induced an even greater effort to escape, prompting Jack to pull his hand away. Peetie would have to settle down in his own time. Jack hoped he would.

Releasing the brake, he allowed the Hummer to coast down the snow-packed driveway. He glanced at the horizon. The elements would challenge his progress north as snow was now falling at a fierce pace. The press of a button engaged the Hummer's four-wheel drive system and a slide of his hand dropped the gearshift into the drive position.

As the vehicle lurched forward, Jack viewed the home as it disappeared behind his shoulder, wishing like hell he'd wake up to find this all to be a nasty dream. Searching his own eyes in the rearview mirror, he struggled with the sudden, overwhelming desire to want to make things right with his family. He had no idea what was ahead, only the direction he was traveling and the exit he was seeking. He also knew Bigsby was going to pay, and his family would be back where they belonged, regardless of the consequences or his past transgressions.

CHAPTER 17

Jack reversed his course south in favor of the Eisenhower Expressway after seeing no signs the Department of Transportation had cleared the roads from the night before. A plodding line of traffic stretching beyond his sight forced the decision and meant he and his companion were in for a long ride.

The strategy proved a blessing in disguise, as much lighter traffic greeted him upon entering the six-lane stretch. Amazing as it was that six inches of snow could cause such disruption and utter chaos, he found it criminal that not a single plow truck was working the roads in the twenty minutes he traversed Ridgeland, the fifteen on the Eisenhower, or the forty-five spent on I-294.

He noticed one orange truck dropping salt on the Kennedy Expressway while passing time battling hordes of holiday travelers desperate to reach O'Hare, where they would no doubt spend Christmas Day in the terminals due to delayed or canceled flights.

Under normal circumstances, the trip to Rockford ran just under two hours. With current conditions as they were, it took twice as long. The duo lost valuable time avoiding skidding vehicles, maneuvering out of the way of 18-wheelers driving as if it was seventy-five degrees and sunny, and plowing through snow falling so fast and hard, Jack swore he was seeing an increase in accumulation at the base of each passing mile marker.

He expected the weather to worsen the farther north he traveled. To his surprise and delight, he found improved roadway conditions at the

Wisconsin border. Able to see the black of the asphalt below, he
concluded the Badger State's DOT was unconcerned about getting their
trucks covered in a little slush.

Three hours into the journey, Jack recognized the absence of the
reverberation in his seat. Just north of Rockford common, he'd caught
a peripheral view of Peetie coming to rest on his belly, his head droop-
ing over the edge of the bucket seat in the direction of a large side panel
speaker near the floorboard.

Jack called out his name in as docile a manner as he could muster but
did not push the issue when tremors resumed. He spent several miles
contemplating the mental damage he'd caused and if it was reversible.

Based on the info provided by the Hummer's navigation system,
Jack determined their travel time was lagging since passing the
outskirts of Madison. Although traffic was thinning, the snowfall had
intensified exponentially, making it impossible to determine one lane
from the next. Had it not been for a rather large and tightly-packed
convoy of semis allowing him to slip in between, he'd have found
continuing an impracticality; fighting both heavy snow from above and
slush being shot from the rigs' tires.

The natural plowing action of the semis proved invaluable, although
he questioned if he were placing his trust in the right hands, since their
rate of speed far exceeded what he'd be doing if traveling solo. No
matter, their travel time picked up, and as the convoy neared the
outskirts of Black River Falls, Jack determined his destination was not
far beyond.

Cradled between a UPS double-hauler and some poor slob humping
a load of Chevy pickup trucks, Jack broke free of his fixation of
keeping the Hummer within the dimensions of the tire ruts to view
through the driver's side window at the ever-darkening landscape.

Watching the white world zip by at sixty miles an hour, he spotted
a lone, magnificent tree positioned 200 yards from the highway. Its

hundreds of branches and offshoots appeared white as human bones, fanning out in a span surpassing the width of a large livestock barn sitting just beyond. Struck by its familiarity, he followed the giant chestnut until it passed beyond his periphery.

The image ignited a recollection of a similar tree from his childhood, one nestled in the middle of old farmer Kell's cornfield just four fields removed from property owned by his grandmother. The kind man allowed him to build a small treehouse high within its massive branches, even supplying the lumber, hardware, and a helping hand.

The secret hideaway proved a safe haven and a place he could dream dreams and escape from the trials of his family life. A smile cracked his lips as he remembered looking over the acres of corn stalks stretching eight, even ten feet high. Pretending they were warriors assigned to protect their king and castle, he would raise a sword farmer Kell had carved from an old pine plank, bark out orders in all directions, and watch as the stalks swayed back and forth in the summer breeze as if responding to his decrees. It was one of but a few recollections he had of normalcy during his childhood. Staring deep into the brown abyss of the UPS trailer, he wondered what it was he did to cause God to dislike him so.

Jack noticed the distance widening between the Hummer and UPS hauler. The rig behind was nearly parked in his back seat. Breaking from the memory, he repositioned in his seat to alleviate a numb tingle dripping down his legs before mashing on the accelerator to close the gap. He engaged the Hummer's automatic phone system requesting the computer redial his in-laws. The connection was barely audible but clear enough to hear the same, recorded message he'd heard several times in the last twenty-four hours. His frustration overflowed at the thought of what his in-laws must be thinking.

"I can see it now," he said aloud, slapping a hand against the steering wheel, glancing out the driver's side window. "Brooke's family all gathered around the kitchen table, her mother sitting, sipping on a cup of coffee, John sitting nearby listening as she explains the situation to her daughters and their husbands as to how she made *every* attempt to get in touch with me but I cared so little I didn't even bother calling them back. I can see it as plain as the nose on your face," he said, pointing to Peetie.

"Of course they'll all jump on the Jack's-a-worthless-piece-of-crap bandwagon and discuss how they all tried to talk Brooke out of making the biggest mistake of her life," he mocked as his voice faded beneath the sound of the Hummer's V-8 block. Peetie arched his floppy ears checking again to see if the comment was directed at him.

"They have to know the weather is the reason why I haven't called, right?" Although he knew John and Anna were very much aware of the storm, they may not be aware of its severity this far south. He also knew the family needed very little motivation to find reason to despise him. Despite his several attempts to call, they would just find him guilty of something else—probably for not being home when they called in the first place.

"There's not one thing I'll ever be able to do that would mean anything to any of them. But, what else is new, right?" he said, realizing the sound of his voice was no longer sending Peetie seeking cover. He expelled a sarcastic laugh.

"At least you listen, I'll give you that," he said. "No offense, but I wish you were Sam."

Sam had swept in and out of his thoughts for miles, resulting in the same reaction—a push of air through his nostrils at the totality of his stupidity. The level of importance and role she played at the office came nowhere close to her value to him as a friend. It was only now he realized he'd never told her. He thought how a body could survive without a kidney but not without its heart. Sam was his heart and right now, he felt the void. He needed to hear her voice. He wanted to talk.

If he called now, she would either let his call go to voice mail or, at the very worst, pick up just to hang up, which would not be a surprise. Either way, he convinced himself he had nothing to lose.

Jack tapped the communication button and barked out the command to call. The system obtained a line and soon, the faint sound of Sam's phone ringing reverberated throughout the cab. Two rings, then three, followed by four then five. Jack grew nervous; his mouth turned sticky. He vowed he'd hold his temper in check even if she decided to take advantage of the situation to ream him a new hole. Losing count of the number of rings, he was set to cut the line. As his thumb moved over the top of the button on the steering wheel, the line picked up.

"Hello," Sam said, more as a statement than a question. Her voice was soft and reserved as it competed with a fair amount of static crackling through a small speaker just above Jack's temple.

"Sam, it's me."

Her response was not immediate. Jack let the crackle settle several seconds before calling her name again.

"What do you want?" she replied.

"Are you in East Alton?" he asked.

"Yes . . . at my parents' house."

"Are you okay?"

"I'm fine. We just got back from the high school . . . the Oilers had a basketball game tonight."

"Another victory for the maroon and gold?" Jack quipped.

"Of course. What do you want, Jack?"

"I just wanted to hear your voice; make sure you're okay."

"I'm fine. You've heard my voice, so goodbye."

"Sam . . . please . . . don't hang up." He paused, waiting to see if she had cut the line.

"Are you there?"

"I'm here . . . but I don't want to talk to you. I want you to leave me alone."

"Sam, please, I was wrong, okay? I was dead wrong. I've made a terrible mistake and I know it. I'm sorry it happened and sorry you got caught in the middle."

His confession surprised her. It was rare he owned up to a mistake and his voice suggested this was not some concoction to appease. Although she wanted to hear more, Sam wondered if he was sorry for the act or sorry for getting caught in the act.

"Staci was a mistake and it never should've happened. I'm not in love with her and have no intention of seeing her again. She offered something I needed at the time and I took it, okay? It was selfish and disrespectful and a hundred other descriptions I'm sure you've already come up with. But I want you to know why. I want you to know why it happened."

"I don't care why it happened. I've washed my hands of this mess and will be happy to move on from it. There's nothing you can say to erase what I saw. There's nothing you can do to restore my faith in you. I don't trust you anymore and hope Brooke comes to the same conclusion. She deserves something so much more than you. I can't even believe—"

"Sam," Jack snapped, interrupting her rant, "have you ever known a woman who was raped?" Sam fell silent. Jack heard what he thought was a gasp.

"Brooke was raped when she was fourteen years old by a member of her own family. Do you know what happens to a woman after she's been through something like that? Do you have any idea?"

Sam did not respond. Her mind connected several dots regarding Brooke's personality that she'd always found strange. Many of those questions added up in the flash of his statement.

"It's been a wedge between us for years. That part of her has never been right and it's caused many problems between us. I know it may not be easy for you to understand and I'm willing to take some blame because I lost patience with it all a long time ago. But there's only so much one can do to help. At some point, she needed to find a way to deal with it and never did."

Sam was stunned. She could not believe her friend had endured something so horrible. She felt sick that she had not been there for her and sorry she had to face the trauma alone all these years.

"Do you have any idea what it's like to go without sex or intimacy?" he said, moving well beyond his comfort zone. "I thought we could get through it in the beginning, but I knew something was wrong because no one could be that shy, frightened, or inept without having suffered something bad. When she told me what happened, it was like she did so just so she'd not have to perform any longer. What was I supposed to do, spend the rest of my adult life in a state of celibacy? It's been complete misery—for the both of us."

Sam's voice began to crack. "So it was okay to get it elsewhere?" she asked, trying gain control of her emotions. "Is that what you're saying?"

Jack held his response. His thoughts drifted to the first time he met Brooke. He could not deny wanting to get her into bed, but also recalled how he fell for her compassion, sensitivity, and the way she made him feel. She was the one woman willing to make him work for her attention and affection.

"Jack?" Sam's voice reeled him back to the conversation.

"I'm not saying it was right. I know what I did was wrong, and I know she will never forgive me for this. I'm not sure I'd forgive me for this. But you have to consider what it's like to be in your sexual prime and have no chance at sex other than taking it. Every time we had sex, including after the girls were born, it felt like I was raping her myself. Who the hell wants to feel like they're raping their own wife? Staci was an opportunity to relieve tension and stress and I took advantage of it. What else do you want me to say?"

"How many other women were there?"

"What difference does it make? Whether there was one or a hundred and one, I know it was wrong."

"How many others?" she insisted.

Jack paused for what seemed an eternity. "Three," he replied.

"I can't believe you. Why didn't you just ask for a divorce if the circumstances were so bad? I know she would've been devastated but at least she'd not have been humiliated and betrayed."

"Because she means a great deal to me . . . she does. I . . . I just don't know"

"You don't know what?" Sam demanded.

Jack paused, unsure if he wanted to go down that path right now.

"What don't you know, Jack?"

"I don't know what love is. I'm not sure I've ever known. All I know is I never wanted to hurt her, you, or anyone. I'm just a screw-up."

Sam was at a loss. She knew Brooke was not alone suffering from a childhood trauma.

"What in the world happened to you?" Sam asked. "I've known for a long time you've been haunted by something. Why won't you tell me what it is?"

"I could tell you everything but it won't change what I've done or what I have to do. This isn't about me anymore. It's about getting my family back."

"Where are you?" she asked, concerned he was in the process of doing something stupid.

"Like I said, I'm going to get my family back."

"Where are you?" she insisted.

"I'm driving to Wisconsin."

"Why are you driving to Wisconsin?"

"Because it's the last place Brooke's family heard from her."

"What are you talking about?"

"When I got up this morning, I got a message from her mother. She told me Brooke decided to drive home and not fly. She spoke with her just before she pulled off the highway to get gas around the Cartersville area."

"Cartersville? You mean the place Bigsby said he was from? That Cartersville?"

"I guess so. What other Cartersville could it be? They got concerned when she and the girls didn't show up on time. I've been trying to call them ever since but the lines are down. I can't get through."

"Why didn't you call them back last night?"

"If I tried to explain to you what happened to me when I got home last night you'd hang up and call the nearest mental hospital. The fact is, I didn't see the answering machine until this morning. It's also when I discovered . . ." Jack paused. The words stuck behind a huge lump in his throat.

"Discovered what?"

"That she'd cleared out her and the girls' closets. Everything is gone."

The two shared a long pause as Sam considered how she should respond. "I'm sorry Jack. I am. I knew this day was coming. I can't believe you would be willing to let all this slip away. And for Staci DiSano? Are you kidding me? I would have been more understanding had you said you'd fallen for a blow-up doll.

"You may not know what love is but Brooke does, and it was you. She loves you so much. I can see it in her eyes when we talk. You were the person she was looking for. How could you not care?" Sam heard him sigh.

"Where are you right now?" she asked.

"I'm a few miles or so from the exit."

"What are you going to do when you get there?"

"I told you, I'm going to get her and the girls back."

"From who, from where? You don't even know for sure she's there. She could have gone to a different exit. She might be at her parents' house as we speak."

"I'm sure she's not. She's with Bigsby. He has her; I know it."

"You mean this ghost that keeps reappearing? Which one do you think has her?"

Jack swiped at his brow, knowing he did not have an answer. He glanced to his right and noticed Peetie staring at him as if he, too, were wondering the same thing.

"Have you lost your mind?" Sam yelled. "All you're doing is chasing ghosts. And by the way, do you have any idea what you're driving into; do you understand what's going on with this storm? All the news stations are claiming it to be the most significant winter weather event this century. They're calling for several feet of snow and ice and you're in a car driving right into the heart of it."

"I know it's going to be bad. It's getting worse every mile I travel, but what would you have me do? Brooke and the girls are missing— this, I know to be a fact. Like you said, I can't call the police, so there's nowhere else to turn. It's up to me. I have to find them. I'm going to find them and bring them home. Whatever happens after that, happens. But it will happen within the walls of our own home."

"What are you going to do when you get there?"

"I don't know. I don't have the first clue. If it means searching from building to building and house to house, so be it. I'm bringing them home . . . period. And Bigsby, well, that asshole has delivered his last message."

"What do you mean?" Sam's concern for his rationale was growing with each passing second.

"This guy's gonna pay; I can assure you. One way or another, he's going to pay."

"Again, what do you mean?"

Jack kept his tongue. He didn't know himself exactly what he meant.

"Listen," he said, "there are few things I know for sure, but one of them is that Brooke and the girls are in danger. I know it; I can feel it. I've got to do this because there's no one else who can. Would you believe any of this if you didn't know me or hadn't witnessed for yourself the goofy shit that's gone on the past few days? No. This is my doing and my problem. One way or another, this ends now."

"Have you given any thought about the email you received? Do you know you're playing right into the hands of the email message?"

"I have no plans of staying anywhere. If I have to, I'll sleep at a rest stop in the truck; Peetie will keep me warm. "

"Peetie? What are you doing with him?"

"When I was leaving this morning he appeared out of nowhere. I had no choice but to take him."

"Oh, I don't know about that, Jack. That sure doesn't sound like Brooke, especially if she were driving. There's something not right about that."

"I know. But, it is what it is."

"Is he okay?"

"Yeah, I think so. It took him a time to settle down, but he's better now."

"Maybe it's an opportunity for the two of you to bond."

"Yeah . . . not a real concern right now. I've got to worry about what's ahead."

"You're crazy. You're absolutely nuts."

"And you sound like you still care."

The line fell silent. Sam cared and she was concerned, but she was not in a place to forgive him.

Jack cleared his throat. "Let me ask you something . . . have I lost you?" He waited as the butterflies redeveloped in anticipation of an unfavorable response. Static filled the cab.

"Did I? Are you gone?"

Her silence was like a knife burrowing its way deep into his chest.

"I trusted you, Jack," she said, much less animated. "For years I've dealt with your ego and insensitivity; the poor way you've treated people and your foul mouth. I've dealt with it all and continued to be loyal to you. You challenge me professionally every day, and I trusted you. I can't work for someone I don't trust or respect . . . no matter how much it hurts to leave."

"Okay. I'm not going to beg. I understand your position and know I have myself to blame. I'm sorry it's come to this. I'm sorry I let you down."

Jack paused to check his mirrors and the GPS display on the dash. He watched as the bright green arrow representing the Hummer passed well beyond the outskirts of Bloomer, approaching another city famil-iar to his conscience, New Auburn. He was hoping Sam would recon-sider, but knew she needed space. He traveled a bit in silence as each waited for the other to speak.

"I need to get off and concentrate on the road. I appreciate you speaking to me. I hope you have a great visit with your family."

"I think you're making a big mistake," she stated.

"There's no other way. This is my fault and it's time to pay the piper. Like I said, I'm putting an end to this, one way or another, right now."

"I'll want to know of any updates . . . I will be concerned."

"I know you will. I appreciate it. I'll call if I can." Jack tapped the button to cut the line.

Sam closed her eyes, still holding the phone to her ear. The position he put her in was unforgivable, yet she wanted to kick herself for not offering help. Her faith and trust in God and all things good was being challenged, but she held steadfast in her belief this was something he needed to make right on his own. Jack remembered passing the bright lights of Eau Claire, prompting a mental image of the newspaper delivered by young Bigsby. In a string of events producing one bizarre nugget after another, the photo on the back of the relic stirred his mind above all others. If he were passing the city during normal business hours, he'd stop by the offices of the Eau Claire Leader, if still in existence, to authenticate the paper. Despite the many scenarios concocted, he could not fathom the reason for his image in the paper.

Although the convoy was moving along at a decent clip, Jack grew antsy after catching a glimpse above the UPS trailer of an overhead sign indicating Cartersville just four miles out. Thinking better of attempting a pass, he remained cuddled in between the two rigs, spending the time working out a strategy.

"We have to assume the conditions when they passed through were a far cry better," he said. "It was still light out and was probably snowing, but even in daylight, I doubt she ventured far from the highway. I guess we stop at the first place serving both gas and food and start asking questions. It's all we can do."

Peetie maintained good eye contact and an attentive position throughout the planning session. Seeing the dog at ease, Jack felt it was time to extend an olive branch.

Peetie kept a concerned and nervous eye targeted on Jack's hand as it moved beyond the center storage compartment. With every muscle set firm, he extended his claws into the seat in the event he needed to spring to the floorboard for cover. As if tracking a rabbit in the bush, he gazed without blinking as his master's fingers extended toward the back of his neck, his eyes growing wider the closer Jack approached. The gesture seemed non-threatening, and in a display of trust, Peetie held his position. The touch of skin on fur induced a ripple across his body but also a slight wag of his tail. Jack dragged his hand from the base of Peetie's neck to down his back.

"That wasn't so bad, was it?"

Peetie remained on high alert in the event the situation regressed. As Jack pulled his hand back across the dividing line, he noticed a quickening of the thumping of Peetie's tail against the back of the leather seat. Although the exchange would not solve any of his current problems, the significance of the moment went a long way in restoring some confidence that poor decisions and bad choices are rectifiable. He hoped for the same opportunity with his family.

With the back of the UPS trailer no longer engulfing his line of sight, Jack noticed a low-hovering, muted bubble of light in the distance off to his right, and as the rig in front pulled away, a large Flying J truck stop sign appeared several hundred feet above all others. He set his blinker, doing so in near unison with the UPS truck. The sight of the truck's bright flashing yellow light brought relief, as he'd not been looking forward to navigating the exit alone. A flashing yellow beacon also appeared in his rearview mirror.

He arrived in Cartersville safe and sound, thanks to his unexpected escort and a potential newfound friend at his side. As the group made its way up the ramp, Jack scanned the right side of the highway for potential targets. A couple of gas stations appeared open on both sides, but he knew the Flying J offered both fuel and food.

He remained in single file as the group of trucks entered the packed property, before coming to rest in a space next to his favorite UPS driver. Shutting down the engine, he scanned the parking lot for the Escalade in hopes Brooke decided to wait out the storm. Several SUV's appeared, though none black in color. Peetie scrambled from the seat to get his bearings. Jack dropped against the headrest, whispering for assistance from no one in particular.

CHAPTER 18

"That sure was one hell of a ride, wasn't it, cowboy?"

Jack exited the Hummer just as Mr. UPS stepped from his idling rig. Decked in dark brown coveralls with a face full of whiskers bursting a shade of orange brighter than the fruit, the hulking man resembled more the part of a conquering Norse Viking than a modern day trucker. With a smile a mile long and a mid-section equal in circumference, he hopped from the last step of the cab with his hand extended.

"Glad you stayed with us, fella. My buddy behind you thought you were gonna try and pass. It was mighty wise to stay right where ya were, guarantee it was as safe as your momma's womb."

Jack accepted the man's hand, marveling at its size as it wrapped around his twice. It stung his skin as if made of steel wool. His exuberance and high energy caught Jack off-guard, rendering him speechless. His smile was a surprising comfort and Jack soon felt a release knowing he was not alone

"I got to tell ya, son, we all appreciate you keepin' up with us like ya did," said a voice from behind. "I almost turned you into a bumper sticker a couple times." Both drivers reacted to the Chevy hauler half-jogging through the snow to join in the conversation.

Now that's a trucker, Jack thought. The man, no taller than a fire hydrant but twice as wide, sported rooster-red cowboy boots, tight blue jeans attached to his waist with a silver-plated belt buckle the size of a football, and a ten-gallon, black cowboy hat pulled low over his brow. Chiseled features and a wide girth suggested he was active in the weight room, or spent his Saturday nights wrestling at his local community center. His smile was eager and his demeanor friendly, but far from submissive. It was clear that underneath the plaid shirt, a wolverine lay in wait, ready to strike if someone dared to provoke.

"I was telling old E-Red I was bettin' your balls were itchin' to get on by him. You were smart to stay put."

Jack stepped back as the two truckers greeted each other with a warm handshake.

"You guys know each other?" Jack asked, pointing a finger in each direction.

"Oh . . . sure . . . for years," said the smaller man. "E-Red and I've been pulling junk down this road for near twenty years."

"E-Red?" Jack questioned.

"Short for Eric the Red, son," he explained. "Just a nickname. This here is Big John Frederikson, and I'm Jimbo Cooper; the boys call me Mule . . . pleasure to meet ya."

Jack grabbed the man's hand, matched his smile then fought off a challenging shake intended to determine who possessed the stouter grip.

"My name's Jack . . . Jack Clarke. I appreciate you fellas allowing me a spot in your line. I don't know that I'd have made it without you."

"It's a pleasure to meet ya, Jack. Glad we could be of service. What-a ya say we step inside and grab some coffee?"

"I'd enjoy it, but I'm in a pretty big hurry."

"You mean you're going back out in that soup?" Big John asked.

"Well, it's somewhat of an emergency."

"I'll tell you what ole' buddy," Jimbo said, slapping Jack on the back, "let's all step inside, grab a quick cup of Joe, and you can tell us all about it. Maybe we can help ya."

"Well, I need—"

"We ain't taking no for an answer, cowboy," Big John said. A wide smile followed.

Jack nodded as the two truckers moved off toward the front door of the large diner connected to the station. After assuring both he'd be right in, he shuffled through the snow to the passenger's side door where Peetie sat watching his every move. Reaching inside, he placed a bright colored collar around Peetie's neck, attached a like-colored leash and guided him out of the truck. Quick to lift a leg, Peetie changed the color of the snow under the trailer of Big John's rig. Jack surveyed the parking lot while Peetie loitered about the immediate area to the length of his leash.

The weather system was producing and dropping precipitation at a staggering rate, and if not for the absence of wind, would classify as blizzard conditions. Viewing a large light hovering above the parking lot and the volume of snow passing through its luminosity, Jack grew concerned he was running out of time if he were intending to question the several other establishments scattered along the exit. He scooped Peetie from off the ground, wiped his paws free of slush, and eased him into the cab. The dog kept a watchful eye as Jack darted through the snow and around parked vehicles toward the diner.

"Jackie-boy . . . over here." The booming voice exploded from Jack's left, but he was unable to locate his newfound buddies through the sea of truckers packing the joint. Scanning through smoke and over a wave of bodies moving between tables, he spied a lone, giant hand waving above the crowd in the back. Zig-zagging between tables, he navigated to a booth where Big John and Jimbo were holding court with two other drivers.

"Jackie," Jimbo said, sliding one space to his left, "come on in here and meet a couple good friends."

Jack eased onto the padded red bench next to Big John.

"This here is Charlie Parker and Clete Gilliam. We call Charlie there John Boy because of them glasses and that stain on the side of his face, and Clete, well, we call him King Clete. He's been haulin' loads longer than any of us've been alive."

Jack offered a wave and a nod. The truckers responded in kind. Big John yelled in the direction of the counter for another cup of coffee.

"You're a mighty big fella," Clete said, looking at Jack as if recognizing a useful plan for him. "I'll just bet you played a little football in your day."

"I did . . . played in college."

"I knew it. Looks like ya took a couple shots to the nose, there."

"Well, the other guys looked much worse."

The comment induced a hearty barrage of laughs; Jimbo buried his elbow into Jack's ribs.

"I appreciate the help you guys gave me tonight," Jack said, "but I need to get back on the road. The snow's piling up and I have a few more miles I need to travel."

"That's fair," Big John said. "We don't mean to hold you up son; just thought it'd be nice to meet you and hear a new story. We've already heard the stories of the rest of these bums."

"I appreciate it. I do. If it were any other time, I'd enjoy the opportunity to hang with you a bit. But, I've got an emergency I'm dealing with."

"Son . . . one thing about us truckers, we stick together," Clete said. "Now I know you don't drive a truck, but these boys here tell me you were in their cradle five hours, and I can tell you this, if they didn't want ya there, they would've passed you, and I guarantee you wouldn't be sittin' here right now. Why don't you tell us what's going on . . . maybe we can help."

Jack was not in much of a mood to share his predicament and was more than apprehensive about sharing his troubles with complete strangers. But he did believe there was power in numbers and had relied on the axiom to his benefit more than once in his career. Looking from the table to across the room, he watched the exchange between the other truckers and their seemingly friendly and trusting nature. Maybe one of them saw Brooke stop. He decided to take Clete up on his offer.

"The fact is, I'm looking for my wife and two daughters. They were traveling up this way to visit family. We lost contact with her last night after she supposedly got off at this exit for gas and food. I'm here trying to find out if anyone saw them."

The smiles and smirks on the faces of his newfound friends exchanged for looks of sincere concern and empathy.

"I have to get to these other places along the highway before they close. She stopped somewhere around here, I just know it."

"I'll tell you what, Jackie-boy," Jimbo said, pointing a finger, "while you question the staff in here, we'll all go out to our trucks, get on the radio and make a call out over a few different channels to find out who passed through last night. There are two truck stops at this exit; this one and another on the west side of the highway. She stopped at one of 'em because there ain't no fuel for another twenty-two miles. What's she driving?"

"A black Cadillac Escalade."

"What's your wife look like?" Charlie asked. "What was she wearing?"

Jack found describing Brooke difficult. Doing so meant she was really missing. An uneasy feeling swelled as several scenarios developed as to her plight. A lump rose in his throat.

"You okay, Jackie?" asked Jimbo, leaning over and speaking in a whisper.

Jack nodded. "I don't know what she was wearing," he said. "But she's about five feet, eight inches tall, thin, with long black hair. My daughters are twins and a little more than four years old. The Escalade has Illinois plates and has a towing package on the back with a Chicago Bears hitch cover."

"Okay, boys," Big John said. "Let's see what we can find out."

The men started pushing their way out of the booth. Jack stepped aside to let them pass.

"Fellas, can I have your attention." Big John's voice shot across the diner, stifling the conversations of all in the room. The man held great respect with the other drivers due either to his mountainous frame or the fact he was just a good and well respected man.

"This here is a good friend of mine. His name is Jack Clarke. He's looking for his wife and daughters. They've come up missing and were said to have stopped at this exit last night. Now, his wife was driving a black Cadillac Escalade with Land of Lincoln plates. I'd like for you all to take a moment and contact some of your buddies to find out if anyone saw her here last night. Okay?"

The place emptied as if it were a sinking ship. Jack brought his hand to his face, wiping at the heavy stubble against his chin. Their willing nature more than surprised. Big John laid his hand atop Jack's shoulder, offered a wink and followed the trickle of truckers out the door. Jack watched through a large window as each jumped into his cab.

It took just fifteen minutes with the staff. No one recalled seeing a woman of Brooke's description at the pumps or in the restaurant. Jack thanked the staff then requested to speak to the manager. Appreciating the truckers' help, he inquired what it would take to pay for all they'd ordered and handed over a credit card to pay for the thousand-dollar ticket.

Upon signing his name, Jack jumped as Jimbo burst through the double set of glass doors hollering like a mad man. "Come on Jackie-boy," he yelled, waving his arm in a gesture to follow. "I think we just got lucky."

Adrenaline raced through Jack's body as he hustled out the door on Jimbo's heels. The two headed for a rig taking on fuel. Several of the men gathered around the cab, including Big John, Clete, and Charlie. As the two approached, the men parted to allow Jack a spot near the door.

"We got some information Jack," Big John said. "Dale here spoke with a guy who saw a woman fitting your wife's description pull into the BP truck stop on the other side of the highway."

Jack shook his head. He saw the BP sign and had failed to make the connection. Of course Brooke would've stopped at the BP; it was the lone gas card she carried in her wallet.

"Dale said his buddy saw a woman park in the greasy spoon on the other side of the station. He said she got out in a hurry and took the girls inside. It appeared steam or smoke was shootin' out the grill. He said he was just about to walk over there to see if he could help, but the woman came out of the diner with a man who walked to the vehicle for a look-see. Thinking she was in good hands, he pulled out and didn't see anything else."

Jack rushed to shake his friends hand and hustled to the Hummer.

"Hey, Jack," Big John yelled, kicking through the snow in pursuit with Jimbo at his side. "Do you want us to come with you?"

Jack stepped from the Hummer. "You guys have already done more than I can ever repay. You got me here safe and you've pointed me in the right direction. I'll take it from here."

"What if we hear of something more?" Big John asked. "We have a lot of calls out and we might get some more information. How can we contact you?"

Jack reached into his wallet and grabbed a couple of business cards.

"My cell number's on the bottom."

"We drive through Chicago all the time; maybe we can have that cup of coffee some other day." Jimbo said.

"You just let me know when and where," Jack replied, smiling. "Thanks again."

"Merry Christmas, Jackie-boy. We'll be praying for ya," Jimbo winked.

Jack hopped into the Hummer, watching through a fogged window as the men retreated to the diner. As they approached, several truckers piled out, handing over a white slip of paper. In a single motion, they acknowledged Jack's deed.

Jack acknowledged the group through the window then engaged the Hummer's four-wheel-drive system. Pulling around Big John's rig, he rushed for the exit, targeting a set of tire ruts formed by a semi that had exited moments before. Heading west on Highway 8, with anxiety at a fever pitch, he fixated on the green and white BP sign, holding out hope he'd caught up to his wife's trail.

CHAPTER 19

The Eat at 8 Diner sat back off the road, surrounded by a large grouping of aged oak and hickory trees, just a hundred yards beyond the property of the BP station. A large neon sign extending the width of the building's stucco-finish front glowed in brilliant red, green, and gold, casting the colors halfway across its lot.

Lights inside burned through several large plate glass windows, illuminating a smattering of patrons of the truck driving persuasion, all huddled around tables, slapping backs, and telling lies.

Pulling in the second of two entrances, Jack conducted a quick search of the BP lot, noticing tractor-trailers parked in three neat rows, appearing as if the operators had settled in for the night. He brought the Hummer to rest on the far side of the lot near an area adjacent to a grouping of picnic tables. Before shutting off the engine, he cracked the driver's side window. Peetie resettled in the seat, unconcerned they'd come to another stop. Reaching behind, Jack grabbed his coat and draped it over the dog's body.

"I'll be right back," he said. "Just hang tight . . . I'll bring you a burger."

A shiver ripped through his body upon stepping into the six-plus inches of virgin snow, as the precipitation bit at the exposed skin just above his sock line. Bounding across the slick surface on his toes, he found relief under a large, green canvas awning stretching along the front of the building's entrance. Grabbing hold of the molding encasing the door, he kicked against the building's stone foundation to clear the snow from his shoes.

The sound of metal utensils clinking against china and an unfamiliar oldie tune blaring in the background permeated the thin stucco
walls. Peeking around a window near the door, he figured the diner
much smaller than the one on the other side of the highway and serving
a great many less. Several booths and tables near the front sat empty. A
long counter, decked in stainless steel and featuring red padded swivel
stools atop black-and-white checkered tile, stretched the entire length of
the far wall. He set his sights on a vacant stool near the counter's center.

With most of the snow from his shoes now scattered across a green
indoor-outdoor carpet, he moved through the front entrance, setting off
a bell hanging on a nail just above. The pleasant chime alerted those
gathered of his presence, prompting an ease in conversation and
sending every head rotating. The aroma of strong black coffee, scrambled eggs and fried meats infiltrated his nostrils. He could hear the echo
of burgers sizzling on a grill in the kitchen. Unlike the truckers at the
Flying J, this group did not seem a friendly sort and appeared annoyed
he'd interrupted their meal.

Jack swung open the door and moved toward the counter, wading in
and around tables of patrons sizing him up and staring him down. He
passed a young couple sitting on the same side of a booth sharing a
piece a cake; they nodded but said nothing.

Reaching the counter, he pulled a leg over an empty stool in
between a coverall-wearing trucker chewing on a corndog to his left
and a well dressed, elderly gentleman sipping on a spoon-full of chili.
Jack bellied up to the bar and nodded toward the man to his right, who
was keeping a sharp account out of the corner of his eye.

Jack searched both ends of the bar but found no sign of a server. He
did notice a woman working a table on the opposite side of the room,
but did not have the nerve to yell across the room to gain her attention.
A voice soon called out, interrupting his search.

"I'll be right with you, sir," a young woman yelled, poking out from behind a wall appearing as a staging area for the kitchen.

Jack waved in recognition. Before he could complete another scan of the interior, the twenty-something woman moved from behind the wall holding a pot of coffee in one hand and balancing a tray packed with loaded plates in the other.

Dressed in a short, pink satin skirt with a white apron pulled tight around her waist, a pink polka dot chiffon scarf around her neck and a matching pink satin beret, she appeared every bit a waitress from a 1950s drive-in. Although attractive, in a Midwest tomboy sort of way, and pleasant facially, everything else about her suggested someone wishing they were somewhere else in life rather than dressed as a clown serving hungry truckers from dawn 'til dusk.

Jack watched as she moved down the line, dropping off pie here, a steak sandwich there, refilling coffee cups, and passing out extra napkins and straws. She looked exhausted. He suspected she'd been there since breakfast.

"Good evening . . . what can I get for you?" she asked. The woman placed her tray on a counter behind then reached for a scratch pad buried in the pocket of her apron. The name on a badge clipped just over her left breast read Katlyn. Deep, beautiful teal-colored eyes dominated a thin, bony face, but were unable to hold the attention of onlookers more than a few seconds due to a sizable burn scar covering a large portion of her right temple. The woman was accustomed to people staring at the crimson-colored mark that presented more like a backlit billboard.

"What can I get for you this evening, sir?" she asked again, deflated and disappointed that the most handsome man she'd seen all day saw her as all others did—damaged goods.

Jack pulled his stare away from the scar. "I'm sorry, Katlyn," he said. The woman's face glowed. It was the first time all day someone had addressed her by name rather than sugar or sweetheart.

"I'll have three burgers to go; one without a bun."

Still enjoying the moment, she hesitated with her response. As she spotted Jack's eyes peeking over a grease-covered menu, the world of waitressing returned in an instant.

"I'm sorry, sir," she said. "What did you say?"

"Two burgers, loaded, one plain with no bun."

"Would you care for some fries or onion rings?" she asked, staring deep into his eyes.

"A diet pop will be fine. No fries . . . I'd also like a glass of water to go."

Katlyn winked and offered a smile reserved for those respectful of her lot in life. She held her position to enjoy a few more moments with this perfect gentleman and specimen.

"Uh, Katlyn . . . before you go," Jack said, aware he'd need to mention at some point he was in hurry, "do you have any knowledge of a woman with two young girls who stopped here last night experiencing car trouble?"

She squinted then bit at her lip. "Um, last night? No sir, I wouldn't. I wasn't here last night. I was off."

"Is the owner here? Could I speak with them?"

"He's not here in the evenings. He opens the diner in the morning. I'll see if the night manager knows anything. She was here last night and may be able to help. Is there anything else I can get you?"

"No, thank you."

The woman retreated toward the kitchen, gazing over her shoulder the entire distance of the bar. Devouring his blue eyes, she recognized the encounter as the best five minutes of her day.

"You lookin' for someone, son?"

Jack swiveled to his right just as the man finished taking a napkin to his chin. The old timer reached for what remained of a toasted BLT, and keeping his head forward, leaned over the counter to insert the final chunk into his mouth. Not wanting to interrupt, Jack waited as the bit of sandwich passed through the man's throat.

"Yes, I am. I'm looking for my wife and daughters."

The man's appearance evoked an aura of experience, common sense, and kindly reserve; something not surprising of someone of his obvious generation. A well-defined depiction of an anchor dominated the nearest forearm, making known his loyalty to the Navy and *U.S.S. Indianapolis* in particular. Jack did not recognize the vessel as anything significant.

Removing his cap, revealing thinning, silver hair, he offered a genuine smile. "Chester J. Walton's the name, son," he said, extending an aged, liver spotted hand. Jack obliged his request, being careful with his grip.

"Pleasure to meet you, Mr. Walton."

"Please . . . call me Chester. Mr. Walton was my father and he was a horse's ass."

Jack laughed; the old man did not.

"You say it's your wife and daughters you're looking for, huh?"

"Yes. She was traveling this way for the holidays and I lost contact with her. A trucker across the way said they'd seen her here last night; said she pulled in with steam spilling out of the radiator."

"I see," the old man said, rubbing under his chin and staring as if catching Jack in a lie. "How did she come to be traveling all this way in this weather alone . . . if you don't mind me asking?"

"Her parents live in Iron River and—"

"Oh, sure, I know Iron River," the man broke in. "Been there many times . . . beautiful country. Thought someday I'd live there myself."

Jack nodded, smiled, and tried to appear as if the interruption was no big deal. "As I was saying, she was on her way up here with my daughters. I was planning to join them Christmas Eve . . . you know, work and all."

"Oh, sure, I know how busy a fella can get this time of year . . . yes sir, I sure do," Chester said, wiping a splash of chili off the countertop.

"I remember being too busy, just like you. I'd just come home from the war over there in the Pacific." The man's voice drifted; his gaze moved to the empty plates scattered in front of him. He rubbed his hands together, nodding.

"Came home angry at the world and everyone around me, including my wife who'd given me a son not two months after I'd set sail from Quantico, Virginia, as a twenty-two-year-old gunnery sergeant. The boy was three when we met for the first time. Didn't know much about being a father; just like my old man. I took on as an engineer with the old Wisconsin Central carrying freight and passengers all over the state and was never home long enough to get to know the boy."

Jack stared with a blank look, wondering when his food would be ready and what he'd done to give the man the idea he was the least bit interested in his life story.

"I'll never forget coming home one day to an empty house. My wife moved out lock, stock, and barrel . . . took the boy with her."

Jack's attention perked.

"Two weeks later, they were both dead. Just riding along in a train, track separates, train derails, and the whole lot of 'em plunge into a canyon—123 men, women, and children; burned and crushed. It's a difficult thing having to identify mangled bodies when it's your own kin. I'll tell you something, son," the man said, pointing a finger, "dying with 'em would have been a helluva lot better than living without 'em."

Jack was unaware to the extent his mouth had fallen open. He could appreciate a friendly, casual conversation. But this?

"Excuse me sir, you were asking about a young woman?" The night manager had stumbled upon the two somewhere just past the middle of the story. She'd heard it relayed many times before from the man considered a regular customer.

Jack pondered the point of the old man's story, as it struck a chord with his own predicament. He invested a great deal of thought about life without his wife and daughters through divorce. He spent no time think- ing about life without them as a result of death. Although he recognized the danger they were in, he did not consider the possibility Bigsby's motives were deadly. The man's story stirred anxiety, prompting a renewed urgency to get some answers.

Jack maintained a puzzled stare at the man who'd found it as easy as a first grade spelling bee to share such a personal story with a complete stranger. As his eyes caught up with the turn of his head toward the night manager, his body jerked at the shock before him, nearly sending him off the back of the stool and forcing a quick and desperate stab for the edge of the bar to maintain balance.

"Grace?" What are you doing here?"

The woman pulled back as if insulted. "I'm sorry?" she asked, shooting a quick glance to Chester.

Jack stared through her as if Bigsby himself were standing just behind munching on a piece of pecan pie.

"Grace . . . it's me, Jack . . . Jack Clarke. We met last night in the lobby bar at the Palmer House Hotel."

A questioning smirk settled across the manager's lips. She brought her arms up in a fold against her chest. "I'm sorry, sir," she said, "you must have me confused with somebody else."

Jack glanced to the old man, expecting him to be as surprised as he was in her denying their meeting. He turned to the night manager with an expression of utter disbelief. Though the name badge pinned above her left breast read Caroline, he did not believe it for one second.

Sitting stiff, in a haze, his eyes confirmed that this was the same woman from the bar last night; close to sixty, slender, dark brown hair with streaks of gray meeting at a bun on the exact same point on the back of her head, weathered skin—olive in color—no makeup, identical height, weight, and facial features. A chill swept his body as he waited for her to end the gag. The two traded looks and facial orientations suggesting each could not believe what the other was claiming.

"I don't understand," Jack said, throwing his arms in the air. "I sat right there at the bar and you served me a drink . . . you spent twenty minutes looking at my old newspaper."

Chester looked to Caroline. He lifted his eyebrows before looking away.

"Old newspaper?" she asked.

"Oh, come on, Grace. How can you stand there and deny it?" he begged.

"Mr. Clarke, my name is Caroline. I'm very sorry but you—"

"Aha, you see," Jack said, jumping from his stool, pointing, "how do you know my name?"

The woman shook her head. "You just told me two seconds ago," she reminded.

The diner fell silent. Realizing the scene he'd created, Jack glanced over his shoulder before settling back atop the stool.

"I'm sure you're just confusing me with someone else."

"You said the same thing last night when I told you how familiar you looked," Jack said.

"Well, if that's the case, then you were here last night, not in Chicago."

"Either I've lost my mind or she has," he said, looking to Chester. "I'm telling you, she served me a drink in the lobby of the Palmer House Hotel in downtown Chicago last night."

"I'd vote you've lost your mind, son," Chester said, smiling. "I was here last night, as I am most every night. I don't believe Caroline's been off a night from this place in five years."

Chester reached into the pocket of his shirt and retrieved a small stash of folded pieces of paper. Thumbing through the mess, he located a particular receipt, and after folding it in half, passed it to Jack under the lip of the counter.

"Here ya go, son," he said, waiting for Jack to accept it. "Take a good look at the date on the ticket and ask Caroline what I ordered for dinner."

Jack took hold of the receipt, unfolded the piece then scanned over the surface. The date was marked December 21; the order handwritten in pen.

"Meatloaf, baked beans, two pieces of corn on the cob, coffee, cornbread, and a piece of cherry pie for desert. The ticket was stamped around 7:30 p.m.," Caroline said.

Frustrated, Jack expelled a stream of air through his nostrils.

"Caroline, hand him the order you wrote for me tonight," Chester requested.

She pulled her order pad from her apron and tore off a slip.

"I just don't get it," Jack muttered, noticing the identical handwriting on both. He looked to Caroline again. A playful, yet tender smile grabbed his attention. That smile, he thought, I know I've seen it before.

"I know your smile," Jack said in a whisper. "I could identify your face anywhere."

"At my age, I'll accept a good pick-up line anytime," she said, smiling wider and winking.

Finding humor in the response, Chester offered a playful nudge to Jack's ribs. The comment further heightened his senses to the fact something was amiss. She'd responded in kind the night before. Sensing the eyes upon him, Jack diverted from the two to conduct a quick sweep of the room.

"Mr. Clarke, you're obviously upset," Caroline said, moving closer to the countertop, enough so to offer a compassionate pat on his forearm. "A woman with two young girls did stop here last night. She was having car trouble and asked for help. She . . . oh, wait a minute," she said, pausing. She glared over Jack's head toward the back corner. "Floyd was here when she came in. He can tell you . . . Floyd," she called out, "can you come here a minute, darling?"

A thick, gourd-shaped man, draped in bib overalls faded from years of use and washing, wiggled his way out of a booth in the far corner of the room. Suffering from arthritis, a bad back, or both, he struggled to his feet before steadying against the seatback. Jack could not tell if he was a trucker, a farmer, or cattle rancher, but he looked like a good 'ole boy nonetheless.

He paused at each table as he waded through the crowd, shaking hands and joking that Caroline was about to ask him for his hand in marriage. The man seemed friendly enough and well liked. A broad smile revealed missing teeth, and wrinkles spread across his face appeared as ripples resulting from a stone hurled into a calm pond. His eyes squinted shut when he laughed. As he approached the counter, Jack rose to his feet.

"Floyd, this is Mr. Clarke," Caroline said. Jack extended his hand.

"Mr. Clarke," Floyd said, grabbing his hand and dipping his chin.

"Mr. Clarke was asking about the young woman who came in here last night with car trouble. You were here, right?"

"Sure was; real pretty woman with long black hair; had a couple little ones with her as I recall."

"Did you speak with her?" Jack asked.

"No sir. I was sitting at this table right here," he said, pointing to a spot not ten feet from the counter. "She came in, got the girls settled, and ordered some food. She asked one of the girls working the counter if they knew someone who could look at her car. Said the engine light'd come on and steam was pouring out the radiator. I figured she lost a belt or had a hole somewheres. I was about to get up and offer some help when this young fella sittin' at the end of the bar walked over and told her he'd be happy to take a look. Said he worked on cars and could give her a tow if needed. Your wife asked him how much he'd charge and he laughed and said 'six bits.' I hadn't heard anyone say that in years. When he told her it was probably just a belt or hose, I felt she was in good enough hands and let it be."

Jack's stomach dropped. "What did the man look like?"

"He was pretty young . . . I'd say early to mid-thirties. Good lookin' young fella; seemed polite and respectful."

"Do you know who he was?" Jack did a double take of the trucker sitting next to him. Now interested in the conversation, he watched with an excited eye as he pulled what was left of the corndog from its stick.

"No sir. Never seen the man before."

"Did you catch his name?"

"No sir."

"How long were they here?"

The man scratched at his sideburns. "Well, they got the young woman's food pretty quick; just a couple of burgers and fries. The man sat down next to the girls and waited for them to finish eating. Sure was a funny sight."

"What was so funny?" Jack asked, his voice accelerating with suspicion.

"Well, those girls took to him like he was their father. As soon as he sat down next to them they all started laughing and giggling like they was at the monkey house at banana time. I saw the young woman trying to call someone on her cell phone, but she hung up pretty quick . . . didn't appear she had a connection. Those girls sure seemed to adore that fella, though."

Jack was certain the man was describing the version of Bigsby from the party. A lump exploded in his throat as he thought how easily Brooke had fallen into his lap. It had to be him.

"Again, how long were they here?" Jack asked.

"Less than thirty minutes, I'd say. The fella insisted on paying the check, and after they collected their things, they all walked out together. The last time I saw 'em was when I got up to use the facilities. I saw the young lady across the parking lot walking a dog. At least I think—"

"What?" Jack bellowed, moving toward the man. "You saw her with a dog?" The man took a step back, uneasy that Jack had invaded his personal space.

"I . . . I think so. It was snowing awful hard, but it sure looked like 'er."

"What kind of dog?"

"Well, I wouldn't know, son. Like I said, it was snowing hard and was dark where she was standing. Whatever it was, it wasn't very big."

"Did you see them leave the parking lot?" Jack asked, still muddling through his mind how Brooke could be walking a dog when their dog was in his truck.

"No, but another fella I know came in not too long after and asked who's SUV it was being towed down the road. I left about an hour later. Didn't see anything. What type of car was she driving?"

"A black Cadillac Escalade."

"Yeah . . . there was no Cadillac of any kind in the parking lot when I left. I'd have recognized a nice vehicle like that."

Jack shuffled backward then dropped on top of the stool. His mind was racing with the newfound information. Maybe it wasn't her. Maybe he was chasing the trail of someone else's wife.

"Do you know what direction they took off in?" he asked, looking up at the man.

"East, back toward the highway. Cartersville is a fair stretch of the legs down the road. If you go west, you'd be driving a long time before you reach any town worth anything, including one with a garage."

"Is there a garage in Cartersville?"

"Yes sir, but that fella don't work there."

"How do you know that?"

"Because my brother owns the one station in Cartersville and has but one partner—his son—and one tow truck which his partner drove into the lake last weekend. That truck couldn't tow a Pinewood Derby car right now. Is this woman kin to you, son?" Jack did not respond.

"They're his wife and daughters," Caroline informed.

"I see. Well, I'm sure they're okay. The man seemed nice enough to me. He was awful good with those girls. He carried both of them out the diner like he was, well, you."

The comment ignited a fire in Jack's belly. He knew the man was unaware of the circumstances and meant no harm. It was Bigsby. He knew it.

Jack thanked the man for the information. Floyd tipped the rim of his red DeKalb cap.

"Thanks, sweetie," Caroline said with a smile.

Jack remained fixed on the man as he hobbled back to his booth. He soon felt a soft touch upon his shoulder.

"Mr. Clarke, is there anything I can do for you?" Caroline's smile burned in his brain. He wished like hell it *was* Grace. At least she was aware of his predicament. How can this not be her?

"Ma'am, I'm certain it was you I saw last night," he insisted. "If this is a joke, it's not one damn bit funny." The smile evaporated from her face.

"Mr. Clarke," she said, planting her elbows on the counter, "I've lived in this area my entire life. I've never once left the state of Wisconsin. Now, this is a simple case of you mistaking me for someone else. I'm sorry for your predicament; believe me, I am. But I'm not this Grace person."

"Did you see the man?" he asked, changing the subject.

"No. I was dealing with an issue in the kitchen last night. Didn't see him or your wife. The girl working the counter told me about it."

"Would she know who this man was?"

"I don't think so. She just started with us less than a week ago. She moved here from a small community about three hours west of here. She doesn't know a soul around these parts."

Jack sighed. "I've got to find my family," he whispered, staring at the checkered floor, speaking to no one in particular. "She has to be close."

"Sir . . . I have your order," Katlyn yelled, rushing from the kitchen with a brown bag in hand. Jack reached to his back pocket but felt a hand wrap around his wrist.

"I've got this one, son," Chester said. The old man pulled out a money clip and dropped a crisp ten and twenty on the counter.

The gesture caught Jack off guard. "No . . . I can't let you do that."

"It's already done, son. Don't you worry about it . . . it's the least I can do considering your situation."

Jack studied the women behind the counter. Both smiled in agreement.

"That's awful nice of you Chester."

"Don't mention it. I'm just paying a debt forward."

"What?"

"I said I'm just paying a debt forward."

"I'm sorry I don't know what that means."

"Well, I remember this fella a long time ago noticed I was in a bad state . . . right here at this very counter, as a matter of fact. I'd stopped by here the evening after I buried my wife and son and this traveling salesman saw I was grieving. He picked up my tab without me knowing it or saying a word. Like I said, I'm just paying a good deed forward. Maybe someday you'll pay this debt forward to someone in need."

Jack returned his wallet to his pocket and extended his hand to the old man. Chester grabbed hold, shook once then pulled himself off the stool. "I wish you luck in finding your wife. If I can be of any help, just let these lovely ladies know. They know how to reach me."

"I will. Thank you."

"Good evening all." With a tip of his cap, the old man waddled toward the door on a set of short, skinny legs so bowed he appeared in a perpetual state of straddling a giant boulder. Jack watched him walk down the sidewalk toward the BP station.

"He's a nice man," Caroline said. Jack nodded in agreement.

"He didn't tell you the full story, you know," she said. "He shares his experience with people he thinks may be taking what they have for granted or feeling sorry for themselves. He's the sweetest man I know."

"What didn't he tell me?"

"Well, it's true he did come back from the war a different man. And it's true he didn't take time to get to know his own son. What he didn't tell you is he was on the *U.S.S. Indianapolis*, along with a thousand others, when it was hit by a Japanese torpedo. Mr. Walton was blown into the water and remained there with hundreds of other sailors for four days. He watched as three quarters of 'em were eaten alive by sharks. Just 316 survived; he was one of 'em."

Somewhere in the conversation, Jack reclaimed his seat.

"He also didn't tell you he was the conductor of the train his wife and son were riding. He did not know they were on board, and had no recollection of the accident or how he survived the plunge. He remembers identifying the bodies at the morgue; it haunts him every day. How in the world he walks and talks at all is beyond any of us. He comes in here every night and is as pleasant as a Sunday preacher."

Stunned as he was, Jack was surprised the first thought bursting forth was of his rude encounter with Mr. McDonald. Somewhere down the road, he knew he'd have to make that right.

"I'm sorry for your situation, Mr. Clarke," Caroline said. "I know what it's like to want a second chance with your family."

"How do you know it's a second chance I'm seeking?" he asked, his speech faint and lethargic.

Caroline smiled. "I can just tell. I see it in your eyes; in your emotion. You're on the verge of losing something very important and you will do whatever it takes to make sure it doesn't happen." She paused as Jack turned away.

"Tell me I'm wrong," she said. He did not respond.

"I had two children once. But I was too late. I missed my chance at reconciliation. I hope you find Brooke. I hope you get a second chance."

"Here's your order, Mr. Clarke," Katlyn said. "I hope everything works out." Jack grabbed the bag of burgers, the diet pop and water off the counter.

"I don't know what's going on here but there's no way you and I didn't meet last night," he insisted. "I realize I may not be the most sane person in the world at the moment, but I'm not crazy."

"Go find Brooke, Mr. Clarke," Caroline said. "Second chances are sometimes what dreams are made of." A silky, knowing smile broke across her face.

Jack did not believe for an instant she was not Grace.

"Good luck kid," said the trucker in a grating, foghorn-like voice, wiping away a face full of dark yellow mustard with his shirtsleeve.

Jack traded glances with those at the counter. The place fell silent. Feeling the eyes of those behind burning a hole in his back, he responded with an accusatory stare. In a slow, untrusting motion, he scrutinized the room from one side to the other.

"I know she's here," he said, pointing a finger, making eye contact with as many as possible, "and I will find her. There's nothing any of you can do to stop me from finding my family."

Jack backed his way to the door like a sheriff dragging out a horse thief from a saloon in the days of the old west. Something was very wrong with this space and the people in it. The way they tracked his retreat stirred suspicion and paranoia. The strange smiles erupting across their faces suggested all were privy to a gag and just biding time for that special moment to occur. Jack turned to the night manager. The woman he *knew* as Grace stood behind the counter with arms folded, smiling and nodding in a manner suggesting it was his destiny to open and walk through the door.

Grabbing hold of the front door latch, he depressed the thumb mechanism and pulled. A fierce suction pulling in the opposite direction contradicted his effort to swing the door open, forcing his opposite shoulder against the molding to gain leverage. He turned to the crowd in a moment of nervous anticipation. Their smiles widened. Leaning hard against the molding with his shoulder and forearm, he pried the door open just enough to feel the suction grabbing at the paper sack full of burgers, his hair and clothes, and extracting into the abyss bits and pieces of various paper products from within the diner.

With the growl of a weightlifter, Jack pulled at the door with his full reserve. The instant his elbow achieved a right angle to his shoulder, the force of the suction beyond collected him like an unused napkin off a table, sending him tumbling through the doorway and into a world more different than he could ever explain.

CHAPTER 20

Sprawled atop the snow-covered walkway, spread-eagle on his face, Jack stared into the gale-force, white onrush of snow as he struggled for a proper breath. Scanning every direction, he searched for any object he could identify. He could not see his Hummer or the other cars parked about the lot. He could not see the BP station to the right, the effulgence of its large green and white sign, or the highway running just beyond the sign's tower. He could not see the running lights of the trucks parked next door or even the yellow glow he remembered emanating through the windows from within the diner.

Jack pulled an arm from underneath his body and was barely able to make out the outline of his fingers. Pushing himself to his knees then to his feet, he brought his body upright and a forearm against his brow, as he pushed into the solid white abyss, with the bag of burgers in hand. The conditions were confounding. He realized his hope of continuing the search was impossible, as the thought of his family being so close yet so far away burned at his stomach lining. The last place he wanted to wait out the storm was inside the diner. Hoping Peetie would be fine for at least a little while longer, he retreated from the snow and sleet slamming hard against his face and worked back toward the front door. Upon making contact with the handle, the conversation with Caroline replayed in full.

He wondered how it was she knew his wife's name. He searched the dialogue for any point he'd mentioned her by name. He was certain he hadn't. He never believed for a second Caroline was not Grace. Now he had her dead to rights and he was eager to confront her.

Jack looked to the picture window to the left. A thick, icy coating prevented a view beyond the glass. Large white lettering spelling out "Mick's" appeared where it had not before. Moving in close, his senses acknowledged a peculiar change coming from within the building. The subdued, half-filled diner he exited just moments before now sounded as if it were filled to capacity. The jukebox blared something from the early days of rock and roll, rising above the raucous sounds of laughter, loud conversation and glasses clinking as if multiple toasts were in progress.

Jack depressed the thumb latch on the door and gave a push. A sudden and violent gust from behind slammed him forward the moment the latch released, forcing the door to sling open, and sending his body spilling across the floor. The instant his face made contact against the cold linoleum, the gale changed directions and sucked the door hard against the jamb,.

A man sitting at a table close to the door sprung to action, assisting Jack to his feet. Two others joined in to wipe snow and debris off his clothes.

"You okay, chum?" a man asked, brushing off a light fringe of snow clinging to his shoulders. "Did you slip on some ice out there?" Someone cut the volume to the jukebox.

Jack hesitated, not knowing for sure what caused the fall. "I . . . I don't know. I guess I lost my balance," he said, brushing the front of his jeans and peeking over his shoulder at the door, trying to hide his bewilderment.

Returning forward, Jack needed the shoulder of the man wiping at his back to steady his body as the shock of what appeared before him weakened his knees. Expecting to see a half-empty space, Floyd in the far corner, the corndog trucker munching away at the counter, and Katlyn and "Grace" attending to customers, he was greeted instead by a completely new cast of characters; not one face in the place appeared familiar.

The interior was from another era. The 1950s counter was no more than a long wooden table with mismatched wooden stools spaced unevenly along its length; no black and white tile, no stainless steel.

He searched the smoke-filled rat-hole searching for anything or anyone recognizable.

"Are you okay, pal?" one of the men asked. Jack's face changed colors three times. "You look like you've seen a ghost, boy."

"Is he drunk, Jake?" a man yelled from the back.

"Naw . . . don't think so." The man leaned in to take a whiff and peek at his pupils. Jack released his grip of the man's jacket.

"I'm okay. I just lost my balance," Jack said, looking to each man with telling suspicion.

"Be careful next time," a man said, handing Jack his sack of burgers.

Jack nodded, scanned the crowd and stepped in guarded fashion toward a single empty stool at the counter. The long row was jammed with men in fedoras and roadster caps sitting shoulder-to-shoulder, smoking cigarettes and cigars, all tracking his stride across the floor. Their dress was peculiar, but more to date compared to what old man Bigsby had been wearing.

Jack settled between two men looking every bit the part of mob flunkies. He placed his elbows on the counter and wiped at his brow. He kept his eyes forward, never once making a move suggesting an interest in exchanging addresses with the thugs.

Jack dragged his hands through his hair. He settled his stare in a large mirror behind the counter, searching into the depths for a familiar face. Every booth was jammed with couples whispering and pointing. As the reality of the circumstance settled, so did a nervous flush. He was laboring to slow his heart rate.

"Sorry about your fall, Mary."

A mouthful of draft shot from the lips of the thug to his right, as the wisecrack ignited a rowdy round of laughter down the line. A stocky, thick-muscled man wearing a sailor's cap, a stained apron two sizes too small, and reeking of stale coffee, sautéed onions, and grease, approached from the left. A rolled-up, white short-sleeve T-shirt revealed a snappy and shapely bare-chested blonde in a hula skirt, burned just below his right shoulder and just above the word "Mother."

Coming to a stop front and center of Jack's position, the man cracked a "whad'ya-gonna-do-bout-it" grin before pulling a toothpick from between his green teeth. Jack kept his head forward, struggling to craft a proper response while inspecting the many moles and liver spots peppered across the man's face and arms. He didn't want any trouble. Another time and place, and the man would be picking his teeth from off the floor. Jack waited for the laughter to run its course.

The man inched closer, settling a roll of stomach fat on top of the counter. He pulled a scratch pad from the pocket of his apron. "What'll ya have, pally?" he said, his voice sounding like a rasp pulled across a metal pipe. Jack set the sack of burgers on the countertop. The room fell silent in anticipation of his response.

"I don't want anything to eat," he said, "I wanted to see if I could speak to Caroline."

"Caroline?" the man, asked, backing away from the counter, taking the roll of fat with him. "How do you know Caroline?"

"Well, I was . . ." Jack hesitated. He traded glances with the two thugs making his business their own. He knew bringing up any discussion of a prior visit to the place was sure to produce a less than desirable outcome. But if Caroline was there, he needed her to come clean. He again searched the mirror. All eyes focused on his person.

"Mister," the man said, "I asked you a question."

"I was in here a few minutes ago speaking to her and Katlyn and I needed to ask her another question," he replied in a rush.

The sarcastic grin evaporated from the man's face. "Boy, I've been here since twenty minutes after my old rooster crowed this morning and I can tell you for certain this ain't the second time you've been in here today. As a matter of fact, I've owned this place going on ten years and I ain't ever seen your ugly mug in here before." The counter erupted in laughter.

"Hey Mick, ya want us to kick his ass?"

"I just want to ask her a question and then I'll be on my way," Jack requested.

The man shot a quick glance to his cronies. Both gave a shrug. He rolled his head and barked, "Car-line. Get your ass out here."

Jack leaned across the counter, as did everyone else, shooting a look to his left. A large rump covered in pink backed out from behind a wall leading into the kitchen. As the woman came to view, Jack shook his head.

"That's not her," he said, "that's not her." He meant for the comment to clear his lips under his breath. The sailor-turned-waiter shot a menacing look. Jack watched the woman make her way to his position.

"Honey, this boy wants to ask you a question . . . said he was just in here talking with you a few minutes ago." The man reinserted the toothpick between his teeth before folding his arms. His grin returned.

The squatty, silver-haired, middle-aged woman sized Jack up and down. Her face was pursed as if she'd been weaned on lemons from birth. Jack found it difficult to look away from a large dime-sized, hairy mole on her cheekbone.

The woman allowed her eyes to wander over Jack's frame. Leaning over the counter, she planted an elbow and released a sultry smile. "Well, how do, stranger," she said, winking. "What can Momma do for ya?" Laughter nearly razed the place. Jack scooted his barstool toward the door.

"I'm sorry," Jack said, with a nervous stutter, "I have you confused with someone else."

"Well, there's no need to be shy," she said, reaching and running a fingertip across his forearm, "I won't bite . . . unless you want me to."

Jack held his tongue as the counter again exploded in hearty laughter.

"Git on outta here," the woman's boss yelled, slapping her on the backside. "I don't know what you're trying to pull, pally, but you weren't in here five minutes ago," he said, leaning hard on the counter with his knuckles. "You ain't never been in here. Now, I don't know who this Katlyn is, and this is the only Car-line I employ. I don't know what you're on boy, but I want you the hell out of my diner . . . and I mean right now."

"I don't understand," Jack said. "I was just talking to her right here."

"I want you outta here right now, or do I have to split your lip first?"

"We'll throw him out, Mick," a voice in the back yelled. The man's eyes intensified.

"No . . . won't be necessary boys . . . he's leaving," he said, maintaining a rigid look that would peel paint off a new car. He motioned to the door with a hitch of his thumb.

Jack pushed away from the counter. Scanning the room a final time, he fled for the exit without looking back.

"Hey, Sonny, I get off in thirty minutes and there's a motel just down the road," the server yelled, sending the place into a tizzy.

Jack clutched the front door latch. He could hear and feel the ferocious growl of the wind beating against the door. Bracing his body as he did in his days on the football field, he snapped the latch, allowed the wind to take control of the swing of the door, then pushed into the tumult toward the general direction of the Hummer. Bent over at the waist, straining against the arctic swirling blast as it pummeled his body, he plodded across the lot in calf-deep snow, keeping his free hand out in front to protect from any unseen objects along the way. His directional senses delivered him within three feet of the Hummer's front grill. Placing a hand on the hood, he followed the outline over the side mirror to the driver's side door. He paused to brush the snow from his shoulders before climbing into the pitch-black cab.

A quick push of the overhead light brought the space into full luminance, including an empty passenger seat. Jack studied his coat and a building pile of snow accumulating through the crack in the passenger's side window. Peetie was nowhere in sight. Making a quick search of the space, he located the dog wrapped in a ball, shivering, on the floorboard behind his seat. Wiping the snow from the passenger's seat, he repositioned the jacket, reached behind and trickled a couple of fingers down the dog's back to get his attention before summoning him to the front.

Peetie was slow to respond. He appeared agitated, but soon jumped over the console and atop the jacket. Jack retrieved the plain burger from the brown sack, quartered it, and placed it in front of his nose. The half-pound patty disappeared within seconds. Peetie wagged his tail in semi-appreciation and buried his nose in his paws.

Jack fired up the Hummer's engine, brushed a few remaining flakes of snow from off his sleeves, and wanting to protect what little cash he had, pried his wallet from his jeans and stashed it in his duffle bag. He leaned against the headrest, absorbing the strain of the dense weight of wasted time. He searched to connect the lost moments between Floyd, Chester, and Caroline.

"What the hell just happened?" he whispered, dropping forward against the cherry inlay wrapping the steering wheel.

Jack closed his tired eyes, attempting to make sense of his extraction from real time. Engaged in something well beyond his own comprehension, he concluded the best plan was to stay the course. He must find Brooke. Whatever plan he concocted, he'd be doing so blinded by weather and a lack of facts, not to mention having no idea if his family, too, was captured in the warp. How this could get any worse, he didn't know.

Jack felt exhaustion gripping his body. Resting against the steering wheel, his body swayed to the motion of the Hummer rocking back and forth as a powerful wind slammed hard against its side. As the pitching intensified, an eerie howling manifested, and frigid air sped over, around, and under the frame of the truck. The sound was unlike anything he'd ever heard and was piercing to the point both man and beast found it unbearable.

Jack released his grip of the steering wheel to mash his palms against his ears. He turned to his passenger just as an enormous burst of air plowed into the driver's side with a force equal to a broadside collision. The four-and-a-half-ton Hummer lifted from off the surface, pitched ninety degrees in the air toward the passenger side, before slamming back down. The two occupants were tossed about like leaves on a windy day. Peetie crumpled in a ball on the floorboard; Jack pitched against the passenger side door, banging the crown of his head against the doorframe. The instant the Hummer's axles steadied to a rest, the world outside fell silent.

With one arm braced against the glove compartment and the other covering the growing welt on his head, Jack held steady several moments to ensure the event had passed. He could hear no sounds coming from beyond the cab; not even ice pricking against the windows. As quickly as the gust developed, it also vanished.

He grabbed the handgrip above the passenger's side window to assist in re-taking his position on the driver's side. Seeing his master secured, Peetie crawled from the floorboard. The two traded a glance as if each were waiting for an explanation from the other. Peetie soon lost interest in their predicament as the smell of food wafted from the floorboard. He stretched from the seat to help himself to the remaining burgers and buns now scattered about.

Aside from a thin, four-inch crack in the windshield, all seemed in perfect order inside the cab. The engine stalled, but a quick turn of the key brought relief they'd not be left stranded. An attempt to clear the windshield with the wipers failed. Jack located the ice scraper underfoot.

"I'll be right back," he said to Peetie. "You stay here." He needed not worry. The dog was well into the second burger and eyeing a few tomatoes and pickles for dessert.

Prepared for blinding snow and arctic temperatures, Jack exited the cab to find cool, not frigid air. A clear sky above boasted a billion stars. The air was fresh, crisp, and heavy with the smell of exposed soil and manure. He pulled in a deep breath, enjoying for a moment its cleansing qualities. He stumbled about confused, wondering how an onrush of weather could disappear in the snap of a finger.

He worked down the side of the vehicle checking for damage to the body and to the inside of the rear wheel well. Retracing his steps to the front, he inspected for scrapes and scratches. As he pulled upright, another shock caused a misstep on what felt like a gravel surface below a thin layer of snow. Holding tight to the driver's side mirror, his mind raced as he assessed what appeared before him.

"What is this? . . . What the hell is this?" he yelled, throwing an arm into the air. His voice echoed over the darkened landscape, reverberating as if he were standing in the middle of a rock-faced canyon.

The BP station was gone—no trucks, pumps, or signs. Just a vast conglomeration of rolling fields hosting the remains of recent harvests covered in snow, reflecting in the moonlight. The Flying J sign on the opposite side of the highway, the one he'd followed off the exit, was no more. Pastures and patches of forest stretched as far as the moon's radiance allowed. The most chilling realization was the absence of Highway 53 and the exit leading to his very position. Everything was wiped clean.

The Eat at 8 Diner—a.k.a. Mick's—remained, but as a shell of its former self. Gone was the green awning, the bright neon light, large plate glass windows, and the swath of trees hovering around its sides

and rear. A large, red brick chimney centered in the middle of the building and, extending fifteen feet above a sheet metal roof, belched white
smoke forty feet into the silvery night sky. A small glass window
littered with red and yellow hand-painted lettering, revealed a muted
glow coming from within. The scene was inexplicable.

With mouth agape and arms motionless at his side, Jack wondered
if the blow to his head was the reason for the trip into the rabbit hole.
He shook his head, attempting to talk himself out of what he was
seeing. The light of the moon reflected off a tin façade and a large white
sign promoting Fossee's Seed and Feed. An eerie chill tingled as he
scanned the landscape in search for something—anything—he could
identify as being present when he first pulled into the lot.

Jack walked several paces in the direction of the road. The two-lane
thoroughfare was no longer. As best he could tell, it was less than a road
now; just a narrow, winding, single lane goat trail. Moving to the rear of
the vehicle to survey the view west, he noticed the absence of the four
picnic tables situated on the grassy knoll. Gone, too, was the grassy knoll.
Reflection off the blanket of white exposed miles of rolling hills and
valleys dotted with farmhouses, barns, outbuildings, and silos. A large,
ominous bank of black clouds stretched across the western sky. They
appeared to be closing in. The view was as stunning as it was disturbing.

Jack stumbled to the opposite side of the Hummer for an unimpeded
view of the building. Its stucco-finish was now skinned in board-and-
batten, so weathered it appeared as sheet metal in the moon's light.
Large, hand-hewed cedar beams supported a tin overhang, which
protected a raised, wrap-around porch guarding the front and both sides.

Several stacks of wood kegs blocked the porch to the left. Four
hitching posts rose from the ground on the right near a black, Model-T-
type roadster which had been backed in along the side of the building.
As Jack moved closer, with caution, he noticed two rocking chairs
under the front window and several farming implements on display for

sale. Nearing the bottom step leading to the front door, he paused as a shadow moved across the small picture window and past a window cut in the door. He wrapped his fingers around one of the cedar beams and pulled himself onto the deck. Wood planks creaked and groaned as he crept close to the small picture window.

Peeking in, he spotted a bank of wood bins stacked six high and stretching the length of the far wall in place of the counter where he'd sat down twice in the last hour. Searching left, he was startled at the sight of a tall, lanky man of middle age standing behind a cash register, illuminated by a triple-wicked chandelier dangling from a beam above. The man peered through wire spectacles counting money and transferring the totals to a logbook. The man appeared to be alone.

Moving a few paces to his left, Jack pulled at the aged screen door guarding the front entrance, as the sound of rusty, unoiled hinges exploded across the porch and into the thin night air. The noise startled the clerk, prompting a quick reaction to stuff the money back in the cash drawer and the logbook to a drawer behind. He reached for something under the counter before proceeding toward the front of the store in double time. Jack's release of the screen door unleashed a discordant whining followed by several intermittent slaps of wood against wood as the rusty spring attached at the top expelled its kinetic energy.

Back peddling off the deck, Jack kept a sharp eye on the front door as he retreated. He soon noticed a gray, almost white face appearing at the top corner of the door window and the whites of eyes searching the length of the porch. The clerk was quick to make eye contact. As their stares locked, Jack raised a hand in a motion indicating intent to ask a question rather than wave hello. The old man swept his view one more time before releasing several latches. Jack saw the strike of a match and another oil lamp burst to life. The door opened with a slow creek; a long black double barrel followed, poking around the screen door toward Jack's general direction. He continued his retreat.

"What you want, boy?" the man barked. A beam of yellow light stretched from the door, covering enough ground to include Jack's body in its luminescence.

"What ya do-en on my prop-a-tee at this hour?"

A graying handlebar mustache spread wide across the man's face added several years to his appearance. Dressed in a starched white dress shirt and tucked tie, suit pants, matching suit vest with a white apron hanging from his waist, he appeared every bit an early 19th century clerk.

"I'm looking for directions," Jack stated. "Can you tell me if I'm close to Cartersville?"

The man surveyed his agitator from top to bottom, looking perplexed at the clothes on his back. "Cartersville? What bidness you have in Cartersville?"

"My business is my own."

"Fine. Mind it and leave me be." The man pulled the barrel of the shotgun across the threshold and slammed the door. Jack scooted forward calling out for the clerk to reconsider. The barrel soon reappeared.

"I'm looking for my wife. I think she may be in Cartersville."

"Maybe she don't wanna be found," the clerk shot back, coughing out a rusty laugh. Jack stretched his back and pulled a palm across his brow.

"That may be, mister. Can you tell me if Cartersville is near?"

"Follow the path east for eight or ten miles. It's on the other side of Brossy's Hollow. Now, this store is closed. I'll be askin' ya to move on and take your contraption with ya," he said, pointing to the Hummer. "I'll call the sheriff or blow a hole through ya myself; your choice."

"No need of either," Jack said, raising both hands in the air. "Sorry to have disturbed you."

The man's eyes narrowed as he stretched his neck around the corner in search of an accomplice. The double barrel disappeared behind the slapping of the screen door, followed by the sound of dead bolts sliding into place. Jack executed a spot-on military-style about face, having no desire to find out if the old goat was a good shot. Regardless, he had found the answer he was looking for.

Jack paused upon reaching the Hummer. Looking east, he inspected the miles of fertile fields stretching and merging with the horizon. Confounded by the disappearance of those things he recalled seeing, he weighed what options remained, given the circumstances. The sound of an owl screeching in the distance supplanted his thoughts of disappearing buildings and highways, names and faces coming and going, and random winds manipulating time and space.

Whatever evil wind had gobbled him up, at least it spit him out in the same location. It was a break, but how big of one he could not tell. He hoped his family had been caught up in the same phenomenon and was waiting for him on the other side of Brossy's Hollow.

CHAPTER 21

Jack sat in the idling Hummer at the far end of the property, surveying the road. He wondered what lay beneath the snow and what type of surface he was getting ready to subject his $80,000 piece of machinery to drive upon. Although designed for moments like this, he doubted the vehicle's engineers intended the non-military models to endure such a potential beating. Cringing at the thought of the possible damage to his ride, he knew one thing—the store clerk was right; this was nothing more than a path.

The wall of clouds he'd seen earlier advancing from the west had overtaken their position, devouring the stars on its trek east. The landscape appeared now in feet rather than acres, as the brightest light in the sky exhausted like a flame pinched by moist fingertips. The hope of only a light dusting of snow faded with each flake that tumbled to the ground, as the precipitation gained in both size and volume. Jack was not the least bit interested in getting caught in another white-out situation. Smooth road, rough path, or rugged goat track, he was ready to get on his way and into Cartersville as soon as possible.

Reaching to the dashboard, he selected the map view button just to the left of the large LED screen positioned above the stereo receiver. The list of tracks off the current CD dissolved from view and was replaced with a solid, electric blue screen. Seconds later, an iconic hourglass dripping sand manifested, indicating the computer was gathering data as to his exact geographic position. Tapping on the steering wheel, he waited for the system to churn through its start-up procedure, glancing in both directions for any sign of life.

He slung the gearshift into park, killed the engine and paused before restarting in hopes the system would re-set. The blue screen and hourglass reappeared. Several moments passed without a response. The system appeared dead.

Jack slapped his hands against the steering wheel. Peetie uncoiled and shot to the floorboard before the echo of his master's expletive dissipated.

"I'm sorry . . . come on boy," Jack pleaded, leaning over and patting the center of his coat.

Taking quick account of the predicament, Jack reached into the front pocket of his jeans, digging deep to retrieve his cell. A GPS app that came standard with the device would be sufficient for his current needs. At the very least, it could assist in identifying street names as he made his way through town. He woke the phone from its slumber, punched in his password and waited. The small screen filled with icons, including several for which he'd found no use. Tapping his index finger atop a miniature globe, he waited for the program to connect. A pinwheel of color rotated in search of a connection. Several moments passed before an icon popped up indicating no available service.

He backed out of the app and tapped atop several others—no response. He brought up the keypad and tapped 911—there was no dial tone.

Jack dropped the phone to his lap and sighed. Bringing a hand against his face, he rubbed at his temples and searched again in both directions.

"Well, boy," he said, looking to Peetie, "I don't know about you, but I'd like to get the hell out of here and into Cartersville."

Trusting the storeowner's advice, Jack dropped the gearshift, engaged the Hummer's four-wheel-drive system and eased the vehicle onto the unknown surface bearing east. He traveled but fifty feet before what lay beneath the snow revealed itself as an uneven, primitive track; maybe gravel, but probably frozen dirt, rutted by whatever vehicles had passed over before temperatures dipped below the freezing point. The

Hummer proved difficult to control atop the surface so battered by expansive potholes and deep crevices. The road was graded to a crown that fell off at steep angles on both sides toward unprotected ditches, sending Jack and his passenger bounding like rag dolls. Shallow tree lines embedded in a briar patch rose atop embankments on either side of the road, separating the path from crop fields stretching in both directions beyond view.

Leaning in toward the windshield, fighting to see through blinding snowfall and slapping wipers, Jack surveyed the landscape, calculating from memory the distance he traveled upon exiting the highway before easing the Hummer to a crawl at the point he recalled Highway 53 running below an overpass.

Coming to a stop, he searched through the thinning tree line at the view south. The highway was just not there. Although plenty of experiences the past few hours rammed home the fact that all was askew, the sight of the missing highway somehow made the predicament more real.

"How could it all have just disappeared?" he whispered, searching through the passenger's side window. Easing the Hummer forward, he stopped again in the general area of the Flying J. A simple barn and silo standing alone against the weather several hundred yards off the road had taken its place. He wondered about the fate of the truckers.

Although the road ahead appeared to flatten, it also narrowed to a fine point before disappearing into a featureless, black abyss he guessed to be some sort of tunnel. The point at which the surface of the road vanished fell just below a thick canopy of low-hanging, tangled overgrown trees and brush, which formed a dense line stretching north and south beyond his visibility. Broken and twisted branches, reminding him of the skeletal remains of human hands, eerily framed the opening as if guarding the very gate of hell. It looked more like a portal for the four horsemen of the apocalypse. Jack leaned into the windshield, staring with a nervous eye, knowing the next rotation of the

Hummer's tires would carry him into uncharted territory. Drawing a deep breath, he reached into a crevice fronting the dashboard to retrieve an object of motivation.

He stabbed blindly for the cabin light, bringing into focus the picture of his daughters. Drawing it close to his face, he paused to absorb the power of their smiles. The thought of their predicament and the potential danger facing them prompted a rabid desire to find them at all costs. Returning the photo to his wallet and his wallet to the duffle bag, he pushed against the accelerator.

As the black hole grew in his windshield, he eased off the gas, uncertain the limited girth of the opening could accept the width of the Hummer. With hands clutched at ten and two, he fought against the vehicle's inclination to ride up one side of the embankment or the other, before bringing the Hummer to a complete stop after noticing an opening framed with dark wood slats rising to a peak well above the trees. The surface beyond the entrance was free of snow and appeared constructed of wood planks.

Relief settled in as he soon recognized the structure as something very familiar from his childhood. It was a covered bridge. He'd spent many a sunny afternoon as a child dangling his feet over the sides of covered bridges near and around his home, fishing until accumulating more mosquito bites than bites against his line. The bridge brought back a bucket-full of memories as he inspected its interior and design, contemplating a crossing. His recollection of the construction methods used to build the bridges included dense, flagstone footings and thick hickory planking; more than adequate to allow farmers hauling loads of grain, pushing livestock or moving heavy equipment between fields to pass without fear of tumbling to the brooks and streams below.

Jack thought the weight of the Hummer probably equaled that of a tractor pulling a topped-off grain wagon. He was most concerned the vehicle was too wide. He let off the brake, allowing gravity to take control. A few remaining branches guarding the entrance scraped against the side mirrors as the Hummer's front tires dropped onto the solid surface. Jack brought the vehicle to a stop as an overwhelming fragrance of pine drifted through the cab.

An initial survey suggested the construction was brand new. Nails securing trim and other finishing features glistened of bright silver in the reflection of the Hummer's headlamps, showing little signs of wear. Lumber throughout appeared hand cut by axe and hatchet. At least twenty, twelve-inch-square pine beams, unweathered and set no less than fifteen feet apart, supported the main structural elements on both sides, including a cobweb network of cross beams and trusses reaching to a significant peak to form the roof.

Jack opened the door to inspect the bridge's surface. Rough-cut hickory planks, a good two to three inches thick, offered comfort that the builders had planned for heavy loads.

Easing the vehicle forward, he could feel the surface bowing under the tremendous weight, causing the Hummer to bob and dip from side to side as its tires passed over each plank. The high-pitched squeaking of nails rubbing against hardwood and the unnerving sound of lumber cracking beneath the seat ripped through an otherwise silent surround, creating enough concern to slow the Hummer to a crawl.

A low-hanging center truss running the entire length of the span and the pine beams jutting out on either side kept his head in constant motion. Perturbed by the unnatural movement and obvious look of concern on his master's face, Peetie retreated from the comfortable confines of the soft leather seat to the floorboard where he secured a more stable stance.

Three sharp pops coming from behind forced Jack to stop the Hummer. With less than a hundred feet of bridge to travel, a sobering feeling suggested the rear of the vehicle was no longer gliding on top. Opening the door, Jack viewed the Hummer's rear tire buried below the surface, having cut through a wood plank. Fearing a slowing of the pace would cause more harm than good, he assumed a resolute grip on the steering wheel as the Hummer bucked in response to an increased speed.

With the vehicle bouncing across the surface, Jack fought to keep it centered in the exit, which appeared a much tighter fit than the entrance. Unsure of the road's condition or direction it would take beyond the bridge, he located the beam supporting the timbers framing the exit. At the precise moment the nose of the vehicle breached the last beam, he removed his foot from the gas and slammed on the brakes.

The front end dropped then leveled. Jack felt the back end swing to his right as it emerged. Seconds seemed like minutes as the Hummer spun out of control before bouncing hard off a tree and coming to rest in a shallow ditch.

The jolt to the rear quarter panel sent Jack bounding off the frame of the driver's side door and Peetie shooting across the floorboard to underneath Jack's feet. With his hand cupping the left side of his head, Jack searched through the windshield and the hard falling snow to decipher his direction. The bridge appeared a few yards in front, well above his current elevation.

"You okay, boy?" Jack asked, reaching down between his legs, patting Peetie's head. The dog was frightened. Cupping both hands around the animal's undercarriage, he pulled him from the floor to his lap. Peetie pawed at his chest as if asking permission to get closer before burying himself between his master's arm and rib cage. Jack ran his hands down the dog's back in an attempt to calm his nerves. He cracked a smile after realizing it was the first time he'd held the dog in his lap.

With the snow gaining in intensity and with the uncertainty of the extent of the damage done to the vehicle, Jack's confidence withered. "There's no way we're going to be able to track them tonight," he said, stroking Peetie's head. "We got to get off this road and find this town." Peetie shoved his head deeper in between his arm.

With the dog secured, Jack pulled the steering wheel hard to initiate the close quarter U-turn. Plowing over a row of small samplings and a sizeable stump, he coaxed the Hummer in the right direction. The surface turned smooth and less slick, allowing for a speed that quenched his thirst for haste. He was anxious to locate a city limit sign.

Stretches of straightaway followed by sharp S-curves traded back and forth before a steep incline up a sizeable hill brought the Hummer to a crawl, its tires clawing and spinning to reach the peak. Once atop the summit, Jack brought the vehicle to a stop. Relocating Peetie to the passenger's seat, he stepped from the cab to survey the landscape ahead.

A deep valley snaked to his right toward the northeast, settling below several descending stair-step fields and rising to a significant peak at a point in the distance. If this was Brossy's Hollow, Cartersville must be over the next ridge.

Moving out from behind the door, Jack guarded his step to the front of the Hummer. The grade down the backside was significant, and at first glance, appeared to descend at a much steeper rate than the opposite ascent. The road was an absolute sledder's dream—no less than eight inches of unmolested snow atop a straightaway spanning at least a quarter mile. He'd raced down hills just like this as a child, strapping himself to anything with a slick surface. A sled or saucer he could control; the four-ton Hummer was another story. An opening in the clouds brought the bottom of the hill into full view. Jack crossed his arms and dropped to his haunches.

A wide, sweeping curve located just at the point where the road leveled off from the grade, banked east along the outline of the valley before disappearing behind another series of small hills. The bank opposite the curve rose well above the surface of the road. A fencerow running atop traced the curve completely. Silver reflectors on the posts glowed in the moon's light.

The steep grade and blizzard conditions would cancel out any traction Jack could hope for, no matter if he engaged the four-wheel drive or not. By the time he reached the bottom, he knew the Hummer would be traveling at a clip he'd have little ability to slow.

"We'll be sliding the whole damn way and there won't be a thing I'll be able to do to control it," he said, whispering. "I hope the bank is dirt covered with snow and not rock, because that's where we're going to end up." The thought that Brooke and the girls were just over the next ridge left no room in his determined and arrogant mind to concede the attempt.

The world beyond the luminance of the Hummer's headlamps soon fell back into shadow, as the moon disappeared in a glob of clouds pushing by. As if a switch had flipped, a frigid gust from the northwest skipped across the hilltop, sending snow from above along with that already accumulated on the ground, whisking sideways to create a blinding condition.

Taking one last look, Jack lifted a forearm across his brow to shield his face from the large flakes, brushed his body, and retreated into the cab. He wanted to put his fist through something soft in response to yet another bad break.

Convinced the temperature was plummeting, the chill in his bones received instant relief upon making contact with the warm leather of the driver's seat. Blowing on his fingers, Jack's mind squirmed for answers as to how best traverse the hill, as he tracked the path of the wipers swooshing across the windshield, noting their ineffectiveness in keeping pace with the snowfall. He also wondered how best to protect his passenger.

Sitting perpendicular to Jack's position, leaning against the back of the seat, Peetie kept a sharp eye on his master's actions. His was a look of total exhaustion mixed with a knowing sense that danger was upon them. Realizing there was no way to strap Peetie to the seat, Jack leaned over the center console, pulled his coat from under Peetie's feet, and stuffed the mass underneath the passenger seat. He drug his duffel bag close behind to form a small well.

Jack relocated Peetie to the secure space, and as if understanding the intent, Peetie circled his position several times before coming to rest atop the carpeted floor mat. Jack secured his seatbelt across his chest.

"Hang on boy . . . we're both gonna feel this one," he said, dropping the gearshift.

With his mouth drying and his heart beating through his skin, Jack eyed the descent, recalling the days of his mischievous youth when the thrill of an adventurous challenge stirred his blood to the core. His memory flashed to the time he dared Boone Early's bull to a race across the pasture. And the time when he hitched up his neighbor's horse to a homemade cart constructed of produce crates and lawnmower wheels and rode off for a spin down his town's main thoroughfare. His blood stirred now, but for a very different reason. There was no thrill in what presented before him.

Jack nudged the gas pedal toward the floorboard, knowing the plight of his family hung in the balance. A resounding crunch followed as the massive tires plowed forward. He kept the gas covered as the Hummer moved over the crown of the hill, moving to the brake the instant the vehicle's nose broke from level.

With gravity clawing at the front end, he eased the brake pedal to the floor, deciding they stood a much better chance sliding down rather than trying to engage the brakes at the bottom. Either way, his lone option to lessen the damage would be skidding into the bank broadside. If the Hummer hit head-on, well. . . .

As the rear of the vehicle cleared the summit, Jack readjusted in his seat and repositioned his hands on the steering wheel as if grasping the guardrails of a roller coaster nearing its most significant plunge. Few feelings in the world muster a sense of helplessness more than the rear end of a vehicle sliding out of control. Jack's grip tightened as the Hummer's back started drifting left seconds after clearing the summit. With the wheels locked and the Hummer gaining speed, he fought his instinct to turn into the slide, keeping his hands level to the dash and the front wheels as straight as possible.

The task was made more difficult by a malevolent tempest slamming hard against the driver's side, causing the vehicle to push right. With eyes glued to the point in the distance where the edge of illumination from his headlights butted against the black of night, Jack scoured the uppermost region of his windshield searching through an impossible onrush for the reflectors he'd noticed on the fence posts. If he could catch their glow the instant his headlights made contact, he could anticipate the point at which he'd need to start yanking the steering wheel.

The increase in speed the Hummer was experiencing with each foot traveled drained his confidence in the outcome. With his senses so focused on obtaining sight of the reflectors, Jack failed to notice the rear end now fishtailing in the wrong direction. If he were to have any chance, he knew the driver's side, not the passenger's side, must make contact first. If not, the vehicle would bounce off and shoot down the road backwards into the valley.

Having no idea how far the Hummer had descended, he manipulated the slide for the first time by sweeping the steering wheel right in hopes of swinging the tail to the left. The action was less than fluid as he fought against the strong wind and a surface marred with ruts and potholes. The Hummer was slow to respond to the command, causing Jack to pull at the wheel much farther than anticipated. The moment he felt the rear slide back to the right, he maneuvered the wheel left of center to prevent it from pushing too far, too fast.

Withdrawing from the view of the passenger's side mirror, two small dots caught his attention very near the top-center of the windshield. Appearing more as enlarged pupils of an animal caught in the reflection of high beams, they morphed in size, shape, and luminance as the Hummer bounced toward the bottom of the hill.

As he centered the steering wheel on the dots, a bone-jarring thud exploded the front, right tire, sending the sound of shredding rubber ripping through the cab. As Jack lost control of the steering wheel, the Hummer bucked to the left, sending the back end sliding well out to the right. With sweat pouring over his face, he slammed his palms against the wheel to re-engage, fighting its torque for control.

A fraction of a second later, clawing at the wheel hand over hand, confused at what direction to turn, Jack was thrust into a moment of slow motion as he felt the cab level off at the bottom of the hill. With the steering wheel yanked as far right as it could go, and the embankment appearing in full view before him, he expelled a horrified groan as the Hummer settled back to dead center.

CHAPTER 22

A more perfect evening it could not have been—a couple's dream, really—crisp December night air filled with snow drifting from the heavens, Christmas lights sparkling against the black of night, blazing campfires scattered about keeping piping hot kettles of chocolate at the ready, ice skaters waltzing and spinning to the sounds of holiday music—perfect.

Her eyes sparkled happy and content, her appearance was stunning as usual, despite the many layers of sweaters guarding her delicate features. Her cheeks glowed bright red, matching the end of her nose and a flowing scarf cuddled against her neck. Her long black ponytail dangled at the middle of her back, whipping around her body as she skated in and around his position. Her laugh was intoxicating; her smile radiant.

He marveled as she passed like an angel in flight, weaving with grace in and behind other skaters. He heard her voice, playful in its tone, almost teasing.

One moment she was near, the next out of his sight, before reappearing from behind, gliding close enough to whisper words of affection into his ear. She reached again, but he did not react; could not react. His legs felt heavy; his skin burned as if rubbing against frozen garments. His arms fell stiff against his side. A chill creeping through his veins from below intensified, but he could not locate its origin. His feet burned as if frostbitten.

She called his name again, this time in a tone causing alarm. Her voice was sharp, stricken with panic but fading as if she were being whisked away in the opposite direction. He rotated in pursuit but a menacing gust blasting snow stopped him cold. Seconds later, silence ensued as the hard rushing wind removed the other skaters from his view. He was alone, surrounded by a wall of white collapsing from every direction.

A distant sound confused his senses; was it a scream or something crying out in pain? With the palm of a hand, he cleared his face of sweat dripping from his brow. The moisture felt heavy, sticky. He opened his fist to see his fingers soaked in blood. Spreading his hand, he watched lifeblood drip to the surface below, staining the snow that had collected atop his shoes. A fleshy, moist object drug across the back of his neck, igniting a shiver.

Within seconds, the sensation struck again, causing an awkward shift of his weight, inducing a fracture in the ice below his feet. Cracks raced in slow motion outward from the epicenter in every direction, causing a thrust of sweeping panic. Water gushed into the soles of his shoes just before the surface gave way, sending his body plummeting through the ice pack and into the black, frigid abyss below.

Although fully submerged, he felt the icy bite only against the middle of his shins. He struggled to remain close to the breach. Within a split second, a swift current grabbed hold and pulled him away. His mind grew confused. Despite being underwater, he could still feel the rush of oxygen entering his lungs. Pounding on the underside of the ice pack with his palms, he noticed a dark shadow moving above the ice, tracking his body as it slid further away from the break. He attempted to slow his drift by clawing at the ice with his fingernails and kicking with the tips of his shoes.

An outline of a hand pushed through the snow and appeared flush against the ice just inches from his face. Frantic swipes cleared an opening. Bubbles of air exploded from his lips; his eyes widened upon seeing Brooke leaning close to the ice, appearing ghostly white and stricken with fear. Tears flowed down her cheeks. Her lips contorted as she screamed, but Jack could hear nothing. His body was sinking. He stretched an arm above his head in an attempt to reach her; she slammed her fists against the ice, ripping open the flesh around her knuckles, screaming something inaudible.

Their eyes locked as his body descended. Her actions turned furious as she punched away at the ice. He watched in horror as the murky water faded her image to black.

A pain-filled yelp followed by another swipe of the fleshy object against his neck broke Jack free of the horrific hallucination. His eyes burst open to a scene his brain could not comprehend. Lying flat on his chest, a canvas of black appeared before him, revealing the faint outlines of a few objects located near his position. Struggling to regain his resolve and some sense of depth perception, he searched the black hole for his wife; her face. His mind was convinced she was near.

A dense haze settled against his pupils, creating a ripple effect flowing toward the outer edges of his line of sight. The abnormality held steady several moments, subsiding only when he flashed his eyelids several times in succession.

Contending with a compressed fog swirling about his head, Jack was slow to react to the utter chaos scattered about him. Unenlightened to a gash running atop his scalp or the stream of blood tracing the outer edge of his right eye to the corner of his mouth, he stared through an opening framed by twisted and jagged metal at a landscape appearing in dark grayscale, as if all the color in the world had been wiped clean. His eyes were heavy, sore and watering. His body was stiff and unresponsive. The landscape appeared in full illumination one second, and solid black the next.

The first sensation to stimulate his cognitive processes was a bitter chill racing up his legs, followed by a severe stabbing pain in his side and shoulder. With each passing second a new sensation broke through the fog, setting off various physical and mental alarms that something was very wrong.

The fleshy object dragged again over his neck. His legs kicked as a result. He heard water splashing and the sting of ice further up his leg. Recognizing he was lying flat atop something hard, his sense of balance told him his body was slanting at a downward angle. His mind raced to catch up with the circumstance as he fought the urge to close his eyes. Frigid water bit at his calves; he could feel it rising up his leg. Another sudden slip and the sound of whimpering from behind prompted his first physical motion.

Lifting his chin from the surface proved difficult. His head felt as heavy as two cement blocks. The move was not immediate, nor was it without excruciating pain. He struggled for breath. The wet object accosting him for what seemed like hours struck again at his chin and upper lip, followed by several rapid jabs near his eye. A cry of pain brought Jack's conscious mind up to speed.

Just inches away, on his side, Peetie lunged toward Jack's face, increasing his efforts ten-fold at the sight of the whites of his master's eyes. His diligence to pull Jack from the unconscious state that had been holding him hostage for more than an hour paid off. Jack gasped in horror as the animal's own predicament came into full view. He could no longer see the many brown and black spots sprinkled atop his mostly white coat. His fur was soaked in blood from head to tail, oozing from a giant gash on his left side exposing several ribs.

The vision sent a wave of panic coursing through Jack's mind. Fighting his own pain, he pulled both arms free from his side, lifted his elbows into the air, and tucked the palms of his hands flush to the surface. The moment the transfer was complete, an intense ripping sensation followed by a sharp spasm shot through his left shoulder and down his arm. The socket was throbbing and swollen to twice its size. He tested its condition by pressing his palms to the surface. The result was a vociferous cry of agony. He knew the injury. He'd separated the shoulder once before.

With his right side now forced to carry the load, Jack commenced a deep pull of oxygen into his lungs and pushed the air back out in an exaggerated exhale as the muscles of his right arm bulged through his sweatshirt, forcing his torso from the surface. Pausing to shift his weight to stretch his lower back and pelvis, the hard surface underneath again shifted to the rear, sliding in perfect syncopation with the sound of metal grinding upon metal. The gravity of their circumstance broke through the fog bogging down the right side of his brain, at the realization the two were still inside the Hummer—what was left of it—and it was upside down.

He recognized their position as in between the first and second row of bench seats. Chunks of debris lay scattered across the space; the odor of gasoline burned at his nostrils. He was confused as to why the Hummer was in such a condition, as he had no recollection of the impact against the snowy bank at the bottom of the hill.

Another slide of the wreckage to the rear stole the breath from his lungs. He peered over his shoulder. The vision was surreal. The front half of the Hummer, up to the dashboard, was missing; ripped away like the lid of a sardine tin. What remained of the floorboard, center console, and front seats lay submerged in black murky water, with large chunks of ice floating on top. He could hear the distinct sound of water bubbling and felt the line rising up his leg to just below his knees as the trashed SUV continued its slide south. The rear of the vehicle was gaining in pitch with each passing second; the Hummer and its passengers were being swallowed.

Clawing at the headliner, Jack stabbed at the surface for anything offering a grip. Finding the broken dome light below the third row of seats, he pressed his fingers inside the metal frame and pulled his legs from the encroaching pool. He felt nothing from the middle of his shins to the tips of his toes. His knees, burning from contact with ice formed underneath his jeans, balked at his first command to bend under his torso. A sharp pain in his side further hindered his movement, sending muscle spasms digging into his back. He grew concerned as to how many ribs he'd broken, and any other internal injuries he may have suffered that were not yet making their presence known.

He coaxed his knees to action, leaned against the center seatback, closed his eyes and paused as the pain from the movement struck with a debilitating force. Knowing their seconds were precious, he willed his body in the opposite direction, coming to rest above his passenger.

Intermittent clouds of condensation leaked from Peetie's nostrils as his breath fell shallow. Jack leaned in close to inspect the damage. The gash snaked from the top of his shoulder blade to under his belly. Blood oozed from the wound at several points along the path, merging with already frozen streaks running down underneath his belly. Jack ran his fingertips down the length of the wound to over his hindquarter, where he felt a bone protruding through the skin.

Another slide of the vehicle pulled his attention from the dog's wound. Knowing there would be no delicate way to extract him from the wreck, Jack flopped the hand of his injured arm against the head-liner near Peetie's breastplate, and placed his other near the dog's tail-bone. Intending to secure him under his sweatshirt and against his chest, he would first have to cradle the dog in his injured arm. No matter the plan, he was certain the maneuver would be excruciating for both.

Taking a deep breath first, and with a quick scoop, he lifted the dog from the surface into his damaged arm. The weight of the animal pulled hard on the shoulder, prompting a deep, guttural howl equal in pitch and intensity to the dog's own shriek. Struggling to breathe through the torture, trying to keep the dog balanced on his arm, Jack dropped his right hand from under Peetie's hind end, grabbed hold of the bottom of his sweatshirt, and with a burst of air and spit shooting from his mouth, drug the cotton canopy over Peetie's head while pushing him up to his chest. The motion sent Jack falling to his back, screaming in pain. The intense burn of ice-covered fur melding against warm bare skin caused a frigid shock.

The two continued exchanging bursts of modulated emotion before their pain subsided enough that each could catch their breath. Jack entwined the ribbing encircling the bottom of the sweatshirt into a ball in his fist and pulled it tight up under Peetie's hind end. With his shoulder taut and in a stable position, he pulled the collar of the sweatshirt up over his mouth with his nose to communicate with his passenger.

"I'm sorry, boy," he said in a slurred, almost drunken whisper into the cotton cavern as he scooted his body toward the rear of the vehicle. "Hang on for me. I'm going to get you out of here."

Shifting the weight of his body to his right forearm, he wiggled over the littered surface, ducking underneath the second row seatback, and bending several sharp metal fragments away from his path. Another push propelled his body forward and under the third row bench seat. The shift of his weight sent the Hummer dipping backward, away from the hole in the ice.

Jack paused to devise an exit plan. Jagged pieces of glass remained intact around the rear window frame, which appeared as if hollowed out by a shotgun blast from a few feet away. Searching through the debris, he located a thin, shiny strip of metal, which he used to clear the remaining glass chunks from the frame.

Jack grabbed hold of the opening and pulled through. Heavy snow pelted his face as he rotated to view the surface. The drop appeared less than three feet but the condition or density of the ice below was anyone's guess. Was it intact or cracked? Knowing he would have to slide out onto his back in order to protect Peetie and his own injuries, he contemplated the results of his 250-pound frame falling three feet onto a questionable surface.

Pushing his hand into his hair, thinking through other possible options, he grew confused at the feeling on his fingertips and the gooey mess on the right side of his head above his ear. The region was painful to the touch and swollen well beyond its natural margins. His sense of touch identified a large gash running from the top of his front temple to just above the base of his neck. He could feel a large flap of skin and hair dangling free of the scalp. Pulling his hand from the mess, he brought it close to his face and fanned his palm. Blood dripped from each fingertip to his sweatshirt; the amount was significant.

The wound caused a great stir of concern; not only inducing panic as to the amount of blood already lost, but how long he could remain conscious once out in the open. Dropping his chin to his chest, he could see the faint expansion of his sweatshirt as Peetie labored to pull in air through his damaged lungs. A long line of blood seeped through from underneath the sweatshirt, outlining the dimensions of the dog's wound. Jack dropped back to the surface, staring at the window over his brow.

The Hummer's design would not provide an easy escape. The over-sized spare tire, located on a mounted swing gate in the center of the tailgate, rose well above the window frame leaving little room for the pair to wiggle out. Knowing he would need the assistance of the tail-gate handle, he slid his body across the headliner as far left as the mangled interior would allow. Making contact with the ice-covered device just inches above the frame, he grabbed hold and began pulling his body forward. Blood flowed from his scalp, dripping from his hair onto his cheek. The growing burn in his side prohibited a normal breathing pattern.

Keeping the sweatshirt tight against his chest and pulling with what little reserve remained, he managed to squeeze his body past the spare tire, through the window. As he rotated his torso to re-establish Peetie to the center of his chest, the change of position caused the Hummer to plunge toward the surface, almost shaking free his grip and unfolding him backwards, before the frame swung up and slid at a sharp angle forward toward the hole in the ice.

The unexpected motion caused his upper body to twist in the opposite direction as he struggled to regain his balance, prompting his left arm to lose grip of his passenger. Peetie's body twisted into an odd angle; the harrowing sound of the snap of a rib set off a blood-curdling howl. Quick to re-establish a secure grip, Jack held tightly to provide as much comfort as he could. As if throwing a switch, the dog's cry fell silent.

With the angle of the Hummer steepening, Jack feared the distance he'd have to free fall to escape had doubled. Fighting wind, heavy snow and pain attacking all points of his body, he tucked his fist under Peetie's hind end. If he broke through the icy surface, he knew they'd sink like a block of cement. Regardless, he was not letting go of the dog.

With a tight grip on the door handle, he maneuvered his body to align the frame of the window to just in front of the bend of his knees. Pulling his body as close to the Hummer as he could, he pumped his arm to gain momentum, before pushing hard against the handle. His grip released at the apex of his reach.

The resulting collision resonated like a wet bag of sand dropped to a concrete surface. The impact extracted the air from his lungs; his body contorted atop the ice as he gasped for breath and fought through intense pain. A limitless repertoire of sounds invaded the space around him. Some seemed strange and unrelated to the circumstance, but all beckoned his senses to react.

With frigid water shooting from below his body near the small of his back, Jack dug hard with his heels, pushing off the surface to scoot the pair as far away from the break as possible.

His kicking and gasping lasted a near eternity before the sensation of water soaking into his clothes exchanged with the burn of snow biting at his skin. The surface below felt solid, but he continued to push across the ice. The sound of water gurgling replaced that of screeching metal.

Jack dropped his legs to the surface and fell limp. His eyes demanded rest. His mind begged for an unconscious state. His skin pleaded for a blanket. Oxygen was slow to refill his lungs, never reaching a capacity considered normal. His breathing remained labored.

Squinting into the heavens through the onslaught of snow, he envisioned Brooke's face against a cropping of thinning clouds passing in front of the moon. How he wanted to place his fingertips against her cheek. In an instant, the clouds reformed and the image dissipated, stirring the recollection of his dream and her screams as he disappeared under an ice pack. The vision aroused his senses to his location and his desire to get off the ice. He knew he must get moving or they would die.

Jack rolled to his right and waited for the spinning in his head to pass, before pushing from off the surface into a half-sitting position. Openings in the clouds allowed for intermittent views of the landscape surrounding them. The lake settled in a basin, guarded on all sides by a legion of quaint mounds and hills merging as one—some heavily wooded, others cleared for pasture. A steep bank appeared several hundred yards to the rear, littered with small trees and brush and rising to thirty feet. The bank traced the curvature of the lake on its easternmost border, losing significant grade as it flowed to his right and beyond his sight.

He reached his knees but not without a struggle and a thunderous groan. Securing the bottom of his sweatshirt with both hands, he brought his body upright, fighting its will to remain on the surface. The pain was excruciating.

Teetering like a man walking a tightrope, he stepped into the gale to view the wreck. Seeing not the first sign of the Hummer, he shuffled a few steps forward, bringing to view a giant, gaping hole in the ice with but a few small chunks of debris sprinkled around the edges.

Jack backpeddled toward the shoreline, digging through his memory to reason why his $80,000 ride and other personal belongings were now at the bottom of this lake. He remembered the Hummer tumbling, but had no memory of an impact.

"How in the hell did I get this far from shore?" he mumbled, quickening his stride backwards. Turning from the rupture in the ice, an eerie jolt struck at the sight of the front end of the Hummer sitting fifty yards away, with headlamps still burning bright. The piece was sheered away at the dashboard, leaving Jack questioning as to how his legs were not lying somewhere nearby. Scanning beyond the wreck, he noticed an open swath beginning halfway down the backside of the embankment, cleared of all trees and brush. He surmised the Hummer went airborne before landing and rolling on its side and onto the lake. Staring at the headlamps, he wondered how he was still alive.

Caught in a moment of awe, he wandered much too close to the chunk and realized his blunder as water rushed into his shoes. Looking closer, he noticed a front tire buried below the ice and redirected away from the wreck. Not wanting to press their luck any further, Jack scanned the landscape east, looking for the best spot to exit off the lake.

Jack aligned his body to a shallow point in the distance and moved toward the shoreline, arcing well beyond the area of the wreckage. The brutal, frigid conditions coupled with clothes frozen stiff against his body prohibited a normal gait. Luckily, the wind was at his back. He could feel snow pelting against his neck and a dull sensation of heat upon his chest. Every other part of his body was numb. He wanted to check his scalp, but dared not pull his hands from under the protection of his sweatshirt. His head was getting heavy and his mind drowsy. He was desperate to find shelter and fast.

Jack fought to remain focused on the shallow point ahead, plodding along fatigued beyond his ability to lift his legs to step. Nearing his target, he noticed a structure taking shape to the right; another fifty feet brought into full view a dock rising well above the surface, projecting several hundred yards from the shoreline. Where there was a dock, there was sure to be a path leading somewhere. A ladder affixed to the end would make his escape much easier than anticipated.

Eyeing the first rung, he grabbed hold of a steel handrail to pull himself from the ice. The action brought a sense of relief and an opportunity for a brief respite to allow the pain clawing at every joint and digit to simmer. Dropping his forehead against the rung, he drew as deep a breath as his battered ribcage would allow. He adjusted his grip on the bottom of his sweatshirt to ensure the dog was secure.

He tugged at the collar of his sweatshirt to check if Peetie was alive. He could feel the faint beat of the dog's heart palpitating against his skin in near unison with the rhythm of his own; warm air exiting the pup's nostrils kept a small spot on the center of his chest at a decent temperature.

Jack pushed to the next rung, fighting the pain of heavy, frozen denim tearing at his kneecaps. Thirteen rungs and twelve feet later, he set foot atop the snow and ice-covered dock. The structure felt solid below his feet, and like the covered bridge, appeared to be of newer construction. Wasting no time, he headed inland.

With his mind leaking cognitive wherewithal and his motor skills deteriorating, he staggered across the surface with the aid of a frozen-over handrail. A slight incline just forward of where the structure extended past the waterline and a wall of machine-cut granite further challenged his waning physical aptitude. Pushing onward to a point that leveled off before dropping to a path branching in three directions, he paused to survey the landscape and plot a course.

The path left wound down to the shore over a slew of jagged rocks, crevices and vegetative stubble. The way forward cut through a dense forest packed with wind-worn pines and low-growing evergreens, snaking southeast toward a large boulder where the path forked. Eager to find cover, Jack stepped from the dock to the path, paying a steep price in the form of pain coming from the joints of his ankles and knees. If it were not for the dog, he'd be doubled over on the ground. A cry of defiance in the form of an expletive kept him moving as he breached the timberline defining shore and forest.

Jack wavered upon reaching the boulder, contemplating the best route. The passage right was narrow, appeared less traveled, and its margins less defined as it ascended the side of the bluff in a haphazard, switchback fashion over rocks and thick underbrush. The way left appeared wide and level and its boundaries better defined, as it cut through a less-packed cropping of red pines of varying circumference. First impressions indicated this path was well traveled and probably the main artery leading to the dock. Regardless, it was flat; he did not have the energy to climb.

The way was dark but less arduous as the large trees offered protection from the bitter wind and blowing snow. The path remained straight and level for the first couple hundred yards, before pitching and switching back and forth every twenty feet traveled.

A large, cubed-shaped piece of machine-cut granite marked another fork, forcing a decision. The way right switched back well to his rear and out of sight. Having no interest in backtracking—not even an inch—he continued left, working through a narrowing passageway guarded by dense thicket and holly berry.

Another fifty yards revealed a one-lane opening through a split-rail fence line separating forest from field. Stepping beyond the protective confines of the red pines, Jack viewed the fence to the right, which ran along the tree line and out of sight. To the left, the fence disappeared into thick brush before angling ninety degrees and continuing along the outer-most edge of a long, open pasture. Following the fence line to the left, he moved in as close as the underbrush would allow, stumbling across a surface rutted and clotted underneath the snow. The way was ascending toward a ridge.

As the grade increased, Jack's pace slowed exponentially. His injuries begged for attention as he struggled to remain in control of his faculties and in motion. Despite the chilled elements benefiting the clotting process to his head wound, the intense burning sensation gripping his legs from hips to toes wrought more distress than his other injuries combined.

His mind swirled with inconsistent and incoherent thoughts of Brooke, his girls, and his own death. He could be dead and at peace by now had the ice but broken under his fall. The misery of his circumstance did not halt the rhythm of his shuffle forward.

Fifteen more feet brought him to level ground and a path narrowing to that of the width of the dock. A natural dam split the center of two sunken valleys on either side. A sizeable frozen-over lake occupied most of the view to the left; to the right of the dam appeared a large field littered with the remains of harvested corn.

Forcing his body forward, Jack kept his focus on the ground to ensure he remained within the margins of the trail, lifting his head every few steps and spying forward to check the distance to the other side. A slight incline worked toward a small peak at the dam's center, and as he reached a point where his line of sight rose above the path's apex, he caught a glimpse of a soft yellow dot burning just off center and to the right of his mark.

His mind did not accept what his eyes relayed as fact, working instead to convince him that he was nearing the end of his existence and would soon succumb to Mother Nature's fury. With head down and his eyeballs jammed to the uppermost limit of their sockets, he watched the yellow dot grow larger with each inch traveled.

Reaching the dam's center, a massive cloud of condensation burst from his mouth as a sense of relief settled. The window appeared to him in full view. Another twenty feet revealed a gabled roofline set at least two stories above the beacon. The warm glow emanated from a position just to the right of a large tubular object extending well into the night sky, capped at sharp angles on both sides with something shiny extending from its center.

With the path descending at a much steeper angle than its rise on the opposite side, Jack's motion slowed despite a desire to run. The landscape to the east and west offered no other signs of life or electrical power. He moved beyond a small depression merging into a field on the backside of the ridge guarding the lake. Another hundred yards brought him to within an arm's length of the red board-and-batten barn.

Jack moved to his left, and pushed up against the window. He pulled his hand from underneath his sweatshirt to wipe at the ice covering the glass. Unable to gain a clear view of the interior, he moved off in search of a door.

Making his way around a massive stone and mortar silo, he located a heavy double-Dutch door encased in thick timber and fieldstone. Pulling hard on a wood block attached to a knotted piece of heavy rope, he eased through the opening and into the space. The improved change in temperature was immediate.

Pulling the door shut behind, he stumbled across the dirt and hay covered floor, searching for the best place to drop. Strong odors of urine and manure filled the air, competing with sweet smells of alfalfa, hay, and fermenting cornstalks. The space felt damp and cool, but not frigid. Eight large stalls lined the left side with an open bay situated in the middle, packed to the rafters with hay. An oil lamp hanging on a hook in front of the window offered the structure's lone source of light.

Jack collapsed onto his knees upon reaching the haystack. He conducted a slight roll onto his back as he fell, enduring staggering pain as his body settled hard against the heavy oak timbers lining the adjacent stall.

Lost in the expanse of the two-story structure, gasping for every ounce of fresh oxygen his damaged ribcage would concede, he swatted hay across his lower extremities before tugging at a horse blanket draped over the adjacent stall. A final tug on its corner to cover the lump atop his chest expensed all remaining muscular and mental reserve, as fatigue, substantial blood loss, and hypothermia conspired in shutting down his systems.

Jack fell limp as his mind spun a grand concoction he was home, lying on *his* hammock, staring into the rafters of *his* barn. He attempted to call out Brooke's name but managed just a slight push of air. As if in the waning moments of an alert state following an intravenous anesthetic, a distinct buzzing settled between his ears, gaining in pitch and intensity with each passing second.

The last visual object making any sense to his mangled and confused mind was the long, muscular head of a solid white Belgian draft horse peeking over the stall. A burst of forced air from the beast's nostrils was the last sound he heard; a growing chill upon his chest where heat once flourished, the last sensation.

Jack's eyelids fluttered and collapsed simultaneous to his head falling off to one side as his world was gobbled into the black hole of an unconscious state.

CHAPTER 23
December 23

"Lad, can you hear me? It's important you wake up. We've got to get you moving about."

The words fell soft as if delivered in the whispers of a pleasant breeze brushing past one's face. The voice, unfamiliar though it was, broke through Jack's subconscious as a trusted confidant extending a compassionate plea. He could hear the words and desired to respond, but was unable to break free of the grasp holding his mind and higher functions hostage.

Lingering in a world of fractured images and bizarre illusions passing in rapid succession, the voice persisted from what seemed a great distance, breaking through the jumbled mess, masquerading as a hand Jack needed only clasp to pull to the surface and into the conscious world. The instant a response seemed possible, the voice dissolved as another dream sequence pulled him under. The plea continued, as did his attempts to break free.

"It's very important you wake, Mr. Clarke. Can you hear me?"

A cold, damp cloth sweeping across his cheek interrupted a dream in which he was tracking through a frosted window Brooke and Bigsby walking hand in hand—each carrying one of his daughters—up a snow-covered porch toward him, smiling at one another as if content; as if in love. The combination of the disturbing image and frigid shock to his skin produced a violent jerk striking with such force, the world holding him hostage was unable to maintain its grip.

Propelled from the deepest region of his mind, Jack awoke to an intense buzz growing in crescendo between his ears and each of his senses fighting to deliver the first cognitive realization. Much like the lingering ringing following the collision of two cymbals, the buzzing drifted into the distance, leaving him to organize the many new, strange sounds flooding in from every direction. An attempt to open his eyes stalled; the burst of bright white flooding through was too much, too soon.

"Easy now . . . it will take time to adjust, so it will. Keep your eyes closed for now, lad. Can you hear me?"

Jack responded with a lethargic, half-nod. Aromas of burning wood and musty fabric converged upon his nostrils, serving as a poor man's homemade smelling salts.

"Good boy. Just relax now . . . you're in gentle hands, so ya are."

The voice was very near his ear. Even in his dazed condition, Jack recognized it as an accent of foreign origination. Did he hear his name called? He was not certain. The cloth continued passing across his cheek and forehead in a soothing, rhythmic pattern from the right, each stroke working in unison with the sound of metal springs creaking underneath in response to someone's weight shifting.

His senses revealed a feather-soft surface beneath him, conforming and supporting every dip and angle of his body. With eyes screwed shut, he initiated a slow roll, moving out of a deep, pudding-soft crevice, all the while attempting to absorb and comprehend the sounds manifesting about.

Voices traded information in whispers in the direction of his feet and to his right, bodies shuffled from one side of his position to the other, pushing waves of cool air across his face as they passed. Water dripped, as if being wrung from a towel; something heavy drug across the floor to his left; the distant bellow of a cow rose above the dialogue. Each second produced improved clarity and cognizance.

"I think he'll be fine," the accented voice proclaimed. "I'm sure his exhaustion is equal to his injuries, so."

"Thank you Doctor Danaher," a soft, female voice responded. He rolled his head in the woman's direction.

"God must be looking down upon this poor soul; I was scared to death I'd be left alone to tend to him myself. I felt the power of the Lord shoot straight through me when Matthew brought us the news of seeing you coming up the road. As long as my days, I won't figure why you happened by the very moment we needed you most. A miracle it was."

"Well, I have a few affairs to attend here," the doctor said, not wanting to expound. "I was in the fancy borough of New Auburn a few days by and resigned myself to making rounds the rest of the week before heading homeward for the Christmas celebration. 'But,' says I, 'do I owe a visit to the widow Pendleton?' So, this morn' I set out early to pay a call. May the good Jesus Christ in all His glory bless her poor, wretched soul."

"Is she doing better?"

"Oh, bloody grand altogether, my dear. The ole' harridan will be fine; sore, miserable, and red-faced as the Union Jack, but she'll be fine. I suspect she'll be meetin' the Virgin Mary herself if she attempts to shoe that ole' mule again. I'm supposin' the dent in her skull will be a permanent reminder. How she talked your husband's kin into selling her such an unruly beast is beyond me. Sure I heard tale of the animal kicking him once, so I do."

"Doctor . . . what should I do if . . . I mean . . . if he gets worse? Doctor Potter won't be back till Sunday next."

"Don't worry your soul. I'll stay 'round overnight and keep a careful watch. Can't say I could do much better than you, but as dawn turns to dusk, the innards of all God's creatures all work the same way."

"I would appreciate it. Anyway, I'm sure it will be less than ideal traveling this evening and I'm guessing you could use a good home-cooked meal."

"Aye, it's a fair swap for the house call, dear one."

"Where's he from, Mamma?" Jack was sluggish in his reaction to the young man's voice. It seemed to originate above his feet.

"I don't know, son. I've not seen him before. Have you, Doctor?"

"Och, no. I'm afraid I've not strayed long enough in these parts to know most."

"He's a big cuss," another, older and lower male voice interjected, this time coming from somewhere behind the woman.

"He bloody well is, lad. I'd say he weighs twice a newborn Angus if he's an ounce. I'd also guess his good physical condition is what saved his life, so it did."

Jack attempted to speak but was unable to pull enough air to start the process. The conversations continued over and around his position, drifting back and forth at a pace still beyond his ability to digest fully. Cattle increased their lonely calls in the distance.

The sound of heavy footsteps approaching from the left induced a lull in the room. Jack lifted his eyelids as far as the light would allow, just in time to catch the outline of a giant of a man ducking into the room under the doorjamb. Although the light was still too bright and his eyelids weighed a ton, he managed to keep them open long enough for a glimpse.

"How's he doin' Doc? Ain't like taking care of an ornery ole' bull, huh?"

The deep, rich voice broke as a baritone in an empty cathedral. The man's presence put an immediate end to all other conversation.

"He's hurt good and sore, so he is." The doctor's brow knitted as he scratched his ginger-colored sideburns with thumb and forefinger.

"Mind you, master darling, his injuries are sure to slow him a bit but he's in good enough shape he'll be up and about soon. It seems he traveled a pretty fair distance on foot, so he did."

"I suspect we'll get some answers later."

"Aye, that we shall."

"Olan, the doctor would like to stay on through the night to keep an eye on him."

The woman laid the palm of her hand across Jack's forehead. Her touch was warm, gentle; her skin callused and coarse, like leather.

"That's a good idea, Mamma. I'm not sure you'd find your way home tonight anyway, Doc. There's a pretty stout wall of clouds comin' in from the west. I'd say more snow is on the way."

"Matty?"

"Yes sir?" Jack rolled back to the center of the pillow as the adolescent voice responded in military fashion.

"I think the doc can get along without you. I need you to finish the woodpile out back then get Jack and London's stalls cleaned and filled. Go on now boy."

"Yes Pa."

Jack followed the sound of the young man's path around the bed and out of the room. Who were Jack and London? The words served as a pull cord to his cognitive function as his brain regurgitated the accident, his escape from the sinking Hummer and trek across the frigid landscape. He recollected a barn, but nothing beyond. Where was he and in whose bed was he lying? His mind scampered for answers but it was all too much.

The cold washcloth reemerged on his neck just under the chin, inducing a shiver. Concentrating hard on the goings on around him, the bitter chill from the cloth caught him off guard, causing his body to twitch and sending his ankles flexing forward into something hard radiating an enormous amount of heat. His lower extremities burned from defrosting, and he felt numb from the small of his back to his toenails. His joints felt as if filled with glue. A rotation of his hips to pull back from the object below his feet triggered an eruption of pain on his left side, forcing a deep groan. Muscles encasing his throat tightened like ropes heaving a loaded dumbwaiter. The woman laid a comforting palm against his naked right shoulder.

"Easy now, lad," the doctor remarked. "You've sustained some pretty hearty injuries to your left side and head, so you have. Try to protect your side the best you can." The doctor offered a compassionate pat atop his chest.

"Do you want to try and open your eyes?"

Jack nodded. The effort to roll across the pillow was slow and not without pain, but it was the most fluent motion completed since regaining his faculties. The doctor repositioned in his chair.

"I'm gonna hold a pillow up to your face to blot the light. Take your time."

Jack drew a deep breath through his nostrils before exhaling the mass through pursed lips. In a slow, deliberate motion, he explored the outside world, fighting a sensitive flutter as his pupils adjusted to the muted colors of the dark green and yellow stripped pillow. Several quick blinks cleared the haze and improved his resolution. Working over and around the design of the fabric covering him, he identified several colorful hand-stitched flower petals of varying sizes and types. A few seconds passed before the pillow drifted from focus and his caretaker revealed himself.

The doctor's face was warm and pleasing. He leaned in close, pushing an affable aroma of peppermint and pipe tobacco, on his way to a thorough inspection of Jack's pupils. Content they'd constricted properly, the doctor pulled away, extending a grandfatherly smile and a friendly wink of a deep green eye.

"Jesus, Mary, and Joseph, you had us worried," he said, adjusting a bright blue and white stripped bow tie under the collar tips of a starched off-white dress shirt. "You'll live to see another day, so ya will."

Jack's mind reconciled the doctor was of Irish descent. Not a little bit Irish or Americanized Irish, but right-off-the-boat-at-the-gates-of-Ellis-Island Irish. The thick brogue was as soothing as the man's smile.

Peering through half-moon lenses encased in gilded wire rims positioned low on the bridge of his nose, the eighty-something-year-old man worked a bucktoothed grin around the room, nodding with relief rather than accomplishment.

Jack worked to achieve total clarity focusing on the man's wizened, spade-shaped face, inspecting every pucker, crease, and wrinkle. Bushy, graying brows arcing high above eyes flanked on either side by deep laugh lines enhanced a warm, trusting look sure to coax even the most introverted personality into conversation. His skin, plum in color, clung snug to his face everywhere but below the chin. Thinning copper-colored hair sprinkled with silver bunched in disorder and was marked by a hat line at the base of his neck. It was a good face. Jack liked it.

The man's garments reminded Jack of Bigsby's—as if drug from a chest tucked away in an attic for a century. A heavy worsted black wool vest with a silver stripe—complete with matching fob pockets—molded around his torso, outlining a portly midsection. A thin, gold chain strung through a buttonhole emptied into the pocket nearest his view. Jack assumed matching pants completed a snappy Sunday-go-to-meeting ensemble. The analysis ended as their eyes locked. The doctor's smile erupted into a full-blown Cheshire grin upon seeing Jack's eyes clearing of haze.

"A cup a tay would crown ya sure me boy, but a wee bit of water would be more fittin' at the moment."

Jack initiated a confused nod. Although appreciative of the doctor's warm ways and pleasing attributes, the peculiar manner in which he looked upon him—the way one eye pushed higher than the other and coincided with a slanting grin—sparked a subtle suspicion the man knew something about him or his circumstance others in the room did not. Jack's mind grew paranoid. *Is he relieved of my improved condition, or pleased he has me right where he wants me?* he thought.

"Sophie dear, let's get some liquid into him, so."

Jack rolled across the pillow in pursuit of the woman.

Close beside him on the bed, sitting with one leg bent at the knee toward her midsection and the other planted firmly on the floor, the woman appeared with a smile equal in warmth to the hand she laid atop his shoulder. Her eyes, wet and glassy, burned a deep indigo blue only a secluded, sun-drenched mountain lake could replicate. The air around her was redolent with the sweet scent of lavender. Her look was one of heartfelt relief and Jack grew curious if she were on the verge of tears.

Smiling wide, she patted his shoulder. She brought her palm into her chest and clutched hold of a crucifix dangling from a string of brilliant-white pearls. Her face was aged, but well kept and drenched in a simplistic beauty striking a familiarity he could not place just yet. Soft dimples immersed in rounded cheeks showed the merest hint of a pale peach color. As her smile grew, her dimples deepened, coaxing a smile from Jack's own lips. Hovering well above and behind the woman, a tall, lean, wide-shouldered young man wearing worn, blue suspender overalls atop a red and black checked flannel shirt, pushed a tin cup full of water past the woman's shoulder. He met Jack's stare with a simple nod.

Jack assessed the young man to be in his late teens, and either a son or hired help. His grip around the cup exposed scarred and disjointed knuckles and fingernails that appeared as having been drug across a grinding stone. He was not thick of body but offered a look that suggested pulling small saplings from the ground—roots and all—posed little challenge. Strange as it was, Jack sensed the two could be friends.

Sophie released the crucifix to accept the tin cup. She eased her other hand behind Jack's neck and in a fluid motion, lifted him from the pillow. The edge of the cup was frigid against his lips, as was the liquid sweeping down his throat. She tilted the cup to just short of upside down, delivering its contents in full. A brush of cloth across his lips collected what trickled away. The water was good. The sensation of cotton clinging to the roof of his mouth and a throat encased in sandpaper washed away with the gulp. A once-over with a toothbrush would be a welcome luxury.

Jack rolled toward the woman. "Thank . . ." his voice was hoarse and cracked as he attempted to speak for the first time. He swallowed deep and tried again. "Thank you . . . ma'am," this time more in a whisper.

"You're welcome, Mr. Clarke. I'm so thankful." The woman again reached for her crucifix. Jack felt a hand fall atop of his chest. He rolled across the pillow with confidence.

"Mr. Clarke, I'm Doctor Danaher." The contented look once sprawled across the man's face muted to a more serious, concerned mien. Scooting to the edge of his chair, the doctor pushed his spectacles up the bridge of his nose with an index finger before moving in closer.

"Can you tell me, lad, how you're feeling on the inside."

Jack took another deep swallow, hoping his voice would not skip. Listing to his left, he drug his right arm out from underneath the covers, stretched his shoulder to the rear before dropping his arm across his chest. The room was cool.

"My left side is very sore . . . constricting when I breathe. I guess I've broken some ribs." His voice echoed like a rasp over steel and was several octaves lower than what he considered normal. The words rolled slowly off his tongue but were clear enough.

"I can hardly move my shoulder. The side of my head feels like it's split open . . . where am I?"

"You've suffered a significant wound, so ya have." The doctor reached across Jack's body to adjust a cotton bandage wrapped around the upper half of his skull.

"Ya've got a long gash running from the crown to behind your ear," he said, making a slicing motion across the top of his own skull. "I managed to stitch the skin back to your scalp, so I did, and suspect you've suffered a concussion of some degree. There may be some nerve damage but I can't be sure at this point."

Jack brushed his fingers across the top of his head. The bandage was thick and well secured.

"Your ribcage took a pummeling, so it did. I do suspect you broke some ribs. Your left shoulder separated but we managed to jam it into the socket once we got you settled in bed."

"Where am I?"

The doctor took a quick account of those in the room. "Well, lad, you're the guest of Mr. and Mrs. Olan Brossy." Jack rolled his head toward the woman.

"That's Mrs. Brossy, Annesophie, to be exact—Sophie for short— and their eldest, Caleb." The woman offered a pleasing smile; the boy another nod.

"To my right is himself." Jack rolled to the left.

The man was seven feet tall if he was an inch and sported a barrel chest as widespread and thick as a cofferdam. Like son, like father, the man offered no emotion, just a simple nod upon eye contact. His face was hard, scarred, and country through and through. Large dark brown eyes fell deep into their sockets, flanking a long Roman nose of stout, crooked bone. A huge Adam's apple sprung from the middle of a thick neck still holding tight to the summer's sunburn. A stubble-strewn chin, carved at the end like a square-toed boot, jutted forward from jaws of granite cut tight to his ears. The man's stare suggested that Jack was more of a foreigner in his home than the doctor. Jack liked the woman much better.

Succumbing to the deep fold of the pillow, he recognized the family name as his mind regurgitated the words of the not-so-pleasant storeowner. "Just on the other side of Brossy's Holler," he remembered the feed and seed storeowner saying. Moving his hand across his chest, he backtracked through his mind the events leading him to this place. His chest was sore; empty feeling. His body stung through and through, as if he had jumped into a hot shower after spending hours buried up to the ears in snow. He worked and stretched his joints, rotated his hips from side to side—despite the pain—and even brought his knees to a slight bend beneath the covers. He rolled toward Sophie but kept his eyes closed.

"Ma'am, what's under the covers at the bottom of the bed?" His voice was improved but breaking through his lips just above a whisper.

"They're bricks, Mr. Clarke. We needed to get your core temperature up and the blood flowing to your feet. Doctor Danaher felt sure you'd be missing some toes, maybe all of them, had you spent another minute in the elements."

Jack felt the woman's hand against his shoulder. Her touch sprung to life a realization they were calling him by name.

"How is it you know my name?" he asked.

The woman shot a glance across the room. "Doctor Danaher mentioned he found your wallet on your person. He placed it in a secure place, as not to lose it. He was afraid if . . . well, if something bad were to come of all this, we'd want to contact your next of kin."

Her answer was reasonable. Jack fell back onto the pillow.

"Are you from these parts, Mr. Clarke?" the woman asked.

"May I have another sip of water?" Jack heard the sound of the tin cup dipped into a bucket behind the woman's position and felt her hand slip behind his neck. A second drenching quenched his thirst. The water was metallic tasting.

"I'm from Chicago."

"Are you here to visit kin?"

"No," Jack said, directing his stare to the beadboard ceiling above. Painted a dingy white, it appeared unusually low and minus any type of light fixture. He dropped his chin toward the foot of the bed. Two large windows centered along the far wall allowed for an expansive view, but a layer of frost a quarter of the way up prohibited seeing what lie beyond. The woman waited for Jack to elaborate. He intended to keep the details of his circumstance cloaked.

"Son, how did you happen to end up in our barn?" Olan asked.

Jack closed his eyes, attempting to recall the exact details of what transpired following the bizarre sequence of events in the parking lot of the diner.

"I remember getting directions to Cartersville from a storeowner over on Highway 8. He pointed me down the road which led to a—"

"I'm sorry son, wha'd you just say?" The elder Brossy uncrossed his arms and moved to the other side of the doctor's chair.

"I was coming from a general store off Highway 8 when—"

"Highway 8? I've never heard of that."

Olan settled erect with fists buried in his hips, looking confused. The doctor leaned deep into his chair, staring at the ground in a way suggesting he wanted no part of the debriefing and wished it would all just end—immediately.

"I'm not certain of its direction from this location, but it's not far."

"What do you mean by not far? I've lived in this area goin' on forty years and I ain't ever heard of a Highway 8."

"Olan, please," Sophie interrupted, "let the boy tell his circumstance. He may not be of right mind," she said, whispering and pointing to Jack's head.

"Aye, Sophie, 'tis true as God's promise," the doctor said.

"Go on, Mr. Clarke," Sophie urged.

The conversation triggered a dizzy spell. "I remember having some trouble navigating a covered bridge and the road beyond winding a great distance before leading to a steep hill. I remember struggling to get my Hummer to the top of the slope before—"

"A what?" Olan asked, leaning in, cocking his head.

"Hummer; it's an SUV."

"What's an SUV?"

Doctor Danaher swiped a palm over his brow and hair, appearing agitated with the line of questioning. Jack found each reaction equal in their confusion.

"It's a sport utility vehicle; it's like a truck but much wider with an enclosed bed."

"Whoever heard of an enclosed truck? What'd be the point of having a truck enclosed? How would ya haul anything?"

"Olan . . . please," Sophie demanded.

Jack continued. "I remember coming to the top of a steep hill. If I wanted to get to Cartersville, there was but one option. I lost control about halfway down the hill and the next thing I remember is waking up, upside down in the vehicle on top of a frozen lake."

Sophie gasped.

"Wow," Caleb responded.

"I got out just before the vehicle broke through the ice then walked across the lake and found a trail leading to a barn."

"Good God, son," Olan said, shooting a shocked glance across the bed to his wife. "You weren't on a lake, you were on what's left of the old Mankato Company granite quarry. They flooded that God-forsaken eyesore two years ago. Why, there are spots in there descending a half-mile deep."

Jack's face paled.

"I think that's enough questions for now, master darling," the doctor said. "He needs to rest a wee bit. There'll be plenty of time for questions later."

"Doctor, if you don't mind," Sophie said, holding up a finger. The doctor conceded.

"Mr. Clarke, were you able to save anything of your belongings other than your wallet?" she said.

"I don't know. There was some debris . . . I think. I just don't know."

"Caleb," Olan interrupted, "I want you to saddle up and take a ride over the south ridge and see what you can see. Don't cut through the pasture. Go around along the dam wall and cut back over Jeb's pasture. You're not to set the first foot on top of the ice no matter what you see, do you understand me?"

Sophie expelled a deep sigh of relief. The murky depths of that disaster of an engineering effort had claimed the lives of several locals over the years—she did not want her eldest added to the list of the missing.

"Is that clear, son?"

"Yes sir; crystal."

Jack watched the scrappy young man move beyond the end of the bed, ducking in behind his father before disappearing down the hallway.

"You're so very lucky, Mr. Clarke," Sophie said. "I'm glad no one else was with you."

The woman's comment sent his head snapping across the pillow. The look on his face caused Sophie to pull back from her position and flash a look of surprise to her husband as if seeking explanation as to what it was she said to cause such a reaction. Jack's lips pursed as the color leaked from his face. The sight frightened Sophie to the other side of the room to a position behind her husband.

Working the palm of his hand faster and faster, Jack grew more agitated with each passing second, stabbing at the middle of his chest as if searching for something that had dangled from a chain around his neck. The three could see his wheels spinning. His eyes darted back and forth at a dizzying pace; his breathing grew heavy.

Doctor Danaher feared his patient was on the verge of hyperventilating. He moved to the edge of his seat in case panic set in. Reaching across the bed he was caught between sitting and standing when Jack, without warning, ripped the bed covers from off his body, catching the doctor with an upper-cut to the chin and sending him crashing to the floor.

A window-shattering groan of agony expelled from Jack's lips as he maneuvered into a half-lying, half-sitting position on the edge of the bed. Caught off guard, Olan was slow to react as Jack worked to achieve an upright position. Thrusting forward, Jack managed to wrap his hand around the near bedpost and pull himself to his feet. With the panic of a trapped animal and his eyes glowing as red as the blood now dripping from the doctor's mouth, he erupted with an emotional burst, stringing together several salty expletives before ripping a four-letter whopper that stopped all in their tracks.

Jack reached the bedroom door, fell against the jamb and yelled at the extent his chest would allow—"Where the hell's my dog?"

CHAPTER 24

"That boy is strong as an ox and stubborn as a ten-year-old mule," Olan said between quick gasps of breath.

"Aye . . . that he is master darling," the doctor agreed, his voice projecting hoarse and airy, sounding as if he were speaking through a bout of laryngitis. "A bullish one, he is."

"Are you okay, Doc?"

"Grand, so I am."

Slumped on the floor with knees tucked underneath his torso and the crown of his head resting against a side rail plank of knotty pine, Doctor Danaher waited for the pounding in his chest to subside. Biding time, he dabbled with a white handkerchief at blood trickling down his chin from a deep cut in his lower lip. With his free arm outstretched atop the mattress, he clinched a wad of quilt, using the grip to prevent his dazed body from falling backward and onto the floor.

Preventing the patient from exiting the room and returning him under the sheets exhausted the strength of both men. Intent on finding his travel companion, Jack made it to the doorway before Olan moved beyond his shock to react with a body block cutting off his path, stalling his progress just beyond the threshold and just in time for the doctor to regain his senses and grab hold around Jack's waist.

The two men pulled, tugged, and pushed in a valiant attempt to harness Jack's intense energy. Had his body been up to the task of taking him where he wanted to go, both fared little chance of redirecting his course. The struggle, seeming as if lasting an eternity, came to a peaceful resolution when Jack succumbed to the pain and a swirling skull before falling sideways across the bed. The doctor ended up where he began—on the floor, on his knees, against the bed frame. Olan maintained a bear hug on Jack throughout the ordeal, somehow getting his arms wrapped under Jack's armpits. With fingers interlocked around his back, Olan rode Jack all the way down on top the mattress.

Bent at the waist, with palms buried in his thighs and working to reclaim the normal breath forfeited in the scuffle, Olan followed droplets of sweat releasing from the tip of his nose to the hardwood floor below, watching as they exploded on contact like heavy raindrops on a car windshield. He knew he'd wrestled tougher men to the ground but could not recall a time he needed help to get one man under control.

"I'll tell you this," Olan said, "I'd sure enjoy having him 'round here for the harvest . . . not so sure he couldn't spare the pull teams by dragging the thresher through the field himself. I bet he could chuck a bale a half mile."

The doctor grunted in agreement, far too winded to string together another sentence and too tired to move from off the floor. The bloody handkerchief remained pressed against his mouth.

A fit man for his age—despite an ongoing battle with arthritis and occasional bouts with gout—the doctor could still hold his own against a stubborn calf wishing to remain in its mother's womb or an angry mare protecting its newborn. Fit or not, trying to harness this beast of a man on a half night's sleep, an empty stomach, and the stinging effects of a sucker punch, took its toll.

Olan collected the sweat on his face with a swipe of a flannel shirtsleeve. He moved toward the bed, stretching his lower back along the way. From behind the doctor, he reached to the floor, and following a deep inhale, pulled with a grunt and deposited the doctor into the chair he'd vacated during the scuffle. He wiped at the back of the doctor's vest and shoulders before spying and retrieving the man's spectacles near the door. With the doctor resting easy, Olan eased against a corner bedpost, watching his wife apply a damp cloth to their guest's forehead. Jack appeared conscious, but groggy.

"Are you okay, Mamma?" Olan asked, noticing her chest heaving at an accelerated rate equal to his own and the void of the soft, warm colors usual to her complexion.

Her hair, silky as a black bird's wing and sprinkled with streaks of silver the color of the spring moon, had untangled from its bun and draped over her shoulders. Long strands trickled across her face in perfect rhythm with the motion of her arms as she wiped down her patient. Her neck shone ashen and spotty.

Sophie was caught between the doorway and her husband when Jack attempted his escape. She took a direct hit from Olan's right shoulder as he plowed through her in pursuit. Like the doctor, she too crashed to the floor, ending up close to the ensuing scrum with the three pairs of legs stomping and jockeying for position very near her face. Her simple, hand-embroidered linen gray dress ripped just below the knee as she scurried out of harm's way. Her apron was situated half-way around her waist and covered in dirt. She'd lost one of her shoes somewhere along the way.

"Sweetheart, are you okay?" Olan's second attempt captured her ear. She twitched as if shaking off a deep thought.

"Yes dear, I'm fine," she replied, dragging a hand through her hair. She flashed an exhausted look before gathering fresh water into the cloth.

"What is it, Mamma?" Olan asked, seeing concern in her eyes.

She placed the cloth to Jack's forehead and released a heavy sigh.

"We have to tell him the truth . . . and the sooner the better," she said. "It's obvious the animal means the world to him."

Olan nodded in agreement. He glanced to the doctor to see what *he* planned on doing about it.

Sitting hunched forward with specs in hand and elbows buried on the top of his knees, Doctor Danaher worked through the words of his pending explanation. He treated the animal; did all he could for the poor beast. He knew it to be his obligation to inform the owner. A nasty part of the job it was, but one he accepted long ago as part of it all. Still, after many years of service in the trade, he could never find the proper words or forget the reactions to whatever news he delivered. From pet goldfish, to prize racehorses, to a lone heifer and sole provider of a family's source of fresh milk, there was no easy way to lessen the strain or pain.

A groan from the patient brought the doctor forward in his chair and the glasses back to the end of his nose. Jack worked to regain his bearings, rolling across the pillow. Sophie continued attending to the sweat dripping from the corners of his eyebrows; Olan remained close, watching his wife care for the stranger as she would one of the boys.

A hard man living in hard times, Olan's rugged and rough exterior was a result of a lifetime spent working the land and other occupations of his youth where a man was made before he developed hair on his chest. At the age of ten, he earned his first saddle and spent the next five years rounding up and breaking wild mustangs for ranchers in the Montana territory. By age fifteen, he was driving mules and horses across the plains to miners in Colorado.

Before his nineteenth birthday, he'd shot and killed his first man fighting off cattle rustlers at the Mexican border. He killed many wild, edible creatures to survive, sometimes with his bare hands, had suffered a broken back, broken bones in almost every limb, gunshot wounds and internal ailments so painful, the devil himself would be screaming for his mamma. He handled it all as a true frontiersman. But seeing someone in pain due to loss or death broke him like a child separated from its mother. He viewed it a cowardly fault over which he had little control.

Sophie watched as Olan turned his stare to the out of doors, his attention drifting as if he were, in some way, connected to the system of clouds rolling above. The very trait he viewed as despicable was the quality she loved most about him.

The doctor nudged the armchair across the floor to reposition near the edge of the bed. He placed a hand on Jack's chest and hacked away a bit of phlegm caught low in his throat. The disturbance recaptured his patient's attention.

Responding sloth-like, Jack fought through a thin layer of built-up moisture to locate the doctor. Allowing a hint of a smile to form at the corner of his swollen lip, the doctor removed his hand from atop Jack's chest, giving him space enough to pull his right arm from underneath the covers. Drawing his hand to his brow, Jack wiped at his soaking wet hairline. Blurred vision gave way to a clearer view of the doctor's face. Jack swallowed deep, fixing on the old man's face.

"I'm very sorry, lad," the doctor said, again removing the specs. He dragged a palm across his cheek before running it around to the back of his neck. "I did everything I could for your wee mate, so I did. The poor beast took a terrible beating. I attended to him the moment we settled you. He was lingering at God's gate the last I looked upon him and would not be surprised if he's passed on. No living creature wee or other could have survived those injuries. From what you described, it's a bloody wonder you pulled him from the wreckage alive at all, so it is."

Jack flattened the palm of his hand against his face. The doctor's words kindled a string of snapshots his mind was eager to process but slow to develop. He remembered locating the dog and pulling him from the wreckage but could not recall his injuries. He was certain he stuffed the animal under his sweatshirt. He recalled seeing the front end of the destroyed Hummer, its headlamps burning toward the sky; the wicked sting of freezing water burning the skin from his bones; his trek across the frozen lake and frigid winter air clawing and slicing at his body. The snippets were breaking through much quicker now—and in no particular order—rushing to the surface of his conscious in great haste. He moved his hand over his face as Sophie continued soaking his neck with the damp cloth.

He recalled the barn; its great expanse and primitive design; the yellow light glowing through a window, serving as a beacon as he moved across the dam. The dock stretching over the lake appeared, as did one of the large boulders marking the trail from the lake. The doctor's voice interrupted.

"I'm heartily sorry I could do no more."

Jack felt the man's hand come to rest atop his bicep. The instant the doctor's fingers flexed in the form of a comforting squeeze another recollection surfaced; one bringing the circumstance to a clear point. Reaching for the top of his chest, he moved his fingers over the area, circling the spot where he'd felt the warm air expelling from Peetie's nostrils. The breath of the dying dog was the lone source of heat against his body as the two fought their way through the frigid conditions. The breath kept his limbs in motion and moving forward, propelling his internal will to find shelter. Bringing his fingers to rest, he contemplated his final moments of consciousness, as he lay half-buried in the haystack. His last recollection was the consistent warm spot having grown cold. The mattress depressed near his right side.

"I'm very sorry, Mr. Clarke," Sophie said. "I know this must be difficult for you but Doctor Danaher really did everything he could. He spent a great deal of time shuffling between the two of you and . . . well, we were more concerned with keeping you alive . . . I am sorry."

Jack rolled across the pillow. He noticed she'd been crying. He moved his hand atop hers and patted, prompting a hint of a smile but one she did not allow to stretch too far.

Centering on the pillow, with his head pounding like a corps of kettledrums, Jack paused to digest the doctor's account. The news worked down his throat like a chugged cup of dusty pea gravel, causing him to want to choke and leaving his mind to contemplate the change of heart he was feeling for this animal. The more he attempted to rationalize the mushrooming ache, the more reminded he was of the night he sent Peetie sailing across the den floor in a drunken rage. He could not shake the sensation of feeling the dog's side caving in against the top of his dress shoe or the subsequent scream of pain following contact. The sound of Peetie's yelp served as a propellant for a low burning guilt building deep within. It triggered a vision buried in the resulting mass of circumstances and experiences endured in the last twenty-four hours.

Jack stared at the ceiling. A vision manifested of the huge gash running down the length of the dog's body; the exposed ribs extruding; his white coat drenched in blood. In a subconscious moment, his thumb worked across the tips of his fingers as he recalled tracing the expanse of the injury to a point revealing the jagged end of a broken leg bone.

Jack brought a hand to his face, working the fingertips deep into the skin of his temples just below the bandage wrap, replaying the few moments he spent navigating his way around the inside of the wreck. He wondered why Peetie worked so hard to save him, especially after the way Jack had treated him. The prospect that the dog's deed could be attributed to unconditional love was laughable. Jack did not believe in the concept, or the theory someone or something could love beyond repeated physical or mental abuse. He mocked at Brooke's insistence Peetie's devotion was a direct result of her compassion in coming to his rescue; giving him a second chance at life. He could understand the dog's devotion, were Brooke in grave danger. Jack wondered what it was that made the dog want to save his life.

The more the question of why Peetie would work to save him swirled, the greater clarity Jack had of a building parallel. Wading through an expanding cesspool of remorse, he wondered how it was possible his own family had stuck with him for so long. Expelling a deep sigh, he searched the deepest recesses for any reason whatsoever why they might love him. His body shifted about the bed as he grew more agitated at the realization of the years of abuse he had inflicted upon them. His treatment of the dog was a mere scratch on the surface of a pattern of physical and mental abuse dished out to everyone around him. He wondered at what point in his life that had become acceptable behavior.

As if his life were flashing before him in a moment eluding death, examples of the years of repeated abuse and deceit swamped to the forefront. He wondered when he'd lost touch with his own humble beginnings, and where mental and physical abuse became as normal a daily routine as brushing one's teeth or eating a meal. Yet he allowed himself to carry on the cowardly tradition set in motion by his own father with his own wife and daughters. He wondered if they still loved him. If unconditional love is possible, could it be so with them? He now wished to believe in the concept.

For the first time since he cowered in a corner of his bedroom at the age of fourteen, dripping with perverted guilt and shame, a tear broke free from Jack's eye, racing over his cheek to the corner of his mouth. He absorbed the drop with the tip of his tongue; the taste of salt was strong. Drawing a palm over his face, he pushed hard to stall additional tears from escaping. He felt Sophie's hand behind his head.

"Here Mr. Clarke, please take another sip of water." The woman eased the cup to his lips. Jack worked to clear his pallet by washing his tongue around the inside of his mouth. The taste of iron was overwhelming.

Sitting on the edge of his chair hunched over with hands interlocked between his legs, Doctor Danaher appeared in deep conversation with something on the floor. Jack watched the old man's lips form complete sentences in silence while he bobbed and dipped in agreement with whatever it was he was attempting to gain favor.

"Doctor?" Jack's voice cracked, forcing a clearing cough before proceeding. "I know it may be too late, but I'd like to see my dog."

The plea brought an end to the doctor's mumbling. Olan turned from the window upon registering the plea. He offered a shake of his head but passed on voicing an opinion. He knew well the condition of the dog and felt it a very bad idea.

Doctor Danaher sunk deep into the back of the chair, eyeing Jack while deliberating the request. He knew the sight of the animal to be ghastly, at best. He sutured the wound but significant bruising left the animal appearing as if bludgeoned from nose to tail with a sledgehammer. He did not have the necessary implements to set the broken distal femur; it remained protruding through the skin, covered by a thin, blood-soaked bandage. The shock could be too much for his patient to handle.

The doctor repositioned again forward, inducing a piercing crack from the maple chair.

"Lad," he said, removing his specs, "I think given your condition it would be best for you to let this go, so it would. If the poor beast is still with us, and I doubt he is, you need to let us take care of what needs to be done. I'm certain he won't have any knowledge of your presence."

"What is it you need to do?"

"If the animal is alive we should put him out of his misery. He's suffering, so . . . nothing more can be done for him."

"What would you recommend? Euthanasia?"

"Any other time and I'd have the proper necessaries . . . unfortunately, I do not have any of the recipe on hand."

"What other option is there?"

The doctor rubbed the stubble under his chin. Olan fled to the window. The awkward actions stirred a rumble in Jack's gut.

"Doctor?" Jack asked. The old man squirmed a bit in his chair and cleared his throat.

"We'd have to shoot him, lad. I have no other means and we cannot let him suffer any longer. Myself or himself will make sure it's a clean shot into his head. On my word, I swear t'ya the poor creature won't even hear the sound of the gun."

The response caught Jack off guard. He paused to halt emotions seeking escape. Sophie moved in close upon noticing his reaction. Jack held his position several seconds, working to get to a place where he could speak without his voice cracking. He wiped again at his face.

"Do you know how my wife found the dog?" Jack asked. His voice was low and hoarse. Doctor Danaher shook his head and eased against the back of the chair. Feeling liquid on his lip, he pulled the blood-stained handkerchief from his pocket and placed it against his mouth.

"She found him half-buried in snow in a ditch after someone had shot him and left him for dead. How can I do the same to him now after he saved my life?"

"I understand your pain, so I do," the doctor confided, stuffing the cloth back into his pocket, "but you'd be doing him no favors keeping him alive. I'm sure he appreciates the second chance your family gave him. But do the right thing now."

Jack could not fathom the brutality or imagery of placing the barrel of a gun to the head of this animal and pulling the trigger. He could not rationalize that to be the right thing to do. The animal saved his life. How could killing him now be best?

"If it were not for him," Jack continued, "I'd be at the bottom of the lake as a frozen block of ice. He woke me up. He's the reason I'm alive. I can't reward him by blowing his head off. I can't kill him."

"You won't be pulling the trigger, son," said Olan, still searching his property for something to occupy his mind, "and I can assure you it would be a single, clean shot. This is my farm. If it must be done—and *this* needs to be done—then it is my responsibility. There's no reason for you to carry any guilt . . . it's just a fact of life."

Sophie's touch provided little comfort.

"I'd like to see him . . . please, doctor . . . bring him to me?"

The doctor expelled a deep sigh, turned to the Brossys in hopes one would offer an objection, but was left disappointed as each adjusted their stares to the floor. He conceded to the request, albeit with great trepidation. Pushing off the arms of the chair, his old bones popping and cracking every bit as loudly as the chair frame, he eased to his feet before grabbing hold of the bedpost to steady his legs. Jack followed the man's lethargic gait to the door. Eager to remove himself from the room, Olan fell in behind, almost pushing past the doctor at the doorframe. Jack watched the two men move down the hallway and out of his sight. He listened as their footsteps faded from his ears. Seconds later, somewhere on the opposite side of the house, a door opened and closed.

Absorbing the newfound silence, Jack pushed aside his swelling emotions by working his eyes around the room, taking in the quaint and humble surroundings. Sophie, having moved off the bed, glided in silence around the frame hunched over, readjusting the sheets and quilts. Watching as she worked, he concluded he'd remained down the rabbit hole, based on the odd way the room presented and Sophie's attire.

The early period clothing was no longer a surprise. He'd witnessed enough in recent days to know all was not normal. The room itself was very small, more so in width than depth and was made to seem even smaller due to a low built ceiling which appeared to be a mistake during construction that was never remedied. Every wall was finished in a dingy, flat whitewash over rough-coat plaster, with an aged yellowing tint overtaking the corners nearer the floor. White molding rose high against the base of the walls with like-painted quarter round resting flush atop hand cut, wide-plank maple wood flooring. The most significant omission was an electrical source. Searching every wall, Jack was unable to spot the first outlet or switch. Nothing in the way of a light fixture appeared against the ceiling. Other than the large windows, an old oil lamp on the night table to his left and a modest wood-burning fireplace in the corner to the left of the first window provided the only other sources of light. Although ablaze, the fire's flames produced little in the way of illumination.

Jack lifted off the pillow to view a large handmade case of dresser drawers set center and flush against the wall. Several family pictures framed in silver displayed in a neat row, angled toward the bed. A large white ceramic bowl and tin pan sat on a matching night table to his right.

Without warning, Sophie untucked the sheets at the foot of the bed, ending Jack's brief inspection of the room. The action sent a wave of cool air racing up his legs, extending the hair from his skin. Refocusing his attention forward, he studied her as she worked around the bed, noticing every few seconds or so, her looking upon him as if wanting to ask a question, but thinking better of it. As she leaned over the foot of the bed with the gray of the darkening December sky back-lighting her position, Jack explored her face in full for the first time. Her look was familiar.

He wondered how it was this woman could bear such a striking resemblance to his mother-in-law. Their facial features were nearly identical as was their respective physical make-ups. The one attribute he recognized as dissimilar was their mannerisms—those were polar opposite. Where his mother-in-law was rigid, Sophie was soft; where Anna was judgmental, Sophie seemed accepting. Her ways were kind and compassionate, yet she conducted herself in a manner that seemed odd to him—almost as if she were the live-in help. She reacted to her husband with obedience and seemed subservient to the other males in the house, yet Olan seemed protective of her feelings and respectful of her wishes. The manner and demeanor in which they functioned as a family unit was foreign to him. No matter, the physical resemblance to his mother-in-law was more than just a little disturbing.

Sophie retrieved the two bricks from under the sheets, placing the burgundy-colored slabs on the floor. She leaned back over the foot of the bed to retuck the sheets. Noticing Jack following her every move, she paused in mid-tuck.

"Is there something I can get for you, Mr. Clarke?" she asked, resuming her work while waiting for his reply.

"No," he said. "It seems you and your family have done enough already."

His voice had returned to pre-accident condition, although he was not yet willing to release it in full. He adjusted his hips to relieve a stabbing pain that was racing down his left thigh and calf. Sophie continued to the opposite side of the bed, fluffing and adjusting the heavy quilt lying on top.

"Are you feeling better?"

Jack stretched his neck and traps. His lips pursed as sharp prickles of pain shot down his spine and into his buttocks.

"I'm very sore," he said, letting out a deep sigh. "My entire left side feels like it's been beaten with a hammer. My head feels like it weighs a ton." Stretching and arching his back, he inquired of the time. He scanned the room for a clock.

"It's almost half past three."

He searched the windows; daylight was fading fast. "Is it the twenty-third?" he asked.

"It is . . . of December."

Jack expelled a deep "oooh" as he lifted and pointed the elbow of his left arm out to the side. His shoulder was stiff, but less painful. He determined the function of the joint at or near seventy-five percent. He continued working the joint to loosen it further. As he stretched, he probed for more answers.

"How did you find me?"

"It wasn't very hard. Our eldest son heard the horses stirring in the barn just past midnight and went to check to see what might be spooking them. He found you buried in the haystack."

Sophie moved away from the bed to the front corner of the room. Kneeling to the ground in front of the fireplace, she stoked the heap before placing another log on the fire. Her voice muted as she spoke toward the flame.

"You're so very lucky to be alive. Not one of us can figure how you managed to find your way from the mine in those conditions. It's a miracle," she said, moving to the foot of the bed with the precision and elegance of a woman bred in the ways of royalty.

"I don't know why you're here, but I'm convinced the good Lord Almighty has blessed you this day. It's just an absolute miracle you're alive."

Jack turned away. His indifference stirred her curiosity.

"You disagree, Mr. Clarke?" He did not respond, deciding instead to roll further from her view.

"Mr. Clarke?"

The echo of her voice drifted about before silence ensued.

"I find it hard to believe a man in your condition, so very near death as you were, not considering God's intervention in your circumstance. Could it be you do not believe in God?"

Jack wondered why his religious beliefs were of concern. His eyes remained low in their sockets, like a child's after being caught red-handed in a lie.

"I don't know," he replied, growing ashamed as a look of motherly shock spread across her face. An awkward silence reminded him of his first trip inside the confessional at St. Bernard's Church when he spilled to Father Prater the details of a Hot Wheels car he lifted from the local

Ben Franklin dime store. Cows bellowing in the distance brought a welcomed break.

"I'm sorry, Mr. Clarke," she said, dropping her hand from the post. She glided to his right. I did not mean to pry. I understand a man's choice to choose God is just that. I just can't imagine, though, how lonely it must be for a body to go through life empty of the Lord's good word and wisdom. As the good book says, 'but if from there you seek the Lord your God, you will find Him if you look for Him with all your heart and with all your soul.' Are you familiar with the verse Mr. Clarke?"

Jack shook his head.

"Deuteronomy four, twenty-nine. Have you ever sought the Lord?"

"I was born and raised Catholic . . . went through the church system most of my youth."

Sophie moved along the bed toward the nightstand. Jack followed her slow, majestic gait. Her ability to quote the Bible—especially a verse from a book as obscure as Deuteronomy—convinced him she and his mother-in-law exited the same womb. Anna was a Bible-toting fanatic herself and could rattle off verse after verse at the drop of a dime, be it in casual conversation or terse circumstance. His experience with those spewing verse was their use of it as a tool of control and means to elevate themselves among others. His mother-in-law was a prime example. Jack didn't buy any of it.

Sophie stood over the nightstand gathering up several cloths used to wipe her patient down during the night.

"I know many people who've not missed a day of church their entire life and are no more closer to God today than their first day kneeling in His house. Going to church and knowing God is not one in the same."

Jack pondered her rationale but held no interest in exploring her views of his religious shortcomings. He wondered how soon he could get up and be on his way; how close he was to Cartersville and if Brooke and his daughters were within his reach. His mission returned in full to his conscience; his mind wandered farther and farther away from the question at hand. Seeing him drifting, Sophie moved on about her work.

With his attention now captured by the fireplace and its bright amber flames bursting toward the chimney, another lost bit of information percolated to the surface as the building ash pile below the fire grate grew. The grayish-white dust prompted a recollection of the charred remnants of the picture pulled from his own fireplace. The significance meant nothing at first until his memory moved to the vision of his dufflebag, and the important bits of information stuffed inside now settled at the bottom of the lake.

He brought a hand over his forehead and shook his head. "Goddamn it."

The word rushed forth in a whisper, but not near silent enough. As his mind registered the gaffe, he rolled across the pillow, keeping his hand stretched over his brow, peeking through the gaps in his fingers. For an instant, he thought the miscue had passed without notice. The look morphing across his caretaker's face indicated otherwise. He hunkered in preparation of the coming lightning strike.

In her shock, Sophie let slip the stash of wet cloths to the floor. Her face went pale; her eyes squinted nearly closed. Jack thought he might wet the sheets. After a long pause and menacing stare, her voice broke forth in a tone diametrically opposed to the calming and compassionate grace with which she had cared for him up to the point.

"We've all had the pleasure of sampling the extent of your vocabulary, Mr. Clarke," she said, closing in on his position. "I credited the earlier outburst to the fact you were not right of mind and under a great deal of stress. However, I can only assume now that repulsive language is more your way than not. Regardless of your situation or misfortune, while you are a guest in this house you will never again take the Lord's name in vain or use such language. I will not permit such vile speak nor the cursing of the Lord in this house. Do you even have any idea what you are saying when you ask God to damn? Are you even familiar with His commandments? In case you are unaware, thou shalt not take the Lord's name in vain falls just after do not make an idol for yourself and just before remember the Sabbath and keep it holy. Have I made myself clear?"

Jack's eyes bulged. He dropped his jaw in an attempt to speak; Sophie beat him to the punch.

"I suggest if you ever decide to seek the Lord and His forgiving nature, you start by guarding what flows from your own lips . . . 'There is nothing from without a man, that entering into him can defile him: but the things which come out of him, those are they that defile the man.' Mark seventeen, fifteen."

Jack contemplated an apology but knew it would do little to repair the damage done.

"Never in my life have I heard such vulgarity," she said, reaching to the floor to retrieve the rags. "Any man who speaks with such discourtesy is destined to—"

The slamming of a distant door interrupted Sophie's rant, sending her body squaring toward the hallway. She traded a quick glance with Jack as footsteps grew in crescendo toward the door. Jack heard the words "oh dear" skim past his ears in a whisper, accelerating a sizeable knot deep in his stomach. He wondered if his request of the doctor was a mistake.

CHAPTER 25

Sophie did not intend for the gasp to escape with such dramatics. The sight of her eldest son approaching from the hallway brought a measure of relief only a mother could know. Concern for his safe return held a great deal of her mind hostage, despite her husband's direct orders he not travel onto the frozen surface and his acceptance of those terms.

Caleb's thirst for adventure and exploration was equaled only by his father's. She knew how difficult it would be for him to remain on the shoreline as instructed. The sight of the young man also took Jack by surprise. He released a sigh, feeling relieved for the stay in facing his dying friend.

"Thank God you're home, son," Sophie said. "Are you okay?"

"Yes ma'am, I'm fine," Caleb replied, a bit out of breath. His face shown bright red from windburn; his lips glowed purple.

Jack slid his body toward the headboard, doing his ribcage no favors, upon noticing his red dufflebag dangling from the boy's hand. The bag, soaking wet and marred with streak marks caused by earth and branch, appeared as if having been sent through a shredding machine. The side nearest his view sported several large, gaping slashes in the heavy denim-like material, revealing the white of his cotton T-shirts and underwear within. A strong pine scent swept across the bed, cutting off the smell of hickory from the fireplace.

"What do you have there?" his mother asked, pointing to the bag.

"I found it on the side of the embankment overlooking the mine. It was buried under some sheared-off pine limbs."

"Does this belong to you, Mr. Clarke?"

Jack nodded, never taking his eye off the bag.

"Did you find anything else, son?"

"No ma'am . . . well . . . there was a lot of debris scattered down the embankment but mostly bits and pieces of metal and junk. The lake is covered with snow; I didn't see anything on the surface."

Sophie locked eyes with her son and dipped her head in Jack's direction. Caleb understood the command and deposited the bag on top of the bed near Jack's hip. Sophie examined the strange word displayed in large, white raised stitched lettering facing her. She spoke low working out the enunciation. "A—di—das."

"Adidas," Jack said, offering the correct pronunciation and cadence. "It's a sports apparel company."

"I've never seen such a travel case," she said.

"I use it for short vacations or trips to the fitness center."

"What's a fitness center?" asked the boy.

Jack exchanged a confused look with him before Sophie intervened.

"Caleb, we must not trouble Mr. Clarke with questions right now. He's still not quite himself. There will be time later. Please take these rags to the mud room and find what's keeping your father and Doctor Danaher."

"Yes ma'am," he said. Jack marveled at the boy's obedient and subservient reaction to his parents' every command. He either had not responded promptly enough in the past and paid a heavy price, or was on some sort of parental remote control. Caleb met his mother halfway around the bed to retrieve the bundle of wet rags wedged in the fold of her arm. Jack stopped his progress with a wave of his hand as he set to exit.

"I appreciate you going out like you did," Jack said, breaking the standoff. "I'm sorry to have caused you the trouble."

Caleb offered an abbreviated nod. His expression conveyed uncertainty, even distrust; Jack wasn't sure. He paused to study the boy's face. There was no question as to whom the boy favored most. Sharp jaw lines, a matching Roman nose and dark-brown sunken eyes aped his father's look spot on. His skin was dark and leathery, his hands large, battered, and callused; a farmer through and through. Curly black hair and a deep cleft in the center of his chin were likely identifying features of the males on his mother's side. Jack figured he was his father's equal in height but much less thick. He was a handsome young man with a face as honest as ole' Abe Lincoln himself.

So why the look? Jack wondered. It sent his mind to racing. Did he rummage through the bag? Did he see the gun? Maybe young Caleb knew a little more than what he'd confessed to his mother. Jack viewed the bag out of the corner of his eye. The young man did not budge; his expression remained intact. Another long pause ensued as each waited for the other to speak.

"You say you saw nothing on the lake?"

"Yes sir." The boy stood at near attention as if Jack were his drill sergeant.

"No sign of a vehicle on top of the ice?"

"No sir. I saw two spots where the snow was disturbed, but there was no machinery of any kind visible. I'm sure whatever was on top broke through and sunk to the bottom."

"When you found the bag, was it open?" Jack dragged his hand along the path of the gash, grimacing in pain.

"No sir. The condition you see it now is the condition I found it."

Jack nodded in acceptance of his answer. "Well, again, I appreciate your trouble."

"Yes sir." Caleb looked to his mother, acknowledged Jack with another nod and exited the room. His eyes followed the young man until he disappeared down the hallway.

"You need not worry, Mr. Clarke," Sophie said, displaying a keen sense of woman's intuition. "He's a good and mindful boy. He does not make a habit of going through property not belonging to him. I'm certain you'll find the contents of your bag intact."

Jack draped his arm over the bag, embarrassed she'd sensed his concern and hoping soon to have a private moment to check its contents.

Falling deep into his pillow, he absorbed the silence and breathed deep the pine aroma overtaking the room. The mere whiff of the scent disturbed his senses. He remembered from his childhood the smell of fresh cut pine as *the* definitive trigger denoting the arrival of the holiday season. His mother insisted the family's greenery be fresh and in place no later than the day following Thanksgiving, which allowed for the heavenly perfume to fill their nostrils through the New Year.

He lamented as he thought of the few early Christmases he experienced as a child that lived up to the expectations and excitement any young boy or girl would dream for the day. He drew in his mind the images of the landscape covered in fresh-packed snow, the family tree and its sparkling lights highlighting presents jammed under its outstretched branches. Christmas morning broke early as his mother's parents arrived before the crow of the rooster, waking him from his slumber to announce the arrival of Santa. He recalled the utter hysteria of opening an autographed official league football or Lionel train set, the mouth-watering aromas of ham, eggs, bacon, and homemade biscuits wafting from the kitchen, and the many friends coming and going throughout the day.

The retrospection stung his heart. So much had changed; so much seemed as if it never was. The once glorious scent of pine was nothing more than a stench to him now; a nasty fume he would flee from if he could. He thought of Julianna and Jordan. How he wished for courage to scatter his past in the wind and make those traditions anew with them.

The sound of shuffling feet and grumbling voices brought Jack's head off the pillow in the direction of the hallway. He could hear the doctor and Olan speaking over one another as they neared. Hunched over the firebox, Sophie jumped upright as the two men reached the bedroom door. Jack watched her face grow ashen. Her right hand, balled in a fist, pressed hard into the middle of her chest as she made her way to the foot of the bed. Her look ignited butterflies in his stomach.

"Let's put him there," Doctor Danaher said. The two men struggled to the edge of the bed and placed Peetie on the mattress just opposite Jack's hip. Stepping back, the doctor buried his hands into his sides, bent backward at the waist and worked to catch his breath. Olan moved around the bed to join his wife. The two embraced. She disappeared into the folds of his huge arms.

"Now mind you lad," the doctor said between short breaths, "we've got him covered so we have, but he's not a site to behold. If it becomes too much for ya, don't be punishing yourself. He's alive—God be it a miracle—but barely."

The pungent smell of dried blood and soiled animal fur rose in an instant, forcing Jack's nose in the opposite direction. He caught Sophie taking a quick peek before turning into her husband's chest. Jack's stomach dropped. Certain now he'd made a mistake, he moved even further away from the growing stench, uncertain if his emotions could deal with what he was about to see.

His courage teetered only because he lacked confidence he could keep his emotions in check. He'd made one teary scene already and did not intend to make a second. Sucking in a deep breath of air, he turned to view his friend.

The shocking image of the animal provoked an instant, uncontrolled gasp of breath pushing out of his mouth from deep in his gut, which he tried to camouflage by pressing the end of a fist to his mouth and forcing an exaggerated cough.

"Oh God no . . . no," he whispered through his balled palm as his eye sockets swelled to their brims with tears. Crushing his eyes closed, Jack turned away. His reaction sucked the very life from those standing near, creating a confused and awkward ambience pushing through the room.

Doctor Danaher retreated to the maple chair, plopped on top of its thin cushion and cupped his brow in his hand. Sprawling his legs outward, he contemplated intervening, but thought it best his patient get his grieving over and out of his system. Olan swallowed deep, before redirecting his attention to the view out of doors. He maintained a tight grip of his wife. Sophie remained face-first against his chest, fighting an urge to come to Jack's side in support.

Jack heaved back and forth, pushing against the headboard and into the wall behind, unable to harness the explosion of emotions. His breath evaporated into unbounded sobbing. With his fist firm against his mouth, his body rocked as he tried to digest the image and the role he played in causing it all.

An unsuspecting, blood curdling yelp erupted above his sobbing, catching everyone in the room by surprise and causing each to jump nearly out of their skin. Doctor Danaher grabbed hold of his chest, as the shock of the animal making a noise at all at this stage of his body shutting down sent his heart racing. Working through blurred vision and the sting of salty tears, Jack could not help but notice how very little the animal looked like the one he'd traveled with from Chicago.

Peetie rested on his side, wrapped in a musty, burlap chicken feed sack, with his head resting atop paws stained by blood discharging from his nose. His paws were missing several nails, each pulled clean from their joint. His eyes remained half-open, although void of color and life, and were caked at their corners with a grayish-green, gelatinous gunk. His mouth opened and closed at a lethargic pace, gasping at breath and almost appearing as if he were some sort of mechanical toy operating on its last thrust of battery power.

Jack stretched to make contact with the crown of Peetie's head. Fanning out his fingertips, he brushed across Peetie's skull and over an ear, before withdrawing.

Staring at his hand, still fighting tears seeking escape, he rubbed his thumb across the tops of his fingertips, growing sick at the absence of heat. The chill lingered on his skin like some heavy gel he could not wipe clean. He swallowed hard at the realization death was near. Reaching again for his friend, he pinched at the nearest corner of the burlap sack just beyond Peetie's neck. The move stirred Doctor Danaher from his sprawled position to the edge of the seat.

"Lad, I beg you not to," he said, raising his arms and flattening his palms in Jack's direction. "Just let it be. You mustn't punish yourself like this."

Jack gained a secure grip on the corner of the sack. Shaking his head, he peeled back the flap covering the length of Peetie's body.

"Oh my dear God," Sophie said, her voice trailing to a whisper.

Upon hearing the doctor's plea, she watched the moment unfold holding out hope Jack would abide by the doctor's request. She closed her eyes and swallowed.

Jack gazed at the dog with his mouth agape. His breath paused and his tears dried in an instant at the shocking, unimaginable image. The gash, sutured though it was, presented as a length of black rope, as dried blood caked to the jagged edges of skin snaking from just under the dog's chin to a position disappearing underneath his belly. He could no longer differentiate Peetie's natural black and brown spots from the stains of dried, pooled blood. His skin, in the areas the doctor shaved, looked as if it'd been spray-painted black with a blue gradient. The bone in his leg remained as it was, broken and protruding from the skin.

Sophie broke free of her husband, moved to the edge of the bed and pulled the sack back across Peetie's body. A quick glance in the doctor's direction left no doubt in her disappointment he'd allowed the scenario to play out.

"Mr. Clarke, are you okay?" Sophie asked.

Jack again placed his hand atop Peetie's head. Rubbing across his skull, he gathered the dog's ear in his palm and caressed it with his thumb.

"I'm so sorry," he said, his voice projecting in a listless, near despondent whisper. "I'm so sorry for . . . for everything. I wish . . . I could . . ."

His words evaporated. He could say no more with the lump in the middle of his throat. Upon releasing Peetie's ear from his palm, the dog opened his eyes to three-quarters, stretched his mouth wide and let go a final, distinct breath. His front paws stretched from his body, as if reaching out for Jack's touch, before recoiling to his chest. As the dog's final breath drifted away, he watched Peetie's front and back legs twitch in a final act of function. A burst of saliva shot from Jack's mouth and mucus from his nose as a new round of sobbing sent streams of tears gushing over his eyelids. He reached for Peetie's front paw as if in some way he could prevent the one link between he and his family from slipping away forever. There was no reaction to his touch.

Counting the seconds to the end, Olan advanced in double time, sidestepping his wife, to reach the edge of the bed. Stretching the burlap sack to cover Peetie's lifeless body, he clutched both ends and moved to the door. His pace quickened upon entering the hallway.

Doctor Danaher situated on the edge of his chair, balancing his elbows on his knees. He worked a thumb deep into the bowl of a briarwood smoking pipe, trading quick glances between his patient and the compressed tobacco makings. His heart grieved for the young man but he was pleased the poor beast expired on his own terms. Putting an animal down, regardless of necessity, disturbed his soul like sin. The lad needed the experience, he was certain of it.

Hunched over the ceramic bowl on the nightstand, Sophie wrung out the last piece of clean cloth on hand. Moving to the bed, she eased onto the mattress and offered the cloth by touching it against Jack's forearm. With her hand cupped against his brow, Jack allowed a few remaining sobs to release before reaching blindly for the rag and pressing it flat against his face.

Sophie laid her hand atop his shoulder. "Mr. Clarke, is there anything I can get you?" She waited several moments for a response but got none. She offered another drink; he declined.

"I'm very sorry," she said.

The scratch of a match head sizzling to life caused Jack to release the rag from his face. He watched the doctor puff away at the pipe, igniting the tobacco. A swift moving odor of sulfur drifted across the bed and past the tip of his nose, gobbling up the stale stench of burlap and wet fur still lingering. A plume of white smoke erupted in front of the doctor's face, as several deep puffs brought the scented cloud billowing from a corner of his mouth. Noticing daylight waning, the doctor pushed from his chair, moved to the nightstand, and with the flame near his fingertips, removed the large Tam-o-shanter crystal shade from off the oil lamp and ignited the wick.

With the pipe clenched in his teeth and a suggestion of cherry mixed with an earthy root now overtaking the smell of sulfur, Doctor Danaher offered Jack a compassionate wink before moving off toward the fireplace. Jack followed the trail of smoke before breaking to view the scene out of doors. Twilight was upon the landscape, but the sky remained bright enough to reveal snow drifting by and sticking to the windows.

Doctor Danaher tossed another piece of split hickory onto the fire, and using a long, cast iron poker, bent low to stoke the logs. A couple of sharp jabs sent burnt remains crumbling below the grate and embers flashing to life. The newfound oxygen produced brilliant orange and blue flames racing high into the box.

Pleased he'd resurrected their sole heat source for at least another thirty minutes, he returned the poker and splashed his hands together to clear debris. Moving in front of the nearest window, he tugged at the gold chain attached to his vest to extract a gold pocket watch. The large, heavy gothic font numerals imprinted on the face allowed for visual confirmation with or without his specs in place. It was quarter to five. The snap of the two opposing cases echoed across the room.

Jack cleared his throat as the doctor reinserted his pipe and moved toward the bed.

"Doctor? I . . . I appreciate everything you tried to do to save him. I know you're not used to such work . . . but."

The doctor pulled his pipe then drug his stare to Sophie. She understood the look on his face, knowing as he did the two had failed to mention his line of work. The doctor moved around the bedpost and eased onto the corner of the mattress.

"I'm sorry I could do no more for him, lad, so I am. However, I would stand a far better chance saving him than you, had you been worse for the wear. By trade, I'm a veterinarian, not a general practitioner. Some principles tend to overlap between the trades, so they do, but I just happened to be the closest thing to a family doc the Brossy's could get, considering the circumstances."

The doctor flashed his palm toward the window. Jack followed the motion and noticed the snow picking up and the muted colors of dusk gaining on the day.

"Did he suffer much?"

"The poor beast was in a great deal of pain when I first arrived. He spent most of the ordeal unconscious, however. I know this was difficult for you, but I'm glad you could be with him as he passed."

"Did you notice his paws?" Jack asked.

"Aye; that I did," the doctor acknowledged.

"I don't understand." Jack dragged the wet cloth across his face.

"I've been exposed to such a circumstance but one other time. A man once brought a young, almost starved to death male coyote to my surgery missing all but a couple nails on both paws. The man mentioned the beast digging into the frozen ground hours on end searching for food. He dug until exhaustion got the better of him, so it did." Doctor Danaher grabbed hold of the bedpost and pulled himself to his feet.

"I don't know how to explain what happened to your mate. It's possible he was in such a position he had to claw his way to get to you . . . I don't know. But it could explain why he was missing the longest nails on both paws.

"You have to understand, lad, your dog was behaving in a manner befitting a pack animal. They're born to a pack mentality and they die by the pack mentality. He was just responding as nature intended. You were his master. "

"I know you both think the dog was special to me," Jack said. "The fact is, until recently, I couldn't stand the sight of him. I even kicked him once for making a mess in the house."

Sophie dropped her hand from his shoulder. Her eyes narrowed.

"Och," the doctor said, speaking in a low whisper, "that would explain it." Jack tracked his eyes as they moved about the room; the doctor recognized the inquisitiveness.

"When I first inspected his wound, I noticed three of his ribs had suffered previous breaks. I was surprised the animal lived as long as he did. One rib in particular was broken at such an angle it would have taken but a wee bloody jolt for it to puncture a lung."

"I wish I could take it all back," Jack said. "I realize the harm I've done him and would give anything to take it all back."

"We all make mistakes. Sometimes we get the chance to make it right and others we're left with to stir for eternity. There's an old Irish saying me Dad told when I was but a wee chiseller—'May you get all your wishes but one, least you have something to strive for.'"

"I don't understand."

"Life lessons come to us in many forms, so they do. The poor beast may have crossed your path for no other reason than provide you an opportunity to reflect on your life or how very fragile life itself is . . . I don't know . . . I do know our blessed Father works in mysterious ways and would not think twice of using whatever means necessary to right one's donkey. But I don't think I have to tell you that," he said, reinserting his pipe.

Jack searched through the windows. The old man was right. He wondered why the animal had to die for the sake of a life lesson.

"'Take My yoke upon you and learn from Me,'" Sophie quoted, "'for I am gentle and humble in heart, and you will find rest for your souls.'"

A dying ember popping from the grate onto the large slabs of slate in front of the firebox caught Jack's attention.

"It's a miracle how one can find such comfort in the Word of the Lord when tragic times darken our souls, isn't it Doctor?"

"True it 'tis, Sophie dear . . . true, indeed."

"I believe, Mr. Clarke, you should lay back now and rest," Doctor Danaher said. "You've had a right stressful afternoon and I'm certain you'll find a little sleep very refreshing."

"I'll stop in a little later to check up and bring you something to eat," Sophie added. She adjusted Jack's pillow and maneuvered him into a more horizontal position. She removed the duffle bag and placed it on the floor next to the bed. Jack watched out of the corner of his eye as to its exact location.

"Are you warm enough?" she asked.

"Yes . . . plenty." With her rant against his curse of the Lord fresh in his mind, Jack marveled at the fact Sophie was still concerned with his condition. It's as if she'd already buried the incident and moved on.

"Just holler if you need anything. The kitchen is just on the other side of the house. I'll leave the door cracked a bit."

Jack nodded.

The old man stepped aside as Sophie eased in front of him to exit the room. A burst of pipe smoke was sucked into her wake as she passed, sending the cloud rolling over the bed and across Jack's face. The scent ignited a memory of his father, who smoked a pipe before progressing to cigarettes and an occasional cigar. The aroma tingled at his senses, conjuring the memory of an old photograph taken when he was but three years old, given to him by his mother, of his old man sitting in his favorite chair balancing Jack on his knee reading *Twas the Night Before Christmas.*

Years later, his mother confessed to it being the one time she recalled his father ever holding him in his lap. He wanted to know what it felt like tucked tight in the fold of his father's arms, but the moment took place too early in life for an eternal stamp.

"Get some rest, lad," Doctor Danaher said, "you're going to need it."

He pulled the creaking door behind as he exited, leaving just enough of an opening one could look in on him without fear of disruption. Jack did not hear the doctor as he exited.

Gazing through the bedroom windows, watching the final moments of dusk, a numb feeling settled over him as he worked to digest the reality of his actions and the vision of Peetie breathing his last. He rubbed again over the tips of his fingers, still unable to release the frigid sensation of death. Uncontrolled sobs volleyed forth at will, as fluid pricked at the backs of his eyelids.

He visualized an outline of Brooke's face. He wondered if she was just a mere mile or so away; how soon could he reach her; could she ever forgive him for his betrayal? Could she ever forgive him for Peetie's death? He swallowed hard as his mind wandered and the battle for control of his eyelids waned. The melodic sounds of popping embers, hard hickory crackling under the duress of widespread flames, and the soft ticking of sleet against the window made for a rhythmic sedative pulling him from the conscious world.

Just prior to his slip into darkness, the faint sound of a child's giggle at his door interrupted. With his mind unable to distinguish folly from reality, he fell into a dream sequence already underway, reuniting him with his just deceased friend.

CHAPTER 26

The thunderous applause exploding around the dining room table seemed equal in decibel to a herd of wild buffalo stampeding through the house—at least upon the ears of a five-year-old.

Barely able to contain his excitement, young Jack pulled his hands up and placed them over his ears. He watched with great delight the animated actions of the adults watching as his father carved around the center bone of a large Virginia ham at the head of the table. Roasted to an amber perfection, the tantalizing aroma of brown sugar, pineapple, and cloves teased the senses and stirred great anticipation as to who would get the first slice.

With eyes the size of silver dollars, Jack—or 'Jack-lantern' as he was called by his uncle Jay—searched each face at the table for amusing expressions, while taking account of the assortment of holiday knick-knacks his mother had scattered between the many baking dishes and serving trays.

In front of his position, nestled between a heaping, steaming platter of scrambled eggs and a basket of homemade biscuits, he followed with fascination a caravan of brass angels pushed by the heat of four thin, white candles round a tall, star-studded golden spire. The delicate sound of their tiny brass rods tinkling against brass bells as they rounded sent a wave of holiday cheer pulsating through his veins.

Jack turned to the opposite end of the table where he spied his mother hiding behind a tall crystal glass of an orange juice mix of which he was forbidden to partake. Her look suggested she was running

thin on patience as she deflected praise from her mother for the beautiful table arrangements and from her sister for the many delectable
entrees spread about.

She eased the glass from her lips after catching her little man's eye;
the expression on her face was unlike any other at the table, causing
Jack to recoil his wide smile. He wondered why she appeared so
unhappy. She was tired, almost the way she looked when coming home
in the evening following her shift at the diner. Catching a hint of a smile
break over her lips, he peeked over his shoulder, unsure if the gesture
was meant for his benefit, his aunt, or someone else down the line.

His mother's look was vacant; he knew something was wrong. The
corners of her lips dipped in the direction of her chin. Her smile evaporated, inducing fear he'd done something wrong; he froze. His face
flushed. Leaning forward, he turned to his father but saw no sign, just
the ham resting atop its silver platter with a large carving knife buried
deep as if having been stabbed with a heavy plunge from above. Blood
oozed from the wound as if the mass were freshly slaughtered rather
than fully cooked. A rush of fresh blood overflowed the platter's rim,
spilling onto the white and green tablecloth and advancing in an even
flow toward him. Jack turned again to his mother.

Now standing, facing the table, she offered her glass into the air
toward his father's vacated position; others around the table joined her.
Touching the crystal to her lips, she drew a small quantity of drink into
her mouth, faced her son, and in a slow, methodic manner, orchestrated
a sinister, almost evil grin. His body shivered. Pushing back from the
table, he watched his mother's mouth purse and reposition to speak.
Jack fell backward to the floor upon hearing the words float in an airy
whisper—"Why did you kill him, Jackie?"

The bawl of a bull trespassing into the space from beyond the
bedroom windows brought Jack's eyes shooting open and his mind
separating from the shadows of the same dream that had haunted him

since childhood. Having rolled onto his right side sometime during the nap, he worked to regain his vision by staring at the chest of drawers and family photos atop.

Fighting through the fog and his mother's devastating accusation, he organized in his mind the actual events of that Christmas morning, sorting fact from folly.

The sequence of events, beginning with the toast and ending with the cutting words whispered from her lips, were nothing more than a conjured twist of the dream world. In fact, his mother had offered a loving smile, representing more an expression that he alone was the reason she existed; he alone was the reason she woke every morning, breathed in air, and continued about her life to help make something of his. When she crossed his mind, it was her warming smile he remembered most.

He often wondered why this Christmas that haunted his dreams was the last Christmas the family celebrated or recognized in their home and what he did to cause the ensuing fracture between his parents.

With residual segments of the dream flashing about, he wondered what time it was, and for the first time in forty-eight hours, felt a twinge of hunger and another surging within his kidneys. He thought of searching for a bathroom. His throat was dry but the feeling of hunger overpowered his desire for something to drink.

Jack separated his legs in a scissor motion underneath the bed coverings. His muscular function had improved, as had the motion in his shoulder. His ribcage was painful to the touch, much like the top of his head, the ache of which was compounded by a substantial pounding headache encompassing the entire right half of his skull.

Continuing to stretch and flex, he reconciled to accept the dream for what it was; a disturbing connection to his past he was sure never to resolve. What he couldn't accept was the last few minutes of Peetie's life and the role he played in the animal's death. He wished to reconcile the moment, but feared the sounds, smells, and images leading to the dog's last breath were burned permanently in his memory.

Rocking across the top of the pillow, haunted by his careless descent down the hill and the ever-present memory of the kick once inflicted on the animal, he replayed the words delivered by the doctor.

"Maybe he's right," he mumbled through a hoarse whisper, "maybe it's something best never forgotten." Jack swallowed deep, wondering what was causing the bull outside the window such distress.

Nearly drifting back to sleep, he stirred at the sound of a young child's playful giggle just beyond the bedroom door. Holding steady, fighting a powerful surge of pain rushing his temples, he brought to view the top half of the heavy wood door, illuminated to an earthy orange by the flame of the oil lamp, expecting it to fly open any moment.

The young voice stirred a familiarity but Jack was unable to place who or why. A slight rustling against the outside door molding brought his shoulder from off the mattress as he worked to gain a better vantage point. Short, heavy breaths burst through the cracked opening near the floor, prompting him to bark out a questioning "hello." The sound of his voice startled the young intruder. A sharp, happy squeal, followed by the rustling sounds of someone getting to their feet in haste, forced a tempered smile from his lips. It was clear he'd not yet met every Brossy.

As the uneven footsteps trampled down the hallway in the wake of a fit of laughter, he heard the sound of china clinking against glass and metal, as if someone was setting a table. His senses also honed to the ambrosial aroma of homemade bread and something fried—maybe pork. He wasn't sure what exactly was cooking, but didn't care. The smell of fresh bread alone sent his mouth to watering.

With his elbow and forearm planted deep into the soft mattress, he completed a slow roll onto his back, exhaling a quick burst of breath in response to the sharp pain piercing his side and surging around the inside of his skull. With eyelids crushed tight, he paused to allow the pain to pass before bringing into view the white beadboard slats of the ceiling and contemplating his chances of getting to his feet without assistance.

He peeked underneath the covers to assess his state of dress. Seeing boxer shorts—appearing to be his own—his mind set to stirring as to who among the Brossy clan assisted the doctor during the stripping and where the rest of his clothes might be currently. The room was cool, but much less so than his first recollection.

The sweet aromas wafting from the hallway were motivation enough to want to crawl from underneath the sheets but so was his growing anxiety to test his condition. Clinching the corner of the bed coverings in his fist, he launched the heap across his body.

Desiring to relieve the cool air pricking against his skin, he remembered the extra sweatshirt and pair of sweatpants packed in his duffle bag, which Sophie placed on the floor near the nightstand. Anxious to feel the soft cotton against his body, he secured a hold of the bedpost above, brought his knees to near his chest and swung his legs from underneath the covers over the edge of the bed. The move did not come without a price. He forced his eyes closed with a crushing wince, attempting to offset the effects of the pounding in his head by pushing the palm of his hand against the bandage wrapping his skull. The wound was sensitive to the touch and swollen to twice its size, preventing him from exerting enough pressure to make a difference. A ringing developed between his ears, as did a nauseous sensitivity. Breathing in short, quick gasps to stave off heaving, he folded his arms around his body to minimize the intense shiver rippling over his skin. The hardwood slabs below stung at the balls of his feet.

Jack held steady, shaking like a child just out of the bath on a cold winter's night, waiting for the pain and queasy sensation to pass. The ringing between his ears eased first, followed thereafter by the unsettling in his stomach. He opened his eyes to the room spinning about but was soon able to work through the spell.

The pounding dulled to a less intense but consistent throb. He noticed the duffle bag within an arm's reach on the floor and a copper-looking bowl on the nightstand appearing very much like an old-fashioned bedpan.

Whether a bedpan or not, he could wait no longer. Easing toward the nightstand, he managed a pain-free maneuver to lift from the mattress. His legs felt heavy and unsteady below him but nothing a little movement wouldn't remedy. Filling the copper basin almost to its brim relieved the stabbing pain in his side.

With his bladder relieved, Jack retrieved the duffle bag, tossed it to the opposite side of the mattress where the glow of the oil lamp would provide a better view, and worked his way around the room, bedpost by bedpost.

His gait improved with every step traveled. At the far post, he released his hand from a thin wood strip connecting the bedposts near their tops and shuffled across the frigid hardwood planks to the open bedroom door. Stretching around its corner like a mob lookout, he glanced down the hallway to the left, seeing nothing but a mass of black.

The way right stretched some forty paces where it ebbed from black shadow to a brilliant amber glow flooding in from an opening to the left. At the very end of the hall, he noticed a lone candle burning bright atop a wood table, just below a diamond-shaped stained-glass window. The sound of voices and metal pricking atop china suggested the Brossy's had sat down for dinner.

Relieved to find the child gone, Jack secured the door against the jamb, moved to the edge of the bed and dropped onto the mattress. He gave the bag a once over, spying the white cotton band of a pair of crew socks through a gash in its side, which he extracted and unraveled. What he thought would be an easy task of getting the socks over his toes and pulled to his ankles proved daunting and exhausting.

Unable to bend at the waist and limited by the use of just the one arm, seconds turned to minutes as he struggled to gain a comfortable position in which to pull his socks over toes glowing purple and ankles a frosty blue. Several failed attempts led to a serviceable maneuver, bringing instant relief. Eager to get the rest of his body covered, he unzipped the bag with a newfound urgency.

He rummaged through the tangled mess, brushing against several familiar items, including the gun and one of its loaded clips. He located his Chicago Bears hoodie and sweatpants at the bottom.

Where applying the socks proved more awkward, getting into the hoodie induced a painful current shooting down his entire left side. Sitting hunched over the edge of the bed, holding tight against his shoulder, he paused through a moment of bittersweet. The pain was excruciating, but the warmth building against his skin was invigorating. Up to this point, he held more concern for the head wound but now conceded the separated shoulder may be the most substantial of his injuries, and the most impeding to his overall mission. He needed a sling.

Jack worked to the bedroom door, cracking it to an eyeball's width to check the hallway. The sounds coming from the other end of the house grew more animated as fits of laughter rose above muffled conversation and clinking china plates. He breathed deep a new aroma joining the tantalizing combination, which his senses identified as apple pie. The accumulation sent his stomach to growling.

Jack nudged the door against the jamb, satisfied of his privacy, stepped to the bed, unzipped the duffle bag and began pulling its contents onto the mattress. Resting sidesaddle on the edge of the bed, he organized piles; clothing to the left, weapon and ammo clips to the right, another pile in front reserved for toiletries.

He stabbed for a couple pairs of green and blue-checkered boxers ensnared in the neck hole of a t-shirt. His motion paused as he spied the manila folder underneath the heap. Tossing the wad of clothing into the wrong pile, he retrieved the envelope, separated the tab and released its contents. The sight of the objects falling free worked like a tablet of ammonium carbonate cracked under his nostrils, as his sluggish mind awoke and was reintroduced to the very real circumstances facing him.

Jack managed with little hesitation the quick connection of a couple of dots. He recalled the contents of the telegram and the strange email received in his office describing directions to his very location. It became clear—the Eat at 8 Diner, Mick's, the old country store—he'd landed where he assured Sam he would not, to a tee, and as the email foretold. He remembered reading about the dock, dam, and a guiding light; all of which he traversed and followed without realizing what he was actually doing. *If the email is so,* he thought, *that means the telegram. . . .*

Looking to the quilt, he fingered over the exposed items to separate the telegram from the other pieces. He positioned it just inches from the lamp.

```
MR JACK L. CLARKE=
1794 M-P-E ACR-S DRIVE    OAK BR-OK    IL-=
YOU MU-T ASCEN--TAIRWAY   STOP
-OOR TO LEFT IS WH-RE SHE LAYS   ST-
I AM NOT THE-E    S-P
TH-Y HAVE BE-N CAL-D BUT SHE M-ST REMAIN   S-
N-T    -E-IV-RY   -O-A-   A-   2 P-
URGENT   STO-
MOD = DEC21-450PM-1923
```

Jack dropped the telegram from the light. Staring at the flame ascending and descending as it gnawed away at the oxygen surrounding its space, he recounted the most recent events and the cast of characters thrust into his presence.

Everything about the Brossys and the doctor now made sense—the manner in which they spoke; addressed one another; the obedience of their sons; the lack of electrical power and traditional lighting; it all added up. Jack repositioned himself next to the dufflebag.

"I'm there," he mulled, "I'm in 1923 . . . sonuvabitch." He looked to the nightstand at the bedpan. "I bet they don't even have indoor plumbing."

Searching the room, he conceded whoever wanted him here had accomplished their mission and done so with such stealth he did not see it coming.

"Now what?" he whispered, looking to the family pictures atop the chest of drawers.

He worked through the message of the telegram again, concentrating on filling in the blanks of the smudged and broken type based on the conclusions he and Sam had reached. Taking into account the location and how he arrived, he absorbed each line as if reading it anew, coming to grips with the fact it was indeed a set of instructions.

"How am I expected to act upon a message written as a riddle?" he whispered, swinging his body again toward the lamp, knowing he was now thrust into the author's timeline. "You must ascend the stairway . . . door to the left is where she lays . . . I am not there . . . they have been called but she must remain . . . who is she? . . . who's been called? . . . who's M.O.D.?"

Jack worked through in his mind the people he crossed paths with since leaving Chicago. He discounted the truckers, those at the truck stop and those at the Eat at 8 Diner; they all appeared to him in real time, other than Caroline. She was a mystery and one he'd have to get to the bottom of at some point.

He recalled the conversation with Chester and the story he relayed. Aside from the fact it made him conscious of what life might be like without his wife and daughters, he could draw no more conclusions.

He was certain he could check Chester off the list as the author of the telegram.

Moving along in his mind to Mick's, he waded through the faces and names of the hoodlum-filled dive, concluding no possible connections in that establishment.

"But how could the Eat at 8 Diner just disappear and why? What was the point?" Other than it being one step closer to 1923, he thought, what was the point?

Trying to find the logic that would lead him to the conclusion stirred his mind to the sudden violent and blinding wind that sent him splashing through the front door of the diner. It was obvious now the freak gust was the catalyst for his journey.

Maybe the place was just the halfway point, he thought. The diner was spot on for something set in the fifties and he guessed the subsequent gust in the parking lot delivered him the rest of the way. It would explain the feed and seed store and why Mr. Brossy had never heard of Highway 8.

Feeling no relief or peace of mind as to how he ended up seventy-five years in arrears, the questions concerning why this needed to be and who in the hell needed him to be here buzzed his conscious mind like a pesky, relentless gnat. He identified the doctor as the lone potential suspect in the bunch; not just because his name included one of the letters in "m. o. d.," but because of the bizarre manner with which he looked upon him.

"What reason would an old Irish country vet have for needing me in 1923?" he whispered. Jack pondered the question before his thoughts wandered to his family. *Where in the hell are they if I'm in 1923? What's happened to them?*

With his mind racing, he failed to recognize the chill against his skin had eased, as the snug-fitting cotton garments worked to bring his core temperature back to a more normal level. Looking to the oil lamp, analyzing the parallel between its bright flicker and the sparkle in Brooke's eyes, he longed to know if she'd ever look upon him again with the same desire or if he'd ever find his way back to her. Caught up in a mental image of her face and mesmerized by the methodic dance of the flame, he was jolted from its rhythmic pattern at the sound of a pop from the direction of the fireplace. He noticed the absence of flame as remnants of what remained in the grate cast a muted glow in shades of fire engine red and burnt orange.

Jack pushed from the bed, paused to stretch his back and neck, and approached the fireplace at a slow shuffle. He pulled a piece of split hickory nestled in a crevice cut into the stone façade and tossed it atop the heap. Red-hot embers peppered across the floor and atop his socks. A quick jab with the poker repositioned the stack enough to allow an influx of fresh oxygen, sending a burst of yellow flame high into the chimney. He extended the palm of his right hand toward the flame—the left as far as he could—bringing relief to parts of his body still seeking warmth.

Staring into the flame, he wrestled with just how much the Brossys knew of his predicament and how he planned to deal with them moving forward.

"They didn't seem to act as if they knew anything at all," he reassured himself, whispering to the flame as he would a confidant. "They treated me like an accident victim . . . nothing more."

He replayed their reactions to every situation as best he could recall. He concluded nothing out of the ordinary.

"If you tell them what's going on, they'll assume you are a lunatic or chalk it up to the head wound . . . there's no way they'll buy any of this."

Concluding less might be more, he felt certain the proper course of action was to say as little as possible.

But what about Danaher, he wondered. Something about him didn't add up, giving cause to believe he knew more than everyone else in the room. Searching the moment when he first came to, he recalled soon thereafter someone identifying him by name and either Mr. Brossy or Sophie mentioning that Danaher had informed them of his identity after finding his wallet.

Jack drew his eyes from the flame to look over his shoulder, as another vision stormed from the depths. Scanning his possessions scattered atop the mattress, he moved from the fireplace to assume a position hovering just above the mess. Flinging the small remaining pile of clothes to the foot of the bed, he searched for the billfold given to him by his girls on Father's Day two years earlier. Having picked through the lot, he grew puzzled at finding no sign. Searching under the duffle bag and the several layers of quilts also proved fruitless.

As a last ditch effort, he flipped the bag upside down, gave it a lengthy shake and tossed it to the floor. His body fell limp as he spied the black leather tri-fold lying unfolded atop his pistol. Having recalled stuffing the wallet into the bag just prior to his descent down the hill, his suspicion was confirmed.

"How could he have known my identity prior to their son retrieving the duffle bag?" Jack chewed on the question but for a moment.

"I knew it," he said, shaking his head. The doctor was the key and Jack grew anxious at the thought of getting him cornered.

Unable to ignore any longer the distinct pangs of hunger clawing at his gut and the smell of apples and cinnamon, he decided it was time to venture from the room and introduce himself to his caretakers. Reaching to the bed, he retrieved his wallet, pistol, and the two loaded ammo clips and secured the items under the mattress near the headboard. He next collected the telegram and antique newspaper—which he searched again for any new clues, before returning the pieces to the manila folder. The black and white photo slipped off the bed to the floor near his feet.

He brought the image into the light of the oil lamp, taking a moment to gaze upon the young girl holding her cat. The resemblance to Brooke was uncanny. Having forgotten the photo was in his possession, he contemplated the girl's identity and the reason for its delivery.

Not wanting the items to fall into the wrong hands, he slid the packet of clues under the mattress along with the rest of his loot. A quick search of the bedroom for his shoes proved unsuccessful. Moving to the door, he took a final account to ensure he'd not left anything exposed.

Jack scooped the lantern from the nightstand and stepped through the door feeling comfortable he'd left the room free of mystery. Banking to the right, he advanced down the hallway, counting on Sophie to have prepared enough food for everyone and hoping for an empty seat next to the good doctor.

CHAPTER 27

"Mama, did you hear the Howards are losing their homestead?" Speaking as he dunked half a biscuit into a bowl of white country gravy, the elder Brossy took advantage of a lull in conversation to deliver the account. The remark sucked dry the upbeat mood in the room and shifted the topic from a spirited exchange concerning the many chores in store in preparation of the family's looming Christmas Eve celebration.

Positioned opposite her husband at the end of the long, farmer's-style table just feet from the archway leading into the kitchen, Sophie froze in mid-motion of pressing a stabbed piece of boiled turnip to her lips. Just visible inside the perimeter of luminance supplied by a large, Victorian-style kerosene chandelier dangling above the center of the table, the family noticed her expression change and the color drain from her brow. Equally surprised by the news, the Brossy boys, seated next to each other at their father's left, both held steady their next bites, trading glances between their parents and knowing all too well the impact the Howards' loss could have on their own farm.

"My goodness," Sophie said, "the land has been in Clete's family since well before we became a state. Do you know of their plans?"

Olan wiped away a glob of gravy from his chin. "Don't know for sure," he said, taking a quick gulp of buttermilk. "John Quincy mentioned they may move to Detroit. Ellie's brother has him a job at one of those automobile plants . . . says he could get Clete on the line; maybe even find him a crop-sharing deal."

Sophie dropped her fork atop the unadorned white china plate left to her by her mother. "That poor, dear woman. And her with the four small ones. I just feel sick for them . . . especially at this time of year."

The family entered a moment of silence, each contemplating the personal impact. "We will all be sure to remember the Howards in our prayers tonight," Sophie demanded.

"Why would God let something like that happen, Ma?" Matty asked. "The Howards is nice people."

The question forced Sophie's eyes from the table as she considered an appropriate response but not before correcting his improper use of the English language.

"Are nice people," she said. Staring into the expanse of the home's open floor plan, Sophie searched her knowledge for an appropriate Bible verse. A warm smile ensued.

"'But if God doth so clothe the grass of the field, which today is,'" she said, pointing a finger to the ceiling, "'and tomorrow is cast into the oven, shall he not much more clothe you, O ye of little faith?' Do you remember that verse, son?"

"Yes, ma'am," Matty replied.

"Do you remember the book?"

"No ma'am." He dropped his head in disappointment.

"It's from Matthew, right Ma?" Caleb's voice echoed low and crisp across the table, much like his father's. If both men were out of her presence, she could no longer tell the two apart.

"Right . . . and it means God will take good care of the Howards despite their troubled times. They *are* good people and God will provide for them. Although He gives us all the right to make our own decisions, He will never abandon us when we stumble along the way. It is, however, our Christian duty to offer prayer for those in need. So you will both remember them this evening."

"Yes ma'am." The boys replied in unison.

"How many does that make now, Pa?" Caleb asked.

Olan pushed from the table, hooked his thumbs under his suspenders, and leaned deep into his chair. "I've lost count, son. Maybe ten, twelve farms . . . I don't know."

The boy was more than just a helping hand around the place; he was a partner now and knew as much about running the farm as he did himself.

"How we gonna replace the feed? We get more than half our hay and almost all the corn from his fields."

"Well, right soon after the first of the year, we'll scout out another supplier. It may be we buy some of them fields and farm them ourselves. We'll just have to see how it all washes out."

"Olan," Sophie pressed, "I don't think this is the time to be discussing their property . . . especially in front of the boys with the land still in their possession."

"These boys need to know the reality of the times we're in," he said. "Besides, it may be I can offer Clete a good fair price before the bankers steal it from him. It'd give him money in his pocket in case they do have to go to Detroit. I guarantee he'd rather see the land go to us than some bank getting it for a song. We're gonna need hay and corn to keep things going here."

"Why are so many of our friends losing their farms, Pa?" Matty asked. He reached across his brother's forearm, just beyond a large carved wood bowl of new potatoes, to grab another hunk of cornbread.

"Well son . . . the world's at peace. During the war, when all the men over there was fightin' it out, them countries in Europe were darn near starving to death and relied on us for their supply of grains; to feed their soldiers, people, and stock. Once the war ended, the demand all but dried up because they got back to farming their own lands. Many of our friends 'round here borrowed extra money to purchase more land and equipment to plant and harvest. So, as things returned to normal overseas, they were left with fields they still owed for, full of crops they couldn't sell, and equipment bought on credit they couldn't pay for. It just caught up with 'em."

"Will we lose our farm?" Caleb stretched an arm across his younger brother's shoulder.

Olan glanced at both his sons then to the far end of the table where he offered his childhood sweetheart a wink. "I don't think so, Matty," he said, "and we have your Ma to thank for that." The boys' view shifted to the other end of the table as if watching a serve rifled across the net at a tennis match.

"Oh, Olan . . . you know that's not true."

"Why it's as true as I'm sittin' here and sure as God has blessed us." The boys followed the return serve back to their father's side of the court. They were anxious for the details.

Olan recognized their interest. "A few months before you and your sister's fourth birthday," Olan said, dropping his elbows to the table and taking dead aim at Caleb, "your Ma and I hit on some hard times . . . I mean some real hard times. We'd just lost your sister and all but a couple of our herd to some sickness we still haven't figured out. We didn't have a paper bill or coin to our name, or the means to rebuild the stock, so I decided no more livestock; we were just going to crop farm.

"So, one night I saddled up the mule, rode over to 'ole Obediah Coble's place and traded what was left of our herd, the mule, and seven month's worth of hay and corn for a Gilpin Sulky plow—which was about ten years old—seventy-five sacks of seed and some other implements. When I got home and told your Ma what I'd done, she listened as calm as an afternoon spring breeze . . . listened to every word and said, 'O,'—she called me 'O' back then—'I'm sure you know what's best for this family and whatever you decide, I'll abide. But what do we have in our possession we don't need that we can sell to buy the horses to pull the plow?'" The boys both laughed. Their mother's grin equaled her husband's.

"So, I went back to see Obediah the next morning, told him I'd made a fool mistake and begged for his pardon. He was a nice old man . . . even told me he hadn't taken me serious because he knew I was red-hot about something. Anyway, your Ma was right, and with God's help, we found our way out of the hole and lived to tell about it."

Matty and Caleb shared a smile. The boys were close, despite their sibling moments, and very aware they'd be farming this land together for the rest of their lives. It was in their blood and both felt relief in their father's confidence in the future of the Brossy homestead.

"Don't worry boys, milk, butter, and cheese will always be in demand in this country . . . you can count on it."

"Regardless," Sophie interrupted, pointing at each of her men, "we will do whatever we can to help the Howards until they decide their future. It's times like this when people need you the most but are most unwilling to ask for help. Caleb, first thing in the morning after milking, I want you to ride over there and ask if they need anything and invite them to join us for Christmas Eve dinner."

"Yes ma'am . . . first thing."

"How were you able to rebuild the herd, Pa?" Matty asked.

"Now that's a right interesting story, son. I think you can credit the Lord working in mysterious ways . . . ain't that right Mama?"

"Isn't," Sophie corrected. "I don't know anything in this world truer," she said.

"One morning, right after Christmas, your Ma and I were in the barn tending to the chickens and milking the few cows left when we heard the dogs start going crazy. When we walked outside . . . well . . ."

The boys watched their father pause to allow a rare bit of exposed emotion to pass. The old man cleared his throat.

"Coming up the road were ten of our friends with ten of their friends, each holding on a rope tied to a Holstein behind 'em. The word spread about our troubles, including your sister's death, and farmers in this community just took it upon themselves to make it right; some of them folk came forty miles. It was a sight to behold for your Ma and I, and one I will remember long past my time on this earth."

The boys stared with mouths wide open. Olan leaned up against the table and pointed a finger in their direction.

"That, boys, is why when a neighbor finds themselves in trouble, the Brossys pitch in to help without question. Don't either of you ever forget it all the days of your life."

Jack leaned against the molding of the archway at the end of the hall, shifting his weight from one foot to the other. He held short, digesting the family's conversation and fighting a nervous tic building over his ensuing grand entrance. The hardwood floor below, cupped from age and the dry winter air, chilled straight through the thin wool of his socks, making it impossible to keep one foot down very long.

He'd crept down the narrow hallway like a thief, with lantern in hand, searching door to door along the way, hoping for a bathroom. He discovered only a few guest rooms appearing as if unused for years. Careful not to allow the glow of the lamp to breach the threshold of the entryway, he placed the antique flashlight on a small stand just beyond the second bedroom door, just past the halfway point of the hallway.

The home seemed in good repair for what he believed to be an early 1800s-something construction. The fact that it was clean did not surprise; he was certain Mrs. Brossy would have it no other way.

Whitewashed bead board paneled the hall's entire length halfway up the walls, pushing a strong scent of oil and lacquer into his path. The ceiling rose to a height much greater than his room. Appearing from out of the gold cast of the lantern's flame, he noticed a large painting hanging crooked above the lamp stand. The colorful oil, nestled in a stained, hand-made frame, depicted a small child strolling at a casual pace through a field of tall grasses in the wake of several cows progressing toward a nearby barn.

Jack broke from the family's engaging conversation to mull which facts regarding his being there he intended to share and those which he would dance around. He gathered already each Brossy held a penchant for probing—Mrs. Brossy specifically. Like his mother-in-law, Sophie intimidated him a bit and was someone he'd rather not spar with. Maybe it was her direct manner or the fact she could sling a Bible verse as would a cowboy with a six-shooter. He didn't know, and didn't care to find out.

"Just think before you speak," he whispered. "Remember what the old man told you."

Jack recollected his first fifteen minutes as an employee of Morgando and Rossi when John Junior shook his hand, welcomed him aboard and said, "Never use ten words when four will do, son."

He was nervous of the family's reaction. Drawing a deep breath, he pushed from the wall and stepped atop the wide plank hardwood opposite the threshold.

The scene beyond appeared as something from an exhibit at a historical museum. Stalling his progress to gaze into the open expanse of the Brossys' parlor, he marveled at its magnificent simplicity and charming yet antiquated furnishings. Any doubt as to the era in which he was now participating was dashed.

A mammoth bronze and brown-colored fieldstone fireplace roaring with flame at full capacity in a firebox cut high enough for a man to stand upright, was positioned on what he guessed was the front exterior wall of the home. At least twice the size of the one he restored in his den, its purpose was well beyond an aesthetic touch, appearing as the family's gathering point during the evening hours. A thick, hand-carved mantle, draped with pine garland and stretching the entire length of the fireplace, rested against the face atop beams jutting perpendicular from the stone.

The family's meager furnishings included a single, simple coffee table nestled between two small deep blue sofas upholstered in fabric plastered with a dizzying floral pattern. Several cushioned chairs, all unique to each other and of the rocking variety, flanked both couches. The ensemble positioned at a slight angle to the firebox, creating a cozy ambience beckoning for a steaming cup of hot chocolate, a quilted throw, and Grandpa's tales.

The atmosphere dripped of family and holiday cheer, enlivened by a massive fir tree decorated with strings of dried berries, popcorn, a smattering of glass ornaments, and every other homemade Christmas trinket imaginable. He noticed an open roll-top desk, stuffed full with stacks of papers, in the opposite corner and a dark-stained cabinet supporting a closed wood box with a polished brass phonograph bell on top.

Kerosene lanterns of all shapes and sizes littered the room; the largest hanging from the ceiling above the couch. The space reminded Jack of an old *Saturday Evening Post* cover he'd discovered in a trunk in his grandmother's attic.

The home's front door, a large hand-cut cherry beauty he assessed to be at least nine feet in height, was positioned to his immediate right just left of a large window encased in a flowery, light blue drapery. To his left, a half-moon shaped wood landing led to a set of stairs rising steeply to a second floor. He could hear the family's voices resonating much clearer and assumed their position to be just beyond the wall rising along the outside of the staircase.

Growing anxious over the looming reception, Jack shuffled to the staircase and grabbed hold of a simple newel post connected to the handrail. Leaning beyond the post, he brought into view the spacious dining area, recognizing Caleb's profile in the foreground and Mrs. Brossy at the far end of the table patting her lips with a napkin. Olan was seated at the end of the table nearest the staircase, facing the opposite direction. He did not see the first sign of Doctor Danaher. Scanning the space a final time, he drew in a deep breath before moving beyond the post and into the family's view. Sophie was the first to react.

"Mr. Clarke, my goodness . . . what are you doing out of bed?" she asked, springing to her feet. Her reaction startled the Brossy men, sending them scrambling to their feet as well. Olan dumped his chair backward to the floor.

"Why didn't you call out? I would be happy to bring whatever it is you need."

Jack paused to refamiliarize himself with the family's faces. He did not notice Matty when first entering the space; the boy spilled out from behind Caleb looking nothing like what he remembered. His surprise was evident as to just how different they appeared to him now. He was wrong about the boys. They were both their father's equal in height; Caleb appeared just as wide with Matty a little less so, but not far behind.

Olan appeared much older but every bit the tough, rugged type he displayed. Even as much time as Sophie had spent in his room, her petite and slender figure surprised him. Her resemblance to his mother-in-law increased with the improved light in the room. Sophie closed in and dropped her hand atop his forearm.

"I . . . I just wanted to get my legs under me. I was getting stiff; smelled the food," he said, pointing to the table, "and thought I should try to move around a little."

"You're hungry? When did you eat last?"

Jack viewed over the top of her to take an inventory of the remaining space. A large opening just behind Sophie's chair led to the kitchen. He also noticed another doorway at the far corner, not ten paces from the roll-top desk. Moving across the space, exchanging glances with each of the Brossy men, he could already see excitement building for the pending inquisition.

"About two days ago, I think."

"Are you sure you wouldn't rather eat in bed? I can bring you a tray."

"No. I'd rather try to eat sitting up if that's okay with you."

Jack appreciated the soft creases and lines of Sophie's face; the way it made her appear to smile when, in fact, she was showing no expression at all. She made a person want to smile, if for no other reason than to acknowledge the soothing comfort and warmth of her face.

"Certainly, Mr. Clarke," she said, patting his arm, "let me get you a plate and some silver."

"Please, call me Jack."

"I'm sorry, Mr. Clarke," she said, smiling, "it's just an old habit from my upbringing I fear I will never be able to break. My mother taught me first names are for family and close friends only."

Jack nodded.

"But I insist you call me Sophie."

"Okay, Sophie," he replied.

Sophie asked her husband as she passed to show their guest to the table. Without a word of contention, he extended a palm to the opposite side of the table from where his boys were standing. Slow to react, Jack dipped his chin in acceptance and followed his direction around the table.

Clearing Olan's position, he uncovered the source of the smells that had been taunting him. Thick sausage links, potatoes, a bowl of something leafy green and mushy, biscuits and cornbread, white gravy, hard-boiled eggs, something yellow chopped in small chunks, and two jars of halved tomatoes. He did not see an apple pie but the aroma of cinnamon hovered over the space nonetheless.

"Let me get that chair for ya," Olan said. Jack dropped back a step to allow enough room for the man to pull an armless high back from under the table.

Olan motioned for his sons to retake their positions at the table. The Brossy men eased into their chairs as Jack struggled into his. The bending motion stabbed at his side, forcing a quick and desperate reach for the corner of the table and a painful wince disturbing the muscles in his jaw. Olan jumped from his chair to place a hand against Jack's bicep, helping to balance him as he dropped to the hardwood seat.

"Okay?" Olan asked.

"Yeah, thank you." Jack brought both arms across his stomach as the pain ripped up and down his left side. Several cleansing breaths helped erase the sting. Olan leaned on the back legs of the chair, folded his arms across his chest and watched Jack work through the misery.

"We've got us a horse named Jack," Olan said. Jack figured the statement for a slight sarcasm and responded in kind.

"Well, I've got a better one for you," he said, rubbing his shoulder, "my middle name is London." The legs of Olan's chair hit hard atop the floor.

"You're kidding?"

Jack shook his head.

Olan planted his elbows on the table. "I named them for the author. Read *Call of the Wild* fifty times. Only book I've ever read complete in my life."

"He was my father's favorite author for the same reason," Jack replied.

"Well, I'll be dogged," Olan said, raking the tips of his fingers across his scalp. Jack winced as another round of pain shot down his arm.

"You have some right nasty injuries there, son." Olan paused for a response but got none. Jack worked to regain a normal breath. "I don't have the first idea as to how you're still alive. If the accident didn't kill ya, the walk from the mine should've."

The very manner of the statement and his suspecting look suggested to Jack the man didn't trust him as far as he could throw him.

"I don't know how or why I survived," Jack said, grimacing, trading glances among the three. "I guess it just wasn't my time."

He was hoping for a reaction from one of them; something indicating they knew the reasons for his visit. They were either well-schooled in the art of the poker face, or as surprised by his presence as he was. No matter, the distrust was mutual.

"Here you are, Mr. Clarke." Sophie moved in along his side to place a plate and silverware in front of his position.

"Now, we have some smoked sausage, biscuits, cornbread and gravy . . . uh . . . garden greens, boiled turnips, and some red potatoes. "What would you prefer?"

Jack gazed at the spread and requested, "A little bit of everything would be great."

"Would you like a cup of tea, buttermilk . . . some water, maybe?" He thought how a cold beer might taste right about now but guessed alcohol to be sinful in this household, even if they owned a refrigerator. He wondered if they'd been invented yet.

"Water will be fine."

"Matty, please go draw Mr. Clarke a glass a water."

"Yes ma'am." The boy excused himself from the table, actually saying the words, before moving off toward the kitchen. A wry smile broke across Jack's lips as he followed the boy's path along the opposite side of the table. The kid didn't so much as hesitate or form a questioning look on his face when given the instruction; his willing nature to serve and obey fascinated.

Sophie scooped and stabbed just enough from each bowl to fill his plate. She grabbed two biscuits and a hunk of cornbread and placed the plate before him.

"Enough for now, Mr. Clarke?" Sophie asked, presenting a plate packed with a healthy sample of each delicacy.

"Yeah, that's fine."

As the words spilled from his lips, Jack noted out of the corner of his eye Olan leaning toward him.

"Now, son," he said, bringing both elbows to the table, "I understand you're unfamiliar with this household and our ways and a stranger to these parts. But as long as you're a guest here you will respond to my wife with a 'yes or no ma'am.' Not 'yeah, yep, okay, nah, or uh-huh.' Do you understand?"

Sophie brought her hand to her mouth. "Olan, please . . . Mr. Clarke has been through a great deal today." Olan flashed the palm of his hand in his wife's direction.

"Mama, I know he's had a right rough day or two, but a man can be polite and respectful even on his death bed and I don't think this boy's dyin' anytime soon." Olan paused to allow his words to sink in. He captured Jack's eyes dead on.

"There's but a few things a man has complete control over in this world; one is his level of devotion to the Lord God, another is his word, and another is the way in which he treats others. I find any man who works to make sure he doesn't fail on those points is a man I can trust and a man I'll aid any time day or night. So, I ask you Mr. Clarke, do we have an understanding?"

Jack paused as Olan's words struck a chord, stirring a voice and an uncomfortable clinch in his left breast. He recalled Sam's crushing diatribe as to her disgust with his language and the manner with which he'd treated people over the years. Never taking his eyes off Olan, he considered the laundry list of things he must change if ever he wanted his family back. He figured he'd better get crackin'.

"I understand Mr. Brossy and I apologize. I meant no disrespect to you or your family."

The calm response caught Olan off guard. Having moved in closer, expecting a challenge, he was quick to withdraw to the back of his chair, and following a long pause, offered a nod of acceptance.

"As long as we understand one another, son," he said, looking with a nervous eye to Caleb as if embarrassed he made such a scene, "I believe we can all move forward. You can start by calling me Olan."

The man extended his hand across the table, which Jack accepted. Olan nodded to his son.

Caleb was next to fire his hand across the table. "My name's Caleb, Mr. Clarke . . . it's a pleasure to meet you," he said.

"Caleb," Jack said, shaking his hand and nodding. "You can all call me Jack."

"Fair enough, Jack," Olan said. "Go ahead now, you dig in."

"Whatever you need, Mr. Clarke, you just let me know." Sophie offered a compassionate tap atop his shoulder and moved to the other end of the table.

"Yes ma'am," he responded.

Jack caught sight of an arm extending past his right shoulder, placing a green-tinted glass on the table near his plate.

"Son, introduce yourself," Olan requested.

"My name's Matt," he said, extending his hand. "It's a pleasure to meet you."

"Pleasure to meet you, Matt. Please, call me Jack."

"Yes sir." Matt walked around his father's end of the table to retake his seat next to his brother. Settling in their chairs, the family enjoyed a moment of silence as each looked upon their guest with a million questions burning in their minds.

"You have fine boys. I'm sure you're very proud," Jack commented, looking to Sophie.

"Thank you, Mr. Clarke," she replied, "it's kind of you to say. They are very good boys. Don't know what we would do without them." She offered a pleasant smile. "You should eat. I'm afraid the food was already cold before you came in. I'm sorry."

Jack grabbed the fork and cut a two-inch chunk off the end of one of the two sausage links. The flavor against his tongue was unlike any he'd ever experienced and something more welcoming than anticipated. A heavy concentration of pepper combined with several herbs offered a spicy kick setting off a hot flash to his brow. A smooth, smoky aftertaste left him anxious for the next bite. He cut another piece, drenching it in white gravy; just when he thought it couldn't get any better.

"Boys, it's not polite to stare," Sophie said, redirecting her sons' attention from their guest. "Please finish your plates. We have a lot of work to do tomorrow and it's getting late."

Jack swallowed a bit of potato before biting off a chunk of biscuit. Both were dry and tasted bland; a quick gulp of metal-enriched water washed them down.

"I was expecting to see Doctor Danaher," he said, wiping his chin. "Has he gone?"

"He took off across the meadow a couple hours ago," Olan said. "One of our neighbors on the other side of the hollow was having some trouble with a horse."

"He felt sure you were going to be okay," Sophie insisted. "I'm certain he would've stayed on if he believed the situation to be grave."

"I hope I get a chance to talk to him. I'd like to thank him."

"Oh, he'll be back . . . said he had some business to attend here but wanted to check up on you before he headed for home," Olan said.

"I take it he's not from around here?"

"Don't know exactly where he lives," Olan said, looking somewhat puzzled as to why that was so. "I'd guess it's a fair distance from here though . . . at least from the way he talks."

"Have you known him long?"

"No sir. He dropped in around here sorta sudden like. It sure surprised all of us. Just one day out of the clear blue sky, we have ourselves a country vet no one knows the first thing about. A blessing from the Lord, I suppose."

"How long has he been in the community?"

"Maybe a month, maybe less. I know he came from Ireland and hear tell has quite a way with livestock. Don't know much other than that."

"I sure am sorry about your dog, Mr. Clarke," Matty said. The room fell silent; all motion at the table stalled.

"Matty," Sophie snapped, "you mind your manners. Now I told you boys to finish your meal and get on about your chores. Caleb, please take your plate into the kitchen and get Roo on upstairs and into bed. I'm sure she's in the mud room pestering those baby chicks."

Caleb excused himself from the table. Matty cleared his plate of a final piece of turnip and tomato.

Jack swallowed deep as the sting of the dog's final moments rifled across his conscience. He knew the boy meant no harm. An automatic reflex to the subject sent his thumb sliding across the tips of his fingers. He wondered if the feeling of life leaving Peetie's body would ever subside.

"I'm sorry, Mr. Clarke," Sophie said, breaking his contemplation. "The boys are fond of all animals and hate seeing anything pass."

"It's okay Matt," Jack said, "I appreciate your concern. I'm sorry too; more than I can tell you. I wish I could take it back . . . I wish I could take a lot of things back," he said, his voice trailing off. Sophie exchanged a puzzled look with her husband.

"Is he buried?" Jack asked Olan.

"I'm afraid not . . . ground is frozen solid. We'll have to wait awhile. Doc wrapped him in a couple potato sacks and tucked him in a safe place where no critters can get to him."

Jack reached across his plate to retrieve the green-tinted glass. As he eased the frigid liquid into his mouth, he caught out of the corner of his eye Caleb approaching from the right toting a small child bobbing up and down just below his hip. Still draining the water into his gut, he saw the boy pause just behind his shoulder.

"Roo, say hello to Mr. Clarke."

CHAPTER 28

Before the echo of glass shattering against china faded beneath the shrill of her youngest child's scream, Sophie leapt from her chair and raced to Roo's side. Sweeping the startled four-year-old into her arms, clear of the hundreds of tiny green-tinted glass shards now scattered about the floor, she did her best to calm her, not knowing if the outburst was prompted by the falling and breaking glass or the shock of their guest's reaction as he came eye-to-eye with the child.

Maintaining a steady balance on the back legs of his chair, Olan did not move an inch from the moment the glass slipped from Jack's hand to watching him nearly fall to the floor backward as he reacted to the introduction. With hands clasped behind his neck, a look of stupor overtook his initial expression of surprise. The change caught Caleb's attention, reminding him of the time he'd confessed to his father that the reason his younger brother had broken his arm was because he had urged the boy to jump from that the hay loft, stating that if he flapped his arms fast enough he could fly.

"Mr. Clarke," Sophie scolded, holding Roo tight against her neck, "please do explain yourself."

Jack's face flushed a deep red as embarrassment mixed with utter shock. With his mouth ajar, he glanced over his shoulder with a nervous eye to Olan before releasing the grip managed at the last second against the tabletop.

"I'm . . . I'm so sorry," he said, looking up toward Sophie. She studied his face; his confusion was real and surprise undeniable.

"I'm truly sorry. She's the spitting image of someone I know. It just caught me off guard . . . it . . . just surprised me." Jack glanced again at Olan; his gaze remained unchanged.

"Is she okay?" Jack asked. The servile look on his face neutralized Sophie's annoyance. She moved the hair from off her daughter's cheek and patted her behind.

"I'm sure she'll be fine. A little shaken is all."

Jack eased against the seatback, cupped a hand against his forehead and pushed a line of sweat toward his scalp. A new anxiety awakened. It was *her*; it was the girl in the black and white photo.

"Caleb, please take your sister upstairs and get her into bed; I'll be up in a bit."

Sophie passed the girl into her eldest son's arms and shifted to meet Matt, who reentered from the kitchen toting a homemade broom and dustpan. Jack stared at the young girl as Caleb passed. Buried the fold of her brother's neck, she made sure to keep her face concealed. He was desperate to confirm.

"I'm sorry sweetheart," he said, hoping she'd lift at the sound of his voice. "I didn't mean to scare you." His plea went unrecognized.

Jack followed the pair as they moved through the parlor. Soon out of view upon their turn up the staircase, a quick redirect brought him again into the crosshairs of the elder Brossy's gaze. Olan dropped the front legs of his chair to the floor. The table vibrated as his elbows planted on the surface.

"Mr. Clarke, why is it you're here?" The old man clasped his hands, settling the balled-up flesh against his lips. Sophie stopped in mid-stroke of pushing another small pile of glass slivers into the dustpan.

Jack mashed his jaw tight, angered over his mistimed reaction. He knew he'd further incited the Brossy's suspicions and would now have to act fast to concoct a plausible explanation. Sophie worked in another push of the broom as the family waited for a response.

"I'm very sorry," he said, looking to Olan. "I had no intention of scaring your daughter. I don't know what came over . . ."

"Son," Olan interrupted, "don't worry, she'll be fine. She's had plenty of scares around this farm and will have plenty more. Why are you here?" His voice was calm; his body language not so much. Jack hesitated, wavering between the best of three white lies he'd prepared. He inspected the soggy mess of his dinner plate before selecting lie number two.

"I'm here to visit family," he said, less assertively than he intended.

"Well, I know just about everyone within forty mile of this farm and don't recall anyone by the name of Clarke. There's a bunch-full of Clarksons on the other side of Breezewood, but I don't know any Clarkes."

"It's my wife's family . . . Mayberry's their name."

"No Mayberrys, strawberries, or any other berries round here." Olan moved his hands away from his mouth.

"They're not from around here. They live in Iron River . . . it's north of here."

Olan crossed his arms and fell against his seatback. "Sure it's north of here . . . 'bout 150 miles worth of back roads and pastures as far as the eye can see. I've fished Half Moon Lake plenty times. How'd you come to miss your mark by such a margin? You'd of had to make several exact turns off the path to find us way over here . . . enough so it makes me think you being here was no mistake."

Jack kept a sharp focus on his plate. If he just knew how easy it was to find this place, he thought.

"How 'bout it, son?" Olan asked.

"I was getting tired and stopped to ask directions to the nearest town," he said, dragging his gaze to meet Olan eye-to-eye. "A man at a feed store pointed me this way . . . said I'd find Cartersville on the other side of Brossy's Hollow."

"Who told you?" Olan snapped, hoping to extract a lie.

"The fella at the store . . . I guess he was the owner. It was late, and he was there alone. I didn't catch his name. I saw the name of the place on the outside, but I can't remember."

"Fossee's?" Olan asked.

"Yes, I think so." Jack moved his hand over the bandage. He replayed again the image of their daughter. The reality of it was haunting; he could feel his skin still tingling under his sweatshirt.

"You're lucky he didn't fill your hide full of buckshot . . . wouldn't be the first time Jed's peppered a stranger hangin' 'round late at night."

"Matty, please take this to the mud room, then I want you to get on upstairs and into bed," Sophie said, passing off the broom and dustpan. The boy obliged; Sophie settled into a chair next to her husband.

"Mr. Clarke," she said, "you were closer to the town of Cameron, why didn't you find a place there to spend the night?"

"Right," Olan agreed. "Seems Fossee would've pointed you there first. Cartersville doesn't have a hotel."

Jack glanced at both searching for his next move.

"Good night Mama . . . Pa," Matty said as he passed the table.

"Good night son. Please make sure Roo is in bed."

"Yes ma'am. Good night Mr. Clarke." Matty sent a nervous glance toward his parents to gauge their reaction. "It was nice meeting you." Jack turned to the boy and nodded.

The Brossys waited for their son to ascend to the second level. With his energy depleting and a pounding returning to his head, Jack wanted nothing more than to excuse himself and retire to the underside of his covers. A quick scan of their faces suggested they were far from satisfied.

"Why Roo?" Jack asked, changing the subject.

"I'm sorry?" Sophie squinted; a puzzled look formed across her face.

"Your daughter's name . . . why Roo?"

"Oh . . . Matty gave her that nickname when she was just a little thing," she said.

"One of my kin ended up in Australia after getting shot up during the war," Olan said, "and came home with a picture of a real-to-goodness kangaroo. He showed the children how the animal hopped around. Well, she took to aping him. She hopped around this place with a potato sack tied to her waist for months on end. One day Matty called her Roo—you know, short for kangaroo—and it's been Roo ever since. Her birth name is Olivia Jean."

"She's a very pretty young girl," he said. "How old is she?"

"Four," Sophie replied, smiling. "Who is it she reminds you of?"

Jack invoked the advice of his boss. "Just a friend of a friend."

"Seems quite the overreaction for just a friend of a friend?" Olan jabbed.

"No, just a friend of a friend. The resemblance is dead on."

"Speaking of the war," Olan continued, "where were you stationed?"

"Me?" Jack asked, burying his index finger into his chest. "I wasn't stationed anywhere. I didn't serve in the war."

"How did such a young, strappin' fella like yourself manage to avoid gettin' drafted? I read somewhere there were more than two million boys drafted."

"Lucky, I guess," Jack said.

"Lucky?" Olan pushed from his seatback to the edge of the table. "Why, they threw me out of the community hall three times before I took no for an answer. They said I was too old to join in the fight." He moved in close and pointed a finger in Jack's direction. "I'll tell ya though, had I been a few years younger, I'd been first in line and had that fight settled in—"

"Olan," Sophie cut in, "reasons why Mr. Clarke did or did not fight in the war is none of our affair. He doesn't owe us an explanation."

Jack released a sigh, relieved for her rescue. He was pleased the subject was moving in a different direction.

"However, he does owe us the truth as to why he's here. Mr. Clarke, God knows I would never turn my back on a stranger in need. As Jesus told His disciples 'for I was hungry and you gave me food, I was thirsty and you gave me drink, I was a stranger and you invited me in . . . just as you did it for one of the least of these brothers or sisters of mine, you did it for me.' Are you familiar with that verse?" she asked, keen to hear his answer.

"No ma'am . . . I'm not," Jack replied.

"Matthew twenty-five, thirty-five. We want to help you because it's God's will. I ask you to respect us by dealing in truth. I know a great deal has happened to you in the past few days but I also know there is much more to your story than you are letting on. We would appreciate the truth."

Jack fell spellbound at the sophistication with which Sophie expressed her thoughts. Her manner calmed and soothed in such a way, his mind was quick to associate it with the rapture he felt for his mother in the very early years of his life. He absorbed Sophie's words and intent. Her power went far beyond the honor and integrity with which she chose to live her own life and influence her family. He could not look her in the eye and lie. He thought of a response but was consumed with wonder as to how this woman could so make him want her respect. He sensed a trust previously known only with Sam.

"The truth is," he started, pausing to consider the can of worms he was about to unleash, "I'm searching for my wife and daughters. She was on the way to visit her family and didn't show up. I set out to look for them."

"You have daughters?" Sophie asked.

"Two. Julianna and Jordan."

"And your wife's name?"

"Brooke."

"What lovely names. I'm sure they mean everything in the world to you."

"Yes ma'am, they do . . . more than anything."

"What makes you think they're 'round here?" Olan asked.

Jack worried one of them would soon ask a question he'd not be able to answer. How could he explain it all?

"Someone told me they a saw a woman fitting her description having car trouble, heading in the direction of Cartersville with a man who appeared to be helping her."

Olan cracked a puzzling smile. "How do you know she wasn't headed for Cameron?"

Knowing he could not explain Jubel Bigsby, Jack said, "I don't. I was just going on what I was told. Is Cartersville near?"

"About eight miles by horse, fifteen by car," Olan said. "I know the town well, if you can call it a town. It's no bigger than an ink blot. I know most of the people too. I was a co-op partner of a cheese factory there . . . 'til it burned to the ground 'bout five years ago," he said, disappointed. "But I am part owner of the Cartersville Farmers' Store and Market Association." His chest expanded as he buried his thumbs under his overall straps.

"I just need to get to Cartersville as soon as possible."

"So you allowed your wife to take your daughters in an automobile this time of year and drive from Chicago to Iron River . . . alone?" Olan asked.

"I couldn't get away from work and was planning on meeting them up there."

"I don't know what kind of automobiles you have," Olan said, "but it'd take the best Model-T at least two days, not counting the snow, the roads and if you were able to find enough gas along the way. And you let her and your daughters go off alone?"

Jack drew forward. The draining expression on his face prompted Sophie to intervene.

"Olan, he told us why he is here."

Olan noticed the change in her demeanor. She was ready to accept his word and move on; he wasn't.

"I'm very sorry about your family, Mr. Clarke," she said. "With all you have been through, I can only guess how concerned you must be. I am certain you will agree there is nothing more you can do at the moment in your condition, and I'm afraid the weather may delay you even further.

"If he is feeling better, is it possible we could get him to the Pritchert farm in the next few days? He may be able to use their phone to get in touch with his family."

"You don't have a phone?" Jack asked.

"I'm afraid not," Sophie said, rolling her eyes.

Olan rationalized her disappointment. "I'm not much for those new-fangled devices they keep comin' up with. Anyway, Fossee's is less than an hour away by wagon if'n there ever was a need to telephone someone. We could go there but would have no chance of getting the team or the truck up Pilot's Peak . . . you know the steep hill I'm talking about. Climbin' the old telegraph pole we used to have in the south field was a lot easier."

It didn't matter much anyway and Jack knew it. Who am I going to call, he thought . . . the two-year-old father or mother of my unborn wife? You don't even know if they were alive in 1923.

"It's okay," Jack said. "My wife's parents don't have a phone either. I wouldn't know who to call who could contact them."

"Then how do you know your wife went missing?" Olan probed.

Jack shrugged. "They must have called me from a neighbor's phone. I didn't ask."

"Well, I guess all we can do is wait out this weather and get you wherever it is you need to go just as soon as we can," Sophie said.

"I'd appreciate it," Jack said with a slight smile. "I'm sorry for the mess on the table."

"Don't worry—it's not the first or last broken glass in this house. I know it was an accident."

"And, again, I'm sorry for scaring your daughter. I will look forward to seeing her in the morning to offer my apologies."

"I would like to know a little bit more about this automobile you spoke of," Olan said, folding his arms across his chest. "A Hummer, was it?"

Jack massaged his thumb and forefinger over his temples; the pounding was gaining in intensity.

"I'm feeling very tired," he said, "I think maybe I should go to bed."

Olan's eyes narrowed. His expression layered with suspicion. Grunting, he said, "Okay, Jack. Maybe we can pick up where we left off in the morning . . . when you're feeling better."

Jack responded with an unconvincing "sure" following a lengthy pause.

"I want to thank you both for everything," he said, directing his comment away from them. "I'm sorry for all the trouble I've caused.

I'm also sorry for losing my composure earlier; I mean . . . with the dog and all. I don't make a habit of doing that."

Staring at his wife, Olan grew amused at the concerned look upon her face. He, on the other hand, refused to believe a man who failed to look him in the eye.

"Why would you think you would need to apologize for your emotions?" Sophie asked.

Jack kept his silence. Light from the kerosene lamp above skimmed off his pupils as he adjusted them toward the floor. Sophie could see they'd grown wet.

"Having or expressing emotion is nothing to be ashamed of, especially over something as traumatic as what we all witnessed. Your reaction was normal." She studied his face. His look troubled her heart.

"Anyway," Jack continued, "I promise I'll be on my way as soon as I'm able."

"As long as it takes . . . there's no rush," Sophie said. "Would you like a little more to eat? I'd be happy to get you a clean plate."

"No ma'am. I think I need to get to bed."

"Would you like me to heat a couple bricks for you?"

Jack scooted the chair away from the table. "No. But I would appreciate an extra blanket . . . if you have one."

"You go on and get settled. I'll bring one to you presently."

Pushing from the tabletop, Jack brought his aching body upright. The movement sent an ice cream-like rush to his head causing a momentary deficit of his equilibrium. Holding tight to the table, he allowed the dizzying wave to pass and the blood in his legs to circulate before stepping away.

"Wait, Mr. Clarke," Sophie said, "you'll need this."

Jack paused as she removed the glass shade off an oil lamp and held it steady as Olan struck a match to light the wick.

"I'm afraid we don't have electric light either . . . maybe someday."

"Electricity costs money," Olan growled. "I ain't never seen an oil lamp which didn't provide all the light I needed."

Sophie smiled, thankful her children were not present to hear their father butcher the English language. Returning the glass shade atop the lamp, she released it into Olan's hands. Olan passed the lamp to Jack, letting go following a lengthy, silent exchange. As if one had called the other following the last draw in a game of stud, each traded a simple nod.

Jack knew the man didn't buy his story. He also knew he had to be on his way as soon as possible.

A light rap against the bedroom door failed to pull Jack from the depths of the black and white picture of the young girl positioned just inches from the kerosene lamp and even closer to his face. Studying every detail, and brooding over doubt now spreading as to whether this girl and Roo were one in the same, he replayed the moment of contact with her, attempting to construct a clearer image.

The shock of their meeting stained his perception. A second and much sharper knock on his door interrupted his reverie, sending him scrambling to stuff the image between his legs under the mattress. Jack grabbed his duffle bag and tossed it to the floor on the opposite side of the bed.

"Mr. Clarke, is everything quite alright?"

"Uh . . . yes ma'am, please . . . come in."

Inching the door away from the jamb, Sophie peeked through the growing crack to ensure their guest was decent.

"I'm very sorry," she said, moving full into the room. "I must apologize. I forgot I'd set your shoes on the stove in the kitchen to dry. Your feet must be freezing."

"No, I'm fine . . . I'm okay."

"Well, here are your shoes. I took the liberty of washing your clothes. I'm afraid I could not get all the blood out," she said, bending low in his direction. Jack grabbed the lot out of the fold of her arm and placed them on the floor near the nightstand.

"I must say, I've not seen shoes or clothes of these types in all my life; not even in the Sears and Roebuck. Where did you find them, if I may ask?"

"My wife bought them for me on a trip out east."

"Not surprising," she said, moving across the room toward the dresser. "Whenever someone has something new around these parts, it seems to come from New York or Boston. I've brought you a pair of long underwear . . . you are welcome to them if you desire."

"I think I'll be just fine with what I have on."

Sophie dropped the dingy white clump atop the dresser. "Well, if you change your mind, I'll leave them here." She placed the extra quilt on the edge of the bed.

"I see you found the bedpan."

"I'm sorry I didn't know what to do. I wasn't sure if there was a bathroom near."

"That's what it's for. We have one bathroom upstairs. It has a tub but no running water or toilet. If you are in need of something more than a bedpan, the outhouse is located just through the kitchen and down a short path. You will see a lantern and a box of matches on the counter by the door . . . if you have the urge in the middle of the night. I will dispose of this and set it outside your door."

Moving to the fireplace, she pulled the poker from its latch and adjusted the logs in the grate. A quick stab released a scent of burnt hickory into the room.

"I want to thank you," Jack said, maneuvering his legs under the covers.

"You've already thanked me Mr. Clarke, and I appreciate it," she said over her shoulder. "Under the circumstances, I'm thankful you managed to find your way to us. Surely you would have been dead had it not been the case. Praise be to the Lord."

"No, you don't understand . . . I want to thank you for not asking me why."

"Why what, Mr. Clarke?"

"Why my wife and daughters were traveling alone." Sophie placed a heap of thatch between the logs. A wave of heavy white smoke preceded a bright ruby flame. She extracted a couple of fresh logs from the bin.

"One does not enter the home of a stranger uninvited. We asked why you were here and you told us."

"So, you believe me?"

Sophie placed the logs atop the new flame, satisfied the lot would offer heat well into the morning hours. Wiping her hands against her apron, she turned to the window to draw a set of corn silk-colored lace sheers across the panes before moving to the end of the bed and grabbing hold of the bedpost.

"I believe you are searching for your wife and daughters."

"So, you don't believe me."

"I believe what you were willing to share. If there is more and you wish to tell me, I will be happy help or lend an ear . . . whichever you require. Beyond that, it is a matter between you and God."

"God," Jack said expelling a sigh. "Why is it everyone assumes God is right here walking alongside of us at every moment? How can you be so sure He or it exists? And if He or it does exist, where does it say He's there for every single person? As I recall, He has a chosen people."

Sophie moved beyond the bedpost and settled on the corner of the bed. The blue of her eyes burst forth from the shadows like precious gems backlit by the summer sun.

"Man is born with the Holy Spirit in his heart," she said, wrapping an arm around the bedpost. "I believe this. And it's up to man to seek out God's glory. It's stated many times and many places in the Bible, but Jeremiah twenty-nine, thirteen is as specific as the Lord can make it. 'And ye shall seek me, and find me, when ye shall search for me with all your heart.' Are you familiar with that verse?"

Jack settled into the pillows situated against the headboard. Sophie moved off the corner seeing his desire to stretch his legs further under the quilts.

"I'm familiar with the reference. I've heard it more times than I can count. I also think it's easy for people like you to point out God's grace and His many wonders and not consider the possibility betrayal goes both ways. God may be perfect in the verses and passages you've engraved in your memory and He may have filled your life with such abundant blessings you have no choice but to sing His praises. But in my world, in my reality, from what I've come from, He's left me to fend for myself. I don't expect you or anyone else to understand."

"If you are such a non-believer, why do you reference His abandonment? If your heart felt no presence in the first place, would not the thought of abandonment be nonexistent?"

"All I know," Jack said, unwilling to look upon her, "the times I've needed His presence in my life, He or it was nowhere to be found. I'm surprised He didn't kill me when He had the chance."

"Mr. Clarke," Sophie shot back. "You should be ashamed of making such a statement. Yours is not a predicament new or extraordinary. No . . . you *have* known God and have loved God before; something happened to change your attitude. Tempting God, however, is blasphemous. 'It is written again, thou shalt not tempt the Lord thy God.'"

"You throw verses around as if it empowers you to evoke change and make everything right. Well, it doesn't and there's nothing you or anyone can quote from the Bible to restore what God stole from me.

"Is it not true if you drug your children out into the middle of the woods and left them to survive on their own you'd be vilified as a monster? Why then, when God does the exact same thing, are we obliged to get down on our knees like dogs and praise the glory of His name?"

Sophie retreated from the side of the bed clutching tight to the crucifix hanging from her neck. The look sweeping across Jack's face stalled her next point.

"You are a very careless and foolish young man," she said, following several moments contemplating her response. "To think you could equate God to a mere mortal being . . . how dare you. God is here. He is with you right now. You have abandoned *Him*. Need I remind you, you called out His very name the moment you saw your dog this afternoon?" Sophie inched closer.

"How are we to grow, mature, prosper, become self-sufficient and accountable if at every turn God pleases our every whim? Are not our struggles, and how we deal with them, a direct reflection of who we become and the character we develop? You can blame God for all the misfortune in your life, Mr. Clarke, but I'm sure even you can dig deep and reconcile a challenging circumstance in which you have made a better man of yourself."

Ready with a rebuttal, Jack opened his mouth to speak but was quick to pull back as her words gave reason for pause. He reckoned his current predicament and the feelings stirring within regarding his family. Unwilling to admit to the validity of her point, he maintained a stubborn air.

"Regardless," he said, taking a nervous swallow, "as you yourself said, you do not enter the home of a stranger uninvited. Well, I'm not interested in the topic of God. God left me for dead," he said, his voice fading. "I cannot praise Him for abandoning me."

"Very well," she replied, wondering what could have happened to foster such hate. Releasing her grip of the cross, she cleared her throat and straightened her body as if suggesting his verbal assault did little to the many layers of religious armor encircling her being. She proceeded toward the door at a snappy clip.

"I will be sure to respect your position in the future. If you require anything further just call to me from the bottom of the stairs. Good night, Mr. Clarke."

Regretting sharing so much, he attempted to stall her exit. "Mrs. Brossy, I'm sorry . . . I did not mean to—"

As the heavy door pulled against the jamb, his voice fell silent. Releasing a sigh, he collapsed against the cold, hardwood headboard, listening as her footsteps faded down the hallway.

"Don't use ten words when four will do," he whispered, rolling across the headboard knowing he had alienated his lone ally amongst the Brossy clan. "Well done asshole. Now you have two apologies to make in the morning."

Jack squirmed further under the sheets, bringing instant relief to the burn in his side and ache in his shoulder. He stretched atop the soft surface, expelling a deep sigh in response to the mounting warmth enveloping his body. He tugged the covers tight up under his chin and searched deep into the bright amber flames shooting high into the firebox. The peace of the flicker and its rhythmic crackling against the dried stack soon rendered his mind a cerebral playground on which spun the confluence of facts, faces, and cryptic instructions that occupied every ounce of his rational thought.

Sophie's words created a stir in his heart, but his predicament offered enough challenges; there were much more important things to digest rather than wasting time explaining or defending his stance regarding the Almighty. The topic of God passed into the shadows of his mind like a fallen leaf floating away on the current of a secluded stream.

Fighting heavy eyelids, he kept the wheels of his mind in motion, exploring the significance of the young girl, her role in the scheme of all things, and the reasons why her picture had been hand-delivered to him.

"What could she have to do with me finding Brooke?" he whispered, recalling their meeting.

Jack was certain he'd not misjudged what his senses first recognized, contradicting his earlier doubt.

"It's her," he whispered, "I know she's the girl in the picture."

Captured by the pattern of the flames, he searched for a connecting dot; it just didn't add up.

He switched his gaze to the silver tint of the moon leaking through the sheers. Relieved the evening sky was clear of the snow clouds that had so dominated the day, he hoped dawn would break with equal clarity. Anxiety seeped into his conscience at the prospects of moving on from the Brossy homestead and making his way into Cartersville.

Losing the battle with the conscious world, he shifted toward the fireplace and the violent combust inside the box, where the image of himself on the backside of the newspaper flashed before his tired eyes. Whether triggered by the smoke billowing into the chimney or the flames chasing just behind, his mind aroused to the picture of himself in the newspaper. An instant later, as he slipped into shadow, a portion of the telegram stirred what was left of his conscious thought: "the room to the left is where she lies."

CHAPTER 29

December 24

Leaning against the chilled fieldstone of the bedroom fireplace, peeking behind lace sheers reeking of must from seasons of permanent placement, Jack scanned over the farm grounds and horizon, falling captive to the utter magnificence of the cloudless, mid-morning sky.

Bursting a deep, cobalt blue, the brilliant tone of the heavens offered a stunning backdrop against the snow-covered gable roof protecting the contents of the Brossys' barn. The muffled bawl of cattle—no doubt in the midst of milking—and the bleating of sheep offered a sense of peace; a sense of home.

Christmas Eve day had dawned bright, crisp, and clear, triggering optimism the weather was ready and willing to cooperate with Jack's desire to flee the farm for Cartersville. Scanning the deepest blue of the sky where it backlit a dense, snow-covered line of pines rising along a ridge to the south, he formed a contented smile in anticipation of continuing the mission. Unable to spot the exact location of the sun, and based on the angle of its reflection against a few barn windows, he guessed the time of day at or near the ten o'clock hour.

Having slept like a fat rock, he awakened when the ambitious aroma of bacon, pancakes, potatoes, and fresh coffee infiltrated the room. Once the haze cleared from his mind, he noticed the blue brilliance bulging through the sheers and moved from his bed to the window as excitement churned within.

His body appreciated the deep, tranquil sleep, as his limbs and joints now moved upon his every command and nearly free of pain. His shoulder was stiff and sore to the touch but the range of motion was improved. A slight headache pushed against his left temple.

Pulling his attention from the sky, Jack scanned the barn, admiring its stunning construction and likeness to the many turn-of-the-century features he recognized in his own restoration project. A fieldstone and mortar foundation, splattered with patches of snow and ice clinging to crevices concealed from the bright sunlight, rose from the frozen earth to a height of four feet before merging to vertical board planks shedding in spots its crimson-colored top coat.

Jack studied the large silo attached at the southeast corner, recalling the sight of the massive structure during his trek from the lake. Setting the silo's height at near forty feet and girth at no less than fifteen, he marveled at its stunning multi-colored stacked stone construction, its tapered design, and the hand-cut cedar shingles capping its top. If his circumstances were different, he'd relish an opportunity to investigate the structure.

Distracted by the aroma, he swallowed deep and released the sheers from his grip. Although eager to collect his possessions and be on his way, he did not know when he'd have another chance to eat. Having not gotten nearly enough of Sophie's home cooked meal down before the chaotic meeting with Roo, he hoped to get an uninterrupted run at whatever was prepared for the family this fine morning, including the leftover sausage and gravy from last evening's menu.

He collected his shoes from off the floor and the items stuffed under the mattress. Wishing to step into a clean pair of underwear, he tossed the manila folder, gun and ammo clips atop the mattress and shuffled around the bed in search of the battered duffle bag he'd tossed to the floor.

His progress stalled upon reaching the dresser and an image of a woman in one of the black and white pictures aligned on top. Snapped from a good distance away and pixilated to the point that identifying specific facial attributes proved difficult, the image featured a family of four, huddled arm-in-arm in front of the Brossys' silo.

It appeared taken on a dark and gray winter day as snow whizzed across the frame as distorted, elongated streaks. The happy group stood in a snowdrift knee high, waving at the camera with mitted hands.

He reached for the frame to bring it close for a more thorough inspection. The woman appeared to be both wife and mother of the others in the photo. Although wearing a long, bulky coat collecting in a heap atop the snow, he could tell she was of slender body.

Her long neckline and dark, straight hair flowing over her shoulders to a length equal to that at which Brooke kept her own cropped, left plenty of room for his imagination to consider the two could pass for sisters. If nothing else, the way the woman's smile positioned, slanted to one side, was a near perfect match.

Jack studied the two children standing in the forefront. They appeared female, similar in age to Jordan and Julianna, and if the photo were taken closer than twenty feet away, he guessed with high probability they were twins.

With a lump growing in his throat, he traded glances between the girls and their mother, recalling a photo of himself and his daughters in the front yard finishing off the middle portion of a snowman.

The man standing to the woman's left, who he assumed was her husband based on how tight around her waist he'd secured his arm, was indistinguishable, due to a large flake of snow drifting across the lens the moment the photographer captured the pose.

Jack returned the frame to the dresser top, growing curious if the family in the photo were friends or kin of the Brossys. He reached to the floor, fumbled through the duffle bag and located his wallet resting near the bottom. Dividing the flap, he pulled from one of the slots the picture of his daughters at Disney.

Footsteps approaching the bedroom prompted Jack to force the photo into the hand warmer of his hoodie. He moved with a silent step to the foot of the bed where he collected the gun and manila folder and redeposited the collection under the mattress. The steps came to a halt in front of his door. Easing back onto his heels, a wood slat below let loose a bellowing snap. A light rap on the door followed in an instant.

"Mr. Clarke? Are you awake?"

Jack grabbed his duffle bag and placed it atop the bed. "Yes . . . just getting dressed now," he said.

"I have breakfast if you're hungry," Sophie said.

"Thank you. I'll be out in just a moment."

"Are you in need of anything?"

"No ma'am."

Jack held steady as Sophie's footsteps faded down the hallway. Releasing a sigh, he reconsidered bagging the gun and documents, deciding instead to tuck them under the mattress for safekeeping until his departure was certain.

Jack managed with little difficulty removing his sweatpants and stepped into his last clean pair of underwear. Still unable to govern full functionality of his left side, he one-armed the quick-change sequence and slipped into his shoes. He fumbled but a moment with the laces before concluding he'd need the help of a Brossy to get them tied. Searching over the room, he primped the sheets and quilts before moving into the hallway.

Other than a rustling in the kitchen and logs snapping and cracking in the fireplace, the Brossy home was void of the bustling Jack was expecting on such a festive occasion. Scanning the open floor plan of the parlor, he noticed a single place setting at the large country table and nothing to indicate anyone but Sophie was up and moving about. Maybe they were sleeping in, he thought as he moved to the large window nearest the front door.

Enjoying the wave of heat radiating from the firebox, he ducked under the fold of the drapery to view the front property. The sun appeared more muted from this angle, as if clouds were settling in. Diverting from the view overhead, he followed the length of the barn to an enclosed, connected pasture where several small bunches of Holsteins huddled munching on piles of hay. Looking further off in the distance, he followed another immense, snow-covered pasture ascending the face of a sizeable hill running northeast, spotting several small herds of solid black and brown bovines milling about along a tree line. His mind wandered back forty years. He'd run through similar pastures chasing after butterflies, jackrabbits, and fleeing agitated bulls.

"Good morning, Mr. Clarke."

Jack spun from the window in a startled rush. Standing in the doorway to the kitchen, Sophie stared out, wringing her hands in a red-checkered towel. Wearing a solid, light blue dress and dingy-white apron, she appeared to have been hard at work for hours based on the muss to her hair and spots of flour clinging to her sleeves. Her eyes looked heavy but determined.

"If you will have a seat, I will bring you some breakfast."

Hesitating, Jack felt concern he would add further burden to what appeared to be an already busy morning.

"That's not necessary, Sophie. I'm not very hungry and it looks as if you've got your hands full."

"Nonsense," she said. "I know you're hungry. You had three bites last night."

"Well, I thought, maybe, if Olan's able, we could get started for Cartersville. It looks like the weather is going to cooperate today and I'm feeling much better."

Sophie motioned with a finger for him to advance toward her. Her body language unsettled his optimism.

"Let me show you something," she said. "Please, come into the kitchen."

Fighting a suspicion something was about to ruin his day, Jack followed her lead, wading into the large space through a wall of baked spices and scents more reminiscent of the bakeries he frequented on Chicago's south side than a country kitchen. As with the rest of the home, the room evoked a charm forcing pause and inspection.

The space centered on a beefy, black cast iron wood-burning oven displaying more knobs, lids, handles, and nickel-plated doors than made sense or seemed reasonable. The room appeared to be the focal point of the family's daily routine and was designed to accommodate a sizeable traffic flow.

Jack followed Sophie across the hardwood floor. They passed a small rectangular table tucked under a large picture window on the far wall and a wood cabinet just beyond the table supporting an iron hand pump—probably the lone water source to the house.

To his immediate right, he noticed an open doorway leading to a large pantry outfitted with shelves, cabinets and counters on three sides, stuffed full of household goods of all sorts. Pots, pans, sacks of flour, sugar, and salt, several settings of white china, and what seemed like endless rows of glass jars packed with various fruits, vegetables, and pickled delicacies, appeared as a self-contained general store.

Several uncooked pies lined the countertop awaiting their turn in the belly of the stove.

"Just over here, Mr. Clarke," Sophie directed, moving past the pantry to another doorway in the far corner. He followed her lead into a utility room connecting the home to a small back porch. The smell of leather and gunpowder was overpowering; several coats and a small cache of antique rifles and shotguns lined the far wall. Their presence excited more than a dozen baby chicks the family was keeping in a homemade brooder box; wee chirps soon grew in crescendo, falsely portraying their numbers as triple. Sophie walked to the back door of the home and pointed to the sky.

"Can you see the sky? In about two hours—probably less—you will not be able to see the hand in front of your face."

Jack worked in close and dipped over her shoulder. Despite having spent the morning sweating over a hot oven and digging up to her elbows in sacks of flour, her scent reminded him of fresh-cut spring flowers.

"I fear this will not be a small affair," she said.

He looked to the northwest sky and felt the excitement for the day release from his body in a rush. From one end of the horizon to the other stretched a massive wall of midnight blue and black colored clouds advancing toward the farm. The ominous rolling action suggested the system was carrying a heavy punch. Mercury in a thermometer tacked to the inside of a post supporting a small wood awning covering the porch held steady at twenty-two degrees.

"This is nothing unexpected for these parts this time of the year," she said, folding her arms across her chest. "I'm certain the mercury will drop soon. It will take Olan and the boys at least another hour to get the milking done and a couple more to get the herd from the upper pasture."

Jack stepped away with his chin buried into his chest.

"I'm sorry, Mr. Clarke. I know you wanted to leave today. I hope, though, you can appreciate our situation. The cows must be milked and we cannot afford to lose any of the herd to a snowstorm."

Jack glanced at the chicks. He nodded. "I understand. I know this farm is your livelihood."

"If your family is indeed in Cartersville, I doubt they will be going anywhere. Whomever they are staying with will know what is coming and not allow them to venture out into it."

"You know, I've ridden plenty of horses in my time . . . would Olan consider saddling one up and pointing me in the right direction?"

Sophie dropped her chin. A let's-be-serious grin spread across her face. She stretched out a hand. "May I please have your left hand?"

Jack's brow crumpled. "Why do you want to see my left hand?"

She extended hers further.

Jack rolled his shoulder in her direction but was unable to lift his hand into hers. A stabbing pain sent his teeth to gritting. Sophie placed her hand under his, grabbed it, and dropped the other on top, patting softly.

"How do you propose to ride a horse through a snowstorm, in twenty degree weather, over unfamiliar territory, to a town near ten miles away when you cannot even lift your left arm?"

Jack shot a quick glance toward the sky. Sophie could see the anxiety building and the wheels spinning as to how he could find a way, any way, to get to his family.

"Patience, Mr. Clarke," she said. A perfect Bible verse came to mind, but she bit her tongue. "Come, now, let us get you something to eat. Once you have finished, I want to get your bandage changed. Doctor Danaher left some extra dressing."

Jack fell in behind, amazed the woman appeared to be holding no grudge, despite their differences regarding God and faith.

"Will we see the doctor today?" he asked.

"We're expecting several at the dinner table tonight," she said, scurrying toward the oven. "The doctor was invited, but I suspect he does not know from one minute to the next where his work will take him. I am sure it also will depend on how bad things get outside. Now, I have some leftover griddlecakes, eggs, bacon, potato cakes, biscuits, and gravy. What would you prefer?"

"It all sounds good."

"A little bit of everything," she said, with a nod.

Sophie snatched a thick towel dangling on a hook against the wall and cracked open the oven door to check on its contents. A wave of heat pushed across the room as did the smell of simmering crust. The aroma emphasized his hunger.

"Strange how the doctor just happened to show up at the right time, don't you think?" Jack searched the room, taking an inventory of the many strange turn-of-the-century gadgets.

"Oh, I don't think so," she replied. "The power of prayer is the strongest force we humans have at our disposal. I prayed for a miracle and one showed up at my front door at the exact moment in time when it meant most . . . nothing strange about a prayer being answered—at least from my experiences. Go ahead now, Mr. Clarke," Sophie said, turning from the oven, "have a seat and I will be there in a minute."

Jack traded a glance between the dining room and kitchen tables. "Would you mind if I ate in here?" he asked, pointing to one of the chairs under the window, ". . . unless I would be in the way."

"Not at all," she said. "Sit anywhere you please."

Jack offered a tempered smile and pulled the nearest chair from under the table. Looking through the large window framing the Brossys' backyard and another grand panoramic of rolling hills and fields dissected by fence and brush, he spied the family's outhouse and delayed taking a seat.

"I think I'd better use the bathroom before I eat," he said, staring at the vertical board-and-batten structure, already feeling the chill of the seat.

"Just follow the path out the back door," Sophie instructed. "I would make a very quick trip of it. This is not the time of season to tarry."

<hr>

The coffee was just horrible, but served nonetheless its useful purpose of providing an early morning wake up. Its gritty texture alone was equal to a punch in the face. Jack held tight to the white china cup, sipping the home-ground brew to allow its effects to erase the chill in his body. Following Sophie's advice on his trip to the outhouse did little to stifle the frigid Wisconsin winter air from settling deep into his bones.

The facility surprised him with its cleanliness and functionality—he'd never seen one designed with three different sized holes—and even offered a fair amount of entertainment in the form of last year's Sears, Roebuck, & Co. catalog and a stack of seed and feed livestock calendars—all, he was certain, meant for extended use in the spring and summer months.

No matter the material the family chose to construct the toilet seats, it would not be conducive to the skin on one's backside in twenty-degree weather. The Brossys' selection of a sanded and stained oak was little better than a carved piece of granite. Jack was certain he'd left some DNA behind.

"Would you like a glass of fresh buttermilk?" Sophie asked, uncovering and stirring a large pot of boiling cranberries.

He separated the coffee cup from his lips. "No, thank you. The coffee is just fine."

Placing the cup atop a matching saucer, he resumed working his way through the pile of food dished onto his plate, being particularly fond of the potato cakes and fresh eggs.

He watched Sophie move from boiling pot to pantry and back again, slaving to ensure her family a well prepared and delicious holiday meal. She was as at home in the kitchen as any women he knew. She flowed with grace, leaving little doubt as to why the men in the family adored her. I bet she could make boiling water taste good, he thought as she pulled two fruit pies from the stove.

"I was noticing the pictures on the dresser in the bedroom," Jack mentioned, interrupting her flow but for a brief moment. "I was wondering who the family was pictured in front of your silo?"

Sophie slipped out of view into the pantry before doubling back toting three more pies.

"That's our niece's family—well, Olan's niece. She's his late sister's child. They will be joining us this evening for Christmas Eve dinner. I expect their arrival any time . . . I just hope they get here before the weather turns."

"She reminds me of my wife. Are the two children in the picture girls?"

"Yes . . . they are twins. Twins are quite common in Olan's family."

"Does he have just the one sister?"

"No, he also has an older sister. He was the baby of the family. She had twins but they died very young. She took her own life not too long after . . . I guess she could not cope with the heartache. Julia is the sole surviving family member of Olan's kin."

"Do you have any brothers or sisters?"

"I have two older sisters, but they were long out of the house by the time I was born. They've both passed as well."

"I'm sorry . . . so, you and Olan also had a set of twins." Jack thought through last evening's dinner conversation not knowing for sure if he'd mentioned his daughters were twins.

"How did you know we had twins?" she asked.

Jack hesitated; the question caught him off guard. He would have to confess to the near fifteen minutes or so he spent eavesdropping as the family ate their meal. "Well, before I entered the room last night I over-heard Olan recalling a story to Caleb, I believe, where he made mention of his sister and their birthday."

"Oh, I see. Well, it was no surprise based on the family's history." Sophie disappeared again into the pantry.

"I'm sorry for the loss of your daughter. I can't imagine how difficult it was for you."

"Actually, April's death was a blessing, Mr. Clarke," she said, her voice muted as she moved deeper into the pantry. "I thank our gracious Lord every day for the time we had with her. She was something very special."

Competing with the sound of tin lids vibrating atop their posts of boiling contents, he said, "You know, this is what I don't understand . . . how you can praise a being who stole from you an innocent life? How did losing your daughter make one minute of your life better? How did losing a part of you improve who and what you are?"

Jack turned toward the pantry anticipating a reply. Getting none, he feared he'd broached a subject too painful for her to participate. Sophie exited the pantry in a slow, deliberate stride. Jack's jaw slacked at her expression. He started to speak but paused, as Sophie broke first.

"I find it very interesting that a man who detests the Lord so continues to bring up the topic after making it very clear it was closed for discussion."

She moved a few steps closer and kept her stare on him for several moments. Her eyes narrowed as she studied his face. "What happened to you?" she asked, surprising him. "Where does all that hate come from?"

Jack froze. He held off a rabid urge to tell her what she wanted to know; tell her everything. He wondered why his senses urged him to trust her; why he felt telling her would somehow dislodge what haunted him. Breaking from her, he sought out a large, crimson-colored outbuilding he'd noticed during his trip to the outhouse.

"Just what I suspected," she said. "I am very willing to accommodate your request from last evening, but don't then open the topic and expect a believer to bite their tongue.

"You so cavalierly ask questions of how and why but are so unwilling to answer the same when the table is turned. My daughter was indeed a blessing. My son Caleb is here today because, for reasons unknown to us, she had the foresight to push him out of the way of a runaway horse and buggy. She was four. Had she not reacted, I would be without both children.

"I thank God because I know she is safe in His arms and He gave us such a fine boy who is now an even greater man. I have faith, Mr. Clarke. I am comforted and at peace because our salvation and ascension into heaven is God's promise to those who believe in His only Son. I will see my daughter again, one fine day, when my Lord calls me home. This I believe and this is what sustains me in my darkest hours."

Jack heard her every word, crystal clear, despite not once wavering from the view out of doors. Sophie's take on the Almighty and faith in general was familiar to his ears. He'd heard similar attestation's from his mother, his wife, even Sam. *Faith*, he thought. *How can faith in God be possible once He's stripped you to the bone?*

"As I said, Mr. Clarke, I am very sorry you don't know the Lord. I have never known the feeling and pray I never will. But, I will say this . . . and it *will* be the last word I speak on the subject." Sophie's tone changed; her exasperation clear. "If you were half the man you think yourself to be, you would look at the trials in your life with an open mind and realize God had nothing to do with them. Free will is what humankind chooses to do with it, and it can be both a curse and a blessing. God is with you whether free will is dispensed or absorbed for good or evil. He does not merely effervesce in the soul and disappear. He is in place for eternity. At least that is what I believe and what I have placed my personal faith in."

Sophie's theory started his wheels spinning. He saw his father's face building in his conscience. Sophie could see his expression change. The pain in his eyes was clear, the anger settling against his brow undeniable. Her natural caring instincts to nurture got the better of her.

"I can help you if you will let me."

Jack felt emotion building in his chest. Sophie believed a breakthrough was near.

"Faith is beyond my reach," he said, his voice cracking and trailing away. "God made sure of that."

Sophie released a long, disappointed sigh. She opened a path but he refused the opportunity to follow. Both jumped at the sound of the back door bursting open.

In an instant, Roo's voice breached the silence, screaming "Mama, Mama," as she appeared from the utility room swinging a wicker basket. Noticing their guest upon entering the room, she slammed on the brakes, causing a brief slide across the hardwood in her snow-covered shoes, almost falling to the floor. She rushed to between her mother's legs at the sight of the man who'd scared her the night before, nearly dropping the basket full of brown eggs. Sophie secured the lot just in time. Jack saw a glimpse of Roo's profile. The light of day proved, beyond any doubt, he was in his possession of a black and white photo of her.

"It is okay, Roo," Sophie said, hoisting the child into her arms. "Mr. Clarke is our friend. Would you like to say hello to him?"

Roo was quick to shake her head before burying into her mother's neck. Unsure whether to sit or stand, Jack rationalized keeping his position for fear of further traumatizing the child with his size. Snow and ice dripped from the bottom of her boots into a pile on the floor.

"She is very shy," Sophie said. "It takes her quite some time to warm to strangers . . . more so toward men. I hope you will not be offended, but I doubt she will say two words to you during your stay."

"That's okay," Jack said. "I don't blame her . . . especially after last . . ." He paused as Roo viewed him out of the corner of her eye.

"You must be freezing, pumpkin," Sophie said, removing her earmuffs and redirecting the hair from off her face. She patted Roo's behind and released her to the floor. Roo removed her coat into Sophie's hands.

"Now I have a lot of work to do, and you still have chores to finish before your cousins arrive. Come now, I want you to say hello to Mr. Clarke."

Roo tucked her arms close to her chest and shuffled in his direction.

"Go ahead, pumpkin, he won't bite."

"Hello, Mr. Clawke," she said sheepishly, missing the pronunciation of the "r" by a country mile. Her voice was gentle as the coo of a dove with a slight lisp created by the absence of a few baby teeth. She brought her fingers to her mouth and pushed into her mother's dress. Jack thought he saw her smile.

He scooted to the edge of his seat. "Hello, Roo," he said, speaking softly. "I'm very happy to meet you. How old are you?"

"Pumpkin, he asked you a question," Sophie said.

She dropped her hand from her and held up four fingers.

"Four? You know, I have two daughters about your age. I think you would like them." A portion of Sophie's apron nudged upward as Roo nodded.

Sophie stroked her daughter's hair, amused at her shy nature. She wondered how in the world she and Olan had produced such an introvert.

"Okay, pumpkin," Sophie said, "I've got to get back to work. Here are some breadcrumbs . . . go feed your chicks."

She reached for a small glass jar on a shelf near the stove. Roo accepted the jar with both hands and turned toward the utility door making sure to keep her eyes glued to the floor. Walking in a wide arc around Jack's chair, she peeked out of the corner of her eye to see if he was watching.

"I like your baby chicks," he said just as she passed. "I think I like the brown ones the most. How many do you have?"

"Sev-teen," she said, looking to the floor.

"Seventeen?" Jack asked. "That's a lot of baby chicks. Where did they all come from?"

She stared at her mother as if seeking permission to answer. Sophie nodded.

"They came fwom the eggs," she said.

"Do baby chicks come from eggs?"

Roo nodded.

"Well, how did you get them out of those tiny eggs?"

She moved a half-step in his direction.

"I didn't get them out . . . they came out all by themselves." Her voice rose in an excited burst.

"Well, what do you do with the breadcrumbs?"

"I feed them. This is not theiw weal food . . . I just give this as a tweat."

"I see. Are you going to feed them now?"

"Yes. They awe vewy hungwy."

"Would you mind if I watched you feed them?"

"Okay," she said. "But I'm the only one who can feed dem."

"Sure," Jack replied, "I don't think I know how to feed baby chicks. Maybe you can teach me."

"Okay. It's weally easy but you have to talk to them while you feed dem."

Roo moved toward the utility room with a skip in her step. Jack eased from his chair and fell in just behind. Sophie noticed a smile on his face. It was a good and handsome smile. She wished she could do something to make it a permanent attribute.

"Mr. Clarke," she said, "when you are done, we need to get your bandage changed."

"Yes ma'am. Thank you."

Nearing the doorway to the utility room, Jack noticed Sophie react to something at the front of the house. He stopped as a woman's voice rang out.

"Hello? Aunt Sophie? We're here."

CHAPTER 30

"I named this one Andwew," Roo said, pointing to a chick in the nearest corner of the cage. "He's my favowite."

"Andrew, huh?" Jack asked, readjusting his grip on the cage as he balanced next to her on one knee. "How can you tell if it's a boy or a girl chick?"

Roo stared with a puzzled look.

"I don't weally," she said, "I named it aftew my fwiend at chuwch school."

"Oh . . . I see. Well, I think Andrew's a fine name for any chick—boy or girl."

"Me too," she said, cautious to select the proper sized breadcrumb for the next chick in line. "My fwiend Andwew has black spots on his skin, too. He was in a fiwe."

"Oh . . . I'm sorry. I'm sure he'd be happy to know you think enough of him to name one of your chicks after him."

"He does. I told him. I'm going to give him the fiwst egg, when-evew it comes out."

"You're very sweet. He's lucky to have you as a friend."

"Yes, he is," she said, matter-of-factly.

"You must like animals. Do you have any other pets? Dogs or a cat maybe?"

"Suwe, we have dogs and lots of cats in the bawn. My favowite is my black cat, Fancy. She's vewy nice. She was just a baby when I found hew."

Jack knew the color of the cat before the words escaped the young girl's mouth. He studied her face as she went about her work. There was an angelic air about her; something suggesting upon first sight she was as timid and gentle a creature as there ever was upon the earth.

Large, chipmunk cheeks and a soft, round nose retaining a constant rosy hue brought an instant smile to one's face and an unavoidable urge to want to pick her up and squeeze. She had Brooke's eyes—large and dark—from which emanated tranquility and peace. Her hair was just as straight and black as Brooke's, although cut much shorter to where it fell just on top of her shoulders. He conceded the facial resemblance to his wife and maybe, if he saw a baby picture of her, the coincidence would usher in greater surprise. The fact was there was nothing obvious about her appearance to explain the hand-delivered picture. He wondered why she was so important. Regardless, something else was there. He could feel a connection where one should not exist. Her aura was mystical.

"She's lucky to have you . . . your cat, I mean. I bet you take good care of all the animals here."

Roo nodded then continued divvying up the mid-morning snack. Her organizational skills amused. She worked in diligent fashion to make sure each chick got the exact right-sized nugget for its body size, and gluttons waited their turn. With the conversation at the front of the house growing more animated, Jack used the moment to excuse himself.

"Sweetheart, I need to find your mother so she can change my bandage, okay?"

She did not respond. Her work was much too important.

"I'll be back in a few minutes." Jack placed his hand atop her head and patted. Her hair was soft as newly picked cotton, producing the same feeling against his fingertips, as did Brooke's. He thanked her for the feeding lesson as he exited.

Jack hovered above the small kitchen table, listening in on the multiple conversations now falling much clearer upon his ears. Olan's voiced boomed above all others as he traded excited, grandfatherly-like observations with a couple of small children. He heard Sophie discussing the evening's menu with a woman whose voice sounded much younger. He assumed the niece and her family had arrived. Taking a quick swig of coffee brought little pleasure, as the once steaming brew had turned cold and tar-like, as if it had never been coffee at all.

With curiosity getting the better of him, he eased across the kitchen floor toward the parlor, hoping to catch a secretive glimpse of the woman in the picture. The dialogue soon grew into fits of laughter, as Sophie scolded Olan for exciting the young children to the point of chaotic squeals. Her annoyance was short lived, as she too could not contain her amusement. Jack held his ground, just out of their view, searching for the young woman's voice through the disarray.

"Where's your husband?" he heard Sophie ask.

"Oh . . . he saw Matty herding in another bunch-full for milking and wanted to help. You know him, if someone else is working and he's not, it nearly kills him to stand by and do nothing."

"Sounds like three men I know," Sophie responded.

"By the way, where is Caleb?"

"I sent him to the Howard's to invite them over for Christmas Eve dinner. Did you hear they are losing their farm?"

"Yes, we did. What a shame," Julia said. "It hurts my heart so many families are struggling."

The woman's voice flowed soft and kind, with a much more predominant northern twang than her kin. Unable to stand it any longer, Jack drew around the corner of the doorway, noticing only Sophie's profile as she stood hovering above the armrest of the couch.

Jack saw no sign of the woman after jutting out as far as he could without taking a step. Easing back behind the doorway, fighting off a sudden and surprising pang of butterflies, he rested against the kitchen wall, wrestling to conjure an excuse to interrupt their conversation.

Taking a quick breath, he pushed his body away from the wall. "Excuse me, Sophie?" he said, stepping in full through the doorway. After clearing the opening, he expelled a polite, excuse-me cough. "I thought maybe we could—"

"Oh, Mr. Clarke," she interrupted, "please . . . do come in and meet our relatives."

Jack noticed immediately the slender woman sitting on the couch.

"Mr. Clarke, this is my niece, Julia."

She kept forward as she rose to her feet. Long, straight, spotless black hair uncoiled from off the back of the couch, spilling down her shoulders to just above the small of her back. A modest green and white checked gingham dress clung to her figure, revealing delicate shoulders and a narrow waist. Her movement was slow, effortless and elegant; as if at some point, the ways of royal graces were introduced and demanded. Her turn seemed to last an eternity.

The instant her image appeared in full, Jack quickened his pace in her direction. Excitement overpowered his senses before his mind processed the moment, prompting a surprising blurt of Brooke's name as he raced toward the woman with his arms extended.

A horrified look splashed across the woman's face, bringing Jack's brain and the circumstance slamming together. He stopped dead as his internal processor rationalized what he was seeing could not be so. Olan, who'd been balancing on one knee on the floor playing with Julia's eldest daughter, scurried to his feet and toward Jack after seeing his niece retreat toward the fireplace in fear.

Jack's expression grew wide and wild; his jaw fell agape. He called out his wife's name in a dazed whisper.

Julia clutched her fist into a ball and planted it in the center of her chest in an attempt to hold back the pounding of her heart.

"Mr. Clarke," Sophie scolded. "This is our niece, Julia. What is the matter with you?"

Jack did not hear a word; his body fell numb. Olan approached to within a foot and plowed his giant fists deep into his hips.

"Mr. Clarke," he said, jutting forward close to Jack's ear without touching, "say hello to my niece . . . right now."

Jack's eyes blinked; his head twitched as if shaking off a blow. Olan recoiled at the sight of the utter confusion and displacement painted across Jack's face. He looked at his wife and shrugged.

Jack rotated toward Julia. She collected her children against her body as protecting them from an advancing wild beast. The girls grabbed hold of their mother's legs. Jack whispered his daughter's names. His mind worked to convince him he was staring at his family; that they were identical in every way. His eyes refuted what his heart wanted to be so. Why were they staring as if they had no idea who he was? The girls buried themselves deeper into their mother's dress.

"Jack . . . right now," Olan demanded.

His body deflated as he discharged an agreeable sigh. "Hello . . . Julia," he said in an airy, confused whisper. Sophie approached from the right, turning toward the kitchen to hide her lips from the children.

"Mr. Clarke," she said, extending onto the tips of her toes to get nearer his ear. "I find your behavior quite shameful. I insist you apologize to my niece and her family immediately."

Jack dropped his chin against his chest. Several moments passed before he nodded in agreement.

Julia was reminded of a silent movie she'd seen in '19 about a young drifter who hoodwinked an entire town into believing he was a returning wounded war hero before cleaning out the town's meager bank. Her mistrust and imagination grew with every second Jack struggled to regain his composure.

"I'm sorry," he said, his voice still distant and foggy. "I don't know how to explain this. I thought you were . . . I mean . . . you look so much like my wife and your daughters look like my—" Jack could not finish his thought. He looked upon the woman and her daughters and wondered how it was possible this was not his family. It was as if they'd been recreated with miniscule dissimilarities to add to his already tortured mind. He was quick to excuse himself.

"Julia," Sophie interjected, "Mr. Clarke found his way to our home after suffering a very serious accident. He is still recovering and not quite himself. I am sorry dear . . . I will explain it all to you later. Olan, please take the girls' things upstairs to their bedroom. I'm sure they would like to freshen up." Sophie offered a smile to the children before following Jack into the kitchen.

"Well, come on ladies," Olan said. "Let's get you upstairs and settled. Maybe you'd like to take a nap . . . gonna be a late evening 'round here tonight."

Just inside and to the left of the kitchen opening, Sophie huddled near the corner retrieving from off a wall-mounted garment hanger the apron she'd removed upon her niece's arrival. Placing the final touches on a bow tie near the small of her back, she stared wide-eyed through a small inlayed diamond-shaped mirror, at the reverse image of the back of their guest staring into the wild at nothing in particular. Seated at the kitchen table, facing an ever-darkening afternoon sky just starting to dump its white payload, Jack sat in silence with hands crossed in his lap, appearing lost.

With the sound of tin popping against copper, Sophie drew into the opposite corner of the mirror, noticing her boiling cranberries very near to escaping from under the lid. She grabbed hold of the bottom of her apron and relocated the contents to a small resting shelf just above the burner plates. Peeking over her shoulder, she noticed Jack's position remained the same. Checking the contents of the other simmering pots, she added a dash of cinnamon spice to a vat of pears, placed two new logs into the firebox and cleared the oven of three more pies, which she hurried into the pantry for cooling.

"Roo?" she called out from deep within the space, "I want you to leave those chickens be for now. Your cousins are here. Go on upstairs and say hello."

"Yes, Mama," she called out.

Sophie returned from the pantry, struggling to hold steady a large black pan. She lumbered across the floor to the open oven where she stuffed in its belly a turkey large enough to feed her family and several neighbors until New Year's. Turning just in time, she caught Roo shuffling toward Jack, holding out in front of her the cup of breadcrumbs. He did not notice the gesture. Sophie attempted to gain her daughter's attention by motioning with her hand to move along. The girl was determined to capture Jack's eye.

"Mistew Clawke?"

Jack did not budge from watching the falling snow, turning only when Roo tapped his forearm. Sophie could not believe this was her child, especially after the jolt their guest had given her the night before.

"Mistew Clawke? Hewe awe the west of my bwedcwumbs. You can finish feeding the chicks if you want. Don't give any to Andwew, though . . . he's had enough." She extended the cup even further.

He offered a reserved smile and accepted the cup from her tiny hands. "Okay," he said with a low and scratchy voice. "I'll finish feeding them for you."

Roo pointed to his bandage. "What happened to you?"

Jack placed the breadcrumbs on the table. "I was in an accident and bumped my head."

"Oh," she said. "I want to be an amnimal doctow when I gwow up."

His smile widened. He was amused by her serious tone. "I think you'll make a very fine amnimal doctor one day." He placed his hand on the side of her cheek and patted. She giggled before bolting toward the den, passing her surprised mother.

Sophie disappeared again into the pantry, relocating the simmering pies to the far end of the space. She retrieved from the lower cabinets a small sampling of veterinary supplies and other products Doctor Danaher had left behind. Scooping the heap, including a large, rolled-up strip of cotton, she placed the goods on the table in front of Jack, brushing his shoulder in the process. The contact interrupted his thoughts of how he might escape to Cartersville despite the weather and the family's lack of interest in helping.

Sophie placed her hands on either side of his face, readjusted forward to initiate the unpleasant task of removing the bloodied and fluid-stained bandage. The cotton strip felt damp against her fingers, and with each layer uncoiled, released a slight odor driving her nose opposite the wound. Growing uncomfortable with the silence, she drew a breath to speak, stalling when Jack inhaled as if intending to deliver a lengthy statement. As the breath drifted from his lips, a new round of reticence ensued.

What a stubborn, stubborn man he is, Sophie thought. The very idea he thought his behavior required no explanation was as foreign to her as if one of her own had misbehaved during Sunday mass. Coming very near the end of the cotton bandage, Sophie could wait no longer for dialogue. She would ease into her targeted topic.

"You have a way with children, Mr. Clarke," she said, leaning forward to catch his eye. "Not that it matters in the least, but I can assure you my daughter does not fall in with strangers."

Jack cleared his throat but said nothing. Sophie peeled back the final eighteen inches of bandage. The area was swollen and rash red, but appeared in good repair. Under the circumstances and conditions, Doctor Danaher had performed masterfully.

"Well, now," she said, "it looks just fine. I do believe our dear veterinarian has outdone himself. That's as fine a stitch job as I have seen." Sophie tossed the dirty bandage into a large tin bucket kept near the oven for items to be burned later, grabbed a clean rag from a pile stacked near the water pump, and summoned a stream to dampen the rag.

"This is going to be very cold, Mr. Clarke, but I need to clean your wound before putting on the new bandage. I will try not to hurt you."

Jack twitched as the frigid cloth connected against his bare scalp. Sophie pulled back before continuing to dab along the length of the wound. She assured him his hair would grow back in no time.

"Would you believe it took my Roo a year before she warmed up to her very own aunt? Would not even allow the woman to touch her until early last spring. I find it mighty peculiar how trusting she is of you after having just met you."

"Maybe she's maturing," Jack responded.

"No . . . I don't think so. I have seen too many examples of her shy nature to believe she has outgrown it. She sees something in you. You know what they say about children, they often have an insight we adults tend to lose somewhere along the way. No . . . you have a way about you. I'll bet your own daughters feel the same way." His shoulders sunk inward.

After discarding the rag into the same bucket, she reached across Jack's body for a fist-sized ball of cotton and a small brown corked bottle. "I am not certain what this is," she said, "but Doctor Danaher assured me it is necessary for your recovery and is extremely painful." Sophie soaked the cotton swab and dabbed along the suture line. Jack nearly pushed the table through the kitchen window as the fluid scalded the wound.

"I'm very sorry . . . almost done . . . there," she said. Reaching for a jar containing an opaque ointment, she assured him again. "I believe this will feel much better." The salve brought instant relief.

Jack released his grip as she began the counter-clockwise motion of rewrapping the wound.

"Mr. Clarke, would you like to tell me what happened earlier?"

"Nothing happened," he said with a touch of defiance. "I watched her feed the chicks for a moment or two then left to find you to see if we could change my bandage."

"Please do not patronize me, Mr. Clarke. You know very well what I am speaking of."

Jack turned toward the window; Sophie was quick to readjust his head forward. She tucked in the final layer of cotton, securing the fit.

"It's not enough you frightened my daughter to the point of tears, but then scared my niece and her daughters to death—and in a place they should consider safe and secure. Why, it was like watching a crazed lunatic who'd escaped from an asylum. You should be ashamed of yourself . . . it is disgraceful, I tell you, utterly—"

Jack interrupted. "Sophie, I'm not from here," he said, his voice raspy, projecting in a serious, eerie whisper.

The remark did not make sense. She moved to the far end of the table and pulled up a chair. "I am aware you are not from around these parts, but what that has to do with your conduct is beyond me."

She watched the color drain from his face. He appeared to be aging right in front of her. As if looking straight through the floor to the cellar dirt below, he seemed stuck and searching for words. He held to a long pause before dragging his eyes to meet hers. His expression pushed her against the seatback.

Speculating the consequences of what would come from the information he was about to share, he thought through Sophie's trust before deciding he had no other choice. He scooted close to her. She felt a cramp settle in her stomach.

"That's not what I mean, Sophie. I mean I'm not from here," he said, fanning the palm of his hand and spreading his arm wide. "I was born in 1961."

Sophie's mouth fell open. She searched his face for any indication he was lying. As if just learning there was no such place as heaven, she oscillated her head in denial.

"Mr. Clarke . . . you have been under a great deal of strain," she said. "You have suffered a very serious accident, a heart-wrenching loss, and have a foot-long gash running from the back of your head to the front. God only knows the potential damage to your brain. You are not yourself. This will pass."

"No, Sophie . . . no. I'm aware of my faculties. I can't explain why I'm here and I can't explain what happened in there," he said, pointing to the den. "That was my wife and daughters in there. That's what I saw and what my mind wants me to believe."

"That is absurd," she shot back. "I have known my dear Julia since she was but a wee babe; I birthed both her babies. She has been like a daughter to me."

"I'm telling you the truth," he said, extending his hand across to the table to grab hers. Sophie withdrew her hand to her chest. "You must believe me," Jack urged.

Confusion swamped her common sense. His look did not project deceit. Whether he was suffering from a traumatic head wound, or was crazier than a three-legged sow, he did not have the look of one telling a lie. Sophie studied his face. She prided herself in knowing the truth when delivered. This man believed what he was saying.

"How can you expect me to believe such a tale? 1961? My niece is your wife? Her daughters are your daughters? You have done nothing but offer half-truths since the moment you came to and now you sit there and want me to believe those outrageous claims?"

Jack released a heavy sigh. His eyes swam about as would an innocent man's on his way to the gallows. His despair filled Sophie with remorse and guilt for the un-Christian way in which she was accusing and attacking. She sighed, and brought a hand against her cheek. Matthew 7:2 came to mind. Unable to overcome the feeling something was taking place well beyond the boundaries of her own faith, she paused to consider the situation if it were reversed. She wrestled with her conscience several moments, wondering how she would feel if she were trying to convince someone of the truth but no one would believe her.

"Okay, Mr. Clarke," she said, dropping her hands into her lap, "it is times like this when we must believe without seeing. I am sorry for the un-Christian manner with which I have accused you. I must say, you are asking me to believe something that is as foreign to me as downtown Boston. You ask me to believe you were born nearly fifty years from where we are at this very moment in time."

An awkward pause forced Jack into the realization Sophie had not asked a question. He eased from the seatback and looked to the floor to contemplate where to begin and how best to explain elements of the predicament he did not understand or believe himself.

"Can I show you something?" he asked.

Sophie readjusted forward in her chair. Jack reached into the pocket of his hoodie, removed the photo of his daughters and pushed it across the table to within her grasp. Sophie bent forward at the waist to gain a better view. Jack anticipated her reaction. She picked the image off the table and brought it close to her face.

"I don't understand," she said, peeking over the picture. "How is this possible? How can you be holding Julia's children?"

"They're not her children. Those are my daughters. The picture was taken two years ago in Florida at Disney World."

"Disney World?"

"It's an amusement park. They have another one out in California called Disneyland."

"I have never heard of such," she said. Jack cleared his throat.

"Sophie, the park where this picture was taken opened in 1971."

"I don't understand how they can be your daughters. They are identical to Sarah and Samantha."

"Precisely why you must believe me. It's why I reacted the way I did. I saw my family."

Sophie dropped the picture to the table. The revelation of it all sent her mind spinning. How could he not be telling the truth, she thought. Who would make up such a story and for what? The photo must be a coincidence. She moved her stare to the window and the falling snow, needing to get her thoughts in order.

Jack leaned forward ready to tell of the strange wind spinning him back in time, when he noticed Sophie adjust her stare at the sound of the back porch door creaking open. Heavy stomping followed, sending the chicks into a tizzy. He could hear the low rumble of a conversation already in progress and watched as a smile overtook Sophie's shock.

"Hello, Jubel . . . Merry Christmas, my dear."

CHAPTER 31

The heat storming through Jack's chest equaled that of volcanic lava rising from within a crater not having rid itself of its liquid center for centuries. Ready to burst forth with a fury leaving all present no doubt as to the state of his emotions, he paused when Olan and Julia entered through the kitchen doorway at the exact moment he pushed from the table to get to his feet. He noticed Julia first.

Her very presence tamed his temper and cooled his disposition to that of a shy teenage boy. Her nature and way pleased him. It reminded of the moment he saw Brooke for the first time. Julia's face was beautiful; her eyes sparkled with interest. She looked more like Brooke now than during their first encounter.

"Mr. Clarke, I would like you to meet our nephew-in-law, Jubel. Jubel Bigsby, Mr. Jack Clarke."

Jack turned from Julia just in time to catch a glimpse of the man removing a Fedora. Jubel exited the the utility room with his right hand extended. Jack's throat constricted, his eyes burned as coals in a blacksmith's forge.

"Hello Mr. Clarke," Jubel said, "it's a pleasure to meet you. Merry Christmas."

The man's voice was identical to that which Jack recalled from the telephone exchanges in his office and as Bigsby fled from the Palmer House Hotel.

Standing a good foot-and-a-half south of Jack's eye level, the man craned his neck upward, exposing an exuberant country smile stretched ear to ear, suggesting a formal introduction was not necessary as the two were already acquainted.

Bigsby closed to within a foot of Jack. His hair, chestnut in color, shown much darker due to the application of some sort of hair goo. Jack remembered well the dead black of his pupils and noticed a deep dent in the side of his head equal to the size and shape of what he remembered seeing on the old man. He spent several moments browsing Bigsby's features, never making the first gesture of accepting his outstretched hand.

He focused on Bigsby's neck. Getting his much larger hand around it could be accomplished swiftly and accurately, and Jack's height and weight advantage were such, he could drop him to the floor and be on top of him before Olan could react. His internal rage ensured there were not enough Brossy men on the property to stop him if he so inclined to commit a murder. The smile faded from Jubel's chiseled and clean-shaven face as he dropped his hand to near his other to secure the rim of his hat.

Olan expelled an exaggerated sigh. "Mr. Clarke, must we go through this again?"

Jack twitched. The muscles encasing his jawbones burst into a spasmodic rage. He appeared as a bull set to charge.

"Shake the man's hand," Olan demanded.

"I'm sorry," Jack said, his speech slow but direct. "I stood up too fast. My head is spinning a bit."

Jack extended his hand. The smile returned to Jubel's face as his hand disappeared into Jack's up to the wrist. His grip was firm; his fingers felt tacky, as if covered in pinesap.

"Pleasure to meet you," Jack said, offering a single nod.

"Matty mentioned your bad luck over there on Pilot's Point. Must've been some ride. Not too many end up in the middle of that pond and live to tell about it—ice or no ice. You're a lucky man." Jubel laid a manly slap against Jack's left shoulder. The blow sent a bellowing grunt from his lungs, his body crunching at his middle from the pain.

"Oh, Jubel, no," Sophie yelled, "his shoulder was damaged in the accident."

Jubel rushed to place his hand on Jack's opposite shoulder, looking to everyone as if seeking instruction as to how he could relieve the pain.

"Oh, boy . . . I'm awful sorry there," he said. "I had no idea your shoulder was busted up."

Jack spoke through winded breath. "I'm okay . . . I'm fine."

"Well, lucky for you I didn't slap the top of your head."

The comment drew a chuckle from Olan and Julia, with Jubel cackling the loudest as if it were a joke told by someone else. It was a younger version of the laugh he remembered spewing from the old man.

"Right . . . lucky," Jack said, accompanied by a blank stare.

"Have you met my wife?" Jubel asked, moving to Julia and planting a soft kiss upon her cheek. Jack rolled his hand into a fist.

"Yes, we've already met," he said. "Ma'am," Jack said, looking to her and nodding. Julia turned away.

"Well, Jack . . . I'm sorry, where are my manners," he said, smiling to his uncle, "may I call you Jack?"

Jubel received a single, stiff nod. Jack was reminded of the old man starting most every sentence with *well*.

"Well, Jack, I'm going upstairs to check on my little jackrabbits and freshen up. I'll look forward to sharing some stories with you later—maybe even tell a few lies," he said, with a hearty laugh. He pecked his wife again on the cheek, squeezed her around the hip, and whispered something into her ear. It brought a glow to her face and a bright white shade to Jack's knuckles.

Sophie kept careful watch of Jack the moment her niece entered the room. She could see his anger building.

"Oh my word," she said, attempting to draw attention from the couple, "just look at the time. I must get busy in here . . . I have a million things to do. Matthew, where is your brother?"

"He's in the barn tending to London. He just rode up as we was coming in the house."

"Were coming," she corrected. "Did he mention if the Howards would be joining us for dinner?"

"No ma'am."

"Did you finish the milking, son?" Olan asked.

"Yes sir. Uncle Jubel helped me put the canisters in the cellar. I think we need to keep an eye on Tangerine. I saw some clots in the bucket and her udders are a bit red."

"Might be a touch of milk fever," Olan said. "I'll make sure to mention it to Doc later. Go on now and get the horses saddled up. We need to get to the high pasture and get the herd down to the barn. Grab your scatter gun."

"Yes, Pa."

"Please find out if the Howards are coming for dinner," Sophie called out.

"How about you, Jack?" Olan asked. "Would you like to join us?" Jack snapped from his thoughts of standing over Bigsby's dead and lifeless body. He heard his name but not the question.

"Oh, no you don't," Sophie barked. "He is not going on any wild ride into the countryside. He can barely move his shoulder—now especially—and would have no control over a horse at the moment."

"That's probably well enough," Olan said. "I'm sure there's plenty he can do to help you here in the kitchen." He offered a teasing smile aimed at Jack's manhood. The insult deflected into the chilled kitchen air as Jack was well into developing his strategic plan for the next meeting with their nephew.

"Julia," Sophie said, "would you please be a dear and get some more kindling for the stove."

"Of course, Aunt Sophie."

Waiting for her niece to clear the room, Sophie claimed the space vacated near her husband. She turned to cloak her dialogue.

"Olan," she whispered, "is there chance of assisting Mr. Clarke to Cartersville today?"

"Today? Sweetheart, we gotta get the herd down or we're gonna be burying some cattle in the morning. It will take at least a couple hours to round 'em all up. Why, by the time we get 'em down you won't be able to see two feet forward. You've seen this weather before; you know what's coming."

Sophie sighed. "Yes, I know . . . I just thought—"

"I mean, I wanna help the boy, but not at the risk of losing stock or one of our own boys. He's just gonna have to wait it out. I promise," he said, looking to Jack, "I'll get you there just as soon as it's safe to do so."

Sophie smiled and patted her husband's chest. "You are right, dear . . . of course you are right. I'm sorry. Go on now. I want you boys back before it gets any worse." Her shoulders disappeared into Olan's hands. He pulled her close and kissed her forehead.

"Go on now . . . I've got work to do," she said.

Olan adjusted his suspenders and excused himself. He grabbed a heavy wool-lined coat, a double-barreled shotgun from a shelf above the utility room door, and a box of buckshot shells from a small cabinet in the corner. He opened the door to the porch, allowing Julia to pass with an armload of chopped maple twigs.

"Be back soon as we can," he yelled. "Tell Jubel to take a look at the corn planter when he gets a minute."

Jack followed Julia's path across the kitchen floor, watching as she filled the wood box near the stove to its capacity. He wanted to help but could offer little assistance with just one arm.

"Mr. Clarke," Sophie said, stirring the pot of pears with a large wooden spoon, "there's nothing you can do in here . . . why don't you make yourself comfortable in the parlor. We can resume our discussion later."

Seeing Julia disappear into the pantry, she summoned Jack closer.

"I will bring you a nice warm cup of tea in a bit," she said, arching to peek around Jack's frame into the pantry. "I'm sorry we cannot get you to Cartersville at the moment. I will talk with Olan again later."

She released the long wooden spoon from her hand, allowing the swirling contents of the pot to take control. She moved to the kitchen table and picked up the photo. "You must put this away and promise me you will not show it to anyone. I do not think either of us wants to be in a position of having to explain this right now," she said. Jack stuffed the picture into his hand warmer.

"Go on now . . . find a nice spot near the fireplace. It will do you some good. I have so much to do to get everything ready for this evening and I am running behind my time. I promise we will talk about all this later."

"I wish I had a picture of my wife," Jack said, taking a quick glance over his shoulder, "then you would understand—"

Sophie felt him drawing near; his expression was troubling.

"What is it, Mr. Clarke?" she asked, tenderly.

Jack peeked again over his shoulder to ensure their privacy. He bent low to her ear. "I've already met your nephew," he whispered.

Sophie's eyes narrowed. "What? What are you talking about?"

"I said I've already met your nephew; four different times before I ended up here."

Jack latched onto Sophie's arm. "I know . . . I know you think I'm crazy, but it's true. He appeared to me three times in person and once as a—" Jack caught his tongue. Trying to describe the specter would be his death knell. "I mean, I also heard his voice on the phone when I was trying to call my wife."

Sophie could not muster a response. Jack kept his hand in contact with her as she backed up just to the edge of the stove. She studied his face. She wanted to put an end to the nonsense but could not get beyond the factual and determined look in his eyes.

"I . . . I just don't know what to say or believe," she said, "I need time to—"

Julia entered from the pantry, clearing her throat. "Aunt Sophie, is everything okay?"

Sophie did not see Julie reappear, despite having a clear view of the pantry opening. She hurried from Jack's grasp to meet her niece halfway across the floor.

"Everything is just fine dear," she said, producing a wide smile. "I was inviting Mr. Clarke into the parlor so he could relax in front of the fireplace."

Sophie wrapped her hands into her apron, working them nervously into the cloth as if drying them. Julia traded a questioning stare between the two of them. Sophie could tell her niece doubted her account, and in an effort to convince, offered an affectionate pat against the woman's arm.

"My dear, would you be so kind as to roll out those four loaves of wheat dough for me? They are on the back counter under a laundry towel."

Julia flashed a knowing smile, making certain Jack caught her suspecting stare before retreating into the pantry.

Sophie ran her hands over her hair in exasperation. "Please, Mr. Clarke, go on into the parlor. I will bring you some tea."

-------∞-------

Jack tested several chairs for comfort and proximity to the firebox before settling on an oversized cherry rocker to the right of the family's Christmas tree. The cushioned rocker proved beyond comfortable and within an acceptable distance from the fireplace, allowing the warmth of the flames to ease the chill, but not so much as to draw sweat from his brow.

A small, circular table to his right hoisted at armrest-level a home-made cradle supporting two smoking pipes and a tin of Dill's Best tobacco. A second tin of Dan Patch Cut Plug tobacco lay near, decorated in bright green and gold. He assumed he'd found favor in Olan's chair.

Centered between the second of two large picture windows, he leaned into the seatback, taking in the beauty of winter's white veil and a towering, magnificent centuries-old oak tree, complete with a tire swing, standing lone against December's bite. Slumping into the cushion, he commenced a slow, even rocking motion, allowing his mind to wander while watching the snow build upon tree limbs, fence posts, and a few Herefords with no sense to take cover. The room smelled ripe with pine and spice.

The easy creaking of the chair and its hardwood runners rubbing atop wood flooring soothed his senses. If he were looking to nap, the room was well prepared. Shadows manifested in all directions along the floor and up the walls as the sky bled its muted sunlight, increasing the effervescence of the fire's glow. A mouse the size of a half-dollar coin scrambled from under the tree to a corner hole where stone met clap-board, stuffing himself through a nickel sized opening.

Lamenting the moment of Peetie's last breath, Jack choked at the thought of the dog's final act where he appeared to stretch his paws to reach him. The imagery was devastating. Why had he been so careless traversing Pilot's Peak? Why had he not secured Peetie better? He wondered why the dog meant so much more in death than in life.

Although he managed to dam the flood of emotion at the first sight of Julia, he could no longer contain the overflow of ache building for his family. He pictured Brooke's face. How could she and Julia not be one in the same? How could those girls not have the first clue as to who he was? How was it possible they could fear him? *That's my family,* he thought.

He pictured the girls' faces as they sought protection from their mother. He knew those looks; he'd seen it many times before, after raising his voice or expelling a vulgarity in a fit of anger. He could see Julianna and Jordan running to Brooke—in fear.

Jack drew the index finger and thumb of his right hand over the ring finger of his left. He'd long since stopped wearing the band of gold, other than on special occasions or to corporate events. He circled the skin where the ring should be, recalling how Brooke stole the breath from his chest when the doors to the sanctuary of Holy Name Cathedral swung open on their wedding day. She appeared as a brilliant star, glistening in pure white, growing brighter as she neared the altar. He didn't understand at the time how he could have gotten so lucky.

Just as he accepted Brooke from her father, he saw her face for the first time through the utter brilliance of the delicate lace veil. It was a moment in a lifetime filled with misery, rising above all other moments, and one worthy of storage in the deepest treasure chest of his mind.

Shifting to the fireplace, watching as bark curled under the immense heat of the flame before falling to the littered brick surface below, he expelled a sarcastic puff as he recalled Brooke's wishes for a smaller affair to include family and a few friends in a tiny chapel in her hometown. He'd insisted on grandeur, celebrity, excess. She agreed with little to no argument. His wishes were more important to her than the wedding of her dreams. *Her* love was real.

"How practical she was," he whispered, referring to her as if she'd already passed.

He recalled how she fought tooth and nail against purchasing the Escalade. How she begged for a van or a smaller, simpler SUV; anything but the overpowered, overpriced tank that she needed an extra cushion on the seat just to see over the steering wheel. How sensible she was to want less, not more.

"You were so right," he whispered, recalling their argument just days before. Brooke's accusations that he'd bought the vehicle for his own image and ego were dead on. She was also right that he'd not cared the least about her feelings.

"I was?" a voice questioned over his shoulder.

Jack shot forward from the chair as the sound cut through his space like a thunderclap, sending him scrambling to his feet in search of its source.

"I'm sorry?" he questioned, seeing Julia standing just behind the chair.

"I just asked you if I was right," Julia said. "I mentioned when I entered the room I had told Aunt Sophie you would probably prefer coffee over tea."

"I'm sorry," Jack replied, "I didn't hear you . . . I was thinking of something else. I'm sorry. Coffee's fine," he said.

Julia's posture was perfect, straight as an exclamation point, as she cradled a cup and saucer in her hand. A small stream of coffee streaked down the side where it overflowed when her hand jerked in response to his surprised reaction.

"Shall I place it on the table?"

Jack situated a hand on top of his head and pushed backward as if matting down his hair. "That's fine," he said. "Thank you."

"Please, sit down . . . I don't want to disturb you," she said.

Jack grew nervous at the circumstance of being alone with her. Julia placed the cup and saucer on the table with the exactitude of an instructor at a school for young women; her fluidity as precise as an atomic clock. He watched her movement through the corner of his eye. She soon excused herself. Jack watched her every move. His wife was beautiful.

"Julia?" Jack said in a quick burst, stopping the woman's progress. She turned.

"Uh . . . I would like to apologize again for what happened earlier. I'm very sorry if I scared you or your children."

"You've already apologized, Mr. Clarke. You need not do it twice."

"Please . . . call me Jack."

"No, thank you, Mr. Clarke. As my Aunt Sophie has reminded me on many occasions, first names are for family and very close friends."

"Yes . . . yes . . . I recall her saying the very same thing."

"Will there be anything else?"

"Well, yes. Would you mind sitting for just a moment? Please," he said, motioning to the couch.

Julia stepped from the landing, walking toward the couch with an irresolute gait. Tucking her dress under her legs, she seated herself prim and proper in the first position just as close to the armrest as she could squeeze her delicate frame. She folded her arms across her chest. Her look chilled. Jack eased into the rocker, crossing his right leg over his left. He coughed to hide the pain of a stab deep in his left side.

He studied her but a moment, recognizing that if she were soaking wet naked she'd be identical to Brooke in both body type and physical features.

"I know this will sound strange to you, but is there any chance you and I have met before?"

Julia was looking beyond Jack to the tree. He wondered if she'd heard him at all. He was set to ask again.

"Mr. Clarke," she said, "I don't trust you. I have seen your type and know the capabilities of such drifters. I don't know what it is you are trying to pull, but I can assure you, you'll not get away with it."

Jack shrank into the cushion, stunned at the accusation. His first instinct was to retrieve the picture in his hand warmer, but he promised Sophie it would be their secret. He could not jeopardize the progress or trust he'd earned with her. He was at a loss for a response.

"You will not find a more honorable and loving family in all the wilds of the northern states. As a matter of fact, you will find most folks in these parts the very examples of what God intended of His flock. You should be ashamed of yourself taking advantage of them the way you have."

"Drifter? Mrs. Bigsby," Jack said, scrapping his informal approach, "first of all, I live in Chicago, Illinois, and I can assure you I have no such intentions. I don't even want to be here. I'm trying to get to Cartersville," he said, pointing out the window, then to his left, "wherever that is. Ask Sophie. If I could walk there right now, I would. I've lost my car, my dog, my wife, my children, and all I want is to find them and go home."

Julia squirmed to readjust her posture. Embarrassment spread across her face. Jack noticed her ears glowing red. Brooke responded in the same manner when saying something regretful.

"Julia," he said, "the last person I'd ever take advantage of is Sophie. I've not met a kinder, more caring woman in my life, other than . . ."—he paused to work out a lump in his throat—". . . other than my wife. I just want to go home."

Julia was growing more uncomfortable with each passing second. She begged in silence for an out and received it.

"Well now, I see you two are getting acquainted," Jubel said from the landing of the stairs. Julia shot from the couch to meet her husband at the corner of the fireplace.

"I need to be a little more careful where I leave you from now on, sweetheart," he said, dropping his arm atop the mantle. "I can't have you unchaperoned around such a handsome man as Jack here."

He wrapped his arm around her and pulled her tight against his chest, expanding her breasts outward against the material of her dress. Jack felt a pulsating heat building at the sight.

"I don't make a habit of chasing married women," Jack responded. Jubel smiled and nodded. The conversation pushed Julia beyond her level of comfort.

"How are the girls?" she asked, initiating the change in subject.

"Fine as pea pods," he said, never taking his eyes off Jack. "Roo has every last one of her baby dolls spread out on the floor and asked me to leave so they could commence with a tea party."

"Maybe I should join them."

"Why, I think they are intending for you and Aunt Sophie to be the guests of honor," he said. Jack matched Jubel's gaze blink for blink.

"Olan would like you take a look at the corn planter when you have a minute," Julia reminded.

"I'll get right to it."

Julia ran her arms around his waist and squeezed. A smile returned to her face. She planted her lips against his cheek and hurried up the stairs without looking again in Jack's direction. Jack loosened the hoodie from around his neck at the sight of *his* wife kissing another man. He noted the hypocrisy of his anger.

Like two rams preparing for collision, the men stared through one another waiting for the other to break. The silence grew uncomfortable; the air charged.

"She's a beautiful woman, wouldn't you say?" Jubel asked.

Jack nodded. "I'd say so. I'd say you were a lucky man."

Jubel removed his arm from the mantle, joined his hands together and rubbed as if washing. "No, not luck, Jack . . . blessed. Luck is but an explanation for those who don't believe in a higher power. The day I met her was the day my eyes opened to the Lord's many wondrous miracles." He turned to the window, watching snow collect against the sill.

"You see, I had no family of my own—orphaned lickety-split the day I spilled from some woman's womb—then passed from foster parents to foster parents until I was 'bout fourteen. Somewhere along the way, I was introduced to the ways of the Lord and the Holy Bible and, well, I prayed every day I'd have a family of my own. Well, brother, did the Lord ever come through for me. Not only a beautiful and caring wife and two of the most kind-hearted youngins an old broke-down cattle rustler like me could ask for, but an extended family as golden as the very streets of our Lord's heaven."

"Well, we all have our own touching stories in life, don't we— some a little better than others," Jack replied. He pushed from the chair to his feet.

"The topic of a higher power doesn't interest you, I guess?"

"No, I'd say it's an interesting enough topic. But not everyone is blessed, as you say and as you have been."

"Oh, Jack . . . I'm surprised a well-booked man like yourself can't see beyond the tree line into the forest right past. It's not a matter of not being blessed—we're all blessed in so many ways there's bare enough time in this life to count 'em all—it just comes down to how each man accepts what's given and takes advantage of what he recognizes."

"That's a very refreshing thought. Did you come up with it on your own?"

"No need to take offense, brother . . . I thought we were just sharing pieces of mind."

"I'm not interested in pieces of your mind. I want to hear your glass-half-full theory the day you lose everything."

"I can see where that might be a right challenge, but the Lord would not have invented steps had He not wanted us to climb."

"What do you mean?"

"It means what it means," Jubel returned.

A blank look fell across Jubel's face. Jack closed in on him to within a foot. He was tired of the man's doublespeak.

"Why don't you and I stop playing games," he demanded.

Although he feared no man, Jubel recognized Jack's size as more than a little intimidating—it would be so to any man. He retreated a half-step. "What?" His face grew puzzled and chalk white.

Jack tempered his voice as to not lure Sophie's attention. "You know very well who I am. What have you done to my family?" He readied for a nervous tic, an uncomfortable blink or a readjustment of the man's posture. Jubel offered nothing; just a look of utter shock.

"What in the world are you talking about, brother?"

"I'm not your brother or your friend. You've appeared to me in the last three days as an old man, a middle-aged man, as your present self, and as a spirit who almost killed me on the staircase in my own house. You've delivered telegrams, photos, newspapers, and answered my wife's cell phone, and I want to know why . . . right now."

Jubel backed up another step. His lips pursed to rip a whistle. "I say," he said, his expression changing to one of fascination, "that's the most interesting tale I've ever heard. What's a cell phone?"

Jack ground his teeth into one another, pushing the muscles of his cheeks nearly through his reddening skin. His fists balled. "You know what I'm talking about," he said, leaning in close.

A devilish smirk erupted from the corners of Jubel's lips, further igniting Jack's internal furry. "Your wound must have done some awful damage, Jack. I'd say it's disrupted the rational side of your brain."

"You're not fooling anyone. I'm going to get to the bottom of this—one way or another."

Jubel didn't waver. His grin widened as if to push Jack's final button. "Maybe you ought to sit a spell and rest. Head injuries can be awful tricky," he said, settling his fingertips against the dent in his temple.

Sophie poked in from the kitchen. "Is everything alright out here?" she asked.

"Just fine Aunt Sophie . . . Jack and I are just gettin' acquainted."

"How nice . . . Jubel, when you get a few minutes, Olan would like you to take a look at the corn planter . . . seems everything mechanical around here can't make it through a single week without your attention."

"Glad to, Aunt Sophie. I'll be right along."

The two men worked through a lengthy pause before Jubel backed away toward the dining room table.

"This isn't over," Jack said. "Not by a long shot."

Jubel expanded his grin.

"You rest yourself, brother," he said, taunting. Jubel turned on his heel and exited into the kitchen.

Jack's rage intensified at the lingering image of the man's smirk. He regretted not wiping it off his face when the chance presented. Little was left to doubt now that Jubel, somehow, some way, was the cause of all Jack had experienced these past few days. He had to pay.

"He's gonna pay," Jack whispered. "He's gonna pay right now." He liked the advantage a peaceful, detached barn offered. With the Brossy men away chasing doggies, he could accomplish what he needed in short order.

Determined to get the confession and explanation he sought, he rushed down the hallway to the guest bedroom. Reaching blindly under the mattress, he dragged his arm across a wide swath in search of his pistol, connecting with just the manila folder. Settling to the floor on his knee, he pushed the mattress up with his palm and searched. The gun and both clips were missing.

Jack slammed the mattress atop the frame. He gazed about the room in a panic, wondering when the culprit had breached the space. His duffle bag was near, which he searched; no firearm. Indexing a list of likely thieves, he ruled out the boys as they were outdoors probably before sunup; Sophie and Roo were in his sights all morning; there was no need for Julia to search anything.

"Olan," he said, "it has to be him."

He wondered what Olan's motive might be and what it meant that he'd taken possession of the weapon. Regardless, if he was going to act, it had to be while the men were away. Staring irreverently at the far wall, Jack concocted his plan. He soon pushed from the bed to his feet, displaying a new sense of calm.

"You don't need a gun."

CHAPTER 32

"And just where do you think you are going?"

Sophie shot from the pantry just as Jack passed. He'd peeked around the corner and noticed the two women facing the opposite direction, forming balls of dough into loaves. He'd hoped to slip out the back unnoticed. A snap of the hardwood floor just on the other side of the doorway brought Sophie rushing from the depths of the pantry.

"I thought maybe I'd step outside a few minutes; maybe watch Jubel tinker with the corn planter," he said. Sophie stepped through the doorway, nudging him toward the utility room.

"What are you doing?" she whispered, her voice anxious.

"Nothing, Sophie. I promise. I feel I've been inside for a week. I just want to get some fresh air and I'll be back in no time. Anyway, I've been dying to see the barn in the daylight." He turned to the kitchen window and the ever-darkening sky. "Well, almost daylight."

"I don't want any trouble between you and Jubel. Are we clear?"

"Sophie, I'll be back before you know it." He flashed his full, natural smile.

It was the first time she had seen his face in such a state of ease and was quick to recognize his pleasant features. She blushed a bit at his handsome appeal.

Sophie glanced over her shoulder to gauge their privacy. "Don't you try and help him, now. Remember your condition."

Jack reached for her arm and offered two playful squeezes in acknowledgement of her concern. "I won't. I'll be back soon."

"You're going to need a coat," she said, pushing past him into the utility room. "Olan has several, grab any one that fits."

"Yes, ma'am."

Jack scanned a long rectangular slab of hardwood affixed to the far wall that held a large selection of winter coats—all gray—and hand-knitted scarves and stocking caps—a deeper shade of gray—all dangling from more than a dozen painted dowels. It's just like the old movies, he thought. They really do live in black and white.

The first coat on the rack appeared the most long-waisted, with sleeves to match, and a nice puffed wool collar. Jack lifted the coat and ran his right arm through the sleeve. In a natural reaction, he attempted to stuff his left arm through as well. The ensuing groan brought Sophie running from the kitchen.

She stood in the doorway shaking her head. "And you want to ride a horse to Cartersville." Pulling the coat from off his right shoulder and arm, she eased in his left arm before encasing his right. She grabbed a scarf, slung it over his neck, and twisted it to under his chin and stuffed the tail into his coat. She buttoned up the front as though she were sending her own child off to school.

"There now," she said, brushing away horsehairs from off his chest, "should keep you plenty warm."

"Thank you."

"Remember, no helping . . . just watching."

"Yes ma'am," he said, smiling.

Jack swung the back screen door open wide, sending the metal spring stretching beyond its normal extension, inciting a grating echo across the grounds. A wave of frigid air circled his body, delivering with it heavy scents of hay, manure, damp cowhide, and wet earth. A growing layer of snow covered the path leading to the outhouse and most every other manmade implement lying about.

The country air with its many fragrances, cleansed the must and city from his lungs as he moved beyond the overhang of the porch to breathe it in full. The fact that the family did not have even one rocking chair on the stone porch surprised him. The view west was sure to offer stunning pre-dusk artwork as the sun fell below rolling hills lined with pines off in the distance.

He released the door and counted the times it slapped against the frame before coming to rest; six whacks. It was a game he'd played as a child and a sound that had burned sentimental in his memory.

Following a fresh set of footprints to the left brought the barn and silo into view. Making the turn at the corner of the house, a large grouping of crows flitted overhead from off the roof, cawing their displeasure as they shot over the barn. Holly berries flashed bright against their green, pointed lacquer leaves in a long heap lining the entire length of the house to its front corner. He counted a half-dozen apple trees planted equidistance apart, their line stretching well into the front yard.

Less than a hundred yards away, built upon ground sloping from the house, the barn positioned facing northeast, separated from the house by a long hedgerow, certain to be of a fragrant species to provide relief to the nostrils during the spring and summer months. The row was well manicured and trimmed evenly down the line, with two aisled gaps cut adjacent to the large, Dutch entry doors at either end of the barn. He followed what was left visible of the footprints through the first open aisle. A small gabled overhang above offered protection from the elements.

Jack peeked through a mutton-barred window caked with dust and cobwebs. It revealed little of the inside's layout. The door itself weighed a ton, and with a sharp grunt, he popped the door loose from its jamb made of heavy, thick oak timber, but held off passing through. Allowing the door to swing just far enough, he stopped short of the threshold to view the interior. His presence sent the livestock to stirring.

The space was dark and damp and reeked of manure, urine and leather. Other than a small brick landing stretching some ten feet forward, the floor itself was dirt, covered in a fine layer of straw. A pinging sound rising above the din of pigs snorting and chickens cackling gave reason for pause. Almost like the tapping of a ball peen hammer, it seemed to be coming from the opposite end of the barn on the second floor.

Jack stepped with caution down the center of the barn, being careful so as not to startle the various collections of animals chewing their mixes of grasses and grains. He spotted the source of the heavy smell of leather, noticing a mile's worth of harnesses, sets of bridles, and saddles stacked on homemade sawhorses against the wall to his left.

Seven stalls were situated against the far wall to his right, the first housed a menacing-looking black Angus bull, tracking his every move and so camouflaged, that only the whites of his eyes shown visible. Two enormous, silver-spotted draft horses occupied the next two stalls, followed by an open space filled with hay Jack guessed was as the stall where he collapsed.

Three more empty horse stalls, two pens housing a half dozen sheep, another holding black and white spotted hogs, and an even larger pen on the far wall filled with roosting boxes for no less than thirty multi-colored chickens, completed the housing on the first floor. Looking to the far back corner of the barn, Jack spotted then hurried toward a set of stairs leading to the second floor.

He grabbed hold of a large support beam posing as the stairway's newel post and eased around the corner for a peek. Seeing the way clear, he turned up the rise to near the halfway point then looked quickly over his shoulder as the second floor opened to his view. The pinging continued at a steady pace from behind. Searching across the space, he spied a metal contraption illuminated by the glare of an oil lamp and a pair of legs squatting on its opposite side.

Jack ascended the final six steps, the boards creaking and cracking with his every movement, trading glances between Bigsby's position and his foot placement. Upon reaching the top of the run, he stood awestruck by the high cathedral ceilings and its magnificent web of hand-cut beams and rafters that ran the entire length of the barn. The air was dry and ripe with the smell of large stores of hay, alfalfa, clover bales, and corn—a sharp and more pleasant contrast to what pricked at his nostrils below.

Affixed on the planter, he noticed a hammer rise above a large steel wheel on the far side then slam down on something equal in material. The second of two large metal canisters labeled in black and orange letters with the maker's marks—David Bradley No. 1 Corn Planter—and secured to the frame just ahead of the wheel, concealed Bigsby's torso.

Jack searched the space while Jubel continued pounding away at the machine. Snow spit at a dizzying pace through a set of large, open double doors centered on the barn's far wall, revealing an earthen ramp leading to the ground. The level appeared reserved for the storage of the winter-feed stash, planting and harvesting equipment, and the many hand tools needed to keep the grounds in repair. He followed the path of an overhead track system supporting a large hayfork attached to the main center beam. Completing a sweep of the corn planter, he noticed movement. Bigsby rose from his crouched position.

The two men locked eyes. Seeing Bigsby had cornered himself between the machine and a wagon stacked high with bales of hay, Jack marched to the front of the planter, cutting off any chance for escape. Bigsby spied over his shoulder, shooting a nervous glance to the floor after realizing his compromised position.

He dropped the hammer into a metal toolbox at his feet. Looking to Jack, he reached to retrieve a kerosene lantern from off the floor, relocating it to the seat of the planter. A large, circular window cut in near the top of the gable end behind allowed just enough daylight to offset the effect of the lamp's flame.

Bigsby crossed his arms over his chest. "Now, why do I get the feeling you're not here to lend a helping hand?" The chill of the air frosted his breath.

Jack surveyed the area and spied a long, open metal box filled with axe handles attached to the front of the hay wagon.

"I wouldn't know the first thing about fixing this," he said, looking to the planter.

"Well, that's not a surprise," Bigsby said.

"Meaning?"

"Meaning I don't suspect you know much about farming or equipment."

"And you do?" Jack mocked.

"Well, I know just a little about a lot of things, I guess. I farm a little, fix folks' machinery a little, volunteer at the county fire station on weekends and holidays. I'm the county cattle inspector and dabble in some of the more common veterinary cases, and I serve as an usher and collector on Sundays at St. Mary's. But, mostly, I just take care of my family the best way I know how."

"Sounds to me you're a jack of all trades and a master of none."

"I suppose," he said, "other than the one, I'd say."

"And that would be?"

"Taking real good care of my family," he said, looking up. "Something I'm sure you know little about as well." The smile ebbed from Jubel's face.

Jack's brow crinkled; his eyes narrowed. The bull in the stall below let out a timely and vociferous snort.

"I'm going to ask you one more time what you've done to my family."

"Or what?" Bigsby tempted.

"Or, you'll tell me the hard way."

Jubel pinched his nose and squinted as if a headache was upon him. "Jack, it just makes me tired all over to hear you talk," he said.

"How 'bout I kick your ass instead."

"Ya see, you haven't learned a thing, have you?" He reached for a shop rag and wiped his hands. "I don't have the first notion as to what you're talkin' 'bout with this business of me appearing as some sort of goblin . . . but I had you pegged the moment we met. Yes sir, I did.

"Now, the way I see it, you've lost something and want it back. But, instead of looking at your insides and accepting why it was you lost it in the first place, you're gonna blame the rest of the world for your mistakes. It's like a squirrel who spends the entire fall playing games with the bunnies and hedgehogs, then comes wintertime, and he hasn't the first morsel to shove into his mouth and he starts stealing from his neighbors. I know you have an eye for my wife . . . and I don't blame you . . . she's a smart looking woman with decency to match. But she's mine and there's nothing you can do it about it now."

"What do you mean by 'now'?"

Jubel shrugged his shoulders and smiled.

"I want my wife and daughters back . . . the ones you stole from me."

"I've not stolen the first thing in my life. And who's to say they didn't want to be found by someone else?"

"You stole them. They didn't come to you on their own. You stalked them; hunted them down and now you've turned them against me."

"Jack, you're looking at this all wrong . . . this is your time," he said, moving closer, "this is your chance to be free; it's your chance to be what you want, do what you want, and not have to worry about a wife who can't satisfy and a couple kids who hate you anyway."

Feeling a burn against his forehead and a rapid pulse blistering inside his ears, Jack gritted his teeth as Jubel's maddening smirk almost dared him to take his best poke. For but an instant, his angered gaze flicked in the direction of the box of axe handles. He wondered how fast he could reach the nearest handle and if Bigsby's first move would be to advance or retreat.

"I'm warning you . . . you come clean right here, right now," he demanded.

Bigsby took another step closer. "How about we make a deal," he said, speaking secretively, "I'll keep what I have and you can keep Staci . . . you don't even got the dog to worry about anymore, since you killed him off." A wink from his eye sent Jack into a rage.

"You son-of-a—" he yelled. The expletive fell short as he lunged for the closest handle nearest his reach. Pulling the piece of ash free in a single, fluid motion, he swung wildly in Bigsby's direction. The butt end of the handle cut a bloody, razor thin line across Bigsby's cheek, just missing burying square into his jaw as he pulled back, ducking just in time. The follow-through connected against the metal canister atop the corn planter, leaving a crumpling dent in its side.

Bigsby fled for the wall behind. Jack regathered a secure grip of the lumber and rushed in pursuit, dusting up a huge cloud of particles as he grinded for traction atop the hay-strewn surface. Both men's breathing intensified, echoing through the ever-darkening space, as white clouds of condensation discharged from their mouths as each struggled to gain an upper hand.

Adrenaline surging through Jack's veins masked the pain in his shoulder, as he grabbed the free end of the handle and advanced toward Bigsby in a bull-rush, holding the wood spoke horizontal in front of him. Bigsby attempted an escape over the top of the planter but missed with his first step. His leg buckled as his shin slammed against the metal frame.

With two strides, Jack was on top of him. Trapped like a rat, Bigsby just managed to get his palms up in front of his face as the axe handle drove toward the base of his chin. The impact sent him crashing against a stud, forcing a bellowing groan. He fought to keep the handle from crushing against his Adam's apple.

Jack's face burned red with rage; Bigsby's white with fear. The two men struggled like beasts brawling for supremacy in a pack, absorbing each other's haste nose to nose, struggling for position and searching with wild eyes for the slightest opening for an advantage. The force of the handle pressed greater to Bigsby's left, forcing his hand down the shaft to the right, where he kept the attack at an impasse. Jack was pushing at much less than full capacity.

"What have you done to my family?" Jack yelled at the top of his lungs, sending a shower of spit into Bigsby's face. The veins in his neck throbbed as blood rushed to support his fury. He repeated the question. Bigsby clamped his jaw tight, unable to speak as the backs of his hands pushed hard in against his throat.

"I love my wife," Jack yelled. "Do you hear me? I love my wife!"

"She's mine now," Bigsby choked, his face growing blue from his inability to draw a natural inhale.

"You stole her from me," Jack yelled, "you came to me as a ghost!"

The quick burst of grunts and groans emanating from both men unsettled the livestock below. Bigsby noticed a figure appear behind them.

"Alright son, that's enough," boomed a voice from over Jack's shoulder. The sound of two hammers clicking back slowed the tussle, allowing Bigsby to push the handle away from his neck and slip below. He collapsed to the floor, sucking in deep breaths to refill his lungs. Jack turned on his heels, his chest heaving in and out like the billows of a blasting furnace, to see the dual barrels of a shotgun pointed at his face and Olan taking dead aim behind the sight.

"Drop it," Olan demanded.

Staring down both barrels, Jack allowed the axe handle to slip from his grip to the floor.

"Jubel? You alright, son?"

Still unable to speak and hidden from Olan's view, Jubel raised a hand and flipped his wrist to indicate he was fine. His arm collapsed back into his lap as he leaned against the wall, still gasping for breath.

"Okay, son," Olan said, jerking the barrel twice toward the stairs, "let's go." Jack glanced at Bigsby out of the corner of his eye. The smirk had reemerged upon his face. Jubel spread the thumb and pinkie of his right hand and drew them to the side of his head, mimicking the receiver of a telephone.

"I told you your wife and daughters returned to me, Jack," he said, whispering in short quick bursts. "Your time has come and gone . . . jack . . . ass."

Jack's face went pale. A brief tremor surged through his body as if touching the wrong wire on a live outlet. The taunting was enough to make him question if Olan would pull a trigger or two if he attempted to finish the man off.

"I said, let's go . . . now," Olan barked.

Jack chose to live and fight another day. He shuffled off with the gun aimed just inches from the back of his head. Olan ordered Jubel to stay put until he returned. With his adrenaline leaking away, Jack grabbed hold of his left shoulder as severe throbbing commenced, working its way the length of his arm to his fingertips. Descending the stairs, he wondered if the pain in his arm would be equal to Sophie's wrath.

———⟨⟩———

The little women in the house, having grown tired of pouring invisible tea and eating imaginary cookies, relocated to the kitchen in search of something more exciting to occupy their time.

With the equivalent of a complete pie shell in leftover dough scraps, Sophie rolled out the remains at the kitchen table. She provided the girls with an ample amount of sugar and cinnamon, setting about quenching their desire to have their hands in something real. Although not her county-famous shortbread and nut cookies, once baked, the piecrust would taste just as good and would prove twice as tasty as what was at their disposal upstairs.

Giggles erupted as the three homemakers-to-be used a dull butter knife to scribe out snowmen, candy canes and Christmas trees. Their jubilance drowned out the sound of the back door swinging open. When Jack appeared in the doorway, their delight paused.

Sarah and Samantha scampered from the table to the pantry where their mother was busy peeling potatoes. Sophie turned from the stove and smiled. She did not see her husband standing behind.

"I knew you would be gone longer than just a few minutes," she said. Her smile eased away upon a double take of Jack's expression. Jack felt the hard steel of the barrels push against his spine. The two moved through the doorway on the command.

Sophie gasped. "Good heavens, Olan," she exclaimed, her voice rushed with disbelief. "What in the world are you doing?" Julia hurried in from the pantry with her girls clinging to the back of her dress.

"Sophie, I want you to fetch the key from my desk for the back bedroom door."

"Olan, what is it, what happened?"

"I'll tell ya what happened . . . our guest here just worked our nephew over with an axe handle in the barn."

Julia let go a blistering scream. Dragging the girls along, she raced from the kitchen to the den, instructed the two to go up to their room before blowing through the front door in the direction of the barn. Sophie sent Roo upstairs along with her cousins. Her head cocked and face drooped with puzzlement as she kept watch of Jack well past the doorway.

Sophie released the apron from her hands. Jack looked away as she approached.

"What have you done?" she said, tersely. He said nothing.

"I already told ya what he done," Olan barked. "I'm gonna lock him up in his room and send for the sheriff first thing in the morning."

Sophie offered Jack another chance.

"You must tell me what happened."

Jack ground his teeth and swallowed deep. "He said something I didn't like and I lost my tempter."

"How bad is he hurt?" she asked her husband.

"Not bad, I reckon. He's got a bit of a cut on his cheek, from what I can tell, and probably some might sore body parts, but he was moving and talking. I believe I got there just in time. We got some fencing down and I came back for some wire."

Sophie stepped to the side without saying another word. Olan offered a nudge with the gun and the two men moved through the parlor. Sophie followed in their wake through the doorway before breaking off to retrieve the key. She rejoined the two in their slow march down the long hallway.

"Now, I don't want to hear the first peep out of you," Olan said, dropping the barrel of the shotgun across his arm and toward the floor. "You'll stay in this room until the sheriff gets here . . . understood?"

Jack positioned himself against the window near the fireplace. He agreed with a shallow nod.

"I almost pulled the trigger, boy. You need to know that."

"Come, Sophie," Olan said, backing toward the door.

"I will be right along," she answered.

"You'll be right along right now," he demanded. "You're not staying in here alone with that crazy animal."

"Oh, Olan . . . please," she said, motioning her wrist toward the ground. "He is no animal; maybe misguided and wrong-headed, but he is not an animal and he is far from a threat to me. You go on now and tend to Jubel. I'll be right along."

"Sophie, this man is a lunatic. Do you wanna know what I heard him say? He yelled something to Jubel about him bein' some kind of ghost—a ghost. I'm tellin' ya, the man's off his nut."

"Olan . . . I will be right along, please tend to Jubel."

Olan backed off. He'd seen his wife drop Hereford calves five times her weight for branding and turn the orneriest, most foul-mouthed, tobacco-spitting ranch hands west of the Mississippi into altar boys. He was less concerned for her safety than he was Jack's. He knew the boy was in for it.

"Okay," he said, "but you make sure you lock the door."

Jack could feel Sophie closing in from behind, the heat of her anger burning against his neck.

"But I say unto you, that ye resist not evil: but whosoever shall smite thee on thy right cheek, turn to him the other also . . . Matthew five, thirty-nine," she said.

Jack sighed.

"Do you realize what you have done?" she asked. "I will have no ability to talk my husband out of calling for the sheriff. He *will* come and get you and he *will* put you in the county lockup. Olan saved the sheriff's life three years back and he will do to you whatever Olan requests. How could you do such a thing? Jubel is as peaceful as the spring. He's a fine husband and father, and one of our most devoted church goers. I resigned myself to helping you any way I could, despite the fact you have stretched my faith and trust beyond any point I have known. But this? I am very sorry, Mr. Clarke, but you have left me no room to help any further." Sophie turned to the door with key in hand.

"Sophie, please . . . wait. I told you, I'd already met your nephew before. He appeared to me several times. He told me my wife and daughters returned to him during a phone call," his voice grew excited as he pointed toward the barn. "He said the same thing to me in there not fifteen minutes ago."

Sophie's expression dripped with disappointment. Jack knew he was losing her.

"I need to show you something." Moving to the opposite side of the room, he shoved an arm under the mattress and extracted the manila envelope. He grabbed at the edges of the black and white photo, turning it against his chest. He hurried to the bedroom door.

"Three days ago, this was delivered to my office in downtown Chicago by a man calling himself Jubel Bigsby. It was the second time I saw him that morning." Jack extended the photo to Sophie face down; she took a step back. The hair on the back of her neck prickled as she fought against her senses to accept his claim. Several moments passed before she reached with a trembling hand to accept it.

Flipping the picture over, she gasped and brought a hand to her mouth

"Why do you have this?" she demanded, her voice choking. Tears streamed down her cheeks.

"I told you, it was—"

"No," she yelled, interrupting. "Why do you have a picture of my daughter? I have never seen this picture before." Sophie released the image as if it were contagious. She brought both hands to her chest and backed herself into the doorway.

"Sophie . . . please . . . you must believe me," Jack begged. "I don't know why it was delivered to me. I don't understand the significance of it either. All I know is it was brought to me by your nephew."

Sophie wiped the tears from her cheeks and straightened her dress in a show of composure. Clearing her throat, her demeanor turned resolute as she reached for the doorknob. The circumstances fished through her brain like an evil disease, nearly forcing her to do something beyond her natural character; become someone she was not. She studied his face and saw truth, yet she wanted to scream *liar*. It was all too much for her common sense to decipher. She needed to leave his sight.

"What I know for certain," she said, "is my husband has a keen eye for people and their dispositions. He's a fair and honest man. He knows what's best for this family."

She pulled the door hard against the jamb. Jack listened for her footsteps but heard none. Her pause was long and silent. He moved a few steps forward before hearing the key engage the tumblers and the mechanism snap to lock.

CHAPTER 33

Clete and Ellie Howard, along with their four children, arrived chilled and snow-covered, just as dusk claimed its stake on the day. With a 650-acre corn field and three-acre lake separating the families' property line to the south, the Howards made quick time of their trip, saving forty minutes traversing the frozen landscape via horse and sleigh rather than following the lone, winding county road between the homes.

Sophie received the Howards upon their arrival, having managed to complete her Christmas Eve dinner menu on schedule, despite losing an hour attending to Jubel's cut cheek and bruised back, and fighting through the burden of Jack's predicament, which tormented and occupied her every thought. With eight children and seven adults assembled for the evening's festivities, she even found a few extra minutes to wrap enough presents so all could partake in the holiday tradition passed down by her mother.

The family had little extra income to spend on store-bought presents for birthdays and Christmas. Sophie spent most of her evenings throughout the year with a set of needles in her hands or peddling away at her sewing machine preparing homemade goods for just such occasions. As the family relaxed away the rigors of farm life each evening by the radio, enjoying the soothing messages of faith and hope from Father Darby St. Patrick on WPAH Waupaca or on occasion—on a clear night—catching *The Eveready Hour* variety show on Milwaukee's WIAO, Sophie settled in her rocker, knitting everything from sweaters to socks.

Olan also contributed to the cache of homemade merchandise with handcrafted wood furniture and toys he constructed or whittled. Many in the community went without. Sophie's diligence ensured her family and friends did not.

The very essence of Christmas and the season—its sights, smells, and spirits—all manifested into a perfect sensation of holiday warmth and cheer inside the Brossy home. Although simple in decorative splendor, Sophie succeeded in creating an exciting atmosphere that filled each soul with anticipation for the evening's fellowship.

The families merged as one around the dinner table, each face erupting with a smile projecting brighter than the candles burning on the branches of the Christmas tree. When Olan counted the place settings, the festive mood tempered.

"Sophie, my dear," he called out, "why are there two extra plates?" he asked. Seated at her normal position near the kitchen opening, she offered a caring smile to her family and guests, each of whom turned in anticipation of a response. She moved her water glass from one side of her plate to the other, adjusting the silverware as she stalled to generate an explanation. Olan crossed his arms in anticipation.

"Doctor Danaher mentioned he may join us this evening. I thought I better be prepared . . . just in case."

"That accounts for one of them," he said, already keen as to her intent for the second place setting.

Her pause was brief. "Well, I just thought we could consider inviting Mr. Clarke to join us for dinner," she responded, looking to her husband with hopeful eyes.

Olan released a sigh. Sophie grew confused over the smile slanting across his lips, not knowing if he was in support of her suggestion or considering sending her to the asylum along with their misguided guest.

Olan still looked upon her face the same now as the day they met. He loved her for many reasons but the compassion with which she dealt with the world—an attribute he lacked on several levels—moved his heart. She was a single rose in a field full of sandburs and he knew, after counting the plates at the table, she meant it as a silent plea to him. Her tranquil way warmed his insides like a gulp of steaming creamy soup on a frozen winter day.

"I don't think it's a good idea, my dear," he said, being cautious with his tone.

"I know, Olan," she replied, "but it is Christmas Eve. I do not have the stomach to be sitting at this table when we have a stranger locked away in a room like a prisoner. Someone who is quite alone, I might add. I cannot even begin to imagine what the good Lord thinks of us right now."

"My dear, he attacked and injured our nephew, unprovoked. I know I'm not the most religious man at this table, but I'm sure God is not holding you responsible for his actions. You know as well as I, he's unstable and unpredictable. I'm not about to let him have another chance at hurting someone. We need to get him out of this house as soon as possible."

"You know Uncle Olan?" Jubel interrupted, "I think we ought to invite the boy out here." Sophie could not have been more surprised.

"Why would you want him out here after what he done?" Olan asked.

"What he *did*," Sophie suggested.

"Well, the way I see it, he's not too familiar with true family ways, and, well, I think it might do him some good to see how a real family spends its time together. As for this afternoon, well, I just got caught in a corner like a badger in a cave's all; had I been paying more attention, he'd a never got the drop on me."

"And you don't think he'll try it again?" Olan asked.

"No sir . . . I don't. I think the boy is going through a mighty stress-ful moment and he just lost his head. Anyway, what could he do against the five of us?" he asked, looking across the table to Caleb, Matty, and Clete. "I know he's a right big cuss, but I think the five of us can get 'em on the ground if need be. I know for a fact his shoulder's still ailing. Surely we can handle a one-armed man."

Sophie extended to pat Jubel's hand. "That's a right Christian way, Jubel," she said, "God is sure to look down on you with much favor."

Sophie could see her husband's mind working. Jubel's words went a fair distance with him. She clasped her hands underneath the table.

"Olan, I know how you feel about this and agree Mr. Clarke's actions were despicable," she said, gaining his attention. "But, think about what he's been through, how he's fretting for his family and what it must be like to be in a strange place alone . . . having no one familiar near you."

She saw the corners of his eyes soften and a push of air coming from deep in his chest. He recalled the days of running cattle and horses across the plains and the piercing lonesome pain he felt sleeping under a black, star-filled canopy without his beloved Annesophie cuddled next to him. He smiled and nodded.

"Okay, my dear," he conceded, "whatever you want."

Sophie flashed a smile, erasing the crinkle above his brow. How he loved how she could change his mind, when she felt in her heart it was the right thing to do.

"On one condition, though," he demanded. "You all are going to move down one space," he said, pointing to the Howards. "Our guest will sit right here between me and Caleb."

Without hesitation, Clete and Ellie corralled their children and moved one space to their left just as Olan requested. Sophie pushed away from the table and walked with an anxious gait to the other end.

She flung her arms around Olan's neck, planted a kiss on his cheek, and whispered something into his ear. Her voice provoked a cheerful smile, reigniting the once festive mood.

Jack had crawled under the covers hoping to find deep sleep upon Sophie's exit, after first having tested the door lock for any potential deficiencies. He found none. Tossing for the better part of an hour, he finally ceded the effort, stacked a mess of pillows against the headboard and readjusted from a horizontal to a sitting position.

Now staring into the fireplace at the dying flames, he worked through a series of possible options on how he could escape prior to dawn, each including busting through the door or breaking a bedroom window—both of which he knew would alert all in the house.

Thoughts of Bigsby, and how he might get at him one more time, interrupted his strategy session often. He recalled his words and repeated them. "Your time's come and gone . . . your time's come and gone."

As much as he wanted to do the man irreparable harm, he lamented it would be at the cost of Sophie's allegiance.

She was now more than an arbitrary character crossing a point in life dissecting his own. Unlike Roo, where he felt a connection almost immediately, Sophie seemed just a slight improvement over his mother-in-law, with similar attributes meant to agitate his very soul. But a connection was brewing with her, and the more time he spent in her presence, the stronger the feeling settled in his gut. It bothered him beyond his rationale that he lied to her and let her down. It disturbed him more that he cared.

The knock upon his bedroom door was a surprise. The cadence and

"Mr. Clarke, are you awake?"

Jack hesitated as he thought through remaining silent and leaving things as they were. With his stomach growling and the possibility Olan had given her permission to offer scraps from the table, he responded.

"Yes ma'am, I'm awake," he replied.

He heard the key enter the lock then watched the turn of the knob. Sophie moved through the doorway with caution. She'd come empty-handed.

Walking straight for the fireplace, she bent low to stir the remnants in the firebox, resurrecting a new flame, before placing three fresh logs on top.

Sophie brushed her hands. "We are just now sitting down to Christmas Eve supper and would like you to join us," she said, her voice stern.

Jack's brow furrowed, as a puzzled look spilled over his face.

"I will not have someone locked in a room in my home, alone, on such a holy night." Her expression offered little in the way of a formal invitation; sounding more like a business proposal.

"I don't think it's such a good idea," Jack said. "I don't mind being alone . . . I've been alone most of my life. I don't mind it at all."

"I'm sure that's what you tell everyone, but I don't believe it for a second. Now, we are all waiting to start our supper and I will not serve the first morsel to anyone until you have seated yourself at that table. If you would like to further ruin this day then, by all means, stay put. If not, the food is getting cold." She motioned her hand toward the door.

"Why are you doing this?"

"As I said, I will not have someone sitting alone, locked in a room in my house like a prisoner on Christmas Eve."

"What about what happened earlier? I doubt very much your niece and nephew want me sitting at the table."

"As a matter of fact, it was at Jubel's request my husband agreed."

"And why would Jubel make such a suggestion?"

"Because he's a good Christian, a forgiving man, and is sympathetic to the circumstances you are facing."

"I'll bet he is."

"Oh, Mr. Clarke, you would be wise at this point to accept an olive branch when it is offered. The ice below your feet is as thin as newspaper. The slightest foul intent on your part, I dare say, will not have a pleasant result."

"I know you are upset with me, but—"

Sophie interrupted, "You lied to me, Mr. Clarke. You promised you would not start any trouble. You gave me your word."

"I know I did and I'm sorry. But your nephew told me my time had come and gone with my family. What was I supposed to do? How would you have had me react?"

"By walking away and being the bigger man. My nephew, God love him, dotes over Julia like a mother hen and he's quite jealous of her. I'm sure he feels threatened by you. We all have our obsessions and addictions; not one of us is perfect. You should have walked away. At least I could be in a position to help you."

"Then why are you helping me now? Why risk something else happening?"

Sophie stalled. She did not want to answer the question but refused the telling of any lie, white or other.

She shuffled to the edge of the bed and stared deep into his eyes. "Because you *will* act the perfect gentleman and behave yourself and . . . well . . . because I believe every word you have told me," she said, her voice accelerating. "I don't know how or why you have come to us but there is a reason God has brought you to our doorstep and I will abide by what He guides my soul to do. If it means to help, then I will help."

Jack sunk deep into the pillow, and succumbed into a silent stare. His shock was evident by the sag of his face.

"Now, I would like for you to get out of bed and join us at the table. Please do not make me ask again."

Sophie stepped to the door, opened it wide and stood rigid as a footman at a five-star hotel waiting for Jack to pull the covers from off his body. He recognized the absurdity of his claims, yet she stood behind him relying on the enormous depth of her faith. Her courage amazed him; her faith stirred a desire deep inside him to want to know how he too could grasp a hold of such power. Regardless of her reasons, her actions shortened the distance between them. Jack followed Sophie into the hallway, pausing after she snapped around to deliver a firm request.

"I demand your very best behavior."

<hr/>

Jack fought butterflies masquerading as hornets as he followed close behind Sophie down the darkened hallway toward the bright glow of the den. He paused at the jamb, losing sight of her as she continued around the corner. The near deafening sounds of life and laughter echoing from the table tempered to whispers as Sophie appeared in full. Realizing halfway across the floor she'd lost her guest, she retraced her steps to the doorway.

"What is it, Mr. Clarke?" she asked, poking around the corner.

"I don't think this is a good idea. I'm just going to go back to my room."

"You will do nothing of the sort," she snapped. "We must all own up to our mistakes and you will do it right now. I think you will be surprised how forgiving family and people in general can be if you give them a chance."

Jack released a sigh and followed the crook of Sophie's finger as she motioned for him to follow. As the two entered the den, his forehead and neck began to roast. He felt as a leper walking amongst the uninfected as every head, other than Julia's, tracked his approach.

Sophie passed her husband and motioned Jack to the empty seat to Caleb's right. Surrounded by Brossy men and Clete, Jack took an account of all present, noticing Bigsby on the opposite side of the table at the far end, two positions from Sophie. He was quick to figure the strategic placement.

Olan sat stiff with elbows on the table and hands clasped against his mouth while Jack seated himself. A bowl filled with homemade wheat bread slices just beyond Jack's plate sent a powerful and enticing aroma plowing into his face. He skimmed to his right, catching Olan doing the same to his left. Neither said a word.

"Well, now," Sophie said, "that's much better."

Jack offered Matty a nod, then to Caleb, who responded in kind. Julia, making a point of ignoring him altogether, rested comfortably next to Matty and to the left of Sarah and Samantha.

Jack's breath shortened at the sight of the three, each dressed in their best holiday outfits, with the girls wearing matching bows in their hair. Their similarities to his own family confused his rational thought, forcing his mind to consider drastic measures as to how he could extract them from the home—by force if necessary.

He scanned down the line, meeting the blacks of Jubel's pupils and a provoking grin on his face. Knowing Jack's eyes were upon him, Jubel ran his arms around Samantha, squeezed her and kissed her cheek. Jack's fists trembled under the table. Seeing the family seated together disrupted his already sinking appetite. He fought against an urge to act, recalling his promise to Sophie.

"Mr. Clarke," Sophie called out, "please do say hello to our dear friends Clete and Ellie Howard and their children, Janey, Marylynn, Nicholas, and Clete Junior."

Jack leaned forward as Caleb drew back. He offered a smile and a hello. Clete extended his hand, which Jack accepted.

"Pleasure to meet you, son," Clete said. The man's flesh felt like worn and weathered leather and ribbed with calluses. The shake was country through and through.

"Are we ready to begin?" Sophie asked.

Instinctively, Jack moved his arm forward to retrieve a slice of bread but paused after noticing everyone clasping their hands or flattening them palm against palm.

"Relax, son," Olan whispered. "It's going to be a couple of minutes."

"Our Father in heaven, Hallowed be Your name," Sophie started. The entire table, including the children, joined in unison.

"Your kingdom come, Your will be done on earth as it is in heaven."

Jack looked among the faces noticing the manner in which they all recited. He knew the prayer; had recited it many times as a youngster, but had long since lost memory of the words. His lips lagged behind.

"Give us this day, our daily bread, and forgive us our debts, as we forgive our debtors. And do not lead us into temptation, but deliver us from evil. For Yours is the kingdom, and the power, and the glory forever. Amen."

"Olan," Sophie called out to her husband, "would you please begin?"

The families remained as they were with hands clasped. Jack's gaze switched from one end of the table to the other, unsure of her directive.

"Lord, I thank You for this day and the two strong hands You've given me so I may provide for my family," he said. "I thank You for our friends and wish You will bless all in this house . . . I thank You for the two fine young men we have raised and my wonderful little bundle of pride and joy. Lord, no man can fulfill his own will without the blessing of a strong and wonderful woman. You delivered my wonderful wife to me and in so doing, saved my life. I praise Your name."

"Matty?" Sophie said.

Jack was relieved the sequence moved to the right.

"Lord, I thank You for this farm, this family, and this life, and pray we may all serve You without hesitation to the best of our ability."

Sophie nodded to Julia. Jack watched her face soften and a smile form. Her eyes were just as beautiful closed as open.

"Heavenly Father, thank You so much for my loving family, my wonderful and caring husband, my two lovely children and the many wonderful blessings You have bestowed upon us over the years. I pray for Your continued blessings for all in this house."

Jack felt a sharp pain pierce his chest. For a moment, he consumed her words as if intended for his ears alone. When she opened her eyes, she turned to her husband, who put his hand to his lips and blew a soft kiss. Jack's throat constricted at the sight.

Sarah was next. "Dear God, thank You for my dog Maxie, my pet turtle Brutus, and my sister."

"Thank You God for Mommy and Daddy, for Aunt Sophie and Uncle Olan and cousins Matty, Caleb, and Roo . . . oh, and for my sister, too," said Samantha, drawing a laugh from around the table.

"Thank you God fow evewyone," Roo started. "Fow Mommy, Daddy, Caleb, and Matty. And thank You fow my new fwiend, Mistew Clawke."

Jack gulped. Every head at the table snapped to attention and toward Roo's direction. Sophie could not have been more surprised. Jack suspected the expression appeared in triplicate upon Olan's face.

The family redirected to view Jack's reaction. Despite feeling like a prisoner caught against a brick wall with a blinding searchlight tracking his every motion, he did not turn from her. Roo offered a playful smile, which he reciprocated.

Sophie cleared her throat. "Heavenly Father, I thank You for this moment, this family, these friends and guests, and for the many tender mercies You deliver daily. You have blessed me so with four wonderful children and I pray You help me teach them the great power of Your love and kindness." She paused and breathed deep.

"Lord Jesus," she said, her voice beginning to crack, "You have the power to give and take away and it is our duty to have faith in the call of Your every action. I pray for all those who have passed into Your care, including our April, whom we love so much and miss so terribly."

Jack peeked to his right. A single streak glistened down Olan's cheek. He angled left and noticed Jubel pinching at his eyes, fighting the same flow. Not a dry eye remained at the table. The family's compassion moved him.

"I pray You have brought her peace and have plans for us all to be together one day again," Sophie continued. "Lord I pray You will provide care and guidance to the Howards as they begin their search for a new life. Please make Your presence known to all those who have yet to feel Your power and bring peace to all who find themselves alone on this sacred day."

Sophie paused to collect herself and passed the baton on to the Howards. The family continued the sentiments of thanks, praising their kind neighbors and praying for guidance as they set out on their new journey. Caleb followed with a lengthy and emotional tribute to his mother and father, which brought the table to tears a second time.

As the final sentiment dripped from Caleb's lips, Jack again felt a deluge of eyes descending upon him as if surrounded prey amongst a pack of hungry lions. A nervous heat rippled against the back of his neck. The hypocrisy of him thanking God in such a moment was a level to which even he could not stoop. He did not move a muscle as the embarrassment of the situation sizzled inside his chest.

"Lord Jesus Christ, the Almighty, we pray You can help Mr. Clarke find what he's seeking. We ask You fill his spirit with Your love, his heart with Your guidance, and his mind with Your faith. We pray You show him Your path to truth and righteousness and deliver him from the bonds of Satan's grip. In Your name we pray."

Jack sat still in his chair, dumbfounded by Jubel's words. He seemed isolated in his surprise by the man's gesture. He was at a loss for words and thought.

"Now, everyone, if you please," Sophie said, "take what you'd like from the bowl in front of you, and pass it to the person to your left. Olan, Caleb, please help Mr. Clarke with the heavier platters."

CHAPTER 34

For an hour-and-a-half, the families fought their way through the bountiful feast, making but a dent in the fare as more time was spent passing the circling parade of bowls and platters rather than inserting fork and spoons into mouths.

Appetites slowed with the delivery of second and third helpings. Each eased deep into their chairs, holding onto their bellies, and complaining of gluttony and the inability to finish that *one* last bite.

Jack enjoyed the roast turkey and smoked ham most, followed by everything prepared with cinnamon spice and some concoction of potatoes, cabbage, and onions originating from Ellie Howard's kitchen. A couple pieces of pie crammed full of raspberries, blackberries, and a berry he could not identify, rounded out the perfect meal.

Jack said little and was asked less during the feast, as he consumed the festive banter detailing Brossy family Christmases past, and stories of simpler times and harder struggles. The conversation tore at his conscience and his heart, as he pictured several times while looking about the table, his mother in Sophie's position and his father in Olan's, and the warmth he remembered from the days when his family shared similar conversations and feasted on similar dishes.

He spent his entire life trying to erase those days from his memory, laboring to build a tolerance to offset the pain. As he listened to their banter, studied their faces, and absorbed the obvious love they held for one another, he contemplated the many years missed in renewing those same moments with his own family.

He studied Jubel's interaction with Julia. The collaboration between husband and wife was as free flowing and effortless as the most sophisticated timepiece. The physical contact between them was often and dripping with a tender passion. Jubel's every touch upon her looked as if he were handling the most delicate of crystal pieces from a curio cabinet stuffed full of the same. When they spoke, they did so as if no one else existed around them. Their faces glowed with a joy and contentment that left him empty. On more than one occasion, Jubel flashed an eye and winked, as if offering instruction.

At one point, while leaning back in his chair, easing the pressure of an expanded abdomen, Jack spied through an opening over Caleb's shoulder Jubel accepting Sarah into his lap and bringing her close against his chest. Jack could see the muscles in her tiny arms constricting as she held tight to his neck. Her loving touch forced Jubel's eyes shut. The look upon his face rendered Jack numb. It was as if he were seeing a reflection in a mirror. His jealousy piqued as Bigsby absorbed the love of his daughter as if a meal in itself. "How can that not be what you want?" Jack whispered under his breath.

The adults moved into post-meal conversation, complete with the mandatory rapid fire round of compliments for having just been the beneficiaries of the finest meal ever prepared. The children, having long since been excused from the table, relocated to the den where they huddled on hands and knees near the Christmas tree, counting the many presents stuffed under the branches and discussing who would be getting the large blue box with the red bow, and the smaller green package with the white ribbon. Being outnumbered and outvoted, the boys were informed they'd be receiving nothing.

Olan stretched his frame horizontal in the chair and dug his thumbs under the lapels of a finely stitched brown dress coat. "My dear . . . that was the finest meal I believe I've ever had," he said, releasing a smack as he sucked a turkey sliver loose from in between his teeth.

"Here, here," Jubel added. "You couldn't get a meal like this in Eau Claire."

"The last meal I got in Eau Claire stayed put for about a half-hour," Clete said, drawing a hearty laugh.

"Mr. Clarke, did you get enough to eat?" Sophie asked.

"Yes ma'am. I've not had a better meal myself." Jack leaned over the table. "Mrs. Howard, your potato dish was remarkable."

"Thank you. I like to use sweet potatoes but we just didn't have any on hand at the moment."

"It was right delicious just as," Olan said, nodding and winking.

"Well, if everyone's had enough for the moment, I best be getting this table cleared so we can open some presents," Sophie said. The announcement brought screams from the children.

"Aunt Sophie, you stay put," Julia said. "You've worked hard enough today. Ellie and I can clear the table and have it done in a matter of minutes. Matty, Caleb, would you boys mind lending us a hand? Girls? Come on now and get your plates."

The brothers eased from their chairs like a couple of old men off a park bench following a day of checkers, grunting from the added weight and newfound lethargy associated with fresh roasted turkey. The kids raced in from every direction, each grabbing a plate and a handful of silverware before following the adults into the kitchen. Despite direct orders, Sophie cleared her end of the table, drawing the ire of her niece.

Jack scooted his chair from the table, readying to assist clearing his side of a few plates, when he felt a tug on his sleeve. Roo stood just behind his chair, holding something behind her back.

She tugged at him shyly and asked, "Would you please wead me this book?"

Sophie reappeared from the kitchen just as her daughter made the request. Olan hurried to dispel her wishes.

"Roo, he just finished his supper. You go on now and help your ma clear the table."

"A grand idea, Roo," Sophie interrupted. "It would be a great help if you could clear these youngsters out of the way for me, Mr. Clarke. I believe things would go much faster."

Sophie's urging produced a wide smile across Roo's face. She tugged again at Jack's arm, exposing a bright red, hard covered book with an artist's rendition of several small children dressed in varying turn-of-the-century pajamas painted various shades of green and red-stripe, carrying stockings to hang on a fireplace mantle.

"This is my favowite stowy," she exclaimed.

"Twas the Night Before Christmas," Jack said aloud.

He inspected the book for several moments. The spine appeared wrinkled and worn from years of repeated use with the book itself aged well beyond Roo's years. The title, in its large, scripted white lettering, forced the recollection of the lone picture he saw of his father holding him. The book in the photo was one in the same, other than Jack recalling a green cover and a picture of Santa's sleigh and team of reindeer planted on a rooftop.

"I know this book very well," he said, speaking to no one in particular.

A tap instead of a tug erased his father's face from his thoughts.

"Would you wead it to me? Please?" Roo begged.

"You would be doing me a great favor." Sophie continued stacking plates atop each other, resolute in her wish he'd grant her daughter's request. Jack flashed Roo a smile and pushed from off his seat; she was quick to take his hand and lead him to the large rocking chair near the tree. Sophie expelled a surprised sigh as her daughter transformed into a socialite right before her eyes. Olan moved from his seat to her end of the table.

"Why would you contradict me?" he questioned. "Does nothing I say hold any merit in this house anymore?"

"Olan, please . . . have you ever in your life seen her respond to an adult like this?" He turned as Roo led Jack by the hand into *his* rocker.

"Look," she whispered. "There is something in that man that she trusts; something she has connected with. I do not know what or how, but just look. Have you ever seen her take an adult's hand before— especially a man's?"

Olan brought his hand to under his chin and rubbed over a hearty cropping of two-day's growth. The more he thought about it, the more he identified with her point. He remembered how Roo avoided his cousin like the plague, despite the fact the man had spent six months on the farm following the war and played with the kids from morning till sundown. He never once recalled the two coming in contact with one another.

"Well, if it's all the same to you, I think I'll just sit by close and keep an eye out."

"Olan, for heaven's sake, he's just reading a book. What in the world is he going to do?"

"If it's all the same to you," he said, with a mocking grin, attempting to reestablish his hold as head of the family. He returned to his place at the end of the table, swung his chair ninety degrees and stretched out with hands clasped behind his head, watching the children gather around Jack's feet.

Feeling awkward at the sudden splash of attention, Jack flipped through the book as a nervous diversion as the children poked and elbowed in their attempts to each obtain front row seating. As they settled, with legs crossed and bodies packed tight against one another in a semi-circle around the rocker, he peeked over the top of the book at the eyes staring back with excited anticipation of the impromptu command performance.

The delight on their faces warmed his soul, but a stabbing also persisted as he looked to Sarah and Samantha, both of whom had muscled their way into the two most forward positions. They gazed upon him as Julianna and Jordan often did. The similarity of their smiles and familiarity of their facial features caused an awakening, paralyzing like a dagger to the spine. He had never held his own girls in his lap and read them a story.

A tap on his knee interrupted the second of two deep breaths he drew to stave off the emotion building. Relocating his arm away from his body, Roo crawled up into his lap, just as casual as a kitten, and without so much as a "please," as if he were Olan or Santa Claus himself.

Her insistence startled him and stunned her mother. Sophie flashed her husband a toothy grin. Her hard-charging man of the house was already fast asleep.

Roo tumbled and flopped about in his lap like a netted trout until she found the most comfortable spot. Jack placed a hand against her thigh and scooted her nearer his frame to ensure her security. The feeling of her sitting bunched up in a ball against his ribs was like a dose of a miracle medicine erasing every known human malady. He drew his nose close to her hair, taking in the sweet smell of the same lavender scent he noticed on Sophie. His heart began to ache.

"Okay, you can wead now," she instructed.

Jack opened the book to page one. Clete and Ellie settled close together on the couch. Matty took up a position on the floor against the corner of the fireplace, leaning against the stone and looking very much like he was about to join his father for a nap. Caleb slumped in a rocker under the window just beyond, having pulled a pocketknife to continue carving at a small stock of wood. Jack did not notice the Bigsbys' occupying a couple chairs just opposite the couch. Julia appeared nervous as a worm in a chicken coop that her daughters were but an arm's length away from him; Jubel appeared quite the opposite, almost as if he knew the moment had to be.

"Twas the night before Christmas when all through the house, not a creature was stirring not even a mouse," Jack began. The entire house fell silent as his voice spilled out deep and rustic. It reminded Sophie of a radio personality she'd heard pitching laundry detergent.

"The stockings were hung by the chimney with care, in hopes that St. Nicholas soon would be there.

"The children were nestled all snug in their beds, while visions of sugarplums danced in their heads.

"And mamma in her kerchief and I in my cap, had just settled down for a long winter's nap."

Sophie eased behind her husband and placed her hands atop his. His body jerked, drawing laughs and the trading of mocking glances from the boys. As Olan focused on the scene before him, he moved toward the edge of his seat as if preparing to advance. Sophie drew her arms around his neck, easing him against the seatback.

Content as a newborn fawn, Roo rested her head against Jack's chest, concentrating on his every word. The children grew anxious with each passage of the poem, conjuring thoughts of Santa's midnight visit and wonder if his reindeers could really fly.

"He spoke not a word, but went straight to his work, and filled all the stockings; then turned with a jerk.

"And laying his finger aside of his nose, and giving a nod, up the chimney he rose.

"He sprang to his sleigh, to his team gave a whistle, and away they all flew like the down of a thistle.

"But I heard him exclaim, ere he drove out of sight, 'Happy Christmas to all, and to all a good-night.'"

Jack closed the book to wild, giggle-induced applause as the children scrambled to their feet, shooting off in all directions seeking out the laps of their parents. The adults reciprocated with a tempered hand, applauding approval in recognition of the beautiful oration and the renewed spirit of holiday cheer it injected into the evening.

Roo squeezed Jack tight around his middle; he leaned over and planted a soft kiss against her cheek then patted her leg. She jumped from his lap and ran straight into the arms of Matty.

Sophie bent low to near Olan's ear. "He's no monster," she whispered, patting his shoulder.

Olan was not convinced. "I've seen wolves in sheep's clothing before," he assured. Sophie knew he was not going to budge from calling for the sheriff.

Anxious to move along with the evening's festivities, Sophie stepped to the middle of the den and announced, "I believe it is time to open some presents." The girls let rip a new round of screams; the boys jumped up and down at their inclusion in the tradition.

Sophie orchestrated a complete overhaul of the seating with the help of Matty and Caleb, shifting the array of rockers and armchairs into an oblong arrangement jutting at an angle from the Christmas tree toward the dining table. She doled out seat assignments; children first and nearest the tree; then by family members. Jack removed himself from the mix, relocating near the stairs, careful not to obstruct as the room transformed.

As the frantic scramble settled, Jack called to Sophie, half raising his hand, but was unable to capture her attention as she bent low under the tree, instructing a couple of her helpers as to which present should be delivered to which guests.

A second attempt brought Sophie upright.

"Sophie, I'm gonna let your family enjoy your Christmas and go on to bed now."

"You will do nothing of the sort," she demanded, throwing her hands against her hips. "I have a present here for you and it's a family tradition we open our presents together."

"No, please, you don't need to give me anything, you've done enough. I'm very tired and should go on to bed."

"Jack, it's Christmas Eve . . . you've been the life of the party so far . . . you should stay. I think you will enjoy this," Jubel said from across the room.

"Please, we'd like you to stay," Sophie said, nodding in approval of her nephew's suspicions.

Jack traded stares between the two and conceded with an accepting nod. The very thought of exchanging and opening presents, or watching others do it, made him sick to his stomach, but he had less of a stomach for disappointing Sophie again. He eased into an armchair next to Olan. As he settled, Roo chugged toward him from her chair near the tree. Her father outstretched his arms upon her approach but she sidestepped his attempt to collect her and jumped straight into Jack's lap.

"Maybe you should sit with your father while you open presents," Jack said.

"I want to sit with you," she said, snuggling tighter against his side.

"It's okay, son . . . this bein' your last night with us and all," Olan said, shooting a reproving look before returning his attention to the shuffling under the tree.

Jack gauged Olan's body language. He knew he'd need to orchestrate a plan for escape to Cartersville well before sunup. He put his arm around Roo; she balled up smaller than a hedgehog.

With Clete Junior and Marylynn serving as Santa's helpers, at Sophie's instruction, the two delivered presents until the space under the tree lay vacant. Jack was hesitant accepting an unboxed bundle wrapped in green tissue paper delivered by Marylynn. He made mention aloud to no one in particular it was not necessary, but his words went unheard to those about him. He tucked the gift under the presents the elves delivered to Roo.

The relative calm that ensued surprised. Jack expected the children to have the tissue and wrapping paper shredded and in piles in the middle of the floor. If it had been his family, this portion of Christmas would have lasted about thirty seconds. Even as a youngster, he wondered what was the point of spending two months getting ready, and in a matter of seconds, the holiday was declared over.

"Okay Janey, why don't you go first," Sophie suggested. The youngest of the Howards' children smiled wide and asked her mother which of the two presents she should open first. Not waiting for her answer, she tore open a rectangular bundle wrapped in red tissue paper, revealing a beautiful pink, hand-knitted sweater with protruding rose buds. What the Howards lacked most was proper winter clothing for their children. The gift was a relief to her parents.

Nicholas Howard was next in line, and calculating that the rectangular object in his lap was a sweater, chose to open the other. The boy's eyes lit like spotlights at the hand-carved steam shovel toy with a working bucket. It was one of Olan's specialties, along with trains and stake-bed pickup trucks, and was in better working condition than most store-bought items of the same device. Nicholas lost contact with the rest of the room as he fell to his knees to discover the intricacies of his new machine.

One by one, each opened a single present to the excited compliments of the others. The process was wearing thin on Jack's emotions. Although he could not deny the excitement on the children's faces delighted him, he spent most of the celebration pushing aside the sickening feeling that Christmas always induced. He and suffered through having to watch Julia interact with her children, wishing all the time, by some miracle, a switch would flip and all would be right with the world. He watched her every move, careful not to let her catch his prying eye. The mannerisms with which she dealt with the girls were indistinguishable from the way Brooke cared for and loved theirs. He'd rather be in the county lockup than watching their interaction from but a few feet away.

"Now, that's a right beautiful gift, Olan," Jubel said, with a bit of quiver to his voice. Jubel extended the item from his body for all to see. "Thank you very much."

The two-inch long wooden cross, masterfully carved from a piece of cherry and in-laid with a thin piece of brass stripping running across both dimensions, was finished to a sheen smooth as glass.

"Well, I couldn't find a proper chain . . . you'll have to steal one from your wife," Olan said.

"I think I know the very one," Jubel responded. "Thanks again."

"Okay, your turn," Sophie said, looking to Jack.

The situation was growing more uncomfortable by the second. Jack wanted nothing to do with opening a gift in front of everyone.

"Maybe we should let Roo open her present first?" he said, attempting a bypass.

"Everyone goes in order . . . go on now."

Roo dug for the present and placed it on top of her lap. Bending low, he whispered into her ear. Not needing a second request, she shredded the paper, revealing a hand-knitted stocking cap and scarf matching perfectly the colors of his beloved Chicago Bears

"I just happened on some yarn that matched your shirt and thought you could use something more to keep you warm," Sophie said, smiling ear to ear.

"It's perfect, Sophie," Jack said with a sigh. "You shouldn't have done this." She leaned back in her chair, pleased he appreciated her work. He wondered how in the world she'd found the time to knit the items and why she included him in their holiday.

Anxious to get the celebration back on track, and without prompting, Roo ripped open her first present, proudly displaying to all a beautiful white-laced dress for her favorite baby doll. Barely able to contain her excitement, she dropped the dress against Jack's chest and under his chin, twisting and turning as if fitting it to her doll. The room burst into laughter.

The families circled twice around as Jack hunkered deeper and deeper into the seatback with each gift opened. Wanting to retreat to his bedroom, he grew encouraged that the festivities might be winding down as Sophie removed tissue paper from around the final gift. Tears flowed as she panned to the group a finger painting from Roo of her pushing her daughter in the tire swing hanging from the large oak tree in the front yard. Even from a distance, the bright colors indicated a beautiful spring day. Sophie swung her arms wide, prompting Roo to jump from Jack's lap. Their embrace forced a smile upon his face.

Jack leveled his arms to lift from the chair, believing the festivities had concluded. He made it halfway out before Sophie announced round two of the tradition.

"Okay everyone," she announced, "it's time for the gift of giving."

Jack stared, puzzled, as each looked to their gifts then to the others around the circle as if trying to make some sort of decision. Jack eased back in his chair, seeing no one else budged.

Sophie noticed the confused look on his face. "This is a time we each pay tribute to our Lord Jesus Christ through the gift of giving. You see, Mr. Clarke, Christmas is not about receiving . . . it is about giving. So, each year, after all the presents have been opened, we each give away something we received to someone whom we think needs it more.

It is just a way to remind us all of the true meaning of Christmas and to always do for others first."

Jack never heard of such. He was shocked less by the philosophy of the lesson than he was at not hearing the first objection from one of the children. Easing into his seat, he scanned the faces as each person sized up someone across from them.

"Who would like to go first?" Sophie asked.

Olan raised his hand then stood. "Sophie, my dear, the hat is beautiful, but I believe Clete will need plenty more of them where he's headed." Olan walked to Clete's position, extended the knitted stocking hat and wished him a Merry Christmas

The giving gained momentum as Olan resettled in his chair. Roo gave her doll dress and sweater to each of the Howard girls, Matty gave his scarf and cap to Clete Junior and Caleb his three new cork bobbers to Nicholas. Julia gave a sweater to Ellie and a pair of mittens to Janey. Sarah and Samantha also gave away goods to the Howard girls. Jubel gave his cross to Roo.

The scene between the families pushed Jack beyond a level of emotion he was willing to share. He felt the room closing in on him.

Sophie lifted from her chair and shuffled through the circle of Christmas paper to stand in front of Jack. She pushed the watercolor painting within his reach. Jack pushed deeper into his chair as if she were getting ready to stick him with a hot poker. His face melted in confusion.

"I would like for you to have this." Jack shook his head. He could not get words to form on his lips.

"Please . . . it will be something to help you remember this adventure."

Not to be outdone by her mother, Roo raced to her side and with an excited eye and twinkling smile, extended the cross from her hand.

"This is fow you," she said. "Now God will be with you no mattew whewe you go."

The expression on her face broke the last bit of resistance he kept in reserve. He could no longer swallow the emotion. Pushing from the chair, allowing his cap and scarf to tumble to the floor, he exited toward the staircase.

"I want to thank you all for everything," he said, his voice cracking, "but I can't do this anymore . . . I just can't. I hope you can forgive me."

Jack fled into the hallway, moving off to the sounds of hardwood snapping below his steps. Sophie placed an arm around her daughter. Roo stared at the now empty doorway leading from the room. As the families traded perplexed looks, the sound of his bedroom door clicking shut drained what was left of the cheer of the moment.

CHAPTER 35

"Jack? May I come in? I would like to speak with you."

Having shrouded himself in a heavy quilt and settled close to the fireplace, Jack traded blurred glances between the orange of the flame and a section of sky where the silver light of the moon pushed its way through an ever-thinning cover of clouds. When the nightlight disappeared behind a passing cloud, he returned to the flame. The exchange dallied more than an hour.

"Jack? Are you awake?"

His surprise did not come from hearing his first name, but from the voice from which it sprung. The thoughts rushing through his mind of Christmas Eve 1967 faded, as Jack unwrapped himself of the quilt and moved across the floor. He cracked the door just enough to allow the visitor a peek inside

"May I please come in?"

Jack swung the door open wide and moved aside. Sophie stepped through, toting the gifts he'd left behind, and a clump wrapped in a small burlap sack. She proceeded to the fireplace. Jack retreated to the edge of the bed and planted himself on the corner.

Sophie pulled a chair close, placed the bundle of items on the floor and resituated, crossing her legs. A momentary lull ensued as she studied the wrinkles around his tired eyes and the gray of his complexion, which she concluded was a residuum of his discomfort during their gift exchange.

"You called me by my first name," he muttered. His speech was slow and drained of all vitality.

"Yes, I know."

"I thought that was reserved for family and close friends."

"It is. I am certain you will find this hard to believe, but I consider you a friend. I want to help you."

"There's nothing you can do for me. But, for what it's worth, I consider you a friend as well."

"Mr. . . . I mean, Jack, I am a simple woman brought up by simple people and have known nothing but cattle, sheep, corn, and wheat my entire life. My father's brother was a newspaperman who traveled a great bit covering events in Europe and Asia. He brought me stacks of newspapers and bulletins from which I learned to read and write. I am not an overly educated woman, but I do know pain when I see it, and in your case, I see much more. I see a man harmed in such a way he has forgotten how to live the very life he was given.

"I see a man searching for something but not having the first idea of how and where to search, or in which direction to walk. I see a man who wants to be more than what he is, better than what he has been, and to be forgiven for what he has done. I see a man who wants to love but does not know how. I see a man who wants to find God but is too afraid to give himself up and allow Him to take over . . . tell me, have I have misjudged you or suggested a false portrayal?"

Jack said nothing.

"I take by your silence you do not refute my assessment?"

"There's nothing you can do to help me. There's nothing anyone can do."

"I know something happened to you. I promise . . . you *can* trust me with your troubles. It will stay between us."

His refusal over the years to discuss his past created a burden so overwhelming he no longer knew how to handle the ever-present rage bubbling just below the surface. The memory of his family's failings was eating away at his insides as if an advancing cancer with not the first hint of a cure. Who would better understand his feelings?

"You know," he said, still looking to the floor, "when I was very little, my family used to celebrate Christmas much in the same way your family does. Friends and relatives popped in and out on Christmas Eve and day. It was always something I looked forward to, as did my younger sister."

"You have not mentioned her before. Is she your only sibling?"

"Yes. Her name is Shannon, and we were very close during those days."

"You refer to her as if she's passed on."

"No, she's still alive—as far as I know. We've not spoken since we were teenagers."

"That is very sad. I am sorry."

He let a few moments slip before continuing. "As I was saying, we celebrated Christmas like everyone else until I was four years old. After that, things changed in our house. It's like the holiday was wiped clean from the calendar. My mother would put up a tree and we'd pass a few homemade presents back and forth, but there were no more celebrations or family gatherings on Christmas Day. It seemed just another day of the week.

"My sister and I were always in trouble, I guess . . . you know, always getting into something or doing things we shouldn't. At about that same time, I remember when one of us got in trouble, my mother and father would fight like cats and dogs. My father was very physical with us. My sister and I usually got the belt, and then he'd go to work on my mom. It seemed like no matter what we did, whether we broke a shoelace or spilled a glass of milk, we all paid the same price. I remember him once beating my sister when she came home from school, after he found out I'd lost my stocking cap on the playground."

Sophie covered her mouth with her hand. She never heard of such abuse. Jack wiped at the side of his face as he struggled to continue.

"When I was seven years old, right after Thanksgiving, my father told my sister and me we would not be celebrating Christmas because we'd not behaved well enough in the past year to earn the *'right,'*" he said, grinning and expelling a sarcastic breath. His voice drifted as he was transported to the moment.

"That Christmas Eve, my mother ran out on an errand and brought back a very small tree, which my sister and I decorated. My dad had gone to a local corner bar and didn't come home until late. He was drunk and angry about something before he walked in the door, I think. But when he saw the tree, he went into a rage." Jack pushed a hand to his face as tears began to flow.

"He beat my mother to within an inch of her life . . . she could not move or speak," he said, his voice cracking and becoming difficult to understand. His breathing intensified.

"My sister ran across the street to a neighbor's house. I was sitting on the couch in the living room, frozen stiff. I just sat there and did nothing. I could hear my mother screaming for help and then—all of sudden—her screams cut off as if someone had flipped a switch. Even though she was no longer calling out, I could still hear my father beating her. I just sat there and did nothing."

Jack covered his face and bent in half. Sophie jumped from her chair as he cried out in pain. She moved onto the bed next to him and threw her arms around him. She rubbed her hand across his back. Jack grabbed at the sides of his head and planted his elbows atop his knees.

"Oh God," he said, pushing in hard against his head. Sophie tried to pull at his arms.

"When he came out of their room he saw me sitting on the couch, staring at the tree," Jack said, his voice rising. "He walked in front of me, smoking a cigarette, looking as if nothing at all had happened. I didn't see the gun in his hand. He flicked his cigarette to the floor, pointed the gun at my head, and told me it was my fault my mother was dead. Then he smiled, jammed the gun under his chin, and pulled the trigger."

Sophie let out a gasp. She could no longer see through her tears. Her throat constricted as his grief spilled.

"His head exploded all over me and his body collapsed on top of me. I went into shock. The police found me sitting on the couch, staring straight ahead with his body draped across mine, covered in his blood."

Sophie grabbed Jack around his neck and pulled him against her chest.

"Oh my dear Lord," she whispered. "You poor, poor man. Shhhhh . . . It is okay."

Sophie placed her cheek against his. She held him tight, rocking back and forth as if holding an infant. He shook in her arms like a mountain succumbing to shifting plates below, compelling her to wrap tighter around him. The warmth of her loving and tender touch broke the very will he used to fight against his demons. In a desperate moment of pure vulnerability and revelation, he thrust his arms around her and held on. Sophie accepted his reach as a plea for help and held him until his sobbing eased. She too drained of tears, as his pain struck her to her very core.

Jack eased his grip after regaining control. Sophie moved from the bed to the washbasin, soaked a rag full of water then returned. She passed the rag off into his hands before easing onto the edge of the chair. As he dabbed at his forehead, she wiped away from her cheeks what was left of her tears.

"I don't have the first idea of what to say," she said, trembling, still reeling from the details of something much less believable than the date of his birth.

Jack cleared his throat. "As I said, not much can be done. I don't know if it will ever pass."

"Please tell me you understand you did nothing wrong."

He swallowed deep but did not answer. The very mention he was guiltless in the matter sent tears spilling.

"Jack . . . you were just a little boy. You cannot blame yourself for the actions of your father. Little boys and little girls get in trouble. It is what they do. They do things they are not supposed to do because they are children. It is the very definition of being a child. Your father was responsible for his own actions. "Jack, look at me," she demanded. "Look at me . . . please." Sophie scooted from her chair to her knees, placing her hands atop his thighs.

"You were a little boy," she repeated, gaining his stare. "You did not attack your mother or your sister, and you did not pull the trigger. You said the other day you felt regret over kicking your dog. Was it his fault *you* chose to deal with your anger in that manner? Whatever it was he did, could you not have dealt with the situation another way?"

Jack nodded.

"So could your father, but he chose not to. You are not to blame. We must all account for our own actions. In Deuteronomy, it spells out God's expectations of our accountability. 'Fathers shall not be put to death for their children, nor children for their fathers; only for his own guilt shall a man be put to death.' Do you understand? It means you are not held accountable for the sins of your father."

Sophie eased into the chair, crossed her legs and brought both palms together against her chin. She was unable to release the image of him sitting on a couch with the bloody remains of his father in his lap. The vision churned a frigid chill inside her even the flame of the fireplace could not penetrate.

"I can't imagine you spending your entire life carrying around such guilt," she said. "What a horrible, horrible burden to carry."

Jack moved from the corner of the bed to the headboard, leaning against the pile of pillows. He winced as he stretched his legs across the mattress.

"So your mother passed?"

"No. My father beat her into a coma, but she survived that attack. She passed a few years ago."

"Where you able to spend much time with her?"

"I left my home when I was fourteen and never saw her again."

"Is that why you also lost touch with your sister?"

She watched his expression change. It was one of humiliation rather than pain. He fidgeted about the bed, trying to avoid eye contact; she waited out his hesitancy.

"The one thing you need to know," he said, pressing a thumb into his palm and rubbing methodically, "the world I have come to you from is nothing like the world you live in today. So many things have changed. There's a great deal of evil in the world; evil people who will stop at nothing to acquire wealth by any means. Even if we had a week, I could not explain it well enough for you to have proper perspective. But, one of those evils is drugs manufactured for recreational use."

"As in medicine?" she asked.

"No, it's like alcohol, but different. They are referred to as recreational because they do not provide a medicinal value. People take them for pleasure because of the effect it has on them; they can become addicted. It can lead to a lot of bad things."

"Why would a person take such products?"

"I could never explain that. Like I said, the world will be very different in fifty years. The point is, when my father died, my mother did all she could to keep a roof over our heads and food on the table. She worked two jobs—at a diner during the day and at a local bar at night—and, well, she just ended up falling in with the wrong sort."

"Drugs?" Sophie asked.

"Well, a man who was heavy into taking and selling them. Because most of these drugs are against the law to use and sell, there's a great deal of money to be made—especially from those who are addicted. There are a great many in the business of selling these drugs. My mother fell in with this man and . . . well, it was very bad. She tried several times to get herself and us away from him, but he threatened he'd kill us if she left."

Sophie grew conscious of the growing tumult in her stomach. She resigned herself not to push Jack for details, but he continued unprompted.

"I came home from school one afternoon while my mother was at work. I found her boyfriend and several of his friends, also drug users and dealers, in the living room taking turns—"

Jack paused to search for words to describe the scene. Drawing his right leg up to near his chest, he rested the ball of his fist against his lips, fighting off a choking spasm and images of the dreadful moment.

"The men were taking turns having intercourse with my sister," he said, his speech quavering. "She was only eleven."

Sophie released another echoing gasp as she rushed to cover her mouth with her hands.

"When I saw what they were doing, I froze stiff with fear. I did nothing to help her. When they saw me, they grabbed me and kicked me around a bit, but not enough to do any real damage." His face dripped with shame.

"The men grabbed my sister and my mother's boyfriend pulled a gun and put it against her head. He told me . . . he told me if I didn't have intercourse with her he was going to kill her. I told him no. So one of his friends lit a match and set her hair on fire. I yelled for them to stop." Jack covered his face with his hands. "I had no choice but to do whatever they asked me to do . . . so I did. They forced the both of us to do . . . well, some very unpleasant things, and just sat there and watched . . . drinking and laughing."

Sophie felt an urge to want to vomit.

"My mother came home during the middle of it all, saw what was happening and ran from the house to call the police. Unfortunately, her boyfriend got to her before the police arrived and beat and kicked her into a coma. She was in the hospital for several weeks."

Jack breathed deep. "As I'm sure you can appreciate, my sister and I could not look at one another or even be in the same room together. I stayed until my mother was released from the hospital and I left . . . forever. I could not stay in the house or in that town a minute more."

Silence settled as the two gathered from opposing perspectives the remains of his account like storm survivors surveying the destruction. Jack puzzled at the cleansing sensation rippling through his conscience. Sophie looked about the room, focusing on nothing in particular, ingesting his words and trying to fathom the immeasurable burden he had lugged around more than half his life.

"Where did you go?" she asked. Her voice did not penetrate his consciousness immediately.

"I'm sorry, what?" he asked, shaking off an afterthought.

"Where did you go when you left home?"

"To a distant cousin's house in Minnesota, until I finished high school. Then I went on to college."

"And you never contacted your mother or sister?"

"I did hear from my mother about a year after I left. She sent me a letter."

"And did you respond?"

"No. I could never forgive her for not protecting us; for not doing something, anything. I heard she bounced around from town to town working as a waitress. She died of a heart attack at work around Christmas one year. The last time I was near her was at her funeral. My sister was there, but I just couldn't speak to her. I saw her, and she saw me, but I walked right by her and said nothing."

"Do you regret not keeping in touch with your mother?"

"I do now. I thought being free from her—from them—was the answer for normalcy. I don't know what she went through. I don't know how painful it was for her—dealing with my father and trying to raise us alone. I wish I had an opportunity to ask her those questions."

"Do you regret losing touch with your sister?"

"I didn't used to . . . I'm not so sure now. I just don't know how I would ever come to face her again. I don't know if I'm strong enough. I just know my heart aches at times at the thought that she dealt with all this pain alone. I ache knowing I was not there for her."

"There is still plenty of life left. You can correct this," Sophie said. "I think one day you will wake up and want to speak with her. What about Brooke? Is she aware of these circumstances?"

Sophie moved from the chair to take a side-saddled position on the edge of the bed near him. "Jack, look at me," she said, reaching to bring his hand into hers. "You have to sit her down and tell her everything. It is not fair to her that you have left so much of your life unexplained. She cannot be whole to you or to the union if she does not know your past. I realize how difficult it would be to tell her the truth, but the events you just described were the results of decisions made by others and out of your control. My Lord knows how horrible it was for you and your sister, but what you did, because you had no other choice, saved her life. Could you have lived your own life had they killed her? Could you have avoided madness with the image of her death along with that of your father's? You must believe . . . none of this was your fault."

Sophie's touch was as soft as her words, and equal in the peace it brought to his troubled soul. His mind opened to her suggestion that he was swallowing more blame than was his fair share. She grabbed his hand.

"I see now why talk of God disturbs you so," she observed, as her face darkened. "I know many who have come to the same conclusion when the floor beneath their feet is swept away."

Jack relayed in detail how he prayed to God for his father's intervention that spring afternoon on the playground when he was overmatched and unprepared to defend himself. How he prayed daily seeking God's protection for himself, his sister, and mother from the brutal, senseless attacks each endured at the hands of his father. How he prayed the night of his father's suicide that God would give him the courage to get off the couch and do something, anything, in defense of his mother. He also spoke of the moment he saw the men raping his sister and recalled not offering the first prayer for God's help or even thinking to ask.

Sophie struggled for the words to respond. She knew faith to be a ring at the top of a lengthy pole that each person must reach on their own, in their own way. She could not think of a single verse to renew his will to reach for that ring.

She released his hand to clasp her own together. "This is what I know to be true. There is but one gift God could not afford not to give us. He gave us the breath of life, He gave us this world and the very

necessities and resources we need to survive, He gave us companionship and the ability to distinguish one sense from another, and He gave
us the ability to reproduce and live on. He also gave us the gift of free
will. Without it, He could not distinguish if our love for Him was true
or because He insisted upon it.

"Your wife loves you because she found love in her heart and she
found it on her own. If you forced her to love you, how would you ever
know if her love was real? The same goes for God. By giving us free
will, He identifies with those who love Him and have faith in Him and
those of the world who have evil in their hearts and love another. It is
the one and only true way He can love and be loved.

"The bully in the schoolyard and your father's reaction to it all was
an act of free will. What those men did to you and your family was an
act of free will. Your father chose a wrongful path as well. God did not,
and does not want you harmed in any manner . . . ever. But, as I told
you, it is what humankind does with free will that makes the world go
round. You must release Him from blame if you want to find Him again.
I promise you, He wants to be found."

Somewhere during the appeal, Jack descended into the blue of her
eyes, allowing her assurances to flow unimpeded. Her ideals, or maybe
the manner with which she expressed them, delivered a link he was
unable to connect previously, cracking a window for reconsideration of
the blame he accepted as his own and what he was dishing out. He
remembered once knowing God and His only Son. He wondered now
if the only way back to his family meant getting right with God first.

"Do you want to find God?" she asked.

Jack kept up his stare. It annoyed his fighting side that he could no
longer control his tears. His voice choked. "I know I don't want to be
the man I've been anymore. I want my wife and children to love me."

"They do love you Jack. You just have forgotten how to accept it.
But you can make it so if you give God a fighting chance to help you.

He wants to help. You cannot go forward any longer on your own. You want Brooke and you will do anything to get her back. Well, God wants you just as much, if not more, and He too will do anything to get you back. Please, just give Him a chance. I promise, if you do, the doors you want opened in your life will open. Would you like to pray with me?" Sophie asked.

Jack nodded, and reached for her hand.

"Heavenly Father, You have a son who wants to return to You. Please help him to find Your guiding light and blessed Spirit so he may know Your love and tenderness. Please lead him back to his family and bring him fulfillment in his desires to be the man he's chosen to become. In Your name we pray."

With little hesitation, Jack reached forward to collect Sophie in his arms. She accepted his embrace as she would from her own son. She whispered that he would always be in her thoughts and prayers. As each released, a summons ripped through the door.

"Sophie, is everything all right in there?" Olan barked. She shot from the bed to open the door. Olan gazed about with a suspecting eye.

"You've been in there nearly an hour. What's the trouble?"

"No trouble. I was just speaking with Mr. Clarke."

"For two hours?"

"He was just telling me a bit about his family. Is everything all right out there?" she asked, redirecting.

"Everything's fine 'cept Jubel needs to leave. Jeff Pruit showed up on the front porch needing his help. His bull is down and he doesn't have the first idea of what's wrong."

"Oh, for heaven's sake," Sophie cried, "that bull is twenty years old if he's a day. Why that man will not let the poor beast die in peace is beyond me."

"Well, I thought you should pack up some food for him. Looks like he's in for a long night. While he's at Jeff's, he's going to call on the sheriff," Olan said, looking over her shoulder to Jack. "I told him to ask the sheriff to be here first light."

"Olan . . . please . . . on Christmas Day? This is all so unnecessary."

"It's done," he said, resolute. "There will be no more discussion about it."

Olan stomped down the hallway, leaving Sophie standing alone in the doorway. She offered a quick prayer on her husband's behalf.

"I'm so sorry, Jack. I do not know what I can do. Once he makes his mind up about something, it is rare I can get him to change it."

"Is the sheriff in Cartersville?"

"No. The county lockup is in Cameron."

Jack released a heavy sigh. His body deflated.

Sophie walked to the edge of the bed and placed her hand on his shoulder. "Just sit tight," she said. "I might have an idea."

———— ◦◦◦◦◦ ————

Having recoiled into the pillows, sucked dry of all vitality from the emotional dump, Jack stared at the ceiling dichotomizing Sophie's words. Although mentally spent, he reconfirmed his desire to want to become a different man—a better man—and tossed about how he could live her philosophies as his own. He dropped against the headboard and found deep sleep within a few minutes of her exit.

A considerate tap upon the door awoke him from an hour-long, dreamless drift. Sophie entered, holding a piece of folded white paper in her grip. She relocated the chair to near the nightstand.

"I am afraid I could not get Olan to budge," she said, her face blazoned with defeat. "He's bound and determined to hand you over to the authorities." Sophie drew in close.

"I have drawn you a map of how to get from this house to Cartersville," she said, whispering. "I am afraid my artistic skills are limited, but I have included several landmarks to guide you . . . even in the dark. There are two turns and the first is down the road a fair bit at a place meeting up at four points near a large red barn. You could not miss it in a blizzard." She handed over the paper.

Jack unfolded the piece and viewed her charcoal pencil outline. It appeared easy enough and something he was sure he could navigate.

Sophie glanced over her shoulder then leaned close to his ear. "On the upper level of the barn, Olan has a truck he uses to deliver milk and curd to the farmer's market. It is a beast of a machine; one I dare say has produced more foulness from his mouth than any other piece of machinery we own.

"I know one person can start it by use of a crank handle located in front. I think, too, you have to get in quickly because it tends to take off on its own. I do not know if they all do that, but this particular model does. Now, all you need to do is open the large barn doors and drive it out. You can be on your way before anyone would have time to stop you."

"I've never driven a vehicle like that . . . I wouldn't even know how to start the thing."

"Well, I've never driven it myself, but getting it started seems quite simple. There is a lever on the left side of the steering wheel you must push upward and one on the opposite side that must be in the down position. I have no idea as to their significance, but it seems those adjustments are vital in getting the truck started. There is also a knob in the front below the . . . below the . . ." Sophie searched for the term she'd heard her husband use a hundred times.

"Radiator," she said, snapping her fingers. "You must pull the knob down then return to the truck and turn the key. You must push the hand crank toward the radiator and crank clockwise a turn or two. Once it starts though, be sure to get out of the way. Those cranks have been known to break a man's arm in half."

"I can't ask you to do this for me. It's not right," he said. "I can't ask you to deceive your husband this way."

"You did not ask me," she said, leaning back into the chair. "And I do not consider this deception. We both know the circumstances well and I see no way of explaining any of this to anyone. Olan will never understand and it is just best all the way around if you slip out before sunup and be on your way."

"But now he'll have me on the hook for stealing his truck," he said, refolding the map.

"Don't you worry. The farmer's market is on the main road just before you get into town. Go straight there and leave the truck in the lot. Everyone knows Olan's truck and someone will get in touch with him. It won't be stolen if you leave it there."

"I don't think the law works that way, Sophie," he questioned.

"There is no other way, unless you want to go in the wrong direction and spend who knows how long behind bars. They tend to forget about drifters around these parts; and they *will* consider you a drifter. I will leave some supplies and food in a sack for you in the cabinet in the mudroom. Be sure to take a coat and anything else you need to keep warm. It is going to be very cold. I'm hopeful the snow will have stopped."

Sophie looked to the floor at the items she'd placed there earlier and brought the heap into her lap. She handed over the burlap sack.

"I took this from your room. I found it quite by accident," she said, looking as if confessing a sin.

Jack unwrapped the burlap to reveal his pistol and ammo clips.

"I checked on you the other night, and while tucking in your sheets, I found it. I grew worried . . . well, with the loss of your dog and not knowing the condition of your family . . . I thought you might use it to harm yourself. I must say, in all the guns I've seen in my life, I've never seen anything like that."

Jack smiled. Had the gun been in his possession, he'd be on his way to the county lockup for sure on a charge of murder. He was glad now it had disappeared from the room.

"I understand. I appreciate you were concerned." He paused to enjoy the smile on her face. "I have too many things left to do to take my own life." Her smile grew wider.

"I think you will need these," she said, handing over the cap and scarf, "and I want you to have these things."

Jack accepted the watercolor painting and wood cross from her fingers. "I can't accept these things . . . I just can't. These are way too sentimental for you to be giving to me."

"It will be something for you to remember your adventure with us. I know Roo would be down in the mouth for weeks if you did not take the cross, especially. She is so very fond of you. I cannot tell you the impact you have had on her."

The very mention of the girl brought his face to glowing. "She's something," he said. "She's beyond special. There is something about her I feel will always be a part of me, no matter where I end up. It's very strange, but I felt it the moment we met."

"Then you will take these things?"

Jack reviewed each item for a moment and nodded. "Okay, Sophie. As you wish . . . and thank you."

Just short of the moment becoming awkward, Sophie stood to excuse herself.

"Well, now," she said, brushing to straighten her dress, "I have guests to see off and children to get to bed." Jack rose from the bed to meet her.

Sophie ran her arms behind him. Her embrace was delicate and motherly. Jack leaned low and placed his cheek against hers.

"I don't know how to thank you," he whispered. "I don't even know how to explain all this but if I were sent here for no other reason than to meet you, it was worth every second."

Sophie patted his back and released from his arms.

"I know you are going to find your family," she said, wiping away tears. "I feel it in my heart your journey is just beginning. When you find them, do not ever let them get away from you again. Tell Brooke everything; be honest with her and let her help you heal. If you give her the chance, I promise everything will work out for the best. And ask God for help, Jack. Put that cross in your pocket and whenever you think God is not with you, put it in your palm and call to Him."

They embraced again before Sophie moved to the door. "Remember," she said, looking over her shoulder, "make sure you leave well before daylight." Jack nodded.

"Thank you Sophie . . . for everything."

Reaching for the knob, she opened the door wide before pausing and pushing it back to a closed position. She turned sharply.

Jack noticed a puzzled look growing on her face. He was certain he knew what was on her mind.

"Jack, if I may," she said, extending a questioning index finger, "what are some things I will see in my lifetime?"

He moved to the bed and planted himself on the edge. "Are you sure you want to know?"

"No, but I am quite curious."

He paused to accumulate a few historical facts. "Well, I can tell you there will be a great advancement in the equipment you'll use in the running of your home and farm. Everyone has running water, telephones, electricity, and natural gas inside their homes. They will invent a machine to keep your home cool in the summer and warm in the winter; pretty much eliminating the need for fireplaces or keeping your windows open in the summer. Most everything you use now to handle your daily chores will run on electricity. A boxed device called the television will be invented, which will bring actual live motion pictures of people and events into your home."

Sophie's mouth fell agape. "Do you know who will be our next president?"

"Who is the president now?"

"Well, President Harding passed away in August and President Coolidge is now in office."

"I'm not certain, but I think he remains in office until around 1930. I believe Herbert Hoover comes next. I will say, though, your coming times will not be easy ones."

"How so?" she asked.

"In about six years, the country will enter a time which the historians refer to as the Great Depression. In late October of 1929, the New York Stock Exchange will crash and send the economy into a tailspin. Millions will be without work and it will take the country a long time to recover. You must do everything you can to protect yourself. I would recommend you urge Olan to start saving every extra penny he can and get out of any long-term loans you may have. No one will be safe from this disaster."

Sophie stood stiff with amazement as his knowledge of the future mesmerized. She was shocked at the manner in which he spoke, in such a factual context.

"The worst of it, I'd say, will be the second World War," he said, with an apologetic tone.

"Oh, my dear Lord," she said, brining her fists to her chest. "They said the past war was the war to end all wars."

"I'm afraid not, Sophie. Germany invades Poland in the fall of 1939. The United States is able to stay out of the fighting for a couple of years, but will get involved in December of 1941 after Japan launches an attack against our naval forces in Hawaii—which, by the way, becomes an official state in the late fifties."

"Is our country invaded?" she asked.

"No, as a matter of fact, in all the conflicts upcoming, our borders are never breached. But more than 70 million are killed as a result of this war. The good news is we eventually defeat Germany and Japan. But it comes at a grave cost. Once the war ends, however, the U.S. economy will explode with great prosperity.

"There is so much more, Sophie, but I fear life does not get any easier. Mankind seems to find a way to reinvent new and ongoing conflicts. I will always wish for your family's safety."

"Good luck to you, Jack," she said, following a lengthy pause. "May God bless. I will not soon forget you."

CHAPTER 36

December 25

Christmas Day 1923 came soft and unassuming as the final stroke of midnight spat from the mantel clock in the den, sending its knelling tone coalescing into the silence now settled throughout the home and forcing Jack's eyes to flutter open. Through a sizeable gap left between the bedroom door and jamb, he woke to a view of the darkened hallway as the crowning chime loitered for what seemed an eternity.

Summoned from a sunken doze, his mind was quick to clear and recognize the nearing hour of his departure. With no cell phone or alarm clock at his bedside, he placed the fate of his escape in an inherited knack for waking to a set mental alarm with the mantelpiece chime as a backup. He found sleep again with relative ease, deep enough he missed the three strokes of the new day's first two hours. The closing chime of three a.m. brought him out from under the covers.

Jack stabbed through the dark, fumbling for, then locating the small box of matches on the nightstand. By the flame of the oil lamp, he worked around the room collecting what little of his belongings remained. Intending to make good use of the cap and scarf, he left those items separate on the bed. He retrieved the other gifts given by Sophie, and enlivened by her advice, placed the wood cross into the hand warmer of his hoodie. He studied the watercolor painting with a fond eye before folding it and inserting it into the manila folder, which he settled flat in the bottom of the bag under refolded, dirty clothes and his pistol.

Stepping to the door with lamp and bag in hand, he searched a final time to ensure he was leaving nothing behind. A thought struck as to how he might explain this encounter to his family, if they were destined to reunite. His eyes immediately drew to the dresser. Retracing his steps, he moved with a renewed energy around the bed where he whisked the center photo from off its top. Bringing it close to his face, he paused to study Julia's image.

As if searching through the plaster of the ceiling to catch Sophie's eye, Jack wondered her reaction to him taking the photo. Believing she'd oblige, but praying for her absolution—just in case—he tucked the frame away. He also removed a picture of her, Roo, and the boys posing in front of the large oak in the front yard, and a third photo featuring Olan, Caleb, and Matty seated atop horses fronting a cornfield. Fearing he'd puttered long enough, he fled the room at a quick step.

Jack slinked through the hallway, avoiding those spots on the floor he'd discovered to be prone to blatant cracks and pops. He worked through the dark toward the kitchen, guarding each stride as if he were the intruding Old Saint Nick himself. The den was cold and damp, with the cooling embers in the firebox providing the lone sign the room was once occupied. The Brossys had returned the furniture to its original orientation with but a single alteration. No doubt at Roo's insistence, a small, round coffee table was placed just to the right of the fireplace, serving as support for a glass of milk, a plate of cookies and a hand-written note.

Inching close to the table, he dropped the duffle bag to the floor and brought the note to within the scope of the lamp's flame. The handwriting presented inconsistent in size and shape, and the spelling was awkward—just what one would expect from a child of four. Jack read the note and smiled. Expecting the young girl to wish for the riches of toys and unnecessary objects for herself, she asked Santa for a new tractor for her father, a new dress for her mother, and fishing poles for her brothers. The last line included a wish for Mr. Clarke to find his family. Jack's heart melted like jelly on a blistering July afternoon. He dropped his hand to his side.

"What a remarkable girl," he whispered. He paused to explore how such a young and inexperienced heart as Roo's could grasp and comprehend what his was now just beginning to understand. He folded the note and placed it in his duffle bag, took a bite out of the cookie and a long swig of the glass of milk to complete the illusion for the family.

Proceeding to the kitchen, his gait slowed at the stark smell of smoke. The scent was overwhelming, enough so that he expected to see visible flames shooting from somewhere, and an intense heat flashing against his face. He saw and felt neither. Visibility was crystal-clear and the room's temperature just as equal to the rest of the home. With curiosity getting the better of him, he brushed the stove with his fingertips, feeling it slightly warm and affirming his assumption the odor was coming from the cooling embers smoldering in the unit's firebox.

Jack advanced to the mudroom, entering the space with caution so as not to startle the chicks. He laid the lamp and duffle bag atop the brooder box and knelt to investigate the cupboards below the counter. Just as Sophie promised, a large, burlap sack settled front and center inside the second door, stuffed full of wrapped clumps of food and supplies.

He retrieved the sack, grabbed the lantern and scoured the peg hanger in search of the coat he'd used the day before. It was buried under a long, heavy brown duster. Performing a quick exchange, he ran his arms through and stretched the new stocking cap atop his head; a perfect fit. Uncertain as to the reliability of Olan's truck and the possibility he'd be walking a good bit of the way, he grabbed two pairs of gloves, an extra scarf and a homemade ear muff, all which he stuffed into the burlap bag along with a box of matches from off the counter. Tossing the bag over his shoulder, he pushed a breath of air into the lampshade then exited through the back door into an arctic breeze.

Spits of snow brushed across his face as he worked his way around the back of the house. The clouds were thinning and detaching, leaving intermittent openings large enough in the starlit stratum for the moon's dull silver to serve as a nightlight as he worked across the frozen yard.

Pausing along the path just short of the hedgerow, the smell of smoke again teased his senses. He searched every direction but noticed nothing. A horse clearing its nostrils in the barn brought a resumption to his step.

The barn door opened with negligible resistance, allowing entry into the space without sending the inhabitants into a tizzy. A silver wedge of light illuminated across the floor twenty feet past, making an easy task of locating a spare lantern hanging on a hook attached to the first vertical ceiling support. Jack fumbled for the matches before setting aflame the wick of an old brass conductor's lantern.

The green, red, and clear glass medallions making up the lantern's shade cast an eerie combination of colors across the space, begetting a scene straight from the imagination of the Brothers Grimm. Numerous sets of eyes of all shapes and sizes flickered like fireflies in the pitch black, watching his every step as if goblins readying a strike. He closed the barn door behind him and entered into a half-jog toward the stairs.

Jack positioned the lantern so one of the two clear glass medallions faced forward. He hurried to the second level, covering two steps with every stride. He reached the top to a view black as coal. For reasons he did not understand, the barn's designer had failed to add a single window on either side of this level, disallowing what little light the moon was casting.

Depositing both sack and duffle bag to the floor, he worked across the space to the opposite center of the barn where he remembered the two large doors. He pushed the first panel open along a lengthy iron rack system belching intermittent squeaks and grating screeches until it fell against a makeshift wood stopper some fifteen feet away. The right side slid open with nary a sound. The bottom half of the earthen ramp shown visible, although an unmolested layer of snow made it difficult to determine how much play was available side to side. He figured he could not go wrong keeping the truck dead center.

He did not notice the truck during his encounter with Bigsby, but knew it was not located near the corn planter. Moving right, he crept close up against the wall before several horse-drawn, rust-covered farm implements forced him back to the center of the floor. Piece after piece lined the wall until the cast from the lantern happened on a black box sitting atop a rickety frame with wheels.

He'd not seen a vintage vehicle such as this up close and marveled at its simplistic design and seeming frailty. Holding the lantern well forward from his body, he inspected the relic inch-by-inch. He spotted the hand crank jutting from the base of the radiator. The cab offered but one glass window in the front, two side mirrors mounted just inches from the roofline and a small side step merging seamlessly with the fender. The truck's bed was lined with pine rails on three sides. Inching closer, he eased the lantern through the driver's side window to take a closer peek at the interior.

He spotted the two levers Sophie had described on either side of the steering column and a toggle switch on the dash he assumed was the "key." Three pedals on the floorboard produced confusion. A long, vertical steel rod projecting from the floorboard near the door appeared to be a parking brake.

Jack opened the door and climbed in behind the steering wheel. The fit was tight and uncomfortable, but a better option, he figured, than saddling up a horse or walking. Like a mischievous child, he maneuvered the levers up and down, worked the floorboard pedals in and out and moved the steering wheel from side to side. He wondered if he could even get the thing out of the barn, and if so, how it would react and handle in the snow. With the instrumentation set clearly in his mind, he adjusted the levers on the steering column as Sophie instructed.

Jack hurried across the floor to the landing, gathering the burlap sack and duffle bag, stopping again to pause as the smell of smoke continued to baffle. A quick glance down the stairs and a view of the other end of the barn produced nothing. He doubled back to the vehicle, settling to one knee in front of the radiator. Running his hand underneath, he located a knob and pulled toward the floor, extending it about two inches. He returned to the cab, tossed his belongings to the passenger side, and turned the key.

His first attempt at rotating the crank produced nothing more than a jarring to his wrist. The shaft failed to move an inch. A second attempt produced the same result. Jack pulled up from his squatted position to study the predicament. Remembering Sophie's instructions, he bent low, placed his hand tight around the handle, and pushed the shaft inward. Feeling the crank move, he braced his legs for a third attempt. Set to put the cold steel shaft in motion, a loud, crashing boom from outside the barn sent his body shooting upright in a blink. He turned sharp toward the west wall.

In an instant, the animals below fell into hysteria. The horses stomped and snorted, some kicking against their stall doors. The bull's bellow sent the cattle in the yard into a panic. Chickens cackled in a crazed rampage; pigs began squealing and sheep bleating. Jack looked about and noticed an ominous orange glow pushing through gaps in the structure's siding. A raging fury of goose pimples shot over his body as he rushed down the stairs to the confused screams of the animals. Turning at the bottom step, he noticed a flickering light shooting through every pane of every glass window. He rushed to the first window along the wall. His eyes exploded to the size of manhole covers at the sight.

Half the upper level of the back side of the Brossy home had collapsed onto the lower as a bank of ferocious flames gobbled away at the structure's second story, sending fire shooting fifty feet into the night sky. The breath sucked from Jack's chest as he watched in utter disbelief. How had he smelled smoke but seen no flame? As the initial shock dripped from his body, he fled for the barn door. Opening it wide, he stood in the doorway watching in horror.

The intensity of the heat blistering against his face and body forced him from the doorway and down the side of the barn. Stumbling on legs that felt liquid, he worked to the second opening in the hedgerow, watching over his shoulder as fire devoured the back end of the house. His traction improved little as he stammered like a drunken man for the home's front porch.

Searching the interior through the large plate glass window just to the right of the front door, he noticed the family's kitchen fully engulfed in flames. In an excited haste, he ripped the screen door from off its hinges, tossed it aside and kicked the front door in with a solid, single blow. Heat and smoke stormed from the opening in deadly measures, forcing him to pull the stocking cap to cover his nose and mouth before proceeding. Within seconds of entering, he heard someone call out his name.

"Jack . . . help me . . . please."

He scanned the parlor and the hallway, but saw no one. Moving to the staircase, he noticed through the smoke an outline of a figure on the landing at the top; behind it, a full view of the night sky where walls and ceilings once merged. Not seeing any visible flames, Jack raced up the stairs on all fours to find Sophie face down near the top step, trapped under a large pile of debris. Acting on instinct, he began clearing away material but paused upon seeing her point to his left. Her hand shook with a violent tremble; her skin was blistered and burned black.

She cried out in a heavy, desperate breath, "She's in there . . . please save her."

"I've got to get you out of here," Jack pleaded.

"No . . . please . . . .Olivia."

Jack turned to his left. A single door remained closed. Crawling over the pile, he stepped with caution atop a small wedge of landing that was clear of debris. Beyond, he could see below the crumpled and twisted mess of what remained of the upper floor. A single, lifeless arm poking through a heap of burning timbers distracted his momentum.

As Sophie again called out her daughter's name in a desperate plea, Jack hopped over another pile to reach the door. With the force of a mule, he kicked against the bedroom door, sending an instant wave of newfound oxygen into the space, igniting flames bursting near his face from the right. As the fire sucked back into the room, Jack dropped to his knees and crawled to the center.

"Roo . . . where are you?" he yelled. "Roo!"

He paused to search all corners while continuing to call her name. A large dresser and small rocking horse set blazing to his right. He noticed the girl's bed to his left—unmolested by flame—and crept toward it on his elbows.

"Roo?"

Nearing the frame of the bed, Jack heard a whimper and noticed a lump on top. He stabbed for it, but felt only a pillow. Dropping to the floor, he noticed through the smoke a white clump under the bed. Smashed against the frame, he reached out as far as his arm would stretch. Finding flesh, he jerked hard and pulled Roo across the floor. Collecting her shivering body into his arms, he pushed the stocking cap against her face and rose to his feet. Not wanting to waste a single second, he ran from the room to the top of the landing, racing past Sophie.

"I found her, Sophie," he yelled, stumbling atop the debris pile, making his way toward the stairs. "I'll be right back for you . . . I promise."

With Roo secured, he worked down the stairway through an increasing wall of smoke, sidestepping falling chunks of burning home before reaching the front door. Racing to the barn, Jack checked along the outside of the structure and saw no signs the fire was spreading. He raced to the hay stall and settled to a knee.

Releasing Roo from his grip, he ripped off his coat and secured it around her. He eased her into a sitting position in the hay pile and draped a horse blanket across her body. He dropped to a crouch and moved close to her.

"Roo, sweetheart . . . everything's going to be okay," he said, holding her shoulders. "I want you to stay right here, okay?" Her sobbing increased.

"Don't move from here. Do you understand me?" She nodded. "I will be back in just a few minutes. Stay right here."

Jack reached in and kissed her on the cheek. Roo flung her arms from under the coat and blanket and wrapped them around his neck and buried her cheek against his. She shook him to the bone as her body convulsed with fear. Jack grabbed her and squeezed.

"It's going to be okay," he whispered. "You're going to be okay."

Releasing from her grasp, Jack quickly repositioned the coat and blanket and raced from the barn back into the burning home.

Flames had spread to the dining room wall side of the stairwell, forcing him against the opposite wall as he made his way back up the narrow staircase. Near the halfway point, the smoke cleared enough for him to catch a glimpse of Sophie, her eyes glistening, staring at nothing, as if already accepting her fate. Jack fell to his knees upon reaching the top step and placed his hand upon her cheek.

"Is she okay?" Sophie whispered, the effort labored.

"She's fine," Jack said. Sophie closed her eyes and released a breath and a faint cough.

Flames were growing to his left. He hurried to scatter bits of lumber from off her body to the yard below; some still aflame, others smoldering. Digging through the mess, he uncovered a large timber two feet square pinned atop the middle of her back. He attempted to push it to the rear, but was unable to brace his body to get enough force behind it.

Jack dug for Sophie's other arm, latched on to both and pulled as hard as he could. She let out a murderous scream as his hands made contact with the burnt flesh. Unable to budge her, he pulled away with the skin of her arms clinging to his fingertips. He attempted another push of the timber, releasing an extended grunt as he expelled every ounce of power he could muster. The timber didn't budge.

In a lethargic cadence, Sophie begged, "Jack . . . please don't let me burn. Please don't let me burn."

The flames building to the left eerily sucked below the floor. Readjusting his position, Jack noticed the greedy pyre had found its way underneath the landing and was now advancing under Sophie's position. With arms flailing, he clawed away the debris from around the timber, attempting to clear enough room to get a better angle at pushing it to the side. Grabbing hold of a smoldering two-by-four, he rammed one end into a small opening wedging it against the timber. Securing his legs against the far wall, he pushed against the makeshift lever with what little energy he had remaining. Nothing.

Tossing the two-by-four to the side, Jack reached through flames now shooting through cracks in the floor, attempting to pull Sophie again by her arms. It was no use. With smoke and flames now over-whelming his position, he backed off in search of another angle in which he could make a run. As he stepped to Sophie's right, she let out a harrowing scream.

"I'm burning . . . Jack . . . I'm burning!" Her eyes drew open wide as flames shot from underneath, wrapping around her body like a glove. "Jack, help me. Don't let me burn."

Jack froze in horror as the flames ignited her nightgown and hair. All went silent in his head. Her eyes bulged and her mouth twisted but he could hear nothing. Time around him stopped; as if a victim of shell shock.

In a desperate act masquerading as an out-of-body experience, one proceeding in slow motion, he reached for the two-by-four used to pry against the timber, and with a single motion, brought the smoldering end of the object down into the top of Sophie's skull. The single, crushing blow sent her eyes rolling into the back of her head and her screams into the abyss. Jack let the stock slip from his fingers as he watched the flames swallow her body. The burning against his own skin sent him scurrying in a daze to the lower level. He reached the front door just as the entire staircase collapsed toward the back of the house.

Moving from the porch, he stumbled across the front yard before collapsing to his knees, choking and gagging on the inhaled smoke and soot. He grabbed a palm-full of snow and shoved the mass into his mouth, allowing the clump to melt before sloshing it about then spitting the blackened mess to the ground.

With the sequence of events chewing at his sanity, he dropped to his elbows, struggling to draw a normal breath while staring at his hands. Seeing remnants of Sophie's skin, the vision of the blow he delivered to her head was more than he could bear. His body shook as tears poured; a groan of anguish erupted from deep within. He called out Sophie's name through a sobbing, screaming voice. As torment turned to anger, he lifted from the ground, leaned back against his heels and with fists clinched, wailed into the night as the home disintegrated behind him.

A final crashing collapse brought his head dragging over his shoulder, extinguishing a lengthy, paralytic gaze of the night sky, as the timbers supporting the front porch succumbed to raging flame and the weight of the roof above. The magnificent two-story structure reduced to a burning pile of kindling.

Pushing to his feet, Jack fell into a stuttered trek across the yard, shielding his face from the intense heat while arcing well around the pyre toward the rear of the property. He plowed flat-footed through the snow in a stupor, looking between gaps in the mangled web of burning and smoldering timbers, two-by-fours, and furnishings for any signs of life.

He passed by what was left of the back porch to just beyond the overhang of the outhouse and paused as the enormity of the devastation cauterized in his brain. Settling against a young maple, spying through voids in the flicker, a jolt rocked the center of his chest as he caught a glimpse of three charred figures, one stacked atop the other, jutting from the scorched remnants of a large upper-story window frame wedged in debris just clear of a portion of roofing.

The sight of the twisted and blackened limbs of the bodies sent his legs buckling from underneath. Crumpling to the ground, gazing in horror, his mind was quick to adduce the victims to be an adult and two small children. With all sense of reality drained from his mangled conscience, he slumped against the tattered slats of the outhouse, calling for Brooke and his daughters through a wrenching breath and stuttered voice.

Broken of mind and spirit, Jack fell forward into the snow with palms buried against his forehead. Stripped clean of the selfdom responsible for the hard shell he'd used to detach from his loved ones, he now begged God to spare those very same lives.

"I'm sorry . . . I'm so sorry; please forgive me," he cried, cowering in a shivering lump. "Don't take them away . . . please give me a second chance."

Over the crackle of flame eating at the hundred-year-old structure, the sounds of popping glass jars and windows, and the intermittent crash of objects falling further through the tangled mess, Jack opened and exposed naked his soul. Through a steady stream of tears and in a pleading whisper, he released his anger, burdens, and fears into God's hands and challenged Him to take complete control just as Sophie tutored.

Lifting and reaching for the sky, Jack repledged his vow not to be the man he once was. God, in all His glory, responded. As he opened his eyes, he gazed in disbelief into the cloudless, starlit sky at hulking flakes of brilliant white snow, originating from nothing, floating gently to the ground.

⌘

Roo had kept her promise. Having not moved an inch from the position in which Jack left her, she lay curled in a ball, half-buried in the haystack, with the horse blanket pulled tight under her chin.

Hovering above, looking upon her through an increasing blur, Jack watched her eyelids and nose twitch in tandem with her breathing, wondering where it was her dreams had taken her, and how he could explain her family's plight. He dropped to one knee at her side.

The unsuspecting, peaceful manner with which she rested splintered his heart into a million pieces. He thought of the world as she knew it and what that same world would look like once she woke to the light of day. He cupped his head as her fate tore away at his heart.

The swell of adrenaline had run its course. Barely able to move his limbs, Jack fell limp atop the haystack on Roo's opposite side, settling in close. He drug an arm over her head and pulled her near with the last speck of energy remaining. Prompted by the motion, Roo shifted under the blanket and buried herself against his chest. With her head tucked under his chin and the smell of lavender replacing that of burnt wood, Jack held her as if she were his only possession left in the world.

Affixing a sleepy stare to a window opposite, watching flames stretching high into the night sky, Jack drifted away whispering the words of the telegram and coming to the realization of its intent.

You must ascend the stairway. Door to the left is where she lays. I am not there. They have been called, but she must remain.

CHAPTER 37

"Get them bodies outta there," a loud, booming voice rang out just beyond the barn walls, jolting Jack from his slumber. "Place 'em over there boys . . . by that tree. Sam, Hank, check the northwest corner . . . there's another body over there."

The man's instructions, coupled with a rush of footsteps sloshing across the yard and a ground-shaking reverberation from horses and wagons descending from the north, launched Jack from a deep impression in the hay into a sitting position.

Looking about in a confused, half-daze, he shot quick glances to both ends of the barn and to his immediate right, shading the glare of the rising sun. Roo remained fast asleep, curled in a small bundle at his side.

Jack repositioned to his knees. His body jerked with surprise as he caught a glimpse of a figure passing and peeking in through the window opposite his position. Topped in a bright red fire helmet painted with a white number seven against a black shield, the man searched the space before meeting Jack's stare. His eyes opened wide. In a blur, he disappeared from view.

"In here, boys," Jack heard the man bark.

He reached to the hay pile to gobble Roo into his arms, blanket and all, before getting to his feet. The motion brought a coo from her lips. In a sleepy voice, with eyes still closed, she asked for her mother.

Jack heard the barn door push open the instant he exited the stall. Three men dressed in antiquated fire gear rushed toward him.

"Are you okay, son?" the man with the number seven on his helmet asked, his voice hoarse and rushing with excitement. "Is she the Brossy girl? Is she the only survivor? Do you know what happened?"

Jack said nothing as the three men closed in to form a half circle around him. He brushed a backhand across his face, removing a solid, black streak.

"Are you burned?" the smallest of the three men asked.

"No, not burned," Jack said, following a long pause, "just sore and tired."

"I'm Claude Colbert, fire chief of Cameron and Barron county inspector."

Jack resituated Roo in his arms.

"Can you tell what happened, son?"

Jack made a round of eye contact with each man, then to Roo. His expression drew a slow nod from the chief.

"Chester, go get my truck and pull it around to the other side of the barn, out of view of the house. Willie, you take the girl and put her in the truck once Chet moves 'er. Now you keep her head covered when you take her out of here," he said, pointing his finger, "I don't want her to see the mess out there. Do whatever you have to do to keep her warm and don't let her get out of the truck. Understood?"

Without a word, both men sprung to action. Jack extended his arms to pass Roo off, but pulled back as her face exposed from under the blanket. She'd fallen back to sleep. Resting his forehead against hers, he closed his eyes to absorb her warmth and scent.

"I'm so sorry sweetheart," he whispered. "I'm so sorry. I did everything I could." He brought her against the side of his face and pressed his lips against her cheek. He would never forget the fragrance of lavender.

Jack thought briefly of taking her with him now that she was all alone in the world. Knowing the situation was impossible, he passed her off with the reluctance of a first-time parent dropping their child off to daycare.

"I'm sorry, son," Claude said, placing a hand atop his shoulder. "We searched all through that mess and found them all, 'cept her. We feared she was still buried or was one of the two small bodies we could not identify. We found them near another woman, but they're so badly burned we don't know who they are or if the children are male or female."

"It's Mrs. Bigsby and her two daughters," Jack said, his voice cracking. He dropped his chin and brought a palm over his brow.

"Jubel's wife?" the man asked, his voice accelerating. "Oh, no. Oh dear God, that means we've got us another body to dig out."

"No, Jubel left the house late last night. I remember Mr. Brossy telling Sophie he was needed at someone's farm . . . something about a bull in trouble."

"Must be big Jeff Pruit. He carries on over that bull as if'n it were his wife. Don't know why the man won't let that poor beast die in peace."

The chief went to the door and yelled for an assistant. Seconds later the man appeared in the doorway. "Hank, get on over to Jeff Pruit's and fetch Jubel. Those three bodies are his wife and daughters. Don't you say a word about it . . . just tell him I need him."

"I don't believe I know you son," the chief said, working back across the floor.

"My name's Jack Clarke."

"Are you kin to the Brossy's?"

"No sir. Just a friend."

"Can you tell me what happened?"

Jack hesitated. Describing what he knew to be true would bring more questions than answers. Knowing the possibility of doing time in the county slammer was still a distinct possibility, he needed to rework the events. His mind responded.

"I was fast asleep in their guest bedroom on the bottom floor. I awoke to a very loud and extended crashing sound. The room was full of smoke. I crawled to the front door and heard Sophie yelling from the top of the landing. She was trapped under a lot of debris. She pointed to Roo's room and begged me to find her. I reached the top of the stairs and saw that the entire back top of the house had collapsed into the back yard. I worked my way into the room and found the girl under her bed. I grabbed her and ran out of the house to the barn. I made sure she was secure before going back. As I neared the porch, what was left of the house collapsed; I was too late."

"Do you have any idea how it might have started?"

"Not the first. Like I said, I was sound asleep. It must have started upstairs because I didn't see or hear anything until the crash."

The chief gave Jack a once over; his eyelids narrowed. "And you don't have any injuries?"

"No sir. Just a few cuts and bruises."

"I see," the man said, looking to the ground and nodding. Jack could tell he was questioning his account.

"Well, because we have casualties, I'm sure the sheriff will want to speak with you. I suspect he and his deputies will be along anytime."

"What's going to happen to the girl?" Jack asked.

"I don't rightly know, son. I suspect she'll become a ward of the state and they'll place her in the county orphanage."

Jack released a heavy sigh. The guilt of Roo not knowing the truth of what happened to her mother and family stung him to his core.

The chief patted his shoulder. "Sounds like you did all you could do, son. At least the girl is alive. You can be right proud."

Both men turned at the sound of the barn door slapping open.

"Chief! Chief! Jubel's coming up the road."

The chief hung his head. "I wouldn't wish this moment on my worst enemy."

He entered into a half-jog toward the exit.

Reluctant to follow, Jack did so only because of his growing concern for Roo's condition. She was certain to be awake by now and more confused and frightened than he could imagine.

A brilliant blue sky and sun-drenched landscape provided little distraction for the surreal scene beyond the barn walls. Stalling at the threshold, Jack fell against the jamb in disbelief of the smoldering pile before him. Men raced from one side of the yard to the other, some dousing what was left of the flames, others searching through cooled sections for anything salvageable.

Exiting into the sunlight, he stiff-armed against the wood slats to maintain balance as he moved toward the opposite end of the barn. Reaching the far corner, he spied several men grouped under the naked branches of the lonely oak in the Brossys' front yard, hovering over seven lumps covered with blankets. The sound of reins slapping against flesh and an anxious driver barking out *"ya there, ya"* pulled his attention away from the group.

Jack stretched his neck around the corner of the barn. He caught sight of a team of four horses plowing up the road with Jubel standing upright in a sled whipping at the reins. Barreling toward the tree, he yanked the reins as far as the bend of his back would allow, causing the team leaders to each rare up and release a piercing neigh. Before the team came to a complete stop, Jubel jumped from the rig into the snow. Three men rushed to offer assistance. Jack fell against the barn wall watching Jubel stumble across the snow, in a frantic rush toward the two smallest humps on the ground.

A knot the size of a fist ballooned in Jack's throat as Jubel released a blood-stirring yell at the top of his lungs before falling to his hands and knees. The men attempted to console and lift him from the ground, but he refused. Screams of denial soon turned to a wail, echoing from all points along the valley.

Positioned just a few feet behind, the chief shuffled forward, fell to a knee, and wrapped his arm around Jubel's neck. One by one, the men removed their hats, walked alongside and placed a hand on Jubel's back; each bending low to offer a word. Jack pushed his hands against his forehead. The loss was biting, the grief real. He focused on Jubel as if staring into a mirror. The pain was all too familiar.

Chief Colbert held on tight to his friend, rubbing the back of his neck, until the initial wave of emotion passed. Addressing his men, they soon moved off in all directions to continue about their assignments.

A small cloud of condensation escaped Jubel's lips, prompting the chief to bend low, nearer his face. The two engaged before the chief nodded and pointed toward the barn. Jubel drew his eyes in Jack's direction. Not knowing what to do with his hands, Jack left them pushed against his forehead. He could see the pain and desperation in Jubel's eyes as clear as the bright blue sky above.

Unable to stomach the sight any longer, Jack fled around the corner of the barn through a small passage separating the structure from the holding pasture in search of the chief's truck. Model-T cars and trucks carrying friends and gawkers alike descended upon the property at a staggering rate. Horse-led wagons and sleds dotted the narrow country road approaching the property from the north.

Several vehicles sat scattered along a small open field, and despite their identical black finishes, Jack was quick to spot the chief's truck; it was the one rocking back and forth on its frame—as if a struggle were taking place inside the cab. Moments later, he heard Roo scream.

Racing to the passenger's side window, he peeked in to see the fireman trying his best to gain control of her. With arms flailing and feet kicking, she was fighting off his grip and screaming for her mother. Jack whipped the door open, causing the man to release his hold. Roo raced across the bench, flung herself into Jack's chest and grappled her way up to around his neck. Her exposed body was shaking with chill and fear; her sobbing intensified.

"I'm sorry mister," the man said, "I don't know what to do with her. She woke up and just went batty. I tried to calm her but she won't stop kicking me."

"Give me the coat and blanket," Jack demanded, his voice agitated. He secured Roo in his arms and kicked the door shut. Roo continued calling out for her mother.

"Don't cry sweetheart. Everything's going to be okay," he whispered. "Your mother's not here right now. I'm going to take you to see your Uncle Jubel."

"Whewe's my mama?" Roo cried. Jack brought her against his neck and patted her back.

Neighbors in overalls and winter garb, officials in fedoras and long trench coats, and even a few newsmen and cameramen all jammed under the large tree, encircling Jubel, the fire chief, and the victims. The front yard looked like an auctioneer's dream as antique vehicles jammed into each other in an uncoordinated mess.

Jack held back as people raced past to get a better glimpse of the carnage. Two men with silver, six-point stars dangling from the lapels of their coats struggled to keep the crowd at a respectable distance. Several women joined hands over the bodies; some wept, some prayed. The newsmen backed Chief Colbert against the tree. One of them spotted Jack.

"There he is, boys," the man yelled. Every eye searched as the reporters raced toward the barn. Jack braced himself against the wall and secured his grip on Roo as the mass formed a tight wall around him, closing off every angle of escape. Mob order and chaos ensued.

"What happened, fella?" a short, pencil-necked man in his later years asked, pulling a writing tablet and number two pencil close to his face in anticipation of a quote. The crowd pushed and shoved their way forward; the circle around Jack ballooned to a dozen people deep.

"Is that the girl?" asked another reporter. "Is that little Olivia?"

A third reporter wearing wire-rim glasses and dressed in a three-piece suit and overcoat pushed his way to the front of the pack. "Is she hurt? What's your full name, fella? Are you the one who saved her?"

"I've never seen him before," a woman said.

"Just look at those clothes," said another.

Questions and comments shot from every direction. Jack tightened his grip around Roo; his head jerked from side to side at the sound of every new voice. He felt like a caged animal.

A man in a black overcoat pushed aside the reporters and dropped a tripod between them. He disappeared under a tan cloth and snapped a photo. "You're gonna be famous, son," he said, pulling from under the cloth.

"Listen son," the man in the wire-rim glasses said, grabbing hold of Jack's arm, "my paper will give you a hundred dollars cash money for an exclusive. What do you say to that?"

"My paper will pay two," said the pencil-neck, pushing closer.

"My column's syndicated, son," the man in the suit said. "Every major paper of consequence in this country will want to run your story."

Jack pressed his back harder and harder against the barn as the crowd inched its way to within a foot. Someone to his left pulled at the blanket in an attempt to expose Roo's face. Jack jerked his body in the opposite direction, nearly falling to the ground. A hush drew over the crowd as a loud, booming voice erupted from behind the mass, sending people scattering.

"Gangway . . . move aside," the man yelled. An opening emerged to Jack's right. A stubby, thick hand shot through the crowd, grabbing hold of a wad of Jack's sweatshirt.

"No more questions, boys. Not until I get a chance to speak to this man myself."

"Awe, but sheriff, we got deadlines," said pencil-neck.

"Sorry, boys. My duty ranks first. You'll get your story . . . but it'll have to wait."

The man looked Jack square in the eye and gave a tug. "Come with me, son," he said. The two men wearing the stars on their lapels parted the crowd, leading the men to safe passage.

"Who is he, sheriff?" a man yelled.

"You all go on about your business now," the sheriff responded. "There's nothing more to see here. I want you all to get in your cars and go on home. We have a lot of work to do and I don't need anyone gettin' in my way."

The sheriff held tight to Jack's arm, tugging him along until passing through a wall of Chief Colbert's men near where the bodies lay. As the two emerged from the crowd, Jack glanced over the deputies and fire-fighters and noticed a familiar face. Chief Colbert appeared deep into expressing his theory of the chain of events, pointing wildly in all directions, as Doctor Danaher followed the path of his finger with a hand supporting his chin. Jubel remained on the ground; now sitting on his heels, slumped at the shoulders as if a fallen soldier waiting for his final breath. It looked as if the man were not even breathing.

Approaching the place where Jubel rested, the sheriff released his grip before peeling off toward Chief Colbert. The smell of burnt flesh was ripe. Jack wanted to look away but fell into a daze upon seeing the outlines of the families' twisted limbs under the sheets.

Just in front and to the right, the man with the tripod hunkered under a sheet behind his camera and snapped a shot. The click of the camera brought Jack's eyes forward. A large black case at his feet lay open with the words Eau Claire Leader painted in large, white block letters on the inside.

"Get on out of here, now," the sheriff yelled, racing toward the man. "I told you no pictures of the bodies or those grieving for 'em. You snap one more and I'll throw your ass in the can. Understood?"

The man collapsed the tripod, grabbed his case and scampered into the crowd like a frightened squirrel.

"Lousy sons of bitches," the sheriff snarled under his breath. "Chance, keep those damn reporters away from these bodies . . . ya hear me?"

Mumbling in disgust, the sheriff retraced his steps and paused to face Jack from opposite the bodies. A thick, bushy, graying mustache falling well below his chin did little to shield those standing within a five-foot radius of spittle ejecting in all directions when he spoke. Brown boots, black pants, and a salt and pepper vest expanding well beyond its maker's intent seemed at odds with the white, ten-gallon cowboy hat situated at an angle atop his head. Well beyond the age of retirement, he looked more the part of a grizzled Texas Ranger than an old country sheriff. Pulling a half-smoked cigar from a pocket inside his vest, he slid the stogie under his nose and inhaled. An associate rushed to his side to offer a lit match. The sheriff drew the cigar to life while working Jack over with a slanted eye.

Roo's sobs, although muffled under the heavy coat and blanket, continued in a steady pattern, drawing the attention of her uncle-in-law.

Jack shuffled backward as Jubel worked to his feet with the rigidity of a man four times his age. He looked beaten to a pulp but without the bruising. His fingers glistened bright blue; his face was sunken and drained to a shade of corpse-like gray. He set his stare square at the bridge of Jack's nose.

A hush developed amongst the men standing near as Jubel, with the assistance of one of his brethren, cut the distance by half between himself and Jack.

He stared to his adversary with a sniper's eye. "I see you made it out just fine," he accused, his body shaking. "How do you explain seven bodies and you with not even a scratch?"

"I did everything I could for them, Jubel," Jack defended. "By the time I knew what was going on, most of the second floor was gone. The fire just spread too fast, they didn't have a chance."

"I don't believe you. You had a good reason for them all to be dead, didn't you . . . especially with me away from the house."

"No, that's not true," Jack said, agitated. "That's not true at all. I tried to save them. I tried to save them all. How would you explain this," Jack said, nodding toward the bundle in his arms. "She was on the second floor with the others."

Roo's sobs continued at a steady pace. Jack adjusted her in his arms. Jubel broke from the assistance of his friend and moved forward with his arms outstretched.

"Give me my niece," he demanded.

Jack retreated a half-step, clutching Roo tighter in his arms, as if not wanting to give her up. Realizing his reaction was wrongheaded, especially under the circumstances and considering Jubel was kin, he passed her into his arms, showing visible signs of regret.

Jubel uncovered Roo's face from under the blanket and kissed her on the cheek. Tears rushed but he did not make a sound. His touch eased her sobbing but not her desire to know where her mother was.

A sharp whistle from the sheriff's lips brought another deputy scurrying to his side.

"Jubel, the Howards have offered to take little Olivia in for the time being until we get things straightened out around here. I think it would be best to get her inside and away from this scene."

Jubel hesitated, but passed Roo off. Jack sunk as the man whisked her away. Peeking around the man's hat, Roo kept her eyes glued to Jack's as she disappeared into the crowd. An empty feeling settled inside at the certainty he'd never hold or see her again.

"Son?" the sheriff interrupted. "I'm Sheriff Hiram J. Ivey. Chief Colbert tells me your name is Jack . . . Jack Clarke."

"Yes, sir, that's right," he replied.

"Well, Mr. Clarke, seems we have ourselves a bit of a problem here."

"I don't understand. I told the fire chief everything I knew. I did all I could."

"Well, it may be, but ya didn't tell him Olan was planning on having you arrested for roughing up poor Jubel here."

Jack wiped nervously at his face, glancing at Jubel.

"Seems to me it'd be real easy to sit and watch a place burn knowing I was headed for jail."

"I tried to save them," Jack yelled.

"Chief also tells me you claim you were in the house when the fire started."

"Yes . . . I was in the very back bedroom on the bottom floor."

"I see," the sheriff responded, kicking away snow clinging to the toes of his boots. His indifference to the response suggested the answer was expected. "So you heard a loud crash, wake up to a smoke-filled room then make your way to the front of the house . . . is that right?"

"Yes sir."

The sheriff pointed to Jack's head. "How'd you come to hurt yourself?" he asked.

"Aye constable, I believe I can clear up that bit of mystery," a voice rang from behind. Having heard enough of Chief Colbert's account of things, Doctor Danaher excused himself the moment Sheriff Ivey sprung into his interrogation. Sidling up next to Jack, he offered a light pat on his shoulder and a familiar wink.

"Howya, lad?" he asked, his voice filled with compassion.

The doctor offered his hand. Deep creases splitting outward from the corners of his eyes suggested he too had seen little sleep. Jack was slow to react as his mind flashed the initials printed on the telegram— M.O.D. If he could just get Danaher alone.

"You know this man?" the sheriff asked.

"Aye, constable . . . well I do. He came to the family after suffering a most desperate accident over near the lake. I happened by along my route and tended to him, so I did."

"Is that true, son?" the sheriff asked.

Jack nodded.

"Well, it's not rightly fair to say you were a friend of the family . . . more like a stranger in need who they befriended. Would you agree?"

"Yes, but—"

"So you make your way up the stairs and into Olivia's bedroom, find her under the bed, take her from the room to the barn."

"That's right . . . and when—"

"And when you came from the barn, you say, the house had already collapsed."

Jack swallowed his response. He did not like the direction of the questioning or the fact the sheriff seemed as if he were going through the motions—as if cued to the alterations in the story. It didn't help that the man refused to look at him. Jack grew concerned the Brossys' front yard was now the Barron County courthouse.

"Sheriff, I did everything I could. If Mrs. Brossy were not pinned and begging I get her daughter, I would have gotten her out as well. All the other rooms were gone. I heard no one else. I saw no one else. I did what she asked me to do."

The sheriff tossed his spent cigar to the ground. Hiking up his pants, he whispered an instruction to a deputy standing near. The man nodded and pushed through the gathering crowd toward the barn.

"Now son," the sheriff said, "I've known Olan Brossy going on fifty years. The man saved my life once and to say we were good friends is an understatement. I've stayed overnight at this house more times than I can count and most often in the very room you say you were fast asleep. I happen to know the layout of this home better than most. You say a loud crash woke you up. You also say when you got to the top of the house the backside was gone. If what you say is so, how is it you're alive to tell this story when the bottom bedroom is under the far back bedroom on the upper floor? How is it the rooms right above yours did not come crashing down on top of you?"

It was now that Jack realized a crowd had gathered—mostly Chief Colbert's men, a sprinkling of deputies with nothing better to do, and curious neighbors. He scanned the group over with a nervous eye. His less than alert state allowed for an obvious and glaring hole in his story.

The deputy sent scurrying to the barn returned, pushing his way through the crowd. Reaching the center of the circle, he passed a beat-to-hell duffle bag and burlap sack into the sheriff's hands. Jack swallowed deep.

"One of my boys found these in Olan's truck," the sheriff said. He lifted both for all to see before tossing them over the bodies to Jack's feet. The crowd around sucked in a collective breath.

"That sack is stuffed full of food. My deputies also noticed Olan's truck was being prepped for ignition. Now, we might just be dumb 'ole country hicks compared to where you come from, but I know when a man's settin' to flee. You weren't in the house, were ya, boy?"

Jack shifted his eyes to the ground. A voice from behind blurted out the question on everyone's mind. "Did he start the fire, sheriff?"

"Jubel, you know I didn't start that fire," Jack pleaded. "You know I didn't do this."

Jubel did not respond. His stare was dead.

"Tell them I didn't do this."

Two deputies emerged from behind, each wrapping a hand around Jack's arms.

"Mr. Clarke, I'm taking you in on suspicion of arson, attempted theft of private property, and assault and battery. Okay, boys, get my car and take him to town," the sheriff said. "I'll be along later in the day."

Jack ripped his arms away and out of the hold of the deputies, advancing several steps toward the sheriff before the deputies regained control with the assistance of a few of Chief Colbert's men.

"Sheriff, I didn't start this fire," he yelled. "Doc, tell them I didn't do this."

Doctor Danaher moved from Jack's side to near the tree.

"I'm sorry, lad . . . I'm but a wee country vet and you have bloody well bolloxed things up right so."

"Doctor. Please tell them I didn't do this. Tell them I didn't kill them."

"No one said you've killed anyone, son—yet," the sheriff said, igniting another cigar, "but it's clear to me you had a good reason for this family not to survive."

"That's not true. I tried to save them," Jack yelled.

"We'll let Judge Cooper decide that. Boys, get him outta here."

Jack struggled against their control. "Jubel . . . Jubel help me."

Jubel turned away; his attention again consumed by his loss. He settled to one knee nearest the first and smallest body in line. The crowed fell into a hush as he cleared a mass from his throat. He turned slowly from the bodies.

"You wished this upon me," he accused Jack, his voice dragging and cracking. "What you've wished upon me, you've wished upon yourself. Now take a good look at what you've done."

Jubel ripped the sheets free from each of the first three bodies. Women screamed in horror; one crumpled face-first into the snow, drawing several to her aid. Men gasped then turned clutching their stomachs. Jack's face exploded in a white flush. The bodies were charred of flesh, face, and hair, exposed gaping cavities that revealed blackened internal organs. Their arms and fingers, burnt to the bone and stretching outward in grotesque configurations, seemed to be still in a struggle to escape the hellfire.

The men summoned to remove Jack began pulling him toward the barn. Refusing their will, Jack struggled to maintain his position and focus on the bodies despite his stomach wrenching and expelling what little remained undigested. Another grouping of men jumped in the middle of the scrum to assist and soon redirected the accused from the scene. Jack bellowed his innocence, demanding Jubel set the record straight, as the men pushed and tugged him across the property before forcing him into the back seat of the sheriff's car. A deputy jumped in alongside with gun drawn; another hustled to the front to unpin the hood to prepare the vehicle for ignition.

Jack crumpled against the corner of the back seat as if shot from behind. His body quivered uncontrollably as his mind frothed with horror. What little hope he harbored of ever finding his family dissipated at the sight of the bodies. His mind swirled with the many clues, warnings, and premonitions plaguing to this point, each now making perfect sense and no sense whatsoever. His spirit was broken and his hope dashed. He dumped his head into his hands.

A push to the ignition switch sent the McLaughlin grumbling to life. The deputy directed the vehicle around the back bumper of Chief Colbert's truck. As the car accelerated, a loud slap bounced off the passenger's side door.

"You'll be regrettin' leavin' these things behind, so you will," Doctor Danaher said, leaning in through the window with duffle bag in hand, peering over his half-moons.

Jack lifted his eyes to view the man who'd refused to collaborate his innocence. The guise fanned out about his face shown livelier than a downed power line. So strangely odd was the expression, Jack's eyes cleared in an instant as he pondered what part of the events of the day would cause a man to appear anything but solemn. The doctor made it worse by offering a wink and a smile. Jack stared in disbelief.

The doctor looked to the driver simultaneous to opening the passenger side door. "Could you be givin' an old, knackered mink a ride to town?" he asked. "I'm gummin' for a pint and know but one who'll serve on such a day for the hay, so I do."

"Sure, Doc," the deputy replied, astonished as anyone the man could be smiling at a time like this.

"Grand so," Doctor Danaher replied.

He crawled onto the passenger side seat, slow and deliberate as an aging man would, dropped the duffle bag to the floor and stretched his forearm across the seatback. He pivoted toward the back left. Jack sat stiff, returning a blank, unbelieving stare. How could the man be grinning?

The doctor reached for and gave a slap to his knee as if the pair where old friends. He smiled wider and winked. "Lack of resource has hanged many a thick eegit, me lad. I'm pleased as the 'morrow's sun you got me telegram."

CHAPTER 38

The ride, Jack concluded, was little better than a wooden wheeled bicycle traveling along a rocked and potted primitive wilderness path. Other than an occasional gliding sensation as the tires skated across slush, the driver managed to hit every bump, pothole, and rut, sending passengers bouncing about the cab. Jack twice caromed off the ceiling as the McLaughlin made its way southwest toward Cameron.

Jack removed his eyes from the back of the doctor's head just once to check the landscape for any familiar landmark. The man's brazen confession to having penned the telegram and the impassive manner with which he offered up that confession sent Jack's mind reeling into a soupy daze and scrambling for answers as to just who this man was.

The doctor settled forward in his seat, bobbing left to right as if whistling a tune inside his head. His body language infuriated Jack. He wanted to grab the old buzzard by his neck and squeeze until the last truth spilled from his lips, but the deputy's pistol residing just inches from his rib cage would put a quick and painful end to anything he attempted.

The pace of the vehicle slowed as the group happened upon a crossroads. Jack noticed a large red barn settled to the right and in an instant, recognized its significance. Sophie mentioned the structure in her directions. Her drawing indicated turning right would take him to Cartersville. The deputy rolled the McLaughlin through the stop and turned left.

As the vehicle straightened, the doctor angled his head to capture Jack's eye, and winked. The moment the driver reached the proper cruising speed for the conditions, Doctor Danaher lifted his arm off the seatback and gave a casual flick of his wrist. On cue, a bone-shaking thud emanated from under Jack's seat, sending the car fishtailing along the narrow path and spinning sideways and coming to rest facing the opposite direction. Each man—other than the doctor—released a deep breath and their grips of the nearest bolted-down vehicle part they'd managed to secure.

"Seems your motorcar has blown a hoof, so it has," the doctor said.

The deputy slapped the steering wheel with both hands then cussed. "Come on Barney, let's take a look. Doc, you mind keeping an eye on the prisoner?" he asked, reaching for his sidearm and passing it by the barrel.

"I couldn't hit the side of a barn with a pint of the plain, but if he makes a break for it, I'll aim for the seat of his britches, so I will."

"I'm sure he'll stay put." The deputy grinned. "He couldn't get far in these conditions." The doctor scoffed at the suggestion, knowing full-well Jack's capacity for trekking across the countryside in sub-zero degree weather.

"I'll be right back," the deputy called out, shutting the car door.

"Off you go me good man and God to ya," the doctor said, flicking a wave.

The instant the deputy in the back exited, the doctor shot across the bench seat like a teenager, jammed the starter switch to the floorboard and pulled away to the yells of the deputies.

"I'd be removin' myself from view of that rear window if I were you, lad," he shouted.

The doctor's words met with a blank stare.

"I'd get down right now lad," he yelled again.

Jack collapsed against the floorboard, wedging his body between the bench seats. A shot from the deputy's pistol pierced the rear glass and exited through the front windshield. Another shot rang out but missed. The McLaughlin gained speed and soon outdistanced the men and the range of their firearms. Jack rose from his position in time to see the red barn passing on his right and a sign opposite pointing passersby toward Cartersville. He peered through the back window to see the deputies chasing then stopping, flinging their arms forward in anger as if throwing rocks. Jack slid across the seat to gain a better angle.

"That was a bloody well-crafted ambush . . . wouldn't you say lad?" the doctor asked, peeking through a thin piece of mirror rigged against the windshield. Jack rested against the seatback, his mouth agape.

Moving well out of the sight of the deputies, the doctor brought the McLaughlin to a stop in the middle of the road, reached into his coat pocket and pulled out a pipe. Another pocket held a smallish tin of tobacco. He stuffed the pipe full, ignited a matchstick, and puffed the lot to life.

He caught Jack's face in the mirror. "Don't be a fearin,' me Jackie boy, I know what I'm doing. Here," he said, reaching across the bench and tossing a dampened towel into his lap, "you could use a good scrubbing."

"Why did you do that?" Jack demanded, wiping at his neck and face. "Who are you?"

With the tobacco burning at a steady smolder, the doctor released the clutch and continued along the blanketed path.

"Lucky I happened by, so it is. I'm told those actin' the lig in these parts are tossed in the hole and forgotten about."

"Where's my family? What have you done to them?"

"What have I done to his family, he says . . . impetuous," the doctor mumbled under his breath. "Your situation is of your own making, so it is."

"Are they dead? Was that my family back there?"

"What if they were, lad? Why are you frettin' over them so? You had plenty of time to fulfill your duty, so ya did . . . and ya pissed it away."

"Are they dead?" Jack yelled.

Doctor Danaher glanced to the passing landscape, measuring his response. "I'm sure I don't know," he said. "That's not my purpose or my business here; Himself reveals only what He sees as relevant."

"Himself?" Jack asked.

"God, lad."

"God? I don't understand. Who are you?"

"Michaleen Oge Danaher's the name. M. O. D."

"Why are you here? Why did you send the telegram?"

"Isn't it plain to ya now?"

"How was it even possible I got it?"

"With Himself, everything is possible. I'm an answer to a prayer, so I am."

"I didn't pray for this. I didn't ask for any of this. Why did I need to save the girl? She and her family don't mean a thing to me or have anything to do with my wife and daughters missing," he yelled, moving to the edge of the seat. "None of this makes any sense."

"I didn't say I was the answer to your prayer, lad."

"Then whose?"

The doctor drew into the mirror. "So the lot of 'em meant nothing to ya, eh?"

Jack readied to blurt the word 'no' but checked himself, as the feeling of Roo sleeping balled against him and the smell of lavender radiating from her hair filled his conscience. He recalled her sweet nature and insight into his own misgivings. He could not shake the feeling she was in some way a part of him. He looked out to view the passing landscape.

The once bright blue sky was washing to gray as another push of winter's wrath approached from the west. What was left of the sun sparkled against icicles dangling from the eaves of humble farmhouses and aged barns scattered along the way. Cardinals and red-winged blackbirds flittered from tree to tree in between dive-bomb runs upon holly berry bushes. Cattle and their hoofed companions bunched in close circles, munching on stacks of hay and thrown corn. Each property passed like a peaceful memory as Jack gazed through the window, conceding the interaction with Roo intensified the realization of the wrongs he'd committed against his family.

"You had to be in the moment, lad," the doctor said, seeing a glistening in Jack's eyes. "You had to be the one to bring her from the house. Himself chose you for the task. It was for your own good."

"I had to be in that moment? I murdered that little girl's mother. Why was that for my own good?"

"You musn't say things like that. You murdered no one."

Jack moved forward, clutching the seatback. "I took a two-by-four and drove it into that poor woman's skull and killed her," he yelled. "Don't tell me I didn't murder her."

"You delivered an act of mercy, so you did. Himself knew you'd do the right thing when the moment called."

"Why? Why was I was put in this position?"

"God does things accordin' to His own time and plans, so He does. He's a purpose not meant for questioning. It was just her time. It was their time . . . but not the wee one's." The doctor peeked over his shoulder. "Why ya worried so? You said yourself they meant nothing."

Jack pushed an angered shot of breath from his lungs. "Sophie," he said, pointing, "is as fine a human being as I have ever known."

"That she is, lad . . . a fine darlin' of a woman."

"She didn't deserve this . . . none of them did. The girl does not deserve going through the rest of her life without her family. They were all good people. What God would do that to prove a point?"

"Himself uses us all as instruments to accomplish His fine work, so He does. I'm an instrument unto Brooke; Jubel was an instrument unto me."

Jack lurched forward. "How do you know my wife?" he demanded.

"I told ya lad, I was an answer to a prayer . . . her's. Ah, she's a fine, darlin' of a woman your Brooke and she's a heart of corn. On my immortal soul, she loves ya beyond what ya be deservin.' She prayed to Himself, so here I am."

"So, you're some kind of a guardian angel?"

"Och, not at all man. That's blather fit for those believin' in the fairies and the Dov Shee, so it is."

"I don't know what that means but I demand you take me to her right now."

"Demand, so ya say? Sorry lad, that's not my mission."

"Mission? What mission? What does that mean?"

"As I said, I'm a mere instrument of Himself . . . as well you are. We're all instruments in accomplishing His wondrous works. You got me telegram, eh? You followed its instruction, eh? Mission accomplished."

"Your mission was to place me in the presence of an arbitrary family some 70 years removed from my time? For what reason? To allow me to see the lot of them wiped clean from this earth?"

"Are ya a lesser man for knowin' em? Are ya a lesser man for knowin' herself?"

Jack turned again to the window.

"Of course not. You've been given a grand gift, so. You accept from the loving God and ya thank Him for the moment. Do ya think the darlin' Brossys are sufferin' now, lad? No. They've arrived at their destination, so they have. They are a part of Himself now and much better for it.

"Look about ya," the doctor said pointing to the farmland spread before them, "this is nothing but a dress rehearsal, so it is. This is all but a brief moment in the glimpse of eternity where you learn from your missteps and prepare for what lies beyond. It's a mog of a bloke who thinks all of this is both beginning and end. Will ya listen to the man? I bring ya the news of more to come. And unless ya be changing your way right straight, you'll be backstrokin' in the fires of the hell as sure as the shamrock grows."

Jack reached into the pocket of his hoodie for the carved cross. The instant he secured the object in his palm, a peace rustled though his conscience, spreading about his body. Sophie's words reassured and the memory of her smile eased the struggle ripping at his insides over her final moments.

"A gift, lad," the doctor said. "Tell me you'll not remember the darlin' woman or the wee one and the tender moments ya shared with them both for the rest of your days. Tell me you'll be forgettin' herself's words of wisdom."

Jack caught the doc's eye in the mirror. He could tell the man knew what he held in his hand.

"For reasons not explained to me, it was important ya knew them all."

"But why is the girl so important? Why can't you tell me why I needed to save her?" A small, homemade road sign caught Jack's attention. Cartersville was but fifteen miles ahead.

The doctor did not answer. He brought the McLaughlin to a stop, dropped an elbow over the seatback and let go a stream of smoke from the corner of his mouth. Jack's nostrils expanded as he drew in the pleasing bouquet of cinnamon and nutmeg. The blend was familiar.

"Remind ya of something, eh lad?" The doctor drew another deep puff and released.

"It was your da's tobacco, wasn't it boy?"

The comment flushed the color from Jack's face and forced him against the back seat.

"How did you know that?" he asked in a whisper.

"I know your people, so I do."

Jack's eyes searched wildly about the cab. He was finding breathing difficult. "What do you mean? I don't understand?"

"Well . . . lad . . . your da was my boy's son, so it where. I held your da in me own arms the very day he clawed from the womb. He was blushin' redder than a lobster and madder than a corner boy who'd spent his last bob."

Unknown to his conscious awareness, Jack crossed his arms and attempted to form a word. He could say nothing.

"I don't wonder ya stare at me boy. It's not every day a man gets to pass tales with a dead relative." The doctor smacked his lips against the pipe and flashed a wink to his great-grandson.

Jack brought a hand to his forehead to wipe away a bead of sweat forming just under his scalp. He searched to either side as if attempting to identify the direction of an unsuspecting punch. The claim was preposterous, yet sure not impossible . . . considering.

Jack's voice cracked as he spoke, "Doctor, where is—"

"Please me lad, we're kin, so it is. You can forgo the formalities."

"Michaleen . . . where is my father . . . I mean . . . is he—"

"It's not for me to say, lad. I can tell ya your da loved ya, so. Like yourself, he just had a difficult time showing it. He was an angry and confused boy from the drop of the gate—although I don't know why— and when he fled for America in his early days, he left behind every piece of his former self recognizable to kin and friend alike. He even changed his name to ensure he'd never be located.

"Of course his da warned him he'd have better luck whistling up a mouse's hole than tryin' a go at America with nottin' but the shirt on his back and a single bob to his name. But, your da paid never no mind. And when he found himself with not even a dog to lick his trousers, he joined the army."

"I remember his uniform, nothing more."

"You should know the war stripped him of everything human; to the point he was unable to function in reality. What he did to ya and your ma was bloody shameful, so it was. But, understand lad, what he done was not a fault of your own. Your da just could not cope anymore and he got out the only way he knew how.

"Ya suffered a right unfair lot, so you did, but Himself saw to it ya had a chance at something your da did not; a chance at life, the love of a darlin' woman, the gift of wee ones about and an extended family, so it were. But even then, you let it slip from your fingers . . . pissed it away good and straight, like a summer breeze sweeping over the willow."

The doctor reengaged the McLaughlin's clutch. The car backfired as it pulled away, sending a grouping of crows scattering from a large tree just beyond the ditch. The sun had all but disappeared behind the clouds of the advancing system and the once crystal blue sky was smeared a dark blue-gray. Despite the surreal presence of a family member, Jack felt alone in the world.

"You know, I never wanted anything to happen to the dog," Jack said.

"What's that lad?" the doctor replied, peeking over his shoulder.

"I said I never wanted the dog to die."

"Didn't ya now?" he quipped.

"I was dead wrong the way I treated him. I wish I could take it back. I wish I could take everything back."

"True it 'tis we sometimes see in death and not in life. A hard lesson it is."

Jack pulled the cross from his pocket and traced along its outline with his finger. He could still see the twinkle in Roo's eyes when she offered it during the family's gift exchange.

"Michaleen . . . I don't want to be that man anymore," Jack said, continuing the trace of the object. "I want a second chance with my family. I want to be to Brooke the man she needs me to be—on all levels. I want to be the father to my children my father never was to me. I'll do anything God wants. I'll get on my knees and pray every day and go to church every Sunday."

"If only it were that easy, me lad," he said. "Himself doesn't need ya on your knees nor goin' to His house as if it were a weekend chore. What He wants from all of us is the very same. He wants your love, your heart, and for ya to be believin' in His only Son. He wants a personal relationship, so He does."

"I don't know how to do that."

The doctor drew his eyes into the mirror. "You start by askin' Him, so ya do. He's right there beside ya, lad. You've spent your life wrappin' yourself in bloody chains and He's been right there beside ya with the key the entire time."

Jack stared at the empty seat next to him.

"Go ahead, boy, ask Him."

The doctor noticed his eyes darting about as if working through a script.

"Ya needn't recite a portion of scripture. Just ask Him. It's as simple as requestin' a second slice of pie, so it is. Are ya willin' to commit to Him?"

Jack nodded. He could not help the emotion flooding his voice. "God, I want a relationship with You," he said, whispering.

"Say it out loud boy . . . it's just the three of us."

"God, please forgive me for what I've done. I want a relationship with You and I want to be what You want me to be. I need Your help. I don't want to be alone anymore. Please help me find my family."

Jack lifted from prayer to the doctor's glowing smile.

"Good boy," he said, returning his attention to the road. Jack looked beyond the windshield through blurred vision. The sky opened up, sending large flakes tumbling across the landscape.

"How do I get to them, Michaleen? How do I find them?"

"I don't know, lad. I don't have the answers for ya."

"What more can I do? How many times must I pray for a second chance?"

"Himself does not answer prayer with a thunder clap or stroke of a scepter. Would none of us learn a bloody thing if that be the situation. If ya seek, ya'll find through opportunity. Himself delivers opportunity and it is up to each man to take advantage of those moments. But opportunity comes not without faith."

The dialogue fell silent as the doctor steered the machine through an ever-increasing steady rush of snow and a winding glen challenging the McLaughlin's treadless tires and unstable axles. Several miles of open pastures spotted with homesteads gave way to a new grouping of farmhouses and outbuildings condensed as if plotted on the outskirts of a larger community. A sudden sharp right-hand turn led to a quick left. The vehicle struggled to crest atop a slightly rolling hill then skated down a shallow grade along a straightaway lined by fence and brush. The doctor let off the gas upon approaching a fork in the road, allowing the McLaughlin to coast to a stall. Jack noticed a small row of wood and stone buildings lining a single main thoroughfare less than a quarter mile down the road. Cartersville appeared even smaller than imagined. The doctor cut the engine.

"Well, me lad, this is where we must part," he said.

"What? Why? Isn't that Cartersville?" Jack asked, pointing out the window.

"Indeed it is. But my journey continues in the opposite direction."

"You're just going to leave me here?"

"Ya don't need me any longer. If ya've made peace in your heart with Himself and your intentions are true, He's the only guide you'll be a needin' from now on. I've other matters to attend, so I do."

"But I have a million questions. There's so much more I need to ask . . . more I want to know."

"I've got nothing more to offer ya, me boy. My time is short. I must be off."

The doctor reached to the front floorboard and passed the mangled duffle bag over the seatback.

"I can't do this alone," Jack pleaded. "I need your help."

"You have to find your own way, Jackie. Just remember, with Himself, all is possible. But if you fail to take advantage of the opportunities He gives ya, all can be just as lost."

Jack settled the duffle bag in his lap.

"Off ya go me lad, and God to ya."

Jack exited into the falling snow, shut the door and stepped back.

The doctor summoned him to the front passenger window.

"Remember, it takes the entire family to make a family. Ya need to find love for 'em all," he said winking, then smiling. "Keep this moment in your heart me boy and don't ever forget what's passed between us."

"I don't understand why you're leaving me."

"You soon will."

"But I wanted to know more about you . . . more about my dad."

"You have a lot of amends ahead, so ya do. Now's not the time to be worryin' about your da. There's always a chance we'll meet again someday . . . but it will be up to you, so it will. God's blessing to your ma."

The doctor mashed the starter to the floor, bringing the McLaughlin's engine sputtering back to life. Jack reached for the door handle as the vehicle banked in the opposite direction.

"My ma? Wait. What are you talking about?" he yelled.

Jack tried to keep pace as the car pulled away but was unable to maintain his grip of the door handle and his balance in the sloshy mess underfoot. A sudden gale whipped snow and ice pellets into a frenzy, pushing hard against his face and body, forcing him in the opposite direction. Quick to bring a forearm to a protective position, he searched into the onrush and saw nothing but a white wall rushing toward him. Fighting against the wind, he tracked the ruts of the McLaughlin forty paces before coming to a point where the roadway lay undisturbed. The doctor and the black sedan vanished into the belly of the wintry mix.

Reversing course, he fixed upon the lone structure he could make out in the swirling blast; a red-bricked building stretching well above the other more modest and less aesthetically pleasing structures making up Cartersville's meager business district. Fighting a severe drop in the temperature culminating with the gust, he moved between the ditches in snow deep enough to bury his ankles. It was as if he were walking from the lake once again only with better visibility and without his injured companion clinging to life.

Ice pellets the size of bb's striking at the back of his legs and head commanded a quicker pace along a surface gaining in grade. Cutting the distance to the town in half, open pastures soon gave way to more wooded ground. From his vantage point, the town appeared uninhabited. Not a single person, vehicle, or beast of burden strapped to a sled or carriage appeared along either side of the street or narrow sidewalks lining the storefronts. A wood-slat farmhouse to his right belched a stream of black smoke and ash from its stone chimney, but offered no indication of occupancy otherwise. A small, white church with a needle spire sat well back from the road to his left, tucked in a web of old hardwoods and appearing abandoned altogether.

A small stone monument marking the town's westernmost border rose from the snow just in front of a wood and stone bridge hovering over a shallow streambed. The landscape below the span flattened in both directions; to the south toward ground occupied by heavy brush and dense forest; to the north toward the property of the farmer's market partly owned by Olan Brossy. Jack paused to note the year chiseled into the face of the rock—1851.

Under an ever-darkening sky and pounding wind gusts, he moved beyond the bridge and through the snow another hundred yards toward the row of buildings on the left. First in line was the town's barbershop, identifiable by a classic red, white, and blue barber pole doubling as a support post for a green striped awning above.

Grabbing hold of the post, Jack pulled himself from the slush onto a set of worn wooden steps, splintered and concaved from years of heavy traffic, and under cover of the awning and onto a wood plank walkway stretching the entire length of the row of buildings. A large plate glass window identified the store as Harvey's Tonsorial Parlor. Smaller lettering at the bottom corner revealed Harvey also served as the town's postmaster general.

Jack peeked through the window and noticed two barber's chairs fronting a wall of mirror, a small counter and office caged in wire framing, and a bulletin board near the front entry plastered with wanted posters and local notices. The room was dark and empty, appearing as if there had not been a lick of trade for several days. He scanned the length of the walkway past the red brick building and the six others making up the row. Signs jutting perpendicular from above each doorway indicated the town had its own bank, building and loan, general store, fix-it shop, and jail.

Jack stepped to the edge of the walkway to view the opposite side of the street. The row of buildings displayed a much greater state of disrepair, as if upon settlement the townspeople had constructed that side first. Clapboards once whitewashed, revealed the silver of aged wood underneath, as years of harsh weather chipped away at the original finish. Jack surveyed the signage above each door. Scanning the length, he noticed a dingy, yellow glow bursting through two windows of the very last building in the row.

Swirling snow and an awkward sight angle made it impossible to decipher the name on the sign affixed flat against the building's façade. No matter, it appeared the proprietor was open for business and a decent chance the space was warm. Hurrying from under the protection of the barbershop awning, he crossed the street to the opposite covered sidewalk. The slats below creaked and moaned with his every step as he worked his way down the row from shop to shop, peeking in through each window as he passed. A law office, a grain and feed store, and a clothing store appeared as if they had seen as much business as the barbershop in recent days.

Crossing over a small alley separating the final two buildings from the others, he paused upon reaching the first—a drugstore and soda shop—to gaze upon an elaborate Christmas display spanning the length of the front window. He marveled at the simplicity of the tin and metal fabricated toys; World War I vehicles, farm tractors, and airplanes. The space beyond the display lay littered with Christmas-themed Coca Cola displays and cigarette and drug advertisements. A long stretching counter, lined with bright red stools and soda fountains, added to the sentimentality of the scene. He recalled a similar location on the main drag of his hometown and the memory of his mother taking him and his sister to see the decorated storefront of the old Ben Franklin dime store.

The yellow light pushing from the window next door grew more pronounced as the gray of the afternoon sky deepened. Continuing down the sidewalk, Jack peeked through the first window, noticing a room full of tables adorned with red-checkered tablecloths, a few booths lining the far wall, and a dining counter located against the back wall. A large man in an apron stood between a wall of mirror and a stainless steel encased bar, perusing a newspaper; a woman of equal age dressed in waitress garb sat in front and to his right on a stationary bar stool, working a fingernail file. He stepped from the building toward the street to catch an angle on the sign—Cartersville Diner.

He moved past the windows undetected, engaged the front door-knob, and with a nudge, entered the establishment to the sound of a single ding from a bell above. The man jerked from the paper; the woman followed with a sharp swivel of her stool.

"I was hoping maybe to get a bite to eat," Jack said, closing the door behind.

The man dropped the paper, rolled it then stowed it under the counter. Jack thought he was standing. He was wrong. When he rose, he extended to near six-foot eight. An obvious omission was his left arm. Man, they sure do grow them large around here, Jack thought.

"We're open, son," the storeowner said with a suspicious air. His voice was deep and intimidating. Jack would not be surprised to learn the man lost the arm in a fight with a grizzly. He pitied the bear.

"Take any seat you like."

Jack nodded and moved to the first of two booths situated at the front of the diner under the second storefront window. He tossed his duffle bag into the first seat then followed in behind. Looking toward the counter, he noticed the man waive off the server as she reached for a menu. Grabbing it himself, he moved from behind the bar. The booth was small but comfortable. Unless a hotel was near, Jack feared it might be his bed for the night.

"Evening," the man said, sliding a menu atop the table. He took in a couple deep sniffs. The smell of smoke was strong.

"Merry Christmas to you."

"Merry Christmas to you," Jack responded. "I was surprised to see the place open, seems all the other shops around here are closed."

"Most everything closes on Christmas Day in these parts. I don't believe I've seen you before."

"No, I'm not from around here."

"What happened to you there, if you don't mind me asking," the man said pointing to his head with the stub end of his pencil.

"I was in an accident a couple of days ago. Lost my car . . . everything. I'm just trying to get back home."

"What happened to your arm?" Jack responded.

The man appreciated the sense of fair play. He nodded and let go a slight grin.

"Lost it in the war," he grimaced. "Got too close to a dirty Kraut in a machine gun nest."

"Sorry to hear it . . . must have been pretty painful."

"Well, I was thinking it'd grow back, but we haven't seen the first sign of progress. Hasn't stopped me from serving the best food around, though. Where's home for you?"

"Chicago."

"I'd say you have a long journey ahead without a car . . . even longer without a horse."

Jack smiled. "How come your place is open?"

"We have some folks here who are widowed; they come in everyday, sometimes three times a day for their meals. My wife and I live above the place, so it makes no never mind to be open."

Jack scanned the menu. The prices were comical; everything but a steak and full order of chicken sold for under a buck. He decided on a steak sandwich and red beans and rice. It did not occur to him how he'd pay or the fact he did not have the correct currency, until the man asked for his order.

He reached for the duffle bag in search of his wallet. Finding it near the top of the pile, he pulled it and opened the fold. His surprise was surpassed only by the storeowner's.

"Well, it looks like you won't have to walk back to Chicago," he said, leaning over the table, peeking into the wallet.

Jack fanned through the wad. It was full of period bills. "Michaleen," he whispered.

"Excuse me?" the man asked.

"Nothing. I forgot my great-grandfather gave me a little traveling money," he said, shaking his head.

"So, what'll ya have, son?"

Jack fanned through the money. He stopped counting at two hundred.

"I'll have a steak sandwich and some red beans and rice."

"And to drink?"

"A pop will be fine."

"A what?" the man asked.

"A soda?"

"You mean a Coca Cola?"

"That'd be fine."

"Coming right up."

The man collected the menu and stepped away.

"Excuse me," Jack said, "any place for someone from out of town to stay the night?"

"No. We don't have a hotel here, son. The closest one's in Cameron . . . about thirty miles west by buggy, forty-five by car."

Jack shook his head, confused with the math. "I know this might sound strange, but any chance you'd let me wait out the night here? I've got no place to go. I can give you a hundred bucks for your trouble," he said, pulling five, crisp twenty-dollar bills from the wallet.

The storeowner's jaw dropped against his chest. Jack was more than a bit surprised at the reaction, not having the first clue as to the present value of a hundred dollars. The man doubled back with a wide smile building across his face.

Knowing the exact present value of one hundred dollars, he could barely hold his excitement knowing an otherwise abysmal day at the register now surpassed the best day he ever had and possibly the best month. "Son, for one hundred dollars you can sit until next week."

Jack slipped the bills into the man's waiting palm.

"I'll throw in a piece of my wife's homemade apple pie for ya and breakfast in the morning," he said. "No charge."

Jack nodded. The storeowner fled the booth, flashing the money at his wife.

Jack turned to the window and watched as snow spat past the rectangle of soft yellow light stretching onto the sidewalk. He drew in a deep breath; the taste of ash and soot remained distinct. His tongue and gums craved a liquid. Flipping the duffle bag on its side, he buried an elbow against the end, cupped his chin in his hand and rested against the back of the booth watching snow pile atop the steps leading from the street.

Before his steak had browned on the grill and his beans fully cooked, he fell fast asleep dreaming of his mother's smile.

CHAPTER 39

December 26

A wild scramble of sounds, any one of a hundred different, could have shaken Jack from the uncomfortable upright position in which he'd found sleep. Whether aroused by the latest "ding" of the bell above the door, or a symphony of forks and spoons dropped upon plates, or ceramic coffee cups chinking against their saucers, the realization that night had passed to day erupted accompanied by a razor-like burn against his right cheek.

Jack had fallen fast asleep with his face flush against the glass. The flesh of his cheek, despite a healthy patch of four-day growth, melded against the frosty surface as a tongue would to frozen metal.

Peeling away, cringing as the skin fought against release, he forced himself upright, rolled his neck in a semi-circle and worked through vertebrae snapping and realigning. The sounds rushing from within the restaurant suggested the place was packed. Subdued conversation, bursts of laughter and friendly banter grew plentiful from the center and sides of the room.

Jack dropped his hands, released a gaping yawn and stretched his arms wide. He conducted a quick inspection of his immediate space. The duffle bag remained at his side, upended. The tabletop was empty. Not a steak sandwich, a plate of beans, or a Coke to be found.

Jack looked to the center of the room. He was not surprised to see every table and booth occupied by Cartersville's early risers. Friends traded comments and laughs across tables and across the room as servers buzzed about like bees, refilling coffee cups and delivering steaming plates of pancakes, scrambled eggs, and biscuits and gravy.

He noticed an elderly man at the table adjacent to his wearing a red-checked flannel shirt, blue jeans, and cowboy boots. His friend sitting opposite wore a light gray sweatshirt and a worn and tattered Green Bay Packers cap low over his brow. The iconic Green Bay "G" above the bill jarred his mind to the fact something was amiss.

Looking about, he saw servers outfitted in Khaki pants, white polo shirts and tennis shoes. Two women in a booth on the opposite wall were dressed in jogging suits. He peeked over his shoulder. A Rock-Ola jukebox bursting with bright colored lights sat against the far wall. A digital wall clock hung just above. A large chalkboard opposite the jukebox revealed the special of the day—two pancakes, two eggs, two strips of bacon, two biscuits, all for under six dollars. Metal framed tables replaced wood-slatted ones. Handmade hardwood chairs had been traded for aluminum-padded high backs. Wide-plank hardwood on the floor for black and white checkered Linoleum squares. George Strait crooned a country ballad out of a center speaker in the drop ceiling above.

The street beyond the poured concrete sidewalk was jammed with cars—real cars—parked perpendicular against concrete pavers. Not McLaughlin's, Model-T's, or horses hooked to sleds or buggies—but real cars, painted real colors. Jack swiped at his eyes and looked again. A silver Ford pick-up was wedged in between a blue Chevy Blazer and white Camry. A bumperless Ford Escort had backed in next to a yellow Volkswagen. The row of buildings across the street were of modern construction—brick, cultured stone, vinyl siding.

A rush of excitement alerted his conscience. Somehow, some way he had found his way back. He brought the butt end of his fist against his forehead. His words to God were brief as reality advanced.

"What about Brooke?" he whispered. "What about the girls? Did they return as well?"

The excitement drained faster than it erupted. He focused on the Ford's license plate. He checked the DMV sticker on the Chevy's plate as well. Both affirmed he had not returned all the way.

His body sunk against the back of the bench. It was as if he was starting from square one. "What now?" he whispered.

"Good morning Jack . . . I've been waiting for you to wake." The soft voice broke from the booth situated in front of him. A single figure rested against the seatback, facing the opposite direction. Black hair massed neatly in a bun revealed a slender, silky-white neckline merging with soft, delicate shoulders covered in white lace.

"Did you get a good rest?" the woman asked.

Not a soul sitting next to him paid attention to the woman or her voice. A server passed without a word to either of them, as if the booth did not exist. Jack waved an arm into the air. The man seated opposite offered no response.

"Would you care to join me?" she asked, bringing a coffee cup to her lips.

Jack hesitated. The woman kept forward.

"Don't be frightened."

Jack slid across the bench. His legs tingled from reduced blood flow caused by the cramped quarters of the narrow space. Extending full into the aisle, not a single eye recognized his presence. The crowd's indifference stoked trepidation.

"Don't worry, they can't see you," the woman said, in between another sip. "You're not even a shadow to them."

A shiver swept Jack's body, agitating the hairs on the back of his neck. Arcing his path as he proceeded forward, he dipped at the shoulders as he passed the woman's seat bench, hoping to catch a glimpse of her face. His body jutted erect as she appeared in full.

The woman offered a pleasing smile. "It's okay . . . you can sit," she said, seeing the declination in his expression. She opened the palm of her hand toward the opposite bench.

Overwhelmed at the sight of her, Jack stumbled, bumbled, and banged his way into the narrow space. He could not peel from the deep blue of her pupils. His breathing condensed; his throat choked as he settled opposite her.

The woman felt his anguish and responded. The warmth of her hand atop his own induced tears. She caressed his fingers and knuckles with the delicacy of a mother's touch. Her smile did not fade.

"How is this possible?" Jack whispered, his voice sputtering.

"All is possible with God," she said.

"I'm so sorry," he said. "I'm so sorry for what I did."

"There was nothing more you could do. You needed to leave. Don't punish yourself."

"But why me, Sophie? Why did I have to be the one?"

"You did what any decent, caring, loving person would do under the circumstances." She pressed her finger deep into his palm. "You saved the most precious possession I had in this world and and you saved me from suffering. What you did had to be done."

"But why?"

"God always has a plan, Jack. You have to trust He has one for you. Faith in God and His plan begins every chapter of every life, is the first step in every journey we take, is the very breath we need to sustain this mortal life. You must turn everything over to Him and believe His will has purpose."

"Why am I here . . . now?" he asked. "Why are you here?"

Sophie smiled and released her hand of his. "I was given an opportunity to assist in your reclamation and accepted without hesitation."

"Is that what all this is?" Jack asked.

"It is whatever you make of it and take from it. Even if it is so, we are still bound by the decisions we make."

"Have *they* returned also, Sophie?"

She reached for her cup and sipped then brought the edge of a napkin tapping against her lips. "I've never in my life tasted anything as marvelous as chocolate and cream espresso. What amazing delicacies man has invented. It's a far cry from what my poor Olan suffered with all those years."

Jack leaned over the tabletop. "Sophie, did I lose them? Have I lost a second chance with my family?"

The smile shed from her face. She spotted a woman walking hand in hand with her child along the opposite sidewalk. Releasing a sigh, she asked, "If I could change anything about your life, what would you have me do?"

"Get me back to Brooke and my girls," he said without equivocation.

"Would it make your life whole?"

Jack's brow furrowed; he twitched with confusion. "I don't understand. They're all I have. I have nothing else. I want nothing more."

"Do you anticipate them forgiving you?"

He flashed a blank look before slumping against the back of the booth contemplating the question. Letting go a shallow sigh, he viewed the street. "I don't know, Sophie," he responded. "I pray they will."

"How can you expect to be forgiven when you, yourself, are unwilling to forgive?" She reached for his hand to recapture his attention.

"For if ye forgive men their trespasses, your heavenly Father will also forgive you. Matthew, six-fourteen," she said.

Sophie brought the cup against her lips, allowing her words to sink in.

"You know," she said, "your mother has been at your side, watching over you since the day she died. What do you remember most about her?"

Jack's brow furrowed. The question seemed out of place. "The way she used to smile at me," he answered. "I will always remember her smile."

"Have you not seen the same smile recently?"

He pitched toward the floor, working his memory backward.

"You see, your mother also was given an opportunity to help you. Although for her, the stakes were much greater. She could have revealed herself to you at any time, just as I have and as did your great-grandfather before me. But hers was a different mission. Tell me, where have you seen that smile?"

"I met two women, both waitresses. They both knew things about me that—"

Sophie smiled.

"My mother?"

"Let me ask you . . . if she were here with us now, and she asked for *your* forgiveness, could you grant it knowing it was true in your heart?"

Jack paused several moments. "I don't know," he said, shaking his head. "I don't know if I could ever forgive her for not protecting us."

"That's why she did not reveal herself to you. If you ever in your lifetime decided to forgive her, she wanted it to be something coming from your heart, not because she appeared to you in death. She is willing to spend eternity without reconciliation rather than force you into doing something contrary to what you believe in your heart. That, Jack, is true to a mother's love."

Jack released a deep sigh. The conflict unsettled him.

"You told me you wished you knew her side and what she went through . . . did you not?"

Jack nodded.

"Have you given thought as to how difficult it must have been for her to be abused as she was, abandoned with two small children to care for, and working two jobs to make sure there were clothes on your back and food on the table? Do you really wish for answers to your questions?"

Jack whispered an affirmation. Sophie placed her hand against his cheek. "Then do so."

A loving glow fanned out across her face. Jack's expression became confused. Sophie turned her head toward the back of the diner; Jack followed her gaze an instant later. An emotional burst escaped his throat. Sophie grabbed his hand.

Standing behind the counter, taking an order, he saw his mother as never before. She appeared frail and old; her face wrinkled with age and hair sprinkled with gray. He pulled in a deep breath to avoid sobbing.

"Go to her, Jack," Sophie said. "This is the moment where you can make this part of your life whole again."

Jack could not take his eyes off the woman he'd not seen since he was fourteen. A patron thanked her for her service; she returned his generous tip with a smile. That smile. Jack saw it in his sleep and could pick it out in the most diverse crowds. He felt a sudden urge to run, but his mind restrained him. Sophie rubbed the side of his arm.

"Will she know everything?" he asked

"She has not yet passed on. Go on now, Jack. You both deserve this moment."

Jack pushed on the seat and scooted to its edge. Standing upright, the man in the Packers hat acknowledged him with a nod and smile. A passing waitress excused herself as she maneuvered around him. A woman to his right winked and wished him a good day. Jack turned back to face the booth. It was empty.

He watched his mother's every motion as he weaved in and around tables en route to the counter. How the years of strife had worked her over. She seemed tired; winded even—just as he remembered as a child. Yet she worked on—also as he remembered.

His mother caught his image upon receiving a stack of pancakes through a small window behind the counter. The plate slipped and shattered at her feet.

She brought a shivering hand to her mouth as she staggered from behind the counter to near the first stool. She attempted to sit but did not have the strength to lift her leg. Her knees weakened and her legs shook. Unable to stand, his mother crumpled to the floor sobbing, shaking. Jack rushed to her side and fell to his knees. Bringing her tight against him, he buried his face in her hair and began to sob. The restaurant fell silent as the two embraced. Waitresses rushed from all points; the kitchen staff followed. Jack held her, rocking her in his arms.

"Oh Jackie," she said through her sobbing. "My dear boy." Jack held on until her shaking lessened. She flung her arms around his neck. He could feel the frailty in her limbs. Her condition troubled him.

He maneuvered to a knee, and with the assistance of her friend, helped her to her feet. Leading her to the first stool at the counter, he guided her atop the padded seat. She weighed less than a medium size piece of luggage. Situating himself on the stool next to her, he wiped at a smudge on her skirt as she redirected hair from in front of her face to behind her ears. She pulled a handkerchief from the pocket of her apron to wipe her eyes. Jack dragged the sleeve of his sweatshirt across his own face. The diner soon returned to its normal operation.

"There's not a day gone by I've not prayed for or dreamed of this moment," she said, still shaking. She cupped both hands over her nose and mouth, staring at him with excited delight.

"It's good to see you, Mom."

She pressed her hands hard against her face. "You have no idea how I've missed you. I love you so much." She breathed deep.

"I know, Mom. I'm sorry."

"No Jackie, please," she said, "you have nothing to be sorry for. Neither of you kids has anything to be sorry about. I'm the one . . ." She brought the handkerchief to her face. ". . . I'm the one who's sorry. I can't even begin to know what you and your sister have been through."

"You've suffered too, Mom," he said.

"I suffer because I did not do the right thing when I had a chance. When your father died, I should have packed us up and gotten as far away as our money could take us. I'm so sorry, Jackie."

"I'm sorry too, Mom. I should have gotten in touch with you long before now."

"I don't blame you, son. I would not have blamed you had you never decided to seek me out. You needed to get away. God knows I didn't do a thing to protect you."

Jack leaned over and collected his mother in his arms. Her body trembled. "I'm here now, Mom," he whispered.

"Can you ever forgive me?" she cried.

Jack searched his heart. Although he could not deny the impact of Sophie's theory regarding forgiveness, his desire to be a better man trumped her words. He was ready to accept God's plan—whatever it was.

"There's nothing to forgive, Mom," he said, pulling her closer. "You are not responsible for those who are careless with God's free will. You did the best you could under the circumstances. I know that now. I would ask you to forgive me for the time I've wasted."

Jack buried his face in her hair and smiled. His body felt cleansed and his heart as light as a feather.

"Emily, are you okay?" one of the servers asked, placing a hand on her shoulder. Jack released his hold as his mother and swiveled the stool in the woman's direction.

"Yes, I'm fine," she said, wiping her eyes. "This is my Jack."

"Well, I figured as much," the woman said. She extended her hand.

"You've made your mother very happy," she said. "Not a day has gone by around here we've not heard your name at least once."

Jack collected his mother's hand into his.

"Since things are starting to die down a bit, Emily, why don't you take your break now and you and your son go settle in a booth," the woman suggested. "I'll bring you both some coffee."

Emily nodded. Jack kept his grip of her hand as she eased off the stool. Placing his arm around her shoulder, he guided her to the front booth where his duffle bag sat, crumpled and unmolested. He helped her in then scooted into the bench opposite. They both looked to the street. The storm outside had intensified.

She studied his face several moments before noticing the bandage. "For heaven's sake, what happened to you?"

"I was in an accident a couple days back. I'm fine . . . just cut my scalp open a bit."

"We're both a sight, aren't we?" she asked. "You bandaged up like a boxer and me with my makeup smeared and looking so unkempt. I hate you have to see me like this."

Jack smiled as she brushed the hair away from her face. "You look beautiful, Mom."

"I just can't believe this," she said. "Am I dreaming?"

"No," Jack said, smiling. "It was time."

"I'm so happy, Jackie. I'm so very happy. I've worried so much about you over the years. I wanted so badly to get in my car and drive until I found you, but knew you wouldn't want that. I've myself to blame; it hurts me so knowing what you children endured . . . you especially. You may have forgiven me, but I will never forgive myself."

"Like I said Mom, you can't be held responsible for what others do."

"No, but I was responsible for your safety. When your father died, it changed me. I lost myself for the longest time. I regret every moment, Jackie. I hope you know."

"I do, Mom. I know you didn't intend for those things to happen. I've been wanting to know for the longest time what Dad was like . . . I mean before he went off to war."

She resituated atop the bench and released a deep sigh.

"Oh, Jackie, your father was such a troubled soul. There's so much you don't know; so much I'd hoped you and your sister would never find out about him. He was never able to find himself again once he got home, but I think he was lost well before he left.

"He was captured less than a month into the conflict and spent four years in a prison camp. Following his rescue, when he returned home, I went to the air base, along with the other wives and families to greet all the men returning. When they came off the plane, he had to come find me because I didn't even recognize him. He was a different man physically and mentally. The things he suffered; the things those animals did to him and the others were just unspeakable. I tried to help him as best I could. I thought just sticking by his side would go a long way to help in the healing process, but there was no saving him. His mind and soul was ravaged. What he did to you in the end . . . well, I'm certain he had no idea what he was doing. That night, he was not a man, just a sick and desperate animal looking to free itself from a cage."

"Do you know much about his childhood?"

"Very little. He spoke very little of it to me. I know he came from Ireland as a very young boy—even changed his name, but he mentioned nothing of his family. He did speak fondly one night about his grandfather, but it was brief. After that, whenever I'd ask about them, he'd become very uncomfortable and combative. We stopped talking about it. I never met a single member of his family in all the years we were together.

"Jackie, your father loved you. You need to know that."

He looked to the street, pressing his thumb and forefinger against his eyes.

"He was so proud the day you were born," she said. "It was just the strangest thing, but the very next day, it was as if he wanted nothing to do with you. I could not explain if I had a hundred years to try. All I know is the war stole every bit of who he was, because he was nothing like that when we first met."

"What was he like?"

"He was very eager to make something of his life; eager to start a family. And he was so handsome. I fell for him the moment we met. But even then, like I said, he seemed never to be able to find his way or fit in. It was like he was just not meant for this world and his life was just one big mistake."

Jack dragged his sleeve across his face.

"He hurt you often, didn't he?"

Emily turned away.

"I'm sorry, Mom. You don't need to answer."

"Have you spoken to Shannon?" she asked.

"No, I haven't."

"I saw her last Christmas and again a few months ago. She stopped by to introduce me to my new grandson. Can you believe it? I'm a grandmother . . . and you're an uncle. She lives in Kansas City now."

"Is she well?"

"Oh, I think so. Her husband is just a fine, fine man. His last name is Reynolds. He owns several banks. He's given her a life I never dreamed possible. You should have seen her holding that little boy. He's the absolute love of her life."

"I'm happy for her. I really am. You know you have more grandchildren," he said.

Jack reached into the duffle bag for his wallet. Unfolding it, he released a grin upon noticing the period bills stuffed inside had replaced with standard currency of the day.

Shuffling through the plastic sleeves containing the few pictures he carried, he retrieved the photo of his daughters at Disney. He slid the picture across to in front of his mother. She gasped.

"Oh, Jackie, they're just beautiful. What are their names?"

"Julianna is on the left and Jordan on the right."

"What beautiful names. And your wife?"

"Her name is Brooke."

"Do you have a picture of her?"

His mother could see his disappointment.

"She must be beautiful."

"She is Mom. I know you would love her. She's a great mother."

"Maybe someday I can meet them all," she said.

"Mom, you don't look well, are you alright?"

"Oh, just old and worn out. My doctor keeps telling me I need to take it easy, but I can't afford to stop working. Shannon has asked me several times to come live with them, but I just don't want to be a burden—especially now with the little one."

"You wouldn't be a burden, Mom. She wouldn't have asked if she thought you would. Maybe you'd like to come live with us?"

"Oh, I don't know Jackie. Anyway, I have many friends here who take good care of me. The waitress you met, she and her husband own the place and are very kind to me. They make sure I have what I need and dote on me as if I were their mother. They said I could work for them as long as I wanted, just as long as I promised not to kill myself trying," she said, laughing.

Jack gazed upon her smile. It filled him to his core. He wondered if the moment Sophie spoke of included changing her history. He wondered if he'd been given the opportunity to extend her life. Jack grew puzzled as he contemplated the predicament. This was not his life, or the life from whence he came. His mind raced through the possibilities. If he stayed, would he lose Brooke? Emily noticed his distress.

"What is it Jackie?" she said, reaching for his hand.

"Nothing, Mom. I'm fine. I was just thinking maybe you could get the rest of the day off and we could spend it together."

She squeezed his fingers. "I'm so happy, Jackie. I love you so much and I'm so proud of you. You've turned into such a good and handsome man. You could never imagine how much it means to me to be with you here now. If my life ended today I could not wish for anything more."

Jack grew uneasy. He was determined to change history.

"Mom, why don't you speak to your boss and see if they'll let you go. Maybe you could show me where you live?"

"I'm sure they won't mind. From the looks outside, we won't be very busy." She patted his hand and inched across the bench. Jack saw the struggle in her arms to pull her own weight upright. He moved to help, but paused as she extended into the aisle. She moved from the booth toward the back counter, taking each step with caution. It was clear to him now her duties consisted of working behind the counter. He doubted she could spend even the breakfast shift walking the floor.

Jack retrieved the picture of his girls, inserted it back into his wallet and readjusted the contents of the duffle bag. As he grabbed the strap, a loud crash erupted from over his shoulder. He turned at the sound to see his mother crumpled atop the floor with patrons and employees alike rushing to her aid.

Jack shot from the bench, catching the material of his sweatpants on the underside of the tabletop and pulling it across the floor as he went. Breaking free, he rushed to his mother's side, pushing and shoving onlookers from his path. He settled on his knees and cupped his hand behind her neck. A trickle of blood dripped across his fingers from where she hit the edge of the jukebox.

"Mom, can you hear me? Mom?"

Her eyes fluttered opened to the sound of his voice. Her breathing was near nothing.

"Mom, please hang on."

Jack watched a smile spread across her face.

"Thank you," she whispered. "You've made me very happy."

"Mom, please . . ." Jack lifted from his crouch. "Did someone call an ambulance?" he yelled. "Mom, please stay with me."

She rolled her head. "Don't worry Jackie," she said, each word separated by a labored breath. "I can go now with a happy heart. Thank you for bringing me peace."

Tears rolled off Jack's face onto his mother's apron. He knew it was her time. "Mom, please don't leave me. Not now. I love you. I will always love you."

She nodded and smiled wider. "I know, son," she said, her voice now little more than air. "Jackie?"

He bent low to place his ear next to her mouth to accept her final words. He pulled from her face, nodding. "I know, Mom, I love you too."

His mother drifted away content and filled with peace in her heart. Her final breath pushed from her lips like a kissing breeze off the ocean. Lifting her into his arms, Jack pulled her tight against his chest. He felt no anger; no guilt. His heart was at peace and his soul bursting with appreciation. He whispered thanks to God for allowing this final moment. He kissed her again on the cheek, whispered something in her ear then eased her body to the floor.

Rising from his knees, he collected his duffle bag and extracted himself from the ever-growing wall of customers closing in around. Heading toward the front of the diner, sidestepping a team of EMT personnel hustling in from the street, he paused after spying the image of a solitary figure seated at the booth. He stopped and smiled.

"Thank you, Sophie," he said

"'For if ye forgive men their trespasses, your heavenly Father will also forgive you,'" she replied, smiling.

Sophie pushed her hand across the tabletop and released a small piece of paper from her fingertips. She nodded for Jack to take it. Reaching over the seatback, he grabbed the slip and brought it close to his face. A ten-digit number appeared in pencil.

"I don't understand," he said.

"Please don't forget what has passed between us," Sophie said.

"I will never forget what you've done," he said. "I will never forget you."

"My time is up, Jack. Good luck to you. Your family is waiting."

Jack collected the slip of paper and smiled. Glancing over his shoulder, he viewed his mother a final time then turned to the booth. Sophie had vanished.

Beyond the large picture window, a rolling mass of solid white precipitation swept in from the west, wiping out what, moments before, was visible. In an instant, not a single car or building was identifiable. Anxious to find a telephone, Jack exited the diner into the white abyss, having little concern for what lay beyond the door unseen.

CHAPTER 40

As the diner door slammed shut, sucked with a crushing velocity toward the street as if to prevent any chance of retreat, a wicked and frigid winter squall ensued in an instant. Reverberating like a diesel freight train churning at high speed, its pummeling force pinned Jack against the building.

Finding he could not move in either direction, Jack brought the duffle bag against his face to shield blowing snow and shards of ice caught in the disturbance—then fell to his knees, quailing against the building's stone foundation.

Jack kept low and his body compact as the sound of breaking glass, structural elements ripping off facades, whole buildings collapsing, and large metal objects tossing about as if matchsticks, raised the fear that a deadly collision was imminent. With a final heavy surge pushing him against the stone, his inner ears ballooned with an intense pressure, and released with a painful pop. Following a brief moment of dead silence, the sounds and odors accustomed to a small town main street returned.

He breathed deep. Exhaust fumes consorted with the delicate aromas of baked goods and the stale smell of dampened brick and concrete. Horns honked, bells above shop doors tinkled as patrons hustled in and out, distant muffled conversations between friends competed with birds chirping and dogs barking. Footsteps passed at close range.

Feeling a warm surge encasing his body and a pleasing glow augmenting, he rolled toward the sky to the view of an infinite canopy of sparkling, crystal blue. The air was crisp with a slight breeze caressing his cheek as it pushed down the street, urging Christmas-themed flags and banners hanging above to whip and ting against their metal lampposts.

Jack stared at the brick-paved sidewalk below; a light layer of snow rested atop what was uncovered nearer the curb. A DMV sticker on the license plate of a pick-up truck produced excited relief. Another one of Mother Nature's crazy furies had delivered him back to present time, unharmed.

Getting to his feet, Jack gave a quick brush of his clothes and adjusted his sweatpants. He paid little attention to a string of townspeople passing by looking at him as if he were a vagrant. The street and a couple of its buildings he recognized, with but a few slight modifications, including a yarn store now conducting business in the space the diner once occupied and a new, three-story brick-faced building on the side opposite hosting the town's municipal offices.

Jack searched the shop signs above each door. The soda shop sharing a wall with the diner remained as it was. He gathered his duffle bag in hand and entered the store.

"Good morning, sir," a young girl with a mouthful of braces said from behind a row of stainless steel soda fountains. "Would you like . . ." She paused in mid-sentence, noticing the bandage and those steel blue eyes. She fell smitten before continuing with a shy reserve, ". . . a counter or a booth?"

Jack flashed a hurried smile then scanned the shop. Tin ceiling tiles and a pulley-driven ceiling fan system enhanced the early twentieth century charm of the place. Stainless steel sparkled from one end to the other, with a row of thirty red-leather-topped stationary stools extending the entire length of the counter. A local police officer seated in the middle of the row sipped on a cup of coffee, reading a newspaper and picking at a piece of pumpkin pie. A wall of mirrors returned his reflection from behind the young girl, who moved from around the fountains to gain a better sightline. He noticed in the mirror an antique, neon Coca-Cola sign with a second-hand clock hanging on the wall just behind him. It was just past eleven.

Jack turned to the girl, catching her staring. "Actually, I wonder if I might use your phone?" he asked.

Embarrassed, the girl guided her auburn colored hair to behind her ears with a nervous stroke. Freckles and a small patch of budding acne concealed under an uneven layer of makeup placed her at no more than a senior in high school.

"Phone?" she asked, trying to hide her braces.

Jack smiled. Her innocence charmed him. "Yes, do you have a phone I could use?"

"We have one, but my mom doesn't like me letting people use it."

"Oh, I see. Is there another store I could—?"

"But she's not here right now," she interrupted, hoping to win his favor.

"I wouldn't want to do anything to get you into trouble."

"If you promise not to stay on long, it will be okay," she said, moving closer to the counter. "Is it a local call?"

"No, but I would be happy to pay. I can give you ten dollars." Jack let the duffle bag slip to the floor and fished for his wallet, struggling to control the anxiety building within. Pulling the ten-spot, he said, "I need to call my wife. It's very important."

The girl's body deflated. Disappointment seeped across her face. She sighed, rolled her eyes, and pointed to the end of the counter, "It's over there. But don't tell anyone I let you use it."

"I won't, I promise. Thank you," Jack said, sliding the bill across the counter.

The girl took in several deep sniffs as he passed. The smell of smoke flowed from behind him like the vapor trail of a high-flying jet. "I suppose you don't want anything to eat," she said, annoyed.

"I need to make this call first." Jack offered a smile and a nod to the officer as he passed.

The girl snatched a bar towel and wiped along the soda fountain, irritated she'd never meet her Prince Charming with those stupid braces plastered across her teeth.

Jack reached for the phone receiver simultaneous to pulling the slip of paper he'd received from Sophie from the pocket of his hoodie. Eager to dial, he punched in the one and area code, before pausing and dropping the receiver back onto the cradle. A massive bout of butterflies erupted in his stomach.

"What if *she* answers the phone?" he whispered. "What do I say?" He dropped an elbow on the counter and worked through the first few sentences he knew would be vital to keep Brooke from hanging up. The young girl popped out from behind the fountains.

"Is anything wrong?" she asked.

Jack was slow to respond as he sifted through potential dialogue. "No . . . everything's fine. I was just trying to remember something."

"Please hurry . . . my mom will be coming back soon."

Jack acknowledged with a nod. Shaking his head in self-deprecation, he spit a mocking laugh upon recalling the one other time he felt the first bit uneasy picking up a phone and calling a woman. Brooke was different. She was the exception. He remembered it taking a week to build the nerve to call her when they'd first met. His stomach wrenched then as if being punched. It was wrenching again now, but a punch he'd welcome. This felt worse.

Jack fished for words he could offer Brooke to make some sense as to where he was and how he'd arrived in Cartersville. No matter, he committed she'd get the complete truth, whether she believed him or not, including the answer to the question igniting the entire, sordid affair.

"No more lies," he whispered.

He lifted the receiver and punched in all eleven numbers. He was determined to live with the consequences. His stomach gurgled and growled as if the desired result of a deposited enema was near. The pause was lengthy before the earpiece echoed with the first ring. A second ring went unanswered. Jack wiped a nervous palm atop his sweatpants. Ring four passed. An instant into ring five, the phone picked up.

"Hello, Brooke? Is that you?" The woman's voice was rushed; her breathing heavy and panicked.

Jack knew her identity in an instant. His stomach shrank.

"Hello? Who is this," the woman demanded.

Jack stopped himself from hanging up. "Anna, it's me, it's Jack," he said, fearing the wrath he knew was imminent. The ensuing pause was lengthy. Jack kept his mouth shut and waited.

"Well, now, isn't this a surprise," she said, scathing with her sarcasm. Jack heard her cover the phone and announce his identity to those standing nearby. "It's him," she said, coldly.

"Where in the world have you been?"

"Anna, I—"

"Three days we've been trying to call you . . . three days. I've left you message after message. Why have you not returned our calls? Do you even care that my daughter and grandchildren have been missing for four days?"

"Anna, please listen . . . let me explain."

"Explain? You mean explain the reason why she was driving in the first place; why she asked me if she could stay with us for a few weeks? What's to explain? It's the same thing over and over again. You don't care about her, you don't care about the girls. All you care about is yourself. And now my daughter and grandchildren are missing and it's all your fault."

"Anna, I didn't get your message until the morning after you phoned. I didn't get home until late from my office's Christmas party."

"So you're out having a good time while my Brooke is driving, alone, six hours with two small children in a snowstorm, and you have no idea she's missing until the next day?"

"I didn't know she was driving. I found out because of your message. I was under the impression they were flying."

"How is it you did not know of her whereabouts?"

"We had an argument," he conceded, "and didn't speak the entire rest of the day."

"You had an argument . . . that's the story of your entire marriage. Why did she ask if she could stay with us for a few weeks?"

Jack did not respond. He wiped a hand across his face.

"I want to know," she demanded.

"It appears she was leaving me. She cleared out her side of the closet and everything in the girls' rooms."

Anna began to cry. "You just remember you did this to them," she said through her tears. "You did this to them." Anna's voice drifted from the phone as one of Brooke's sisters offered a comforting plea. The phone passed into the hands of someone standing near.

"Jack, it's John," Brooke's father said. "Have you spoken with her at all?"

"No, John, I haven't. Not since the day she left."

"Where are you now?"

"I'm in Cartersville."

"Cartersville? What are you doing in Cartersville?"

"When I got Anna's message, I took off to find them. I've been here for three days."

"Why haven't we heard from you?"

"I've not been able to get a call through because of the weather. Every time I tried, I got a recording saying the lines were down."

"Well, there was some hit-and-miss service the first night, but it was restored in full the next afternoon. If you were trying to call, seems you would have gotten through the next day."

"I don't know what else to say, John. I've been trying since I left Chicago."

"I see," he said, his voice filled with doubt. "What have you been doing to find her? Have you made contact with the local police or highway patrol?"

"No, I just got into town. I was in an accident a couple of days ago and lost everything; my car, my cell phone and . . . well, everything."

"You just told me you've been there three days, now which is it?"

"It's a long story, John. You wouldn't believe me if I told you."

"If you've done something to hurt her I will spend the rest of my life making sure you pay."

"What are you saying, John? You think I would hurt her or my daughters?"

"I don't know what to think. How do you expect us to believe anything that comes out of your mouth anymore? How are we to trust you? You've done nothing but cause our daughter pain and confusion from the day the two of you met and now she's missing. I'm sorry to say it, but if she was leaving you, I think it was long overdue."

Jack could hear Brooke's sisters yelling in the background in support of their father's opinion. John expected another one of his son-in-law's well known blame-it-on-the-rest-of-the-world rants. What he got in response surprised.

"I can't and won't disagree with you, John," Jack said, releasing a heavy sigh. "I've not held up my end of the bargain as a husband or a father. I don't expect you, Anna, or your family to believe or forgive me for who I've been or what I've done. I understand and accept it. But, I do love your daughter. I love her more than I can describe and more than my own life. When I find her, I will beg her for one last chance, because I'm not going to need another. I'm not the man I was four days ago. I can't explain to you why or how it came to be. As I said, you wouldn't believe me if I told you. But my life's mission moving forward will be what Brooke and my girls want and need me to be."

John held his tongue. The line fell silent as he absorbed the words. He was quick to wonder if this indeed was his son-in-law. He never heard the man speak of his daughter or his grandchildren with such passion. He wanted to like the man; wanted to trust him. There had just been too much chaos in their marriage.

"Where are you calling from, Jack?"

"Hold on," he said. Jack placed his palm over the mouthpiece.

"Miss? Miss?" he called out. The girl approached. "What is the name of your restaurant?"

Her look suggested he was an idiot, "the Cartersville Soda Fountain."

"I'm at the Cartersville Soda Fountain. It's on the main street here."

"You say you have no transportation?"

"None. I don't know if I can even rent a car."

"How did you get this number?"

"What? I don't understand."

"This is Anna's new cell phone. Brooke's sister Erin and her husband Bobby gave it to her yesterday. How'd you get the number?"

"I just managed to get it somehow."

Jack could hear Brooke's father sigh. "You really do everything you can to make it tough on yourself, don't you Jack."

"John, please. You would not begin to believe what has happened to me since I got here. I've been stranded for three days. I've a single pair of clothes, my ribs are smashed up, I have a slice across the top of my skull about twelve inches long, I'm tired, I'm hungry, and I just want to find my wife."

"Just sit tight. Bobby, Jeff, Darrin, and I are coming to get you. We'll search the area ourselves. The roads have cleared . . . we can probably make it in a couple hours. Just stay where you are. Don't make me have to come looking for you once we get there."

The phone clicked dead. Jack held the receiver tight against his ear, stunned at the turn of events. Upon dropping the phone to the cradle, he buried his hands inside the front pocket of his hoodie and deflated against the bar. How he wanted to hear Brooke's voice. How he needed to tell her he loved her. He released a deep sigh.

Noticing his dejection, the waitress shuffled from the soda fountains, wiping at the counter and staring.

"Are you okay?" she asked. Her voice was soft and delicate. Gone was the edgy tone.

"Yes, I'm fine," he replied, his forehead still resting atop the counter.

"Were you able to speak with your wife?"

"No—couldn't get through."

"I'm sorry. Can I get you something to eat?" she asked.

"Yeah," Jack said, resolute. "I'd like the biggest burger you have, with everything, an order of fries, a diet Coke, and a chocolate milk shake," he said.

The girl smiled. "Would you like to sit here?"

"No, I think I'll grab a booth. Looks like I might be here a while."

The girl retreated to the kitchen. Jack slid from off the stool and walked toward the officer.

A large shield patch on the shoulder of his black leather jacket indicated his affiliation with the Cartersville police department.

"Excuse me, officer," Jack said.

The man finished a final paragraph before closing the paper. "What can I do for you, son?" he said, his voice snappish and his body language suggesting he did not appreciate the interruption.

"Have you heard any reports in the last few days of accidents or any persons stranded due to car trouble?"

The officer bit at his lower lip. "There was an accident out on 53 a couple nights ago, but wasn't much of anything. A tractor trailer slid off the road; driver wasn't hurt none."

"Anyone from out of town you know who might've been having some car trouble?"

"No one comes to mind," he said. "You lookin' for someone?"

"I'm trying to find my wife and daughters. They were coming this way for Christmas but did not make it to her parents' house in Iron River. Her mother told me they pulled off at the exit on Highway 8 to get some food and gas. We have not heard from them since."

The officer reached inside his coat and extracted a pocket notebook and pen. He flipped open past several pages to reach a blank space. "Give me their descriptions and I'll pass it along to the dispatch and have the information sent out to the other agencies in the area."

"I'd appreciate that," Jack said. He described Brooke and the girls in detail, including the identical moles located at the center of each of his daughters' chins. Jack thanked the officer again.

"Where can I reach you, in case we hear anything?"

"Well, I'll be here at least for the next couple of hours. I'm waiting for my father-in-law."

"Okay, son. I'll let you know if I come up with anything."

Jack selected a booth offering a clear view of the street. He tossed his duffle bag to the bench opposite and settled in. Still reeling from exhaustion, he rested against the seatback. Outlining Brooke's face in his mind, he imagined placing his hands against her cheeks and pulling her close. He wondered if she'd ever allow him to kiss her again. He'd settle with just staring into her eyes. Close to dozing off, he thrust forward at the sound of china and silverware clinking from behind his booth. The young girl soon appeared at his table; burger, fries, Coke, and shake in hand.

"Here you are, sir," she said with a glowing, closed-lip smile. Jack matched her smile, thinking it funny how she recalibrated her attitude now that a tip was possible.

"Thank you, Kari," he said, looking to the badge attached to her bright green shirt.

She unloaded the tray and reached to the next booth to retrieve a full bottle of ketchup. She turned as the officer slid from his stool.

"Goodbye, Mr. Miliken. Thank you," she said.

"Goodbye, Kari. Say hello to your mother." The officer resituated his cap. "I'll let you know if I hear anything, son."

"Thank you," Jack replied.

The man touched the bill of his cap, nodded, and eased through the soft mechanical chime of the front door.

"Are you in some sort of trouble?" the girl asked.

Jack grabbed at a napkin and unrolled it to the silverware folded within. The burger, a triple-decker and loaded with cheese, set his mouth to watering. "No . . . no trouble," he responded, "just looking for someone who might've stopped in town the last few days. Do you know of anyone who might have been from out of town having car trouble?"

"No one comes to mind," she said.

"Could you ask your parents for me?"

"Who is it you're looking for?"

"Well, I haven't heard from my wife and kids for a few days. We're just a little concerned."

"I'm so sorry," she said, taking an interest, then a seat in the booth opposite.

"Would you like to sit down?" Jack teased.

"How do you know they stopped here?" the girl said, not catching in the least his attempt at humor.

"Well, we think she stopped around here for gas and food. Maybe your mom or dad might know something."

"I'll ask my mom; I can't ask my dad."

Jack looked up after taking a bite of burger. It tasted better than a burger. "Is your dad not here?" he asked, still chewing.

"No. He left Mom and me about eight years ago."

Jack set the burger back on his plate and wiped his mouth.

"I'm sorry, Kari," he said, wiping pickle juice from the corner of his lip. "That must have been hard on the both of you."

"It's been much harder on Mom. I miss not having a dad, but he wasn't very nice or much of a father. It was almost a relief when he left."

Jack froze at her expression. He could see her pain despite whatever relief she said she felt. Her plight struck him close. He envisioned Julianna and Jordan someday relaying the same sentiments to their friends. "I'm really sorry, Kari," he said, reaching across the table to pat her hand.

"It's okay," she said. Her smile dimmed. "I sometimes dream he will come back someday a changed person and we could be a family again. But, it will never happen. It doesn't matter anymore, anyway. Mom and I are a good team. We have this shop and we do just fine . . . at least enough to pay all the bills. She even said I might be able to go to junior college next fall."

"You want to go to college, huh?"

"Well, a junior college is better than nothing. I always dreamed of someday going to the university but we couldn't come up with the money in a million years."

"The university?" Jack asked.

"Of Wisconsin . . . in Madison."

"Oh, of course," he said.

"They have a great journalism school there." Kari smiled, then turned away. "I want to be a writer."

"Well, you know, history's littered with authors who did not have a formal education beyond what they learned at home or in grade school."

"Oh, I know . . . I just thought . . . well . . . maybe I'd like to be a news reporter or TV anchor, something in television, maybe."

"Well, you're pretty enough," Jack said, smiling, "and you have the right personality."

Kari blushed. She turned so Jack could not see the silver through her smile.

"You know, I wore braces until I was a sophomore in college," he said, smiling. "I was glad I did, too. It made a big difference."

Kari released her lips. Her smile was beautiful. Jack hoped someday she'd find her way to Madison.

The chime above the door caught their attention. Jack grabbed another bite out of the burger in between stuffing a couple steak fries into his mouth. Kari jumped from the booth.

"Kari, haven't I told you to leave the customers be?" the woman said. With both standing within view, Jack made an easy distinction. The girl was a younger version of the woman approaching.

"Go on now, get behind the counter."

Jack traded a smile with her. "You're going to be just fine," he said. "I'll look forward to reading your first novel."

Kari smiled and scooted off to behind the counter.

"I'm sorry ma'am," Jack said. "It was my fault. I asked her to sit."

Smelling smoke, the woman drew in several sniffs before turning to the window behind the counter exposing the kitchen.

"Well, she'd talk the shine off a dime if I let her," she said. "Is there anything more you need? Maybe something more to drink?"

"No ma'am. I'm fine. I *would* like to know if you've happened to run across anyone in town the past couple of days who was stranded because of car trouble?"

"No. Not that I can think of. Sorry. And I know just about everyone in town."

Jack nodded.

The woman readjusted the several bags in her arms. "Well, if you don't need anything else, I need to get back to the kitchen."

"Nothing else. Thank you."

Finishing off the last bite of burger then sipping a long, creamy stream of chocolate shake, Jack thought of commandeering a ride to the intersection of Highway 8 and Interstate 53 for another search of the area, but decided the situation would best be served if he remained where he told his father-in-law he'd be. The last thing he needed was to not be the first person the ex-marine saw upon arriving to town.

Jack stuffed the last two remaining fries into his mouth and pushed the plate away. A sudden wave of downtown shoppers and local employees entered for the noon-hour rush. Several breezed past his booth, smiling, nodding, and sniffing. His bandage drew long stares and private whispers.

Stretching his legs as far as the booth would allow he leaned deep into the seatback wondering why Sophie felt it necessary he make contact with Brooke's family at this moment. *Does she not know how much they hate me,* he wondered. *What good could she have seen coming from this?* He recounted the rocky relationship with the family, especially with Brooke's mother. Losing himself in the pedestrian traffic hustling by along the sidewalk, he allowed his mind to open and consider for the first time his longstanding opinion, and oftentimes unfair assessment, of his mother-in-law's personality. Anna, too, in her own way had attempted to enlighten him as to the ways of God and family, and in many instances, with more subtlety. He contemplated several minutes why Sophie's perspectives of the same had cracked his shell and Anna's had not. He could never deny, without lying, that his in-laws were good people.

Jack brought a hand against his mouth, and rubbed at the stubble surrounding his chin. He worked across the large plate glass window as he considered for the first time his role in the tension and distrust between them. He recognized the Mayberrys as very caring, giving, and loving people. In the few times he'd been exposed to them collectively, including his sisters and brothers-in-law, they tried hard to make him feel welcome; even harder to make him feel like one of them. The man they knew, he knew all too well, and it did not take long for the picture to become clear. The barriers he set, he did so on purpose. His actions toward them left them with no room to accept him. He wadded then tossed his napkin across the table on top of his plate, recalling one of Sam's many assessments of his personality.

"She was right," Jack whispered, "you never gave them a chance."

Jack folded his arms over his chest and smiled as the messages and intentions of Michaleen and Sophie danced about his conscience. He knew now the way to Brooke was through her family. Without them—all of them—there was no way the two could ever be whole. He wondered if he'd have the courage to face them all and ask for their forgiveness. No matter, he hoped the opportunity would present itself soon.

"And I say unto you, ask and it shall be given to you; seek and ye shall find; knock and it shall be opened unto you" (Luke 11:9).

CHAPTER 41

Kari stared into her palm wide-eyed. "I just don't know what to say."

"You don't need to say anything," Jack replied. "It's not much, but it may buy you a book or two next fall."

"Not that much? I don't think my mom will let me accept this."

"This isn't for your mother, it's for you. I'm the customer, right?"

"Well, yes, sir."

"You would expect a tip for your work, right?"

"Yes, but ten or fifteen percent is customary around here."

"Well, I think you did an exceptional job. Anyway the customer's always right."

"But, five hundred dollars?" she asked.

"It's okay, Kari. Don't worry about it."

"But it's everything you had in your wallet."

"It's just money. I have a couple credit cards if I need more. Just take it and put it to good use."

"I just never . . . thank you so much Mr. . . ."

"Jack . . . my name is Jack," he said.

"Thank you so much, Mr. Jack. I don't think I've ever held this much money in my hand in my life."

"Just promise you'll put it to good use."

"My mom started a savings account for me two years ago. As soon as I go on break I'll walk across the street and deposit it all."

"Good girl," he said, sipping the final draw of milkshake.

She slipped a yellow copy of the receipt into his hand. He folded the paper across handwriting wishing him a blessed day and signed Kari Goodman. He placed the receipt into the now empty fold of his wallet.

"It's just the nicest, kindest thing anyone's ever done for me," she said, her sincerity far exceeding what one would expect from a girl her age.

Jack stretched an index finger. "Don't make me out to be some kind of hero, now. I can tell you I'm nowhere near close to the many back payments I owe to a lot of people."

Jack reached across the tabletop for his duffle bag. Feeling an immediate bite, he pursed his lips and slipped back against the seatback grabbing hold of his side. Although his injuries were on the mend, his rib cage reminded him limitations still existed. Seeing his failed attempt, Kari assisted in retrieving the bag. She was the first to notice the white, snow and slush-splattered SUV pulling into a vacated parking space just to the right of the diner's front door. A dark blue Suburban pulled alongside.

An elderly, gray-haired man whose facial features reminded her of a black and white photo of a spit-and-polish army general she'd seen hanging in the classroom of her third period history professor, exited in haste from the front passenger's side door of the white vehicle. Outfitted in black jeans, cowboy boots, a brown leather jacket, and a green, faded John Deere cap, he looked every bit a local from top to bottom. Quick to dispose the classroom image from her mind, Kari resumed her assumption he was just another customer that would help her and her mother make ends meet.

Jack drew his stare up as the magnetic strip above the door separated from the frame, releasing a chime. Before the glass door swung open, he straightened his spine against the bench and stiffened as the man pushed his way through.

He had not seen Brooke's father in some time—maybe two years. The man looked worn; desperate. Deep crow's feet stretched from his eyes, adding twenty years to a face already subjected to two brutal wars and years of bitter, biting winds and baking sun in the corn and wheat fields from which he made his living. He was much thinner, but still advanced with the same determined and confident gait that earned him recognition as a leader among men with his military superiors.

John caught Jack's eye the instant he passed beyond the threshold. His pace slowed upon observing the bandage and his overall condition. Approaching with a cautious look about him, he removed his cap, served Kari a grandfatherly smile then planted his fists into his hips as he gave his son-in-law a thorough once-over.

"What on earth happened to you?" he asked.

Jack cocked his head and scrunched his brow. John's surprise puzzled him.

"I told you I was in an accident," Jack said.

"I recall," he said, easing into the seat opposite and dropping his cap atop the table, "but I didn't think you were mangled. What happened? Do you need a doctor?"

"No," he replied. "I'll be alright. I'm feeling much better than I did a few days ago."

John sniffed. "You smell like smoke. Your clothes . . . they're stained with soot. Is that blood?"

"Well, there was a fire. The home where I was staying following the accident burned to the ground yesterday morning."

"Good Lord, was anyone hurt?"

Jack turned away. "Yeah, a few."

"I guess you weren't kidding when you said a lot had happened since you got here. What have you done since we last spoke?"

"I've done nothing. I stayed right here to make sure you didn't have to come looking for me."

"You've not even walked up or down the street or contacted the police? You know we had to report her missing, right?"

"I assumed you did, yes," Jack replied.

Feeling the tension brewing between the men, Kari backed away from the table. "Mr. Jack, thank you very much," she said, smiling and flashing the wad of bills in her hand. "I could never repay you for this. I promise I'll use it just as we discussed."

Jack stretched out his arm, collecting Kari's hand into his. "Good luck, Kari. Remember, when you get your first novel published, I want an autographed copy." He settled his business card into the palm of her hand.

Kari smiled wide, forgetting altogether the bright metal radiating from behind her lips. Jack gave a squeeze and released her hand. She offered John something to eat or drink and moved off to another table following his decline.

"You mean to tell me you've just been sitting here, doing nothing all this time?" John asked, leaning over the table.

"I gave a description of her and the girls to a police officer who was taking a break and asked him to check if anyone fitting their description was stranded due to car trouble."

John pulled back, satisfied he'd at least made some attempt. The two men squared their stares.

"That looked to be a right healthy tip, Jack," John said, never missing the chance to let others know very little escaped his observation.

"She's just a young girl hoping to go to college someday . . . it was the least I could do."

"I've never known you to be so generous with your money—at least to others." He flashed a saucy grin.

The man he knew himself to be would have made strong suggestions as to where the old man could stick his comment. The man he intended to be moving forward was better—much better.

"I suppose you're right," he said. "There's no excuse for it. I can assure you it won't be the case moving forward."

The grin melted from John's face in an instant. His eyebrows crumpled. "What is it you're trying to sell me, Jack? All of sudden, you're a new man?"

"I'm not trying to sell you anything. I told you on the phone, a lot has happened . . . I don't want to be the man I was any longer. I would hope you and your family would give me a chance to prove it but I don't expect it. And I won't blame you if you don't. You've every reason to doubt me because of what I've been. I get it."

"What happened to you?"

"Let's just say *I* was revealed to *me* and I didn't like what I saw."

John folded his arms across his chest. "I know for a fact if Brooke went to the length of clearing out her and the girls' closets, she has no intention of returning to you. I know for a fact how much she loved you—although I don't know why—and how hard of a decision that must have been for her . . . and for her to take that step . . . well."

"That may be," Jack said, nodding, "and I may have to live with that consequence. Regardless, if she returns or not, I need to make changes in my life and I'm going to make those changes with or without her. I may lose her and that will be tragic, but the fault will be my own. I have two girls who are going to need me the rest of their lives and they're going to have a father they can count on and rely on no matter what."

John sighed. "You know, that's the most mature thing I've heard come out of your mouth since you first introduced yourself to the family."

"I've made a lot of mistakes, John, more than I deserve to be forgiven for. But I believe God will show me the way."

John drew in his chin, surprised by the reference. "So, am I to surmise you've found God in all this?"

"No," Jack said, "God found *me*. He got my attention in ways I could never describe or explain."

John softened; his posture eased. He grabbed and began to fiddle with the bill of his cap. "You know, just before I shipped off to the South Pacific, one of my drill sergeants gave me a bit of advice. He said only trust the fella sitting next to you in the foxhole if you can see in his eyes what the enemy would fear. I've spent most of my adult life trusting what I see in a man's eyes. When your very life depends on it, it becomes a habit. The problem here is we've given you chance upon chance to prove you have the best interest of our firstborn at heart. I've waited a long time for you to display in your actions and words just a speck of maturity."

He leaned across the tabletop.

"I trust what I'm seeing in your eyes. God help me, but I believe you're speaking from the heart. I believe in second chances. In your case, we're pushin' a half-dozen, but I know how much Brooke loves you. She's never loved like this before and no matter what happens now, she'll never love like this again."

John leaned back against the seatback, caught off guard as Jack wiped at his eyes.

"Because of her love for you and for the sake of her future, I'm willing to wipe the slate clean between us. But this is it, Jack. There won't be another chance after this—that is, if she decides to return to you. I won't allow you to betray her again. If at any point I hear you've breached her trust or hurt her or the girls in any way, I'll pull them out of your house myself and our relationship will cease to exist without the possibility of repair. Do you understand?"

Jack nodded. "I understand, John. I appreciate the chance you're giving me to make amends and to prove my worth. We will not have to have this conversation again."

"Fair enough," John responded. He extended his hand. Jack accepted it.

"Now, I should warn you, you might not find the rest of the family so willing to forgive and forget—especially your mother-in-law. She and I . . . well we have a different way about ourselves—a different way of handling these types of things—the least of which is the vast difference between a father and his daughter and a mother and her baby. I have to be honest, I don't know if that relationship is repairable at this point."

"I would not direct an ounce of blame in Anna's direction and would understand if she never wanted to see me with her daughter again. Maybe time and my actions can heal the strain. At this point, though, none of it will matter unless we find Brooke."

"Where do you suggest we begin?" John asked, centering his cap atop his head.

"I think we need to get back to the exit and retrace the path from there. When I arrived the other night, I stopped at a truck stop right off I-53. A truck driver said he saw Brooke's Escalade at a diner on the opposite side of the road spitting out steam. I went to the diner and asked the staff and they said a woman and two little girls left with a man who said he could fix the car. Not long after, I had the accident and have been laid up ever since."

"Do you know the way?"

"I'm so turned around right now I doubt I could find my way down the street."

"It doesn't matter. Bobby's got a pretty snazzy GPS in his car. I'm sure we can find the intersection."

"Well, let's get going," Jack suggested, reaching for his duffle bag. John held his position. A strange look floated over his face.

"What is it?" Jack asked.

"I was not very successful in keeping this a small search and rescue mission."

"What do you mean?"

"Well, as I mentioned in our phone conversation, my intent was to have Bobby, Jeff, and Darrin along. Unfortunately, your sisters-in-law took issue."

Jack swallowed. "You mean they all came?"

"Well, not all of 'em. Gina stayed behind with my sister and brother to watch all the kids. Anna insisted on coming and the girls followed her lead."

"They're all outside?" Jack asked.

"In two vehicles."

Well, you asked for it, Jack thought. He counted in his head the total number of Mayberry family members waiting just outside the door.

"I'm sorry, Jack, but by all rights, I can't expect them not to want to help. They're all very concerned. I couldn't demand they stay behind."

"It's okay. I would've been more surprised had they all wanted to stay home. I don't blame them for wanting to come. I've got to face them at some point. Now is as good a time as any."

"I've got to hand it to you . . . it takes a lot of guts to stand up and face the music like this. Only you won't be going up against a string quartet. It's an entire orchestra out there and they'd not mind one bit seeing you disappear."

"They've earned the right to dislike me. I've given them no reason to feel any different. Are you ready to get going?"

John nodded. The two men slid from the booth and moved toward the door. Jack searched the diner over his shoulder for Kari. He caught her eye as she attended a customer at the far end of the counter. She offered a wave and a less-than-enthusiastic smile, knowing she'd never see her new friend again. Jack winked before exiting the diner on John's heels.

He spotted Erin's husband Bobby first, stretching across the steering wheel of his white Tahoe, pressing close to the windshield to gain a better view. He appeared stunned at the sight of Jack and was quick to turn to the driver's side window to gauge the reaction of the Mayberry women. Jack followed the swing of his head. The Suburban rocked on its axles as Erin, Faye, Diane, and Kaye fell across each other's laps checking his condition. Jack took a half step toward the vehicle upon seeing Anna seated in the front passenger's seat. Her arms folded against her body, her stare boring resolute into the vehicle's floorboard. She refused to look in his direction despite Faye's husband, James, serving as chauffeur, patting her shoulder and pointing in his direction. Diane swiped at the rear passenger's side window at the condensation collecting from the comments traded between them.

Jack scanned the sidewalk east to its end, before viewing the opposite direction. The blue of the sky had deepened; a mild breeze remained persistent. Those areas doused in sunlight tickled the imagination with thoughts of an early spring—or at least a short winter. He breathed deep, expanding his lungs to twice their limit. The smell of manure hovered for a tick before whisking away with the breeze, replaced with the fried odors venting from the diner's grill.

"Why don't you sit up front Jack . . . you can help Bobby navigate," John suggested, opening the door. Jack stepped off the curb and reached for the handle. Both men turned at the sound of a voice calling from across the street.

"Son . . . wait just a minute," the man yelled, skirting around traffic as he advanced toward them. Jack recognized the police officer in an instant. He moved past John to the end of the parking space.

"I've got some good news for ya, son," he said, out of breath. He waved a slip of pink paper between his fingers. "I spoke with our captain and he made a few calls. Come to find out, the son of a nephew of someone the captain knows took in a woman and two young girls a few nights ago between here and Cameron."

John slammed the car door and advanced on the conversation, pushing in between the two.

"Anyway, I have the address where this fella lives," the officer said, extending the slip.

With hands shaking, Jack snatched the paper from the officer's fingers. Adrenaline raced through his veins; the whites of his eyes shone two blocks down the street.

"Captain tried to call 'em, but they still don't have telephone service out there from the ice the other night."

John grabbed at the back of Jack's neck in an excited burst of relief. Jack studied the handwritten note while raw emotion flushed through his body.

"If you got a GPS, you should be able to find it in a snap. It's not but fifteen miles or so from here, near the old quarry lake."

"Quarry lake?" Jack asked.

"Yeah. The old Mankato Company granite quarry; near highway 113."

Jack knew the area, the lake in particular. He raised the slip of paper, jerked his hand forward simultaneous to gritting his jaw and, with an airy, emotionally charged breath, offered thanks to the officer for his help.

"Let's go, Jack," John said, grabbing the slip out of his hand and passing it to Kaye's husband, Darrin, who'd exited the vehicle unnoticed.

"Get the address into the GPS and let's go get my daughter." Darrin smiled and handed the slip to Bobby who punched the coordinates into the dashboard system.

John rushed to the opposite side of the vehicle, tapped against the glass, and announced they'd been given an address. Joyful bursts caught the attention of those walking along the sidewalk. Anna buried her face into her hands and began to sob.

"Just follow us," John instructed. "The officer said the house is about fifteen miles from here."

Jack waited on John to return before climbing into the passenger seat, lugging along his duffle bag without the first offer of assistance from his brothers-in-law. He nodded to Bobby then glanced over his shoulder to view Jeff and Darrin in the back seat. The men said nothing. A tap on the passenger side window provided a distraction.

"Kari, what's the matter?" Jack asked, opening the door.

"Oh, nothing. I just wanted to give you my home address . . . you know . . . just in case you're ever up this way again, you could stop by for a visit."

"Thank you," he said, accepting the index card. "I'll be sure to look you up . . . if I'm ever up this way again."

"Thanks again for the money. I hope you enjoyed your time here."

Jack turned as his brothers-in-law behind reacted with quick bursts of snide laughter.

"Boys, you don't have the first idea what that's all about," John defended. "I'm not in the mood for any nonsense from any of ya's. Got it?"

"Thank you, Kari," Jack said. "You take care of yourself."

She smiled and waved as he closed the door.

"Is the address punched in?" John demanded.

"It's right here," Bobby said, pointing to the map embedded in the dash. John and Jack both studied the red flashing destination marker.

"Then let's get to it."

James backed from his slot first, giving Bobby a clear path and protection from oncoming traffic. Heading east, the convoy reached the last traffic light marking Main and Sixth, before making a U-turn at the request of the soft, pleasing voice emanating from the GPS.

The slow-moving traffic was reason for concern. Jack's knuckles glowed bright white as he tightened his fingers around the handgrip above his head. His opposite palm grew hot from friction caused by a nervous tic of rubbing it back and forth atop his thigh. *What if the officer's wrong?* he thought, counting the passing shop windows as they crawled along from one red light to the next. *What if it's someone else?* He knew the letdown would be crippling.

"But what if it is her?" he whispered. "What do I do? What do I say?" His thoughts grew confused; sweat beaded along his forehead. Releasing from the handgrip, he collected the moisture in his palm. As he swiped a second time, he felt a hand grab and plant atop his shoulder, pulling his body toward the seatback. John drew forward, leaning and squeezing between the headrest and window.

"If she's not there, it won't mean we're finished," he said, concealing his comment from the others. "We'll search as long as it takes." John squeezed and released his hand.

Jack agreed with a slight nod. He appreciated the supportive words, but wondered what the reaction of the rest of the Mayberry clan would be if indeed their lead was a dead end.

Passing through the last intersection marking the town's main drag brought the group passing over the old fieldstone bridge. Although Jack had entered Cartersville over the very same span—some seventy years ago as it were—many of its original features remained preserved, including the chestnut and silver-colored stone columns serving as supports for the split rail system protecting from the drop below. The bridge was wider and layered in blacktop rather than the wood slats he recalled. A shallow concrete aqueduct rested below the span, stretching in both directions out of his view. As the vehicle reached the opposite side of the bridge, he caught a glimpse of the original stone marker displaying the town's founding year.

The two-lane road leading from Main Street, having received a recent resurfacing, felt smooth as glass under the SUV's tires, unlike the bone-jarring experience Jack remembered while traveling in the McLaughlin. The town had razed the property where the old white church stood, making room for the county's high school—home of the Fighting Minutemen.

A weather-induced line of demarcation appeared just as the SUV passed the property boundaries of the school. As if township responsibility switched to county, the roadway turned treacherous and was made passable only by the deep ruts cut by other vehicles in well over a foot of snow. Their progress slowed to a much slower pace than they experienced navigating Cartersville's main drag.

Jack noticed a road near the spot where he parted ways with Michaleen now led into a large subdivision. A bright yellow sign just beyond the entrance advised there was no through outlet. As Bobby continued along the very path down which Michaleen disappeared into thin air, Jack took view of the GPS map. Their current path would snake along in a southwesterly route for another thirteen miles before reaching their destination. He idled the time glancing between the slow passing landscape and LED display counting down the distance to their target.

"Looks like your accident was pretty intense, Jack," Darrin said, breaking the awkward silence.

Jack glanced over his shoulder. The comment did not surprise. By trade, Darrin served as an EMT responder for his hometown fire department. Of his four brothers-in-law, he and Darrin had hit it off best. The two shared an equal passion for sports—football in particular—and even hooked up for a long golf weekend several years earlier when Darrin visited the Windy City for a fire and rescue conference. The few rounds together set their friendship on a solid foundation—until Jack sent Brooke fleeing from their home after hitting her. By order of Darrin's wife, their relationship was iced.

"It was one for the books," Jack responded.

"Were you driving the Hummer?"

"Yeah."

"Was it totaled?"

"Every square inch."

"Wow, what a shame. That sure was a nice vehicle. How'd it happened?"

"I was trying to drive down a pretty steep hill and lost control on the snow. I hit an embankment, rolled over it and tumbled down another embankment before ending up upside down in the middle of a frozen lake. I managed to get out of the cab just before the whole thing broke through and sank."

"God, Jack," Bobby said, breaking concentration from the road. "What the hell were you trying to do?"

"I was trying to find Brooke. There was but one way to go, and it was down."

"I'll take a look at your wound later, if you want," Darrin said, pointing to the bandage.

"I'd appreciate it," Jack said.

"Sounds like you're lucky to be alive," Jeff added. "Why do you smell like smoke?"

"The home I was staying in following the accident caught fire . . . it's a long story."

"I sure hate to see you lose the Hummer," Darrin quipped. "I always did like it. I remember driving it from the golf course that one time and thinking how similar it was to driving the rescue truck."

"Well, it's the least of the things I lost."

"What do you mean?" Jeff asked.

Jack turned to the window, watching barns and silos pass at a snail's pace. The mere mention of the topic ignited the sounds, smells and visions in an instant.

"Brooke's dog was with me. He didn't survive." Jack released a sigh and brought his palm against his forehead.

Bobby turned with a quick stare. The three behind stared at one another as the cab fell silent for nearly a half mile.

"Wow, Jack, that's a tough break," Darrin said. "Brooke . . . well, she loved the dog like it was her own child."

Jack nodded. "I know. It's going to devastate her. I can't believe it happened. He survived the initial impact, and if it were not for him licking and waking me, we'd both be at the bottom of the lake. I got him out and managed to find our way to a farmhouse a mile or so from the lake. The family did everything they could to save him, but the injuries were just too much. It was horrible," he said, his voice drifting.

"If I remember, Brooke said you hated the dog," Jeff said.

"I don't think this is the time," John suggested.

"It's okay," Jack replied, his voice somber. "It's not altogether untrue . . . at least before this trip. I'd give anything to get him back.

Not just because he meant a lot to Brooke, but because his last conscious act was to save my life."

Jack brought a hand to his face and wiped at his eyes. Darrin looked to Jeff then to John, expressing utter shock at his tears and the emotion in his voice. This was a side of him none of them had seen. John raised a palm to the two and shook his head. The men let it be.

The pumping of the SUV's brakes brought everyone's attention forward as Bobby slowed for an approaching four-way stop. A small, two-pump gas station occupied a plot to their immediate right, an old general store—now pushing local antiquities—set opposite the intersection also on the right. Jack viewed the opposite corner. A large, red barn, crippled by years of exposure to the elements and not the first caring hand, rested in a heap appearing two parts rubble and one part salvageable structure. It was *the* barn. He remembered it from Sophie's map and from passing it twice. A sign located a hundred paces to the right indicated Cameron was ten miles away. It was from that direction Michaleen and he dumped and fled from the deputies. Jack scanned the dash with a hurried interest. The marker on the map was placed several miles straight ahead. Its position spooked him.

John leaned over the center console, noticing the change in Jack's demeanor. "What is it, Jack?" he asked.

Jack knew the location. "Nothing," he responded. "I thought this intersection looked familiar."

"Bobby, can this view pull out any further?" Jack asked, pointing to the map.

"Just toggle down the joystick with the red dot in its center. It's directional, so you can move it across the map to the area you want to view. If you push it in over a location, it will give you an address or reference point."

Jack reached for the switch and toggled down. He repeated the motion a second, then third time. Moving the crosshairs south and west, he located a large, blue mass near the upper right hand corner of the map. The marker dotting their location remained in his view at the far left. Scrolling over the blue mass, he pushed in on the toggle switch. The words "Quarry Lake" appeared in large white lettering in the middle of the crosshairs. Jack studied the distance from the lake to their destination. Toggling the switch up, bringing the map to near street level, he scrolled over the marker.

"It can't be," he whispered. "This can't be the same property."

Jack kept a close watch of the map.

"What's the matter?" Bobby asked.

"Nothing . . . just trying to get my bearings."

Jack tracked the marker on the screen as the SUV covered six miles with each man concentrating on his own thoughts.

Bobby maneuvered the Tahoe through a sharp left turn along a treacherous decline. Clearing a dense grouping of large trees packing along both sides of the road, the land gave way to various groupings of homes and subdivisions. Jack recalled the beauty of the valley and felt regret the land had been parceled out for development. The pastures, fertile wheat fields, and quaint homesteads were gone.

As the female voice announced their destination as less than a quarter mile away, Jack moved forward in his seat searching out mailbox numbers. The address given by the officer specified box 771. Number 776 passed on his right. Bobby released his foot from the gas pedal. Box 775 appeared on the left . . . 774 to the right . . . 773 . . . 772 . . .

Bobby brought the vehicle to a stop just past a green box in the shape of a tractor, with the number 771 painted in large black letters. Jack crossed over Bobby's lap, straining to get a better view. The property appeared unfamiliar. There was no sign of the barn, not even a hint it ever existed.

"This can't be their property," Jack said.

"Whose property?" John asked.

Jack did not respond. His every sense was occupied. The property in relation to the lake seemed spot on. Nothing else appeared familiar. Bobby pulled into the driveway, followed by James, who'd been tailing like an undercover agent from the moment the group crossed the bridge leading out of Cartersville. With tires spinning, he eased the Tahoe up a slight incline, keeping aligned with a set of double-wide tire ruts blazing the trail. As the vehicle crested the hill, Jack felt the wind exit his lungs. A single landmark affirmed what he thought impossible. He knew he was in possession of something that would confirm his suspicions.

Reaching for and unzipping his duffle bag, he worked through the mess in search of the framed pictures taken from the dresser of the Brossys' guest room. Viewing each, he pulled a frame containing the photo he knew could prove or dispel his suspicion. Paying no attention to Bobby keeping close track of his every action, Jack brought the frame from out of the bag and up close to his face, studying its subjects and switching his view to the massive oak tree standing alone just off to the right. Bobby noticed Jack's cheeks draining of color.

Jack felt an empty feeling gathering as he studied the smiling faces of Roo, Matty, and Caleb gathered arm in arm on a bright sunny day in front of the massive oak positioned not fifty paces from the Brossys' front porch.

CHAPTER 42

Bobby led the group deeper into the property past the oak to a point where it appeared to split; to the right toward a detached garage and to the left, unmolested by tire ruts, toward a small, two-story red brick home facing at an angle to the road. He opted left.

Jack scoured the horizon searching all points for any sign of Brooke's Escalade. The garage nestled to the right under a canopy of soughing pines whose slim trunks seemed to stretch out of their bark in an attempt to inch as close to the winter sun as possible. A single set of tire ruts extended from the first of two garage doors, merging with those leading out to the road. An orange, three-point tractor tucked under an overhang attached to the garage was the lone vehicle visible. He looked to the oak and drew his eye to where the Brossy home once stood. He could see the magnificent, two-story farmhouse still.

In the distance, beyond the garage, a large barn situated to the right atop a knoll. Pastures continued past, bringing a semblance of peace. The land remained as he remembered. Jack wondered if the current owners held papers for the Brossys' entire, original plot.

Bobby brought the SUV to a stop in the middle of a patch of yard enjoying the full vigor of the sun, a hundred paces from the corner of the home's front porch. Before the vehicle came to a complete stop, Jack dropped the duffle bag to the floorboard, too anxious to re-zip and conceal its contents. He opened the door to a rush of crisp winter air and the scents of various hardwoods burning in the chimneys scattered about the valley. Shading his face from the bright glare bouncing off the canopy of white, he pivoted in every direction, searching the property like a crazed man.

Equal to his urgency, the Mayberry women abandoned their vehicle, advancing toward the lead car determined to bring their sister home and passing Jack without nary a look or word to recognize his existence. Kaye trailed the group and offered a faint smile and shallow "hello" that fell well out of the range of her siblings' ears. She did not wait for a response.

The second oldest, Kaye resembled Brooke the most. Their smiles were identical; their eyes proportioned and colored exact. She was even blessed with Brooke's long, bristly black lashes and coal colored hair. Despite her similarity to Brooke, Kaye favored another even more. Jack eyed her as she passed. It was as if Jubel's wife had returned to the scene of her demise. He allowed an eerie feeling to pass before pivoting and continuing down the side of the SUV toward the Suburban, intending to survey the opposite side of the yard for any signs of the former barn.

Anna remained fastened in her seatbelt, staring out the passenger side window, shaking uncontrollably. Cupping her hands against her mouth, she appeared almost to be gasping for breath as tears exploded down her cheeks. The sight brought Jack to a standstill. James reached across the console to place a hand atop her shoulder. His lips mouthed a concerned plea but she did not respond.

He caught Jack's eye through the windshield and shrugged in a gesture suggesting confusion to her reaction. Surmising John should know the situation, Jack turned in search of him and noticed he and Darrin were now surrounded by Erin, Faye, and Kaye, engaged in conversation with Bobby. Looking over the top of the vehicle, he saw Jeff and Diane approaching the home's front porch.

James exited the vehicle, keeping a close eye on Anna as he kicked through the snow toward Jack.

"I don't know what happened," he said, blowing breath into his cupped hands. "I made the comment I was disappointed in not seeing Brooke's car and she just lost it. Maybe I should tell John."

"That's probably a good idea," Jack said, the cadence of his voice snail-like as he watched Anna struggle with her emotions. Her pain hit him hard. For a brief second he saw Sophie and the shattered look upon her face the instant before he dropped the two-by-four on top of her. He looked toward the horizon, feeling remorse for the pain he'd caused her and her family. He wished to erase it all with a snap of his fingers.

"How are you, Jack?" James asked.

"I'm alright," he said.

"I've seen you looking better."

Jack nodded. Despair lurked as the reality of not seeing Brooke's Escalade anywhere about the property settled in.

James leaned in close to cloak his words. "Just so you know, I don't have a horse in this race, other than the fact my wife despises you and Brooke deserves a little better, but if you need someone to talk to, let me know."

Jack knew James the least, but knew him to be the lone brother-in-law who walked down the middle of the road on all topics and subjects, and was the least fearful of his wife. Unlike Darrin, whom Jack liked the least, James refused to stir the family pot and was least thrilled when a member became a target for kin retribution. Faye was the most outspoken and demonstrative of the Mayberry women and James managed to keep her on a level keel with the non-combative, logical style with which he expressed his opinions and offered solutions. Jack respected him and appreciated his desire to remain friends.

Patting his shoulder, James moved off toward the sound of Faye's voice requesting his assistance. Anna remained with her hands cupped against her mouth, although her sobbing had eased, she appeared lost in another place and time. Jack wanted to speak to her and provide some comfort, but knew this was not the time. If she was ever going to speak to him again, he was certain it would take more than a prayer to the Almighty to make it happen.

Jack searched the side yard, dumbfounded he could not identify the first piece of evidence of the barn or silo. The low rumble and grumble of an engine under stress caught his attention, approaching from the same direction the group had just traveled. Whatever the vehicle, it was not a car and sounded as if it were pulling, pushing, or carrying a load. Jack passed between the two vehicles and worked to the back bumper of the Suburban to get a clearer view of the road. A row of snow-covered evergreens aligned to the right of the mailbox allowed just a hint that a vehicle had come to a stop on the other side. Jack shuffled forward a few steps, anticipating in another second or so a gap in the shrubbery revealing the vehicle and the driver's intentions.

As if stopping first to check the address on the mailbox, the driver idled for several moments before engaging the gearshift, sending the sound of grinding and clicking mechanical parts echoing across the open land. The red and black nose of a truck appeared first then its bed. As the driver pulled from behind the evergreens, Jack's chest tightened and his legs liquefied at the sight of a black, four-door SUV strapped atop the truck's bed.

On cue with the driver gunning the engine to meet the incline of the driveway, screams from behind sent Jack pivoting toward the house. Stepping away from the Suburban, he saw a rush of Mayberry women and their husbands racing toward the porch toward a woman with long, coal black hair hanging and holding on to Diane.

Jack was stunned to a point that all sound around him ceased. His first steps landed awkward and heavy, as if his legs were encased in a suit of knight's armor and tied from behind to a tree. Needing the assistance of the Suburban to keep his balance, he moved unsure at first, gazing ahead in disbelief, staring at the woman and her long black hair, not believing for a second it was Brooke or that she was just yards from his arms. His legs could barely hold his weight. He wanted to run, but stumbled along instead as would an intoxicated man.

In an instant, his in-laws had surrounded her. With her out of his sight, he hurried as best he could, moving more laterally along the driveway than parallel, as shock toyed with his equilibrium. Reaching the middle of the yard, some twenty paces from the porch, he stopped as an opening manifested, giving him a clear view. It was her.

Brooke released from the arms of her father, turned and faced the yard and nearly fainted at the sight of her husband, standing as a statue with a bloodstained bandage wrapped around his head, looking nothing like the man she left five days earlier.

Jack succumbed to the emotion and exhaustion of the ordeal as his wife came full into his view. His legs buckled, sending him driving into the snow on his knees. Brooke broke forward, as if wanting to run to his side, but felt her father's grip tight around her arm. Jack dropped his hands atop his thighs and broke apart like a newborn.

The family stood silent atop the porch, watching in disbelief. Brooke started shaking. The sight and shock of her husband sobbing uncontrollably in front of her, in front of her family, paralyzed her thoughts. This man who'd epitomized grit and defiance had not shed a single tear when they wed, when their children were born, or when his only surviving relative passed. It was beyond her immediate capacity to reconcile the actions and emotions of this man she did not recognize. With tears flowing, she watched, knowing something beyond his open display of emotion had changed.

Darrin, standing closest to the door, was the first to react to something brushing against his leg. Erin let go a faint, surprised screech as she too felt a bump from below. Before Brooke or those standing forward on the porch could react, the dog zipped by and shot down the porch steps and into the front yard in a blink.

Unsuspecting, and still trying to regain his composure, Jack was bowled nearly onto his backside as Peetie flung himself into his chest, barking, licking, and wagging his tail as if it were Jack who'd given him his second chance at life. Catching the dog in his arms, Jack inspected him from top to bottom, not believing he was real. He whispered his name then pulled him tight against him. Burying his face into the back of his neck, the two looked as if they'd been reunited following years of separation. Brooke's hands dropped from her face. Her mouth flew open. A stir worked through her siblings and in-laws at the utter deception each was feeling.

"I thought you said the dog hated him, Brooke," Faye whispered in her ear.

Brooke did not respond. She watched in awe, trying to figure out herself what was taking place before her.

"John, didn't Jack say . . ."

"Yes, yes he did," John interrupted, in an angry, cold tone.

Brooke questioned her father's comment with a look.

"Sweetheart, you should know by now your husband is nothing but a liar."

"What's going on here?" Brooke asked, staring blankly at them all. "What's happening here?"

"All we care about is that you're safe and unharmed. We've been worried sick about you. Why didn't you call us and let us know what happened?"

"There's been no phone service here because of the snow and ice and I've not been able to get a cell signal," she said. "The snow just stopped this morning and it was going to be the first chance to get my car back. I was going to call just as soon as I got back on the road and got a cell signal."

"How did you end up here?" her father demanded.

"I left the highway to get some gas and the girls something to eat. Just as I pulled into the parking lot of a restaurant, my engine light went on and steam started shooting from the radiator. It was just by luck a young mechanic was inside eating. He towed the car to his shop and brought us here to wait out the storm. This is his parents' house."

"We're so relieved you're safe," John said, wiping his brow. "That's all that matters now."

Jack held onto Peetie as if he were saying goodbye rather than hello. As Brooke pushed forward from the group, Julianna and Jordan burst from within the house, past the adults, and into the front yard screaming, "Daddy! Daddy!"

Jack released his hold of Peetie and crawled forward through the snow on hands and knees to meet his daughters halfway. Screaming and giggling, the girls bounded into his arms, each pressing hard against his cheeks. He collected them in one fell swoop as they flung their arms around his neck. Their bodies were warm and their skin as soft as butterfly wings. Tears rushed as he repeatedly thanked God for the moment.

Brooke searched the faces of her sisters and brothers-in-law for any expression that might explain what she was seeing.

"Merry Christmas, Daddy," Julianna said. "I knew you'd come to see us for Christmas."

Jack squeezed tighter.

"Merry Christmas, sweetheart," he said. "Oh, I love you both so much."

Brooke grabbed hold of a support beam. The moment was like a storybook. She could not stop shaking.

The girls hopped from his arms and stood in front of him. He looked each up and down, smiled wide, and clutched Julianna's face and kissed her. Jordan was next. He couldn't believe how beautiful they were. He grabbed their hands into his and brought them against his lips. His sobbing resumed.

"Daddy, why are you crying?" Jordan asked.

He released their hands and wiped away the blur. "I'm sorry, sweetheart. I'm just so happy to see you both. I've missed you so much," he said, his voice choking.

"It's too bad you missed Christmas; you should see some of the presents Mommy got us," Julianna said.

Jack laughed. Her smile warmed him like hot bricks under a sheet. "Maybe we could celebrate it again tonight?" The girls screamed and jumped up and down with delight.

Jack brought them both close. "I promise you," he said, "we will never spend another Christmas apart again, okay?"

The girls nodded and flung themselves into his arms. Jack's heart was beating like a kettledrum.

"It's cold out here girls," Jack said, patting their behinds. "Why don't you go on inside . . . I'll be in soon, okay?"

Both girls planted a kiss on his cheek and skipped across the surface to the porch. Jack pulled himself off the ground, brushed away the snow and rubbed both sides of Peetie's ears before the dog scurried off in pursuit of his playmates.

Regaining his legs, he held both hands against his face, clearing his eyes, then pushing through the snow to come within a single step of the porch. Brooke's family closed in around her. John stepped in front of his daughter, descending to the first step.

Speaking over his shoulder, John called for Bobby. He pushed through the family and delivered Jack's duffle bag.

"You've made a fool of me for the last time, son," John said.

Brooke shook off the thoughts swirling in her head. "Daddy, what are you doing?" she asked, breaking from the hands holding her back.

"Sweetheart, a lot has happened and I think it's only fair you know the truth. You need to know what a liar your husband is."

Jack searched their faces. His sisters-in-law smiled with delight. Jeff and Bobby nodded only because their wives were doing the same. Darrin turned away. James folded his arms across his chest, disgusted over the unfair inquisition.

"Go ahead, Jack, tell everyone how difficult it was for you to see Peetie die. Tell us again about the fantastic accident; how you almost drowned in a lake and how Peetie saved you from death. How did that story go?"

"Daddy, what are you talking about?" Brooke insisted. "What are you doing?"

"Ask your husband, sweetheart. Ask him to tell you the story he told us. Ask him to tell you how he's a changed man and how he's never going to hurt you or the girls again. Even better, ask how he's found God."

Brooke could see the anger in her father's eyes. She did not know the man to tell a lie. Her voice became shallow. "What's he talking about, Jack? What's happening?" she asked, turning toward her husband.

Jack was not surprised at their accusing him without first giving him a chance to explain, but was disappointed they'd decided to rummage through his personal belongings as if he were a convict. If they looked through the bag, they'd seen everything. There was no way to explain. His word was all he had, but that ship had sailed long ago.

He studied the curves of Brooke's face as if seeing her for the first time. All he wanted was to place his hands against the delicate skin formed around her cheeks. "My God, you're so beautiful," he whispered.

Brooke balled a fist against her chest. Her breath grew short.

"Oh, come on, Jack," Faye yelled. "How ignorant do you think we are? Do you think you're going to toss out a bunch of lines and lies and everything will be alright?"

Jack said nothing. They had a right to hate him. They had a right not to trust him. They had a right to protect their sister. The assured expressions on their faces faded with the understanding smile forming across his lips.

"You think this is funny, son?" John asked.

No more lies, Jack thought. No more.

"I know it's real easy for all of you to act as judge and jury against me," he said, looking over the group. "I know I've not helped my cause one bit and you have the right to hate me. I will not deny any of you that right, because I know I'm the cause of it all."

"Just more of your crap, Jack, and you know it," Diane barked out from behind her husband.

"May I suggest we at least give the man an opportunity to say his piece?" James announced. "There's still plenty of daylight for the tar and feathering."

Faye shot a nasty, menacing glare at her husband. James avoided her eye contact, remaining resolute with his opinion.

"I just want an answer to two things," John said. "I want to know the meaning of these items in your bag, especially why you have a framed picture of that very tree over there, and why you told us Peetie died in the accident. I don't care if you claim to have found God or not, because God knows a liar and a sinner."

Jack scoured the faces of each family member before settling his stare upon his father-in-law. His reticence gave way to his promise of no more lies—regardless of the circumstance.

"Okay, John," he said, nodding, "I'll tell you what happened. I told you when we spoke on the phone something had happened you would never believe. When I found out Brooke went missing, and after not being able to connect with you, I took off in search of her."

Jack recounted the story from the beginning, skimming over names and the few intimate moments he shared with his mother and Michaleen. He spoke of strange characters at his doorstep, disappearing horses and carriages, mystical, transporting winds, a near-death experience, the spectacular accident, raging fires, daring rescues, death of beast and man, God, and miracle encounters. When he completed detailing his return to real time in the diner, all fell silent other than the rustling of the north wind whistling through the surrounding trees and the distant holler of a Holstein. Brooke, her father and all there stood stunned, staring wide-eyed.

"Oh my God," Erin yelled, breaking the silence. "Brooke, are you kidding me? Are you going to keep listening to this nonsense?"

"God, Jack, you really do think we're nothing but a bunch of idiots," Diane said.

"You're crazy," Faye charged. "You're absolutely stark, raving mad."

"You're such a liar, Jack," Bobby said. "Why don't you do us all a favor and get lost."

Jack offered not the first reaction to the barrage of insults. James studied him closely, watching his every movement as Jack swung his head in the direction of each discourtesy. James had witnessed the man come under attack by the family before and was wondering at what instant the dam would break and his salty language and conceited air would commence to bloodying ears. He was mystified at the man's phlegmatic stance. The manner with which Jack was accepting the assault, like a heavyweight against the ropes whose tank was on empty, did not mesh with someone attempting to lie their way out of a situation. He offered not the first reaction. James whispered to Darrin that Jack was either suffering from the effects of a severe brain trauma or believed exactly what he'd recanted to the family. Not knowing why, James suggested he felt the latter to be the case.

"I've had enough of this," John yelled. "Brooke, get yours and the girls' things together. There's no way this man deserves you or this family. Give him the keys to your car and let's get you home."

Brooke stood paralyzed, grasping the support beam, staring at her husband, startled and questioning. His account confused her due to more than just the mere fantasy of it all. She knew him to tell a lie if it meant avoiding confrontation, but this just didn't make sense. He was way too intelligent to relay such a careless tale and there was no reason for it. He'd not even asked if she'd consider taking him back. Her mind was saturated with doubt. Something wasn't adding up.

A slam of a door brought every head turning toward the parked cars.

"Momma," Faye screamed. The charge in her voice sent the family scurrying from the porch. Anna stumbled alongside the SUV toward them, struggling for every step and holding at her chest as if straining for breath. Jack followed in behind the family as they rushed to her side.

John was the first to arrive, collecting her into his arms. Falling against him, exhausted, she buried her head into in his chest. Her breathing was short; her body shook. Bobby whisked the coat from off his shoulders and covered her.

In an instant, the Mayberry women surrounded her, each jockeying past the other to check her condition and offer pleas of concern. Spotting Brooke, Anna grabbed at her sweater and pulled her close. Both began to cry as they embraced.

"She'll be alright," John announced. "This has just been too much for her today. Everybody step back. Let's give her some air."

Jack approached the group from the rear, coming to a standstill between the two vehicles.

Faye exploded. "This is your fault," she yelled, pointing. James pulled at her waist but she refused to temper her anger. "You're not wanted here anymore. You're nothing but a lying piece of crap under a rock and you've hurt this family for the last time. All you care about is yourself. You're such a coward."

Brooke broke free from her mother's grasp. Turning sharply, she centered on the sister whose eye she once blackened for throwing a rock at a squirrel in their front yard.

"I'm tired of the way you're speaking to him," she defended, displaying an irritation to the surprise of everyone, including her father. "I'm tired of the way you *all* are speaking to him."

"Brooke, he doesn't give a darn about you or the girls; he's done nothing but hurt you. How can you defend him?" Diane questioned.

"You know less about marriage than anyone I know, Diane," Brooke shot back. "I would worry about your own marriage before you start giving others advice."

"The man's been cheating on you, Brooke. You told me yourself two weeks ago," Faye added.

Brooke turned to James and Darrin. Both offered looks suggesting their wives were right—this time. Finally submitting to the truths she knew he could not deny, she paused and looked to Jack. Her eyes filled with despair and a longing for him to make it all right.

"You're right, Faye. I am a coward," Jack said, putting an end to the lively banter. "I've spent my entire life hiding behind my inability to deal with the truth. As I said before, I've made it very easy for you all to judge me and I don't blame any of you. This moment was going to have to happen, and if this is where it has to take place, then so be it.

"Brooke, I love you more than I have words to describe."

"Brooke, please . . . don't listen to this," Kay pleaded.

"Again . . . let the man speak his piece," James barked. "Even a convict on death row gets a freakin' opportunity to say something before he's juiced."

Jack offered James an appreciative nod before stepping closer toward his wife.

"I didn't know six days ago what I'd done. It was just in the past three days that I managed to figure all this out. I've never given you or your family a chance—not from day one. I've not given you or them a chance to know the real me because I've been living a lie my entire life. Our entire marriage has been based on the unknown." Jack had captured his in-laws' undivided attention.

"The lies are over, sweetheart. You have the right not to trust me and I apologize for putting you in that position. There are so many things I've just now been able to rise above. It's easy sometimes to look upon a man and judge without knowing. It's the easiest thing in the world to do. And we are all guilty of having done it at some point in our lives. But I never afforded you the gift of honesty. You were never playing on level ground."

Jack took a deep breath. The chill gaining with the setting sun along with his intent to come clean, sent a quiver racing through his body.

"When I was seven years old, my father came home Christmas Eve after spending the day drinking. He was a mean and nasty drunk and, well, that night he raped then nearly beat my mother to death. I was in the living room, listening to the entire affair, unable to move or speak, when he came in, naked from the waist down, pointed a gun at my head and told me it was my fault he had to kill her. He told me I was a coward and put the gun under his chin and blew his head off. He didn't kill her that night, but he put her into a coma."

The family drew in a collective breath. Tears exploded as Brooke cupped her hands around her mouth. Her sisters stood frozen. Their eyes began to glisten.

"Then, when I was fourteen, my mother got involved with a real bad man," he said, smiling and letting go a humbling laugh. "He was a serious drug addict and dealer and had drug parties in our home at all hours of the day and night. One afternoon, I came home from school and found him and some of his friends raping my younger sister."

"Sister? You have a sister?" Brooke asked, choking through her sobs.

Jack kicked at the snow on the ground, unable to look his wife in the eye.

"My mother's boyfriend pulled a pistol and put it against my sister's head and said he'd kill her if she and I didn't "put on a show" for them. When I refused, they set her hair on fire. He put the gun to her head and started counting down from ten. I figured the only way I could save her life was to do what he said. So he forced me into having sex with her.

"Do you remember the woman at my mother's funeral?" Jack asked, looking to Brooke. "Well, that was my sister. Her name is Shannon."

Brooke's shoulders bobbed up and down as her sobbing intensified.

"I left home two weeks later and never saw my mother again. I've not spoken to my sister since. I've spent my entire life on my own trying to conquer this world. In the process, I lost myself and developed some very bad habits of which you took the brunt of all these years. I'm so sorry, Brooke."

Jack moved closer to her, but not to within reach.

"I have cheated on you Brooke. I've been unfaithful. I've not handled the situation we have between us very well. I regret every action that has caused you and the girls pain. I don't expect your trust ever again; I have no right to ask. What I know now, and what I'm more certain of than anything in my life, is that the man you knew—the man you all knew—is no longer. I don't want to be that man anymore. And whether I have you back or not, I'm still not going to be that man anymore."

Brooke's sisters worked at wiping away the tears pushing down their cheeks. Her brothers-in-law each searched in opposite directions, fighting guilt and contemplating how they would've handled similar burdens.

Having backed a few paces from the group, John held Anna close as she whispered something into his ear. An instant later, the family's matriarch collapsed into the snow.

CHAPTER 43

John followed his wife to the ground, patting at her face. With twenty years of emergency room nursing under her belt, Kaye reached her mother first, grabbing at her hand and checking for a pulse. The others opened a hole for Darrin, then surrounded. Before having a chance to lay her flat, Anna jerked from the benumbed state, organizing which daughter was near her side and the identity of the man on his knees inspecting her. Before Kaye could get a good read, Anna placed the right name with the right face.

"Let's get her up," Darrin said.

Jeff helped John to his feet. Bobby assisted in delivering Anna back into his arms.

"Are you okay, hon?" John asked.

"I'm fine," she said. Her daughters expressed concern over the tears still streaming down her face.

"Momma, what's wrong?" Brooke asked.

"Why are you crying?" Diane followed.

Anna leaned against her. John bent low. She whispered again into his ear.

"Sweetheart, you must be making a mistake," John insisted.

She rolled her head in disagreement.

"Are you certain?"

Anna nodded and whispered, "I've never been more certain."

John pulled upright, looked in the direction of the Suburban then to Jack. "Bobby, bring me that duffle bag," he said.

Always eager to please the marine, Bobby rushed passed the others to deliver the duffle bag into John's grip. Dropping it to the ground, he removed the picture frame sitting atop the pile of personal belongings and handed it to his wife.

"This bag belongs to Jack," he said. "We found this inside."

With her sight blurred by tears and having left her bifocals in her purse, Anna brought close to her face the picture of Roo, Matty, and Caleb posing in front of the oak tree. Inspecting the photo, her sobbing intensified and her hands began to shake, creating a rattling as the glass securing the image ticked against the silver frame. Seeking Jack's location, Gina, Faye, and James stepped to the side, giving her a clear view.

Jack saw pain rather than anger in her face. Regardless, he felt her stare as a noose cinching around his neck, prompting a confused expression of his own, which he directed to his wife.

"Momma, what's wrong?" Brooke demanded.

"Where did you get this picture?" Anna asked, her voice faint.

Jack stammered hoping she'd address her daughter first. Her eyes never strayed. "From the family who helped me following my accident," he responded.

"What was the family's name?"

"Brossy . . . Their name was Brossy . . . Olan and Annesophie."

John's mouth dropped open. Anna's legs buckled. Darrin was quick to grab her from behind, Brooke from the front. The picture frame slipped from her fingertips, glanced off the side of the bag and into the snow. John recollected Anna in his arms. A look of utter shock spread over his face; a look unfamiliar to his children and one he hoped to leave behind in the jungles of the South Pacific. The impossibility of Jack's response urged Anna to want to get nearer him. Pulling her husband along, she stumbled toward Jack to within an arm's length. The family moved along in stride, tightening any route for escape.

Anna's voice cracked. "What are the names of the children in the picture?"

Jack swallowed. "Matty, Caleb, and Roo," he said.

Coming just short of his chest, Anna crooked her neck as if staring up into a tree. The hard lines outlining her face and cheekbones softened. Her eyes glistened against a small swath of sunlight poking around Jack's shoulder. She nodded.

"It was you," she whispered.

"Momma, please, what is this all about? What are you talking about?" Brooke urged.

"It was you," Anna whispered again, staring deep into Jack's eyes.

Jack shook his head. "I don't understand."

"Anna, you don't have to do this," John said, "not here, not now."

She wrapped her fingers around her husband's wrist. "It's time they knew the truth. I've put it off much too long." She patted his hand and allowed a slight smile to crack her lips.

To the befuddlement of everyone, Anna secured Jack's hand into her own.

"My name is Olivia Jean Brossy."

Anna felt the jolt shoot through Jack's body. His mouth fell open and his eyes widened. He searched her facial features for anything to remind him of the girl who'd softened and stolen his heart. He peeled away the wrinkles, erased the lines moving outward from her eyes and lips, and the deep rolls of crevices stretching across her forehead. He envisioned shorter, coal black hair and added youth to cheeks cachectic with age. It *was* her, it was Roo. He could see the young girl staring back just as she did as she disappeared into the crowd the morning of the fire.

"You're Roo," he said, assured of the assessment. What made no sense, now made perfect sense. The journey he took, the reasons why things happened as they did, was as clear to him now as the growing smile spreading across his mother-in-law's face.

Jack stumbled to accept Anna's arms around his waist. Their embrace nearly stopped time. Nothing the girls would ever see again could be more surprising than their mother wanting to embrace *this* man. Her daughters flew into a tizzy, demanding an explanation.

Releasing from Jack's arms, Anna reached for Brooke's hand as her daughters surrounded, looking each one in the eye.

"This land you're standing on belonged to my mother and father," she said, scanning across the horizon west, the purple of the waning winter sky reflecting off her pupils. "This was my home. I was born here."

"But Momma, you told us you were born in California," Erin said.

"You said you were adopted," Faye added.

"That's right, I did," she said. "I told you because I didn't want to face the truth. It was all just too painful to relive. Since it has now come full circle, it's time you all knew the truth about my life.

"As Jack has so bravely admitted to all of you," she said, patting his forearm, "I too have been living a life of lies." Anna slid into the arms of her husband. He collected her and kissed her forehead.

"When I was four years old, I remember my mother and father finding a man in a haystack in our barn a few days before Christmas. It was 1923. The man had suffered a horrible accident and my father was certain he'd not survive the night. There were no doctors nearby in those days, so we were left to our own remedies and means. It was our good fortune the county veterinarian happened along and managed to stitch him up enough to stop the bleeding.

"I forgot his name and face not long after—until now."

The claim coerced a reaction from each member of the family—some gasping, some shaking their heads, some standing rigid, dumfounded.

"I remember my brother running into the house and yelling for my father . . ."

"You have a brother?" Kay interrupted, her voice bursting with surprise.

"You had two uncles," she said, "Caleb and Matty. Also an aunt—April—but she died before I was born. I remember Caleb yelling, and my mother pulling me through the snow toward the barn. When we arrived, the man was unconscious and bleeding from a wound on his head," she said, pointing to Jack's bandage. "Blood was everywhere; on his face, his hands, his clothing.

"The sight of it all was very frightening," she continued. "I walked closer when I noticed a large lump under the man's shirt. When my father looked, he found a dog spread out across the man's chest, clinging to life. I remember screaming and my mother pulling me up from off the floor and taking me back into the house."

Anna paused to collect a tear at her chin.

"A few days later, early Christmas morning, a fire broke out in the house. I remember seeing flames coming out of a small closet and from under the floorboards in my bedroom. I was scared and crawled under my bed. The room filled with smoke and I remember not being able to see a thing. All of a sudden, I heard a voice calling my name, and the next thing I knew, someone grabbed hold of my arm and pulled me out from under the bed. It was this man. We rushed out of the bedroom and all I remember was seeing my mother at the top of the landing, trapped under debris, extending her hand toward me as we descended. It was the last time I ever saw her. The man took me to the barn then ran out again. I did not see him until I woke the next morning.

"My entire family perished—Caleb, Matty, my mother, father, my aunt, and two cousins."

The girls surveyed the smear of mascara on each others faces. They'd never known of uncles, great aunts, or second cousins on their mother's side.

"I don't understand any of this, Jack," Anna said, "I don't know how or why but I believe in God and I believe God performs miracles every day. Some happen right under our very noses, others from a distance. But I do believe they happen in some form every day. Just so we can all put to rest any doubt as to the validity of your claims, can you tell me the names of the other three who perished along with my parents and brothers?"

"It was your Aunt Julia and your cousins Sarah and Samantha."

Anna nodded. "Do you know the name of Julia's husband?"

"Jubel . . . Jubel Bigsby," Jack replied.

"That's right," she said. "And it was my Uncle Jubel who took care of me until I met your father. We were all each other had. He changed my name to Anna and took me to California for a few years to avoid having the state place me in a foster home. When I was fifteen, we moved back to Wisconsin. I moved away from him soon after.

"One more thing," Anna said, "just in case there's anyone here who needs further convincing, I remember when we were exchanging gifts Christmas Eve, giving this man a wood cross my Uncle Jubel gave to me that my father gave to him.

"You see, my mother had a tradition that once all the presents were open, each family member was to give away something we'd been given to someone we thought needed it more. It was her way of ensuring we all kept the intended meaning of Christmas true in our hearts. I remember, for some reason, knowing our guest needed this gift more than I did. It was very strange, but I knew it in my heart. I have to ask you, Jack, do you know what I'm speaking of?"

Jack allowed his smile to widen. Reaching into the hand warmer of his hoodie, he retrieved the cross, securing it in his palm and concealing it from view as he pulled it free. Extending his arm, he released his fingers. Gasps spewed as the family huddled in close for a better view. Anna picked the piece from his palm. Brooke knew for a fact her husband had never owned a cross.

"You should keep it," Jack suggested, as she inspected the relic. She brought the cross close to her face, studying its delicate curves and the bright copper inlay tracing its outline.

"I gave it to you," she said. "It may still do you some good yet."

"Your giving it to me was all I needed. It's a moment I will never forget. Besides, it's a product of your father's own hands. I can't think of anyone here who needs it more than you do. That was the point of your mother's tradition, right?"

Anna nodded. She brought the cross to her lips and kissed it.

"You know, it was your uncle Jubel who started this. And I know, no matter how the words come from my mouth, it will always sound unbelievable, but he paid me a visit the morning Brooke and the girls were set to leave."

"Is that why the front door and garage door were left wide open?" Brooke asked.

"I didn't realize I'd left everything open. I saw the man leaving on a horse and carriage of all things, and took off to chase him down. It was the craziest thing I'd ever seen—at least since the police busted our neighbors across the street for breaking into their own home."

"You mean he's still alive, Momma?" Diane asked.

"No, sweetheart. Uncle Jubel died in 1950."

Another round of gasps and shocked statements fluttered into the crisp winter air.

"But, it was your mother . . ." Jack paused to catch his voice, bringing a palm against his lips. "It was Sophie who helped me find me. I want you to know that. She was an amazing, incredible woman."

"Maybe you and I could have a nice, long chat," Anna said, smiling.

"I think the sooner the better . . . about a lot of things," he said.

"But Momma, how was it that you've never recalled Jack's name or face, I mean, with him being in the family for so long?" Faye asked.

"Sweetheart, the mind is a powerful thing. It can wipe clean any memory if we want it wiped clean. There are just some things and moments so painful you erase them forever. I could not put the loss of my family into words. I still can't. I don't ever recall hearing his name mentioned in my presence. And, too, I was only four at the time. He was just a blur that passed before us like a flash. I so never wanted to relive that moment of my life. The only bit I have in my memory is bright flames and seeing my mother trapped under debris. Everything else about that time is but a blur."

"Jack, I'm afraid I don't know what to say," John said. "I just don't know how I'm going to apologize."

"How can you apologize?" he replied, searching their faces. "How can any of you apologize? I'm still having a hard time accepting what happened. But I believe it and I believe it happened to benefit many— not just me."

Jack approached Brooke. He placed both hands on the sides of her face. The warmth of her skin melted the sting from his fingertips. Her eyes sparkled as diamonds under bright light. Her scent was exhilarating and he couldn't breathe deep enough to consume all he wanted. He could have held her like this forever.

"I am not who or what you remember me to be," he said. "I have failed you and the girls so many ways and so many times I will never hold it against you if you decide to leave. But I'm asking for you to forgive me one more time—the last time—and for a chance to love you again. I promise you, your family, our daughters, God, and my mother's soul I am not that man anymore. Let me prove it to you. Let me be what you need me to be and let me love you like you deserve to be loved."

Streams of tears flowed across his thumbs. "I'm so scared," she said. "I'm scared I can't ever be the woman you want and need me to be."

"You will never have to be scared again," Jack said, resolute. "The woman you are right now is all I want. All of our issues . . . we can work on those, but we need to do it together. No more lies, no more hidden files. I don't want to spend another second of my life without you or the girls. Please tell me you haven't left me."

Brooke lunged against his chest, throwing her arms over his neck. Anna placed a loving touch upon her back as the two embraced. He pulled her as close as his cracked ribs would allow, buried his face in her hair and whispered his love and promised their life would be different; better. Pulling his head from off her shoulder, he wiped her tears and leaned in. The feeling of a silk glove sliding over one's skin for a perfect fit could not compare to the feel of her lips against his own.

Their embrace released as both pulled away to exchange smiles. Jack stepped to Brooke's side, settled his arm tight around her waist and faced her family.

"I don't want to be your enemy anymore," he said, looking to each sister and brother-in-law. "You don't owe me any apologies. I would just ask you to forgive me, and give me a chance to be a part of your family. You're all I have."

Faye was the first to break. Eyes welling with tears, she pushed past Diane and Erin and wrapped her arms around his neck. The others followed in behind, each hugging him then their sister, reminding them all of the small receiving line at their wedding. Darrin, Jeff, Bobby, and James followed with handshakes and light grips of his bicep. John brought up the rear.

He extended his hand first and drew Jack against him with a hug. "I'm sorry. Your slate is still clean with me."

Smiles and laughter ensued. "Let's go home," Anna said, patting Jack's arm. He stretched both arms and pulled both her and Brooke close to his side.

"Momma, why did Jack call you Roo?" Kaye asked.

"It was my nickname, sweetheart, but for the life of me I don't remember why."

"I know," Jack said. "I asked your mother the very same question. Your brother Matty penned that name for you. A relative of your father's, stationed in Australia following the war, spent some time at the farm before returning home. He brought pictures of kangaroos with him." Anna bobbed her head as the memory returned.

"Your father said you'd hopped around the farm for three weeks like a kangaroo."

Anna ran her arms around Kaye's waist, laughing and enjoying the fond recollection as the group followed the others toward the house. Jack kissed Brooke against her temple. Her heart was beating as it did the day they met.

"Hey," he whispered, "by the way, do you recall seeing a manila envelope on the kitchen table with your name on it?"

"No, I don't think so," she responded.

"Well, again, I know this sounds crazy, but . . ."

Brooke stopped and grabbed at the front of his sweatshirt. "You don't have to qualify your experience to me anymore," she said, smiling. "I believe everything you've said, okay?"

He nodded and smiled. She could never know his relief.

"When your mother's uncle came to the house," he continued, "he delivered an envelope for you and one for me. I tossed the one for you on the kitchen table—not knowing at the time what was going on. I have no idea what's inside it," he said, with a nervous twitch.

"I don't recall seeing it, but if it was on the stack of magazines and mail, I grabbed the entire pile and tossed it in my shopping bag. It's in the car."

The two peeled off from the others as the family worked out seating arrangements for the ride back to Iron River. Having just completed removing the final towrope from under the vehicle, both Brooke and Jack thanked the mechanic for his help then rummaged for the shopping bag full of magazines. Scattering the lot across the back bed, the aged envelope was easy to identify.

Jack felt an uneasy surge as to the uncertainty of what Brooke's great uncle intended for her view. He thought to offer a disclaimer but held his tongue, hoping Brooke would understand—regardless of the contents—and hoping he'd satisfied what Jubel, Sophie, Michaleen, and his mother had intended.

Brooke inspected the envelope. She noticed the letter "e" was missing from the end of her name. Glancing at her husband with a mysterious gleam in her eye, she slid a finger under the flap and sliced away the seal. Reaching inside, she pulled a color print from the depths. Rotating the image right side up, the couple inspected the image before trading shocked stares.

"I don't understand," Brooke said, shaking her head. "How is this possible?"

"I don't know," Jack replied. "I pulled that same picture from the fireplace in our bedroom."

Brooke turned from his stare. "I know," she said, her voice splashed with regret, "I'm very sorry."

Jack placed his hand against her cheek and drew her face to meet his stare. "You don't need to apologize for that. I understand and I don't blame you one bit. Besides, this one's even better."

"How is it possible? I know that photographer took just the one picture and it was in black and white. This is color."

"I don't know. All I know is it falls right in line with everything else that's happened."

Jack drew her close against his body. He stared deep into her eyes, brushing back her hair. "It doesn't really matter anymore," he said, "I will never need pictures from our honeymoon to remind me how important you are and how much I love you."

Brooke placed her hands against his cheeks. Their kiss ignited a passion neither had felt in years. Upon hearing the echo of Anna's voice, their lips separated.

Ever the organizer, Anna instructed Darrin he would drive Brooke's car back to the farm because she and *her* son-in-law had a lot of catching up to do.

<hr>

The two and a half hour trip to the Mayberry farm disappointed because it wasn't a four and a half hour trip. Tucked in the back seat between her eldest daughter and son-in-law, Anna spent the many miles absorbing Jack's every word, asking for a detailed account of everything he saw, heard, felt, and smelled from the time he arrived to the moment he was hauled away by Barron County's finest. Relieved he was not behind the wheel, John spent the entire journey facing the back seat hanging on Jack's every word.

The details of his adventure pulled nuggets from the deepest recesses of Anna's earliest childhood memories, prompting tears at many points and blank stares at others. Despite the emotional toll reliving the final moments of her mother's life took, Anna assured she understood Jack did all he could to save her and thanked him for not letting her suffer. Her heart filled with a peace she'd never known when Jack described his encounter with Sophie in the diner, knowing that she was happy with the wonderful life her daughter was living.

Jack emptied the contents of the duffle bag, minus the dirty clothes, his pistol, and a piece of folded paper, explaining to them the succession of clues he'd received. Of what he'd accumulated, they all agreed the newspaper was the most eerie and definitive piece of corroborating evidence in his possession.

Nothing Anna ever received at any point in her life compared to the pictures Jack placed in her lap. Brooke stumbled for words twice—first upon seeing the resemblance between herself, her great-aunt Julia, and their daughters, and again upon studying the black and white photo of her mother sitting on the front porch. Anna was quick to point out she was in possession of an identical photo of Brooke on or around the same age.

With the sun long having since slipped below their half of the world, the families entered the long, quarter-mile gravel driveway leading to the Mayberry homestead, riding a high and a growing anxiety to partake in the Christmas feast they had decided to forgo until the entire family could sit and eat as one.

Passing a stable to the left, just forward a rolling knoll splitting the property's front third in half, Jack leaned across Anna's lap toward the center console to catch the beautiful panoramic view he remembered at the crest. As the vehicle leveled, the farmhouse appeared, sending a beacon of holiday colors splashing against the windshield from stringed lights outlining every eave and window on the two-story home. Jack felt a warm tingle caressing his core, refilling in his soul what he'd lost somewhere along the way. The festive glow of traditional green, red, orange, and white lights, accented by deep purple bulbs draped across the shrubbery, brought a peace that invigorated a desire to never stray from his family again. He reached across Anna's lap to take Brooke's hand into his own.

Abuzz with a rejuvenated holiday spirit, eager to fellowship as never before, the families settled together around a large country table situated horizontal to a long bank of colonial-style windows spanning and providing a view of the front pastures. Live garland draped above on two large, sparkling crystal chandeliers, pushed an overwhelming scent of pine into the room. Jack inhaled deep, finding the fragrance as pleasing as the country ham, fresh turkey, and rows of potted delights spread to both ends of the table.

"Do you think we should offer a prayer this evening?" John asked to a round of laughter from all points around the table.

"Well, if you insist," he said, bringing another barrage. "I think I'll pass the torch tonight. Jack, maybe you'd like to say a few words."

Embarrassed already, having lost his clothes at Anna's insistence, and seated dressed in a t-shirt two sizes too small belonging to Bobby, sweatpants too short belonging to Darrin and an old hunting jacket of John's falling eight inches shy of his wrists, Jack looked to his girls, then to Brooke, seeking their approval. Brooke grabbed his hand, prompting all at the table to do the same. Her loving stare brought him to a pause. He soaked in the beauty of her face.

The room fell silent as each family member bowed. His words were brief.

"Heavenly Father, I beg for Your forgiveness for the time I've wasted. I thank You for Your power to forgive and the opportunity to be forgiven. May You bless all in this house."

The group was slow to react as his words settled upon their ears. He opened his eyes to a tableful of smiles and nods for a job well done. As arms outstretched for the nearest serving platter, Anna tapped a knife against her water glass. All paused and turned their stares toward her position.

"I know you're all very hungry but I thought it might be nice if we carried on a favorite tradition of my mother's in which we go around the table and each express something we are thankful for. And if you don't mind, I'd like to start things off."

Still holding her husband's hand, Anna worked her eyes around the table, making contact with each daughter, son-in-law, and grandchild. Her heart was bursting at the sight of her entire family sitting about her.

"I'm thankful for this moment," she said, glancing to both sides of the table. "And I'm thankful for having been given the opportunity for this moment."

Following the feast, the sexes separated. Brooke and her sisters spilled about on the floor around their mother near the fireplace, enjoying her recollections of life growing up on the west coast, and the many other early memories regarding her family she'd kept private over the years. The men retired to the den for a sampling of John's infamous holiday hot toddy and a rousing bout of pocket change poker. Jack declined an invitation to join both groups.

Although fascinated by the many unknown facts her mother was sharing, Brooke found it difficult to focus her attention in full. Trading stares between her mother and husband, she often caught herself nearly choking with emotion at the sight of her daughters cuddled in their father's lap.

Tucked away in a rocking chair in a corner near the tree, with Julianna and Jordan nestled under his chin and their cousins settled at his feet, Jack read one story after another, soaking in the warmth of his girls' smiles and the joy of their giggles. After reciting nearly every childhood Christmas story of notable importance, Jack and the girls drifted off to his gentle rocking and the soft echo of the holiday music in the background.

Noting the late hour and her desire to spend some time alone with her husband, Brooke excused herself from her sisters, woke Jack with a soft kiss on his cheek and collected Jordan into her arms.

"Momma," Brooke called, "We're going to go to bed now."

Anna pushed from her chair and followed them to the stairs leading to the second level.

"Now, I want you two to sleep in as long as you like. Breakfast will be ready whenever you wake."

"Thank you, Momma."

"Anna, I want to show you something," Jack said, pulling a folded piece of paper from a jacket pocket.

She peeled back three folds. Her complexion burst with delight.

"Do you remember?" Jack asked.

She nodded and brought her hand against her mouth.

"Your mother gave me this picture. Of course, at the time, I had no idea why she would give it away to a complete stranger. It just seemed so wrong. It makes perfect sense to me now. It was something that meant more to her than anything. Would you mind if I kept it?"

Anna laughed and shook her head. She passed to Brooke the finger painting of her mother pushing her in the tire swing hanging from the oak tree. She reached up to take hold of Jack's hand.

"There's no one else I'd rather have it," she said, keeping hold of his hand. She looked away as if gathering a thought.

"What is it, Momma?" Brooke asked.

"I'm so sorry for the burdens you've been carrying, Jack," she said. "Although I don't accept it as an excuse for how you've treated Brooke—and I know now you don't either—I do want you to know how very sorry I am. I'm ashamed for the way I've judged you because I should have known better, considering my own history."

"You judged me fairly, Anna, you all did. I'm the one who's ashamed. I just hope you can forgive me and give me time to prove your daughter married the right man. Nothing means more to me now than proving it to her and your family."

"I have no doubt you will be true to your word." Anna smiled and patted his hand. "You two sleep well. We'll talk more in the morning."

"Good night, Momma," Brooke said.

Arm in arm, the two ascended the stairs to a second level bedroom once belonging to Brooke. Settling the girls atop the large, feather bed, Jack helped navigate their limp arms and legs into their matching pajamas, while Brooke arranged then unrolled their sleeping bags. Turning down the cover on the bed, he placed the girls side-by-side and pulled the covers snug under their chins. Within seconds, the girls were fast asleep.

Kneeling next to the bed, brushing away hair from Julianna's face, he ran his fingers through her hair, staring as if never having seen her before. Having completed situating their sleeping bags, Brooke shuffled against him from behind, rubbed across the width of his shoulders, watching him as he watched their daughters.

"Are you ready to put them in their sleeping bags?" she whispered into his ear.

Jack smiled. "What would you think about forgetting the sleeping bags just for tonight? The floor just seems so far away."

CHAPTER 44

December 29

Jack rolled across his pillow, looking to the clock at his bedside, wondering how it was he'd failed to remember to turn off the alarm. As if just another day, the clock pushed from its speakers a light, but upbeat jazz melody at the precise moment needed to ensure he'd get to the office on time. That was not a priority today.

He brought a hand from under the covers to against his chin. It was sore, as if bruised. The sudden and unexpected introduction of the jazz tune was not the catalyst that shocked him from his slumber. He'd been introduced to the dawn of a new day in a variety of ways in his life, but never by a kick to the face.

Now staring wide-eyed into the expanse of a ceiling that was more familiar to him, he strained to temper his laughter, trying hard to avoid waking those nestled very near him.

Following an unsuspecting jolt that chased the sleep away from his head, Jack rolled across his pillow to investigate. Jordan remained fast asleep near the bed's center, her nose twitching and eyelids flittering as her breathing fell upon his ears as a sweet, soothing wave breaking against a distant beach. Brooke lay rolled on her side facing him, just beyond the pink of Jordan's cheeks. Julianna, well, she'd somehow managed to flip and flop enough during the night to end up facing the wrong direction under the sheets. Jack lifted the covers to find two very small heels and ten toes resting near his chin. He began to laugh at the sight, wondering how it was she accomplished the feat without waking the entire bed.

As the beat of the jazz tune intensified, piano, bass, and sax coming together in an organized frenzy, Brooke woke to the view of her husband holding a fist against his mouth, his chest heaving in a fit. She brought a hand to her face to wipe away the sleep. Her movement caught his eye.

Jack pulled the sheets from off his chest to reveal the two small feet protruding in the wrong direction. Brooke let go a quick burst of air before covering her own mouth. They stared into each other's eyes, laughing and heaving in silence under the sheets of their own bed, in the comfort of their own master bedroom, in the privacy of their own home.

Although Jack had desired to spend more time with his in-laws, he appreciated his wife's insistence they return to Chicago, considering their need for some time alone and an opportunity for his wounds to heal. Anna was gracious in her understanding and overly supportive once they promised a return visit following the holidays.

As their laughter waned and each gained control, Jack reached across his daughters' bodies to place a hand against Brooke's face.

"What can I do for you today?" he whispered, his smile expanding.

Brooke breathed deep, shivering from his tender touch.

"Just tell me I'm not dreaming," she whispered.

"This is no dream," he replied, extending his fingers through her hair. "This is just the beginning."

"I know, in many ways, I've not made your life easy. I know I've failed you as a wife."

"Please," Jack whispered, shaking his head, "don't equate my impatience and being selfish with you failing. You needed me and I abandoned you. I failed you. I will never really know the pain you carry, but

I'm certain we can get through it together. You will never again look over your shoulder and wonder where I am."

"What about her, the others?" Brooke asked, hoping not to ruin the moment but desperately needing some assurance.

"They were nothing more than a selfish and arrogant means to an end. I've never loved anyone but you. I've never felt for anyone what I feel for you. I promise, there will never be another," he said, clutching tight to her cheek. "Whatever transparencies you need from me to be comfortable and confident, I will gladly give. No matter what it is you need me to do, just say the word and it's done. I want the chance to prove I'm still the man you thought you were marrying."

Her smile stretched into the folds of her pillow. She wrapped her fingers around his wrist.

"I too, want to be the woman you were expecting to marry."

Jack pulled at her hand and brought it soft against his lips. "When God led me to you, He knew what He was doing. I could not have found you even in my dreams."

Brooke offered a slight shake of her head then touched his face. "What would you like to do today?" she asked.

"Well, I want to go into the office just for a little while. I have some fences to mend there and it cannot wait. I owe some apologies and I don't want to waste a single second."

"I understand . . . if it's something you must do."

"Then, I was thinking, later this afternoon, you and the girls could meet me at the train station and we could go car shopping. I think it's time we get you a minivan."

"Really? Do you mean that?"

"It's long overdue."

"Are you going to replace the Hummer?"

"No, thought I might find me a nice old pick-up . . . and I'm not keeping the Escalade. I thought I would take it to work. There's someone there I'm certain who could use it more than us."

"You know someone who wants to buy it?"

"No, she could never afford it."

"You mean you're just going to give it away?" Brooke asked, surprised but tickled at the thought of it.

"Yeah," Jack said, smiling, tempering a laugh. "What do you think?"

"Well, sure, if that's what you want to do."

"You remember Sandra, our lobby secretary?"

"The one whose husband passed last year?"

"That's right. Well, she's been in a bad way and I think it's the least I could do for her."

Brooke rubbed at his wrist then placed her hand against his face. "I think it's a wonderful idea. I can't imagine her surprise."

"It's the right thing to do. Anyway, it's not like we can't afford it."

She traced the outline of his jaw. "I love you so much," she said.

"I know you do," he replied, "and I love you, too. I promise, you'll never question my love for you or the girls another day in your life."

❦

Jack pulled into the underground parking garage, noticing only a smattering of employee vehicles as he searched out his private space. He removed a few personal items from the Escalade, insured it was clean, and moved off toward the elevator. He spotted Sam's car near the end of the row.

Reaching the corporate lobby, Jack paused just in front of the lobby desk, waiting for Sandra's usual wish for a blessed day. She turned from her computer screen and flashed a blank stare as her eyes drew to the bandage on his head.

"You didn't say anything," Jack said, catching her off guard.

"I'm sorry, Mr. Clarke?"

"You usually wish people a blessed day."

"Well, yes sir, but you're almost always in a hurry and don't hear me anyway . . . what in the world happened to your head?"

"Just a little accident, no big deal," he assured. "The truth is, Sandra, I have heard you. I've just been too much of a pompous ass to reply. I want to apologize. There's no excuse for my past behavior and I want you to know how sorry I am."

"Well, thank you, Mr. Clarke," she said, unsure of his sanity. "I appreciate that. Of course I forgive you."

"Thank you. Now, I'd like to give you something," he said.

The woman pulled her headset and stiffened in her chair as Jack dangled the keys of the Escalade in front of her.

"I don't understand."

"My wife and I bought an Escalade a couple of years ago and it just doesn't make sense for us with the girls. We'd like you to have it. It has eight-thousand miles on it but is in pristine condition—not a scratch inside or out."

"That's very kind of you and your wife, Mr. Clarke, but . . ."

"Sandra, please, no more 'Mr.' between us, okay? Please call me Jack."

"Okay, sir, but, well, I couldn't afford a new car if I sold everything I owned."

"I'm not asking you to buy it, Sandra. We want you to have it."

"What?" she said, shooting from her chair.

"We want to give it to you. And I want to pay for your insurance as well. It's the least I can do. I didn't help you when you needed it most last year and I want to make that right."

The woman began to cry. "I don't know what to say," she said, bringing a hand to her mouth.

"You don't have to say a word. If you want, you could sell it and get something more economical or just keep the cash. Either way, I want to pay for your insurance and maintenance, no matter if you keep this, get a new car or keep the one you own currently. I have a friend who owns and operates the best repair shop in town. Any problems, maintenance, oil changes, whatever, you just take it there and he will take care of it all at no cost to you."

Jack extended the keys in her direction. "It's parked in my spot in the garage. If I were you, I'd drive it first before you decide to sell it," he said, winking.

Sandra accepted the key ring into her shaking palm. She wiped at her eyes. "Thank you so much, Mr. Clarke . . . I mean Jack . . . I . . . I just don't know what to say."

"It's you I hope has a blessed day, Sandra," he said, smiling. "My day was blessed when I woke up this morning."

Sandra leaned over the counter and hugged his neck.

Jack whispered into her ear. "If there's anything my wife or I can do for you, I will expect you to let me know—no matter what the need."

Sandra's sobbing intensified as she patted his back.

"Merry Christmas," Jack said.

Sandra thanked him and hurried to replace her headset. Her family would not believe the good fortune.

Jack passed through the security door and into the long hallway. He noticed the door to Sam's space ajar. A wedge of light extended into the hallway. A passing shadow broke across its path, suggesting someone was moving about inside. His palms felt clammy; a bit of sweat beaded just under his hairline.

Peeking around the doorway, he noticed three open boxes sitting on top of her desk. Above a low rustling of papers, he heard Sam's voice, mumbling as if engaged in conversation with someone standing near. Pushing at the door, he saw a black ponytail bobbing behind her desk near the floor. He pushed forward into the room.

Sam jumped at the sound of the door brushing across the carpet. She appeared as if she'd not slept for days and was either suffering from allergies or had spent a good deal of time crying. Jack smiled and said hello. Sam dropped a load of paperwork, sprung from her knees and raced around the desk. She flung her arms around his neck and pulled him close and hugged. Her chest and shoulders heaved to the rhythm of her sobbing.

Jack patted her back, but said nothing.

She separated from his embrace. He did not expect or see the first balled fist slam against his chest.

"Why didn't you call me?" she yelled. "Do you have any idea how worried I've been? Do you have any idea how sick to my stomach you've made me?" Another balled fist connected just above his left breast. "I've not slept for three days worrying about you . . . you stupid, stupid jerk. You promised you'd call me. Why didn't you call?"

Jack managed to secure her wrist before she planted another forceful blow. She fell against his chest.

"I'm sorry, Sam," he said, wrapping his arms around her. "If you knew what had happened, you'd understand."

"Where's Brooke? Where are the girls?" she asked, her voice muffled.

"We found them. She and the girls are safe. They're at home."

Jack felt a sigh release from her chest. Her sobbing eased. Pulling back, she wiped at her face and moved back around her desk. Her outfit surprised him. He'd never seen her in anything less than business casual—even when working on Saturdays. Sneakers, sweat pants and a matching sweatshirt meant something else. He looked about her office. She was clearing out her belongings.

"What happened to your head?" she asked, reaching for a Kleenex.

"I had an accident. That's why I wasn't able to call you. I lost everything, including my cell phone." Jack kicked at the carpet as the conversation stalled.

"So, you've decided to leave?" he said, still with his chin buried in his chest.

Sam pushed a box from off her chair and sat down. Burying her face in her hands, she wiped her eyes again and readjusted the band securing her ponytail.

"I don't want you to go. I need you."

Sam glanced in his direction before looking away. "I can't do this anymore, Jack," she said, her voice exhausted. "I can't deal with you and do this job at the same time. It's just too much. I can't live like this anymore."

"What if I told you I'm not the man I was eight days ago. Would you believe me?"

"No, I wouldn't. Your word doesn't mean anything to me anymore." She reached for the folders on the ground and dropped them into a box on her desk.

"Okay . . . I understand. I know I'm to blame for that. The least you could do is hear me out and let me explain some things to you. Just give me a few minutes of your time . . . that's all I'm asking." He moved past her desk and opened the door to his office. "Please, just hear me out."

She released a heavy sigh. "It's not going to do any good, Jack. I told you, I don't trust you anymore. You blew it and all I want to do is get out of here as quickly as I can."

"I understand you want to go, but I also know you love your job and you care about me and my family. I just want to tell you the truth of what happened these past few days so you know before you go. That's it."

She turned away to consider the request.

Jack pleaded. "Please, just for a few minutes."

Sam pushed from her seat, expelling an exaggerated sigh, and followed him into the office. She broke from his wake to take a position on the couch opposite his desk. Jack turned one of the leather chairs facing his desk toward her. Knowing his ribs still did not appreciate the sitting position he eased into the chair and crossed his legs. Sam grabbed a tissue from a box on the coffee table.

"You asked me a question a few days ago I would now like to answer," he said. "You asked me what my problem was with Christmas."

"I don't care, Jack. You don't like Christmas, Thanksgiving, Easter . . . whatever. You told me you were going to tell me what happened with Brooke."

"I need to start at the beginning. You'll not understand any of what I'm about to tell you otherwise."

Sam huffed and looked to the window. Ice covered the lake halfway to the horizon. A teal sky and bursting sun made a prolonged stare difficult.

"You need to know what happened on Christmas Eve when I was seven years old."

For nearly two hours Jack relayed every detail of his life and the search for his family. Learning the tragedies of his childhood was enough for Sam to move from the couch to a chair next him. Going through the entire box of Kleenex, she sat on the edge of her seat, paralyzed by his words and the details of his adventure. Never had she shed so many tears.

"I asked Brooke and her family to forgive me, I told them I was not the same man and that I wanted another chance to prove myself. I think they're giving me that chance," he said.

"I just don't believe it," Sam said. She fell against the back of the chair, staring wildly, yet having a much better understanding of his claim of being a changed man. She shook her head as she filtered the information into something sensible.

"Sam, I need you to know I've made the decision to change my ways—all of them. I'm ready to be a better person, a better man, a better husband, and a better friend. But I can't do it without Brooke and I can't do it without you. I need you with me.

"I don't expect you to believe any of this, so I'm willing to make you a deal. I want you to come with me this afternoon. Brooke and the girls are picking me up at the train station. You get the story from Brooke as she herself witnessed it. If you still don't believe what I'm saying is true, I'll help you finish packing your things and give you ten grand out of my own pocket as a bonus on your way out the door."

Jack grew anxious at her pause. "Do we have a deal?"

Sam traded stares between him and the lake. She nodded. "Okay, Jack," she said after several moments, "you have a deal."

"Do I have your word?"

"You have my word."

"Fair enough," he said, smiling. "Now, since we've negotiated a stay in your departure, I'd appreciate your help with a couple small matters. First, I'd like you to speak with Mr. McDonald to see if he'd be willing to meet me for lunch one day next week. I owe him an apology and want to make it in person."

"That would be great, Jack. He's a very good man and I know he will appreciate the gesture."

"I'm sure he is. I'm hoping . . . well . . . maybe he'll forgive me, and at some point, he and I could become friends. I think I could learn a great deal from him."

"I know he'll like you. I know a lot of people who'll like you if you give them the chance."

Jack pulled a slip of paper from the front pocket of his blue jeans.

"I'd like for you to call the University of Wisconsin and find out how much it would cost to send an in-state student there for four years. Here's the name of the young lady I'd like to arrange this for. Find out how I can pay on her behalf."

"The girl from the soda shop?" Sam asked.

"That's her. She's such a sweetheart and has no shot otherwise. Actually, she reminds me of you. She wants to be a writer and I want to help her."

Sam drew in her chin. The request surprised her. "I don't know what to say, Jack," she said. "That's such a generous and incredible gift. It's going to change her life forever."

"I just appreciate the chance and having the means to help. I should've been doing this for others all along."

"I'll get right on it," Sam said, lifting from the chair. Jack met her upright, offering an appreciative smile. His face was different, his body language much less imposing. Sam stared into his eyes. She knew he had something else on his mind.

"What is it?" she asked.

He dropped his chin toward the floor. "There's one other thing," he said, swiping a foot across the hardwood. "I want you to know how . . . how sorry I am for the way I've treated you at times."

"I know . . ."

"No, please let me finish." He took a deep breath. "It's important you know how much you mean to me. I know I've never said it to your face, and this is very hard for me, but . . ." He paused and turned toward the lake. Sam grew amused at his squirming.

"You're the best friend I've ever had and the most loyal person I know, and I . . . well, I want you to know how much I've appreciated that. How much I appreciate you sticking by me all these years. It has meant everything in the world to me. And, well, I want you to know, too, how much . . . I mean, how much I love you."

Sam could not stop the smile spreading across her face or the tears building in her eyes. She moved forward and grabbed his neck. He returned her embrace and let go a relieved sigh she could feel to the core of her soul.

She pulled from his embrace, traded a smile, and dropped a hand softly upon his forearm. "I'm going to unpack my things," she said. "Tell Brooke we can do lunch after the holidays."

***

Jack leaned against the window behind his desk, studying the landscape as if having never seen it before. Commuters inching along the snow and slush splattered surface of Lake Shore Drive did so not knowing the incredible miracle that had taken place.

He pondered the oddity of it all, wondering how it was possible the old city continued about its business—status quo—when life, as he knew it, had changed, never to be the same again. He felt blessed, empowered. His heart skipped in anticipation of spending the afternoon and the remainder of the week with Brooke and the girls.

"Thank You, God," he whispered, his eyes welling as he drew his head to the heavens. "Thank You for finding me and bringing me home."

"God didn't find you, Jack." The voice from behind shattered his muse. Jack turned. His eyes expanded and his jaw dropped.

"Whether you know it or not, you knocked and the door was opened. You sought and you found. You asked and it was given to you."

"Jubel," Jack said in a dazed whisper.

"It also didn't hurt that my great-niece has found much favor with the Lord," he said, lifting from his seated position. He adjusted the Fedora on his head. His long, black duster unraveled and settled to near his ankles. Jack could see the outline of the couch through his body.

"I can tell you, Jack, with great certainty, Brooke is one of His favorites. And she loves you so much. You see, she too knocked."

Jack buried his fist atop the desk to remain upright. He recovered from the initial shock and proceeded to the center of the room. "Jubel . . . I don't know what to say . . . I owe you so much. I don't know how I could ever repay you for . . ."

"I'm not here to collect a thank you, Jack," he interrupted. "We each have a right to be happy and fulfilled in our lives. Your happiness and fulfillment is just as important to God as Brooke's. I'm just grateful for the opportunity to help my family and the confidence He had in me to do His will. No, I'm not here to collect a pat on the back. My work is far from over."

Jubel stepped forward, closing to within an arm's length. Jack felt a soothing peace envelope his space; a radiance he could not explain. The sensation enveloped his entire body. His every sense drew to a perfect purity, as if it were God himself standing before him. The glory was overwhelming.

Jack wanted to look away, but could not. Jubel inched closer. Jack could still see the couch through Jubel's body.

"I'm here to ask you a question," he said. "I'm here to ask if your life is now fulfilled."

Jack closed his eyes and searched his soul. He opened them to a rush of tears. With his complexion draining, he shook his head.

A warm, caring smile eased across Jubel's face. "God knows the pain in your heart, Jack. He knows how much you've suffered. But she's suffered too. More than you can possibly imagine. God wants you to be happy. He wants her to be happy. The time has come for you to make your life whole, make her life whole. God will give you the power and courage to do so."

Jubel brushed against Jack's shoulder as he passed. Jack turned and watched as the phantom drifted to the corner seam of the office behind his desk, never blotting out the buildings opposite the window. Jubel gazed across the expanse before turning and pointing at the desk.

"It's right there, Jack. The decision is yours."

"Jubel," Jack called out, walking toward him. "Thank you . . . thank you for everything."

"Don't thank me. Thank God, then thank Brooke. Thank her every day. It was her love that made your redemption possible. By the way," he said, winking and pointing again to the thank-you-note-sized envelope on the desk, "you owe me six bits." At that, Jubel touched the bill of his Fedora, nodded, and stepped through the corner seam, dissolving into the landscape just beyond.

Jack stared several moments absorbing his words and allowing the shock of the encounter to ease. He soon broke the stare and looked to his desk. A pink envelope lay atop his blotter with his name scribbled in bright red ink. Settling into his chair, he retrieved a single note card from the envelope, pulled it close to his face and recited the ten-digit number in a whisper. He turned to the lake. A blinking light entered his line of sight, which he followed across the horizon while waiting for a nervous flutter to develop or his stomach to knot; neither happened. The aura of peace that had flowed from Jubel remained intact. Jack rubbed his thumb against his forefingers. He no longer felt the chill of death. Jubel was right. The time had come.

Swiveling and drawing near to his desk, Jack picked up the phone and tapped out the ten-digit number. The first ring sent a wave of excitement racing through his veins; the second, a cleansing rush.

He closed his eyes as the line picked up. The woman's voice broke with the serenity of a springtime sunrise.

"Is this Mrs. Reynolds?"

He could not help but smile at hearing the affirmation.

"Shannon, it's me, Jack," he said. "I wanted to call to say hello and wish you a Merry Christmas."

The End

ABOUT THE AUTHOR

Michael Ringering is a native of East Alton, Illinois, and a 1989 graduate of Murray State University. He and his wife, Teresa, reside in southeast Tennessee, where he is working to complete his next novel.

To learn more about Michael and the novel, *Six Bits,* visit online at:
www.michaelringering.com.